DASHING DUVAL

OR THE

LADIES' HIGHWAYMAN,

Presented Gratis with Nos. 1 and 2 of DASHING DUVAL.

The most interesting and thrilling story ever presented to the Boys of Albion.

DASHING DUVAL ROBBING THE MAIL.

"Without a moment's hesitation Duval faced the villain. Two sharp reports rang out, and the fellow fell back into the coach."

London: PALMER & CO., BOLT COURT, E.C.

DASHING DUVAL;

OR,

THE LADIES' HIGHWAYMAN.

CLAUDE LEVELLED HIS PISTOL AT THE DIM GHOSTLIKE FORM.

CHAPTER I.

THE RACE ON THE HEATH—THE ROBBERY—THE PURSUIT—THE HAUNTED MILL—THE ROADSIDE INN—THE STRUGGLE ON THE ROOF—THE ESCAPE—HURRAH FOR THE ROAD !

IT was on a dark tempestuous night at the end of August, year 166—, that a solitary horseman at mad speed tore over the wild, open, dreary heath of Barnet.

The day, hot and sultry, had closed with every indication of a storm.

The wind in hollow gusts soughed over the wide open expanse of heath, ever and anon shrieking wild and shrill across the bleak dreary waste.

Clouds in thick heavy racks hung overhead, through which at times, for a short space, the moon glinted with cold spectral rays on the lone heath.

Unheeding the wildness of the night the traveller, mounted on a beautiful bay mare, raced across the open waste as though on an errand of life or death.

No. 1 & 2.

Price One Penny.

"Hillio ! away, lass ! Show them what you can do, my pet ! Ho ho, Jane ! we shall outrun them yet ! Sacre ! if I'm not ever with Jonathan Anstey, the runner, for this night's work, may I never see sweet France, the land of my birth, or my pretty blue-eyed Dora Devereux, again ! Ugh ! it's a wild night, and a dark one. Good ! 'twill enable me the better to elude my foes !" muttered the horseman, who, now turning round in his saddle, peered intently back through the thickening gloom.

A thin pale ray of moonlight at this moment lighting up the heath, the rider of the bay mare discerned afar back a troop of some dozen horsemen, several of whom, e'en in that dim light, it could be seen were accoutred as mounted dragoons.

"Hem ! they keep well up with me ! Those fellows have good mounts 'tis certain ! I fear we have hot work before us, Jane !" The rider here patted the neck of his handsome steed, a token of regard that was acknowledged by a whinneying sound from the dumb animal.

Casting his eyes up at the thick heavy clouds, and then once more at his pursuers, the horseman, with muttered anathema, again urged the brave steed by voice and touch to renewed exertions.

On, on tore the horse with its rider, the ground flying from under the feet of the bonny mare.

"Hillio ! hi ! hi ! away ! who shall stop us, lass ? Ha, ha, ha ! Hurrah for the road !" The horseman here broke out into a snatch of song, his voice, rich and clear as a bell, echoing far and near over the heath :

" Hark the sound of rattling coaches !
  The hour of attack approaches :
    Ready, pals, and load !"

A loud laugh and shout of defiance at the end of his song here burst from the mouth of the lone rider.

It was a strange wild scene.

Onwards over the heath tore the gallant steed, whilst in the far distance, hanging sleuthhound like upon the track, came the pursuers.

Hollowly the wind moaned across the waste, and now, to add to the grim scene, a broad vivid streak of lightning quivered in the air, lighting up every bush and hollow near.

"Ventre bleu ! a thunder storm ! Better and better ! In the coming tempest, it's hard if we don't give my enemies the double, my bonny Jane ! Hallo, a wayfarer in the distance ahead, and on a good mount, too ! Sacre ! that horseman should carry a full purse by his appearance. I'll e'en stop him and weigh its contents, come what will !"

Coolly checking his steed in her headlong career, the hunted horseman, drawing a richly silver-mounted pistol from his vest, cocked it, and halted on the heath as a stranger came galloping up in the opposite direction.

Nearer, nearer, meantime, came that troop that had followed so pertinaciously in his track.

One glance at their forms, fully revealed in another glare of lightning, and then, as the new-comer dashed up, in a loud ringing voice, he cried " Halt."

"I halt at no man's bidding," replied the stranger ; then, sighting the pursuers, he exclaimed, " Ha ! what is this ? mounted police and dragoons ? I can guess your calling ! Well, with your enemies hanging so closely in your rear, methinks 'tis folly attempting to carry out your nefarious business. Remove from my path, scoundrel and highwayman !"

"Not till you have handed me your purse and that gold repeater, so ostentatiously displayed," said the knight of the road, for such indeed he was.

"Neither purse nor watch do you get from me," shouted the stranger, who, snatching a pistol from his holster, fired at his bold assailant.

There was a ringing report, which was echoed by a laugh of scorn ; and in another moment the highwayman, who had successfully ducked the shot, that with a sharp ping whistled by his ear, now with his clenched fist caught the traveller a fearful blow in the face, that sent him, with a scream for help, tumbling headlong from his saddle.

To dismount from his own steed, and plunder his victim of his valuables, was, to the hunted and daring highwayman, the work of a few moments.

"Villain ! thief ! robber ! you shall hang for this."

"Don't get excited, my dear sir. I hope you are not hurt ! Kindly inform my friends, who are shouting themselves hoarse, like unfledged schoolboys, that you have lent your purse and your watch to help me on the road. Tell them also that Claude Duval is not to be caught this time.

Au revoir ! Allons ! I must on, for I have to meet a pretty mistress, who is pining my absence."

With a loud laugh, the daring highwayman vaulted into his saddle, just as the foremost of his late pursuers, mounted on a powerful grey horse, dashed up. He gave his faithful steed the rein, and was off like the wind.

"Thank you, Jonathan Anstey, not this time," he shouted, derisively, as the enraged runner, for such he was, fired his pistol at his retreating form.

"Ha, ha, ha ! Jane, we've done the trick ! Penniless one hour back, thanks to my luck I am now in possession of funds. Diable !—that shot from my friend Jonathan's pistol winged unpleasantly close to my chapeau ; but a miss is as good as a mile. We will now see if we can't double on our foes. Sacre ! they are again in the saddle ; they have not lost much time with that gent, anyhow. This is a long chase, and a stern chase, Jane, my girl ! So ho, so ho, my bonny girl ! you are still hale in wind and limb ; but I would I could give you a rest, for all that. We have had a long ride of it. Confound that fellow, Anstey, how he sticks, leech-like, to his purpose ! Well, if he has vowed to take me, I've sworn he sha'nt, so we must show a clean pair of heels."

At mad speed the highwayman once more tore across the heath.

The blue forked lightning, that ever and again flashed from the inky clouds, fully revealed to the eyes of the flying horseman the forms of his pursuers.

With compressed lips and knitted brow he saw that his foes were determined to hunt him to the death.

Merely caressing the neck of his noble steed with his hand caused the faithful and sagacious animal to fly onwards at a maddening speed.

The dumb brute knew what was required of it.

It was a brave sight—that horse and its rider.

Her glossy coat not turned a hair—despite the lengthened chase, the bonny mare held on in her course.

A grim smile flitted across the handsome features of her master, as tearing onwards a low dull tramp, and jingling clinking noise of steel clashing against steel, was borne to his ears.

His enemies, the police-officers and the dragoons, were still hot in pursuit.

Shaking back the glossy ringlets of dark curling hair that, like a woman's, clustered about his neck, and hung about his collar in the manner of the times, the bold rider drew a couple of pistols from his vest and carefully examined the priming ; then tightening the waistbelt, from which depended a handsome rapier, the highwayman gave utterance to a loud laugh as a peal of thunder was followed by a perfect deluge of rain.

"So the storm has burst ! Good ! If it spoil my best suit—diable ! it may also serve to damp the ardour of my friends. By heavens, it's a wild night ! I would we were under shelter, my bonny Jane," exclaimed the daring knight of the road, apostrophising his sagacious steed as they swept onwards amidst the frenzy of the howling storm.

Looking back once more, as he left the heath and bore down a narrow lane lined on either side by a thick copse, the highwayman discovered that from some cause his enemies had paused for a time in their pursuit.

"Some accident—a saddle-girth broken perchance ! Good ! Ventre bleu !—a few minutes' more start may enable me to reach unperceived Joe Jennings's crib at Finchley—"The Ostler's Rest"—which, by-the-by, old Joe might with more reason style " The Highwayman's Rest." Let me see; by this handsome repeater, presented me a little while back, it is close on twelve," muttered Duval, as by a vivid blazing glare of lightning he discerned the hands of the costly gold watch he held up to his face. " By Jove ! if we push on, my bonny Jane, I shall be in time to meet my old pal, Gentleman Jack, who promised to be at Joe's to-night provided he got safe away from the arms of the pretty Mabel Merriton—that enchanting little actress of the Duke's Theatre, Bankside. Hillio, away lass ! our enemies have caved in for a time, and yonder, by good luck, looming through the darkness, methinks I can sight a shelter from the pelting of this pitiless storm."

Shivering slightly with the cold, his rich velvet coat soaked through and through, Duval here leaned over the neck of his mare and peered intently through the inky darkness.

Another quivering blue glare from the leaden clouds now revealed to his eyes, some half-mile ahead, standing a little away from the high road, an old ruined mill, the pool which formerly with its waters working the wheel glistening like silver as the lightning played over them.

"Not a very inviting shelter; but, as the sailors have it, 'any port in a storm,'" exclaimed Duval, as dashing up to the old water-mill a fresh hurricane and deluge of rain caused him to leap hastily from the back of his steed.

Taking the reins in his hands, the highwayman unhesitatingly led his brave mare up to the entrance of the ruined mill.

It was a dark gruesome shelter—a shelter, and nothing more.

All was ruin and decay.

Black, bare, and desolate.

Rearing its height up in the air the old mill looked like some huge gaunt spectre standing there alone in the desolate waste.

Following her master, the mare, bending sagaciously her slender neck, stooped and passed with him the narrow entrance to the old mill.

The doorway and other portions fronting the road had long since fallen to decay, leaving a space just sufficient for Duval and his steed to enter.

Here for a brief time was a little shelter from the fury of the storm.

"A nice place, I must confess. Ugh! what a disagreeable odour—a smell as of a charnel house! Well, give me Joe's snug parlour to this; but the present howling storm not even I, dashing, reckless, devil-may-care Duval, care to brave. Sacre! it has already spoilt my best coat and my chapeau. Well, that like the old mill is a perfect ruin!"

With a grim smile our hero, here pulling his Spanish hat from his head, essayed to shake from its drooping ostrich feather the raindrops which had caused it to cling like a wet rag to the fine glossy felt of which the cap was composed.

Squeezing the worst of the wet from it, Claude now once more placed the cap jauntily on his head, and then, gazing out of the mill, discovered to his chagrin that the storm of rain was, if possible, more of a deluge than before.

"Confound it! if it don't give over presently I must e'en face it, or my friends will be gaining upon me unpleasantly close. What an ugly old den this is! It looks for all the world just like a place where a dozen murders might have been committed."

With a shiver he could not control, Duval here gazed around that portion of the old mill in which he had sought shelter.

The flashes of lightning, now incessant, made all as light as day, though in the moment of time that ensued as the electric fluid ceased, all was black, inky darkness.

In one of these fitful blue flashes of vivid light, Duval discerned a ladder at the further end of the lower or ground floor of the mill, which apparently led to an upper chamber above.

Impelled by an irresistible curiosity he, leaving his docile steed, made for the steps.

Placing his feet upon the lowermost rounds, he found, as he expected, that they refused to bear his weight, the wood being rotten and falling to decay.

His hands upon the sides of the rude means of ascent, Claude involuntarily cast his eyes up at the open trap.

A fresh blinding blaze of lightning at this moment quivered through the broken casements and interstices of the old mill; but not the gloomy ruin, not the weird hour, not the howling storm was it that caused the blood of Dashing Duval, the bold highwayman, to run through his veins like ice!

His tall form, drawn to its full height, his head upraised with staring eyes, Claude remained at the foot of the ladder, glaring up at the open trap above.

Did his eyes deceive him?

Was he the victim of a wild delusion?

For a second of time all was darkness.

In that moment of dreary profound obscurity, Claude could hear the beating of his own heart, whilst a shiver of terror, even he the bold daring highwayman could not repress, passed through his frame as he fancied, in a pause of the howling winds without, that he heard a heavy, deep-drawn sigh.

Again a blaze of light from the riven clouds.

A blaze of light that revealed to the staring eyes of the knight of the road a something looming down upon him from the open trap above—

A ghastly livid face!

The pallid face of a corpse, with eyes like pieces of polished tin.

Eyes that stared out of the livid face into his with a gaze of devilish malignity.

For a minute of time the bold highwayman glared up at the hideous face, frozen with terror; then, upon a sudden impulse he could not control, he snatched a pistol from his belt, and fired. There was a bright flash, a loud, stunning report—then all was still.

A cold shiver shook the frame of the bold highwayman as, once more enveloped in impenetrable darkness, a something a moment after came with startling abruptness full in his face!

A something soft, clammy, and cold.

A cry of alarm, changed however to an ejaculation of disgust, as, by a renewed flash of lightning, he discerned the loathsome form of a huge bat, that falling from above now lay in death at his feet—the bullet from the pistol fired a moment before having robbed the hideous thing of life.

"A bat! my bullet found some mark then! But, grace ciel! how about that death-face? I shudder with horror now as I think of the steady stare of those glassy eyes; but, come what will, I, who fear no living man, am not to be frightened by a shadow or trick, perchance practised to play upon my credulity! Be it man or devil, ghost or banshee, Claude Duval is not the man to flag! So ho! Steady Jane; steady, my girl!" Claude here strode over to his horse, and petting the animal, who was somewhat restive, at once, by his voice and hand, restored her to quiet; then, without a thought of his enemies, made his way again to the ladder, and at danger to his neck, and not without considerable toil and trouble, mounted the frail support, while his head was on a level with the fatal trap!

On a level with that opening at which, a few minutes before, he could have staked his life he saw a pale ghastly face, the face of the dead, with the wide, staring, glistening eyes of the living.

Not without a tremor did Dashing Duval force his way through the small opening of the trap into the upper chamber.

Scrambling through, he at length stood in the apartment.

An apartment small, drear, ghastly, and weird in its utter ruin.

The storm now at an end, all was quiet.

The hollow winds moaned sorrowfully through that lone chamber of the old mill.

All was thick darkness!

A darkness black and heavy.

Groping his way to a tiny narrow casement Duval now gave a look out, making the discovery that the small loophole like a window overlooked the mill stream, the waters of which, black as the night, lay sluggish and dismal below.

Placing his hand too heavily on the narrow sill, a crash of decayed wood was followed by a sudden plash as the framework of the casement fell into the sullen depths below.

Peering through the gloom without Claude perceived no signs of his pursuers.

All was dark and drear,—the summer moon emerging from the heavy clouds for a moment adding only to the dreariness of the scene.

"It's strange, very strange! There's some fiendish jugglery in this, or else"—

Scarce had the last words issued from his lips, as he turned from the casement, ere he was started by a deep-drawn sigh!

A sigh as of some one in deepest pain or sorrow.

With wild, staring eyes, Claude peered through the darksome chamber of the old ruin.

Nought met his startled gaze however.

The wind moaned in hollow gusts, the decaying timbers that yet clung together gave out a disagreeable creaking noise; but no hideous form, no weird spectre met the gaze of the highwayman, who, with an oath, now made his way to the trap, and, scrambling through, was presently on the floor below.

Patting his steed, which he found trembling and bedewed with a sweat as though she had but just forded a river, Duval hastened from the old mill, and, leaping into his saddle, was about to gallop from the spot, when, rein in hand, he was startled from his purpose by a strange phenomenon.

The thick, heavy darkness that enshrouded all about the old ruin was less dense in the vicinity of the mill dam.

Over the silent waters hovered a strange shadowy light!

A pale thin bluish haze!

Stronger, brighter grew the light!

A horrible chill crept through the frame of Claude as he beheld the blue-like mist spreading itself over the darksome pool. Patting his bonny mare, that shook and snorted with terror, Duval uttered an exclamation of surprise and alarm as he beheld in the thickening mist or blue haze that hovered over the mill stream, a human form—shadowy and ill-defined, yet the form and figure of a young girl—young and beautiful, pale and wan. Another figure, now emerging from the old mill, made straight for the edge of the dam, with eyes in which there was no lustre, and which, turned on the horse and its rider, shone like pieces of glass; the strange form, that of a young man, stood apparently intently watching the surface of the waters.

For a moment of time Duval, sitting forwards in his saddle, gazed spellbound at the strange vision. Then, as his steed, with a snort of wild terror, roared high up, nearly throwing her rider, he drew a pistol from his belt and fired.

Scarce had the echo of the report died away ere, like the figures in a dream, the vision vanished, whilst a loud shout, a tramp of horses, and jingling of spurs informed Claude of the vicinity of his foes.

Too long had he remained at the mysterious ruin.

With a curse at the folly and imprudence that had chained him to the spot, he now turned and fled!

Fled as a shout of triumph, of exultation, rang in his ears.

Unknowing what he did, in the excitement of the moment Duval pricked his steed with the spur, causing the faithful brute to dash forward at such maddened speed as bade fair to soon leave the foe far behind.

Over hill and dale, through brake and brier rode the bold highwayman, dazed and confused by the incidents of the past hour. He tightened not the rein, but at her own free will allowed his bonny mare to gallop madly on.

The moon now breaking out from a bank of clouds, and throwing a dim light upon the scene, revealed to the eyes of the hunted horseman the spire of a village church.

Glancing back, a cry of exultation escaped the lips of Claude.

His enemies were for a time out of sight.

The terrific speed of his bonny mare had told.

For a little time he was safe.

A deadly cunning enemy was on his track; had traced him from town the preceding day; and all the highwayman's nerve and audacity were required to outwit and elude this foe.

Halting not in his mad career Duval dashed on, and was presently within the precincts of the village the church spire of which he had sighted a few minutes before.

"Safe at Finchley! Hurrah, my bonny Jane! We will play the double on them now or I'm wonderfully mistaken," exclaimed Claude, as hot and panting with excitement he pulled up at the door of an inn, that, standing just without the village, bore a sign swinging from its porch, called "The Ostler's Rest."

"What ho! House! House! Within there! Wolves are out and the hawk's on the wing!"

"Loud and long was the summons made upon the door by the impatient applicant for admission; then, as a head was thrust out from a window above, he exclaimed: "Now, Joe Jennings, bustle, old man, unless you want to see me trapped like a fox under your very nose!"

"What, Duval! my prince of cracksters, my pink of high tobymen, is it you! I'll be down in the shaking of a whisp of straw."

The head disappearing, the casement was slammed to; whilst a minute after the rattling of bolts and clank of a chain were preceded by the opening of the door.

Emerging into the moonlight, the landlord, a red-faced, bald-headed, jolly-looking fellow, without ceremony, seized the horse's bridle and exclaimed,—

"Get on in—one of the family is in the Blue-room! I'll see to the mare." He thrust his early visitor into the passage, and, banging to the door, disappeared with the horse down a narrow lane that ran along the side of the house.

Involved in darkness, Duval remained for a time motionless in the passage of the old inn.

Intently he listened for any sounds from without.

All was quiet, however.

For a time he was safe.

His foes were yet some distance in the rear.

A pale yellow light now shone in the darkness.

The pale flicker of a candle in a horn lantern, borne by the red-faced landlord, who, hurrying forward, exclaimed: "I've put Jane into No. 2!"

"Right you are, Joe! She needs looking after."

"She does so! Why what the deuce have you been doing with her! She's dead beat."

"I had to put her on her mettle, Joe!"

"So I should think! However, Humpy Bill will see to her. But tell me who's after you!"

"Jonathan Anstey."

"Whew! he's a nasty customer."

"Sacre! he is so. He dropped upon me in Alsatia yesterday, and I had warm work to elude him; he meant making my bed in Newgate to-night, but I was too smart for him."

"Well; you want your peepers wide open, and your wits at work when playing with that gent, Claude!"

"Yes, Joe; you are right! But I think I've done him this time."

"Guess you have; he's sharp, indeed, if he noses you out here, Claude."

"Rather; but didn't you say you'd one of the family here already, Joe!" said Duval, who, having followed the landlord into the bar parlour, coolly took up a bottle of brandy from a side table, and pouring out a tumbler half-full, drank it off at a gulp.

"I did tell you one of the family was here, Claude; and it's one you'll be glad to see!"

"Who is it!"

"Gentleman Jack!"

"Ventre bleu, I thought so! he told me he meant dropping in here yesterday."

"Yes, confound him! But the next time he does business in this neighbourhood I'll thank him to return to London, or things may get too warm. Hallo! there's your friends."

A loud authoritative summons now sounded on the outer door.

"It's my foes, sure enough."

"Yes. Why, confound it, Claude, there's soldiers with them," said the landlord, as the clanking of sabres could be heard from without.

"Oh, yes; Anstey came across some dragoons, who joined in the hunt."

"Well, if they get the fox out of this hole they're clever, that's all!"

"Where's Jack!"

"In the Blue-room."

"Good! I'd better join him."

"Just so! You know the way."

"I rather think so!" said Duval, who now hurried out of the bar parlour, the landlord going to the door and asking who was there, a question that elicited a volley of oaths from some one without.

Leaving his friend, Joe Jennings, to parley with his foes, Duval now started down a long narrow passage. At the further end was a strong oaken door.

Unlocked, it yielded to the touch.

On the other side of the door was a steep flight of stone stairs.

Down these steps in total darkness Claude descended.

Reaching the bottom he found himself in a large cellar, only partially illumined by a small oil lamp, that rested in a broken box.

The oil, low in the little lamp, gave but a faint light through the cellar.

Casks, cases of wine, and old lumber were alike piled together in that underground place without an attempt at order.

A cask, empty, here rolled on its side, whilst near it was a perfect stack of empty bottles. Passing the chaotic mass, Duval made for a huge butt at the further end of the cellar.

Voices, loud and in anger, accompanied by the tramp of feet above, told him his enemies were in the house.

In haste Claude now sprang on to the top of the large butt.

It was empty. Evidently aware of this he unhesitatingly lowered himself into it, and, turning to that portion that rested against the wall of the cellar, he pressed a small iron knob that was let into the wood.

With a creaking, grinding noise the whole side of the butt

that rested against the wall now slid back, disclosing a narrow archway. Into this aperture Claude stepped; then, as the little door, so artfully contrived, slid back, he pulled an iron ring in the flooring of the passage, and immediately a loud rush of water followed.

There was now an effectual barrier between the passage and the butt, the latter filling rapidly with water.

Passing along the passage, some eight or ten feet in length, Duval gained a low, narrow door, turning the handle of which the tinkling sound of a bell rang in the air.

A moment after, the door opening apparently of its own accord, Claude stepped out of the passage into a comfortably furnished chamber, the walls, furniture, and ceiling of which were all of the same hue!

A pale blue!

Blue, pinked with gold.

Seated at a table in the centre of the secret chamber was a tall, handsome man, of some one or two and twenty years of age, who, smoking a richly silver-mounted pipe, without turning his head to look at his visitor, exclaimed, "Now, Joe, you infernal old cuss, you wine-bibber and ci-devant knight of the road! where the devil have you been?"

"Playing at hunt the stag! I was the stag, and Jonathan Anstey and his runners were the hounds."

"What, Duval! is it you?" The stranger here started up from his seat, and, darting forward, seized the intruder by the hand, then, with a nod at the door, exclaimed, "Where is Joe, and how the deuce did you come here?"

"By the usual way, old pal, the waterbutt; as for Joe, he is bamboosling the men of the law."

"You have been chased to the house, then, Claude?"

"I have so—by our particular and mutual friend, Jonathan Anstey, who is at this moment outside the house with his infernal myrmidons and some half-a-dozen mounted dragoons into the bargain."

"The devil!"

"Yes. But old Joe is a downy bird. He told me I should find you here. I don't think we shall be troubled by any intruders in the Blue-room, Jack."

"Well, no, Claude; they will have sharp noses to fox us out here. But hark! there's some one at the door now; there goes the bell."

A tinkling noise of a bell now sounded through the room, and scarce had the echo died away ere the door started open, as Duval pressed his hand upon a spring communicating with the lock.

"Proper contrivance this of old Joe's," exclaimed Claude, as, the door swinging slowly open, a short, bullet-headed man, with bumpback, and one of his eyes afflicted with a diabolical squint, hastily made his way into the room.

"It's all up, Duval! Anstey and his Bow-street men have smoked us out at last! Oh, lord, here's a go!"

"What, in the name of all that's infernal, do you mean?"

"Diable! are you going crazy, Humpy Bill?" said Claude, as his companion, who had seized the intruder by the throat, made as though about to pitch him headlong into the vaulted passage without.

"Gentleman Jack, if you will take your hand off my throat, I'll tell yer what's up."

"That's it! Sacre! out with it, man!" exclaimed Duval, as the hunchback, free of the other's grasp, had rushed to and closed the secret door.

"Gentlemen knights of the road, 'The Ostler's Rest' ain't no rest for you now. The devil Anstey has somewhere heard of this 'ere secret chamber. I fancy, leastways master does, that Jem Hornby, him as got a lifer (transportation for life) for the attempted murder of his blowen (mistress), has rounded on us, and let out about this 'ere snuggery. Any way, Anstey knows all about it, and will be here in a few minutes."

"Confusion!"

"Yes; and I've come to bid you make a bolt of it."

"I say, Claude, this looks serious!"

"Rather!"

"What the deuce is to be done?"

"Well, I must make myself scarce! devil take it! I've done a hard run already, and my poor beast is hardly breathed yet."

"And I've left mine at Highgate, padding the hoof from there to the inn here last night; but as I don't fear master Anstey, I'll face him, Duval! Do you cut stick with Humpy Bill, and I'll humbug Jonathan and his men, which will give you five minutes' start."

"By Jove! a good idea Jack! things are hot for me just now! I'll away at once."

"Have you any thought of where to go?"

"No, Jack."

"Then make all speed to the old Tree Cave."

"Will you join me?"

"Yes!"

"I will await your coming."

"Right! away; for, by heavens, the enemy are even now in the cellar!"

"Is it safe to leave you, Jack?"

"Confound it, yes! Anstey has got no warrant out against me. Away, man, while you have a chance."

"Blessed if the chance ain't almost lost!" exclaimed the Hunchback, as a loud crash and sound of voices echoed without.

"Lead on, Bill! Au revoir, Jack, dear boy!"

"Good-bye Claude! The old Tree Cave, mind; you'll be safe there!"

"Right, dear pal! Diable! I don't like this running away, though," muttered Duval, as his fingers convulsively closed on the hilt of his rapier. He followed the Hunchback through a low narrow door that fastened with a spring he had opened a moment before.

Waving his hand in adieu to his friend, the highwayman, closing the secret entrance after him, followed his companion down a long narrow low-roofed vaulted passage.

Not a moment too soon had Duval and the Hunchback quitted the secret chamber; for, even as they hurried along the underground labyrinth, the sound of angry voices came plainly to their ears.

"Ventre bleu! They are in the Blue-room, Bill."

"Yes, worse luck! That there fine little snuggery arn't a nest no longer for such as you. Oh, if I only had that cove Hornby—him as nosed on this crib of our'n—blessed if I wouldn't give him what for," muttered the Hunchback, who, hurrying along holding in his hand a small lamp, now paused, as they arrived at the bottom of the narrow passage.

Breathless, the two men stood in the underground retreat listening for any sound of pursuit.

All however was quiet.

The secret of the passage had not yet been discovered.

"Come on, captain, it's all right for the present! Another minute will take us into the governor's bedroom. Once there, all will be right. You can drop from the window; and, as quick as you are there, I'll be outside with your mare."

"Good, Bill! Here's a guinea, old man; on you go! I wouldn't fall into Jonathan Anstey's hands this time for a trifle! To be run in now would be too provoking."

"Ah! I thinks as we've doubled on him this time, captain," said the hunchback stableman, who, pocketing the guinea handed by Claude, now unlocked a strong oaken door which had barred their further progress.

On the other side of this door was a steep flight of stone steps.

Up these stairs the highwayman and the Hunchback now made their way.

All was dark, dismal, and drear in the underground place.

A damp earthy odour was in the air.

Hastening on up the stone staircase, upon reaching the summit Duval's conductor paused.

They were now standing in a narrow passage, the walls on either side lined with lath and plaster.

A low humming noise now fell upon their ears!

The sound of voices!

Voices low and muffled!

Mummuring and indistinct!

"Them's your coves, captain," said the Hunchback in a whisper to his companion.

"So I suppose, Bill! Where abouts are we now?"

"Alongside the bar parlour."

"The devil we are!"

"Yes! and the police and the dragoons are getting jolly over some of old Joe's old port."

"Confound them, yes! But on you go, Bill; let's get out of this, the dust and air of this secret way is not at all pleasant."

"More pleasant than the air in the Stone Jug, though, captain," exclaimed the Hunchback with a grin, as, lamp in hand, he once more hurried on.

Gaining the end of the narrow passage another staircase or rude ladder was reached.

It was a strange wild place, that secret way in The "Ostler's Rest." The house, formerly belonging to an old Cavalier family, had been contrived to hide its guests from the eyes of the Roundheads, and, could the walls have spoken, would have disclosed many a tale of terror and suffering, sorrow and crime.

Ascending the narrow winding stairs, the dust and cobwebs falling in clouds about their ears, the companions at length gained a second passage or corridor, scarce four feet in breadth. Along this they proceeded with great caution, while the faithful servitor of the old inn halted at a portion of the wall which was composed entirely of wood.

"Now's our time, captain! Here's the secret door of the governor's bedroom, known only to him and me. In you go!"

With a grin the Hunchback, now pressing a brass nail that projected out of the wall, a small door opened inwards; and squeezing through, Duval and his conductor were presently standing in a comfortably-furnished bedroom.

"A pleasant change after those cursed cobwebs and family of spiders," said Claude, as he shook the dust from his clothes.

"Well, yes, this ere is summat more Christian-like, Master Duval. All seems pretty quiet; I'll cut downstairs and see what's up; I daresay as old Joe 'as made your friends pretty comfortable like by this time."

"I've not the least doubt of it, Bill."

"Ah! Joe Jennings knows his book, he does! Catch a weasel asleep, not old Joe! Howsomever, I'll bolt now, captain; that there window opens on the yard; there's not much of a drop from it on to a shed, and when you're in the yard a little wicket gate will lead you into the kitchen garden, over the wall of which you're in the lane where I'll meet ye with the mare."

"All right, Humpy Bill. Tell Joe I shall come and see him to-morrow, when the hawks are on the wing."

"Right you are, captain," said the Hunchback, who now having closed the secret door stepped over to the one that led from the chamber to the landing without.

Listening for a moment intently, and finding all was quiet, with a grin the stableman left the room; Duval at once hastening to the window.

A thin white light was now stealing into the chamber: The light of early morn.

A golden ruddy russet tint was gathering in the eastern sky.

Another day was about to break.

With a shiver as he recalled the strange wild incidents of the old mill, Claude Duval was about to throw up the casement, when, glancing into the yard below, he started back as though stung by a serpent.

The clank of arms had fallen on his ears, whilst in the grey light of the approaching morn he discerned five or six dragoons and a couple of police grouped about the yard.

"Well, I'm in for it nicely this journey, it appears. Jonathan Anstey told me a month back he would follow in my steps like a bloodhound till he brought me to the scaffold, and it appears he intends to keep his oath."

"He does so. Ha, ha, ha! Caged at last. Good morning, Cavalier Duval—dashing, daring knight of the road! I think I am one too many for you this time!"

With wild staring eyes, and his hands convulsively clutching the butt of his pistol, our hero stood spell-bound by the casement, glaring at a tall, broad-shouldered, herculean man who, having softly opened the room door a moment before, had stolen in unperceived.

"You don't seem to appreciate my kindness in looking after you. Your friends, Joe Jennings and Master Gentleman Jack, wanted me to believe that you had quitted the inn abruptly, but I wouldn't believe you could be guilty, after all my affectionate solicitude, of behaving with so much rudeness. And now, tell me Duval—how is it to be?" exclaimed the officer (for such he was), as he dropped his bantering tone and strode towards the highwayman. "How is it to be—are you coming with me quietly, or am I to put the bracelets on?"

The runner here pulling a pair of handcuffs from his pocket coolly shook them in the face of his victim.

"Jonathan Anstey!"

"Well?"

"What is the reason of this venomous and bitter persecution? Why your oath to follow on my track till you bring me to Tyburn—an oath I fancy you'll find me clever

enough to prevent you carrying out? Still, though prepared to thwart you in your kind intentions, I would wish to know, Jonathan Anstey, the cause of your enmity to me, as apart from your calling compelling you to pursue me when wanted? I am perfectly well aware there is some private grudge."

"There is."

"I thought so."

"Then you thought right! Shall I tell you, Claude Duval, why I have sworn to know no rest until I have brought you to the leafless tree? Shall I tell you why I hate you, Dashing Duval, as you are called, with such a hate as only your swinging on the gibbet can allay?"

"Say on, my amiable friend! Don't grind your teeth, and make faces, Jonathan. You are not a pretty man, and, sacre! when you roll those eyes of yours like that under your beetling brows, ventre bleu! you look demmed fiendish."

"You take it coolly, Claude Duval."

"Why not?"

"Because the prospect of Newgate, and Tyburn tree to follow, is not a pleasant one."

"Well, no! But I ain't at the first place yet, leave alone the second!"

"But you soon will be."

"Perhaps!"

"Ha, ha, ha! Good! You think, then, with my men below—the mounted dragoons, to say nothing of myself—that you will escape me!"

"Ma foi, yes!"

"Claude Duval, you are mad—as mad as you were when you stepped between me and the girl, Kate Annersley."

"Oh, sits the wind in that quarter? Parbleu, the cause of your enmity is now explained! Sacre! I had forgot how a few months back I bore the little Lamb from the grey old Wolf. Would you like to know where little Kate, pretty little Kate, with the blue eyes and fair hair, is now, sweet Jonathan?"

With a smile of triumph Claude gazed at his foe, whose dark evil-looking face turned livid, whilst the cunning beadlike eyes glistened beneath a pair of bushy beetling brows like live coals.

Duval's taunts had told.

Jonathan Anstey, the Bow-street runner and thief-taker, was goaded to fury at the coolness of the bold and handsome highwayman.

"You do well, Claude Duval, to remember me; how you crossed my path in my pursuit of the girl Kate Annersley; it reminds me of the debt I owe you. What was she to you that you should interpose to snatch her from me?" exclaimed the runner, who, with a malicious scowl of triumph, now placed the handcuffs on a table near, and coolly pulling a pistol from his vest, put it on full cock.

Duval, with a light laugh, his back to the casement keenly watching his enemy, exclaimed, "Look you, Jonathan Anstey. The girl Kate Annersley was nought to me. I knew her not until that night by the old Bankside and found the helpless orphan struggling with yourself and two of your myrmidons. I objected to the rough treatment you were subjecting her to, and, not knowing who or what the poor girl was to you, wife, sister, or stranger, I knocked you down, and sent your worthy followers after you. Kate Annersley, whom I then discovered was but a poor little waif whom you were persecuting with your odious addresses, and with whom, when I surprised you that night, you had proceeded to open violence, accepted me as her cavalier, and pretty Kate is now in a safe retreat. Ha, ha, ha! wily Jonathan, the Dove is safe from the Hawk; you'll never see lovely Kate again, old man."

"Indeed! We shall see. With her bold cavalier, her highwayman protector, safely caged in Newgate, methinks it will not be long before the Dove is once more in the power of the Hawk; you understand?"

"Perfectly. You'll put me away first, and then hunt up pretty Kate."

"Just so."

"Well; the most difficult part of your task has yet to be performed."

"You mean your capture?"

"That is just what I do mean."

"Well, daring, dashing Claude Duval, I don't see that will be so difficult a task; a cry from my lips and the report of my pistol will bring my men from below in a moment."

"Very likely. But before they are here you may find a blue pill in your inside that won't be easy of digestion." Claude, with a laugh, here snatched both his pistols from his belt, presenting them full at the head of the astounded runner.

A deep-breathed curse escaped the lips of Anstey, who, his own weapon levelled at the highwayman, slowly moved away towards the door.

The wily thief-taker, aware that Duval was a dead shot, cared not alone to face the deadly tubes levelled at his head.

Intending first to rush upon his man, his over-confidence and bantering exultation and triumph had led him into the mistake of giving Claude time to think and act.

For the past few minutes Duval had been revolving in his mind how he could best escape from his certainly very critical position.

With a grim smile and curl of the lip, that fully disclosed his large white and wolfish looking teeth, the Bow-street runner edged his way towards the door.

Duval, hesitating to fire, and not wishing the thief-taker's blood upon his hands, yet inwardly vowed that he would not be taken.

Nearing the door, a loud laugh now escaped the lips of the officer!

A laugh of triumph, as the shadow of a human form darkened the entrance to the chamber.

"Ha, ha! We have you now, clever Duval. Drop your barking irons, man; it's no use, you can't escape us!"

"I beg to disagree with you; I think he can," said the new arrival, who, seizing the thief-taker by the arms, and tripping him up, brought him with a crash to the ground.

To wrench his pistols from his hands and gag the enraged officer was the work of a moment.

In dazed astonishment Claude, during the scene of the runner's discomfiture, remained standing by the casement.

His eye beaming with a lurid light, whilst the veins in his forehead stood out like whipcords from suppressed passion, the baffled thief-taker lay now bound and helpless on the floor.

"What, Jack, is it you?" at length said Claude, as, recovering from his surprise, he stepped forward.

"It's even I, Claude."

"You arrived in the nick of time, old pal!"

"Well; yes! What a sell though for Anstey!"

"Yes; he mistook you for one of his friends."

"He did so."

"What are they all doing, Jack?"

"Getting blind drunk over old Joe's best port."

"Good! how came you to seek me here!"

"Why, I had the office from Humpy Bill, and managing to elude the redbreasts (officers) downstairs, I hastened here, as it happened, in time to stop Anstey's pretty little game."

"Well, having defeated him in his kind intentions, we will leave him to chew the cud of sweet and bitter fancy and o en clear out, Jack."

"Yes; I think that is what we had best do, Claude; but we must act with caution, for those infernal dragoons seem more wideawake than the officers."

"Confound them! yes."

"I learned downstairs that Anstey promised them half the coin to be made over your capture."

"Oh, he did that, did he? That accounts for the presence of the soldiery then!"

"He would like some of them here now, Claude! Don't he look bilious?"

"Parbleu, he does so, poor fellow! He is getting black in the face, his blood wants circulating," said Duval, who here gave a not very gentle kick with the toe of one of his jack boots full upon the hindermost part of the bound and helpless officer.

A smothered moan and writhing of the limbs followed.

Leaving the infuriated captive laying in the centre of the chamber, the companions now made for the door.

All appeared quiet.

Save an occasional shout and chorus of a song that echoed from the rooms below, there was no sound to cause alarm.

"Come on, Jack! I think it's all right."

"What do you propose, Claude?"

"Why, to make our way upstairs and reconnoitre the aspect of affairs from one of the front windows."

"Well, I suppose that is the only plan."

"I dare not go downstairs."

"Well, no."

"Nor can I escape by the yard."

"Confound it! no, Claude. Those infernal dragoons are there."

"Exactly. We must make a bolt of it now, together, as Anstey can clap the darbies on you for aiding in my escape."

"Well, so he can."

"We therefore leave 'The Ostler's Rest' in company."

"Just so, Claude. And I don't care now how soon we get out of it."

Making their way along a corridor, the companions now ascended a flight of stairs at the further end.

Loud shouts of laughter and clinking of glasses sounded plain in their ears from below.

"They are hard at it, Jack!"

"Yes, not much danger from them in a very short time if they continue their present game!"

"No; but we shall have to reimburse old Joe his lost wine."

Softly gliding up the stairs, the companions now gained another landing, and opening a door on their left, entered a large, comfortably-furnished bedroom that, let out to travellers, was upon this occasion tenantless.

"Here we are—the second floor front! A glance out into the road will show us what chance we have."

"Right you are, Claude!"

Hurrying across the room, the friends, reaching its only casement, through which the early morning sun was throwing a broad flood of golden light, stared cautiously out into the high-road below.

A simultaneous curse escaped both their lips.

In front of the inn stood the horses of the dragoons, guarded by one of the soldiery.

"A wholesome look-out, Claude!"

"Very!"

"What the devil shall we do?"

"Sacre! I know not. We are hemmed in!"

"It looks infernally like it."

"I think you had better run down and see how things are below. I don't suppose they will interfere with you."

"Well, no! The idea is a good one. I'll go at once. Will you wait here?"

"Yes, just see what the enemy are up to, and then return and report."

"All right, Claude. Confound it! I wish we were both safe in the old Tree Cave."

"So do I; and, ventre bleu! it shall go hard with me if we are not there in the course of the next hour. Allons on you go! This inactivity is putting me in a fever."

"Same here, old pal; better a bold dash than this!"

"Right you are, Jack! and it's just what I expect it will come to."

Duval, as his companion quitted the room, now took another glance through the diamond-paned casement.

An ejaculation of joy escaped his lips.

In eager tones he called his friend back.

Gentleman Jack, however, had departed hurriedly, and was beyond the reach of his voice.

"Perhaps it's just as well as it is," muttered our hero, who, with eyes fastened upon the scene below him, beheld with delight the dragoons, seven or eight in number, preparing to mount preparatory to quitting the inn.

"Ma foi, they are tired of acting the police business, and wily, cunning, astute Jonathan Anstey will lose his allies. Once they are away, I care not. Half-a-dozen of those cursed soldiers are worth twenty redbreasts. Sacre! once they are off, parbleu, it's not the Bow-street runners will long detain me from pursuing my journey!" With a smile of intense satisfaction Claude now heard the officer below give orders for his men to start.

In another moment the clatter of their horses' hoofs rung loud and clear upon the hard road. With a sigh of relief Claude, about to turn from the window, was startled by the weight of a heavy hand on his shoulder; then, as his eyes alighted upon the figure of a stalwart herculean man, he was felled to the ground by a stunning coward-blow, delivered with fearful violence, full upon his head.

With a sickening, buzzing noise in his ears, and a dazed, dreamy sensation, Claude for a moment lay helpless upon the floor. Then a low, chuckling laugh, and the jingling clanking of fetters, as a pair of handcuffs were about to be thrust upon his wrists, startled him once more into life.

With a gasping cry of fury, he sprang suddenly to his feet, and, clutching wildly at his foe, endeavoured to hurl him to the ground.

Duval, however, was dealing with no ordinary antagonist.

The man, tall and of stalwart proportions, was as a giant to the slim, slender, graceful form of the Frenchman.

The highwayman, exerting all his strength, which was far greater than would have been supposed, was yet no match for his brawny adversary.

Wildly the two struggled round the chamber, Duval growing furious as he found his energies failing him.

"It ain't no use, my beauty; it would take a dozen such as you, Claude Duval, to lick Blue Peters, the runner. Anstey told me he'd land five guineas to the one as copped yer; and I am the one as intends to have the sugar (money)."

"Diantre, bleu! you havn't earned it yet, Blue Peters," gasped Claude, who here, by a twist of his foot as he caught it in the outstretched leg of his herculean foe, sent him with a thundering crash with his head on the edge of the large solid mass of stone that ran about half a foot high round the fireplace.

"So, not this time, my friend; you'll have a headache the rest of the day, I'm afraid," said our hero, as he observed a thin stream of blood trickling from the temple of his enemy, who, now stunned and helpless, lay prostrate upon the floor.

Darting to the door, as he heard voices without, Claude was now met by two new comers, the foremost his enemy Jonathan Anstey, his face livid with fury, with an oath firing a pistol at the bold highwayman.

There was a bright flash, and a sharp ping, close to Duval's ear, as with a bound he dashed out of the room, hurling his enemies to the ground.

Met in the passage without by three or four fresh arrivals, escape seemed hopeless!

Glaring wildly round Claude now bounded up a flight of stairs before him.

There was a yell of voices and stamping of feet as his enemies rushed after in pursuit.

"We've got him!"

"It's all right, Anstey!"

"He can't escape!"

"He's mauled Blue Peters: let him have it!"

"After him!"

"Ten guineas to the one who secures him," yelled the infuriate Anstey, his voice ringing high above the cries of his men, who, shouting and yelling as they rushed up the stairs after their flying victim, were close upon his heels.

"Breathless and panting with the effects of his recent struggle, Claude, inwardly cursing his forbearance in not planting a bullet in the head of his relentless enemy when he had him in his power, now gaining a short dark narrow passage at the top of the staircase darted down it.

A door at the end partly open was his only refuge.

His yelling pursuers, only some few yards behind, making sure of his capture, gave a wild shout of triumph.

"Morbleu, you dogs! I'm not run to earth yet," muttered Claude savagely, as he dashed through the half-open door and banged it to after him.

Lock there was none.

A slender bolt, the only fastening, was shot to as the yelling runners dashed up.

Well Claude knew the bolt would not long keep his foes at bay.

The door shook and creaked as the enemy threw themselves against it.

Glancing round the chamber in which he now found himself Duval discovered that it was one used as an old lumber or store-room.

Broken tables, chairs, old benches, and other articles were jumbled together in wild confusion.

To drag a huge solid oaken bench to the door was but the work of a minute.

Not too soon was the barricade dragged to its place; for even as Claude drew back and darted to a narrow little casement at the further end of the room, the bolt that held the door fast gave way.

There was a yell of triumph, which had scarce died away ere it was echoed by one of pain, as a foremost runner, about to scramble over the door, now lying on its hinges, was stretched bleeding on the floor by a bullet from the pistol of Duval, who sinking down amid a mass of old furniture was enabled to fire at his enemies, himself unseen.

Another shot, and a cry of rage and pain from a man who staggered with his left arm swinging useless by his side, warned the eager crowd back.

For a time there was a cessation of hostilities.

The enraged runners drew back to the further end of the passage.

Duval coolly, and with the utmost deliberation, reloaded his firearms.

Peering through the chinks of the mass of tables, chairs, and piled-up lumber near the casement, and behind which he had sunk, he beheld Jonathan Anstey at the end of the passage, now joined by the fellow called Blue Peters.

It was not with surprise that a moment after Claude heard a simultaneous discharge of pistols.

Crashing among the lumber one bullet, unpleasantly close, raised the skin off his wrist, whilst others pattered on the walls and passed out at the casement.

"Good, all their firearms are empty; now's my time," muttered Claude, who, rising up, and with his own pistols in both hands, boldly darted to the door.

There was a volley of oaths and cries of alarm.

The two wounded officers, with a yell, started back in such precipitation that they sent their companions who were behind tumbling head over heels down the stairs upon the verge of which they had stood.

Duval, with a laugh and shout of defiance now exerting all his strength, seized hold of a massive oaken chair the back of which was broken, and hurled it with a crash into the passage without.

A cloud of dust as the decayed wood splintered to pieces, and a yell of pain, told that the novel shot had taken effect.

"Rush in upon him! Are you all afraid of one man!" yelled the officer Anstey, who, with Blue Peters, was the only one to be seen.

"Well, if they are afraid, you are not! Come on," said Duval, with a sneering laugh which burst into a roar, as, firing one of his pistols, the two who had remained in sight now disappeared down the stairs.

"I must follow this stampede up, and effect an escape on to the roof in the confusion," muttered our hero, who now seized upon several articles of lumber and hurled them into the passage without.

Crashing down the staircase, with a grin Claude heard oaths and cries of rage as the broken boxes and other missiles disappeared.

Aware that his enemies would presently return in force with loaded firearms, Duval, seizing a small broken table upon which was a large glass lamp, broken wine-glasses, and tumblers, with some old-fashioned vases, boldly lifted it up and stepping on the bench by the door hurled the lot into the passage.

Roaring with laughter at the infernal din which followed; a din above which could be heard loud oaths; he now darted to the little casement, forcing it open and boldly scrambling through, he then found himself upon a narrow coping of stone that ran round the roof of the old inn.

"Safe, so far! But a fall from this height to the ground below would not be conducive to health! By heavens, Humpy Bill, takes in my position at a glance! Ma foi! He sees me! The ladder at the end of the yard he now secures will reach the roof; and I shall be able to give the runners the go-by! Ventre bleu! Jonathan Anstey will not have me in Newgate this time."

Peering down into the yard at the back of the house, Claude now beheld the faithful servant of Joe Jennings, running along with a ladder, which he, perceiving our hero when he scrambled through the casement a moment before, had motioned he would place against the wall to aid his escape.

Intently watching the movements of Humpy Bill, Duval had forgotten his foes.

Leaning half-over the parapet he was now nearly hurled from the dangerous height as a heavy grasp was laid upon his collar.

Large bony fingers fastened with ferocious grip round his neck.

A choking, stifling sensation seized upon him as the grip grew stronger, fiercer.

Wildly Duval turned upon his assailant:

The runner, Blue Peters.

Creeping quietly through the casement, he had seized upon his victim unawares.

His eyes like pieces of polished steel glared into the face of our hero.

"You were one too many for me by your trick in the

The Dance with Claude Duval

COLONEL BLOOD, SWORD IN HAND, DREW BACK.

house! But I think I can repay the compliment now we are on the roof of it," exclaimed the runner in a voice hoarse with rage.

Vouchsafing no reply, Duval husbanded his strength.

The least mistake and he was lost.

It was a terrible scene!

On the verge of the roof the two men gripped each other with the firm grip of hate.

Three or four faces, blanched with fear, peered out of the adjacent casement.

When first sighting Humpy Bill, the stableman, Claude had drawn away some two yards from the casement.

Thither had he been followed by the runner, Blue Peters.

Clutching each other by the collar the two now rested half over the coping of the roof, their feet in the gutter that

received the drainage, about two feet of brick work alone saving both from crashing below.

" Will you come quietly? I've sworn to take yer, Duval, give in."

" Never !"

" Then I must make yer."

" You'll want to cut you eye-teeth first."

" Shall I ?"

" Yes; over this parapet we'll go together, Blue Peters; the sun up there is the last we shall see unless you let go your hold."

" Ha, ha, ha !"

" Will you release me !"

" Will you follow me quietly through the casement if I do !"

"No !"

Loud, clear, and defiant rang the voice of Duval.

With a giddy stare, his face flushed, first with passion, then with a pallor of fear as he gazed into the depths below, the runner held on with tenacious grip to Claude's collar.

Duval, his arms now entwined round his adversary's waist, refused to let go, and thus holding together and with eyes of hate and rage, the two stood upon the roof of the old inn.

Two or three officers remained by the casement, rooted to the spot in a fascination of horror.

Even the ruffian officer, Jonathan Anstey, gazed spell-bound and speechless at the grim foes.

For a moment of time the two men, with their lives upon a thread, remained motionless, inactive.

Duval, the first to commence hostilities, now suddenly shifted his grasp, and threw both his hands round his enemy's neck, and drawing himself up, to the horror of all, let himself fall over the parapet.

With a death grip he held on to the neck of his enemy.

But even in that moment of deadly peril, Claude, who had staked his life upon a chance, felt a something catching against his feet.

Dangling over the coping, his finger with deadly grip twined in the neckerchief of the runner, Duval was aware that, if he let his foe loose and caught at the coping, his feet would rest below upon the uppermost rounds of a ladder.

Unknowing this, his eyes bloodshot and starting from his head, whilst his face became purple and dark from the deadly grip around his neck, the man Blue Peters began to sicken with horror.

"Let go your hold !"

In choking, gasping accents the words issued from the mouth of the runner.

With eyes of grim defiance Claude hung on.

"Do you fear death ? Sacre ! 'tis only a fall—a smash, and all will be over ! Lean over, man ! Quo, cela senisse ! We shall be locked in a deathly embrace when they pick us up."

"Let go your hold, Duval ! God of heaven, I cannot die !" gasped the runner, as, not daring to move, he grasped at the coping, having taken his hands off the throat of his enemy.

Duval now, his feet resting on the ladder, a human hand upon his ancles, having a moment before placed them there, suddenly let go his hold of the man Peters's neck, and shifting it to the coping, gave a warning cry, and letting go placed his hands against the walls of the house as he round by round descended the ladder which rested its topmost step about two feet from the roof.

Below, with a grim smile upon his face, was Humpy Bill, who shortened his progress to the ground by placing his legs round the ladder and sliding down.

Duval, looking up as he descended, observed the senseless figure of Blue Peters dragged through the casement by his companions !

He had fallen back senseless, when released by Claude in the excitement of the moment, at his escape.

The safety of our hero was scarce noted by the runners until he stood in the yard below, when, discerned by Jonathan, a howl of fury escaped the officer's lips.

With a loud, defying shout, Claude, following Humpy Bill, presently gained the kitchen garden, from thence issuing through a gateway into a narrow lane he found Gentleman Jack with his bonny mare awaiting him.

"Into the saddle with you, Claude ; they'll be after you presently like bloodhounds ! Let our meeting-place be the old Tree Cave, or The Devil's Punch Bowl at Westminster !"

"All right, dear pal ! we shall meet within the hour."

"Aye ! I but wait here to see the fun out, and then will hasten to the Cave."

"Good ! Au revoir ! Ta ta ! Bill ; tell Joe I'll run down here in a day or two !" exclaimed Claude, who now, once more in the saddle, shouted with wild glee, as, giving his mare the rein, he darted at lightning speed along the high road.

CHAPTER II.

THE DISCOVERY IN THE BARN—A TALE OF SORROW—MEETING WITH COLONEL BLOOD—THE DUEL—THE HUT IN THE WOOD—A TERRIBLE MYSTERY.

In highest excitement at his escape, a shout of wild triumph ever and again burst from the lips of Claude as he sped on.

The inn left far behind, for a time he was safe from pursuit ; well he knew that his friends would delay the departure of his foes.

Bright and beautiful shone the sun that early morning ; the breeze, laden with the perfume of the hawthorn and honeysuckle, that in wildest luxuriance grew by the wayside, invigorated both horse and rider.

Claude, his handsome face flushed with joy and exercise, his rich curling hair flowing over his shoulders, and his symmetrical form with ease and grace poised in the saddle, looked indeed the beau-ideal of manly strength and beauty.

Strange and sad that a wayward fate should have led one gifted with such gentlemanly exterior, and who, with a free and easy disposition, combined a kindness of heart with boldness and daring that might have become the most courageous warrior in the battle-field, to become an outcast to society, and banned by its laws, ever with the fearful prospect of the prison and the scaffold looming terribly in the future !

Despite the danger of his adventurous calling, Claude Duval, however, was light of heart, careless, and free.

Singing snatches of song, and caressing his brave steed, on, on flew the highwayman, his breast devoid of care and forgetful of the fearful perils of the past night.

Emerging from a long lane that, with a thickly-wooded copse on either side, had presented many glimpses of wild scenery to the rider's eyes, Claude now came again upon the high road.

Slackening his speed, he now rode slowly along, and presently paused as he neared a large barn.

Some half-mile ahead, a low range of buildings, with a white stuccoed front, met the eye. This place Claude rightly conjectured was a farmhouse.

"Here's a pretty rural spot. Egad ! I'll e'en visit the farm ; 'tis not likely that my clever and kindly friend Jonathan Anstey will happen on me there. Any way, rest and refreshment I want, and rest and refreshment I'll have."

About again to urge on his steed, Claude was startled by a low moaning sob !

A cry as of some female in terror and distress !

The sound coming from the barn, Duval, unhesitatingly leaping from his saddle, drew his bonny mare on to the rich velvety turf that lined the roadside, and at once made for the lone building.

The sun shining brightly threw a ruddy, golden tint upon the old barn, up the sides of which clustered thickly the wild honeysuckle and clematis.

Passing through a gate, which, half off its hinges, allowed easy ingress, Duval now made for the entrance to the barn.

Again came the low sob of sorrow, plainer and more heartrending in its sound.

In wonder and amazement, Claude, about to enter the barn, now started back :

Started back, as a female figure, ghostlike, glided out and stood before him !

Very beautiful was the young girl who, with eyes yet dimmed with tears, with a startled cry of terror, drew back, staring wildly at our hero.

"Be not alarmed, dear girl ! I would befriend, not distress, you."

In mute admiration, Claude now fastened his eyes on the beautiful form before him.

Very lovely was the young girl ; a true type of our English maiden.

Scarce seventeen, her figure was firmly and fully developed, a tight-fitting bodice of muslin showing off to advantage the rounded bust, whilst the arms, bare, were of loveliest symmetry and contour ; a rich olive-tinted complexion was enriched by the combined hues of the blush rose ; the lips, somewhat too full and red, when opened, disclosed a set of pearly teeth, even and without a blemish ; brown hair in richest luxuriance fell upon the dimpled shoulders, which, the bodice of the dress cut low, were left fully revealed. Of middling height, the young girl's frame was supple, and cast in graceful contour.

His long and fixed gaze Claude now noted caused a crimson glow to replace the pallor of a moment before ; then, about apparently to return to the shelter of the barn, a wild, hunted, startled look gathered in the beauteous eyes ; whilst with the soft dimpled hands clasped in despair the poor girl moaned the words, "They come! they come! Heaven aid me!"

"Whom, what do you fear, dear lady? Pray, be not so alarmed. Sacre! the man had best beware who attempts to lay hand upon you against your wish whilst I am here." In pity and admiration Claude gazed upon the affrighted girl, who with eyes blinded with tears exclaimed—

"Oh, kind sir, you know not my foes! Nor dare I hope your proffered aid would avail to save me from those who pursue me with their odious attentions. In the charge of a cruel stepfather, I am ordered to wed with a man whose very presence is distasteful to me. Fleeing an hour back from the farm, I wandered hither. He whom I fear and loathe, with his friend, even now approaches to compel my return; for this very day am I to become the bride of Miles Ellerton. Death itself were preferable, for mother, father, both dead, I've no hope, no friend!"

"Nay, say not so! I, though a stranger, would be your friend; allow me to offer my protection! If you fear, dear girl, to return to yonder farm I will gladly take you whither you will; in all honour will convey you to some place of safety." Claude here lifting his hat drew near to the distressed maiden, whose cheeks turned of a deadly pallor as two strangers now appeared in the distance.

Both on foot, the new arrivals hurried along the road towards the farm.

"Have no fear; I will protect you, young lady, from insult with my life."

Conducting the trembling and terror-stricken girl through the gate, Claude now paused by the side of his horse!

Paused, with kindling cheek and knitted brows, as the two strangers, with loud and angry cries, dashed up.

"How now, Maude Mayburn? what means this? who is this fellow?" The youngest of the arrivals, a tall, dark-complexioned man, with not unhandsome features, but of sullen and disagreeable cast of countenance, here drew near as though about to lay hands upon the shrinking girl, who now cowered by Claude's side as if for protection.

"Stand back, sir, or the fellow's rapier may find a passage through your ribs."

Duval with heightened colour here drew his sword from its scabbard, flashing the trusty steel in the eyes of the stranger.

"Blood, do you hear that?"

"S'death, yes; the gallant wants a lesson, and, egad! Colonel Blood is the boy to give it him."

The eldest of the two strangers—a stalwart, burly, herculean, coarse-featured man, with a very rubicund visage, large grey eyes, a low receding forehead, and heavy bushy brows, his thick sensual-looking lips nearly covered by a huge moustache—here with a laugh strode up to Duval, and plucking his sword from its sheath threw his burly form into fighting attitude.

"Yes; I perceive you understand the use of the rapier, Colonel Blood. I can tell that from your guard. But don't you think it will be out of place to show off your abilities in that line before a lady?"

"A coward, Miles! Do you seize the dainty Maude; I'll chastise the impertinent interference of this idiot."

"Stand back! or I'll put a bullet in your skull!" Claude here to the astonishment of the strangers pulled his pistols from his vest; then replacing them as the young girl, her face colourless, threw herself on her knees beside the horse, he exclaimed—

"Look you! Miles Ellerton, and you, too, Colonel Blood! the young lady whom you would take away with you is for a time under my protection. Attempt to lay a finger upon her, and your blood be upon your own head!"

"Pshaw! upon him, Blood! Pink him! Let out some of the puddle that runs in his veins."

"Since you will have it, bully Blood! Sacre, be it so! En garde!" Claude here, as a scream issued from the mouth of the affrighted girl, crossed his sword with that of the herculean stranger.

With folded arms the man Miles stood glaring at the scene that now took place.

Duval, after the first pass, found that his burly adversary was no mean combatant.

As if to measure his distance, Colonel Blood made two or three slight passes over his guard, and then, grating his blade against Duval's with that peculiar motion that makes attack, he fixed his eyes on our hero's, in an endeavour to draw off his attention from an intended thrust.

With wary eye Claude watched his enemy.

The quickness and facility with which his weapon changed from side to side, the easy motion of his wrist, and the skilful firmness of his arm, all showed to Claude, himself no mean swordsman, that he had now met his match.

Claude soon saw that his adversary's forte lay in the long-meditated attack, where each movement was part of an artfully-devised series, Blood allowing him trifling advantages by way of giving him a false confidence. Claude's strength was in the skirmishing passages, where most men lunge at random. Here, however, no matter how confused the rally, our hero was as cool as in the salute.

For some time Claude permitted his adversary to play his game out; nor could anything be more beautiful than the passes he made over the hilt. Twice the man Blood planted his point within an inch of his bosom, and nothing but a spring back could have saved him.

The terrified Maude Mayburn, with wild staring eyes, and lips moving tremulously in prayer, remained kneeling by the horse within a few yards of the swordsmen.

The young man, while forgetful of all else around, with flushed face and exultant smile watched the clever swordsmanship of his friend.

"Pink him! Kill—kill him, Blood!"

An exclamation of fury now escaped his lips, as Claude, making a feint within and then without the guard, touched his friend's sword-arm above the wrist.

"A touch, Miles—nothing more!" muttered Blood, the while a crimson stream trickled down his arm and oozed between his fingers.

"S'death, you fence well, sir!" Then as Claude, lunging in and twisting his sword dexterously from his grasp, sent it flying in the air, a fierce oath escaped the lips of Blood, who, biting his lips till they ran with a thin red stream, drew back, acknowledging a defeat.

"But he is not to carry it thus! Upon him! Let him not escape! I command you, Blood, to secure that mad girl, and convey her to the farm."

A fierce, dark look here gathered upon the face of the man, Miles Ellerton, as he glanced at his companion, who in sullen silence snatched up his sword where it had fallen, and rushed once more upon Claude.

"Stand back, man! I'm not to be trifled with. I've defeated you fairly; and if, goaded on by your dark-visaged friend there, you dare to interfere with me and this lady here, by the bright sun that rides in the heavens above us I'll plant a bullet in your skulls!"

Claude here, his back to his brave steed, presented his pistols at the heads of the companions as they dashed forwards.

"Upon him! seize him, Blood!"

"If Blood or yourself don't quit this spot in another minute, I'll fire, so help me Heaven!"

A glittering light in Duval's eyes, a hectic spot upon either cheek, intimated he would carry out his threat. With deep-breathed curses his assailants drew back.

Claude now, in a whisper, bade the young girl mount his horse; then, perceiving she was sinking with terror, he lifted her in his arms, placed her supple form in the saddle, and at one bound seated himself behind her.

A wild yell of fury escaped the lips of the man Miles Ellerton.

A yell that was answered by our hero with a shout of laughter.

"Au revoir, Miles Ellerton! Allons! I must away. Parbleu, Colonel Blood! don't look so glum; we shall meet again, man; and whenever that may be, ventre bleu! we will e'en play again a game of carte and tierce. You handle your rapier very prettily; but are too excited in the rally. Take my advice, colonel, when you are fighting, always keep your temper."

"One word ere you go. S'blood! stop my vitals! you are the only one that has yet beaten the sword out of my hand, and pinked me fair and clean. Let me know to whom I owe myself indebted."

"You would know my name! I can't oblige you at present, colonel; but when next we meet, I may perhaps be in a position to satisfy your curiosity. For the nonce know me as Captain Hawk! If you wish to repeat the little exercise of this morning, a line at any time will find me at The Devil's Punch Bowl."

"The Devil's Punch Bowl, in Westminster!"

"The same!"

"S'death! I know the house and its landlord, Jem Noggins."

"Very good! Then when you want to meet Captain Hawk a message with Jem will affect your object."

Claude, amused at the earnest manner of his late antagonist, with a smile, lifting his cap gaily from his brow, gave his steed the rein; the brave animal, with its double burthen, flying at a clashing pace along the road.

With his arm clasped about the waist of his lovely charge, Claude could not repress a thrill of pleasure darting through his frame; then, as he gazed upon the beauteous face now wearing the livid pallor of death, a cry of alarm escaped him.

No reply was there to his startled ejaculation:

No answering voice to his.

Like a corpse the beautiful girl reclined in his arms.

The lips, pale and colourless, the face of an ashy pallor, whilst the beautiful eyes were closed as if in death.

Wildly Claude pressed the lovely stranger to his breast.

In the frenzy of the moment he placed his lips to hers; then, as he thought of the helpless position of the unhappy girl, with a flushed brow he drew back, and, glancing round, hoped to detect some house where he might procure aid for his senseless burthen; for, with a feeling of intense joy, he now made the discovery that the lovely Maude was but in a faint.

No habitation, however, met his earnest gaze.

All was open country.

A narrow winding road, lined with a thick copse or wood on either side.

Touching his brave mare in the flank with his heel, the sagacious brute bounded on at frantic speed.

Like a corpse Maude Mayburn remained senseless in the arms of her protector.

An ejaculation of alarm from Claude's lips now changed to a cry of joy as he perceived an opening from the high road leading into the woods was worn with the track of wheels and hoofs, whilst some quarter of a mile beyond in the copse he detected a thin bluish haze hovering over the trees.

Turning his horse's head Claude now diverged from the road and cantered into the pathway through the woods.

A strong smell of burning now led him to proceed at greater speed.

With a hope of finding some lodge pertaining to some adjacent estate, he hurried on—

Stronger each moment was the smell of burning wood.

With anxious eyes, Claude glanced around.

As yet no habitation was in sight.

No sign from whence the fire proceeded; then, as he was about to halt, a loud hallo echoed through the woods; and down a narrow turning in the copse, shaded by an avenue of trees, he now discerned a rude hut.

To dash down this open space occupied but a few minutes.

Drawing up as the vegetation grew too thick for further progress, Claude slid from his horse, and, with his still senseless charge in his arms, hurried towards the lone hut.

A few yards only intervened from where he had left his steed to the door of the humble dwelling.

Placing the unfortunate Maude Mayburn upon the greensward, Claude now hammered loudly at the door of the hut.

No reply was there to his rude summons.

Save the chirruping of the feathered songsters, and the buzz of the winged insects that in swarms hovered around, all was quiet.

"Devilish strange! But, sacre, this won't do! I must gain an entry! The cool shade of this hut and a draught of water may restore her who, left longer now, may perish."

With a glance full of alarm at the pallid face of Maude, Claude, now darting back, threw himself with all his force against the frail door, which with a crash gave way.

In another moment he was in the hut.

As he expected, it was tenantless.

With a cry of joy, perceiving an earthenware jug upon a little shelf, he hastened forward and secured it.

As he had hoped, it was half-full of water.

Water, bright, cool, and limpid, drawn from a neighbouring well.

Rushing from the hut he, now lifting the hapless Maude in his arms, brought her in out of the burning rays of the sun.

Bathing the brow of the senseless girl with the grateful fluid, Claude presently beheld the lovely blue eyes once more open, whilst a tinge of colour returned to the pallid features.

"Where, where am I?"

With a friend, Miss Mayburn— one who will serve you to the uttermost of his power!"

"Oh! I remember now! You are he who risked his life to rescue me from Miles Ellerton! To-day was to have been my marriage day, but better the bride of death than of the wicked Miles."

A strong shudder here shook the young girl's frame, whilst, perceiving the ardent eyes of Claude fixed upon her, a crimson flush dyed neck, brow, and bosom.

"When, and how did we get here?" at length she exclaimed, casting down her eyes and hiding her flushed face.

"I came hither to seek aid! You fainted whilst in my arms upon horseback; I was alarmed and sought out this refuge! Thank heaven you are now restored once more to life! We will leave at once if you wish, though I would advise a little rest ere our departure."

"How can I ever repay your generous aid! I cannot find words to express my grateful thanks, and dare not trespass upon you further. I will but ask you to put me on the London road, or tell me where I may procure a conveyance thither. I have a person in town who will give me shelter till such time as I determine on my future course," exclaimed the blushing girl, as she rising placed her hands imploringly in those of her preserver.

"If you will yet further place yourself under my guidance, Miss Mayburn, I will this very day convey you to London. My horse can as before carry double. 'Twill be but till we reach the village of Highgate; at that place I can procure you a steed."

"As you like. Yet I am ashamed at giving to you, a stranger, such great trouble."

"Name it not. Call not that a trouble which, believe me, I esteem a pleasure; and now, pardon me, may I ask whither you propose to go on reaching London?"

"To a faithful old servant, who left the Home Farm, as my late old habitation is called, upon my poor mother's wedding with Percy Dalton, five years back.

A sob and heavy sigh here broke from the poor girl's bosom.

Claude, pressing her warm, soft hands in his, endeavoured to console the sorrying girl; then fancying that it would be more agreeable to her if he at once pushed on and hastened their departure, he now, telling her he would return in a moment, hurried from the hut—his quick ears had caught the sound of a footstep without; and not knowing who might have tracked him to the place, he was desirous to reconnoitre.

All was quiet, however, without.

No human being in sight.

Glancing down the avenue of trees, Claude now looked for his mare.

With a nervous thrill he could not repress, he found she was gone.

Darting in mad haste down the pathway, he gained the spot where he had left his bonny steed half an hour before.

But in vain he searched around.

The horse had gone.

No sign was there of the animal's presence.

Wildly Claude ran hither and thither, the perspiration of alarm and fatigue trickling down his brow.

His horse had strangely disappeared.

But where? How?

Well Claude knew the faithful brute had not of its own accord left the spot.

Some strange hand had led it away.

Who, then, was it?

For what purpose had the dumb brute been removed!

There was only one solution to the query:

To prevent his flight:

To prevent his further progress.

Who, then, was the next question Claude inwardly put to himself, had decoyed away his steed?

Maude Mayburn's enemies or his own?

Had the runners tracked him to the woods?

Or had Miles Ellerton and his associate, Colonel Blood, searched him out?

As Claude stood by the tree where he had left his horse, ruminating on the danger that now threatened him, he was startled by a loud scream:

A scream that woke up echoes in the wood, and caused his blood to rush like ice through his veins!

With a bound he rushed down the avenue.

In a moment he once more gained the lone hut.

All was still, not a sound was to be heard.

"Maude! Maude! Miss Mayburn! where are you! Tonnerre de Dieu! gone! gone! Mort de diable! but I'll have a bitter reckoning for this!"

Wildly Claude searched the hut.

With clenched hands, and the veins upon his forehead standing out like whipcords from the excess of passion, he glared around.

Like his faithful steed the unhappy and persecuted girl, Maude Mayburn, had strangely, mysteriously, disappeared.

Striking his brow with his fist, Duval gave way to a storm of passion, a torrent of oaths issuing from his lips; then in a few minutes growing calmer, he drew his pistols from his belt, carefully loaded them, and then, drawing his sword, was about to leave the hut, when a something caught his eye that caused him to stay his steps.

With a thrill Claude started forward.

Upon the floor close by a door leading to a small inner compartment of the hut was a glittering trinket:

A small brooch set with diamonds, the gems sparkling and glistening in the sun's rays.

With shaking hands Duval held the brooch up to the light.

He had, in a moment of time, recognised it as one belonging to the unhappy Maude.

When clasping her in his embrace he had noted the valuable.

A grey livid pallor stole over his face as he now found his fingers that held the trinket were smirched and smeared with a dark red stain!

Splotches of blood!

The under part of solid gold, in which the diamonds were set, was clotted with blood.

Bending down, Claude now made the discovery that he was standing in a small puddle of the same terrible fluid.

Gasping with terror, sick, faint, and giddy, he glared at the flooring, which, at this part, was covered with blood!

Blood that was trickling from under the door opposite to which he stood!

A small door that apparently opened on a little chamber, or closet, belonging to the hut.

Wild with rage, and shivering as he thought of how he had left the lovely girl, Maude, full of life and health a quarter of an hour before, Claude now placed his hand upon the handle of the door.

As he suspected, it was fast locked.

With knitted brow, and trembling with passion as he thought of how he had been tricked, and how perchance the young girl in whom he felt a greater interest than ever female had before excited in his bosom may have been basely murdered, Claude stood for a moment irresolute, and then with one kick sent the frail door flying from its hinges.

No cry of alarm, no sound, save the crashing of the splintered wood, fell upon his ear.

The door falling aside revealed a dark closet or chamber about half the size of the one he was then in.

This inner compartment of the hut was almost in darkness; a thin ray of light, from a crevice in the wall, the only gleam of the outer air that could gain admittance.

With a shiver, Claude peered into the room.

There was a strange kind of smell, an unearthly odour in the place!

The strange horrible odour of a charnel house!

Sword in hand, and ready for any surprise, Claude now stepped into the darksome chamber.

It was a strange, wild scene.

The broad light of day streamed into the hut, the birds carolling merrily without, and all so dark, drear, and terrible in that little chamber.

Boldly Claude passed over the broken door:

Passed with beating heart into the inner room.

His eyes now gradually got accustomed to the dim light.

Searchingly he cast his eyes around.

Near the door he had shattered from its hinges, was a richly laced velvet coat and satin vest, both lying on the floor.

About to pick them up, Claude started back with an exclamation of disgust.

The garments were reeking with moisture:

Were saturated, dripping with blood!

"Great heavens, what foul den of crime is this a cursed fate has led me to! Dear Maude, Heaven shield and guard her! 'twas her shriek of course that rang upon my ear a short time back! But now that those hideous garments have met my eye, I yet have hope that she still lives. The brooch I have secured may have dropped when she was seized hold of by the murderers who inhabit this den. Yes, yes! it must be so! They have taken her hence, fearing the foul evidence of this crime might meet her eye. If they cross my path, sacre! Heaven have mercy on them, for I will none!"

Standing inactive for some little time, Claude, his eyes growing accustomed to the semi-darkness of the place, now peered eagerly round in search of any further clue that might guide him in his pursuit of the unhappy Maude's abductors. Nothing of moment, however, met his eyes, until at length, about to make his way once more to the outer chamber, he was startled by catching sight of a human hand!

A human hand, white and ghastly, and clotted with blood!

A human hand in horrible mockery sticking up out of the floor as though beckoning him to follow!

Like one in a dream, Claude Duval, bold, daring, and defiant as he was, stood rooted to the spot, with distended eyes glaring at the hideous sight.

Was he mad, or dreaming!

The hurried events of the past few hours dazed and bewildered him.

His narrow escape from The Ostler's Rest, the meeting and duel with the man Colonel Blood, his flight with the beautiful Maude Mayburn, and the young girl's mystic disappearance, with the grim horrors of this lone hut in the wood, confused and confounded him.

With staring eyes Claude for some few minutes stood glaring at the ghastly hand; then, at length, breaking the spell of horror that had chained him statue-like to the spot, he with an oath strode forwards:

Strode forwards to where the blood-stained hand appeared to beckon him away!

Not without a strong shudder and a feeling as though all the blood in his veins was turning to ice did Claude stoop down and seize the grim hand in his.

It was cold, damp, and clammy!

The cold, clammy, horrible chill of death!

The terrible evidence of foul murder Claude now discovered was fixed in the floor!

Fixed fast and firm.

Stooping down to unravel the dread mystery, he found that a small trap in the flooring was partially open.

Between the insterstices it was that the horrible hand was thrust.

Boldly Claude now seized in his grasp the edge of the trap.

It moved readily to his touch.

In another moment it was raised, and like a flash the horrible blood-stained hand disappeared:

Disappeared in the grim darkness below; a low dull thud falling upon the ears of the highwayman as he bent down and peered into the inky gloom at his feet.

Fascinated with horror Claude stood beside the open trap, and then upon a sudden impulse stooped; and, moving his fingers round the edge, as he expected, discovered the topmost round of a ladder.

Unhesitatingly descending he found himself in a kind of cellar.

All was inky darkness.

But not the black horrible gloom of the cellar was it that caused him to turn sick and dizzy.

The air was foul and fœtid;

Horrible and charnel like;

Thick and heavy with the odour of death.

In nervous haste he now with the implements he carried for his pipe struck a light.

Anon a dull faint yellow glimmer shone through the cellar.

Sick with dread he peered round.

The horrible fancy had seized him that perchance he might discover the mangled form of the poor girl in whom he now took deepest interest.

With a sigh of relief, however, he discovered only the half-naked figure of a cavalier lying soaked in a pool of blood at the foot of the ladder.

Grim, horrible, looked the corpse with its wide staring eyes —a round hole in the very centre of the forehead, from which a stream of blood still oozed, showing where the fatal bullet had traversed in its errand of death.

Casting his eyes around, and discerning nought else in the cell save the dread corpse, the victim of foul murder, Claude was about to ascend the ladder when he was startled by the sound of voices without:

The voices of several men in loud converse in the front chamber of the hut.

With the speed of thought he darted up the steps.

Too late, however.

Through the semi-darkness at the entrance of the inner chamber he beheld with dismay four or five men.

Gliding down the ladder Claude now with beating heart stood sword in hand in the horrible cellar there beside the bleeding corpse of the murdered one.

To emerge from the trap in face of the strangers he knew would be madness.

In the funereal darkness of his retreat he might escape and perchance glean tidings of her he sought and the nature of the enemy he had to contend with: in this conjecture he was not mistaken.

Breathless at the foot of the steps he listened eagerly for any sounds from above.

The tramp of feet overhead now informed him that the strangers had entered the inner chamber.

With an involuntary thrill and grasping his sword yet tighter Claude now discerned the outline of a human figure:

A figure of a man bending over the edge of the open trap.

"Well, do you think the dead Aubrey Singleton will jump up, Miles Ellerton, and demand justice on his murderer?"

"I murdered him not, Ralph Adams: he died in fair duel."

"Indeed! I think you'd find a difficulty in proving it. However we won't dispute the matter: you've paid me well for aiding you in your trouble. Let not shut down that trap, and for the folly of leaving it open I will punish severely master Andrew Masterton, when I meet him at the Grange. Giles, Humphreys, and you Gregory, see to the burial of the dead cavalier! He won't find himself alone; for in that cellar lie two of our own pals and Josh Miller, the gamekeeper, who lagged me five years back for snaring a hare."

With a volley of oaths the speaker here with his foot thrust back the trap, leaving Claude, now in utter darkness, spellbound with awe and amaze.

The figure that had loomed before him a few minutes before was, then, the villain Miles Ellerton!

Accompanied by the owners of the hut he had doubtless secured the unhappy Maude.

"By heaven, I see it all! I was tracked to the woods, my horse informed them of my proximity, and securing my bonny mare they hastened hither by another path than the avenue of trees, in my absence seizing upon the poor girl. Well, if I'm not even with you for this, Miles Ellerton, sacre, may I never more do a bold canter o'er Hounslow Heath! Parbleu, I like not my company here; but, methinks, I am safer here than with those pretty members above," muttered Claude to himself as he now with utmost caution drew himself up the ladder, the voices of the strangers falling with a dull hum upon his ears.

With his head almost touching the trap, Claude strained his ears to catch the purport of the murmured converse above, but in vain.

A confused buzzing of voices alone reached him.

Congregated in the front chamber of the hut, the hum of converse sounded but faint and indistinct.

With an ejaculation of annoyance, Claude once more descended the ladder.

At any moment his foes might return and re-open the trap.

Regaining his wonted courage, though sick and faint from the bad air he was forced to breathe, Claude now saw to the priming of his pistols, then, girding his waistbelt more firmly, awaited the departure of his enemies.

At length the humming buzz of voices ceased.

Once more he ascended the steps.

Placing his ears against the trap, with beating heart he listened for any sound from without.

All was now quiet.

Not a sound could be heard.

The villanous troop had departed.

Slowly, cautiously, Claude lifted the trap.

A thin ray of light flashed in his eyes.

A cool draught of fresh air wafted in his face:

Cool, refreshing, and sweet after the charnel vapour of the terrible cellar.

Higher, still higher, he raised the trap.

All remained quiet.

Save the carolling of birds in the wood without the hut, all was still.

With a pistol ready cocked in each hand, Claude now drew himself slowly, cautiously, through the opening in the floor.

A warm glow diffused itself through his veins as he now once more stood erect in the inner chamber of the rude abode.

Free, safe out of the dread charnel vault below.

"So far so good! but confound the luck that prevented me gleaning tidings of my bonny steed and the pretty Maude; and, ma foi, I give not up the chase till I have discovered both!"

Boldly stepping forwards, Claude now made for the outer chamber.

Gaining the door, which, half off its hinges, he had burst an hour before, he now passed its threshold, and in a moment, ere he could raise hand to fire one of his pistols, found himself confronted by a tall, dark-visaged man, who, of herculean build and proportions, gave evidence of possessing immense strength.

"Trapped! Ha, ha, ha! Giles! Gregory! What, ho! The bird is here!"

With a horrible oath, the stranger, dashing upon Duval, hurled him with a crash to the ground; the while two fresh arrivals darkened the outer door or entrance to the hut.

Wildly Claude wrestled with his burly antagonist, his lithe frame twisting like an eel from his fierce grip.

Gaining a temporary advantage, he now buried his knuckles in the neckerchief of his adversary, who under his slim and agile figure, writhed and blasphemed with fearful fury.

Despite his superior strength, Claude promised to become the victor. Tugging now with savage force at the ruffian's collar, his face purpled and lips grew blue and swollen—then, as with a grim smile he snatched a pistol from the villain's belt, intending to slay him with his own weapon, a stunning blow at the back of the head caused a thousand lights to flash in his eyes; whilst, with a low moan, he slipped off the panting form of the man, he, in another moment, would have hurled into eternity.

With a dazed, sickening feeling, Claude sank back.

Three or four dark figures appeared whirling round him.

Then the hut seemed as though lifted up from the ground, a rushing roar as of water in his ears, then all a blank!

CHAPTER III.

THE VAULT OF DEATH IN THE MOAT MANOR HOUSE—THE CONFLICT IN THE STREAM—THE PISTOL SHOT—A FRIEND IN NEED—THE RESCUE—THE ESCAPE TO THE OLD TREE CAVE.

When once more returning to consciousness, it was with a wild dazed feeling that Claude opened his eyes and stared around him.

Was he the victim of a hideous nightmare?

Was it all a dream?

Or had he indeed fallen a captive to the murderous denizens of the hut in the wood?

With a dull aching pain in the head, and a brain dazed and confused, he glared around.

His limbs at liberty, he now staggered to his feet, feeling strangely sick and faint.

With the impulse of a man accustomed to danger and self-defence, he sought for his arms.

They were gone.

Pistols, sword, had alike been removed.

Unarmed and defenceless, he was a helpless captive:

The captive of men, whose hands were stained with blackest crime.

A nervous thrill shot through his veins.

Far more perilous was his position than when at the inn of his friend, Joe Jennings.

The laws then pursued him.

But men who would not hesitate at cold-blooded assassination were now his captors.

Shaking off the feeling of faintness, Claude now began to minutely survey his prison.

He discovered that he was in a long, narrow chamber.

Singularly narrow, and with its walls of bare brick, looking gruesome and prisonlike.

Standing in the centre of his strange abode, Claude, stretching out his arms, found that he could almost touch either side of the apartment with his hands.

At the far end a thick wainscot ran up to the roof, which, like the walls, was of bare brick.

Near where he stood was a low door of solid oak, which, on pressing himself against, he found hard and fast, doubtless bolted and barred without.

Glancing down upon the floor he found that, like the door, the wood was of oak.

It was not without a shudder that Claude discerned upon the flooring several dark red smears, whilst in parts the walls, especially the further end, which was of wood, were alike covered with patches and splotches of the same hue.

Grinding his teeth and then biting his lips with suppressed passion, he glared wildly round his prison-house.

Was there no means of escape?

Was he, after all, to perish in some low den of crime, never to be heard of more?

Eagerly he scanned the singular apartment anew.

Nought fresh, however, did he discover.

He tapped with his knuckles the further end of the strange prison, the oaken wainscot giving out a dull echo.

There was some other chamber, then, on the other side, though exit by this end of the place there was no sign of.

Stooping down upon his hands and knees, he now examined attentively the flooring.

In the middle of the narrow chamber he fancied the boards shook as he knelt upon them; but, though keenly searching them, he found no indication of a trap.

About to rise once more to his feet, he started and listened.

A low murmuring noise sounded from below:

Placing his ears to the boards he now listened intently.

He was not mistaken.

There was an unwonted, strange sound beneath the boards on which he laid:

A rushing, roaring noise.

What was it?

It sounded like a rushing stream, a body of water running in a subterranean way.

It was so; he could not be mistaken.

He recognised without a doubt the sound from below:

The rushing roar of water.

A stream, a heavy body of water, was running beneath his feet.

He knew not why, yet a strange thrill of horror darted through his frame as he listened to the gurgling rush below.

Might not the darksome stream be intended for his shroud?

The only light that entered the narrow prison was from a small iron grating that was fixed in the wall over the door.

To reach this and gain a glimpse into the corridor without was impossible.

Not a single article of furniture was there in the weird-looking prison.

All was bleak and bare:

Drear and repelling!

With a curse at the folly and curiosity that had led him to remain in the lone hut until his enemies secured him, Claude now folded his arms and awaited his doom.

He could not hide it from himself, that he stood in greatest peril:

Greater than any he had yet encountered.

A sound as of footsteps without now fell upon his ear.

With a start he drew back:

Drew back as the door of the strange chamber was thrown open.

Wildly Claude glanced upon his foes, four in number, then a smile darted across his features as he with flashing eyes and with a mocking laugh exclaimed—

"What, four to one! Ha, ha, ha! You fear then your unarmed captive, it seems."

"We fear you not, Claude Duval! aye, you see I know you now," said the youth Miles Ellerton, upon whose entrance at the head of his foes Claude had started, biting his lips with rage and suppressed passion.

"So then, cur, cowardly reprobate, who would war upon a poor weak girl, it's you, is it?"

"Yes, it's even I, Miles Ellerton, from whom you snatched my future bride, the beautiful Maude Mayburn, this morning, Claude Duval—dashing, daring, Claude Duval, knight of the road, highway robber, and knight errant to distressed damsels; but your knight errantry is at an end. Prepare to leave this world, brave Duval; you are far too clever to remain in it! They want clever people in the other sphere: we can do without them here! You see you know our little secret of the hut in the wood; and as dead men tell no tales we have had you brought hither to the Moat Manor House, a curious old house belonging to no one in particular, but now in chancery. We—that is, I and my friends here—have found out a few of its secrets; mayhap if ghosts walk you may in your rambles about the old place find out more; we shan't ask you to come back and make us acquainted with them, however."

Claude, his chest heaving heavily whilst the beads of perspiration from excess of passion trickled down his brow, glared savagely at his mocking enemy, and then, his voice cool and without a tremor, exclaimed—

"Miles Ellerton, think not I shall die unavenged; such crimes as yours will meet their reward!"

"Ha, ha, ha! the devil preaching morality, the highwayman in the pulpit."

"Rail on, assassin, I care not! Sacre! I can but die, and will show you how a brave man can face death. Come on, gentlemen! Parbleu, I'm ready!"

Proudly, defiantly, Claude gazed at his foes, one of whom, the same tall herculean man who had seized upon him in the hut, exclaiming—

"Ten thousand devils, he is a plucky one; 'tis a pity he knows so much. Death, and the devil! he deserves to escape."

"Don't talk like a madman, Rupert Harborough! The fellow dies!"

"Well, of course, that's right enough; but I admire pluck, whether in friend or foe."

"Thank you, Rupert Harborough, since that's your name. If I escape this tussle, I will remember you, my man."

"If you escape! Ha, ha, ha! Claude Duval, you'll never leave this house; your bones will bleach in the stream that runs in the vaults beneath! And I—well, it may pleasure you to be informed, that whilst you lie, stiff, cold, stark, like my former foe, Aubrey Singleton, at the hut in the wood, I shall be blessed in the arms of Maude Mayburn. Her bright eyes were suffused with tears, as on her knees she entreated you might be spared, when half an hour back, in this very house, I told her that to-night your body would be floating in the waters beneath! Egad, I think I have a rival in you, Claude Duval, for the smiles of my beautiful bride; and, as the young lady cannot have us both, I think you are the one can best be spared!"

"Coward! murderer! I am not yet removed from your path! You don't yet know me," his eyes fairly blazing. Claude, who had been calling all his energies to his aid, now dashed upon his foes, who, standing some two yards away, never dreamt of any resistance from their victim.

Duval's idea (that like a lightning flash had darted through his brain) of a sudden rush startling his foes was a correct one.

Astounded for the moment at the onslaught, no great effort was made to seize him, and ere they were aware of the fact, two pistols, torn from their belts by the maddened knight of the road, were fired upon them.

There was a loud yell of fury, followed by the noise of a terrible struggle.

"Open that panel, Giles!"

"Out with him!"

"Slit his weasand (throat)!"

"No, no! throw him into the stream; let him swim for it!"

"Rupert Harborough, are you mad? Damnation, put a bullet in him! I hear voices without; some one is in the house. Officers, by——" A fearful oath here escaped the lips of the villain Miles Ellerton, as four or five Bow-street runners, followed by a ferocious bloodhound, dashed into the chamber.

The scene that ensued appeared to Claude like a wild, horrid dream.

During his brief conflict a low door had been opened by a spring at the further end of the chamber.

To this opening he had, despite his struggles, been dragged.

In the grasp of the man Harborough and another, his attempts to escape were futile.

With a wild, startled shriek he could not repress in that moment of horror, Claude had felt himself hurled through the opening:

Hurled into space:

Hurled into darkness, to meet a horrible death ere the posse of officers had appeared upon the scene.

Claude heard not the fierce oaths, the reports of firearms, and sounds of a terrific conflict as he found himself launched into space.

For a moment of time he felt himself whirling through the air, then with a plash he was tossed and battling in a mass of ice-cold water.

The stream, strong and swift, and running he knew not whither, whirled him along with a rush that rendered all attempts at swimming futile.

In pitchy darkness, with a moan of despair, he gave himself up for lost:

Gave himself up for lost as he felt a sharp pain run up his arm as he struck against a hard substance in the dark.

Wildly Claude threw both arms up out of the water.

A cry of joy escaped his lips.

His hands came in contact with a flight of steps:

Steps that apparently led to the roof of the chamber above.

Drawing himself from the rushing stream that he had feared would be his shroud, Claude now clambered half-way up the rude stairs, nearly falling back into the inky swirling mass he had escaped as a broad flash of light shone suddenly overhead:

A flash of light that rendered him for a few seconds unable to distinguish objects around.

In a moment of time, to his surprise, he found himself in the grasp of a tall, sinewy man, who, sliding down the steps from the open trap above, seized him in his arms.

"It's no use, Dashing Duval! give in, your wanted!"

"Am I?"

"Yes; you'd better come quietly; Anstey's upstairs."

"Is he?"

"Yes; in coming after you, we didn't expect to cop (secure) Master Rupert Harborough; but we've got him!"

"Have you, indeed? then, I hope you'll keep him."

"Now then, down there, how goes it?"

"All right, Blue Peters; what, are you here, too!" cried Claude, as glancing up at a large trap the officers had discovered and forced open, he beheld the flushed, angry face of the Bow-street runner, who, pistol in hand, was leaning forwards glaring into the darkness.

"Oh! you're there, Duval, are you? Good! you're booked for the Stone Jug now, my clever high Toby!"

"Am I? Say you don't know."

"Pshaw! bring him along, Sowerbury."

"He'll find himself a very Sowerbury if he tries to. Take your hands off me, man, or I'll hurl you into the water: I will, by the Lord that made me!"

"Duval!"

"Well, Blue Peters, what is it?"

"If you don't come quietly, I'll put the dog on to you."

"Sacre, bang the dog, and you too!" Duval here determined to make a last effort to escape, shook himself free of the grasp of the daring officer who held him, and dashed up the steps.

There was a bright flash, and a sharp report, whilst the ping of a bullet whistled by his ears; then Claude, caught from behind, was engaged in a desperate struggle with his late assailant, who, catching at the ladder, had drawn himself from the waters Claude had hurled him into a moment before.

A deep-mouthed bay was echoed through the subterranean way, as a huge bloodhound, scrambling down the steps, attempted to seize Duval in his grasp.

For a moment of time Claude beheld the fiery red eyes and the inflamed jaws; then, with a curse, striking at the ferocious beast with the butt of his pistol, he sent it toppling, with a hoarse bark of fury, into the stream.

"So much for the dog, now for its master!" Claude, now, with his doubled fist here sent the astounded Sowerbury again into the water, and leaving him and the yelling bloodhound, rushed up the steps.

With a deep drawn breath he scrambled through the trap, prepared for a struggle with with the runner, Blue Peters.

To his surprise, however, he beheld that officer rendered perfectly hors de combat, lying bound and helpless in a corner.

A tall handsome man standing by the door of the chamber with a brace of loaded pistols now darted forward, and exclaimed—

"Claude, brave heart, haste with you, lad! We've not a second to spare."

"What Jack, you here?"

"Yes; and the sooner Jack gets away from here the better he'd like it! Come on, old pal!"

"Where is Jonathan Anstey, and his men, Jack?"

"In the forecourt of this cursed rookery, seeing after his prisoners."

"Prisoners! what prisoners!"

"Oh! a gang of poachers, or something worse, headed by a fellow named Rupert Harborough."

"Hark! by all the devils, they are having a fresh scrimmage. Do you hear their popguns! Come on, Claude; it's an ill wind that blows nobody good; in the melée we shall escape unnoticed."

"Right you are, Jack, lead on! We will compare notes on the road, for I'm all anxiety to know how you ferreted me out, old pal."

Dashing down a long corridor that led from the dread chamber in which he had so nearly met his death, Claude, with Jack, was startled by a loud, piercing shriek:

A shriek of dire woe:

Of utmost terror!

Both the friends paused:

Paused as they gained a flight of stairs:

A flight of stairs, at the bottom of which they beheld a young girl struggling in the grasp of a man.

Two ominous red spots gathered upon the cheeks of Gentleman Jack as he exclaimed, "Well, if I don't give that whelp something to remember me by, may I never kiss a pretty lass again!"

"Hold, Jack, you must leave that to me."

"As you like, old pal."

"Do you see to the girl, Jack!"

"Right you are."

"I owe that man a heavy debt, and I'm going to pay it."

To the no small astonishment of his friend, Claude, now placing his arms upon the polished oaken banister of the staircase, slid, in a moment of time, from top to bottom.

A trick which Jack immediately followed.

The stranger, unheeding the two highwaymen, was now hurrying along the landing with his hapless victim senseless upon his shoulder.

A startled cry of fury escaped the abductor's lips as Claude darted up, and, with a blow that would have felled an ox, stretched him upon the ground, Gentleman Jack catching the girl as he fell.

"Bravo, Claude, that's good! let him have it."

Claude, who, at the top of the stairs, had recognised the villain, Miles Ellerton, in the young girl's foe, knew not that it was even the unhappy Maude Mayburn who was struggling in his grasp.

He had scarce dared to hope that good fortune would again put it in his power to save her.

Gentleman Jack, holding the fainting girl in his arms now apprised Claude that he had better follow, and either stol his enemy at once or leave him to another opportunity.

Miles Ellerton, livid with fury, had now risen to his feet.

"Hold, Claude Duval! thief! highwayman! robber! Give up that girl! you shall not drag her hence. Even now the runners are in the house; you cannot escape."

"Indeed; you think so! Stand on one side; I don't want to spoil your beauty, but I'm afraid I shall if you don't make yourself scarce."

"Come on Claude. Let him have it!"

"He shall not go hence! What ho, help, help!" With a scream of rage Miles Ellerton here flew at his enemy.

Claude ready for the attack at once closed with his antagonist.

"Away with you, Jack! I'll settle this whelp, and join you anon."

"Confusion! here's one of Anstey's men. If we don't get away at once we shall be trapped after all."

Scarce had these words escaped the lips of Gentleman Jack ere a tall, powerfully-built man, darting along the passage, bounded upon Duval.

Encumbered with the senseless form of the lovely Maude Mayburn, Gentleman Jack was unable to aid his friend.

Struggling to free himself from the grasp of Miles Ellerton Claude was now dragged to the ground:

Slipping upon the polished oak flooring as the runner, with a grin of triumph, pulled a pair of handcuffs out of his pocket.

"Hold on, Ellerton! Now we've got him."

"Have you, then mind you keep him," shouted Jack, who, having laid the unfortunate Maude upon the floor, rushed forwards and catching the exultant Bow-street officer a blow under the ear with his doubled fist, sent him stunned and rolling into a corner.

DASHING DUVAL;
OR,
THE LADIES' HIGHWAYMAN.

CLAUDE NOW STRUCK OUT AT THE RUNNER AND DARTED UP TO THE TRAP.

Claude now, with a cry of rage seized Ellerton by the collar, and, shaking him to and fro in wild fury, hurled him against the wainscoting of the corridor.

"I cannot murder him in cold blood; but I'll mark him for life," said Claude, as with a fearful blow he caught his astounded foe full between the eyes as he rose to his feet, and following it up, as he staggered back, again struck him on the jaw with the butt of his pistol: the wretch, with a groan, sinking down deluged in blood.

"One on the nose, and down he goes. Come on, Duval!"

"All right! Do you lead the way, Jack."

Taking Maude Mayburn from his friend's arms, as her eyes once more opened to the light, Claude, his heart beating proudly, hastened after his companion, who, darting down a narrow passage, was presently descending a second flight of stairs.

Reaching the bottom, a short landing or corridor was passed, a door at the further end of which, forced open by Jack, led them into a large garden at the back of the house.

"Here we are, right and tight, Claude! The enemy are all in the front! We've beat the grabs (officers) this time!"

"Thank heaven, yes! And this poor girl is, mon Dieu! once more safe from that devilsblood, Miles Ellerton!"

"Who, what is she, Claude?"

"I will tell you all by-and-bye. Only let us get from this infernal place, Jack."

No. 3 & 4.
Price One Penny.

"Right you are, my flower! Where shall we go?"

"Anywhere out of this! Would to heaven we had our horses!"

"Don't bother about them, Claude, old pal. They ain't far off."

"What? You are jesting!"

"Devil a bit!"

"You mean to tell me you have your horse with you, Jack, and that you have found my bonny Jane?"

"Just what I do mean! That's to say, I've got your bonny mare, Jane; and a kind friend has lent me a horse as good as my own!"

"My dear old Jack, I scarce can believe my ears!"

"Can you your eyes, Claude? There you are!"

With a grin at the amazed and delighted face of his friend, Gentleman Jack, who had pushed his way followed by Duval through a mass of shrubbery, here pointed to a tract of lawn, upon which, patiently grazing, was the missing mare and a fine handsome horse, with a skin black as jet and smooth as velvet.

Hastening forwards, Claude was received by his steed with a whinnying sound of recognition.

Maude Mayburn, now able to walk, stared round in wild amaze.

Duval, forgetful of his foes and the horrors he had lately gone through, for a time stood by the side of his mare, and gazed into the soft eyes of the lovely girl, oblivious to all around.

The golden sun sinking to rest threw a heavenly lustre upon the scene; whilst the carolling of the feathered songsters, as they flew from bough to bough, woke up pleasant echoes through the deserted grounds of the old house.

Recalled to the perilous proximity of their enemies by the deep baying of a hound, Claude now started, and, pointing to the gabled roof of the house, just discernible through the trees, exclaimed:

"Jack, lead us out of this! Sacre, it will never do to linger longer in the tiger's den!"

"I was just going to hint as much! We must walk our steeds out of the grounds till we gain the broken-down portion of the fence by which I entered."

"All right, you known the way, lead on!"

"Where do you propose to go?"

"Well, I don't know."

"What do you say to the old Tree Cave?"

"The very place, Jack! That retreat will be safe for an hour or two; and at dark we can push on for the long village (London)."

"Exactly! That was my idea."

"Allons, then, forward!"

The young girl, Maude, with a bewildered air, clinging confidingly to the stranger who again had rescued her from her base persecutor, exclaimed, "I never thought to see you more! Miles Ellerton told me he had caused you to be assassinated! He told me, too, that you were hunted by the laws; that your name was Claude Duval! Is that so?"

"Aye, Miss Mayburn, he told you truly! I am that same knight of the road, of whom doubtless you have heard; but, highwayman as I am, I am prepared in all honour to see you in safety where'er you wish."

Tears started to the young girl's eyes, as she noted the flushed face and detected the tremor of her protector's voice.

"Oh, believe me, I care not though all the world were banned against you; though you be indeed that Claude Duval of whom I have heard. Heaven forget me if I, Maude Mayburn, forget the one who, to rescue me from the power of a villain, risked his life in my defence! Claude Duval, good kind protector; would I could, by other than weak words, testify my gratitude!"

"You can, dear girl," exclaimed our hero; who, about to snatch the soft hand of the blushing Maude to his lips, was recalled to their yet dangerous position by the hoarse bay of a hound.

"They have started that dog on our track."

"Confound them, yes! Have we much further to go, Jack?"

"A few steps through that copse there, and we gain the broken fence."

"Good! Once in the saddle I care not."

"Will Miss Mayburn ride with you?"

"Yes, Jack."

"Very good; then I will hang in the rear; and if that infernal dog gets too close will drop a blue plum into him."

"I must see to the brute: he might nose us out at the cave."

"The very thing I was thinking of."

"He seems close upon our heels."

"Confound him, yes!"

"Your barking irons all right?"

"Yes, Claude! I'll drop something into his carcase will stop that pretty note of his before long!"

Hurrying on, the little party now forced their way with their steeds through a thick mass of copse and bramble, presently after emerging close to a portion of park railing that, fallen to decay with time and neglect, lay prone amid the tall rank grass and wild growth of vegetation.

"Here we are, Claude! now's our time. Into the saddle with you!" exclaimed Jack, as he carefully guided the horses over the fallen fence.

Duval, now lifting Maude Mayburn on to the back of his brave mare, at a bound himself followed, then, bidding the young girl hold fast to him, prepared to quit the spot.

"All right, Jack?"

"Not yet, my girth wants tightening."

"That beast will be upon us in a moment."

"Yes; his hoarse roar sounds uncomfortably close. Do you know I think we had better wait and double him up here?"

"As you like."

"I don't fancy the thought of the brute hovering at our heels."

"Nor I. Is your hand steady, Jack?"

"Oh yes, I think I can hit my mark."

"Good! if you fail to wing him I'll let fly."

"Right you are!"

"Let him have it between the eyes, Jack."

"Oh, I'll give it him fair and straight Claude, never fear!"

Leaping into his saddle, the highwayman now reined his horse up at the side of his friend.

Loud, fierce, and angry; closer yet closer sounded the bay of the hound.

Firm and erect in their saddles sat the two friends.

A shade of pallor crept over the face of Maude Mayburn as, looking back through the copse they had torn their way through a few minutes before, she beheld a dark brown mass crashing on towards them.

A short sharp click now sounded as a pause in the hoarse barking of the hound took place.

"Ready, Jack?"

"Yes."

"Fire low."

"All right!"

"The runners are close after the beast!"

"Yes! I hear their voices, Claude! But they don't expect to find us mounted."

"No; there's the sell."

"Won't Jonathan Anstey swear!"

"I fancy he will, just a few!"

"There's the dog! a nice youth for a family party."

"Yes! he's got sore eyes."

"There's a 'tater trap! What a dentist's shop for a chap's calf."

A low laugh here escaped the lips of Gentleman Jack, who, coolly leaning forward in his saddle, waited until the bloodhound, a huge beast with eyes of flame and wide-mouthed open jaws of a dull crimson tint, dashed up.

"There, he has it!"

There was a sharp report, followed by a howl, that in its intensity far exceeded the former savage cries of the infuriate beast; then, blinded in blood, the ferocious animal bounding heedlessly forward fell in a death agony among the tall rank grass.

"So much for the hound."

"Now for its masters, Jack!"

"Here they come!"

"Yelling like schoolboys out for a holiday."

"Don't they think they've got us?"

"Rather!"

"There's not one mount out of the lot, Claude."

"No. They made sure of us! The dog was to do the trick."

"But he did'nt."

"No, Jack! you did it instead."

"Here they are!"

"Don't let them get too close."

"All right, Claude; they can't wing us very well now we

are in the saddle. I must give sweet Jonathan a bit of chaff; he will look so amiable when he finds the sell."

"Parbleu, right, Jack! Sacre! they are here."

A wild shout of fury now echoed from the mouths of some four or five Bow-street runners, who, headed by the officer, Jonathan Anstey, dashed up to the spot, gazing with looks of amazement and rage—first, at the mounted men whom they had made sure of capturing, and then at the blood-hound, which, stark and stiff, with a bullet-hole in its skull, lay an inert mass upon the grass.

"Good evening, Anstey!"

"We are going for a ride."

"I say, Jack, Anstey looks cross."

"He's down on his luck."

"He thought he'd cotched a couple of lambs."

"Instead of which, he finds two old foxes."

"Ha, ha, ha! Good-bye, Johnny!"

"When next you are after two flats, be sure and bring your horses with you!"

A volley of oaths here escaped from the officers, whilst the report of two or three pistols echoed in the air.

"Dont waste your powder, boys."

"Do you want a race?"

"They don't see it, Claude; they've got bad feet!"

Hillio! away, away, Jane! Au revoir, Jonathan Anstey! we shall meet again."

"Yes, in Newgate," screamed the infuriate officers, who, as the friends gave their horses the reins and dashed away, fairly danced with rage.

"Bilked the grabs that time, Claude!"

"Yes, didn't Jonathan Anstey look vicious? He'll be more my foe than ever now. But, ma foi, I care not; and now tell me, Jack, how came you to find me out in that infernal Moat Manor House, as they call it; but for you I might have been either food for the rats in the running stream, or a captive in the hands of our mutual friends, the redbreasts. Whilst dear Miss Mayburn here, ugh! it makes me shudder and grind my teeth, as I think of what might have been her fate."

"A fate I would have ne'er outlived," murmured the young girl, who, her soft round arms clinging to her pre-server's waist, looked up with eyes that beamed with grati-tude and thanksgiving into his.

A warm flush mounted into the face of Claude as he rode slowly on, his friend Jack now for a moment dropping in the rear.

With mingled feelings of pain and pleasure, Duval gazed into the liquid depths of the beauteous eyes, that in all con-fidence and gratitude were bent upon him.

"What," he asked himself, "was he going to do with his fair charge?"

"Take her in safety to London, leave her with the person who would be prepared to shield her from harm, and he, her preserver, never behold her more?"

Such ought to be his course.

But against this was a feeling of something akin to love he now felt for the beautiful, friendless girl.

Then a spasm of pain shot through his breast, as he asked himself, "How could he, a knight of the road, a high-wayman, a man against whom the law had set its ban, the law which he hourly, at risk to life, defied—how—how could he dare to seek a young, pure girl's affection?" With a sigh dismissing the dream of bliss he had for a moment indulged in, Claude, now beckoning Jack to follow close on beside him, asked the beautiful Maude how she had come to again fall into the hands of her villain persecutor, Miles Ellerton.

It then appeared, from the account given by his fair charge, that after he, Claude, had left the hut, she was startled by the sudden appearance of the man Rupert Harborough, and his companions, who, seizing roughly upon her, demanded how she came there? About to falter forth an explanation, a wild scream escaped her, as the villain, Miles, followed by two others, dashed suddenly in with the information that they had secured the highwayman's steed, and thus prevented his further progress. It was then agreed between Miles Ellerton and the man Harborough that she should be conveyed to the Moat Manor House, as it was called—a deserted tenement, distant about a mile from the hut. "My prayers and entreaties availed me not, my dear preserver," continued Maude, shuddering, as she continued the recital. "I was at once dragged away and conducted to that terrible house, and was a little time after informed of your capture and intended destruction.

Giving myself up to despair, and murmuring a prayer to heaven for aid, I was startled by a loud noise in the house and sounds of deadly conflict, in the midst of which, my door was dashed open, and, caught in the arms of the villain Ellerton, I was, in the passage without, again rescued by you. Nor can a lifelong gratitude repay what I owe."

"Nay, talk not thus, dear girl. I were not fit to bear the name of man, had I not, when first we met, attempted to protect you from a coward and a villain. And now, Jack, I am yet in the dark to account for your sudden and oppor-tune arrival."

"'Tis easily explained, dear pal. I knew your road for the old Tree Cave, and, on foot, hastened after you; in passing the barn, where you had gone through a little carte and tierce, I came upon sweet Miles and the fellow Colonel Blood; from them I learned all that had passed. The two worthies, hastening to the neighbouring farm, pro-cured horses, and followed on in your track. Undecided what course to pursue, I was startled into activity by the appearance of Anstey and his runners. Keeping out of their sight, I, cursing the mischance that had left me without my steed, came suddenly across a sour, elderly old gent, mounted on this piece of black stuff (here Jack, with a grin, patted his steed). The old gentleman at first made a bother about lending me the animal, but necessity knows no law; the horse I wanted, and the horse I was determined to have; and as the gent preferred to part rather than receive a bullet in his brainpan, why he lent the animal, which I promised to leave for him at the livery stables the other side of Highgate; and I'll keep my word!"

"Ha, ha, ha! quite an adventure. Go on, Jack, what next?"

"Not much; I am near the climax. I need not say, I was not long after I got in the saddle before I pelted away. Nearing a turning on the high road that led to that copse, in the centre of which the hut is located, I was astounded by running across a gipsy-looking sort of vagabond, half-poacher, half-footpad, seated like a lord upon your mare. I knew her in a minute; and Jane knew me too, didn't you lass?" Claude's steed here tossed her head and whinnied slightly, as Jack placed his hand upon her neck; each party now walking their horses across a broad tract of heath slowly to suit the purpose of converse.

"I suppose you soon settled the fellow, Jack?"

"I wasn't long about it, I can tell you."

"What passed?"

"Everything that was satisfactory to me, though more t'other to bonny Jane's rider. Says I, 'Hallo, old fellow! where did you get that horse?'

"'Do you wish pertickler to know?'

"'I do so.'

"'Well then, as I arn't inclined to tell yer, find out!'

"'Oh, that's your game, is it?'

"'Yes,' says the fellow, with a grin, pulling a pistol from his pocket and snapping it in my face. His powder was damp, or my luck was in, Claude, for the weapon flashed in the pan; and the fellow's eyes flashed fire, or I'm awfully mistaken, for I shot out my right full and fair in his face, and sent him clean out of his saddle into the road-way. Jumping off my borrowed bit of ebony here, I now coolly searched the fellow's pockets, but, to my disgust, only found a shilling on him, and that a bad one. Says I, 'You scurvy thief, now tell me, where did you get that horse?'

"'Find out!' the blackguard here spitting out two of his teeth, looked as savage as our friend Jonathan, when he found us mounted just now.

"'You won't tell me where you got that mare?'

"'No, curse me if I do!'

"'Very good, do you see those teeth?'

"With a grin, anything but pleasant, and then a scowl that sent a pair of bushy eyebrows down on his cheekbones, the fellow, with an oath, said, 'Yes, them's my ivories, and you'll have to pay summat smart for knocking 'em out of my jaw, afore I've done with you.'

"'Very good!' says I. 'Now look here, old man, as I've got to pay for two, I think I'll have all you've got. I dare say you'll expect no more for the lot than you will for those! I don't care about buying, for they are very dirty and are much worn. But if you won't answer my question, darn me, all your teeth I'll have, and no mistake about it!'"

A loud laugh, in which the pretty Maude joined, here burst from the mouth of Claude as his friend humorously related his adventure.

"What followed next, Jack! Did you go in any further for the dentist line?"

"Listen, old pal, and I'll tell you! Of course when I now laid hands on the cove he tried his strength against mine; but the dirty vagabond found it was no go! I could have muzzled two like him! I gave him one on his conk that tapped his claret pretty freely, and, a moment after, one under the lug (ear) that sent him to grass like a stone; in fact, for a moment I thought I'd done for the fellow; finding, however, that he presently came too, I coolly loaded one of my barking irons before him, and when he had once more fairly recovered his senses, pointed the barrel fair between his shaggy eyebrows. 'Now look here,' says I, 'if you don't tell me all about that mare and its owner, by the sun that rides above us I'll put my bullet in your skull, as you meant to put yours in mine!'

"I was getting vicious now, and the fellow saw it! I had tampered with him so far, as I wanted to ascertain from him what was the danger that had befallen you!

"'Now then, I give you one minute: where did you get that mare?'

"'From the Captain!'

"'And who, in the devil's name, is the Captain?'

"'Rupert Harborough!'

"'Then I don't know him; if he's as pretty as you he's a stunner! But your present information amounts to nothing. Who and what is this Harborough? where does he hang out? and how did he come by this mare? Out with it, no prevarication, my fingers are twitching, and this barking iron of mine may go off suddenly, and if it does you'll pretty soon be off too!'

"'Well I suppose,' said the fellow, 'I must tell you all!'

"'I think you had better!'

"'Well then, we collared the mare in the woods near a lone hut; soon arter that the Captain and one Miles Ellerton, a friend of his, nailed a gal! and then they napped the owner of that cussed mare! They have now gone to the Moat Manor House.'

"'What, that old deserted building about a couple of miles from here?'

"'The same,' said the fellow who, now thoroughly cowed, at my bidding led the way, first to the hut, and then to the house, which on reaching I was confounded upon finding surrounded by Anstey and his men, who were after this very Harborough it appeared, as well as you. I allowed my guide, minus two of his teeth and a battered mug, now to depart, and going round to the rear of the place discovered that break in the fence that runs round the grounds; making my way into the house, I, guided by the noise of firing, gained the secret chamber where they were trying to put you out of the way. The rest you know."

"Yes, Jack, dear pal! and am not likely to forget! But see, we are close to our retreat; another half-mile will bring us to the old Tree Cave."

"You think of putting up there for a while?"

"Well, yes; it won't be dark yet for a couple of hours, during that time the road between this and our destination, Highgate, will be well scoured by the enemy, who will have given up the search by the time we are about to quit our hiding place."

"Very true; there's plenty of refreshment in the cave, too, so we shan't want for anything."

"Good! go on ahead Jack, and give Luke the warning."

In some surprise, which was depicted in her face, Maude Mayburn listened to the above brief colloquy of the friends.

Noting her astonished looks Claude with a smile exclaimed, "With your permission, dear Miss Mayburn, I am about to sojourn in a place of safety for an hour: you will accompany me, will you not?" a reproachful glance from the fair girl was the only answer; and Claude, now pointing with the handle of his riding whip to a thick coppice near, exclaimed, "There is our retreat!"

"But I see no dwelling: there is nought before us that I can see likely to hide us for a time from our enemies save that copse."

"And in that copse is our secret habitation."

"What mean you, dear Monsieur Duval? you are jesting with me."

"Ma foi, not I, dear girl! But, hark! there is the warning cry that all is clear."

"I heard nothing but the hoot of an owl."

"And there is the very bird," said Claude, with a smile, as Jack, who with his horse had just before disappeared in the copse, now came forth on foot.

In wonder and surprise Maude now cast her eyes around in search of some hidden habitation in the copse, through a bare part of which, Claude, dismounting, now led his horse. Sign of house, however, there was none.

A high hill, clothed to the summit with the hazel, the blackberry, and a mass of furze and pollard oak, alone met her sight.

With a smile at her evident surprise, Claude preceded by Jack had now gained an open part of the copse in the centre of which stood a blighted withered oak.

Riven by lightning the bleak bare boughs of the old tree looked sad and weird as they waved to and fro in the breeze.

All around was one mass of bright green verdure—trees and bushes alike covered in their leafy foliage, the riven oak alone standing there in the copse in its naked ruin, a sad memento of the powers of the storms.

"Is Luke ready for the horses, Jack?"

"Yes; he is waiting with mine at the foot of the hill."

"Good! go with him and see the cattle stabled, and then, join me and Miss Mayburn in the cave."

"All right, Claude!"

Taking his friend's mare by the head, Jack now disappeared along an open track in the copse, whilst Duval, to the astonishment of Maude, stepping into the side of the riven oak, which on close examination, proved to be quite hollow, exclaimed: "Now Miss Mayburn, if you will follow me I will introduce to you a retreat that has oft saved me and my friend from capture! Have no fear! Come, dear girl, and in three minutes we shall be safe in the old Tree Cave!"

CHAPTER IV.

THE SECRET CAVE—A SNUG RETREAT—THE CONFESSION OF LOVE—A MAIDEN'S GRATITUDE—THE DEPARTURE—THE MOONLIGHT MEETING—THE DEATH FACE—THE MYSTERY OF THE PINE WOOD—THE ESCAPE—HURRAH FOR THE ROAD!

As the last words issued from the mouth of Duval, to Maude's astonishment, her protector began to disappear: Began to disappear in the hollow of the tree.

In another moment he was completely out of sight.

Standing by the tree, Maude now discovered a large opening inside:

A darksome cavity deep down in the earth.

From this aperture Claude's voice now ascended.

With words of encouragement he bade her descend.

Not without a slight tremor as she glanced into the darksome depths, Maude at length stepped into the hollow of the riven oak.

To her surprise, she now found she was standing upon the topmost round of a ladder.

A bright gimmering light flashed from below.

Slowly, cautiously, encouraged and emboldened by the voice of Duval, she now descended the subterranean way.

In a few moments, to her surprise, she reached the bottom of the rude ladder, which, planted upon the ground beneath, just sufficed to reach to the opening above.

Claude, the instant his fair charge was in safety, ascending the steps, now pulled an iron ring, that hung from the roof. A heavy trap, covered with earth, grass, and moss, immediately sliding back in a groove, fitted exactly the hollow of the oak.

Any person now from without glancing into the cavity of the blighted trunk could have no suspicion of the subterranean passage to a cavern below.

"A neat contrivance, is it not, Miss Mayburn!" said Claude, who with a smile, now taking the young girl's hand in his, led her away, as Jack, making his appearance, seized the ladder and placed it in another part of the cave.

With a wild, wondering stare, Maude now glanced around:

Forgetful of the fearful incidents of the day, dismissing from her mind the strange, peculiar nature of her position; alone with the two friends in that underground retreat, she was lost at the fairylike scene before her.

The secret cave, some twenty feet in length, presented a strange, unwonted aspect to the visitant who might cast a glance up at the roof.

Long tendrils of all shapes and thicknesses hung from above, entwined and laced in a perfect network.

Observing her eyes fastened on the phenomenon, Claude informed the wondering Maude that those snake-like creepers were nothing more nor less than the roots of trees above, that, sunk far down in the earth, penetrated roof of the cave.

"What a wonderful place!"

"Yes, it's a curiosity, is it not?"

"It is, indeed! Have you been acquainted with the secret of this cavern long?"

"About a twelvemonth. Accident revealed it to me one day, and, consulting with my friend Jack, we agreed that it was a nice little hermitage and safe retreat in time of danger."

"How strange such an underground place should be in existence!"

"Well, yes, it is; and its existence, and my good fortune in discovering it, has served me in good stead."

"So I suppose! Think you it has been long like this?"

"Doubtless; yes, for many years; probably was fashioned and contrived by some rude outlaw of old. The aged oak may have originally led to a small space which, enlarged, grew into the dimensions of a cave."

"'Tis a wild, romantic spot! I see you have not forgotten contrivances to make the abode habitable."

Maude here, with a smile, pointed to a table and two or three chairs, rudely fashioned of logs; an iron lamp, depending from a large mass of root above, that cast a broad yellow glare through the cave, also being noted by the fair visitant.

"Yes, we have made the 'old Tree Cave,' as we call it, pretty comfortable."

"There is, I presume, no other outlet but the tree."

"Oh, yes there is! but as it is not so hidden from view as the blighted oak in the copse, and is more inconvenient of access, we do not as a rule make use of it, though our boy Luke does."

"Luke! and who is he?"

"I forgot; you are not yet au fait of all our accessories here. Luke is our maid-of-all-work! Come, I will show you the cave whilst Jack, who I see is busy, prepares a slight déjeûner. We shall come across Master Luke presently."

Claude now, taking his fair and wondering charge by the hand, led her to the other end of the cave.

A low narrow opening here disclosed a small outer cavern.

Into this they both passed, and, proceeding onward, Claude, with a hand-lamp that lighted them in their path, now conducted the young girl along a narrow winding passage that was in parts so low that neither could walk upright.

A cool, refreshing air that coursed down the narrow underground passage led Maude to conclude they were approaching the other outlet from the cavern.

Her surmise, upon questioning her conductor, she found was right.

"In a few minutes, Miss Mayburn, we shall be once more in the woods. Hark! I hear Luke, he has heard our footsteps."

A low note of the cuckoo now sounded close at hand, and, emerging through a mass of tangled briar from the narrow passage, Maude was surprised to find herself a moment after on the brink of a small stream, which, some three or four feet in depth, meandered through the coppice.

The sudden change from the darkness of the cavernous retreat for a moment prevented Maude easily distinguishing objects around her.

A low laugh at length escaped her lips as her eyes fell upon an uncouth figure of a ragged boy, who, shoeless and hatless, was setting over the water, laving his feet in the stream.

The lad, with a broad grin, pulling a tuft of red hair, jumped up as Claude strode forward, and exclaimed:

"Heard yer coming. Knowed it was you. Jack's put the horses down yon." The lad here pointed down the stream, grinning and showing a set of teeth white as pearls, as he cast his eyes upon the face of the amused and wondering Maude.

"I suppose this is Luke?"

"Yes, Maude! and I can assure you he is as great a curiosity as the cave. Now, Luke, pay your respects to the lady."

"All right, Captain! Happy to see you, Miss! We don't often get angels from the skies to visit us here. Whoop! I'm poor Luke, the fondlin; was born in the streets, and cradled in the gutter! No one cared for me, till one day I met the Captain in the heart of Alsatia. Eh, eh, eh! The grabs were arter him. I tooked him into a crib one way, and slanted him out another. Whoop! While the hossifers was a hunting we was a bolting, warn't we, Captain?" The lad here, his broad red face expanded into a grin, worked his red eyebrows in a mysterious manner till they nearly reached his shock of hair that hung over his forehead. Then, as he observed his master and his fair companion smiling, he gave a jump some four feet from the ground, dancing madly round them, twice winding up his exciting performance by standing on his head—a proceeding that caused the pretty Maude to laugh more heartily than she had done for many a day.

"I told you Luke was an oddity."

"You have not belied him; poor fellow, I suppose he is very fond of you?"

"Fond of me? The boy would give his life for mine. But come, we must return, or Jack will fancy we have come to harm. Keep a sharp look out, Luke!"

"Right, Captain! Hawks are abroad, Jack told me. Eh, eh! You're the boy, though, to astonish the grabs!

"For a moonlight chase on the heath so free,
Who so merry and bold can be
As Dashing Duval, that merry wight—
Who follows his prey on the wildest night,
Slashing, Dashing Claude, so free—
Who so daring, so brave as he?—
Who so daring, so brave as he?"

With a wild shout and scream of laughter that startled the feathered songsters in a neighbouring tree, causing them to wing their way over the adjacent copse, Master Luke, upon finishing his rude, doggrel lines, which he had sung in a sweet-toned voice, now, at a bound, cleared the stream, and, dashing into the woods, was in a moment lost to sight, Claude, as he disappeared, with Maude returning to the cave by the way they had come.

Upon re-entering the cave they were received with a cry of welcome by Gentleman Jack, who, pointing to the rude table, bade them fall too.

"Now, my dear young lady, here's white bread of the best, a nice cold fowl, a jug of ale to wash it down, and some good old port, if you prefer it to malt. Sit down. Now fall too, Claude; do the honours, I can wait no longer. I'm as hungry as a hunter. Miss Mayburn, you will find our humble repast very decent, and, as Shakespeare as it, 'May good digestion wait on appetite, and health on both.'" With a grin, and a nod at Claude, Jack here began to make heavy inroads on the fare that, in their absence, he had placed upon the table.

Dismissing a momentary shyness that had caused her to draw back, at the earnest entreaties of Duval, Maude now seated herself at the table, and, forgetting her anomalous position, and put at ease by the winning manners of her protector, made a fair repast.

The slight refreshment at an end, Claude now asked when she would like to depart?

"When it pleases you. But pray let not thought of my safety interfere with your plans. We are not far from Highgate; once there, I can make my way to London."

"Well; yes. So you can, under charge of the son of my old friend the landlord of 'The Cat and her Kittens.' If you will allow me to arrange this I shall be happy."

"As you will; I shall never, I fear, be able to repay the debt of gratitude I owe you."

"Say not so! All I ask you, dear Miss Mayburn, is that you will let me know if you can rest in safety with the person whom you are about to seek. A line, a message sent, and I will immediately come to you. You know to whom you are indebted. Perhaps 'twould be most generous of me to desire that you never see me more. But I cannot call upon myself to forego the delight of beholding you once again. And, while I think of it, here is a diamond brooch lost, dear girl, in that lone hut; 'tis yours. I picked it up, stained with blood. But, thank heaven, my then dread fears proved groundless."

"You had thought then that violence had been offered me. In that trying hour, your steed stolen, you thought but of me!" Tears here trembled in the young girl's eyes. Then, as Claude glancing round perceived that his friend had left the cave, he, unable to further control himself, sank upon his knees.

"Maude! Maude! Miss Mayburn, be not angry with me; think me not base and unmanly that I throw myself thus at your feet and proclaim that I dared to love. From the moment that I gazed upon you, dear girl, at the barn, when in wild terror you were fleeing from the wretch Miles Ellerton, I dared to love you; you know I'm banned by the laws, that man's hand is raised against me! But, oh! indeed, dear girl, I can, if it p'eases you, prove that circumstance—not a vile inclination, drove me to my present life."

"I can well believe it, my brave preserver," cried the blushing girl, bending low her head as Claude, no longer master of himself, covered her soft dimpled hands with kisses. "Rise! oh rise! kneel not to me, Claude Duval! Do I not owe to you my life? Have you not saved me from worse than death? Am I not frendless and alone in the world? If I cared not for one to whom I owe so much, gratitude alone would bid me tell you that—that I will try to like you!"

In wild ecstasy as these words faltered on the lips of the blushing and trembling girl Claude sprang to his feet, and exclaimed, "Mon Dieu, dear Maude! I am a wretch to talk to you thus and here! At a more fitting time and place I will remind you of this converse; for the present forget that which my impetuous tongue gave utterance to. Sacre bleu! here's Jack! Come, Maude, we will now away; for I am more than ever anxious to see you hence!"

With light heart, forgetful of everything but that he was not distasteful to the beautiful Maude Mayburn, Duval, now following Jack, conducted her once more through the cavernous passage leading to the stream. Gaining its banks the "tu whit tu woo" of an owl now sounded clear in the night air, and, pursuing a rou h eaten path by the side of the rivulet, the little party at length came to a halt before a mass of tall furze that seemed to bid defiance to their further progress.

"Here we are, Claude!"

"Are the horses ready?"

"Yes."

"All clear?"

"Aye; Luke says there's not a soul on the road."

"Good! Half an hour's gallop will take us to Highgate."

To the on small surprise of Maude, Claude, now assisted by Jack, pushed aside the mass of furze which reared itself up in their path, and which it appeared had been placed there by human agency.

Passing onwards the friends presently reached a small open space that, shut in on every side with copse and furze, was hidden from all chance passers-by.

In this open space stood the horses belonging to the highwaymen, whilst, perched up in a pollard oak near, was the uncouth figure of Master Luke, fully revealed by the moonlight, that in a flood of silvery brightness poured over the copse.

Jack, the first to mount, now proceeded to lead the way back; Claude, having placed Maude in the saddle and himself seated beside her, following his friend, whilst, having glided from the tree, the boy Luke brought up the rear, carefully replacing the furze bushes as the horsemen cleared the stream and made their way slowly through the coppice to the high road beyond, leaving the eccentric youth to return to the cave, the echoes of his voice following them through the woods as he shouted out the lines of his favourite song.

"Poor Luke! is it not strange that one bred in the heart of London's busy town should be so light-hearted and joyous, leading a hermit's life in that secret cave, Claude?"

"Well, yes, it is a mystery, Jack! Poor fellow, I think there can be no doubt that he is a little faulty in the brain-pan."

"He seems happy, Claude! and is, I suppose, to be trusted?"

"Aye, to the death, Maude! I would place my life in his hands!"

"Does he ever come across of any your enemies?"

"The officers? Yes; and well they know it!"

"What mean you?"

"Why, my dear Miss Mayburn, as much as you hate the villain Miles Ellerton, poor half-witted Luke holds in his hatred the Bow-street runners; many a scurvy prank has he played upon them. From all I have heard his wretched parents were criminals, who suffered the extreme of the law; possibly their fate is indelibly fixed upon the poor fellow's brain, hence his rage at the sight of a redbreast, as the officers are termed."

"Poor soul! no wonder he feels embittered against them all, if your story is a true one! How bright and beautiful the night! I feel happy now I've quitted the roof of my wretched stepfather! But for you, Claude,"—the lovely girl's voice here faltered, as she clung to the man to whom she, despite his dangerous calling, had given up her young and spotless heart—"but for you, what misery I should have suffered!"

"Think not of it, dearest Maude! For e. Providence,—has ordained that you should not become the prey of the villain Ellerton! That heaven I crossed your path this morning! Ventre bleu! monsieur Ellerton had better in future play with a venomous serpent than with me! How now, Jack, what is it?"

A warning cry from his friend, who was in advance, had caused Claude to dash forwards.

"I fancied I heard the sound of horses' hoofs in front!"

"Nonsense, man, you are mistaken; there is no one in sight!"

"Isight, Claude! but a whole regiment of dragoons might be drawn up in that pine grove, a quarter of a mile ahead, and we should not see it." Gentleman Jack here pointed to a thick heavy grove of dark pines, fully revealed in the broad white light of the moon.

"You are right, Jack, and I'm a fool! We must act with caution."

"Yes, we know not who may confront us when we reach the pine grove! and you have some one to shield from harm!"

"Sacre bleu, yes! A stray bullet!" a shudder here passed through the breast of the bold highwayman, that not an army of foes would have invoked had he with his friend been alone. The fear of injury to the lovely girl seated before him unnerved him, and caused the dashing knight of the road to peer forwards with anxious eyes, as Jack, putting spurs to his horse, dashed away, being presently lost in the thickness of the adjacent grove of heavy pines that fringed the roadway on either side—a mass of wild copse or wood stretching beyond.

Not without an involuntary thrill was it that Claude now found himself alone.

He knew not why, but a feeling of some impending danger seized upon him.

So fearful was he of danger that he almost wished his fair charge was still in the confines of the secret haunt, the old Tree Cave.

Slowly and with caution, Claude now drew near the beginning of the darksome pine grove.

All around and behind him was wide open heath interspersed with wood and copse.

Before him the dark avenue of pines, passing through which the high road to London was gained.

Drawing up his steed, Claude now listened for some signal from his friend.

None, however, came.

All was deathly still. The moon glinted strongly on the dark summits of the pine trees, giving them a ghastly weird look; whilst the soft breeze moaned with a soughing dirge-like sound over the open heath!

"Diable, I like not this! Confound it, what has become of Jack?"

About to dash forward boldly into the dark grove of pines, Claude was astonished by the report of a musket, the shot from which whistled unpleasantly close to his head.

"That was a cowardly shot, and well meant! But, parbleu! Claude Duval bears a charmed life, you curs!" Wildly he now shouted as, with his sword he had drawn from his scabbard flourished over his head, he dashed forwards at a strange horseman, who, with cry of fury, had galloped out of the grove.

"You bear a charmed life, do you? This to test it!"

With a mocking laugh, the horseman here presented a pistol full at the head of Duval.

There was a slight fluff; a momentary gleam of yellow light; then all was still!

The powder of the stranger's pistol had flashed in the pan!

With an exulting laugh, Claude now leant forward over the neck of his steed, and, whilst a wild shriek burst from the lips of Maude, buried his sword to the hilt in the body of the stranger!

There was a heavy groan; then the pistol that had failed to send forth its leaden messenger of death fell from its owner's grasp, the man, deluged in blood, falling from his horse.

With a wild stare, Claude, incapable of thought or action, glared at the quivering frame of his assailant.

His peril, the safety of Maude Mayburn, now half senseless in his arms, were alike forgotten:

For in the face of the wounded man he had recognised one he had seen before:

Seen under circumstances peculiar and startling.

Once, and only once before, had those wild eyes and hideous face been seen by Claude :

That face now upturned with a ghastly pallor to the moonlight.

For a moment of time the place where the stranger had been seen was forgotten; then, with an exclamation of surprise and awe, it was remembered !

The face, now white and ghastly, the wide staring eyes seemingly glazing in death, was the same he had beheld peering down upon him through the open trap in the haunted mill.

For a moment Claude remained bending over the neck of his brave steed glaring at the grim body, that, sopping in a pool of blood, lay an inert mass upon the turf ; then, as a loud hallo sounded from the pine grove, he raised himself up in the saddle, and with one arm encircling the waist of the fainting Maude and the other flourishing his sword, the blade of which yet reeked with the blood of the stranger, on he dashed in mad haste into the darksome glade.

All was quiet in the dark grove.

The thick foliage of the pine tree avenue meeting overhead, all was intense darkness ; not a single ray of moonlight penetrating the topmost branches of the pines.

Gloomy woods on either side added to the dreary aspect of the place ; whilst huge bats, whirling in the air, ever and again came with a blind rush full against the horse and its rider, as they slowly coursed down the centre of the grove.

With beating heart and with a nervous tremor he could not control, Claude pursued his way.

Straining his eyes, he in vain endeavoured to pierce the inky darkness in search of his friend !

As near as he could guess Claude had now reached the middle or half-way down the avenue :

A thin ray of light at either end giving token of the extremity !

Not a sound had awakened the oppressive stillness of the scene !

The loud hallo that caused him to rush boldly into the grove was not repeated.

Bringing his brave steed to a halt, Claude now debated as to his next course.

A shout to his friend might bring armed foes upon him.

That something strange had happened to Jack, Claude was sure.

Boldly would he have got off his steed and searched the woods, on either side, in an endeavour to seek out the mystery, but for the young girl, whose arms he felt even now closing in terror around him.

Undecided how to act, he was suddenly startled by a cold hand being placed upon his.

In a moment after a pair of brawny arms dragged him from his horse, a wild shriek of terror pealing from the lips of the unhappy Maude as she was borne off.

Dazed, stunned, and confused by the suddenness of the attack, Claude, seized by apparently a dozen rough hands, was now dragged through the thick mass of copse.

A second wild shriek now woke up loud echoes in the pine grove ; then all was still !

Mad, infuriated at the thoughts of the dangers that surrounded Maude, Claude struggled violently for freedom ; but, held in giant grip, he was dragged along through brake and briar, bush and bramble !

Passing through the tangled copse, Claude's captors now emerged upon an open space :

An open space, near which was a steep hollow, at the bottom of which a large fire was burning, thick volumes of smoke ascending into the air.

A strange wild scene was it that now appeared to the the eyes of Duval.

Grouped round the fire below were some half-dozen brawny men, whose faces, black with grime and smut, looked like elves or demons as they stood in the hollow.

The pale moon's rays, throwing a blue ghastly glare on the scene, added to its wild horror !

Lost in amazement, Claude was now dragged along the precipitous sides of the steep, and at length was hurled amid a mass of wood and bramble deposited by the fire, the heat and smoke from which was stifling and intense.

Scarce could Duval believe his eyesight when—bound and helpless, within a few yards—he beheld his friend Jack ! About, at all hazards, to attract his attention, he was startled from his purpose by the sudden appearance of two brawny ruffians, carrying in their arms a human form.

Slowly the men descended from the copse above—the sides of the hollow, steep and precipitous, not easy of descent when encumbered with a load.

The group gathered round the fire now started forwards.

A loud cry now escaped their lips :

Cries of fury and surprise !

Apparently forgetful of their prisoners, the strangers all hurried to meet the two bearing between them a livid ghastly figure :

The figure of a man whose clothes were dripping with blood :

Dripping with blood, that issued from a gaping wound in the chest !

The opposite of the uncouth half-naked blackened men around, the wounded stranger was habited in a rich velvet coat, whilst a rich lace cravat (now sopped with blood) was fastened to his collar.

All in apparent rage and grief gathered round the ghastly and bleeding stranger !

With a nervous thrill Claude recognised the senseless form as that he had left upon the verge of the pine grove.

The wounded or dying man was the same who had assailed him on the heath :

The same, who, with livid face and wide staring eyes, had glared upon him in the haunted mill !

For a moment of time Claude in wonder gazed at the strange scene, then, rising from where he had been thrown and apparently forgotten, he glided over to his friend.

Jack, with flashing eyes and in mute silence, held up his wrists !

They were fastened with stout cords :

Cords drawn so tight that they were buried in the flesh !

To sever these with a large clasp knife he snatched from his pocket, was to Claude the work of a moment ; then, also, slashing at the ligatures that confined his feet, Jack found himself free !

The two friends now sank down in the thick shrubbery that lined the sides of the hollow.

The darkness of night with the smoke now entirely hid their persons, whilst the crackling of the burning wood drowned the crash of their footsteps as they scrambled on up the sides of the hollow.

Still intent upon the wounded and senseless stranger, the black-visaged group below heeded not the flight of their prisoners !

Nearer and nearer, Claude, followed by Jack, reached the top of the hollow.

"Another moment, old pal, and we are safe from those black dogs !"

Parting with exertion and excitement, the companions now gained the summit of the hollow.

All was quiet below.

No sound, no loud outcry indicative of their flight reached them.

Save the moaning of the wind over the copse and crackling of the burning wood, nought could be heard.

"It's all right, Claude ; but, by heavens, it was a close affair."

"Sacre, yes ! Curses on them ! they have that poor girl still in their power."

"Who, what are they, Claude ?"

"Heaven knows ! they bear the outward appearance of charcoal-burners ; but that trade, methinks, is a cover."

"Very likely. Where did they surprise you, Claude ?"

"In the very middle of the pine grove."

"That's where they trapped me. A cloth was hurled over my head, and I was dragged off my horse in that cursed dark grove before I could fire a shot.

"Well, pardieu, we are out of their hands ! But I've lost my sword, and my barking-irons, and my bonny steed : nor care I to leave this infernal place till I have secured them, and likewise rescued from the power of the vile horde poor Maude."

"I join you in that. I cannot call upon myself to leave that poor girl in their power !"

"We will risk all, Jack, to snatch her from them !"

"We will ! I'm with you, Claude, to the death !"

"Allons, then ! let us to business."

Followed by his companion, Duval now crept back to the edge of the hollow and glanced down below.

To his unbounded surprise, not a living creature was to be seen !

All the ruffianly troop had disappeared.

"Well, Jack, this mystery confounds me."

"It's very strange!"

"Where the deuce have they got to?"

"They've vanished?"

"Ma foi! yes, like a vision."

"Perhaps, like us, they have got a cave."

"Not they, Jack, confound them! they puzzle me. I don't like this infernal mystery."

"Nor I. What's to be done?"

"Blessed if I know! We are in utmost danger—may be seized upon any moment whilst we loiter here; but, to save my life, I can't go till I learn the whereabouts of poor Maude."

"Nor I."

"Hist!"

"What is it?" said Jack in a whisper, who, crouching beside Claude, here followed the direction of his friend's hand, which was pointed to a dark moving mass in the shrubbery near.

"One of the enemy, Claude!"

"Yes; keep quiet, take no notice, I'll be down upon him."

"Don't hurt him!"

"Oh, by no means!" Claude here, with a frown, drew the knife from his pocket, and, with a dangerous glitter in his eye, suddenly sprang upon the crouching figure of a man that with a pistol in his hand, was just about to fire upon them.

There was a smothered curse, followed by an ejaculation of fury.

"Attempt to move, utter the least sound, and, by heavens, I'll put your own bullet in your brain!"

Savagely Claude gazed upon the prostrate figure of the man beneath him.

A livid tint could be detected gathering under the black grime that smirched the ruffian's face.

The glitter of his enemy's eye, the broad blade of the knife directed at his throat by Jack; whilst the cold steel barrel of his pistol was pressed hard by Claude against his temple, told the discomfited villain that death was hovering near.

"Now, you black-faced cur, answer truly the question I am about to put, or, by the bright moon that rides above us, the knife held by my friend shall be drawn an inch deep across your throat."

Hissing these words in the terrified villain's ear's, Claude now pointed to the hollow, and exclaimed:

"Who, what are those fellows, your companions?"

"The Black Band."

"Good! Don't press too heavy with the knife, Jack; you're letting out the fellow's blood; and as I think he means to speak the truth I don't mean to kill him! Now tell me, who is that man that was brought with a hole in his side into the hollow?"

"That was the Captain's brother, Vampyre Vaughan."

"Oh, that was Vampyre Vaughan, was it? Well, he will have to get some more blood to-night, for he has lost a dose; and now, pray, who is your Captain?"

"Red Rufus."

"Good! Where does he hang out? where's your hiding-place?"

"We've three."

"Name them!"

"I dare not!"

"Dare not?"

"No; if I was discovered to have informed living man of our retreat they would swing me from the highest tree."

"Indeed!—Jack!"

"Well!"

"Give him the knife!"

With set teeth and livid face the man stared up at his foes: a bubbling cry only escaping his lips.

"What's he saying, Jack?"

"Trying a prayer, Claude."

"Is that so?"

"I'm sure of it!"

Turning once more to the wretched man whom he had left as he gave orders to Jack to slay him, Claude, now bending over him, exclaimed:

"Well, as you were prepared to suffer death rather than name your retreat, I will let that pass! I don't wish, nor did I intend, to play informer. But now tell me where is that young girl who was with me?"

"She has been carried to London."

"You are speaking the truth?"

"As death stares me in the face, yes."

"To what place have they taken her?"

"The Devil's Punch Bowl!"

"In old Westminster?"

"The same!"

"Good! I will make all speed to London, and as you may be risking a lie, you must go with me."

"I am telling nothing but the truth, so help me heaven, Claude Duval."

"Ah! you know me." Claude here started, gazing keenly into his captive's face.

"I know you. Yes, Duval! To Red Rufus, the Captain, and his brother, the Vampire, you are also known; but to none other of the band."

"You say the Vampire, as you term him, is acquainted with me?"

"Yes; and holds you in his hate."

"For what?"

"I know not."

"'Tis strange! There is a mystery in all this I like not! Where are your companions, those fellows that were in the hollow awhile back?"

"They have dispersed."

"Dispersed?"

"Yes; they have all gone to the Long Village (London), leaving me and another behind till the fires are out."

"Indeed, and where is your companion?"

"Asleep in the hollow."

"What brought you up here?"

"I was desirous of looking round to see if I could trace you. I suspected you were close at hand."

"Hem! your suspicions have been verified. But you've not gained much by your move; and now tell me where are our horses?"

"I don't know! when we captured you in the pine grove the animals bolted."

"A very clever proceeding on their part. Come on, Jack! do you see to the safety of our friend, whilst I go ahead and look out for our steeds! I'll warrant that they're not far off."

Claude, now quitting the vicinity of the hollow, made his way through the copse in the direction of the pine grove, Jack following slowly after with the man they had captured, and at whose head as they walked along he ominously presented his pistol.

CHAPTER V.

WHAT DUVAL AND GENTLEMAN JACK SAW IN THE PINE TREE GROVE—A SURPRISE.

Slowly, cautiously, Claude made his way through the copse, intently peering round for the lost steeds.

A gloomy darkness hung over the woods:

An increased darkness that preceded the coming dawn.

With an exclamation of disappointment at his non-encounter with their horses, Duval, now once more gaining the precincts of the pine grove, came to a halt:

Came to a halt as Jack, with a curse, darted forwards with the information that his captive had contrived to slip from his grasp a moment before, and like a fox had torn through the thick copse, disappearing in an instant in the heavy gloom.

"That's unfortunate, Jack! I meant to compel the fellow to go up to London! and failing to find Maude Mayburn at the Punch Bowl, why, sacre! I'd have put a bullet in him."

"Confound him, yes! I'd no idea of his attempting to slip us in these infernal woods."

"Well, no matter, Jack! We are freer to work without the custody of our black-visaged friend; and, by-the-by, respecting the information he favoured us with, do you know I think I've heard old Joe Noggins, at Westminster, speak of a gang called the Black Band?"

"So have I, Claude! They are composed of the vilest of the vile. There's not a knight of the road amongst them."

"No! they are cracksters, footpads, and river pirates; fellows who haunt Alsatia and the purlieus of Westminster, and who, in their devil's deeds, hesitate at nothing. Well, since they have crossed my path, I shall speedily prove to them that Claude Duval is not one to be interfered with! If their Captain, this Red Rufus as they call him, refuses to give up the pretty Maude, I'll e'en stick him as I've done his relative, the Vampyre."

Claude, now with Jack by his side, stood ruminating as to their course in the centre of the pine grove, near the spot upon which the struggle had taken place a little time before.

DUVAL, LEANING FORWARD, THRUST HIS SWORD TO THE HILT IN HIS ADVERSARY'S BODY.

To the gratification of the friends a thin white light now began to steal through the grove:

The light of approaching dawn.

"Morning will soon break, Claude!"

"Yes; we shall be able to see where we are presently."

"I hope we shall tumble on our horses. Where the deuce can they have got to?"

"Oh, they are not far off, depend upon it! We will leave this infernal grove, and very likely may find our brave steeds doing a comfortable graze by the road side."

"I hope we may! I promised to leave the horse I borrowed at Highgate; and though the animal is a good one, I'll keep my word given to it's owner, and restore it; nor

shall I be sorry when I am once more seated astride my own bonny mare! Lead on, Claude, let us get out of this dreary avenue of pines."

"Hold, Jack! What the deuce is that?"

"What?"

"Why, that glimmering light moving to and fro in the copse!" Duval, here seizing his companion by the arm, pointed to a yellow glimmer that shone strangely in the woods against the light of the coming dawn.

Motionless the companions stood within the precincts of the dark avenue of trees, peering intently at the pale yellow rays of a lamp that shone in the copse beyond.

What did it mean?

Impelled by a devouring curiosity the friends now, without a word, quitted the grove once more, winding their way slowly through the copse.

Bright and clear shone the yellow light before them.

All was silence in the woods, not a sound breaking the stillness around.

Slowly and with extreme caution the friends pushed on towards the light.

Pale and sickly it now looked as day began to cast a broad white gleam overhead.

It was in utmost surprise that, gaining a clump of dwarf oaks that surrounded an open space in the woods, Claude and Jack now discovered that the lamp, the light from which had attracted them, was hanging from the branch of a tree.

This tree, almost opposite to where they stood, was bare and bereft of foliage.

Strange and sad the withered oak, scorched and scathed with lightning, looked as it stood there the only one of the many trees around naked and decayed.

Not the blighted oak, not the lamp that swayed to and fro in the soft murmuring breeze, however, was it that chained the companions to the spot.

Hidden by the copse and the trunk of the tree against which they partly leant the friends gazed in speechless wonder at the scene before them.

At the foot of the scathed oak rested the body of a man.

Lividly pale, the horrible pallor of the grave, was the face of the stranger who at this moment slowly began to rise to his feet.

A short gasp of surprise escaped the lips of Claude as in the livid face before him he beheld that of his assailant who had fired upon him some two or three hours before:

The mystic comrade of the Black Band:

The man upon whom was fixed the horrible cognomen of Vampire Vaughan.

Scarce could Claude credit his eyesight as he gazed upon the hideous death face before him.

A low hoarse chuckle now escaped the strange man's lips as he stood at length upright, then, a moment after giving utterance to an exclamation of joy, he sank upon his knees:

Sank upon his knees by the foot of the tree.

In nervous haste he now began to remove the turf with a large knife that he drew from his vest.

Intently, scarce daring to breathe, Claude and Jack watched the stranger's actions.

They perceived his intentions at a glance.

He was about to make a hole at the foot of the scathed oak:

Was evidently going to bury some secret hoard.

Ever and again a low chuckle would escape the man's lips.

Once or twice he turned his head round, revealing to the friends his hideous death-pale face.

With sharp quick glances he seemed to pierce the thickness of the copse.

No token of alarm escaped him.

Screened by the huge trunk of the tree against which they leant, the spies were not detected.

With bated breath and distended eyes the friends glared at the strange scene:

A scene of wonder and horror!

Having apparently dug deep enough for his purpose, the man now paused.

Once more he cast his eyes with a keen swift glance around.

A low chuckle, a hoarse wolfish hyena-like laugh escaped him:

A laugh that revealed the large fangs, that, white and animal-like, projected from the thin pallid lips, like the teeth of a savage cur.

Bold men were Duval and his friend; yet they could not control a slight shudder of horror, as, with beating hearts and bated breath, they beheld the hideous stranger draw forth from the bag a human hand:

The small beautiful dimpled hand of a woman!

Bright luminous sparks, coruscating gleams of light, seemed to flash from the long taper fingers of the dead hand.

This in a moment of time the spies discerned proceeded from several rings, which, set with precious stones, were thrust in profusion upon the stiffened fingers.

For a brief space the hand was held up, a low guttural laugh sounding in the air; then dropping the ghastly object into the earth, the wretch Vaughan filling up the hole in mad haste, darted to his feet as the crackling of wood and tramp of feet sounded in his ears.

With a blasphemous oath, his keen black eyes rolling like beads of fire, whilst his livid face was contorted with rage

and fear, he, with a last glance round, bounded into the thickness of the wood:

Disappearing in the tangled copse, as Duval and Jack found themselves surrounded by a posse of officers!

CHAPTER VI.

THE RUINED HOUSE AT VAUXHALL—MAUDE AND HER CAPTORS—THE SECRETS OF THE BLACK BAND—MYSTERY AND CRIME—THE ESCAPE.

In the days of which we are writing, there stood by the side of the river near Vauxhall, a large old-fashioned rambling pile of buildings called the Ivy House.

It was a gloomy, weird, dreary-looking place.

The front of the house, which faced the river, was thickly covered with ivy, which grew in wild luxuriance against the walls, and from the extravagant growth of which the building took its name.

A large garden at the back of the house was bounded by open fields and meadows.

It was a bleak, bare, open spot, near which stood the old Ivy House.

There was a dark tale in connection with the place.

A cruel murder had been perpetrated in the abode; and, left for some years without a tenant, the house had bade fair to fall to utter ruin, until at last a stranger took courage and rented the place. But in a short time occurred a dispute about the property, and, the occupier leaving, the old building had fallen into chancery.

Year after year now passed away, the Ivy House falling more and more into decay.

The winter storms wreaked their fury on the old building; the rude blasts from the river blew shrill and wild over the ruined tenement, increasing the decay of all around.

The casement beaten in, the chimney-pots torn from the roof by the wintry winds, wretched and repelling indeed looked the old house by the river.

On the night following the capture of Maude Mayburn in the pine tree grove, near the woods at Finchley, a vehicle drew up in the front of the lone dwelling.

From this vehicle two men staggered forth carrying between them a young and senseless girl.

Steeped in a senseless lethargy the unconscious victim was removed into the gloomy old dwelling, the outer door of which closed after the entrance of the strange visitors, sounding dismal and hollow as it woke up echoes around.

Having made their way into a large hall, the two men gave their senseless burthen into the charge of a wild-looking lad, who, lamp in hand, stood shivering by the door, which, in answer to a rude summons, he had opened a moment before.

"Here, Timothy! take that girl to old Mother Barlow, below, and tell her to put her to bed. Let her have some brandy: she is under the influence of a dose. Look alive! Red Rufus will be here soon, and 'twill be worse for you if you ain't sharp in your movements!"

The two men, leaving the lad to execute their bidding, now ascended a flight of stairs at the end of the hall, and passing along a passage or corridor that, even in that summer night smelt mouldy and mildewed, pushed open a door to their left, and were presently seated in a small chamber overlooking the back of the house.

All about the apartment, like the passage without, gave token of neglect and decay.

The gold beading around the ceiling was now black and tarnished, and in parts falling away; the oaken wainscot of the chamber was covered with dust and cobwebs; the floor in many places having, too, been eaten into holes by the rats, the scampering feet of many being heard as the two men entered the room.

The shrill winds whistled and screamed round the gables of the old building, seeming as though singing a mournful dirge over the ruined dwelling.

"A queer den this, Alick!"

"Yes; pah! it smells like a vault! Give me the Moat Manor before this!"

"So say I! But the infernal runners have done us out of that crib for a time."

"They have so! I'm sorry Harborough is run in."

"Yes; he's a decent fellow. As for that cursed Vaughan, with his dead-alive mug and spiteful ways, I'd as lieve have the devil himself for a lieutenant as he."

"That too would I, Jem! Red Rufus is a demon; but t'other—well, there is something infernally unnatural about him."

"So there is, Alick! I often wonder if he is what they call him."

"What's that, Jem?"

"Why, you know, a vampyre."

The two men, here speaking low, gazed in terror round the chamber, which, only lighted by the rays of the moon that crept in through the broken casement, appeared to them peopled with dark shadows.

"I say, Alick!"

"Well!"

"I think the least we say about Vaughan the better! He is a mystery."

"By Satan, you're right, Jem! But, I say, what will be done now Harborough is captured? Will his adherents leave the Band?"

"Not they."

"But you know his pals don't like Rufus or his brother."

"Well, no! But they'll have to now! They dare not turn against the Band though Harborough swung to-morrow."

"Well, I suppose you are right; but if there ain't a split among us over this job of Miles Ellerton and his girl I'm mistaken."

"I think the wench had been best left alone! Here's Andrew Masterton frantic about her."

"How?"

"Why you know he hates that fop Ellerton; and now that Rupert Harborough is out of the way, depend upon it, Andrew will try and do as he likes."

"Possibly."

"I am sure of it."

"Masterton seems almost to defy our leaders, don't he?"

"Well; yes. It has often surprised me that Vaughan has put up with him; but, hark, there's the signal of a fresh arrival!" About to pass through a small door at the further end of the room, the man Alick here hurried from the chamber, followed by his companion, the two returning to the lower part of the house by the way they had come.

Reaching the hall below they were encountered by two strangers, who, merely recognising them with a nod, passed in, and entered a large chamber at the further end of the passage, that, in the days long gone by, had served as a dining-room.

Closing the door after them, the two new arrivals drew near a large fire that, even in that summer night, looked bright and cheerful, dispelling slightly the gloom of ruin and decay.

"Well, Andrew Masterton, you persist in your intention of defying this Miles Ellerton, and taking from him his purposed bride?"

"Aye! If he objects, he can go and complain to his particular friend, Rupert."

"And do you also insist upon demanding the vacant leadership held by Harborough over that portion of the Band known as the Moat Manor House men?"

"I do."

"Nothing can divert you from your purpose?"

"Nothing you can put forth. Look here, I'll be interfered with in this matter by none!"

"Indeed!" The man, the taller of the two who had been seated by the fire, here looked up hard into his companion's face.

There was a snaky, fascinating glitter in the dark eyes that for a moment startled the other, who, jumping off his seat, exclaimed:

"Look here, Vaughan! don't fasten your infernal murderous gaze upon me. I'm not to be frightened by your death's head. I know too much for you, Vampyre!"

"You've said it. Yes! And therefore must perish! The time has come!"

A low grating laugh here escaped the lips of the man, as he again fixed his beadlike orbs of fire upon the flushed, angry countenance of his companion, who, with an oath, snatched a pistol from his vest and levelled it at his head.

"Put down your barking iron, Andrew Masterton; it can't hurt me!"

"Pshaw! You don't put me from your path that way; I am not to be humbugged with the tale of your charmed life."

With a fierce oath the man here stepped back, and, taking aim, fired.

There was a loud, deafening report, the chamber becoming filled with smoke; then, ere the echoes of the pistol-shot

had died away, a low chuckling laugh sounded through the chamber.

"Well meant! you intended it that time, Andrew Masterton! But, eh, eh, eh! you see I do bear a charmed life! The tale is a true one. Here's your bullet. Put it back in your weapon, and have another fire."

With a loud laugh, a bullet, flattened as though it had been sent against a stone wall, was here thrown by the man Vaughan at the feet of his companion.

In wild, stupefied amaze the latter stared upon the livid face of him whom he had daringly attempted to destroy; then, as, throwing away his pistol, he was about to dash from the chamber with the howl of a fierce wolf, the other sprang upon him, bearing him with a crash to the ground.

"Your time has come, Andrew Masterton! You've attempted my life! I were mad to let you live!"

With a snarl, which disclosed, horribly, a set of white and wolfish-looking teeth, the man Vaughan here sprang upon his enemy as he was about to stagger to his feet; and, with the quickness of thought, slipped a handkerchief he drew from his pocket round the other's neck; then, grasping the ends tightly, pulled with all his force.

A low gurgling cry escaped the lips of the doomed man, his face in a second turning a purple tint.

Convulsively he drew his legs up and down in dying agony.

The merciless foe, however, held on, tightening the kerchief round the neck of his victim.

No sound now issued from the blackened lips of the dying man, who, with a fearful tenacity to life, struggled on.

The face of the wretched man was now hideous to behold.

But calm and unmoved the murderer knelt upon his chest, holding on with a fierce grip to the instrument of death.

The face of the helpless man now turned from purple to black, whilst a strong shiver appeared to dart through his frame; then all was still.

The murderer's work was finished!

The wretched Andrew Masterton was no more!

With cool indifference, his eyes having in them a baleful, fierce glitter, the assassin now rose, muttering:

"'Tis a fine trick that of Thugging! Fool, to dare me as he has done!—me, Van Vaughan, before whom the Black Band to a man doth quail! I would have spared the fool had he not so oft reminded me of the past! The old well in the cellar beneath shall be his resting-place! I will remove the corse at once, and then will pay a visit to the girl in the rooms above! She is young and beautiful; making her mine, renewed life will be endowed me! I will this night, this hour, secure her!"

"No you won't, Vampyre Vaughan!"

With a start, and his livid sallow face convulsively contorted with passion, the murderer drew back, dropping the body he had seized upon the floor.

"Rupert Harborough, you here? How came you to escape?"

"It matters not how! I have, you see! What have you been doing to Masterton? Upon my honour you have not increased his beauty! What are you going to do with him?"

"Convey him to the dry well. He defied me, and has met his doom!"

"So I perceive! Well, he is a ruffian less in the world! But ere you convey him to his final resting-place, tell me where have they put that girl of Ellerton's?"

"In the Tapestried Chamber."

"Good! I will go and visit her anon, but will first see the lads in the long room! Go, tell them, Vaughan, that I have escaped; prepare them for my coming; and let me bid you beware how you attempt to molest the pretty Maude Mayburn, or I will, as I've oft threatened, put a bullet in your skull, drive a stake through your carcase, and bury you at the cross roads, going upon the supposition that what they say about you is true! I believe that is the only burial that effectually prevents a vampyre rising from his grave, ain't it?"

A horrible scowl gathered upon the repulsive features of the man Vaughan, as his companion, with a meaning look, quitted the chamber.

"Would that I could compass his destruction! but he is ever on the alert—cool, courageous, and defiant! Even I, who fear none of the Band, care not to risk the consequences of an attempt upon the life of Rupert Harborough, and not the deed!"

Seizing the horrible disfigured corse of his late companion

by the collar of his coat, without a symptom of repugnance or remorse the assassin now dragged it from the chamber.

Whilst the scenes of terrible crime were enacting below, the young girl, brought captive the early part of the night to the lone house, was in a state of distraction, pacing the narrow limits of a small chamber situate at the back of the building on the second floor.

With clasped hands and face of marble whiteness, Maude Mayburn, for it was she, in wild frenzy paced backwards and forwards, seeking in vain an outlet for escape.

The door, hard and fast, resisted her utmost strength to force its fastenings.

Casement there was none.

A small hand-lamp cast strange fitful flashes of light through the room.

The remains of a large piece of tapestry that covered the walls, now hanging mildewed and rotten, added to the dreary aspect of the chamber.

Wildly the unhappy Maude glared around.

There was no chance of escape:

None !

Moaning and sobbing she gave up all for lost.

Even he, her preserver, the brave Claude Duval, she had in that fatal pine grove beheld dragged from his horse and made captive. Nor did she now dare to hope he would ever see her more.

"I am lost ! lost !" In a paroxysm of grief, the poor girl, who for hours the day before had been oblivious to all around, the effects of an opiate adm' istered by her abductors, now sank down upon a seat, ever and again gazing in startled horror around her lone prison chamber.

Dismal, horrible as was the place, she dreaded the moment that would behold her led forth to be handed over to the villain Ellerton.

Hollowly the wind moaned and whistled as it careered round the house.

Strange shadows were cast upon the floor of the tapestried chamber by the pale flickering rays of the lamp.

Her eyes, red and swollen with weeping, Maude, now sinking on her knees, prayed earnestly for aid:

Prayed, too, for him who had risked his life in her defence.

With throbbing, beating heart she asked herself where was he now.

In agonising despair, at length rising to her feet, she staggered to the door.

A cold chill of fear darted through her frame as her ear detected a noise without.

Her ruffian abductors have then come to take her hence :

To give her over to the power of the lothed Miles Ellerton :

To put upon her a doom far worse than death !

A wild shriek escapes her lips as the door swings open.

Mad with terror, she flies to the further end of the chamber.

"Hist, hist, pretty lady ! be not alarmed ! 'tis I, Timothy Tack ! If you would escape from the Ivy House, follow, follow me !"

With mingled terror and surprise, Maude gazed upon the strange being, who, light in hand, now stood before her.

It was the figure of a boy grown prematurely old.

There was the staid look of age with a thoroughly youthful form.

Long elfin locks hung over the brow of the strange being ; whilst a shifting glance and occasional nervous start showed him accustomed to emotions of fear.

Stepping forwards her mysterious visitor now approached Maude and seized her hand, then, pointing without, exclaimed :

"They are in the long room ! If you would hence, dear lady, follow me, ere it be too late ! I have promised I would aid your escape, and Timothy Tack never breaks his word to friend or foe ! Come ! come, lady, come !"

Walking as in a dream, her brain dazed, a sick, giddy feeling upon her, Maude followed with trembling steps her strange conductor, who led her at once from the chamber down a long narrow passage, and from thence through a door into the hall, at the further end of which was the means of egress from the old house.

"Hush ! tread softly ! should we be intercepted now, death would be my doom ! Hark ! those sounds below ! they are breaking up the meeting ; another moment and

we may be too late ! Haste ! Tell him whom you will meet upon the river's bank, that this night may doom me to a horrid death ; but that I have risked all, and my debt is paid !"

As these words fell from his lips the strange lad with feverish impatience unlocked the door of the Ivy House, thrusting the bewildered Maude out into the darkness of the night, and softly closing the door after her.

Dazed, confounded, the young girl stood for a moment incapable of thought or action.

She was now free :

Safe without the walls of that drear old ruin, the haunt of crime, the hiding-place and abode of men whose hands were ready for any deed of rapine !

Wildly Maude stared around her !

She was now alone in the large garden that stretched before the front of the old house !

In the distance were the dark flowing waters of the Thames !

All was pitchy darkness !

Only from the lights on the decks of the craft that rode upon the waters did Maude make out the direction of the river.

Huge black clouds hung low overhead, whilst the wind, blowing chill, in hollow gusts moaned shrilly over the open waste.

Fancying that she beheld a dim muffled figure stealing behind one of the gables of the building, Maude, with lightning speed, and on the wings of fear, darted like a frightened fawn from the precincts of the ruined house.

On tore the affrighted girl ; a stifled shriek once rising to her lips as she stumbled and fell, staggering up with the the thought that a grim dark form was standing beside her.

The lights upon the river were now plain and distinct.

Despite the darkness of the night, Maude, with a cry of joy, now traced out the surface of the waters. The ground over which she was passing was soft and damp.

The gardens of the old house were now left behind.

In mad haste Maude flew on :

Flew on over the meadows that fringed the river's bank.

Ever and again the feet of the fugitive plashed in a pool of water.

The fields over which she was now hastening, oftentimes at high tide being flooded, were very marshy and covered with pools of water ; tall bullrushes and stunted willows flourishing in the moist soil.

It was as she darted past one of these patches of marsh, overgrown with rushes and tall rank grass, that Maude was caught in the strong arms of a man who, ghostlike, started up in her path.

A wild piercing shriek in a moment of time was changed to a cry of joy, as her captor, in a voice she recognised as that of a friend, exclaimed—

"Be not alarmed, dear girl ! Thank heaven you are safe ! Your escape will be brave news for the captive in his Newgate cell !"

Scarce comprehending the words that fell upon her ears, with a sick dizzy feeling, Maude, her frame exhausted by her recent captivity, sank fainting in the arms of her supporter.

The words "What mean you—where, where is Claude ?" dying in a whisper on her lips.

When returning once more to consciousness, she discovered that she was reclining at length in the bottom of a wherry which, rowed by her preserver, was shooting with the tide in the direction of the old Bridge of Westminster, the lights from which glimmered faintly in the darkness of the night. An exclamation of joy escaped the lips of her protector as, ceasing to bend at the oars, he slipped them in the rowlocks and stooped forwards to gaze with evident pleasure at her return to consciousness.

It was with a wild stare of astonishment that Maude now recognised in her companion the friend of Claude Duval :

The light-hearted, daring Gentleman Jack !

CHAPTER VII.
THE VILLA AT KENNINGTON—MAUDE MEETS WITH A FRIEND—LOVE AND FIDELITY.

"You are better now, Miss Maude, are you not ?" As these words issued from his lips, Jack took a quick searching glance over the river, and, noting a boat leaving the shore adjacent to the lone house, he once more seized the oars, and sent his own little craft at terrific speed over the waters.

With flushed face and beating heart, Maude gazed for a moment speechless at her protector, and then, stooping forwards with clasped hands, exclaimed, "Tell me—tell me, where, oh where, is Duval?"

"Well, he is in the hands of the Philistines, dear Miss Mayburn! But don't be alarmed; if he ain't safe out of the jug (prison) by this time to-morrow, I'll forfeit my good right hand. I have a plan for his rescue that cannot fail."

"He is in prison, then?" With white face and pallid lips these words were uttered by Maude in a tone indicative of sorrow and despair.

"Well, yes; they have him safe in Newgate at present, Miss Mayburn; but if I don't help him soon to get safe out of it, put Gentleman Jack down for a double-distilled fool, that's all."

Viciously the highwayman here pulled at the oars, as he thought of the friend who, at that moment, was lodged in a prison cell.

For a few minutes Maude sat still and silent, then, suddenly looking up, in a voice choking with suppressed sobs, asked how it happened that Duval had been captured.

Resting on his oars, and allowing the boat to drift down with the tide, Jack now related facts already known to our readers. When surprised by the officers in the copse, after the disappearance of the man Vaughan, there was a desperate struggle, in the course of which Claude was overpowered; Jonathan Anstey, the leader of the runners, directing the exertions of all his men to the capture of Duval alone.

Finding that but little efforts were made to detain him, Jack, seeing no hope of aiding his friend, had been able to make good his escape! "My idea was that I could be a deuced sight more serviceable to my pal outside the jug than in it! He has had note from me that I am at work; and his only trouble, as I heard from one who saw him this very day, is your captivity in the hands of the unscrupulous members of the Black Band. Your escape made known to him on the morrow, will give him heart to use all his wit and cunning to get out of the hands of his foes, or I'm much mistaken," said Jack, who here, having drawn the boat up to the stairs at Westminster-bridge, assisted his fair charge to get out, the two presently after hurrying over the water in the direction of Southwark.

"Have you any place you would like me to escort you to; or shall I conduct you to a snug retreat, the habitation of one who owes much to my friend, and a lady who I'm sure will do all in her power to serve you?" said Jack, who had paused by the Dog and Duck Gardens (the spot where Bethlem madhouse now stands) and stood awaiting the reply to his question.

Placing her hands confidingly in those of her protector, the young girl, in a low voice struggling with emotion, stated that she could not rest in quiet with any mere acquaintance unknowing the fate of him to whom she owed a lifelong debt of gratitude! "Take me to his friend," she exclaimed, "be she whom she may; with her I shall be able to converse of him—shall know if he escapes from his dreadful prison! A strange fate has thrown us together, and may Heaven desert me if I desert one to whom I owe so much!"

"Spoken like a true British maiden! and, though a knight of the road, Claude Duval, Miss Mayburn, you will I am sure find, is a thorough gentleman. He is my dearest of pals—my life I'd give for him; and in storm or sunshine we are on oath to remain steadfast and true to the end."

Jack here, drawing Maude's arm in his, proceeded onwards along the high road leading to Kennington.

To an interrogation now put to him as to how he had discovered her recent place of captivity, he informed her, as they hurried on, that he had visited an inn at Westminster known as the "Devil's Punch Bowl;" from its landlord he had learned that members of the Black Band could be found at the ruined house at Vauxhall. Making his way to the lone building, Jack had been so fortunate as to come across the boy, Timothy Tack, whose life it appeared had, upon an occasion, been saved by him. From this lad he not only learned that she whom he sought was a prisoner in the den of crime, but also gained upon him to effect her release! "Poor, half-witted fellow," said Jack in conclusion; "I trust no ill may come to him for his timely aid!"

Reaching Kennington Common (at this period a large open tract, with a few houses sparsely scattered here and there) Jack now turned off down a long country lane, lined on either side by the hawthorn and blackberry.

The moon, now bursting from a bank of cloud, made all as light as day.

With some surprise Maude, who expected no habitation near, discovered, half-way down the narrow lane, a pretty cottage or villa, that, standing back on their left hand, appeared surrounded by a most beautiful garden.

In a moment after Jack paused at the gates of the house.

Pulling a bell, to the tinkle of which now sounded the bark of a dog, a light presently appeared at a little casement above.

Presently, after the door of the house was thrown open, an elderly woman, a lamp in her hand, making her appearance, to her interrogation as to who was there, Jack replied with a loud laugh.

"What! don't you know me, Mrs. Hunter? 'Tis I! hurry up! I have a lady here who needs rest and refreshment."

"Good heavens! Is it you, Captain? And where may be the master?"

The female who had hastened forward now unlocked the gate.

"Why, Claude will not be here for a day or two, perchance! In the meantime introduce this young lady to Kate; they are companions in misfortune!"

"Poor thing! come this way, my dear."

The old lady, a motherly dame, stout and pleasant-looking, here conducted Maude to the porch, outside of which was now standing a pretty, petite, fair girl, with blonde hair and laughing blue eyes, who, in merry tones, exclaimed, "Heyday, Master Jack! who have you here! Where is Claude?"

"He'll not be here to-night, Kate!" exclaimed Jack, who here, taking Maude by the hand, in a few brief sentences made the blue-eyed girl acquainted with her misfortunes! "See to her, Kate! You are sisters in trouble, and whilst Dashing Duval and Gentleman Jack draw the breath of life, let them injure you who dare!"

The little party now entering the villa, the door was carefully fastened to, all being presently seated at a table, upon which were the remains of a comfortable repast.

"We have just finished supper, Captain, and Kate, fancying a stroll in the garden, has kept us most fortunately up late," exclaimed the housekeeper, Mrs. Hunter, who here bustling about soon set Maude at her ease.

Winding her arms around her neck with sisterly affection, the young girl Kate entreated her to dismiss all trouble from her mind, that no one could harm her there.

"I'm so glad you've come!" exclaimed the light-hearted girl. "Dear old Mrs. Hunter, she is very kind; but she can't play the piano, she can't sing, and can't even play cards!" A pout of the lips here added to the piquant beauty of the young girl, who, scarce fifteen, seemed a little wayward thing, unknowing and uncaring of the troubles of life.

With a smile Maude gazed upon her future companion; at a first glance conceiving towards her feelings of love and friendship.

It was with a happy heart that Maude retired that night to rest with the pretty Kate Annorsley, the fair and beautiful girl, who, but for Duval, would have become the victim of the thief-taker Jonathan Anstey.

Early the following morning, the little party at Jessamine Villa, as it was called, were up betimes conversing together. The young girls grew more and more attached: their position so like, both orphans, both pursued by men whom they loathed, drew them together in the closest bond of friendship.

For their preserver the fair girls had the deepest reverence and love.

It needed no inquiries from Maude to discover that the pretty Kate had surrendered her girlish heart to the handsome daring friend of Dashing Duval, Gentleman Jack.

Artlessly relating incidents in their past brief career, the young girls wandered in the grounds of the cottage, and but for the absence of a man to whom they owed so much would have had no alloy to their happiness.

Joined just before the breakfast hour by Gentleman Jack, they received an intimation that on the morrow they might expect a visit from the one they were both so anxious again to see, then, with a warning to keep within the house, nor venture forth from its roof, the two girls were left alone, Jack informing them that he was about to keep an appointment with his friend.

CHAPTER VIII.

THE MEETING IN THE CELL—A FRIENDLY WARDER—THE
MYSTERIOUS LOAF—WATCHING FOR MIDNIGHT—A FIGHT
FOR LIBERTY—THE ESCAPE—THE PURSUIT—DASHING
DUVAL AND THE YOKEL—ANSTEY OUTWITTED.

Newgate, that dark, grim, and dreary pile, with its solid
masonry and innumerable narrow and barred casements,
was, in the time of which we write, almost more repelling
than now.

Black, morne, and sombre looked the dread prison-house,
without the walls of which hundreds of unhappy wretched
criminals were strangled out of life ; not as now, for grim-
visaged murder, but for petty robberies and forgeries !

The common thief, stealing an article of a shilling in
value in the good old times of Dashing Duval, swung at
Newgate, Tyburn, Kennington Common, or some bare
desolate heath, side by side with a man whose hands were
crimsoned in human blood !

Newgate, what hideous tales could not those terrible walls
give forth !

What dread scenes have not passed within and without
the gaol !

Black Monday, or Hanging Monday (now, thank heaven,
passed away), was a day of high revelry at Newgate !

The morning that Gentleman Jack left Maude Mayburn
and Kate Annersley at the villa near Kennington Common,
was Black Monday.

All within and without the dread prison was in excitement
and confusion !

Discipline at the hour of an execution in those days was
somewhat lax.

This Gentleman Jack, with a smile and chuckle as he
neared the goal at seven o'clock that summer morn, was
perfectly well aware of.

Not without a shudder did Jack, with his features disguised
by a patch over his eye, and a wig of fiery red hair which
covered his own rich auburn locks, look up at the grim
ghastly gallows erected in the roadway facing the gaol.

A large fighting, yelling crowd was gathered outside
the prison-house.

Here men, women, and children, some of the former gin-
mad, were in their thousands congregated round the gallows.

It was a wild terrible scene :

A scene out of the power of historians or romancists to
properly pourtray !

Bright and beautiful, the sun shone on the dial of St.
Sepulchre's :

St. Sepulchre's, that church, the bell of which has knelled
to death its thousands.

Pushing his way through the noisy, screeching, yelling,
and cursing crowd, Gentleman Jack made for the visitors'
entrance of the great prison-house :

Habited in the garb of a decent tradesman, with the
patch on his right eye, his fiery red wig the hair of which
covered his forehead, and a diabolical squint he contrived
to make with his remaining optic, drawing such jeers and
shouts of laughter upon him from the crowd as convinced
him his disguise was perfect.

" Well, with an accomplice in the goal and a pal without,
I think you will be tricked this time, Jonathan Anstey !"
muttered Jack as he at length, perspiring at every pore,
gained the door at the wicket of which a gaoler was staring
with a grin at the mob without.

" Well, carrots, old man, what is it ?"

" I want to come in !"

" Then you'll have to want," said the custodian of the
gate with a grin.

" But I wish particularly to see one of the prisoners.
The fellow robbed me on Hounslow Heath a month back,
and I swore I'd come and see him when I heard of his
capture."

" Indeed ! what's the fellow's name ?"

" Duval "

" Duval ! what, Dashing Duval, the knight of the road !
Well, you can't see him now ; you must call another time !"

" But I can't ; I'm going to Marseilles to-morrow."

" You can go to Marseilles to-morrow, and you can go to
the devil to-day ; but you don't come in here !"

" But I want to bully this fellow, Duval ; I want to exult
over his capture ! I want something for my fifty guineas and
my gold repeater !"

" Well, I understand your wishing for a grin over him, old
man ; but, if you put it off a little while, you can see him
outside here in a week or two, when, I've no doubt, like

Bill Harvey, Joe the Magsman, and Jim Conner the Water-
man, who will be topped presently, Master Duval will draw
together plenty of friends !"

" You won't let me in, then ?" said Jack, here pulling out
a guinea and passing it into the other's hand through the
wicket of the gate.

" Well, yer see, I can't: it's as much as my place is worth !"
exclaimed the fellow pocketing the coin.

" Is Tony Whiffles inside ?"

" Tony, the warder, do you mean ?"

" Yes."

" Oh yes! he was here a minute ago ! There he is
crossing the hall ! Tony, Tony! here's a cove here as
wants to speak with yer."

" Right you are, Bob ; I'll come." In another moment the
cautious custodian of the gate was joined by a tall red-faced
man, who looked more like a well-to-do yeoman than a
warder in London's principal gaol.

A slight sign of recognition was passed between Jack and
the fresh arrival ; and, the moment after, upon receiving a
whispered ejaculation from the new comer, the gatekeeper
unlocking the wicket allowed the applicant for admission to
enter.

Having passed the portals of the prison-house Jack now
kept close beside the man Whiffles, who in a whisper bade him
follow, nor take note of any one whom they might come
across.

" I'm playing a dangerous game. But your price will
enable me to quit England for the Forests of Canada. I'm
sick of this life, and risk all to be free of it." These words
were uttered in low breathed accents by Jack's conductor,
who, hurrying him first down one passage and then another,
at length halted in the middle of a short corridor, on either
side of which three black doors let in the walls denoted as
many cells.

" Here we are, Jack ! your pal's cell is No. 2."

" All right, Tony ; you received the coin last night all
safe ?"

" Yes, Jack ; you've acted your part, I'll carry out mine."

" Have you arranged about the loaf ?"

" Yes, that is all settled ; he'll have it in soon."

" Good ! You've acted fair and square, and I hope you'll
get on across the water !"

" Thank'ee, Master Jack !"

Having unbolted and unlocked the ponderous iron door
of No. 2 cell, the warder now pushed it open, and in another
moment the two friends had once more met :

Met in a prison chamber :

The one a helpless captive, the other in dire danger, his
only shield from which a clever disguise and the assistance
of the man Tony Whiffles !

" Well, how goes it brave heart ?" said Jack, seizing the
hand of his friend in his as the warder now left them alone,
closing the door carefully after him.

" As well as can be expected, dear pal ; from your message
I was led to look for you this morning."

" Sacre ! would I were free of this accursed cell, breathing
once more the fresh air of liberty, once more seated astride
my bonny Jane, coursing like the wind o'er hill and dale,
heath and road !" With gloomy brow Duval here threw
himself into the one seat the little narrow dungeon boasted,
gazing with longing eye at the gleam of sunshine that
glinted through the iron bars of the small opening in the
walls of his cell, looking out on the courtyard at the back of
the gaol.

" Don't be down on your luck, Claude ! remember, dark
is the hour before the dawn ! rouse up, man, I've good news !"

" Good news ! the news I care for you cannot give me,
Jack," said Duval despondingly.

" Indeed ! perhaps I can."

" What mean you ?" exclaimed Claude, now starting
hastily from his seat and seizing his friend nervously by the
arm,—" you do not mean to tell me that you have brought
me tidings of her ? Do not tamper with me, Jack, dear old
pal ; but have you indeed any news of poor Maude ? I will
tell you the truth, Jack ; I love that poor, unprotected
girl ; and, highwayman as I am, will do aught to serve
her."

" I know it, Claude ; rest content, she is safe !"

" Safe ?"

" Aye, along with Kate Annersley."

" What, at Kennington ?"

" Even so. The two roses—happy the man who secures
them for his own—are now anxiously awaiting my return to

Jessamine Villa with news of him for whom, egad, I believe both would give their lives !"

"This is news, indeed, dear Jack ! By heavens, I shall go mad if I escape not hence to-night !" exclaimed Claude, glaring wildly with glistening eyes at the narrow barred casement of his cell.

"Have no fear of that ; you will be with us on the morrow."

"You speak hopefully."

"I know it."

"Buoy me not up with false hopes, dear Jack ! Behold those bars high up above my reach. I have no means of forcing them—not a knife, not an article with which to carve a way to liberty."

"Perhaps Providence may send you some aid. Hush ! the warder returns ; he is my friend. I can no more ; but in conclusion remember my parting words. Eat your bread to-night, 'twill give you strength to gain your freedom."

With a smile Jack now turned to the door, at that moment thrown back on its hinges by the friendly warder.

Starting forward Claude wrung his companion warmly by the hand, who, smiling upon him and raising his eyes to the little narrow grating of his cell, stepped into the passage without.

A moment after the door banging to with a loud clang was carefully bolted and barred, our hero once more finding himself alone !

Moodily he sat, glaring up with longing eyes at the ruddy rays that poured in through the grating of his prison chamber.

Anon a dark cloud gathered over his brow.

A loud hum of voices was now drowned by the deep, sonorous tolling of a bell :

The bell of St. Sepulchre's :

The bell sounding the death note of the doomed !

With a shiver he could not repress, Claude, starting up, glared wildly at the grating through which streamed the bright rays of the morning sun.

Three fellow-creatures without were gazing their last at that orb of day.

Listening intently for the sounds from without, Claude was now startled by a noise at the door of his cell, and turning round found himself confronted by the thief-taker and Bow-street officer Jonathan Anstey.

"Do you hear that bell, Claude Duval ?"

"It's not lately come to my turn to be deaf !" exclaimed Claude, coolly, at the same time seating himself unconcernedly, and staring his questioner insolently in the face.

"Oh, I see ! Two days' confinement hasn't taken the pluck out of yer ! Ah, we shall see what a week or two will do ! Let me see, I think I can bring your affair off in a fortnight ; and if I play my cards properly I shall be in a position to twist the hemp that will hang you."

"Dear me ! you don't say so ! ain't I frightened ?"

"Duval, this bounce don't impose on me !"

"Don't it ?"

"No ! your acting a part."

"Am I, really ?"

"Yes ; when I first came in you were listening to the sound of that bell !"

"Dear me !"

"Yes ; and you were asking yourself how soon it would be when it tolled out for you !"

"Jonathan, you are quite a prophet ! I was listening to the bell ?"

"Of course you were !" said the thief-taker, with a chuckle.

"Oh, yes, I don't deny it ; but you are out, sweet Jonathan, in diving for my thoughts ! Now I will tell you what I really was thinking—where I should be when that same bell strikes eight to-morrow morning."

"Ha ! ha ! ha ! as Shakespere says, Duval, ' It needs no ghost from the grave to tell us that.'"

"Don't it ? allow me to disagree with you !"

"Oh, perhaps, you think you'll escape ?"

"I'm thinking I shall."

"Good ! Well if you do I'll admit you're clever !"

"Thank you, Jonathan ; your opinion one way or the other will not be valued by me !"

"All right ! But now cease this banter : I've come here on a special mission."

"Have you, really ?"

"Yes ; you are well aware that if I chose you should get off, you'd get off safe enough ; but that if I put on all pressure, I can send you to the gallows !"

"I'm not so sure of that !"

"I am !"

"Very good ! may a difference of opinion never alter friendship !"

"Now look here, Duval," continued the thief-taker, drawing nearer, and unheeding the other's sneering manner, " if you will give to me the address of that girl, and interfere no further between us, I'll guarantee you shall be miles from this by to-morrow."

"Jonathan Anstey !"

"Well ?"

"Allow me to observe you're an ass ! You ask me for the address of some girl, never telling me whom you are alluding to."

"You know well enough !" said the thief-taker, scarce able to control his temper at the cool impudence of his prisoner.

"The deuce I do ! You know a good many girls, Jonathan ; perhaps you mean squinny-eyed Sal or pock-marked Bet of the Saloop Stall ?"

"Claude Duval, the girl I mean is Kate Annersley. She whom, in your knight errantry, you snatched from me, and whom you now have somewhere in hiding."

"Jonathan Anstey, have you read the old fairy tale of ' Little Red Riding Hood '? Of course you have. Very good ! Little Red Riding Hood was eaten by a nasty old wolf ; and I mean to take particular care that my little Kate shan't be devoured by a nasty grey wolf. You understand, sweet Jonathan ?"

"Perfectly. You defy me, fool, idiot, dolt ! you but give me the trouble to hunt up the girl you removed from my path ! It shall not be long ere I have the dainty Kate in my arms. This day fortnight, Claude Duval, shall behold you swinging outside to the sound of those bells that now clang upon the air. To-morrow you shall be heavily fettered ; this night the governor shall know that you have boasted of and meditate an escape. Farewell, my bold highwayman, get out of this if you can !"

"Undoubtedly I will, Jonathan Anstey !" muttered our hero as the enraged thief-taker, glancing fiercely upon him, quitted the cell.

Scarce had the door closed behind his enemy ere it was again thrust back upon its hinges, the warder, Tony Whiffles, appearing with a jug of water and a brown loaf. Placing the articles upon the small table that stood in the centre of the cell, he then left, carefully bolting and fastening the door after him.

Once more Claude now found himself alone.

Remembering the instructions of his friend an hour before, and the look that accompanied his words, not without wild hopes of assistance was it that Duval placed his hands upon the loaf just left by the warder.

A thrill passed through his frame as he lifted it from the table.

It was heavy, and felt like a lump of lead in his hands.

With beating heart Duval broke the loaf in half.

An exclamation of wild joy escaped him.

With steadfast gaze he remained for a moment staring at the bread he held in his hand.

Imbedded in the dough was a pair of minute and exquisitely silver-mounted pistols, loaded and ready for use ; beside these was a coil of silk with a hook at the end ; on unrolling this latter, Claude discovered that it formed an ingeniously contrived ladder. This, together with a small file and a knife, made up the inner portion of the loaf.

"A bold device, and a successful one, Jack !" ejaculated Claude, as he proceeded to hide the different articles about his clothes, then, sitting down, began to ruminate upon his plan of operation for an escape.

Well he knew that nought could be attempted until night had fallen.

Slowly, wearily the hours flew by that livelong day.

Never to the anxious, excited captive did it seem as if it would end.

At six o'clock the last visit was paid by the warder, Tony Whiffles, who appeared to glance meaningly and encouragingly at the captive as he bade him good night.

Slowly the hours wore on, whilst, like a caged tiger, Duval paced backwards and forwards the narrow limits of his cell.

Twelve o'clock at length chimed from the prison bell.

The noise of bolts, rattling of keys, and murmuring voices of the warders died away, and all was silence.

Every cell was locked up for the night.

All was quiet, still as death, in the dreary prison-house !

Scarcely had the last note of the midnight hour ceased to ring upon the air, before Claude, who had been listening at the door of his cell, started back and prepared for the task he had before him.

The grating of his cell, through which the silvery moon-beams now glistened, he found by the help of the table even, he could not conveniently reach : resorting to his silk ladder, he contrived after several efforts to make the hook catch in the bars, then, standing on his table, Claude, winding the silk round one arm, with his right hand free, was able to attack the iron that, fitted in the masonry, prevented his egress to the courtyard without.

With utmost joy, and scarce able to refrain from uttering aloud his exultation, he now found upon attacking the iron bars that they were both rusty and decayed.

Obliged to pause and rest from his labours, and working slowly, so as to make as little noise as possible, it was some hours ere he contrived to remove two of the bars.

The moon, with a broad, bright glare now darted into the cell.

Dropping the two bars of iron he had removed cautiously upon the floor at his feet, Claude, who had sunk down upon the table, now clambered again up the rope, and slowly and carefully thrust his head partly through the grating, the opening being, he found, barely wide enough to permit him passing through.

"Sacre ! it will be a tight squeeze and will spoil my jacket, and, I doubt not, tear the skin off my shoulders ; but, parbleu ! better that than a rope round my neck."

About now to drop once more back into his cell an exclamation of despair escaped him, as he glared into the courtyard of the goal.

A dark look of vexation—of despair—rested on his features.

Pacing up and down in the moonlight below was the figure of a man.

There was a watch, then !

Here was an obstacle not thought of by himself or friend.

For a few moments Claude remained irresolute, glaring out into the moonlit courtyard.

Slowly, and with a dull, heavy tramp, the watch paced backwards and forwards in his round.

Biting his lip with suppressed rage, Claude at length drew back, and was presently once more standing in his cell.

Moodily he glanced up at the casement, then, as he thought of those who were awaiting his arrival, who were, doubtless, that moment praying for his escape, a smile lit up his countenance.

"Worse dangers than this have been surmounted ; I must, I will be free ! Let me see : I have to cross the courtyard, mount the wall, and all is over ; but, to do this, I must avoid being seen by the night watchman below, and in the broad glare of the moonlight how I'm to manage this is a mystery. There is one way, certainly."

A dark look here gathered over the brow of Claude, as he furtively handled the knife he had drawn from his pocket, then replacing it, he muttered—

"No, no ! I must not do that. I must not have the poor wretch's blood upon my hands ; his life must be spared. But I must at once to my task : a struggle—a blow under the ear will soon settle the matter. 'Twill be hard if I cannot render him unfit to raise an alarm, or follow me in my escape without actually slaying him !"

Carefully Duval now once more mounted the table and from thence, by aid of his silken ladder, drew himself up to the grating.

Slowly, and with beating heart, he now, clinging to the edge of the masonry, passed his ladder through the opening till one end fell into the courtyard without.

Fixing the hook to the grating he then began the most dangerous part of his enterprise, first, with an exclamation of thankfulness, noting that, the moon now sinking in the horizon, the courtyard without was enshrouded in darkness.

Dawn near at hand, for the next half hour a semi-darkness would hide his movements.

With beating heart he now prepared to pass his supple figure through the grating or opening he had made by the removal of the two bars.

All was quiet without.

With a last look at his prison chamber, Claude, with drawn breath and compressed lips, gradually squeezed himself through the small opening he had made.

Grasping the ladder with convulsive grip, he at length was free of the prison:

Was dangling some twelve feet from the ground.

Warily, searchingly, he cast his eyes around.

To his intense relief, he now discovered that the watchman had left the vicinity of his cell, and was standing, his figure scarce discernible, in the gloom some two hundred feet away.

Slipping rapidly down the ladder of silk, Claude, gaining the ground, sank down in the shadow of the walls:

Sank down, with a throbbing heart and a nervous thrill, as the night-watchman once more began to pace back towards the vicinity of his late prison chamber.

With gleaming eye and with deep-drawn breath, Claude now cowered down, awaiting the man's approach.

Tramp, tramp ! his head turned up at the cloudy skies, the watchman, unknowing the danger that impended near, now drew closer, yet closer, to the escaped highwayman.

Like a tiger on the spring, Claude glared at his foe.

Another moment and he would be discovered !

Yet no ! Casting his eyes up at the morning star, now bright, large, and glittering like a diamond in the skies, the man retraced his steps when within two yards of the escaped prisoner.

With a sigh of relief at the respite, Duval rose up :

Rose up as the watchman's form began once more to grow dim and indistinct in the gloom.

Stealthily now Duval, not without some trouble, unhooked his silken ladder from the grating above. Coolly as though he were quite alone and in no danger, he pursued his task until at length success crowned his efforts. Gathering up the silk rope as it fell at his feet, he then turned, and, like a fawn, darted across the courtyard.

Scarce had he gained the high wall which, with a row of long bristling spikes above, appeared a formidable barrier to a further escape, when a loud spring of a rattle woke up echoes in the courtyard.

He had been perceived by the lynx eyes of the watchman.

In another moment Claude found himself caught in a pair of strong brawny arms.

Desperately he struggled with his captor.

"It arn't no use, Claude Duval ! you've tried my grip before !" exclaimed the man, who by the dim light of dawn, which like a white veil now overhung the prison, our hero perceived was the herculean runner, Blue Peters. "Jonathan Anstey, a wide-o' bird, put me on the watch, my bold highwayman. It's no use ; give in !"

Claude with a thrill remembered that in point of strength he was no match for his adversary ; but not without compunction was it that he feigned sudden submission.

A trick alone could save him !

In a low, panting voice, ceasing to struggle, he now exclaimed : "All right ! Peters, let go your hold, and I'll return !"

With a grim smile of triumph the officer, releasing his captive, drew back, and snatched a pair of handcuffs from his pocket.

"I must shove on the darbies, Duval !"

"When are you going to do it ?"

"Why, at once. No nonsense, or down you go ; you are no match for me, and you know it !

"In strength no ; but what I lack in bone and muscle, I make up in cunning. Stand back, Blue Peters, or by the Lord that made me, I'll put a bullet in your skull !"

With a curse, the runner started back, as Claude, levelling one of his pistols at his head, drew yet closer to his late assailant.

For a moment of time the man stood irresolute, then darting away, shouted loudly for help.

He cared not to encounter a determined desperate prisoner, who faced him with loaded firearms.

There was that in the eye of Duval that informed the worthy Blue Peters that, driven to necessity, he would keep his word and fire upon him.

An alarm had now spread through the gaol.

Lights could be seen flashing through the gratings and windows.

Flying to the wall, Duval, now in nervous haste threw up his ladder ; a cry of joy escaping his lips as he perceived, at the third attempt, that the hook had caught in one of the iron spikes.

Just as this feat was accomplished, a side door of the gaol at the east end of the courtyard was opened, and half-a-dozen officers rushing out, pointed at the figure of our hero, and began to climb his frail ladder !

DASHING DUVAL;
OR,
THE LADIES' HIGHWAYMAN.

THROWING OFF HIS DISGUISE, CLAUDE GLARED DEFIANTLY AT THE RUNNERS.

"Ha, the bird not yet flown!" shouted the ruffian Anstey, who headed the warders. "Upon him, lads, let him not escape; fire upon him; dead or alive he must be ours!"

Not this time, Jonathan Anstey! Ha, ha, ha! Catch me who can!

With a loud defiant laugh Claude, with the agility of a squirrel, here hand over hand ascended his frail support; the bullets from the firearms of his enraged enemies pattering like hail around him!

Reaching in safety the top of the wall, another derisive shout escaped his lips, as an officer made a fruitless attempt to snatch the ladder which Duval drew up in safety after him.

"Not this time, dear boy. I can't let you have it, cos want it!"

Coolly, deliberately, Duval now fastened the hook afresh, and lowering the invaluable silken ropework into the thoroughfare without, disappeared over the wall, giving a last defiant shout at his infuriated foes.

Scarce had his feet reached the ground, ere a hand was laid upon his arm, while the voice of his friend Jack rang cheerfully in his ears.

"Welcome, welcome, dear pal! So you've done the trick, and slipped the grabs! But hark, by the devils, there goes the alarm bell; we must make ourselves scarce!"

The loud sonorous bell of old Newgate now with a clang sounded clear and ominous in the still morning air.

No. 5 & 6.   **Price One Penny.**

The dawn had now fairly broken, a thin grey light in the east changing to a ruddy golden russet tint as the orb of day rose up in the skies.

Hurrying along, Duval with his friend was about to dive into a narrow turning, when they were suddenly faced by some half-dozen Bow-street runners, who, with loud yells, rushed upon them.

"We shall have them, lads!"

"Seize them both! That other fellow's wanted."

"Down with them!"

"Get the darbies ready!"

"Here comes Jonathan Anstey! It's all right, Anstey, we've got him."

"Then mind you keep him," shouted Claude, who, here struggling in the grasp of two officers, contrived dexterously to slip from his coat, leaving the garment in the hands of his enraged antagonists, who had made sure of his capture.

Like a hare Claude, followed by Jack, who had also eluded the thief-takers, now bounded away.

"You'd better leave me presently, Jack; it's no use your keeping me company! I'm fleeter of foot than you! They are not particularly anxious for your capture; it's me they want, and it's me they won't have," gasped Claude, as he dashed wildly on, the enraged officers, like bloodhounds, following in his track.

"I don't care about leaving you, Claude," gasped Jack, who, perspiring at every pore, could scarce keep up with his companion, who was flying along like the wind.

"It's no use your keeping with me! I must double like the fox on the yelling hounds behind! I bet I'll beat them all at this game! Leave me, Jack; I would rather be alone! I can the better evade my pursuers; if you give in I must stand by! Sacre, take the next turning, I don't want us both to fall into the hands of our foes, and we shall, if you don't evade them; you are already winded."

"That's true, Claude; damn it, how you do cover the ground! I'll follow your advice, dear pal, down the next street I'll turn off! I think you'll beat them at this fun! If all goes right we meet at Kennington."

"Yes, at night, when it's quite dark."

"Good, luck attend you, dear pal! I'm dead beat." Jack, here reaching a narrow lane or alley, darted down it; Claude, meanwhile, still tearing along the high road at headlong speed.

The officers, in a yelling pack, as Duval expected, heeded not his companion, but kept on in their chase after him, their numbers now increased by one or two pedestrians.

"Stop him! Stop thief! Stop thief!"

Wildly the shouts rang in the quiet morning air.

With the speed of a hare Claude bounded on. He had now reached the bottom of Snow-hill, and, turning to his left, made for Holborn. There were but few passengers about at that early hour, but here and there a solitary watchman crossed his path; these Claude either evaded by a feint, darting past them like a hound, or else with his clenched fist striking them to his feet, and then again darting on.

The top of Holborn-hill was at length gained.

Claude here paused to gather breath.

The perspiration in beads now trickled down his brow.

Half-way up the hill behind him were some dozen Bow-street runners, headed by the inveterate Anstey; while about two dozen passengers followed in their wake.

Rattles sprang loudly on the air, mingled with shouts and wild cries from the excited pursuers.

"Stop him! Twenty pounds to the man who brings him back!" yelled the enraged Jonathan Anstey, who began to fear his victim would escape.

Once more Duval rushed on with teeth set grimly, and an angry frown upon his brow.

He inwardly vowed he would not be retaken, and nervously felt for his pistols as he tore on. They were safe, and he knew were loaded.

He held at least two lives; and if it came to a struggle one of these he determined should be the thief-taker Anstey.

Tearing wildly on, his pursuers far in the rear, Claude was suddenly faced by a tall, stalwart, herculean man, a butcher, who, hearing the shouts of his pursuers, darted out of a narrow court.

"Hold on, my hearty! or I'll seize and throttle you like a rabbit!"

"Stand on one side!"

"Not if I knows it! There's twenty goldfinches (sovereigns) hanging to your capture: and curse me if I don't have 'em!"

With a rush the burly butcher here darted upon Claude, seizing him in his herculean grasp.

"Let go your hold!" exclaimed Duval, with a muttered curse, striving to free himself from the other's determined grasp.

"Let go? Not if I knows it! Your friends is a-coming, and I'll have the goldfinches."

"Let me go! Release me, I say!"

"In course I will presently: here they is!"

There was a rush of officers, who now tore up to the spot. A loud cry and heavy groan accompanied by a brief fierce struggle, and, a moment after, once more free of his determined foes, Claude at mad speed was dashing like a fawn along the road, followed by the infuriated Bow-street runners.

A startled group staying behind gathered round the insensible form of the butcher, who, bathed in blood, lay helpless and an inert mass upon the pavement where he had been struck down by the enraged highwayman a moment before.

"Stop him! Stop thief!"

Rattle, rattle, rattle! How the quiet of the early morning was broken by the watchmen who here gathered in the pursuit, and the yells of the gathering crowd!

How exciting to hunt thus a fellow-creature!

How brave to thus chase a single man by an unruly unthinking mob and blood-thirsty revengeful myrmidons of the law!

"Stop him! Stop him!"

Bravely the hunted highwayman sped on in his race for life!

Wildly, madly, he rushed onwards in his course:

Like sleuthhounds the police following in his track!

Loud and incessant were the cries of Stop thief! stop thief! that rang in the ears of the hunted man!

Looking back once or twice, Claude discovered the foremost of his pursuers to be the persevering Jonathan Anstey!

Fleet of foot, and with revengeful feelings urging him on, the enraged runner still kept close on the track of the flying highwayman!

Up one turning, down another, Duval kept on at his fearful speed in the direction of the North road!

His pursuers still kept up the race: some few, however, falling back from sheer exhaustion; others taking their place in the crowd which increased in number as the morning advanced.

With a chill feeling of rage and despair, Claude became now aware that he could not much longer evade his enemies, unless some means of escape presented itself to him.

His limbs were becoming stiff and cramped. His hair in dank wet masses clung to his brow, whilst his breath came short and thick, his chest heaving like a forcepump with the effects of his fearful race.

He now clutched the knife and pistols concealed in his vest with the firm grip and frenzy of despair.

Hunted thus, like some beast of prey, a feeling of dire revenge against his foes took possession of our hero's breast!

He vowed as he ran panting on to escape or perish; he would not be taken with life.

Turning round once more as he held on his maddened course, he discerned far behind the yelling shouting crowd.

Not the hoarse yells of the mob, however, was it that caused Claude, like a tiger at bay, to glare wildly round:

Further escape seemed hopeless!

Jonathan Anstey, who had halted outside an inn a few moments before, was now with two of his men mounting horses!

The cunning thief-takers had procured steeds!

The race was at an end!

Here was a danger not dreamt of!

His enemies would now run him down in a few minutes!

There was no chance, no hope of further escape!

In a few moments more he would be struggling in the grasp of his foes!

Words of despair issued from his lips!

Wildly Claude now glared round to discover if there were any means of eluding his pursuers.

At one moment he was about to come to a halt and sternly face his savage foes. Still racing on, however, he had now arrived at the corner of a street off the Oxford-road, and with a thrill of joy fancied he saw a chance of getting rid of his pursuers.

Leaving the high road, Duval now darted down this turning.

He might elude his enemies yet; he might even now foil them when they had him all but in their hands.

The yells and clattering of hoofs that now sounded in his ears told him the final moment had come.

His enemies were close upon him though not yet in sight.

Half-way down the street Claude, a moment before, had discerned a cornchandler's, next to which was a loft, used for the stowage of hay and straw.

Outside this loft stood a cart with a load of hay.

In the vehicle was a tall pig-headed-looking country lad, with a red flannel cap on his head, and a face as red as his cap. This youth, at the moment that Claude darted up, was engaged in pitching in with a pitchfork trusses of hay into the adjacent loft.

To mount the cart, to the no small astonishment of the yokel, was to Claude the work of a moment.

With his usual daring in an emergency, Duval had conceived a plan for an escape, and prepared without scruple to carry it out.

"Now, my lad, in with you into that loft, or I'll cut you up into mincemeat!"

Flourishing the knife he drew from his vest in the lad's eyes, the horrified youth at a bound sprang out of the cart, quickly followed by his strange visitor, whom with a shudder he took for an escaped madman.

Once in the loft, Claude cared not.

For a time he was concealed from his foes.

He had feared the runners would reach the top of the the street before he gained his present refuge.

Fortune, however, favoured him.

Only as he disappeared in the loft did he hear the angry shout of his pursuers as they noted that he was no longer in sight.

For a moment of time he had thrown them off the scent.

Dragging the horrified country lad up in a corner, Claude now stripped him of his smock frock and cap, then twisting a handkerchief round his mouth hurled him down, placing a truss of straw over him first with an oath, bidding him take no heed of what he might hear, or attempt to move until he had permission under penalty of instant death.

"Lie there quiet, or I'll make you swallow your own pitchfork!" said Claude, as drawing away, he now quickly put over his coat the lad's smock frock, and then, with the the red cap drawn far over his forehead, and a hunk of bread and a piece of fat bacon he found on a shelf in his hand, coolly awaited the turn of events.

Not for long was the bold daring Duval left in quiet in the loft.

Once a smothered groan in the corner drew forth an oath and an admonitory kick, which immediately procured silence: a silence that was presently broken by a loud shout. The enemy had arrived. The moment of trial was at hand. With the bread and bacon crammed into his mouth, Claude, now, pitchfork in one hand, made for the little door of the loft, through which he had made his way from the street a few minutes before.

Loud voices rang without.

"He's in the hayloft!"

"We've run the fox to earth!"

"Oh, we have got him now!"

"He can't escape!"

"Not he!"

Cool, calm, and collected, Duval glanced upon the scene without.

Standing by the cart were the officers, Jonathan Anstey, their leader, glaring fiercely up at the loft.

Scattered about were some few of those who, from mere curiosity, had followed in the pursuit.

Anstey now (detecting the person of Duval, who, munching at the bread and bacon, gazed vacantly at the enraged officer) exclaimed, "Hallo! who the devil are you up there!"

"Eh! eh! eh! I be Giles Jolter, I be! Get away from ma cart, thee'll froighten ma mare!"

"Damn your mare!"

"Wall, if it be all same to thee, mon, I weant she be a rale good 'un in harness, and a danged sight prettier nor you to look at, old pimple face!"

"Look here!"

"Ise looking, mon! and I can't say as I thinks much o' thee. Thee be'est an ugly cove, anyhow!"

Bridling his rage, as a loud laugh emanated from the crowd, Anstey, in as unconcerned a tone as he could assume, exclaimed:

"Have you seen a man pass here?"

"A mon?"

"Yes!"

"What sort o' mon?"

"Why, a dashing, handsome-looking fellow."

"Were he a tall mon?"

"Well, yes."

"Good-looking like?"

"Yes, just so! a smart, dashing sort of chap!"

"I see,—a Lunnon cove? Did the mon come down here?"

"Yes!"

"Were he running?"

"Yes he was! where did he go?"

"Well I don't noa, for I arn't seen him!"

With an exclamation of rage, Anstey turned away, whilst Claude, squinting diabolically and his mouth crammed with the bread and bacon, stood gazing at the crowd below, chuckling at the rage of the infuriated officer.

"Well, lads," exclaimed the enraged runner, "it appears our man has outwitted us. I can make nothing of that bacon-eating lout! The fellow, I'm sure, is laughing at us; but cunning Duval cant be far off. Owen, and you Hatley, guard the end of the street here; it has no thoroughfare; we may catch our bird yet."

"Well, he has given us a run, Anstey; he's a sharp customer!"

"He is so, Peters; I think you've found that out."

"I have so; I'm as eager now as you can be, captain, for his capture."

"Well, I fancy we shall nail him this turn yet he shall not find it an easy task to play his fox-like tricks on me. I'll pursue him to the death. I've sworn to bring him to the gallows, and I'll keep my oath! But come let us search the houses in the street; he must be lurking somewhere, and cannot be far off!"

"Help! help! dang moy buttons, I won't be robbed I won't! Help! help!"

Loudly the cry for aid sounded from the loft.

Anstey, starting round, now suspiciously gazed up.

The country boy had now disappeared.

Whilst from the loft still came a smothered cry for help.

"Our man for a thousand, Peters!" exultingly exclaimed Anstey as he clambered up into the van, and from thence made his way into the hayloft.

A posse of runners were now soon congregated in the place.

A hurried search drew forth a shout of triumph.

Two men with exulting cries, seizing upon a human figure that lay kicking and struggling under two or three trusses of hay, dragged it forwards to the light.

With a cry of malicious triumph, Anstey seized the struggling form in his iron grip.

"Ha! ha! ha! So then clever, funny, astute, cunning Claude Duval, we have got you after all hard and fast?"

"Let ah goo! let ah alone! domn thee, willee let I goa!"

"Ten thousand devils, what is this?" exclaimed the confounded officer, as releasing his hold of the figure he had held in his savage grip he started back.

"A rum go, a trick of the cunning highwayman," muttered the runner, Blue Peters, who, with the rest stared in unqualified amaze at the object shivering and shaking before them—the wretched cowboy, half dead with fright, seeming as though meditating a bold leap into the roadway without.

Anstey, now controlling his rage, stepping forwards, in stern accents exclaimed:

"Who, what are you, fellow? Speak! what is the meaning of all this? who are you?"

"Why, I be farmer Jenkins's mon, I be! I ah been robbed and murdered! Somebody a' stolen ma cap, ma smock, an' ma bread and boarcon! Dang moy buttons! What be I to do? Ah gotten nothing to eat, now I beant!" said the youth who, with the recollection of his lost dinner, appeared to lose his former fears.

Guessing in a moment the trick that had been played off upon him, Anstey, his face flushed with passion, exclaimed "Look you, my lad, you shall be well paid for what you have lost, and shall have something too besides, if you answer my questions truly! Now, tell me where has the man gone who robbed you!"

"Darg moy buttons, that be more nor I can tellee ! He stole ma things ! knocked I down ! shoved I under hay, and ate ma bearcon !"

"Is there any means of quitting this loft besides that door ?" said Anstey, pointing to the opening that looked out upon the street.

"E'es, there be the trop, mon, that leads to Measter Muggins's stable !"

A loud shout escaped the officers :

A shout of rage and indignation as they darted to the far end of the loft pointed out by the cowboy.

"Ten thousand devils, Peters ! we are sold ; the bird has flown !"

"Safe as the bank, governor !"

In another moment with wild shouts the excited and enraged runners were making their way through an open trap which led to some stables below.

CHAPTER IX.

THE PURSUIT—THE STRUGGLE IN THE YARD—THE FLIGHT OVER THE HOUSETOPS—THE BEDCHAMBER AND ITS INMATES—DUVAL AND THE SERVANT MAID—THE FIGHT ON THE STAIRCASE—THE ESCAPE.

Upon Jonathan Anstey turning away with his men from the cart a short time before, Duval, aware that any moment might reveal the trick that had been played, prepared to fly. Scarce, however, had he discovered the trap at the top of the loft, ere he was startled by a loud cry for help from the mouth of the indignant and enraged countryman, who contriving to crawl from under the hay that had nigh smothered him, despite Claude's recent warning, cried lustily for aid.

Duval at once, in feverish haste, lowered himself down through the trap he had found to the space below.

Reaching the ground, he found he was in a small stable.

Hiding-place in this there was none.

Hearing the shouts above of Anstey and the officers at their discovery of the fraud that had been practised upon them, Claude now darted in haste through a door at the back of the stable.

To his chagrin he now found himself in a large yard which was surmounted by a high wall.

A servant wench, with a scream at his sudden appearance, now darted wildly from the yard into the house, slamming to and bolting the door after her.

"Pleasant ; very !" muttered our hero, who, trying the only means of exit from the place, stood gazing in despair around him. "Like a fox in a hole I seem run to earth ! Confound it ! to be caged like this after escaping so far is positively maddening ! Ah ! that ladder ; it will aid me to leave this infernal hole."

Claude now darting forwards to a ladder that rested against the walls of the house attempted to remove it ; but in vain.

Placed there by workmen repairing the roof, the means of escape he had thought to secure was held hard and fast at the top and resisted all his efforts at removal.

"Done again ! No matter ! I'll up at once ; better luck there, perhaps, than down here !"

With his foot on the lowermost round, about to hasten up, Claude was now staggered by receiving a fearful blow on the head.

With his brain in a whirl, and a feeling as though the whole place was swimming round with him, our hero sank back upon the ground, still clinging to the ladder with a nervous grip.

In that moment of pain and terror he retained consciousness enough to know his peril :

To know that capture was imminent ; but that a chance yet remained in gaining the roof of the house.

Like the sound of a trumpet the voice, full of exultation, of Jonathan Anstey now sounded in his ears.

"We have him now, lads ! That stone was well thrown, Owen ! Whilst he lies stunned and helpless shove on the bracelets !"

"Not this time, you don't ! and for your dastard shot take that one, Mr. Owen !" shouted Claude, who, staggering once more to his feet, pulled one of his pistols from his vest and fired at the runner, who, with a laugh of exultation, had darted forwards to seize, as he supposed, upon a senseless man.

There was a sharp report and a bright flash, then came a wild screech and the sound of a heavy fall as the man Owen, huddled up in a heap, stumbled back at the feet of his comrades.

With a shout of defiance Claude now darted up the ladder. Up, up he mounted.

Once the ping of a bullet whizzed past his ear ; a moment after, with a shout of triumph, he gained the roof.

Glancing down Claude now perceived Anstey, his men, and a group of people gathered together in the yard below, whilst rapidly nearing the summit of the ladder was a runner who had daringly followed thus far the hunted highwayman.

With a fierce oath Claude leant over the parapet, glaring viciously at his enemy.

Nervously he clutched the knife that he had drawn from his vest.

There was an ominous look in his eye that caused the officer below to pause in his ascent.

Fascinated with horror the wretched man glared at the one whom he had hunted almost to the death.

Coolly, calmly, with a stare of deadly purpose, Claude now drew his knife backwards and forwards across the rope that fastened the ladder to the coping.

In a few moments the ladder would be loosed.

The house was a high one ; the ladder hurled back instant death must take place to one who, like the wretched runner, had nearly gained the top.

A wild cry of horror escaped the officer's lips.

Duval had now divided the rope, the frail support shaking to and fro as he pressed against it.

"Help ! mercy, mercy ! spare me ! my wife ! my child ! oh, mercy, mercy, Duval !"

In abject terror the Bow-street runner here glared up at Claude, who, with quivering voice, exclaimed :

"What mercy have you shown to me ? Make your way down, you cowardly hound, and forget not that you owe your life to the man whom you have assisted to hunt to the death !"

Needing no second bidding, pausing not to descend step by step, the officer placed his arms round the ladder and slid rapidly down to the ground, which he had barely reached ere Claude, with a crash, sent it hurtling over against the wall of the yard.

Pausing not to look back he now made his way over the roof of the house.

It was a dreary prospect he had before him :

A row of houses some four storeys high, and with no possible or apparent means of descent.

With wild haste, and in desperation, Claude made his way over three of the roofs.

As he stood taking a survey, and irresolute as to his further course, he discerned the figures of his implacable foes appearing on the summit of the first house.

Coolly glancing round he now drew his loaded pistol from his pocket, murmuring :

"At least they shall join me in my journey of death ! but I will not pause till I can go no further ; at the last moment some means of escape may open to me."

Claude now hurried on, his retreating figure discerned causing a loud shout from the officers.

The sun, now well up in the horizon, threw a golden lustre upon the scene.

Heeding not the beauty of the summer morn, or the ruddy golden-tinted clouds, the runners, like ill-omened birds of prey, hurried over the roofs in pursuit of their victim.

Duval proceeding on at length reached the last house in the row.

Behind him were his foes following like bloodhounds on his track.

In front was a depth of many feet to the street below.

With a feeling of utter despair Claude now made for the back of the house, on the roof of which he stood.

Wildly he glared into a piece of garden ground below ; there was no means of descent.

Escape seemed hopeless.

With a sigh he now drew back.

There was no possible means of descent to the ground below ! no trailing growth of ivy by which, at risk of life and limb, he might have quitted the roof, on which he stood like a tiger at bay.

With bated breath and flushed cheeks he now awaited the coming struggle.

He registered an oath not to be taken with life.

He would escape or perish.

Already he could perceive the foremost of the runners rapidly approaching.

In the bright glare of the sun he recognised the man's features.

It was his deadly determined foe, Jonathan Anstey.

Raising his pistol with a grim muttered "Sacre!" Claude prepared to fire, but was diverted from his purpose by catching sight of an opening in the roof, which, in his first hurried search he had failed to discover.

An exclamation of joy escaped him.

He might yet escape.

He would beat in the trap before him, and gaining an entry into the house, perhaps yet elude his enemies at the last moment of despair, when all hope had left him.

Hastening forward, Claude, his movements hidden by a tall stack of chimneys, now squeezed his thin and supple figure through the opening in the roof.

Replacing the trap which he found in the loft he now stood in, Duval, effectually hidden from his foes, searched eagerly for an opening into the garret of the house.

In total darkness he groped blindly about for the trap that he knew must lead from the loft to the garret beneath.

Anon he heard the tramp of feet upon the roof overhead.

His pursuers had arrived:

Were searching for him without.

At this moment with a thrill of joy he discovered the trap of which he was in search.

He pulled at it with all his force.

It resisted his utmost efforts.

With a muttered curse and exclamation of despair he sank back.

The trap was fast secured, the bolts refusing to give way.

Claude gnashed his teeth with rage and fury at the thought of his helpless position.

He now heard the officers conversing on the roof.

In a few moments more his retreat would be discovered.

With the last effort of despair he knelt down, and using all his strength essayed to move the trap. For a few seconds it resisted his attempts, then suddenly, with a loud snap, the bolts that fastened it gave way, and the trap, torn from its place, was left in his hands.

With a cry of joy he now lowered himself into a chamber which he discovered was a sort of lumber room.

Seizing an old pair of steps which he perceived resting against the wall of the garret, Claude now placed the second trap in its former position; then shooting one of the bolts back, fast driving in the nail that held the staple, he jumped down and took a hasty survey of the apartment in which he stood.

It was evidently used only for old lumber, being filled with a heterogeneous collection of goods that fairly surprised the intruder. Old helmets, foils, swords, gauntlets, faded velvet finery, paint pots, and articles of every description, met the eye.

With a smile and a look of wonder Claude now picked his way through the rubbish that filled the chamber, and boldly opened a door that he discovered led to a landing at the summit of a flight of stairs without.

Fancying that he heard the officers trying the trap opening into the chamber on the threshold of which he then stood, Claude hurried forward to descend the stairs, when he was startled by beholding a young girl making her way up.

To make his way down without being seen was impossible.

Should he attempt it and boldly descend, an alarm would be raised that would lead his enemies to the spot immediately.

They had not yet made their way into the chamber he had left. For a few moments longer he was safe.

The young girl ascending higher and higher would presently face him. With a quick sharp glance Claude now cast his eyes round, and detecting a small door opposite to the one he had just fastened behind him, darted forward and placed his hand upon the lock.

Room or closet he cared not which it was so it hid him for a time; turning the handle with joy he found it yielded to his touch.

The door was unlocked.

With a smile at the novelty of his position, and forgetful of his foes, he glided in through the door and now found himself in a neatly furnished bedroom.

Articles of female attire were scattered about the chamber telling at once the sex of its occupant.

A large four-post bedstead stood in the centre of the apartment, hung round with coloured curtains.

The room, neatly and comfortably furnished, looked out upon the front of the house.

Darting to the casement, Claude, lifting it up peered forth.

Pacing up and down the street without, were four or five stalwart, stern-looking, ill-featured men.

These, Duval knew, were Bow-street runners.

One of them, he at a glance recognised as the man whose life he had spared when clinging to the ladder at the rear of the cornchandler's dwelling.

"They are on my track, and are, it seems, prepared to follow me to the death. Well, we shall see. I have baffled them as yet, and my usual good fortune may not desert me. Once I elude them, and gain the villa at Kennington, I care not, from thence I will make for the old Tree Cave, keeping quiet for a day or two! But, from this day, I swear to follow recklessly the path I have selected. I am a marked man—a hunted felon! Be it so, Jonathan Anstey! The wily cunning thief-taker is my sworn and bitter foe; he has vowed to bring me to Tyburn Tree! Let him look to it, for, by the heaven above me, I'll spare him not, should he cross my path! From this hour I'm his relentless foe, and he is mine!"

A light footstep on the landing without at this moment recalled Claude to himself.

Without pausing to close the casement, he darted behind the bedstead, the curtains of which he found would effectually conceal him.

Scarce had he sought this refuge, when he heard the door open, and the young girl, the same he had shortly before beheld ascending the stairs, now entered the room.

"Dear me, I have left the window open; how careless of me to be sure!"

With a smile, Claude now beheld the casement shut to.

At present he was rather pleased with the novelty of his situation.

The little servant-girl was young, plump, and pretty.

His enemies had not as yet forced their way into the house.

For a time he was safe.

Securely hidden by the bed curtains, Claude gazed at the girl, his own presence not suspected.

Singing a snatch of a song, the little servant maid, for a few moments, glanced carelessly out of the window, starting suddenly and looking round the chamber in alarm.

There was a strange unwonted sound in the other room:

The murmuring of voices and trampling of feet.

A deadly pallor now gathered on the young girl's cheek.

About to totter towards the door she staggered back with a half-shriek as Duval, darting from his concealment, rushed to and turned the key in the lock.

"Pardon me, dear girl! Be not alarmed! but if you would save the life of the unfortunate man that stands before you, pray hear me! by those bright eyes and pouting lips I know you are one that will not only listen to, but will aid me in my peril.

"Who—what are you?"

"One who is pursued by the myrmidons of the law! Even now they have burst their way into the house to drag me from my hiding-place to imprisonment and death! But you, sweet girl, will save me; you have but to deny my presence here, and all is safe!"

A crimson flush suffused the young girl's cheeks as Claude, here kneeling at her feet, caught her plump soft hand in his and pressed it to his lips.

We have said our hero was of handsome form, his rich chesnut curling hair resting upon his shoulders, his dark and sparkling eyes, and the smile upon his manly features as he gazed up at the pretty servant maid, completely secured now the young girl's heart, and won upon her to listen to his entreaties.

"I—I don't know what Mr. Avery would say!" said the artless maid, hesitatingly. "Dear me, the idea of—of a gentleman in my bedroom!"

"And a very pleasant place too, my dear, for a young man to be in. But, hark! my enemies are even now at the door! Say, dear girl, where can I conceal myself?"

Claude now cast his eyes hurriedly round the room, but no hiding-place could he discover.

The officers now, too, were hammering loudly at the door, demanding in imperative tones instant admission.

"Open, open in the king's name!"

"Burst the door!"

"Down with it!"

"He must be here!"

"He can't be far off!"

The little servant girl, as the shouts of the officers without rung upon her ears, was now thoroughly alarmed.

Motioning Claude back she gave utterance to a shrill scream.

"A gal is in the room, Anstey."

"Girl or no girl, I'll have the apartment searched!" shouted the enraged thief-taker.

"Murder, murder!" cried the pretty little maid, as, urged by their chief, the runners now made a fierce attack upon the door.

"Open the door, wench, or we'll burst it open!" yelled Anstey in answer to the girl's frantic shouts.

"Me open my bedroom door to a lot of male wretches; I'd like to see myself! Go away! Fire, murder, thieves! Joe, dear, here's some housebreakers as wants to assassinate and ruinate me!"

"All right, Jane; I'm a coming! Now then, Mr. Black-muzzle, what's your particular identical little game?" ejaculated the rough voice of a man in answer to the shrill screams for help uttered by Claude's fair protector.

An animated and yet not very amicable conversation took place now between the Bow-street runners and the new arrival.

"It's Joe; he'll give it to 'em!"

"And who may Joe be, my dear! Not the possessor of the heart that beats in your fair bosom, I trust!"

Master Claude here forgot himself whilst gazing into the liquid depths of the pretty little Jane's bright eyes, the young girl blushing the hue of the damask rose as the dashing handsome knight of the road cast his admiring glances upon her.

Jane was a young girl from Somersetshire, and was not accustomed to the high-flown flattery of cavaliers!

Poor Jane, she learnt full soon the flattery of man.

Scarce could the little maid now keep from shouting with laughter, as Claude who had darted to a wardrobe in a corner of the chamber began to array himself in some female apparel.

In a few minutes the costume was arranged?

Stepping now to the toilet table Duval busied himself at the glass!

At this moment the door was burst open with a loud crash!

Giving way at length to the repeated attacks of the officers!

A crowd of four or five men now darted into the room!

Pushing past a tall thick-set fellow, who, habited as a man-servant was addressed by the pretty Jane, who now rushed to his side, as her dear Joe:

"Turn these ruffians out, Joe, or I'll never speak to you never no more!"

"All right, Jane! I'll cussed soon give 'em what for!"

The man-servant here with an ominous frown, spitting in the hollow of his hands, clenched his fists and assuming a sparring attitude exclaimed:

"Now, gents, one at a time, or all at once, out you goes!"

With a blow of his right which the expert Joe (evidently an adept at boxing) shot out with sledge-hammer force, the foremost runner was knocked completely off his feet, the chamber echoing with shrill screams as Joe fearlessly darted in at the enemy.

"Don't holler, Jane, I won't kill 'em!" exclaimed Joe, who here landed officer number two one full on the nose which caused the assailed one's conk to run with no end of claret.

"Two to me!" yelled the excited boxer as he darted like mad at the bewildered officers. Then as he was about to land his left in the face of the enraged Jonathan Anstey, the belligerent man-servant suddenly paused:

Paused as his eyes alighted upon the figure of Claude, who, an amused spectator, had been gazing admiringly at Joe's sparring performance.

"Why, Jane, who the devil's this you've got in your room?"

In unfeigned astonishment Joe here eyed Claude up and down.

In vain the frowns of the pretty Jane, in vain the fore-finger held up warningly; her lover didn't understand the presence of the stranger, and allowed his surprise to be noted by the officers.

"Zounds, I think we are in the right track now, Owens!"

"So do I, Anstey!"

"I smell a rat," said the runner Blue Peters, who grinned maliciously over at Claude, who stood quietly by the table undecided how to act.

"Owens! Harvey! Get the Darbies ready."

"All right, governor!"

"You, Peters, stand by the door."

"Right you are!"

"I say, my dear," said Jonathan with a spiteful grin at Claude, "would you like a walk?" No reply. "Poor thing, she's bashful; she's ashamed like; she's a strapper too, not very delicate looking is she, Peters?"

"More t'other! Now then, marm, don't you hear our governor talking to you? As you don't care for a walk, why we are all on us fond of the ladies, come along with us and we will give you a ride in a coach free, gratis, for nothing!"

"We will so!"

"And won't take no liberties!"

"On no account!"

"Not by no manner of means!"

"We wouldn't be so rude."

"We'll treat yer like a lamb, marm."

"Just so, behave to yer like gemmons!"

"No mistake about us!"

"That's the sort of men we are!"

Low chuckles and smothered laughter here escaped from the officers.

Poor Jane, who had taken a fancy to the bold, dashing figure of our hero, stood trembling and gazing with no pleasant looks at the runners, which the redoubtable Joe perceiving doubled his fists and seemed preparing for a fresh assault.

"Shall I let 'em have it, Jane?"

"I won't never go out with you never no more if you don't."

These words, uttered in a terrified whisper, was enough for Joe.

With a loud cry he rushed at the foe.

"Clear out!" With this ejaculation Joe now made a savage onslaught on Blue Peters.

Here, however, he had met his match, and had got his work carved out before him.

Claude, as the man-servant again attacked his enemies, now threw off the women's habiliments that disguised him, and, starting back, snatched his pistols from his belt, presenting them at the head of the exultant Jonathan Anstey.

"It's no use, Claude; put up your barking-irons; you can't escape."

"You lie! Stand back from that door, or, by the Lord that made me, I'll fire!"

"Fire and be damned!" shouted the officer, who here with a bound sprang at his victim.

A fierce struggle now took place.

Wrestling desperately with his foes, things were going queer with Claude, when another figure appeared upon the scene:

The figure of a young man with a drawn sword, who dashed in with a loud cry into the chamber.

"Zounds and the devils! What is this uproar that frights the house from its propriety? Jane, what knaves are these?"

"No knaves, sir, but officers, so please you!" exclaimed Blue Peters, with his left eye bunged up, and his nose looking as if he had just dived it in a jam pot; the while Anstey, starting from the floor where Duval had thrown him a moment before, exclaimed:

"My man speaks truth; we are officers, sir."

"Officers, indeed! and may I ask what the devil you are doing in my house?"

"We came here to secure an escaped felon."

"By which way?"

"The roof."

"Indeed! well that is a nice piece of intelligence, truly to own you've forced your way into a man's house through the roof of it!"

"We were racing after our man who had sought this means of escaping us."

"Oh, indeed! and where is this wretched criminal?"

"There, beside you."

Starting round the young man here took a keen survey of Claude, who lifting up his hat exclaimed: "He tells you truly, sir; I sought safety here from those who have hunted me like bloodhounds. That man there pursues me with deadly hate, not for what I have committed against the laws but to gratify a private revenge. On my soul, sir, I am telling you the truth; I've sworn that I will not be dragged back to a prison cell, and with heaven's aid I'll keep my oath!"

"Well, Mr.— Mr.— what's your name!" said the owner of the house, who now turning from Claude, addressed himself to the officer.

"I'm Jonathan Anstey, Bow-street runner, at your service!"

"Well, look here, Jonathan Anstey, Bow-street runner, the sooner you get out of my house the better I shall like it; and allow me to observe, if you don't draw these bulking ruffians away, I shall be under the painful necessity of kicking you downstairs!"

"Are you aware, sir, that to aid and abet a criminal lays you open to prosecution?"

"I am aware from your own lips, that you have with your men, forced your way into this my residence through the roof, and for aught I know, you may be housebreakers instead of officers. Joe, show this black-muzzled blackguard the door!"

"Oh, this won't do! I'm not to be bullied out of our quarry like that. Seize Duval, lads! I'll settle this fellow."

"Will you? how?" The young man here throwing down his sword, stepped forwards and drawing his slim form up to its full height launched his fist out with such force as took the burly thief-taker completely off his feet.

This was the signal for a general assault.

In another moment there was a melée between the officers, Claude, the belligerent Joe, and his master, the latter as expert a boxer as his servant.

In the course of the scrimmage, whilst Blue Peters was groping blindly about, his other eye quite closed by the fist of his former adversary, Claude was hurried through the door by the proprietor of the house, who had for a moment effectually silenced Anstey by knocking him into the fireplace.

"I think you'd better be off! I know not if what that fellow told me be true. I like not his face, and I found four or five to one, and Herbert Clavering always sides with the weakest party. Away with you!"

"How can I ever repay you; how thank you! exclaimed Claude, who wrung his preserver warmly by the hand.

"Name it not! talk not of it! Away with you! I and my Joe, who is good with his mawleys, will keep your foes at bay till you've a start! Farewell! off with you!"

"Au revoir! we shall meet again!" said Claude, who now dashed down the staircase before him, whilst his generous protector starting round confronted one of the runners, who, followed by pugilistic Joe, was groping his way blindly about the landing where Herbert Clavering had drawn Duval, when hurrying him from the scene of conflict.

It was not long ere our hero was able to repay the debt of gratitude he owed the stranger.

The fates of Herbert Clavering and Claude Duval were strangely interwoven.

CHAPTER X.

THE RUINED HOME—THE WHITE FACE IN THE MOONLIGHT—THE PISTOL SHOT—A NARROW ESCAPE—THE OATH OF THE FRIENDS—THE PURSUIT.

It was as the hour of ten was chiming from the tower of old Lambeth Palace, that Claude (who had been in hiding during the day at a humble public in Westminster) made his way hurriedly along the Kennington-road, pulling his cap low down over his brows; our hero, casting keen glances around as he passed a glare of light at the entrance of the Dog and Duck gardens, quickened his pace, fearful that even in the darkness his enemies might be on his track.

It was a beautiful moonlight night, the sky, without a speck of cloud, one sea of azure blue.

Hurrying on, Claude, ever and again casting a searching glance around, at length gained Kennington Common.

Passing the open waste and bearing to the left, he presently made his way down the country lane, in the centre of which was the lonely villa.

It was with an uncomfortable nervous thrill that he discerned no light in the pretty little diamond-paned casements of the house.

He had expected to be greeted with a shout of welcome.

His foes, the officers, knew not of this secret retreat, which he had oft kept aloof from in fear of discovery and only in extreme cases visited in the broad day.

In some alarm Claude now gazed before him:

In vain his eyes sought out a single light:

All was black and drear.

No shadow of female form appeared before him in the moonlight.

All was quiet around, the note of the nightingale alone waking up the stillness of the scene.

With a fear and a dread of he knew not what Claude hurried on:

Hurried on with beating heart and in nervous dread.

Something was wrong he was assured.

His escape from prison known, he would ere this have been met by either one of the girls whose safety he was so anxious about, or by his friend.

For a moment the thought that Jack might have been captured seized upon him, to be dismissed, however, upon a little reflection, as he remembered that all the officers had followed on that morning in pursuit of him alone.

Nearing the house, he now paused:

A something terribly unusual struck him as appearing about the villa.

Staggering with a sick dizzy feeling up to the little white gate, he stared with maddened gaze before him.

The moon in a broad flood of silvery light shone upon the scene:

A scene of drear dire desolation.

With wild staring eyes, Claude glared up at the casements.

They had gone! disappeared! the moon's rays darting through the huge apertures and showing a bare ruin within.

Drawing his hands over his brow, like one in a dream, he fastened his eyes upon his beautiful villa now a wreck—a ruin!

Of the pretty house the walls alone stood!

It was completely gutted by the ravages of a fierce fire!

All was black, bare, and desolate!

Tottering forward, he now made his way close up to the porch:

The porch beneath which, a few evening before, he had left the light-hearted beautiful Kate Annersley.

A pile of bricks, loose mortar, and smouldering rubbish now alone met his gaze.

A few sparks occasionally flickering up in the air, showed that the ruins were still alight.

The dread demon of conflagration had effectually carried out his mission.

Of the once beautiful villa the four bare walls alone remained!

Not the scene of desolation before him, not the destruction of the secret home was it, however, that caused the life-blood in Duval's frame to course like ice through his frame.

"Where, where can they all be? The girls, Kate, Maude, and Jack too! Where are they? Surely the fire has not devoured them besides all else! No, no; it cannot be! the conflagration must have taken place early in the day No harm could have happened to the inmates. My brain is in a whirl! Let me, let me think!"

Dazed, bewildered by this fresh calamity, Claude here drew away from the walls of the ruined house and walked slowly along the garden behind a side door formerly leading to the back of the villa, now like all else lying half-burnt and smouldering upon the ground.

With his eyes bent upon the gravelled path, Claude unthinking, with dizzy brain, wandered on till suddenly a something glittering in the moonlight caught his eye.

With a shiver and a nervous thrill, he stooped and picked it up. A low gasping exclamation of surprise and alarm escaped his lips, as, holding up the object he had discovered in the moonlight, he found it was a string of blue satin, embroidered with gold, the dainty article of female adornment being in a moment recognised as a present from himself, a few days before, to the pretty Kate!

"Great heavens, what can have happened! what does all this portend! How? why is there no one here to meet me! If, if this be the foul work of an enemy, I will follow him till I have a fearful reckoning, though the pursuit and my revenge put the rope round my own neck." Wildly, excitedly, these words fell from the lips of the bewildered and furious knight of the road, as, the little ribbon fluttering in his hand, he glared fiercely round at the ruin of his secret home.

About at length once more to pass on, Claude, happening to cast his eyes at a mass of tangled shrubbery, started and slowly thrust his hand into his vest.

Glaring fiercely upon him were two fiery eyes:

Eyes glittering with deadly purpose:

Eyes low down in the shrubbery fastened upon him with savage ferocity!

A low guttural laugh now sounded in the startled ears of Duval, then a moment after a face, white, livid, the livid pallor of the grave, appeared before him !

For a moment the livid face was fully revealed as it peered forth from the shrubbery, then disappearing, a sharp report echoed in the air, whilst Claud felt the ping of a bullet as it whistled by grazing his ear and causing a pain as of the prick of a hot needle.

With an exclamation of rage he, now darting forward, fired both his own pistols he had snatched from his vest at the spot where a moment before the glistening staring red eyes had been fixed upon him !

No cry of pain responded to the sharp report of the firearms.

Save the sighing of the breeze and rustling branches of the trees, nothing could be heard.

Claude, astounded and enraged, now boldly dashed into the mass of shrubbery before him.

With a wild horror that had caused his blood to almost freeze within his veins, he had a moment before recognised the death face that for a few seconds had appeared in the moonlight :

It was the face of the apparition at the old mill :

The livid death face that had appeared before him in the pinetree grove :

The face of the man upon whom he had inflicted what he had thought a mortal wound :

The hideous stranger Vampyre Vaughan !

"Does the wretch bear a charmed life ? If so, what can he be ?"

A strong shudder shook the frame of Claude as he asked himself this question.

Beating about the shrubbery, in vain he sought for his enemy !

The wretch had strangely disappeared !

No sign of his recent presence could Claude discover !

With beating heart and a cold damp prespiration bedewing his brow, Duval, now reloading his pistols, was suddenly started by a well-known sound :

The tramp of horses' feet.

Hastening from the garden, he now made once more for the front of the house.

Horses were approaching down the lane.

Perhaps the wretch Vaughan had villain associates awaiting him in the neighbouring !

Cool, calm, collected as always in the moment of danger, Claude now stooping low so that his figure should not be discerned in the moonlight, crept slowly along the front garden of the villa, at length pausing as he reached the gate.

To his surprise he now beheld a mounted horseman rapidly making his way down the lane, leading by his side a steed without any rider.

"Ventre bleu ! Providence favours me ! I want a horse and, parblou ! I'll borrow one of this stranger's ! Sacre ! he can't want two. Some groom doubtless ; but, no matter whether he be groom or master, a horse I want, and a horse I'll have !"

"Hold, man ! you can go no further, here's a toll here !"

Bounding over the gate, Claude now presented both pistols at the head of the lone rider :

Instead of a cry of alarm, he was, however, astonished by a shout of laughter.

With an oath, Duval raised his pistols in a level with the stranger's face, and exclaimed :

"You'll find it no laughing matter with me, my friend ; I want a horse, and as you've one to spare, why I'll borrow it ; and as you seem so particularly jolly, perhaps you've some spare cash to help a fellow on the road !"

"You can take the bit of horseflesh ; it ain't mine. But as for coin, you'll get none out of me, Mr. Highwayman !" exclaimed the stranger, who, with a loud laugh, here pulled from his face a pair of huge red whiskers, at the same time snatching off his hat and displacing a wig of the same fiery hue.

A fresh shout of laughter now escaped the stranger's lips, as Claude in stupefied amaze glared upon him.

"What, Duval, old man, don't you know me ?"

"Jack ?"

"Jack ! yes, of course its Jack ! Who, the deuce, did you think it was ? But I forgot, dear old pal, the scene you have returned to has robbed you of your usual coolness and nerve ; but the thought of your stopping me to rob me of your own bonny mare was so very rich ! I could not help laughing, though I haven't much to be merry upon just now, Claude !"

Jack dismounting from his horse now placed his hand upon the arm of his friend, and, pointing to the house, with a sigh exclaimed, "It's a sad tale, though short, I have to tell. I can understand your silence ; I can read the whirlwind of passion that takes from you the power of speech, Claude !"

"Be brief ! Tell me all, Jack ! Who has done this ?" In a low hoarse voice of wild fury the words hissed through the set teeth of Duval.

"I know not : I can but guess the perpetrators of this hellish act."

"Whom do you suspect ?"

"The Black Band."

"You are right."

"How ?"

"I have seen the fiend Vampyre Vaughan here."

"Then my suspicions were correct. We must hunt down this villain, who is more deadly dangerous than even our mutual foe, Jonathan Anstey."

"You are right, Jack ! the one is human ; for the other, diable ! I know not what to think of him. But come, tell me all you know ; I am getting cooler, clearer in the head, now ; I know the worst—the poor girls are carried off ?"

"No ; one escaped."

"Good ! and that one Kate Annersley ?"

"Yes, Claude."

"I though so ! Well, thank heaven, there is one less in the power of that dire fiend ; and now, ere we quit this spot, just make me acquainted in a few words with the terrible events that have taken place since I saw you !"

"It is soon told, Claude. Upon escaping Anstey and his men this morning, I returned here to find the villa a blazing ruin ; a few labourers gathered round informed me that a young girl had been brought out of the house by several men, who, placing her in a carriage had driven off. In fury and alarm I remained for a time by the smouldering ruins of our retreat when I was joined by Kate, who, poor girl, crept only from the shrubbery where she had been concealed when she saw I was alone."

"From her you had an account of this dastard villanous business !"

"Yes ! It appears that at about four o'clock in the morning the girls were awakened by a loud noise and a smell of fire. Hurrying from their rooms, in the passage leading to the staircase, they were met by several men with black masks on their faces. These fellows seizing upon them despite their shrieks carried them down below. Kate, in the garden without, managed to free herself from the ruffian who held her, and, flying to the shrubbery, effectually concealed herself from the search that was made for her. Here she watched the burning of the home in which she had spent so many happy hours. Poor girl ! she was frantic with grief about Maude ! Half-dressed as she was I at once hurried her away, and procuring a coach, took her to Highgate ; from thence I conducted her to the old Tree Cave, and was pleasingly surprised to find that Luke had come across your bonny Jane, whom he found wandering near our cunningly-contrived stables in the copse. Leaving Kate safe with Luke I returned to Highgate, secured my steed, my brave Starlight Nell, and, waiting till night, made for Kennington, where I knew I should find you when darkness had fallen."

Jack, my dear pal, you have acted well and wisely, and with the greatest foresight ! It is a great relief to me to learn that poor Kate Annersley is in safety ; and, for Maude, woe to the villain Vaughan and the Black Band gang if they have wrought her harm ! By yonder bright moon, by the Creator of all, I here swear to know no peace till I have hunted this child of Satan from my path ! Jonathan Anstey, bitter as is his enmity, whitens in his villany beside this master fiend ! Come, Jack, my nerves like steel are now strung to their utmost tension ! I must be away, up and doing ! to linger longer here is to give fresh time to the enemy !"

"Right, Claude ; where do you propose to begin our search ?"

"At the Devil's Punch Bowl !"

"And from thence ?"

"To the ruined house in the Vauxhall-road ; failing there, the hollow by the pinetree grove."

"And supposing, which heaven forbid, we should learn nothing at these places Claude ?"

"Why, I shall then make for the Moat Manor House and the mill near Barnet heath !"

"Good ! I scarce can think, that boldly making our way into these retreats, but what we shall hear something of poor Maude Mayburn !"

"Heaven grant we may ! Allons ! let us forward and God speed our mission !"

WITH A STEEL-LIKE GLITTER IN HIS EYES, THE VAMPYRE FACED THE HIGHWAYMEN.

Seated once more in the saddle, a look of stern, settled purpose shone in the face of Duval.

With a farewell glance at the ruined villa the friends now giving their steeds the rein dashed up the lane, in a moment of time gaining the high road.

CHAPTER XI.

THE DEVIL'S PUNCH BOWL—THE VAMPYRE AND HIS VICTIM—A TERRIBLE PROPOSITION—THE THREAT—THE DEFIANCE—THE LEAP INTO THE WATER—MAUDE MAYBURN'S PERIL.

Old Westminster, at the period of our life romance, like its twin sister, Alsatia, of Whitefriars, contained some of the vilest dens in the metropolis.

Many a foul deed of crime was committed nightly in the purlieus of Westminster.

Dark narrow streets with murderous-looking tenements met the eye at every turn.

Hundreds of the gloomy, dingy, squalid habitations looked as though in the last stage of ruin and decay.

Dirt-begrimed and reeking with foul odours were the majority of the houses situate in Old Westminster.

Oft grim-visaged Murder, with dire yells, woke up echoes in the silent night.

No inquiries were made, no attempt at interference, though the last dying shriek of a victim rang in the air, was ever thought of in the confines of Old Westminster.

London, two centuries ago, contained, among others, thee

popular haunts of crime --viz., Alsatia at Whitefriars; the Old Mint at Southwark; and the neighbourhood of Old Westminster, part of the latter being at times under water from the rising of the tide.

The houses situate close to the river were, if possible, dirtier and more squalid than the rest.

All was dark and drear in this abode of crime on the banks of the Thames.

A few sickly oil lamps here and there scarce dispelled the gloomy horrors of the place.

Gutters, in which were strewn rotting vegetables and decaying matter of every description, sent forth a pestilent odour in the air, carrying death and disease around.

Housebreakers, footpads, highwaymen, pickpockets, and criminals of every grade made the vile dens in Old Westminster a place of common resort.

The murderer and robber alike sought safety here as in Alsatia.

It was close to the river bank that a large red-bricked tenement, known as the Devil's Punch Bowl, was wont to stand at the time of which we are writing.

It was a darksome, squalid, murderous-looking den, but was frequented by all who resided near to or visited the neighbourhood.

A strange-looking sign hung without the building, consisting of a horrible rude painting of a wretched criminal on his road to Tyburn receiving a last drink from a huge bowl:

A sign rather ominous, but quite in keeping with the class who frequented this, the largest public in the neighbourhood.

A thriving roaring trade was carried on at the Devil's Punch Bowl.

"The Bowl," as it was sometimes called, was the resort and favoured rendezvous of the vilest criminals in London.

The most daring officers of the law hesitated ere they ventured within the doors of the Punch Bowl house when in search of an assassin or felon.

The dirt-begrimed windows of the old inn forbade all attempts at an insight of the place from without.

Nought could be descried save by passing its portals.

It was at about the same time that Claude and Jack left the ruins by the villa at Kennington Common that a tall muffled figure of a man, casting a quick searching glance round, dived suddenly through the swinging doors of the Devil's Punch Bowl.

Pushing his way through a motley, noisy, swearing crowd, the stranger, whose face now partly disclosed seemed pretty well known by the frequenters, passed through the large bar, presently making his way into a small chamber some six feet by ten, and in courtesy called a parlour.

Throwing himself into the only chair and resting his arms on the only table, the man in a loud domineering tone called for the landlord.

A few minutes after the proprietor of the Punch Bowl, a sturdy-built red-faced man with one eye, but who, despite his intense ugliness did not carry in his features the murderous hang-dog look that rested upon the countenances of the majority of his customers, bustled forward, and, descrying the face of his visitor by the sickly rays of an oil lamp that hung from a ceiling black as jet, exclaimed:

"Hallo, Mr. Vaughan, is it you?"

"Yes, it's me, Jem Noggins; and how many more times am I to caution you about blurting out my name for the benefit of any passing stranger?"

"Very sorry, forgot at the moment, Captain! And now what can I do for you?"

"Why, you can fetch me a glass of your best brandy—pure mind!—no cursed water with it for me! But, first, tell me how fares the girl I brought hither this morning?"

"Bad enough! I think the sooner you get her out of here the better!"

"I remove her to-night!"

"I am glad of it, poor thing."

"How so?"

"Why, I think a night here would do for her."

"You seem to feel pity for the wench."

"Well, I do."

"Hem! has it lately come to your turn, Jem Noggins, to feel for anyone but yourself?"

"Well, Van Vaughan, Captain, Lieutenant, Vampyre, or whatever else you choose to be called, I can go years back, when I had a girl of my own—that was, before I got my right eye gouged out. I had a wife then, and a pretty one, and for the daughter she gave me I'd have given my life! That girl upstairs puts me in mind of those I have lost; and the sooner you take her away the more I shall be pleased."

"Jem Noggins, you are getting old and soft!"

"If pity for that poor child upstairs is what you term being soft, well, damn it, I am! But look here, Vaughan, it won't do for me and you to quarrel; get the girl away before worse comes of it!"

"What do you mean?"

"Well, if you will have it, she's in danger here!"

"Danger! how?"

"Why, a hightobyman (highwayman) caught a glimpse of her this morning, and swears he'll have her though Satan stood forth to snatch her from him!"

"Indeed! who is this spark?"

"Oh, a devil-may-care blade, a dashing fellow! he was brought here or came here with Colonel Blood."

"That bullying swashbuckler! Said they aught in converse respecting the girl?"

"Yes; I overheard Blood caution the stripling knight of the road not to attempt any interference in that quarter that the girl had been secured by the Black Band for the arms of one who had paid a good sum for her abduction."

"What said the bold knight of the highway to this?"

"He, with an oath, averred the girl should be his; and for the Black Band, he rated them as the lowest cads and sneaks in the kingdom."

"He said that, did he?"

"Aye, and added that he owed you a debt and meant to pay it!"

"Indeed! he knows me then?"

"Oh, yes; he has seen you, it appears, several times, and upon one occasion you helped his capture, he said, by the grabs (officers)."

"What is the fellow's name?"

"Paul Clifford."

"Hem! I do remember the boy, for boy he is and nothing more. But since he barks thus I must pay heed, and have a care that he doth not bite. You can go! Never mind the order I gave you; but now I will at once visit my prize. Have you the key of her prison chamber?"

"It is here." The landlord, pulling a key from his pocket, here handed it to his companion, who, a moment after, strode from the chamber.

"Curse on that fellow, how I hate him! 'Soft,' am I? 'Sdeath, he shall find me out yet; an' he mind not! Look to it, Vampyre Vaughan, or Jem Noggins may prove a serpent in your path! I will go at once and tell dashing, rattling, law-defying Paul Clifford all that has passed! I like the lad, and, dammo, would give something to lay this this viperous Vampyre by the heels! Confound him, his death-face always puts me in a shiver when I look upon it with one eye! Lord knows how they feel who gaze upon it with two!"

Muttering and swearing the landlord now left the parlour, being presently after in deep converse with a young man who was busily engaged sitting on a stool in his private sanctum polishing up and cleaning a pair of pistols.

When leaving the bar parlour a few moments before, the man Vaughan, ascending a flight of ricketty stairs that creaked and groaned at every footstep, made his way up to the second floor of the old house.

Scarce did the oil lamp he had secured when leaving Jem Noggins serve to light him up the rude wide staircase.

All was black, drear, and horrible.

The wind from open doors below rushed up with a strange, sighing sound about the staircase.

Like some hideous being of another world was the man Vaughan, his eyes glistening and rolling horribly in their sockets as he halted at the strong oaken door of a room on the floor he had now reached.

Placing the key noiselessly in the lock he, pausing for a moment, listened for a sound from within.

All was, however, quiet, not the slightest token of living being in the chamber could be heard.

"Hem! she sleeps. Well for her, perchance, if she slept till the day of judgment! Doubtless she would prefer grim death to the love of this Miles Ellerton or mine."

A grin of a satyr here stole over the hideous face of the man, who now softly and cat-like stealthily crept into the room the door of which he had unlocked.

All was quiet.

The chamber, a large one, lighted only by the silvery rays of the moon, looked weird and ghostlike in the gloom.

A small oil lamp, at this moment just dying out, shot up a last yellow gleam, revealing the form of a young girl, who, on her knees by the open casement at the further end of the room, had fallen asleep in the attitude of prayer.

With a devilish look in his corpse-like face the wretch Vaughan now strode forwards.

Placing his lamp on the table, he for a moment with folded arms gazed upon the figure of the hapless girl, who, worn out with horror and despair, had fallen into a fitful slumber.

"She is very beautiful! young and innocent! too lovely to fall the prey of the creature, Miles Ellerton. 'Tis strange the mad infatuation I have for this maiden! I, Vaughan the Vampyre, as they called me, feel towards this girl as I never felt towards woman before! How fair and white her skin! how beautiful she is!"

With his eyes gleaming like polished steel, and his lips drawn up, showing his wolfish-like fangs, a terrible passion seemed to possess the unscrupulous wretch who now bent forward to seize the hapless girl in his grasp, when, with a wild heartrending shriek of horror, she started to her feet.

"Be not alarmed, Maude Mayburn! 'tis only I!"

In wild horror, with a look of intense loathing, poor Maude (for she it was who was now a captive in the terrible Punch Bowl House) started back, leaning upon the ledge of the open casement for support.

The moon, shining through the casement, threw a ghastly blue light upon the contorted hideous features of the villain before her, whilst the lamp that gave out a feeble yellow glare behind, added to the weird gloom of the vast chamber, strange shadows seeming to hover upon the dark oaken panellings of the room.

"What is your purpose? what would you?" gasped Maude, shivering and turning faint and giddy as she gazed into the burning snake-like orbs of the intruder.

"What is my purpose, fair Maude Mayburn? what should it be, but to take you hence?"

"Where? oh, where?" In wild trembling accents, in a hoarse choking voice, the words fell from her lips.

"Where, dear girl? why to the man who loves you, even to your affianced Miles Ellerton. You shudder, you turn away, you hate, detest this man! Is it so? I see your eyes proclaim what your tongue refuses to utter, 'tis well I will save you from him!"

"You?" For a moment of time a hectic flush gathered in her pale cheeks, whilst a gleam of hope appeared in the eyes of the captive; then, as the steel-like orbs of the hideous villain before her were fastened upon her with a satyr-like stare, a cold icy feeling, as of death, darted through her frame.

"Maude Mayburn, hear me!" In a hissing whisper the words fell from the thin white lips of Vaughan, who, drawing near, evoked a scream of horror from the unhappy, terrified girl. "Nay, be not alarmed, I would not hurt thee; what I have said I will carry out; I will free you of this hated Miles Ellerton—he shall trouble you no more. I will slay, kill him! but in return would ask the love you have yet to give; for I, Vaughan, one of the leaders of a band of men for whose crimes the law would condemn to the scaffold, love, aye love you, fair Maude! Consent to be mine, and I will give up all; will quit the kingdom, and in another clime give you such wealth as a princess might envy; refuse to comply, and better death than what shall follow!"

"Then be it death, horrible being! The hated detested villain Miles Ellerton were preferable to thee!" In a low husky voice, panting with terror, Maude leant back against the casement, glaring with wild eyes at her hideous companion.

A guttural chuckle now escaped the lips of Vaughan, who exclaimed:—

"Be it so! You scorn, you loathe me! You freeze with terror at the sight of the man who has sworn to make you his! Ha, ha, ha! Maude Mayburn! had you known me better you would not have spoken out your detestation thus. Girl! know you where you are? Do you know that not your wildest shrieks can bring you aid? You are in a house where none dare come to snatch you from my grasp."

"Wretch! there is one who can even now foil you in your threatened purpose."

"And who may that be, sweet Maude?"

"A power that you will laugh to scorn, but who, if it will, can save me now."

With blanched features, her eyes glistening with wild affright, Maude here pointed up to the star-lit skies, a low mocking laugh escaping the lips of her persecutor.

"Heaven, you would intimate, can save you then! If there indeed be such a place, let it exert its power now in thy behalf; for I'll make thee mine, Maude Mayburn, aye, and within the hour! Methinks your soft and dainty form will put new life-blood in my veins! Ha, ha, ha! you shall be the Vampyre Bride! the cold moon our bridal couch! blood, instead of the rich red wine, our banquet!

A horrible, fiendly, ghastly glitter now shone in the eyes of the wretch, white flecks of foam gathered on the thin lips; the wolfish teeth fully exposed gnashed sharply together; whilst the long skinny fingers seemed grasping at the air, as the arms thrown up, the hands were stretched out as if to clutch the victim, who in wild terror now leaned half-out of the casement.

In maddened horror Maude Mayburn glared at the fearful being before her.

Nothing human was there now in the aspect of the man Vaughan; as though possessed by a demon he fastened his eyes, which shone like pieces of polished steel, upon his terrified victim, low guttural sentences escaping ever and again from the thin drawn-up lips.

"Mine, mine! She can't escape! Oh, oh! A fair bridal! What so fitting for the Vampyre Bride as the bright moon—the moon so lustrous and cold? I love the moon! It gives me life! Come, dear girl! Within the hour! I have said it! Mine, or death!

For a moment Maude, in wildest terror, glared at her maddened enemy; then, casting her eyes without, they were fixed upon the waters below.

Now high tide, the river many feet in depth laved the walls of the Punch Bowl House.

Almost on a level with a casement on the ground floor below had the encroaching waters now risen.

With a wild thrill of speechless agony Maude Mayburn glared at the waters, which glistened like a sea of molten lead in the bright rays of the moon; then a frenzied shriek escaped her lips as the hideous creature Vaughan darted forward to seize her in his grasp, snapping like a wolf with his teeth at her fair white neck, fully exposed as she leant back over the casement staring in horror at her foe.

For a moment of time Maude gazed with horror at the mad horrible being before her; then, with the name of the all-wise Creator issuing from her wan lips, she threw herself out of the window, slipping from the clutch of her foe, and whirling shrieking wildly into the rushing waters below.

CHAPTER XII.

BARNET HEATH—THE MIDNIGHT MEETING—A LIGHT AND A RESCUE—BROTHERS OF THE ROAD—A STRANGE STORY.

Barnet heath!

The hour midnight!

Bright and beautiful shone the moon upon the figure of a solitary horseman, who, drawn up in the centre of the wide open tract seated in his saddle, gazed anxiously in the direction leading to the village of Barnet and the great City beyond.

"Sacre! why comes he not? Parbleu! I wish I had not let him visit the vauxhall den alone!" muttered Claudo; for it was he who, seated upon the back of his bonnie steed, remained motionless and inactive in the centre of Barnet heath at the midnight hour.

Like a statue was the figure of horse and rider as they remained there, motionless on the moonlit heath.

Giant shadows of both were thrown behind; the breeze at times lifting the feather that was looped in the hat of the highwayman, making it assume the shape of a huge gaunt arm beckoning from the spot.

Wearily Claude passed his hand over his brow; a heavy sigh escaping his bosom.

Sad and sorrowful he gazed around.

Life for a time with our bold hero had but little charms.

The girl to whom he had solely rendered up his heart, whom he loved with all the ardent passion of his nature, was lost to him.

As yet no tidings had he gained of her, who in his honest true passion he would have shielded from harm with his life.

Known to the lad Timothy Tuck, Gentleman Jack had entreated Claude to allow him to visit the ruined house at Vauxhall alone.

Claude, when they had left the villa at Kennington, had hastened to the Devil's Punch Bowl; here, however, he had learned nothing; Jem Noggins had been called out and of no one else could Duval venture to make inquiries.

Little did he know that at that moment she whom he sought was a prisoner in the house.

No warning voice whispered in his ear the vicinity of his deadliest enemy, who, as he hurried through the crooked ways of Old Westminster passed him muffled up, and making for the place he had left a few minutes before.

Jack, who had gone to Vauxhall to loiter about for a meeting with the boy Jack, had arranged to meet his friend by twelve o'clock on Barnet heath.

Claude, the first to arrive, in anxious suspense now awaited his companion.

Peering eagerly across the moonlit waste a cry of joy suddenly escaped his lips!

Afar off was a horseman making straight for the spot upon which he stood.

Nearer, nearer came the stranger, who on a splendid mount tore at wild speed over the heath.

In a few minutes more a loud hallo echoed across the waste; a shout that was responded to by Claude, who, now giving his own steed the rein darted forward to meet the stranger.

In another moment the riders met:

Met in full career upon the heath.

"Jack?"

"Duval, dear boy!"

"Any news?"

"None."

"Diablo, I shall go mad! Have you learnt nothing?"

In wild despairing tones Claude addressed his companion.

Jack, with looks of pity, slowly walking his horse beside that of his friend, now exclaimed: "Give not way to despair, Claude, all may yet be well! I have seen Timothy at Vauxhall, and he tells me that Maude has not been taken there; and as of course you gained no tidings of her at the Bowl House, why we may possibly find her again a captive in the Moat Manor."

"Why should we hear of her there any more than at the other places?" said Claude, despondingly.

"Because they may reasonably think that they will be left more undisturbed out of town than in it."

"True, Jack, I did not think of that," ejaculated Claude, ready to catch at the slightest ground for hope.

"I now propose that we make from here to the pinetree grove."

"Very good, dear Jack; I see nothing else for us to do."

"Exactly; failing to find any news in the hollow used for charcoal-making by the Black Band, we will hurry on with all speed to the Moat Manor, looking in upon Luke and Kate at the old Tree Cave."

"Good, dear old pal! capitally arranged! Let us on! I'm in feverish haste to continue our search."

Touching their sagacious steeds with the reins, the companions now raced at good speed over the heath.

It was a lovely night:

Light as day, everything bathed in a silvery glare by the rays of the moon.

On, on, over the moonlit waste, rode the friends.

Exhilarated by the race, Claude once more began to feel himself.

The feeling of depression that had weighed his spirits down the live long day now left him.

Hope once more entered his bosom.

He could not think that one so good and beautiful as the hapless Maude would be deserted by a merciful Providence, and left to become the victim of a villain.

With these fresh hopes kindling in his bosom, Claude, shouting wildly with joy, tore on over the heath, free of his foes, Jonathan Anstey and his runners! Free of his darksome prison cell, our hero, for a time light-hearted as a schoolboy, galloped on, ever and again, by word and caress, urging forward and encouraging his bonny mare, that, like the wind, bounded on over the springy turf.

It was while pursuing thus a mad career, their blood up and excited, and fit for any daring deed, that the friends were suddenly startled by the report of firearms:

The sharp ringing report of pistols that woke up echoes in the silent night.

Gaining, at this point, a verge of the heath, the comrades pulled up.

Just before them was a clump of tangled furze, hazel, and blackberry bushes.

On the other side of this was the high road:

From the high road had echoed the report of pistols.

Pursuing a slight detour, a free way was open from the south to the highway.

With a glance, first, at the barrier before them, and then, with a nod one to the other, the friends boldly urged their steeds to take the leap.

The loud jar of angry voices, and clashing of steel now rang in the air.

With shouts that echoed above those proceeding from the combatants, Jack and Duval now dashed forward at terrific speed, both, at one moment, bounding over the thick tangled furze into the centre of the road on the other side.

A strange scene now met the eyes of the two friends.

Some hundred yards or more down the road they beheld five men, who were attacking with fury a slim youth who, dressed in a costume half-cavalier, half-military, from his appearance, seemed scarce able to defend himself ably from one, leave alone the fearful heavy odds now against him.

No cry for aid, however, escaped his lips; whirling his sword over his head, anon lunging and parrying, the brave stranger for a time held his own.

"Jack!"

"Duval!"

"I can't stand this!"

"Nor I!"

"On to them!"

"That's the ticket!"

Giving their steeds the rein the companions now dashed forward, their sudden appearance stopping the fray.

Leaping from their horses, Claude and Jack now addressed the strangers, speaking in no measured terms of their cowardice in thus attacking and throwing themselves on one man.

"And pray, gentlemen, by what right do you interfere?" exclaimed a stout, broad-shouldered man, habited in black, who now, sword in hand, advanced upon Claude.

"By what right do we interfere? why, by the right of humanity, fatguts!" exclaimed Duval, who, annoyed by the stranger's threatening demeanour, coolly darted upon him, and wrenched the sword from his grasp.

This was the signal for renewed hostilities.

In another moment Jack and Duval, with the young man whose part they had taken, were fencing and struggling with the foe.

Not for long did the affray last.

Jack and Duval, the most expert of swordsmen, soon rendered the five strangers hors de combat.

Finding themselves beaten, they now, with one accord, flew towards their horses, which were quietly grazing further down the road.

"Hold, gentlemen! come back, a word with you! Sacre! if you don't return I'll put a bullet in your brains!" shouted Claude.

With downcast look, and glancing at each other in dismay, the would-be fugitives now came back.

"Well, sir, having taken up arms for that thief there, I think you had better go your way, nor further molest me and my friends! Perhaps you are not aware that you are aiding and abetting a highwayman, which, I take it, is a criminal proceeding," exclaimed the stout stranger, who undertook, it appeared, the office of spokesman for the rest.

"I don't care what the young man may be! You are a set of cowards to hurl yourselves on one; and I am very glad that I and my friend happened to come up."

The stout one, who, by his face, evidently did not coincide with Claude on this point, now exclaimed:

"Well, sir! having prevented us, as was our intention, capturing that fellow, and placing him in the hands of the officers of the law, what may be your further purpose with us? What do you require of us now?"

"Oh! merely a souvenir that may remind me of our pleasant rencontre."

"Sir, I don't understand you!"

"Well, you see, it's something novel to behold five men all attacking one; and as I should like ever to bear in my remembrance such bold heroes, I require some little article from each as a memento mori, such, for instance, as a watch, a snuff-box, or a purse:"

"Well-filled with coins? imprinted with the head of his august Majesty, eh, Claude?" exclaimed Jack with a grin.

"Exactly so; you've hit it," said Duval, laughing loudly at the looks of horror that now gathered in the faces of the fat one and his friends.

"You, you are highwaymen, then?" gasped the strangers in a breath.

"Highwaymen, gentlemen! oh dear no! we merely levy

taxes on his Majesty's subjects that pass this way!—Now Jack, we must skin the lot. They are cowardly fellows, and deserve to be punished."

"Will you allow me to assist in the pleasant operation?" said the young man whom Claude and Jack had rescued from the travellers.

"Certainly, my dear boy! Ma foi, you of all others must decidedly have a hand in plucking the pigeons that a kind and munificent Providence has thrown in our way!"

With pistols cocked and presented at the heads of the enraged strangers, a general process of turning pockets inside out now took place, the performance being carried on by Claude, Jack, and their new-found companion, with much laughter.

Loud cries and threats of future vengeance escaped from the travellers as they beheld themselves rapidly despoiled of their property.

"We shall see you hanged at Tyburn, you rogues!" exclaimed the stout gentleman, who, with fury beheld Claude place in his pocket a little canvas bag he had snatched from him a moment before.

"Thieves! robbers! villains!" shouted the others.

Paying no heed to their cries, Claude and his companions carried on the work of pillage till they were certain they had effectually cleaned them out.

"Now, gentlemen, in spite of your naughty language, we will allow you to depart." Duval, with a grin, here pointed to the youthful stranger as he added, "But for your bad cowardly conduct to him, why who knows your pockets may still have been full! You see Providence, who watches over the weak, aided him at the last moment and meted out punishment. Go! Allons! may you become better and wiser men!"

Screaming with laughter, Jack and the young stranger fairly danced with merriment at the oaths and cries of fury uttered by the fleeced travellers, as, rushing away to their horses, they swore to know no rest till they had had revenge.

"They are considerably chawed up, Claude."

"I fancy they are! So, Jack, would you be if you had lost all your coin!"

"True for you there, Claude! But see, our young friend looks on at us with rather a mystified air, and seems in a brown study! A penny for your thoughts, lad!"

"I was thinking how strange, under the circumstance, was our meeting," said the stranger, who, stepping up to Claude and placing his hand upon his arm, added, "Your comrade there has once or twice addressed you as Claude. Can it be possible that I have been rescued from those vagabonds, saved, perchance, from imprisonment and death, by Claude Duval? Tell me, is it to that dashing knight of the road I am speaking?"

"Yes, lad, I'm Claude Duval! and yonder friend of mine is Gentleman Jack! and now, ere you speak further, ma foi! am I not right in conjecturing you to be also a High Toby—one of those bold hearts who gather gold by the light of her ladyship the Moon?"

"Yes, Claude Duval, I am what they call a highwayman. The world would not let me live in honesty; and, as I was not inclined to starve whilst others feasted, I then took to filling my purse from the pouches of those who are blessed with more than they know what to do with."

"Spoken well, and with excellent cunning! Parbleu! we should be better acquainted. What is your name, brother of the road?" said Claude, eyeing the open handsome face of the young stranger with admiration.

"I am he whom men call Paul Clifford!"

"Paul Clifford! he whose favourite haunt is Hounslow Heath and the North-road?"

"The same."

"Welcome, brave heart! We have often heard of your exploits, have we not, Jack?" said Claude, who here wrung their new-found friend warmly by the hand.

"By Jove, yes, Paul! I and Claude have often laughed over that affair of yours with the grazier, that got talked about all over the town. But, tell me, have we not seen each other before? Now I look at you closely, I could swear your face is known to me."

"I can tell you, at Jem Noggins's" said the young highwayman.

"The Devil's Punch Bowl?"

"Yes, at which place I had a wonderful adventure an hour or two back—an adventure in which you are strangely mixed up, Claude!"

"An adventure in which I am mixed up. What mean you, Paul?" exclaimed our hero, who, with Jack, here gazed in some astonishment at their new companion.

"It's a strange terrible business that I have to relate; and delighted I am to be of service this night to you, Claude, who, unknowing me, rendered me aid in the hour of need."

"Parbleu! I do not understand."

"I will soon enlighten you, Duval! Do you know a demi-devil called Vaughan the Vampire?"

With a start Claude now drew near to Paul, and in an agitated voice exclaimed, "Great heavens, yes! but what do you know of that fiend?"

"Enough to possess the desire to slay him had he a hundred lives."

"You know the man well, it seems?"

"Yes, and he shall know me well, Claude, before I've done with him! But I've strange news for your ear, and will at once relate it. You must know then, when half-an-hour back I was set upon by those fellows, one of whom I may mention recognised me as the party who eased him of a watch a few weeks ago, I was on my way to a certain rendezvous called the old Tree Cave."

"Our secret retreat! who told you of this?" In wild astonishment Claude with his friend here gazed upon their companion.

"Listen, and I will tell you; and to ease your mind, at once, touching a trouble that I know weighs upon and oppresses you, know that to-night, whilst sitting at an open casement on the ground-floor of the Punch Bowl, a wild and terrible incident occurred."

With wide staring eyes and with beating heart, Claude now gazed at his new-found friend.

A something in the tone of Paul Clifford's voice assured him that a surprise was in store; but not in his wildest dream of hope did he realise the truth.

"Speak on! Mon Dieu! say on, Paul!"

"It was, I believe, near upon eleven when, as I have told you, I was seated at the casement of a room of the Punch Bowl overlooking the river. I was thinking, to tell you the truth, of a certain lady who, young, fair, and lovely, had struck my boyish fancy, when I was startled by a piercing heartrending shriek. Starting up, I threw the casement open to it furthest limits and looked out upon the moonlit waters, when a large object flashed before me, and in a second of time I beheld a human form struggling with the tide.

"For a minute the figure was lost to my sight, when, straining my eyes over the rolling waters, I once more caught a glimpse of the unfortunate; for a second of time the fair and lovely face was revealed to me, then, as I recognised in the agonised features those of the poor girl of whom I had shortly before been thinking, I dashed from the casement into the bubbling waters; a bold, strong swimmer, I dived deep down, and was fortunate enough to secure the drowning girl. Too far out in the river now to return to the Bowl House I hailed a passing boatman, and with his aid saved the poor girl and myself. Rowing to the nearest stairs I then had my prize taken to an inn by the waterside, where, under restoratives, she was brought back to consciousness."

"Brave lad! you are a good one and true, Paul!" exclaimed Jack, eying the young highwayman with admiration.

"Pshaw, I did but my duty. But see, our friend Claude appears strangely disturbed!" said Paul, with a smile of hidden meaning, as he gazed at the pallid face and glistening eyes of our hero, who, now catching him by the arm, exclaimed:

"Who? what was she? this girl! Where did you take her?"

"Softly, my dear Duval, and I will tell you! You must know, that all the return I got for my ducking was to hear from the pretty one's lips, the moment she returned to consciousness, that she loved and was betrothed to another! Some, upon this, would have left her; but I, smothering my passion, not only conducted her to a place of safety, but told her I would hunt up her lover."

"Hunt up her lover?" Mechanically Claude echoed the words, staring the while at the narrator, who with a smile, heeding not the interruption, resumed his story.

"Giving the poor girl assurance of my protection from the fiend Vaughan (in escaping from whom it appeared she had been prepared to meet death), I then conveyed her from London to Highgate."

"To Highgate?" reiterated Claude.

"Yes! where I have left her in good hands. This girl, whom I have saved from the river, and whose lover I promised to bring to her side, is now under the charge of Jenny Dunning, the pretty daughter of old Dick, the landlord of The Cat and her Kittens."

"And the girl's name, Paul! said Jack with a smile, as he brushed a gathering tear from his eye.

"Maude Mayburn, Jack; and to her must I conduct her truant lover, Dashing Duval."

CHAPTER XIII.

THE MEETING AT THE OLD INN—A CONVIVIAL PARTY—THE SURPRISE—THE FLIGHT—THE PURSUIT.

"Paul Clifford, how can I thank you?" exclaimed Claude, as, catching the hands of his new-found friend in his own, he wrung them with hearty, earnest warmth.

"Thanks, be bothered! Have you not already wiped out any little service I may have done you by rescuing me from those skunks just now?"

"Name not that, dear Paul; the service was nought to that which you have done for me; you have saved a young girl, whom I love as I never loved woman before, from a horrible death; and I trust that some day I may be in a position to prove to you my gratitude."

"Look here, Claude! if you talk any more about the matter I shall jump on the back of my bonny mare, Brown Bess, and leave you and Gentleman Jack to yourselves."

"You'll do nothing of the kind, Paul; my pal here and I will now hasten with you to Highgate, and we three from this time forth must work together."

"With all my heart," said Clifford, as, following the example of his companions, he vaulted into the saddle.

Presently after, at a slashing pace, the friends were careering across the heath.

His breast relieved from further anxiety respecting the young girl who, in her innocence and beauty had gained his whole heart, Claude Duval now, as his steed bounded on, gave utterance to shouts of glee.

With full purses and light hearts the companions raced on over the heath.

It was about half an hour after their encounter that the three friends gained the then village of Highgate.

Pausing at a substantial well-built inn, just without the village, which rejoiced in the sign of The Cat and her Kittens, the midnight travellers thundered loudly at the doors for admission.

"What ho! house, house!"

"Wake up Dick, old man."

"What is it? Who knocks so loud?" exclaimed the landlord, a fat-faced, rubicund-visaged old fellow, who, at that moment, slowly and cautiously slid back the bolts of the door, at once giving admission to the friends.

"So, so; you've met the pals, then, Paul! How do, Claude? Glad to see you've done the grabs again! Ah, Jack, saucy, handsome Gentleman Jack; how goes it? There's a girl up stairs wants to see you."

"A girl wants to see me? You make a mistake, Dick, old man; Duval is the happy rascal."

"Indeed, I make no mistake at all, Master Jack," exclaimed Boniface, with a grin, at the same time handing to the friends some wine he had just poured out. "There are three young ladies upstairs."

"Indeed, Dick; and who may they be?" said Claude.

"Nay, one is a lady whom, methinks, you'll be happy to meet again; whilst the others—well one is my own daughter, my bonny Jenny, who anxiously awaits a certain gentlemen named Paul Clifford, and the other is a lady named Kate Annesley."

"Kate, is she here?" exclaimed Jack.

"Yes, the young lady is upstairs, my dear Jack! You needn't look so astounded; it's a fact!"

"How, when did she come?"

"About an hour back, in company with your boy, Luke, Claude. It appeared Miss Kate was anxious to know how things were going on, and called to learn some news, being pretty well convinced that you would call at The Cat and her Kittens on your way to your retreat, the old Tree Cave."

"By Jove! this is a surprise! When can we see the ladies, Dick?" said Claude, gulping down his wine and moving anxiously towards the door.

"At once; they are all up expecting a visit; I'll just run and tell them you are here."

With a grin, the worthy landlord now hurried from the parlour in which the friends were seated; returning in a few moments with the intelligence that they were at once to hasten to the drawing-room above, where their arrival was anxiously looked for.

It was with beating heart, that Claude, some five minutes after, was straining to his breast the fair and lovely Maude Mayburn:

She whom the day before he feared he had lost perhaps for ever.

It was not without a shudder that the young girl detailed to her lover the dread scene she had gone through at the Bowl House, at Westminster.

Standing by a casement overlooking the porch projecting from the outer door of the old inn, she detailed at length her sufferings since her abduction from the pretty villa at Kennington.

"Borne off by the horrible man Vaughan, a creature whom I scarce can think is human," said Maude with a shudder, "I was taken to the house in Westminster. Visited there yesternight in a dark gloomy chamber by the villain who had torn me from you, dear Claude, I, in a frenzy of terror, as the wretch sought to clutch me in his arms, leapt wildly from the window into the river that ran swiftly below. Ere I had gained the waters I was bereft of all consciousness, and but for that dear friend yonder (Maude here pointed to Paul Clifford) should have perished in the tide I sought in preference to the loathed arms of the wretch whose very name I scarce can force my tongue to utter without a shudder."

"Think not of the villain, dearest; I will exact from him a heavy price for his daring! He shall not find Claude Duval a man likely to forget an injury. He shall pay for his villany ere the week is out. But we will all retire now, for yourself and Kate must need rest. For a time we will leave you here; Jenny Dunning will see to your comfort, and in the course of a few days I will get ready for you, dearest, a new retreat in some pretty rural spot, where you and Kate can remain in safety until such time as enough can be amassed to take us over to the land of my birth, la Belle France."

"And you, will you take me there?"

"That will I, my pretty Maude! but, come, I must insist upon your seeking your couch. Now then, my friends, the ladies are about to retire. Let us descend below, where we can converse upon our future movements," said Duval, who with Jack and Paul at once prepared to leave the room.

The friends then bidding the young girls adieu, were soon after engaged with Dick Dunning, the landlord, in discussing a supper he had prepared—a repast they were all ready for, and which they much enjoyed.

Hot punch following, it was late in the morning ere the convivial party laid down for a short repose.

Sleeping soundly, the sun was pouring full into the little back room of the old inn, in which the friends lay, ere they rose to go below.

Hot and feverish from the effects of the potations they had a few hours before so freely imbibed, Duval and his companions once aroused were not slow in hastening to the breakfast table.

Here, with the jolly Dick Dunning, the knights of the road were soon discussing some broiled ham, with new laid eggs and hot tea, the latter flavoured with a dash of brandy. Finishing the repast, and about to join their fair charges, Kate Annersley and the lovely Maude, Duval suddenly bounded from his chair as if he'd been shot.

"What's that, Dick?"

"Philistines, for a thousand guineas!" said Dunning, as again the rude summons that had startled our hero was repeated without.

Not the application for admission from a traveller was it that was continuously kept up at the door, but a loud banging, above which the companions presently heard the cries of several men.

"It's the officers, Duval!"

"Damnation, yes!"

"How the deuce have they found us out?"

"Diable! I don't know, Jack!"

"It may be, though they are evidently enemies outside, that they don't actually know we are here."

"You are right, Paul," said Duval, who with the other was busy buckling on his sword and seeing to the priming his pistols.

"Right or wrong, lads, I must see to them, or they'll have

the door down. You'll find your horses safe in the stable; and I think you had better get away."

"How about the girls, Dick?"

"They will be all right, never you fear. Jenny shan't leave them for a moment. But away with you, your beasts are all ready; you can lead them out through the back gate, and be a mile away before there is any pursuit."

"Right you are, Dunning, old boy! You're are not half a bad sort."

"No; don't suppose I am. But I must cut it, or, damme, those cusses outside will do a bust in."

With a grin, the landlord hurried to answer the door, whilst the friends made their way from the kitchen in which they had breakfasted to the garden at the back of the inn.

Lifting their eyes up to a casement above, they beheld the fair faces of three young girls peering down upon them.

Aroused by the noise, in alarm the pretty Maude and her companions had thrown open their window.

Waving an adieu, and shouting words of encouragement, the highwaymen now darted to the stables and presently appeared, leading their horses along the garden to a gate that opened out upon some fields at the back.

To throw open the gate was the work of a moment; then, as the three friends passed into the meadows beyond, each turned, and, waving a final adieu to the young girls, who, with anxious riveted gaze were watching their every movement, vaulted into their saddles, and at mad speed galloped from the spot.

Not too soon had their escape from the inn been effected.

A hoarse cry of rage rang in their ears as they dashed away:

Jonathan Anstey and his men, bounding out through the gate and gaining the meadow as the highwaymen galloped from the spot.

"Anstey is sold again, Claude."

"Yes, don't he look vicious?"

"Rather!"

"They haven't got their mounts."

"No, Paul! they are in the front of the inn."

"Of course—I had forgot. Well, we shall have a good start."

"Yes; but they will be soon after us."

"They will so; but we will give them a good race."

"That we most certainly will."

"Where shall we go to, Duval?"

"Why I think we had best make for the open country; don't you think so, dear pals?"

"Decidedly! It's no use our going to the Long Village (London) with those bloodhounds at our heels," said Jack, who, with Paul Clifford, galloped on beside their friend.

"Do you think Anstey will attempt to follow now we have got such a start, Claude?" exclaimed Clifford, as he coolly drew a pipe from his pocket, and proceeded to fill it with the fragrant weed, preparatory to a smoke.

"I have no doubt but that our enemies will follow till their horses are blown. See, parbleu! they are now hot in pursuit."

Our hero, here turning in his saddle, pointed at some half dozen horsemen, who were rushing on madly in their track.

"Jonathan means it, Claude!"

"He does so! But we shall beat them in a race. We could give them ten to one and win; there is not one of them with such a mount as we each have."

"No; that's right enough, Claude; we will lead them a dance this journey."

"We will so. Thank heaven the girls are all right! I have no anxiety respecting them, and am just in the mood to oblige my particular friend, Anstey, to a race!"

With loud shouts, the three friends, now giving their brave steeds the rein, tore on along the highway like the wind.

The morning now wearing on, the sun, bright and glorious, shone like a ball of burnished gold in the skies.

A light gentle breeze fanned the topmost branches of the trees by the wayside.

A delicious coolness was there in the air that sunny morn.

The birds, twittering merrily in the bright rays of the sun, added to the cheerful scene.

There was a beautiful lovely calm in the aspect of the green lanes and country roads, along which the pursued took their path, that contrasted strangely with their positions.

Hunted like beasts of prey, they urged on their panting steeds in their race:

The race of life!

Well Duval knew that nothing but the halter round his neck would satisfy the deadly enmity of his foe—the fiendly thief-taker.

He had openly defied him:

Had torn from him a girl upon whom he had the vilest designs:

Had outwitted and escaped him upon several occasions.

Duval was now well aware that with the Bow-street runner, Jonathan Anstey, it was revenge a la mort.

With a smile, Claude, as they dashed on, ever and again glanced back at their pursuers.

They were falling back each minute.

The runners failed to gain upon them.

As Claude had predicted, their horses could not attain the speed of the noble beasts upon which they were mounted.

Each moment the distance between pursuers and pursued was increased.

The Bow-street officers were falling rapidly in the rear.

A village was now reached, passing through which again miles of open country stretched before the riders.

On, on they flow, a warm glow kindling through their frames as they tore along, nought for a time sounding in the air save the clatter of their horses' hoofs.

For an hour or more the race was kept up.

The officers, now far, far behind, were scarce to be distinguished as they slowly dragged on in the distance.

Gaining the summit of a high hill, the companions paused for a time.

Some mile and a half behind, coursing onwards along the road, which, zigzag and serpent-like, looked like a mere pathway as seen from the hill, appeared the vindictive men of the law.

"They won't give in, Claude."

"No, Jack, they follow us up. That villain Anstey shall have my bullet in his head before I've done with him."

"Damn him! he seems bent upon your capture."

"Yes, he has a private feeling in the matter, Paul."

"Exactly; but you are too smart for a wooden-headed Bow-street runner."

"No go! yes. But come, our steeds are breathed now, let us on."

"Right, Claude! Our pursuers will have a job, I reckon, to get their horses up the hill," said Jack, as with a grin he pointed to their pursuers, who were crawling along, their horses quite spent.

Descending the hill the friends now made rapid progress towards a little village or hamlet they discerned some two miles ahead.

A thin haze hanging over the place gave token of the vicinity of various habitations, whilst the spire of a pretty country church rearing its height up in the sky could now be seen.

Chatting gaily and laughing loudly as they beheld their pursuers like dim specks now stationed at the top of the hill, the friends, patting their steeds, hastened on to the adjacent village.

It was when within half a mile of this place that our adventurers, drawing in their reins, came to a pause.

Slowly approaching them were two horsemen.

Some mile and a half behind were the inveterate and determined runners.

With a smile Claude, pointing to the approaching strangers, exclaimed, "We must have speech with these gentlemen!"

"Yes, Claude; we must ask them the time of day!"

"Exactly."

"They are hurrying on now they see we have paused."

"Yes! Perhaps they are not aware that there is a toll here."

"Possibly not."

"We must make them acquainted with that, Jack!"

"Just so!"

"Paul!"

"Yes, captain."

"Do you with Jack remain here in the road keeping watch upon our friends behind; I will hurry on and meet the strangers; and if Anstey and his men get too close before I've done with the travellers, why, give them a volley."

"All right, Claude!" Seeing to the priming of their pistols, Jack and Paul now slowly rode back as though about to meet their enemies approaching.

That apparently startled the runners, who could be seen drawn up in a group a mile along the road, for a time pausing in their pursuit.

Duval, patting his bonny Jane upon the neck, at this moment dashed forwards to meet the strange horsemen.

A loud cry escaped the lips of the foremost rider as Claude dashed up :

A cry of malignant fury :

A cry followed by the report of a pistol as our hero in startled amaze glared with eyes of astonishment before him.

Recalled to himself by the ping of a bullet from the stranger's pistol as it winged unpleasantly close to his ears, Duval, with an oath, now leaning forward in his saddle, grappled with his adversary.

A thrill of rage, of mad fury, passed through his frame as he glared at the face of his enemy :

The villain Van Vaughan !

CHAPTER XIV.

THE STRUGGLE ON HORSEBACK—A DEED OF VENGEANCE—THE HUNT IN THE WOOD—THE VILLAGE CHURCH—A BURIAL—PURSUED BY THE ENEMY—A BOLD EXPEDIENT—THE VAULT—DEPARTURE OF THE RUNNERS—LEFT ALONE—A NIGHT OF MYSTERY—THE MOONLIGHT VISION—THE DEAD ALIVE.

"So, hell fiend, we meet again ! I have a score to settle with you !" exclaimed our hero as, his horse side by side with that of his foe, he, gripping him by the neckerchief, essayed to drag him from his saddle.

In his fury at the sudden rencontre with the man who had rased his dwelling at Kennington to the ground, and who had for a time subjected his lovely Maude to horror near ending in death, Claude forgot the presence of the villain Vaughan's companion, who, gliding up behind him, raised his pistol to fire at his unsuspecting victim.

Another moment and the career of the dashing Claude Duval would have come to end ; but, even as the finger of the cowardly assailant was on the trigger of his weapon, a loud report echoed in the air, and, his own pistol falling from his nerveless grasp, bathed in blood the man tumbled headlong from his saddle.

"Done for him ! You nicked him that time, Paul," said Jack, who now dashed up.

Discerning the danger of Claude, Paul had hastened forward just in time to save his friend.

During this brief interval, unknowing the danger he had escaped, Claude, in wild fury, clung to his man.

"Your end is nigh, Vampyre Vaughan ! I mean to slay—to kill you !" In a hoarse whisper the words issued from the lips of the enraged highwayman.

Claude's blood was fairly up.

He determined to have the life of the villain who had done him such foul wrong.

Wildly Vaughan, his livid face contorted with passion, struggled with his youthful and enraged antagonist.

Swaying to and fro in his saddle, each moment threatened to behold him fall beneath the hoofs of the trampling steeds.

Hoarsely bade to stand back by the infuriate Duval, his friends, in greatest excitement, watched the struggle, anon glancing nervously at the Bow-street officers, who were now creeping closer up to them.

"Finish him, Claude !"

"Put your knife in him !"

"I've a bullet for him !"

"Anstey and his men are close upon us !"

Heeding not the excited cries of his friends, Claude, who had been attempting to tear the villain Vaughan from his saddle, at length effected his purpose.

Locked in the grasp of deadly hate, in vain the wretch, who had inflicted such irreparable wrong upon our hero, strove to get free.

Thrown across his saddle, Claude, his fingers twined around his neck in wild fury, caused the livid face of his enemy to assume a purple tint ; then, as the voices of the thief-taker and his myrmidons rang in his ears, with a touch of his heel, he caused his bonny mare, carrying double, to dash at wild speed from the spot.

A few pistol shots, causing no harm to either side, were exchanged by Paul, Jack, and the officers ; then, as the latter endeavoured to urge on their beasts, now dead beat, the friends galloped after Claude, who was now some distance down the road.

"Haven't you finished him ?"

"No ; but I am going to," said Duval, his eyes blazing with fury, as his friends rode up beside him.

Struggling feebly in the grasp of his enemy, Vampyre Vaughan glared with deadly hate around.

Released from the other's strangling grip, he was able to breathe once more :

Once more Claude beheld a red tint gather in the face of the wretch he had sworn to slay.

The livid pallor that had always been noted by Claude was this morn replaced by the hectic flush of health.

With the eye of a fiend, his great tusk-like teeth snapping together like that of a wolf, Vampyre Vaughan glared into the face of his foe :

No mercy was there there !

A dark savage glitter shone in the eyes of our hero.

Drawing a knife from his vest, Claude, using all his great strength, held in deadly grip the slim form of his victim.

"'Tis useless to struggle ; if you escape me, my pals have each a bullet in readiness for you !"

"We have so, Claude, say but the word !"

A ominous click of pistols here took place.

In wild fury Vaughan glared around.

He read his doom in the eyes of all his three foes :

Death ! instant death !

A long narrow lane thickly wooded on either side was now reached.

For a time the officers who still pertinaciously pursued the highwaymen were lost to sight.

"Better do it here, Claude !"

Jack and Paul had found out an open glade at the beginning of the lane.

"Yes ; I'll send him to his brother-fiends, where he can take a last look at the bright skies and the summer's sun the orb of another day he'll never see !"

"Don't suppose he will ! How's it to be, knife or bullet !" said Jack with a grim smile.

"I had intended to bury this knife in his ribs," said Claude as he flashed the keen blade of a dagger in the air. But he can have his choice.

"Let me die by the bullet then," said Vaughan, whose face had once more assumed the leaden corpse-like tint so usual in his features.

He saw, knew, there was no hope in the eyes of his foes His death was decreed :

In a few moments he would be no more !

The shining barrels of three pistols gleamed in his eyes.

Foam speckled with blood now gathered about his lips ; then, as the sound of approaching horses came gently on the air, the doomed villain raised his hand as the click of the pistols of his executioners rang in his ears :

"Hold, Claude Duval, one word with you !"

"I'll not deny you speech ; but cut it short ; think not to dally the time till the arrival of the officers ; you shall be riddled, ere they could get to your side !"

"I wish no delay. You are bent on my death. But, mark me, Claude Duval, we shall meet again !"

A fierce baleful glitter here shone in the eye of Vaughan.

"Is that all you have to say ?" said Duval with a grim smile.

"No ; I would ask a favour at your hands !"

"A favour ?"

"Yes."

"Name it, though, ma foi, dog, you deserve none, even in this dying hour from me ! But say what is it ?"

"Will you keep your promise ?"

"If I give it, yes !"

"Well ; 'tis but a trifling favour. I do not, for certain reasons, wish my body to fall into the hands of the man Anstey and his runners."

"Is that all ! You don't suppose we have time to dig a grave for you, do you ?"

"No."

"What do you wish, then !"

"Merely that—that, when I'm dead,"—a strong spasm here shook the frame of the villain, who glancing around on either side, beheld the glittering barrels of the pistols of his executioners—

"Say on, time passes, man !"

"Well ; promise, Claude Duval, that you will drag my body into that knoll there, where I am little likely to be seen by the officers !"

DASHING DUVAL;

OR,

THE LADIES' HIGHWAYMAN.

DEFIANTLY DUVAL GLARED AT HIS MYSTERIOUS FOES AS THEY POINTED THEIR SWORDS AT HIS BREAST.

Vaughan here pointed to a little rising hillock some few yards to the left which, enshrouded in shrubbery, would scarce be noticed by a passer-by.

"You had my promise. Ma foi! I suppose you want to be, like the babes in the wood, covered with leaves by the feathered songsters! But enough of this! I give you one minute, Vampyre Vaughan! take your last look at the sun, you will not see the morrow's."

No reply fell from the lips of Vaughan.

His face deadly white, his hands clenched, he glared wildly at his foes:

Grinding his teeth savagely together, he glared with deadly hate into the eyes of Claude, who, monotonously counting the seconds he had allotted his enemy, stood pistol in hand ready to fire.

"Fifty-eight! Fifty-nine! Sixty!"

With deadly purpose Claude levelled his weapon at the head of the villain who, pointing to the little knoll near, in a hoarse cry gave utterance to the word "Remember!"

In another moment there was the sharp stinging report of three pistols.

With a wild cry of pain Vampyre Vaughan swung his arm up in air, then turning round and struggling like a drunken man, he fell prone to the ground.

Stark and rigid, with his hideous contracted face turned up to the sun, lay the fiendly member of the Black Band.

"Is he dead, Claude?"

"Yes, he's gone safe enough!" said Duval who having started forward here knelt beside his late foe thrusting his hand in his breast.

No pulsation of the heart was there now.

The mass of evil passion, with all his sins upon his head, had been sent to his account.

Not without a shudder did our hero and his companions gaze upon the hideous corpse before them.

The eyes, the bold vicious eyes, were now glazed in death.

The horrible face, of a deadly livid hue, was streaked with dark stains of blood : blood that welled out from a bullet hole near the left temple !

The white gleaming tusk-like teeth projecting from the mouth looked horrible as the death face was turned upwards to the sky.

For a moment the friends gazed at the hideous corpse ! then, as the sound of hoofs came plainly to their ears from the high road, they with one accord seized the rigid form by the heels, and dragged it through the brushwood to the adjacent knoll.

"He has his last wish ; though it's more than he deserves !" said Claude, who, picking up a miniature that fell from the pocket of the dead man, was surprised to find it was the portrait of a young and beautiful girl. Placing the trinket, after a glance, in his vest, Duval, with Jack and Paul, now hastened away from the grim horrible corpse, and, vaulting into their saddles, the three presently after were at high speed dashing down the lane.

"Well, that was a deed I joined in with little scruple," said Paul ; "but the looks of the wretch as he stared round at us ! ugh, it makes me shiver now !"

"He was a fiendly-looking ruffian ! Do you know, you'll laugh at me, but if we had had time I would have put the wretch under the mould !"

"Why so, Jack ? He did not ask us to bury him," said Claude, with a smile.

"No ! and for that very reason I'd have put him under the turf."

"Well, the wretch has gone now !"

"I suppose so !" said Jack, with shudder.

In surprise his two friends stared round at him.

Cantering on slowly as they found they had left their pursuers again far behind, the friends had time and opportunity for converse.

With a smile, Duval, now pressing to the side of Jack, exclaimed, "You surely don't think for one moment that my late fiendly persecutor is not dead ?"

"Oh, no ! He is dead enough !"

"Well, I should think he was !"

"Yes, of course !"

"Good ! and as you grant he's dead, why there's an end to further trouble with the wretch, unless you think that he might take it into his head to come to life again ?"

"He might do that !"

"I say, old man, are you going out of your mind ?"

"No, Claude ! I was never more sane in my life !"

"And yet in well-measured voice you inform me that you think a dead man might revive !"

"Just so !"

"Look here, are you talking serious ?" Duval here gazed uneasily into the face of his friend, who, returning the glance steadfastly, said, "I will be candid with you, Claude ! Listen, Paul !" Jack here gazed with eyes of startling earnestness into those of his companions, exclaiming in a low hushed voice :

"Have you ever been in Hungary ?"

In mute amaze, and in some concern, Claude peered into the countenance of his friend.

With a smile, Jack, who perceived the look of uneasiness, placing his hand upon his companion's bridle, said, "Look you, Claude, dear pal, I am sane enough, and serious, though I see from the glances of yourself and friend Paul here you think I'm going mad. I now repeat my former question, 'Have either of you ever been in Hungary ?'"

"No," replied Duval and Paul in a breath ; a something in the manner of their friend, at the same time that it reassured them as to his perfect coolness of mind, causing them anxiously to listen to every word that now might fall from his lips.

"You have not been in Hungary ? Well, I have, I was there when a boy."

"Indeed ! Well, what of that ?"

"Listen, and I will tell you !"

"Say on."

"It was some seventeen years ago, when a boy of nine years of age, I was in Hungary, with an uncle, a man of much learning, who travelled on the Continent in the capacity of clerk for a foreign house in England here. During our travels many strange and wild adventures befel us. Child as I was, some of these adventures are fixed indelibly upon me. Some day I may relate one of which my deceased relative was the hero. But to the point : amidst all the strange scenes we passed through, and the many stories we had heard, nothing took so great a hold of my childish imagination as a certain superstition we learned had full credence in Hungary."

"And what was that, Jack ?"

"Why a ghastly, horrible belief, the substance of which is, that a person who is dead, no matter how or by what means he or she may have perished, will, if laid in the moonlight, where the full rays of the silvery orb of night can shine full upon them, return again to life !"

"I have heard of this dread superstition, Jack," said Claude, with a shudder.

"So, too, have I," ejaculated Paul.

"You know, both of you, what these persons are called ?"

"Vampyres !" In a low, hoarse whisper, the words fell from the lips of Claude. There was a startling earnestness in the voice of Jack that confounded and alarmed him.

"Aye, vampyres, that is the name ! a vampyre shot, or killed with sword, or hung from gibbet, will return to life if laid in the moon's rays after death ; returning thus to life, his means of sustenance is human blood, blood drawn from the veins of his living victims !"

"How horrible !" said Paul.

"Yes, it is horrible ; you say right !"

"But you surely don't credit this wild dreadful superstition ; you have no belief in it ?"

"I had not."

"How do you mean, had not ?" said Claude, as he emphasised his friend's words.

"Why, I did not, though it took hold of my boyish imagination, place any credence in the grim and ghastly superstition years back ; but I do now."

"You do now ?"

"Yes."

"And why now ?"

"Because I believe we have all three encountered one."

"Encountered one ! What a vampyre ?"

"Yes, I have said it !"

"You allude to the wretch Vaughan," said Claude, with a shudder.

"I do. He has not, depend upon it, got the name he bears without there being something in it !"

"Great heavens, Jack ! Mon Dieu ! you do not serious-ly mean to intimate that the villain Vaughan is really and indeed a—a—"—the concluding sentence here died on the lips of the startled highwayman.

"A vampyre ? Yes ! Is he not called Vampyre Vaughan ? Are not his features alway of the leaden hue of the grave ? Has he not returned to life after wounds that would have laid either one of us low never to rise again ? Did he not," said Jack, excitedly, "recover from the deadly thrust of your sword that night in the pinetree grove ?"

"And so he did," gasped Claude, who, with a shudder, recalled the scene of the old mill, and the livid face that had peered down upon him from the trap above as he had sought shelter in the lower chamber from the storm.

"If you are right in your terrible idea, Jack, the wretch will appear again before us !"

"I should not be surprised, Paul !"

"But there are means of effectually destroying such monsters, are there not ?"

"There is ; and if I am right, and if I discover Vampyre Vaughan, as he is called, to be indeed a vampyre, I'll lay him low yet ! Did you note his anxiety to be placed upon that hillock in the glade after death ?"

"Yes ; Claude promised him his wish should be carried out."

"Of course ! There, in the moon's rays this night he, if he indeed be the horrible being I suspect, will recover ! The moon is at the full ; its rays will restore the wretch to life !"

"I pray heaven not, Jack ! I care not for any man on the face of the earth ! But, ugh ! a creature of the other world ! My blood runs cold to think of it !" said Clifford.

"Though I shrink with horror at the thought, Mon Dieu, I'm inclined to think you are right, Jack !" at length said Claude, after a few moments' deep reflection.

"I fear I am right ! Would we could get back to where

the corpse of the villain was left; but our cursed foes are close upon us! Cannot we shake them off by any means, Claude?"

I was just asking myself if such a thing could be done, Jack!" The adventurers now coming suddenly to the end of the lane down which they had pursued their way, found themselves close to the village, the vicinity of which they had discerned an hour before, when, descending the hill, ere meeting with the wretch Vaughan.

The dull, solemn clang of a bell was now borne upon the breeze.

Slow, and with lengthened pause, the chimes rang out from the little tower of the ivy-covered church, the spire of which the friends beheld bearing its height up in the air.

A quarter of a mile from the end of the lane, where the three friends had come to halt, was the little village, the smoke from which dimmed the azure blue of the sunlit skies.

A golden lustre, soft and radiant, shone upon the ivy-covered tower of the church :

An old time-worn building of solid grey stonework, that had stood the storms of a century or more.

Winding its way from the adjacent village towards the holy pile was a long funereal procession.

The mourners, with white ribbons round their arms and in their hats, and the velvet pall with knots of the same descending from its corners, as it lay in graceful folds across the coffin, gave token that some young and spotless maid "had gone to that bourne whence no traveller returns."

How sad and solemn was the slow chime of the bell, with the dreary pause between each stroke!

Slowly the sad procession moved onwards, followed apparently by nearly all the inhabitants of the village.

The hapless victim of grim death was evidently loved, revered, and respected by all.

The coffin, borne by four youths, now nearing the church, was lost to the sight of the friends.

Forgetful of their enemies, and deeply impressed by the solemn scene, the adventurers hurried on, presently pausing as they gained the vicinity of the churchyard.

An old grey-haired man, noting their arrival, at once pushed forwards, and in answer to an interrogation from Claude, volunteered to give the particulars of   sad scene before them.

It now appeared that the funeral was that of a young girl in her sixteenth year, the only daughter of a farmer living near. A fit, brought on by her attempted abduction by a stranger from her father's house had, it seems, led to her untimely death !

"And the villain, the cause of the poor girl's decease, has he not been discovered?" exclaimed Claude.

"Alas, no ! Nor could poor dear Miss Ruth Redland give any clue to the ruffian ! A tall, hideous man had, she said, entered by the window of her chamber. She then shrieked, fainted, and knew no more for a time. Consciousness would return at intervals," pursued the old man, "then fit succeeded fit—the poor child was called away."

With tear-dimmed eyes Claude and his companions listened to the recital ; then, giving their horses in charge of a countryman near, who, at our hero's desire, took them to a thick copse that grew behind the church, the three prepared to enter the building.

"What are your intentions, Claude?" said Jack.

"To play a ruse on the grabs (officers)."

"Why have you sent away the horses?"

"For the best of all reasons, Jack ; for the moment they are in the way."

"You are bent on some plan to mislead the enemy, and throw them off the scent?"

"Exactly."

"Do you think that fellow will stop in the copse with our steeds?"

"I'm sure of it."

"But suppose Anstey should discover the animals?"

"We must chance that."

"It will be a fine thing to throw them off our track."

"Just so ! failing to find us here they will hurry on."

"Exactly ; and we can return."

"Precisely ! this poor girl's funeral must aid us to elude our foes."

"But how do you propose to escape the lynx eyes of Jonathan Anstey?"

"By entering the church."

"But, confound it, we shall soon be discovered there !"

"Yes, if we stopped there, which we shall not !"

"And where the deuce shall we stop, then ?"

"Why, in a place where our foes will never think of looking for us."

"And where's that," exclaimed Jack and Paul in a breath as they hurried with Claude up to the church door.

"Why, in the vaults !"

"The vaults ?"

"Yes, the vaults ; and, by Jove, we are none too soon here, for, parbleu ! my inveterate enemy and his myrmidons are even now at the end of the lane," said Claude.

Glancing back the adventurers, with rage and chagrin, beheld Anstey and his men making for the church.

"Failing to find us ahead they will inquire here ; before they go further, come in," said our hero, boldly making his way into the sacred edifice, his companions following at his heels.

On gaining the interior of the building the companions cast their eyes upon a group that stood by the wall to their left.

Making their way to this spot they observed a deep dark cavity in the flooring near where the people were assembled.

"The entrance to the vaults," whispered Claude. "Come !"

Coolly pushing their way through the crowd, which at that moment was turning away, the three friends unnoticed descended unseen the stone steps that led down into the gloomy vaults of the church.

They had hardly reached the bottom ere the minister, coffin bearers, and mourners appeared making their way along from the further end of the vault.

Darting away and stooping down beside a pile of coffins the companions now beheld the funeral train ascending the steps leading to the church.

In another moment they were alone :

Alone in the darksome vaults :

For a few moments nought could be heard by the friends save a confused humming sound which proceeded from the crowded building overhead.

This low hushed noise was, however, broken suddenly by the unusual tumult of voices high in dispute :

The voices of enraged, unruly, men.

"Our foes are in the church, Claude."

"Yes ; but they will not, I take it, attempt to penetrate here."

"I am not so sure of that ; for my part I think Jonathan Anstey capable of any vile act."

"True, Paul, you are right ; but it will be precious dark down here presently, it's gloomy enough now, and the sun is only just declining in the horizon," said Claude, as he pointed to a small iron grating that looked out upon the churchyard, and through which the golden orb of day now shone with thin streaks of fading light.

Anxiously the companions awaited the movements of their foes.

The tumult above dying away, all was quiet. However Anstey and his men appeared not.

A quarter of an hour passed, but no sign of the thief-taker or his myrmidons !

"They have given it up !"

"Yes, Jack, I think we have done them this time."

"I fancy we have. Hallo! what on earth is that ?"

Paul Clifford, who stepped from their hiding-place behind the coffins, here gave a nervous start.

A low rumbling noise sounded for a moment from above :

A rumbling noise, succeeded by a loud jarring sound that echoed hollowly through the vaults.

All was now thick darkness save for the thin ray of light that glistened through the grating.

The broad flood of light from the opening above the the stone steps leading to the church was now shut out.

With an exclamation of alarm Claude and his friends started forwards and groped their way to the steps.

With a thrill they each divined the dread truth.

The slab of stone covering the opening to the vaults had been replaced.

The friends were, for a time, close prisoners ;

Prisoners with the dead ;

Immured in a living tomb ;

Shut out from life ;

They were alone ;

Alone with the decaying dead :

With beating hearts the companions stood by the stone steps.

All was impenetrable gloom :

Darker, yet darker each minute grew the vault ; paler, yet, paler the thin thread of light that shone through the grating.

"Well this is a nice position, Claude !"

"You don't like this prison !"

"No, confound me if I do !"

"Well, you can soon change it for another !"

"How do you mean ?"

"Why, sing out blue murder, give a good yell, and Jonathan Anstey will deuced soon release you !"

"Thank you for your advice !"

"No thanks, my dear fellow, I give it you gratis."

"Well, I shan't avail myself of it."

"You won't !"

"No !"

"What say you, Paul ?"

"Oh, I'm for a stay down here."

"Down among the dead men !"

"Exactly !"

"I say, Claude !"

"Well !"

"Can I have a smoke !"

"Certainly ; I don't object, and I don't suppose our friends around us will."

"I calculate not. What's your next move, captain !" said Jack, who with Paul now lighting a pipe, began vigorously to puff away, as he said, "to keep the stink out of his nose."

"May I propose to stop here quietly for another half-hour ?"

"Well !"

"Well, then, I calculate by that time our enemies will have sheered off."

"Exactly."

"Very good ! We will then attempt to make our escape from our present dismal quarters."

"How !"

Why, by removal of the stone slab, which our united strength may succeed in moving, or else by the breaking away of that iron grating."

"Capital ; you are a first-rate general !"

"Well, yes ; you can't say if I lead you into a mess I don't contrive to get you out of it."

"No, captain, you are too smart for that ; but how dark it is getting !" said Jack with a little shudder.

"Yes, the day seems to have slipped away ; we spent some time in the lane, and then the poor girl's funeral prevented us noting the lapse of the hours ; but hark, Jack, what is that ?"

Breathless and shivering with the deathlike chill of the vault and their fear of they know not what, the bold adventurers stood peering intently through the thick heavy gloom of the old vault.

A pale steel-blue tint now succeeded the golden light of half-an-hour before, as the moon, broad and lustrous like a huge shield of silver, mounted in the sky and threw a ghastly light on the grim abode of the dead.

Night had fallen ; and, save the spot where the grating was situated, all was pitchy darkness in the vault.

"Well, the sooner we get out of this, Duval, the better I shall I like it !"

"Patience, man, is a virtue. You surely, who fear no living man, have no fears of dead 'uns ?"

"Well, no ; only the place is so horrible and the nasty damp earthy odour! it chills my blood !"

"The charnel-house is certainly not over sweet-smelling ; but, allons ! we will go ! Come on, lads ! Get your barking-irons ready in case of surprise ! Now follow up the steps. I'll go first then, heave-ho altogether, ma foi ! and we may soon get out of this, and be astride our bonny steeds."

"Suppose our horses have gone, Claude !"

"Suppose they are not ! One supposition is as good as the other."

"Well, yes !"

"Sufficent for the day is the evil thereof, Jack. If our horses are gone, we must find them : failing to find them, parbleu, must find some one else's !"

"Philosophy in a vault !"

"And a very good place for it, too, master Paul !"

Claude, who endeavoured to cheer his comrades, having now made his way more than half up the stone staircase, bade them, with him, press against it.

Exerting all their strength the three now endeavoured to move the solid slab of stone.

All their efforts were however useless.

Firm and fast as a rock, it refused to move an inch.

"It's no go !"

"I feared not, Claude."

"Well, we must try the grating."

"And if that fails ?"

"It won't fail, Jack ! The iron is old, rusty, and eaten with decay, as is the masonry round it. It will give way easy enough, I warrant. I only tried the slab here first, as a less troublesome means of escape than the other."

"Well, let us tackle the grating at once : I'm sick of this !"

"So, too, am I, dear pal ! But slow and steady must be our motto."

Groping their way down the steps, for all was inky darkness, the companions were, a few minutes after, standing in the centre of the vault. About to move over to the wall towards their only means of exit, they were startled by a low muffled moan of pain :

A wild hollow moan, as of one in a death agony !

"Claude !"

"Jack !"

"Did you hear that ?"

"Great heaven, yes !"

"Paul !"

"What is it !" gasped Clifford in a choking voice.

"Just flash your pistol in the pan : its momentary gleam may reveal something."

"Right, Claude ! By all the saints in the calendar I wish we were well out of this !"

Removing the charge from one of his pistols, Paul, now pulling the trigger, caused a slight momentary flash to show up in the vault.

Eagerly Claude and Jack peered through their dread prison.

Save the coffins, however, ranged all around them, nought met their sight ; and about to turn their attention once more to the grating again, they were harrowed and startled by a kind of horrible muffled shriek.

Duval, a bold and fearless man, could not avoid an exclamation of terror escaping his lips, whilst the perspiration of fear trickled like rain down his brow, his blood like ice crawling through his veins !

Wildly the adventurers glared round the vault, each expecting to behold some hideous vision or spectral form from the other world.

In breathless awe the daring knights of the road stood in the centre of their terrible prison house.

Again a harrowing muffled shriek echoed through the vault.

"Duval ! what means it ! Are we the sport of fiends ?"

"No, Jack ; that fearful cry was from some one in torturing agony !"

"But we are here alone, Claude !" gasped Jack. "We are here alone, surrounded with the dead !"

"Still I say that cry came from a living being !"

"What think you of it, Paul ?"

"I know not what to think."

"Did you note in what direction the horrible cry came, Jack ?" said our hero.

"Yes ; from yonder corner."

"You are right ; it did so. That wild shriek we heard but now emanated from a coffin placed on the top of five others—a coffin covered with blue cloth and white nails !"

"The same we beheld brought down here as we entered the vault ?"

"Yes."

"And which contains the corpse of the ill-fated girl, Ruth Redland."

"Even so."

"And you think, Claude, that that cry of dire agony issued from her coffin ?"

"I do."

"God of heaven, should this be so ?"

"Should it be so ! Then is the fate of that hapless doomed girl more dreadful to contemplate !"

"How quiet now is this dreadful vault !"

"Yes ; the stillness strikes us more after those hideous shrieks."

"What are you going to do now !" exclaimed Jack, as our hero moved away."

"Why, I am going to drag that girl's coffin hither."

"Are you mad, Claude?"

"No! I'm sane and determined! A something tells me that that wretched girl has been buried alive, and, come what will, sacre! I quit not this vault till I have forced the coffin that contains her."

"By heavens you are right, Claude; and I, who would have fled the place, am a cur!"

"Should your suspicions prove correct, we yet may save her!"

"Yes, Paul; but, mon Dieu, I scarce hope to find the wretched girl alive!"

Groping their way along, the bold companions at length found the dread receptacle of the dead for which they were in search.

Placing his hands upon it, Claude gave a start and uttered an exclamation of horror.

"What is it?"

"What have you discovered?"

"Why, that the coffin has evidently shifted since it was placed here; 'twas never left thus I am quite sure," cried our hero, who had found the coffin all on one side.

Trembling with excitement, and in nervous haste, the friends now lifted the dread abiding-place of the dead, and carried it over to the spot where, from the grating, a thin ray of moonlight streamed into the vault.

Placing the coffin upon the ground Claude now, his face looking ghastly pale in the blue rays of the moon, prepared to force the lid.

No easy task was this, as it was firmly screwed down.

Finding that nothing could be done in haste, our hero now slowly and laboriously began to loosen the screws with a large clasp knife handed him by Paul.

In speechless awe, their faces blanched with terror, his companions knelt beside him looking on.

It was a strange scene:

That drear and grim vault with those three men engaged in the dreadful task of forcing open the last tenement of the dead.

Pausing from his labours, Claude suddenly gave a nervous start, as the chimes from the church tower sounded hollowly from without.

In silence and awe the companions listened to the sonorous tones of the bell.

All giving a shudder as they counted out aloud the last stroke of the hour:

Twelve o'clock!

Midnight!

"Mon Dieu! I would our task were over; but we were dastards indeed to give in now!"

In desperation he here bent once more to his work.

The while Jack and Paul, with glaring eyes, gazed upon the coffin, the lid of which they knew would presently be raised.

The last screws now drawn forth, the companions, with faces ashy pale, leant forwards.

A low cry of horror now escaped their lips as the lid of the coffin was thrown aside.

Streaks of blood covered the shroud that enwrapped the form within—streaks of blood plainly visible to the eyes of the beholder by the light of the moon.

All bent forward to peer into the face of the lost one.

The features of the poor doomed girl, however, could not be seen.

A hand white as marble could be discerned clutching a piece of white serge or cloth:

A part of the shroud:

Torn and covered with blood!

A mass of bright golden hair was also dabbled in the ensanguined stream!

Claude, at a glance, understood too well the horrible sight.

The unhappy, miserable girl had been the victim of a trance.

Buried alive!

The moans and piercing shrieks were now explained.

Duval, with cooler, wider head than his companions, had divined the truth.

With an exclamation of sorrow, Claude now gently removed the shroud which covered the dead face.

Bold, daring men were the three knights of the road; accustomed to encounter wild adventures, and ever with a violent death staring them in the face; but never in their many bold deeds, never in their greatest danger did they feel the horror that oppressed them as they now gazed upon the cold marble features of Ruth Redland, the farmer's daughter.

The face of the doomed girl, colourless as Parian marble, was speckled with blood.

Her bosom exposed by part of the shroud being torn away, was also stained with the crimson tide.

Long wavy masses of golden hair rested about the neck and shoulders.

Even there, enshrouded in her coffin, beautiful, most beautiful, was the poor unfortunate.

"Is she dead, Claude?" In a faint hoarse whisper the words fell from the lips of Paul Clifford.

"Yes, she has gone! Poor girl, what a hideous fate!"

"Hideous, indeed! What must have been her horror in awaking from her trance!" he exclaimed, as the tears he was not ashamed of poured like rain down his cheeks.

"Heaven rest her soul! Would—would I could meet with her destroyer! my life would I devote to his distruction. This fell deed must consign the villain after death to the lowest pit of the accursed! I would give something to know the man who brought thee to this, dear girl!" Stifling a convulsive sob that rose despite all his efforts to his bosom, Duval, now pressing his lips reverently to the marble forehead, carefully replaced the lid of the coffin.

"What do you propose to do now, Claude?"

"Shall we inform the villagers of that which we have discovered?"

"No! Why rack the hearts of those who love her with such a tale of horror?"

"You are right, dear Claude. We will replace the coffin where we took it from."

"Yes, Jack; it were best to keep this dread occurrence to ourselves; the tale of the poor girl's fearful doom would drive her unhappy parents into madness!"

"And so it would!"

Jack, now shifting the lid, took one last sorrowful glance at the poor pale face, which looked peaceful and happy in the bright rays of the moon. Upon the point then of covering up from sight the poor pallid corse, an exclamation escaped his lips, and leaning over, to the surprise of his companions, he minutely examined the neck of the doomed girl.

"What is it, Jack?"

"What on earth is the matter?"

"Nothing!" was the reply, given in a quivering voice. "I only was asking myself how those punctured wounds came in the poor girl's neck."

Jack here pointed out to his companions two tiny wounds in the fair white skin of the throat:

Two tiny punctures, blue and scarcely cicatrised.

"Why those marks look like a bite, Jack!"

"Yes; and it has been a bite! Those punctures were caused by a couple of teeth!"

"Its very strange!"

"It is strange, Claude! But my brain whirls with all this horror! Come, let us hasten from this hideous vault! The air is foul and foetid, I feel as though I should choke! Come, Claude, come, Paul, let us away!"

As if overcome with the scene they had gone through, Jack now, his face as pallid and ghastly as that of the doomed girl, staggered to his feet and rushed to the grating.

Claude, concerned at his friend's evidently excited and nervous state, bidding Paul cover up the coffin, hastened at once to the grating, and vigorously applied himself to the task of forcing it away.

As he had predicted the removal of the iron bars was easily effected.

The masonry crumbling to decay, and the grating rusted and worn, was soon displaced, and in a few minutes the opening was eligible for passing through.

"Now, Jack," said our hero, as he finished his task, "we will replace that poor girl's coffin, and will then away!"

"Claude!"

"Yes, Jack!"

"We will let the resting-place of Ruth Redland remain where it is."

"What, on the floor of the vault?"

"Yes."

"But it will be discovered."

"Just so! I have been thinking, Claude! We will inform the minister of this! 'Tis fit that he should know He can then decide as to what further should be done

"Well, perhaps you are right, Jack."

"I am sure I am! You will be guided by me in this! You will let me have my own way!"

"Certainly, dear Jack! Now then, Paul, off is the word!"

"All right, Claude! I am not sorry to quit this horrid place." With a sigh of pain, and a last look at the little coffin in its blue cloth and gilt nails, Clifford hastened to the opening made by the removal of the grating, and scrambling through was presently after standing in the grass-grown churchyard without.

Claude and Jack, following the other, were soon after gazing up at the ivy-covered tower of the revered pile.

The moon, large, bright, and lustrous, made all as light as day.

Woods, village, and all around was bathed in a sea of shining radiance.

"It's a beautiful night!"

"Yes, Claude! And the moon shines brightly!" a visible shudder here shook the frame of Jack.

Glancing at his companions with some concern, Claude now proposed that they should get away from the place as quickly as possible.

"Where do you suggest we should make tracks for?"

"London, Paul; or our hiding-place, the old Tree Cave, near Highgate. The young ladies Kate and Maude are safe for a time at Dick Dunning's inn, The Cat and her Kittens; we will to London or the Cave and rest quiet for a day."

"Good!"

"First, we must learn what has become of our horses."

"Just so! Had not one of us better make for the village inn?"

"Well, yes, Paul! be that your task, and at the same time inform the landlord of all that has past; but tell him we cannot for our own safety's sake stop here! Let him know we are flying from the limbs of the law. I care not! it will show him that the imperative necessity of our getting from the place!"

"Exactly; I'll be explicit with him, never fear!"

"Right!" said Paul.

"Well!"

"Just bring Jack some brandy with you."

"All right! you think one only had better visit the inn?"

"Decidedly; off with you!"

Needing no further directions, and anxious to get away from the neighbourhood where they had encountered such horrors, Paul darted off at a run, soon disappearing in the village.

Moodily and sadly Jack gazed up at the tower of the old church.

"You seem more upset than either I or Paul, Jack!"

"I am, Claude! I cannot get this poor girl out of my mind!"

"Nor I; but 'tis useless brooding over the shocking occurrence; it will quite unnerve you, Jack! Sacre! what would I give to know the monster that caused all this horror!"

Taking his handkerchief from his pocket, Duval here wiped away the perspiration that at the recollection of the hideous scenes of the night bedewed his brow.

It was as he replaced his handkerchief that he was startled by a cry from his friend:

A loud cry of horror, of surprise!

"What is it now, Jack?"

"How! where got you this?"

In a tremor of excitement, with ashen pale lips, Jack, who had picked up a miniature that had fallen from Claude's pocket, here held it up to his gaze in the moonlight.

A blood-red glow now marked the face and brow of Duval—a hectic tinge that changed a moment after to a deadly white!

No sound issued from his lips; only the nervous twitching of the mouth and the knitted brow told of the storm raging within.

With clenched hands, and with a fixed, strong stare, he riveted his eyes upon the miniature held up before him:

The same he had the preceding day taken from the vest of the wretch, Vaughan, after he had been shot down in the glade.

With a wild stare, Claude remained in speechless horror gazing at the portrait:

That of a young and lovely girl

A sweet, fair face:

A face that once seen could not be easily forgotten!

"You—you know these features! You recognise these lineaments, pourtrayed with cunning, faultless hand! You have seen this young girl!" said Jack, his voice hoarse and trembling with excitement.

"Yes, yes, Jack! Mon Dieu! where will this horror end? this picture is a marvellous likeness of her whom we have just left in her tomb."

"Even so! This miniature is that of Ruth Redland."

"It is."

And you found it upon the person of him whom we slew? You took this portrait from the vest of the fiend Vaughan?"

"I did, Jack!"

"I know! When the trinket fell from your pocket but now, I remembered seeing you secure it yesterday from the body of him whom we left dead in the glade!"

"You are right, Jack!"

"Claude!"

"Well!"

"Can you not guess now who is the murderer of Ruth Redland?"

"Aye, the monster Vaughan." A dark grey shadow here gathered upon the handsome features of our hero, the while his fingers convulsively twitched with the hilt of his sword.

"Know you how he killed the unhappy doomed girl?" Jack's eyes here fairly blazed with fury and excitement. "Shall I tell you how that doomed one perished? She fell a victim to a demon: her lifeblood was drawn from her veins! I can read all the hideous truth now, Claude! The man who, in the darkness of night, gained an entry into Ruth Redland's chamber was your enemy Vaughan! Not robbery was it that led him there, but a fiendly craving, a thirst for human blood! The truth struck me but now in the vault! Those punctured marks on the poor girl's throat were caused by human teeth, the fangs of the hideous Vaughan! I am not mad or dreaming; but, Claude, 'tis useless to hide the horrible truth! He whom we left for dead in the forest glade a few hours back is doubtless now restored to life: our mutual foe, whom we must devote our lives to exterminate from the earth, is in verity that which I shudder to name, a vampyre!"

"Then you think that fell fiend will again cross our path?"

"I am sure of it!"

"But, say your dread surmise is correct; supposing indeed that the man is what you say, is there no way of ridding the earth of his presence?" said Claude, in a shiver of rage and horror.

"There are ways yet."

"Name them."

"One is this: Had we, at the midnight hour, buried the accursed at some cross-road, with a stake driven through his body, he could not have again arisen into life; whilst another mode is to put the corpse in a coffin, placing the same in a church—while a minister exorcises the demon, stout nails must be driven into the coffin, it being afterwards at midnight buried in the consecrated ground."

"This, then, must we do. The business of our lives must now be to rid the world of this monstrous fiend!"

"Yes, Claude, we know all the hideous truth. To be forewarned is to be forearmed! We have to deal with one possessed of infernal powers! Be it so; we know full well what we have to do!"

"And with Heaven's aid we'll execute our mission!"

"We will, dear Claude, to the death!"

With eyes upraised to the moonlit skies, the friends here made oath to know no peace, to leave nothing undone that would help to enable them to carry out their mission of vengeance.

They kept their vow!

Talking over the dread incident, it was with pleased surprise that half-an-hour after they perceived Paul hurrying forwards with their horses in company with two strangers!

The foremost of these, hastening up to Claude with white pallid face, proved to be the landlord of the village inn!

Upon questioning the excited and worthy boniface, Duval found that he was determined at once, unseasonable as was the hour, to visit the minister, whose residence was close to Farmer Redland's, about three quarters of a mile from the church.

Promising to visit the place in a few days, Claude, his companions already in their saddles, mounted his steed, the adventurers as they cantered away receiving a god-speed from the trembling lips of the horror-stricken landlord.

CHAPTER XV.

THE MOONLIGHT RIDE—THE MISSING BODY—SUDDEN APPEARANCE OF THE VAMPYRE—THE CHASE—THE ESCAPE.

"Well, thank heaven, we are well away from that place, anyhow !" said Paul Clifford, as, trotting down the lane at the other end of the village green, he turned in his saddle and gave a last glance at the ivy-covered tower of the church.

"Well, I'm glad to get away, I must confess ! And now tell us, Paul, how found you our horses ?"

"Easy enough ! Upon leaving you I made for the village, and with some trouble succeeded in arousing our friend the landlord of the Wheatsheaf, in the back yard of which, in a large shed, I discovered our beasts."

"Who had taken them there ?"

"The fellow we left them in charge of, who, it seems, stayed in the copse awaiting us for hours."

"How about Anstey and his man ?"

"Oh ! they gave up the chase and returned to London !"

"Hem ! that was a blind."

"Well, I think so. I don't think Anstey would have given in like that."

"Nor I," said Jack, rousing up from a train of thought. "It's one of Jonathan's ruses. He's hanging about the village, ten to one."

"That's most likely, Jack !"

"Of course it is ! we know the man."

"Where are we off too now, Claude ?"

"Well, I think we had better return to Highgate !"

"By the same road we traversed yesterday ?"

"Yes, Paul !"

"Good ! we may come across the sweet defunct Vaughan."

"No fear, Paul !" said Jack moodily.

"What do you mean ? You don't suppose he has walked away, do you ?"

"Possibly, he may have done that !"

"Ha ! ha ! devilish good joke, Jack !"

"I'm not jesting, Paul !"

"What ?"

"I was never more serious in my life."

"Claude ! The incidents of the past day have quite upset our pal !" said Clifford, who here cast an anxious glance at his companion who rode beside him.

"You are mistaken in supposing that Jack is ill. Tell him all, dear boy !"

At a nod from Claude Jack here related to the astounded young knight of the road that which is already known to the readers. "It's no comtemptible foe we have to cope with, Paul," said Jack in conclusion. "The fiendly Vaughan must be attacked with all cunning ; and measures must be taken that will ensure his final destruction."

"Great heavens ! If this be true, to what horror was dear Maude Mayburn subjected when within the wretch's power !"

"Had I known then what I know now, Paul ! Diable ! I should have gone mad," said Claude, with a shudder.

"Well, if Jack is right, our bullets were of no avail yesterday !"

"We shall soon know."

"How ?"

"Why, we shall, in another ten minutes, reach the spot where we left his rigid corpse ! If Jack's horrible surmise be correct, as I cannot now doubt, the body will be no longer there !"

"By heavens, no !"

Without further speech the adventurers now pushed on.

It was a glorious night ; the moon, round and shining brilliantly, being at the full.

Swiftly galloping on down the lane, their vicinity to the spot where they had carried out a deed of vengeance the preceding day was presently recognised.

A blighted and withered oak stood grim and sad-looking near the hillock upon which they had left the body of the wretch Vaughan.

The bare bleak branches of this tree could now be discerned in the moonlight.

Drawing in their horses, they now proceeded slowly.

A canter of a few moments would bring them to the spot. The open glade could now be seen.

A flood of silvery radiance rendered all as light as day.

Without a word Claude now brought his steed to a halt :

An example followed by his companions. Dismounting, each now tethered his courser to a tree.

They were now within a hundred yards of the open glade :

The scene of the execution of the morning before.

With grim looks, and with knitted brows, the bold adventurers now strode forward.

Bold, daring men as they were, it was not without beating hearts that they neared the spot where they had some hours before left their victim.

Claude, the first of the party, hurrying forwards paused as he reached the open glade :

With stern eyes and muscle, pointing to his feet, he drew the attention of his companions to a red, stagnant, horrible puddle :

A puddle which the moonbeams revealed as a pool of blood, clotted and horrible.

"The spot where the fiendly villain fell ! Now for the mound behind yon shrubbery where we placed his hideous corpse ! Come Jack, come Paul, follow me !" exclaimed Claude in a hoarse whisper.

Some five minutes afterwards the three adventurers were standing upon the adjacent hillock.

But the body of the villain Vaughan was no longer there. It had gone !

Save here and there a smirch of blood, showing hideously upon the greensward, nought was there to give evidence that the corpse of the accursed had ever been there.

"Said I not truly ? You see the wretch has disappeared ! the cold luminous rays of yon bright shining moon hath restored the Vampyre to life !" A dark frown here gathered upon the brow of Gentleman Jack, as he ground the heel of his boot in the soft turf and bit his lips with passion.

A fierce oath escaped the lips of Claude, as he thought how easily the fiend in the morning of the preceding day, had gained upon him to carry out his dying wish that he might be laid there where the silvery moon at night would shine upon his corpse.

"You were right ! Mon Dieu ! 'tis with a vampyre, not mortal man, we have to deal, in coping with this villain leader of the Black Band !"

"But with all that, with Heaven's aid, we may conquer the accursed !"

"Well said, Jack ! But, come, we will away : 'tis no use lingering here !"

About to turn from the spot the friends were at this moment startled from their purpose by a sight that caused the blood to dart like lightning through their veins, whilst their frames grew icy chill, a damp perspiration breaking out upon their brows.

Rooted to the spot, they gazed spellbound at a gaunt shadow : the gaunt shadow of a man thrown from behind an adjacent tree far out upon the greensward.

Strange and wild were the contortions of the hidden wanderer.

The form of the man hidden behind the trunk of the tree, the shadow only could be seen by the three comrades.

Wildly a pair of arms were thrown up towards the sky, the fists clenched as though in the act of defying the one above.

Recovering his momentary surprise and alarm, Claude now in a hoarse whisper bade his companions move not, nor utter a sound.

"What think you it is, Claude ?" said Jack in a hushed voice.

"Mon Dieu ! even him we seek !"

"Vampyre Vaughan ?"

"The same ! Do you stay here, get your barking-irons ready, whilst I glide up to the tree. I'll have a fire ; and be he man or devil, he will scarce escape the shots of all."

"Mine shall find its mark," muttered Paul.

"And mine," said Jack ; and if we indeed lay the fiend low, I'll have a stake in his cursed carcase this time !"

Pressing his comrades by the hand, Claude, pistol ready cocked, with soft stealthy steps, now glided from the mound towards the adjacent tree :

From behind which the gigantic shadow was still thrown.

A low moaning noise now fell upon the highwayman's ears :

A guttural sound as if a human being in pain.

Brightly the moon shone over the woods.

The shadow of the hidden stranger was still revealed to the eyes of Claude, who, ghostlike and with the stealthy tread of a wild Indian, stole towards the tree.

Cool, bold, and determined, with compressed lips and a savage glitter in his eyes, he crept on towards the spot where he was convinced was hidden the wretch of whom he and his companions were in search

A few paces more and he was leaning against the trunk of the tree:

Upon the one side of which was the one whose figure in strong relief was thrown upon the sward.

With beating heart, his hand rigid as death, as with nervous grip he held his pistol, Claude now, inch by inch, leaned his head forward round the trunk of the tree.

His heart for a time almost ceased its pulsations.

With pistol raised, he, soft and tiger-like, shifted his position, slowly sidling edgeways round the huge trunk of the aged oak.

Glancing keenly round, a gasp of horror now escaped his lips, as suddenly, without any warning, he felt the icy grasp as of a dead hand upon his throat:

A fierce, deadly grip of some foe who had started upon him from behind.

In another moment, with a crash that nearly stunned him, he was hurled to the ground:

Hurled to the ground with a force that nearly shook all the breath out of his body:

Whilst his pistol, his means of defence, was torn from his nerveless grasp.

A low hissing sound, the noise as of a serpent, now rang in his ears.

With wild, staring eyes, Claude gazed up at his assailant.

A cold chill as of death stole over him.

His blood, in a second of time, seemed turning to ice within his veins.

The hissing noise was now increased.

A heavy figure thrown upon his labouring breast, Claude could not move.

All power seemed to have forsaken him.

His limbs appeared palsied.

He was helpless:

Helpless, and at the mercy of his foe.

As in a dream, Claude now glared up at a hideous face that was placed close to his own.

He beheld a countenance hideous in its contortions, horrible in its livid pallor:

While gleaming tusks, like teeth, snapped wolfishly at him.

The hissing sound that emanated from his assailant's lips now changed to a guttural cry of fury.

Frozen with terror Claude gave himself up for lost!

The hideous form of one he had left some hours before for dead was now full of life and strength before him.

He was at the mercy of the demon Vampyre Vaughan.

For a moment of time, Claude beheld the flash of a bright steel blade as, waved before his eyes, it glittered in the moonlight; then, as it appeared about to descend into his bosom, he was restored from a deadly feeling of approaching insensibility by the loud report of two pistols!

Simultaneously with the ping of the bullets, one of which was buried in the trunk of the tree beside him, came a wild frantic yell on the night air; then, as the hideous being who had so near destroyed him sprang up and darted away. his friends, with loud cries, bounded forward.

"Claude, Claude, are you hurt?"

"No, thank heaven; though, mon Dieu, another second and all would have been over!" gasped our hero, who, the first terrible shock passed, was now restored to his former vigour and thirsting for revenge.

"Our horses! follow, follow, he can't escape!" shouted Paul excitedly.

Tearing through the thickets, the friends, a moment after, gained the lane.

To mount their steeds and gallop after a flying figure the moonlight revealed some quarter of a mile ahead, was the work of but a few seconds.

Wildly, excitedly, the adventurers rushed out of the lane.

The high road was now reached.

Bounding along with incredible speed, was the wretch of whom they were in pursuit.

With loud shouts of exultation the riders dashed on after the flying form.

Scarcely a quarter of a mile was there between the pursuers and pursued.

"We shall have him!" yelled Jack.

"Not bad sport. Sacre, this is new, hunting a vampyre!" said Claude, with a grim laugh.

"How he flies along."

"Yes, the accursed being's speed is indeed marvellous."

"I bet he don't keep it up! Ten to one we run him down half-way up the hill!

"It ain't good enough, Paul; I shan't take yer!" exclaimed Jack, who, holding the reins in his mouth, now coolly cocked one of his pistols.

"Don't ride so fast, pals; don't spoil sport; let's have a pop or two at him!"

"Right you are! Ventre bleu, he can't escape!" muttered Claude, as, close upon the heels of the fugitive, they slackened their speed.

"I bet I wing him!"

"What odds, Jack!"

"I'll give yer three to one!"

"Done! let fly!"

There was a bright flash and loud report as Jack, leaning forward, now fired at their horrible foe.

"You've hit him!"

"Guess I have!"

"He falters; he'll be down in a minute!"

"Not he; sacre, he's off again like the wind!" shouted Claude excitedly, as, at mad speed, the flying wretch before them bounded like a hare up the hill.

"After him! he can't get away!"

"Not he; I've lost my bet, Jack! you winged the beggar," said Paul, as stooping in his saddle, he pointed out a series of dark patches that lined the wayside.

"Ma foi, aye! you have hit him, Jack! his blood pours out at every step!"

"Thank heavens! If we secure him now, I'll end his career for ever!"

The companions here nearly came to a halt, as they observed their victim pause.

Gaining the brow of the hill, the hideous being, his form drawn up to its full height, stood defiantly before them.

The moon shining brightly upon the wretch revealed his livid features contorted with demoniacal rage.

A loud yell burst from his lips as he shook his fists in impotent fury at his pursuers; then, as the friends dashed forwards, he disappeared on the other side of the hill.

In a second of time the horses were upon the spot where a moment before the hideous being had stood in defiance.

With one swift glance the pursuers discovered their victim had escaped.

Exclamations of fury now escaped the lips of the highwaymen:

Their terrible and mysterious foe had, indeed, escaped them!

The man, Van Vaughan, the Vampyre, was no longer to be seen: he had strangely disappeared!

CHAPTER XVI.

CLAUDE DUVAL FALLS INTO STRANGE HANDS—THE SECRET BROTHERHOOD—A RIDE WITH THE DEAD—THE BAND OF THE CROSS AND DAGGER.

"Well, he's slipped us!"

"Sacre! yes!"

"It's no ordinary foe we have to deal with here," said Clifford, with grim, troubled visage, staring far ahead, his anxious gaze, however, only discerning the tortuous winding of the road.

"No, Paul! Vampyres arn't human creatures!" exclaimed Jack. "Anyway, if I'm not upsides (even) with him yet, put me down as a fool! I'll have a stake run through his carcase yet!"

"There's no doubt as to the nature of the foe we have to deal with!"

"Not the slightest, Paul!"

"Ventre bleu! Jack, this is a horrible matter! Sacre! I can hardly now credit it!"

"It is a horrible matter, Claude! but you must recall to mind the words of Will Shakespere."

"That there are more things in this world than are dreamed of in our philosophy?"

"Exactly."

"Well; I suppose we had best now push on!"

"Yes; it's no use our waiting here!"

"Not a bit!"

"Vampyre won't turn up again here!"

"Not he!"

"Allons! then let us on! After the horrors we have gone through, I shall be glad of a little change and excitement in the town."

"Right you are, Claude! To London we will at once then make our way!"

THE VILLAIN LA TOUCHE NOW HALTED AT THE DOORS OF THE LONE CHATEAU.

"Yes; but we must make a halt at Highgate."

"At The Cat and her Kittens ?"

"Yes."

"Right you are! Now, Paul, her ladyship the moon is sinking in the horizon—morning is at hand; let us have a race! 'Sdeath, I'm getting peckish, and the sooner we have our legs under Dick Dunning's mahogany the better I shall like it !"

"Ditto, Jack !"

The three friends, now giving utterance to a loud shout, at full speed dashed down the hill, soon at a rattling pace gaining the vicinity of the pine wood near the old Tree Cave.

Claude as they hurried on suggested a call at their secret haunt, but not without a shudder was it that the companions made their way through the darksome pine grove, the place where some days before they had encountered the members of the Black Band.

"Do you remember this spot, Claude ?"

"Should say I did, dear pal !"

"I say, Claude !"

"Well !"

"Do you remember the light in the wood near here ?"

"Sacre ! yes !"

"And the dead hand ?"

"Mon Dieu ! yes, Jack !"

"Suppose we hunt up the burial-place !"

"Ma foi, I've no objection !"

"Have with you, then ! Paul, do you canter on to the end of the grove, and there await our coming !"

"Can't I go with you?"

"No, dear boy, we could not get our steeds through the copse."

"All right; I'll go on ahead then?"

"Yes, do, Paul!"

"You won't be long?"

"No; we are only going into the copse to search out a matter in connection with the villain Vaughan."

"Good! May luck attend you in your project!"

Claude and Jack, who had paused in about the centre of the grove, had now dismounted, and whilst their companion hurried on to the further end of the avenue they scrambled through the wood, making their way in the direction of the forest glade, where, in its ruin and decay, stood the withered oak:

The tree at the foot of which they had, unseen, gazed upon the wretch Vaughan burying the dead hand.

Not without some trouble did the friends, winding on through the almost impervious recesses of the copse, at length gain the little glade or hollow surrounded by dwarf oaks.

Oddly enough, they arrived almost upon the same spot as when, guided by the rays of the lamp from the branches of the blighted oak, they had stood on their first visit.

As upon that occasion, too, the dawn was just breaking.

A broad white light was now thrown over the scene.

All was quiet in that sylvan spot; no sound save the note of the thrush and cuckoo breaking upon the stillness of the scene.

Gaining the well-remembered glade the two friends impulsively darted forwards to the scathed tree.

Sinking down upon their knees they now searched the ground at its roots.

Not without surprise did they discover that the dust had been apparently only recently removed.

"Some one has been here before us!"

"Parbleu, yes, Jack!"

"Perhaps the wretch Vaughan himself!"

"Possibly."

"We are foiled in our purpose!"

"Diable! yes, there is nothing here!" exclaimed our hero, who, turning up the ground with his knife discovered that the dread hand of the dead of which they were in search was no longer there.

"We are this time, Claude!"

"Yes, and only recently, I believe within the hour has some one been here!"

"Aye, we are just too late! Well, no matter; it is not of much consequence! Come, let us get back, or Paul will think there is something up!"

"So he will! Ventre bleu, I am annoyed that nothing has come of our visit to this spot!"

"So am I; but it's only another link in the chain of mystery that is linked with the monster Vaughan!"

"Just so!"

With exclamations of disappointment the two friends now turned away and were presently once more threading the intricacies of the woods.

Brooding over their disappointment and muttering sundry anathemas as they pushed on, they were now startled by the sudden report of firearms.

"Sacre! diable! what's that?"

"I hope nothing's wrong with Paul!" said Jack, as he made a dash through a mass of brushwood. About to follow, Claude, catching his foot in the root of a tree, came with a crash and a muttered curse to the ground. Staggering up he now found that his companion had disappeared!

Jack, bounding at mad speed through the copse, had left him behind!

With curses at his accident, Duval now tore his way through the bushes, following, as he supposed, the footsteps of his friend.

In his discomfiture, however, he went wrong.

With the utmost annoyance he presently found himself bewildered in a thick growth of wood through which he could scarce make way.

"Confound the thing! I've lost myself now in the mazes of this infernal copse, and Paul and Jack will be uneasy if I do not presently shew up! Ventre bleu! where the devil have I got to?"

Thoroughly bewildered now, Duval gazed around.

So thick and tangled was the undergrowth about the spot where he had come to a halt that he was obliged to use ere attempting to push on further.

Whilst standing thus in doubt and perplexity, Claude was suddenly startled by the sharp report of a pistol; a report that was succeeded by a wild, ear-piercing yell, as from one in dire agony or affright.

With quickened pulses our hero now once more dashed, despite the prickly tangled briers, into the heart of the woods.

As near as he could guess he made for the direction of the report.

All was now quiet.

Not a sound broke the stillness of the scene

On went Duval, cursing and anathematising the ill-fortune that had parted him from his friend.

Tearing on through brake and bramble, he at length again came to a halt.

He had now arrived out into a kind of natural pathway through the woods:

A small open space that ran some quarter of a mile either way.

On either side of this lane or avenue in the woods was a row of pollard oaks.

It was in emerging from the almost impervious undergrowth in which he had got meshed that Claude, upon casting his eyes up at one of the adjacent trees, gave utterance to an exclamation of horror.

Swaying to and fro in the air, from a stout outstretching branch, was the body of a man.

Grim and ghastly looked the wretched corpse as it sidled backwards and forwards in the breeze.

The rising sun threw a ray of golden light upon the horrible face, fully revealing the contorted blackened features.

Strangled out of life, terrible and grim looked the sad remnant of mortality.

Starting forward, Claude, without hesitation mounting up into the branches of the tree, cut down from the pendant limb the hideous fruit that depended from it.

Descending again to the ground, he now made a hasty search of the body. The hands and ghastly face, scarce yet cold, told that death had not long claimed the doomed man for its own.

"Sacre! the howl I heard following the report of the pistol doubtless emanated from this unhappy creature's lips! This is no suicide; the wretched man has been hastily strung up and left to perish! Parbleu! these woods appear to be the haunt of fiends. Ha! what have we here?"

Kneeling over the corpse of the hanged man, Claude now drew from the innermost part of his vest a packet of papers!

At first about to throw them aside, he, being struck by their yellow and time-worn appearance, placed them in his pocket.

Then coolly securing a handsome gold repeater and a well-filled purse that he also found upon the corpse, he rose to quit the spot.

"It is newly come to me to rob a dead man; but, ma foi! riches are of no use to him now, and I see not why I should not be his heir," muttered Claude, who, placing his prizes carefully away with the nonchalance due to the nature of his calling, which so often presented him face to face with death, gave a last look at the swollen features of the dead, and turned to hurry away, when he was confounded by the sudden appearance of some half-dozen stalwart strangers, who sprang upon him from the adjacent copse.

Borne to the ground, without power to strike a blow in self-defence, Claude was made captive and a prisoner:

A prisoner in the hands of he knew not whom:

Half military, half civilian in appearance. With a wild stare of astonishment, Claude glared at his captors.

No violence beyond securing him was used by the strangers, who now coolly, despite his remonstrances, bound and gagged him, effectually preventing any attempt at colloquy on his part, had indeed his sudden capture and fresh danger left him inclined to converse with his mysterious foes.

Fierce savage looks were cast upon the dead man; then glances of anything but kindly intentions were bent upon Duval, who, inwardly cursing the folly that had placed him in the hands of his unknown enemies, lay bound and helpless on the greensward there beside the strangled victim.

Enraged and helpless, Claude was struck with fear and horror as he was now borne off through the thicket, the horrible corpse of the hanged man carried side by side with him.

What was the purpose of these saturnine strangers?

Who, what were they, Claude asked himself?

As the thought darted through his brain that they might, perchance, be a portion of the Black Band, a fear crept through his frame that nought else would have aroused within him.

The horrible mystery that enshrined one of its principals, the wretch Vaughan, caused Claude to hold the grim Band more in fear and abhorrence than he otherwise would have done.

If, indeed, the gloomy, silent strangers who had waylaid him were members of Vaughan's band, well our hero knew that he was in a critical and dangerous position:

One of extreme peril:

Of deadly danger!

There was but one chance of release:

A bare and slender one:

The possibility that, in alarm at his absence, Jack and Paul might make search for him.

And even in the event of their crossing the path of himself and his captors, Claude shivered at the thought of what might follow.

His new enemies were tall, stalwart men,

And who appeared well able to cope with twice their own number.

What chance, then, would there be in a contest of two only against them?

Claude, now counting his abductors, found they were no less than seven in number.

With a thrill of fear he gave himself up for lost.

There seemed no hope:

None!

After all his escapes and dangers he now seemed doomed to perish by the hands of he know not whom.

Slowly the men traversed on through the woods; not one word since his capture had Claude heard fall from their lips.

At length the leader, a grim-looking herculean man near six foot in height, a perfect Hercules in appearance, now held high up his right hand.

This, it appeared, was the signal for a halt.

The procession had now gained the high-road:

The road down which Claude with his friends had passed only an hour before.

With a moan of fury he glared wildly round, the perspiration of rage and fear starting out like rain upon his brow.

How he cursed the fatal curiosity that had led himself and Jack to penetrate alone into the woods in a fruitless endeavour, as it turned out, to unravel the villain Vaughan's secret:

The secret of the dead hand!

With horror Claude now found he was about to be blindfolded.

Advancing towards him, the leader of the silent band, holding forth a white kerchief, signified that he must bind it over his eyes.

In vain Claude, with a mute glance, implored mercy and freedom.

In grim silence he was now even deprived of the slight consolation of seeing whither he was borne.

The handkerchief, fastened tightly round his brow, he was lost to sight of all around.

He was now bound, helpless, and in darkness.

Scarce had this fresh indignity been passed upon him, ere a loud whistle sounded in the ears of the captive—a whistle, followed a moment after by the grating rattle of wheels upon the hard road.

In another moment Claude felt himself lifted into some vehicle.

With a thrill of horror he also became aware that another human form was laid beside his own!

It needed not the movement of his outstretched manacled wrists towards his dread companion.

With a shudder and moan of horror he now heard the first words that had fallen from his captors:

Words that told him he was about to ride with the dead!

"Drive to the Crow's Nest, and use all speed when there! Give one passenger six foot of earth, and take the other to the Council Chamber!"

The reply to this order was lost in the sudden clattering of horses' hoofs.

Duval now felt a thrill of maddening fury pass through his frame as a well-known voice sounded in his ears:

The voice of his friend, Gentleman Jack!

With beating heart he listened to the anxious inquiries as to whether he had been seen. His blood fairly boiled in his veins with suppressed passion as he heard the reply of his captors that they could give no intelligence, that the person described had not crossed their path.

The wild fury, the tempest of rage which the gag prevented him giving vent to, caused a species of vertigo to seize upon Claude.

With a humming, buzzing, noise in his ears, and a sick, dizzy, feeling, he relapsed into partial insensibility:

When returning once more to consciousness, he found himself still enshrouded in darkness:

Still gagged, bound, and helpless:

Still riding:

Riding with the dead!

The rattle of the vehicle upon the road, along which he was borne, was the only sound that fell upon his ears.

With sick feeling and dizzy brain, Claude now tried to think.

The shock of his sudden capture and stranger horror of his situation wore off.

He began to ask himself, Was there indeed any great danger to be apprehended from his mysterious enemies?

If not in the power of the murderous Black Band, there was some hope.

There was no cause for the mysterious strangers to slay him.

But why had they seized upon him thus? why had he been torn from his friends?

Did not this portend dire ill?

With his brain in a whirl, Claude asked himself these questions as the conveyance which held him prisoner rattled on—on—on its seemingly interminable journey.

For hours it appeared to the bold and dashing knight of the road, was he captive thus with the dead!

At length, with a sigh of relief rising to his gagged lips, Claude felt the vehicle stop.

He was presently after lifted out.

A cold, sharp breeze was wafted now over his heated brow.

He was now conscious that he was being carried by four of his abductors up some height, for, over and again, they paused to rest.

No sound of voices broke the monotony of the journey.

In grim silence he was carried on.

After a time, the breeze ceasing to fan his face, he knew that his enemies had entered some building; no slamming of doors, however, echoed in his ears.

Only the steady tramp, tramp, of his abductors could be heard by the bewildered Claude.

What did it all mean?

Who, what were those men who conveyed him thus in secret from his friends?

What was their object?

Not murder apparently, for long ere this, without trouble, could the deed have been effected.

What then was their purpose?

In vain Claude revolved the question in his brain.

The intentions of his daring captors were impossible of conjecture.

The whole adventure was shrouded in mystery.

Ceasing to have fear of his life, Duval coolly awaited the issue of his mysterious abductors.

Some little time now would possibly give him to know his fate.

For himself he cared not; he felt almost assured his life was not in great jeopardy.

But for Paul, Jack, and his loved Maude, with the pretty Kate Annersley, he was much concerned.

What would they think of his strange absence?

They would fancy that he had fallen into the hands of the horrible Vaughan.

The thought of the misery and anxiety of his friends as to his fate, alone, was it that caused Claude to pray fervently for an end to his wild and mysterious adventure.

It was with the greatest relief that our hero now discovered his captors had come to a halt.

Placing him at their feet they proceeded to remove not only the gag but the kerchief that bound his eyes.

With a muttered prayer of thankfulness Claude, his eyes relieved of the bandage that had covered them, cast a quick, searching glance around.

For a moment, so long kept from the light, all was a confused haze or mist, deep, bright, and lustrous.

In awe, and not without a feeling of fear, as once more he gathered in objects around him, did Claude stare upon the strange wild scene now presented to his gaze.

Assisted to his feet, the ropes that had confined his ancles removed, our hero, in wild amaze, stared around.

His eyes were now getting accustomed to the glare of light which had at first dazzled them.

With an exclamation of awe Claude gazed at the scene before him:

One of wild mystery:

Of strange and deadly import:

With a nervous thrill he now discovered that he was standing in the centre of a vaulted chamber:

A chamber, the hangings of which were draped with black hangings of velvet.

From a sconce or candelabra that depended from the roof came a glare of light.

By the wax tapers burning in this, the vast chamber was fully illumined.

With surprise Claude noted that the drapery upon the walls had worked upon it a strange device in white:

The device of a cross and dagger, with, underneath, the hideous insignia of a skull.

A group of some dozen masked men were gathered round him, and with a nervous thrill Claude observed the long black cloak that enshrouded each form was wrought with the mystic device of the skull, cross, and dagger!

In wild amaze Duval, bold and daring, at first alarmed, now regaining his wonted courage, was the first to break the silence that, almost oppressive, hung in the chamber.

"What mummery is this, may I ask, gentlemen? May I, a stranger, dragged here like a felon and assassin, beg to know the meaning of this lugubrious masquerade?" Bold, loud, and defiant the words issued from his lips, at the thought of the cowardly way his capture had been effected in the woods, and the suffering of his friends; passion and a longing for revenge upon his abductors rose in his breast.

"Claude Duval! highwayman! knight of the road! we are aware that you are bold and cunning; but boldness and cunning will not avail you here! At a word from me a dozen bright swords would be sheathed in your bosom!"

In surprise and terror, Claude heard his name fall from the lips of the tall leader of the strangers.

He was known then!

Was he, after all, in the hands of some of the confederates of the fiend Vampyre Vaughan?

It would seem so.

A cold, deadly feeling seized upon our bold hero as he asked himself this question.

With a wild stare he gazed at the masked strangers, who now each drew forth a sword from beneath the cloak that enveloped them, and held them forth threateningly at the breast of their unarmed victim.

"Brave fellows! strike! Do that of which you may be proud! Ma foi! I'm at your mercy! Mon Dieu! give me but a prayer! Slay me not like a dog, and I will thank you!"

Scarce had those last words issued from his lips when, as if about to lean forward and bury their weapons in his breast, the masked men fell back:

Fell back as a pale, lovely girl, like a being from the other world, glided from behind the hangings at the further end of the mystic chamber!

No cry was there from the young girl's lips.

Like a vision she glided swiftly forwards, and, darting through the ring of masked men, knelt at the feet of the astounded highwayman.

Almost did Claude imagine himself the victim of a wild dream.

So quiet was all around, so full of mystery, that with a dazed, stupefied look, he could scarce imagine its reality.

For a moment of time deepest silence hung in the weird vault-like chamber.

Then the voice of the leader of the band rang upon the air.

"What means this, mad girl! What do you here? Away, this is no scene for thee!"

Stern and fierce was the voice of the herculean stranger, as, rising from her knees, the beautiful but pale-faced intruder remained proud, motionless, and defiant before him.

"Did you hear me bid you hence, Clotilde?"

"Aye!"

"Then why linger—you know the penalty of disobedience?"

"Yes."

"Why, then, do you stay?"

"To prevent a foul wrong!"

"How say you?"

"To prevent a foul wrong—the murder, perchance, of an innocent man!"

"Pshaw, girl, you are mad!"

"No, I'm sane enough, Pierre la Roche."

"Remove her!" exclaimed the leader of the band, whose mask now falling from his face, revealed features deadly pale and convulsed with passion.

About to lay hands on her fragile form, the lovely girl who had interceded for his life now started close to Claude and, snatching a dagger from her bodice, exclaimed:

"Stand back! You all know me! Approach another step and I'll bury this weapon in my bosom!"

"Hold, Clotilde, mad girl!"

In an agony of alarm, apparently, the tall stranger now held out his hands appealingly to the beauteous and determined maiden.

"Stand back, Paul, and hear me! If you do not assure me on oath that you mean no harm to this bold cavalier, whom you have so basely entrapped and brought hither, I will end all between us! You know that what I threaten I am prepared to carry out! I am almost sick of this business, and would it were well over."

"Clotilde, hear me! I promise you nought of harm shall befall the man for whom you intercede. We meant not his life, foolish girl!"

"Then why bring him here?"

"To prevail upon him to carry out for us a secret mission you wot of."

"Is this so?"

"On my soul, yes!"

"You will swear it, Pierre?"

"As I hope for mercy in the world to come!"

"'Tis well! What is this cavalier's name?"

"Claude Duval, at your service to the death, fair lady!" said Claude, who in awe and wonder had listened to the foregoing colloquy between his lovely protectress and the grim stern leader of the secret band.

"Claude Duval! You are a Frenchman, then?"

"Aye, fair mistress!"

"Methinks the name is known to me!"

"Ma foi, it may be so!" murmured Claude, a flush mounting to his brow, as he recalled to mind the man Pierre La Roche had made him aware, a few moments before, that he knew of his bold vocation. Did this fair girl, she who had saved his life, likewise know of this? Whilst these thoughts had darted like a flash through his mind, his beautiful questioner was gazing keenly upon him; her scrutiny ended, she now, pointing to the stalwart leader of the mystic band, exclaimed:

"He has assured me your life is safe, nay more, has brought you hither to execute for him some secret mission—a mission of danger and enterprise, that will require cunning and audacity in the carrying out—is it not so, Pierre?"

"Aye; for this reason were you brought hither, sir cavalier! We all here know that, whate'er your faults, you lack not boldness and audacity; is it not so?" With a grim smile the tall leader here cast an admiring eye upon the form of Claude, as, bowing low, he exclaimed:

"I think no man dare impugn my courage. In this secret service, since 'tis one of danger, I can feel but honoured that I have been chosen for its execution, though I would have wished a more straightforward manner might have been pursued in procuring my presence here."

"I understand you, sir cavalier; but we had no time to stand upon idle ceremony. I, with my assistants, beheld you in the early morning gazing upon the body of a traitor, whose death-wail had drawn you to the spot. Your face was known to me. I knew a price was offered for your apprehension, Claude Duval; nay more, I knew that officers were on your track. Knowing your boldness, and requiring a gentleman with nerve and courage to execute for me a mission of importance, I conceived the thought of securing your services. With me to think was to act. I had you conveyed hither; and now would ask if you will, for a good round sum, undertake the work we have in hand?"

"Parbleu! how can I refuse? You have pitched upon me for the task, in admiration of my courage. Ma foi," said Claude, with a smile, "I will not do otherwise than continue to deserve your high opinion of my prowess. This task, whate'er it be, I will undertake! I would but first seek my friends, who, in my prolonged absence, will be suffering the cruelest anxiety."

"Trouble not for them: they know you are safe!"

"Ventre bleu! what mean you?"

"Why, your friends are now aware that you are in safety!"

"Diable! how came they to know my true position?"

"From a messenger I despatched to a certain inn."

"The Cat and her Kittens?"

"The same!"

"How knew you they were there?"

"By watching the movements of your companions, Gentleman Jack and Paul Clifford, who surprised us whilst we were putting you into the carriage that brought you hither."

"Morbleu! you have been prompt in action!"

"As those must ever be who mean to attain their desires!"

"What said my friends to your messenger?"

"You have your answer; 'tis there!"

To the surprise of Claude the man Pierre La Roche here held out to him a letter.

At a sign a moment before he had been released from his ligatures and was now free. Stretching forward his hands he eagerly seized the note and devoured its contents: it was brief, but assured him that his friends were easy as to his welfare; the person sent by Pierre La Roche, a minister, had, it appeared from the hurried lines scrawled by Jack, been successful in making them perfectly easy on his account.

"This seems to be a good thing, Claude. 'Tis perhaps as well that you should be away for two or three days. Your disappearance will both astonish Anstey and the moonlight member. We had a hint that you would be compelled to execute the task put upon you. Knowing you are able to take your own part in an emergency we are not now anxious. Anything but Jonathan and Newgate, dear Claude! Au revoir! with love and kisses from you know who!—Yours till death, GENTLEMAN JACK!"

Such was the contents of the note received from his friends.

In wondering surprise, now that he knew no danger was to be expected from the strange band of men into whose hands he had fallen, Claude, not without a natural curiosity, followed La Roche and the fair girl Clotilde from the secret chamber into a long dark passage without.

His hand held in that of his conductor, Claude was led on till at length a flight of stairs was reached: ascending these, a short corridor traversed at the summit, a door on their left opened, and in another moment they were seated in a small but comfortably furnished apartment where, to the surprise of Claude, a sumptuous repast awaited them.

The young lady, who had evinced such alarm on his account some little time before, now bowing her head to the dashing highwayman, left the room.

In another moment our hero was alone with the mystic leader of the secret society, the man Pierre La Roche.

CHAPTER XVII.

THE CONFERENCE—THE TITUS OATES CONSPIRACY—A DANGEROUS SERVICE—THE VOYAGE TO FRANCE—A PERILOUS JOURNEY—MONSIEUR LA TOUCHE—THE MAN WITH THE EVIL EYE—THE DEFIANCE.

Despite the strange nature of his position, Claude at a nod from his host now set to and made a hearty meal.

The day far advanced, the sun sinking in the skies in a golden setting, told our hero how far he must have been brought by his captors, and upon inquiry with astonishment learnt that he was at that moment located in a village on the Kentish coast.

Beckoning him to the only casement the chamber contained, his host pointed out a dark belt of water that could be traced plainly some quarter of a mile away.

The house in which Duval so strangely found himself a guest and not a prisoner, built on an eminence, overlooked the winding waters of the coast.

"I suppose this is the Crow's Nest?" said Duval with a smile.

"Well, yes! I presume you overheard my orders this morning that you should be brought here?"

"I did."

"Are you now prepared to hear what I require of you?"

"Oh, yes, but must advise you that I must have rest ere I start upon my journey, where'er it may be!"

"Certainly. There will be some hours for you yet before you start."

"Where have I to go?"

"St. Omer."

"I know it."

"Reaching this place you will make for the College."

"Yes."

"And inquire for a student named Titus Oates."

"Well!"

"This youth will give you the address of a person upon whom you will have to call."

"Residing also, I suppose, at St. Omer?"

"Yes."

"And the name of this other person?"

"Monsieur La Touche. From this party you will receive a packet of papers, that you must bring back to me, and guard as you would your life!"

"It shall be done!"

"Nothing must lead you to part with these documents."

"Rest content; nothing shall!"

"Good! execute your mission well, and upon your return I, Pierre La Roche, will hand you a hundred li. (pounds)!"

"I will do your bidding to the letter!"

"You will have to take a packet of papers with you."

"Very good; when do I start?"

"You will leave this place for Dover early to-morrow. Can you be ready?"

"Yes; I only want rest, for I was up the entire of yesternight."

"Indeed, then, you must want repose."

"Well, I do. I am worn out with fatigue."

"You must be! but you must bear with me a little longer."

"Don't name it! I am no puny whipster to give in when my services are required!"

"I am sure of that; now answer me truly. Should you not see me on the morrow do you think you could execute my mission? Will you in the morning carry in your mind all that which I have told you this night?"

"Oh, yes! my memory is not a treacherous one."

"You are sure of this?"

"Quite sure."

"Good! Here then is the packet which you will hand to the student, Titus Oates." Claude, here now rather interested in the strange business, took from the man La Roche a small bundle of letters, carefully fastened round with a skein of silk.

"You understand you are to give those letters into the hands of the student of St. Omer and no other?"

"It shall be done."

"Upon visiting Monsieur La Touche you will tell him what you have done."

"Will not Titus Oates be with me?"

"No! You will call upon La Touche alone."

"Well!"

"From him you will receive some such packet as that you have just taken from me."

"Very good!"

"This letter you will guard with your life."

"I will; the packet shall be well cared for."

"Lose it, Claude Duval, and I will not answer for your head! A higher power than mine might take it from your shoulders!"

With a start at these words, our hero now divined the danger of the mission that he had accepted.

He was about to engage in a political plot:

A something against the State.

He could not doubt it.

But, though reading the errand he was upon, he would not now retract.

What was State or King to him?

He was banned by the laws; the wretch Anstey had sworn to bring him to Tyburn; why then need he hesitate to undertake a task that might lead him to the Tower?

He was rather pleased than otherwise at the adventure that had opened to him.

Little recked Claude Duval, however, the dread convulsion that was to follow this the first step in a plot that was to doom good men and true to the block.

Sooner would Duval have that instant yielded up his life

than have become an agent in the first steps taken by the
originators of the Popish plot.

It was, as Claude was carefully placing the papers for
Oates in his pocket, that his hands came in contact with
those he had filched from the body of the wretched man he
had beheld that morning hanging in the woods. He now
asked his mysterious employer who and what the
unfortunate was; and the crime that had doomed him to
the rope ?

"He was a traitor, Duval," exclaimed La Roche with
knitted brows.

"Knew he ought of this ?" Claude here tapped his
pocket containing the paper handed him just before.

"Aye ! and meant to betray the community of which he
was a trusted member !"

"You discovered his treachery, then ?"

"Yes, Duval; as we should yours or any other messenger
whom we entrusted with the task you have in hand should a
double game be attempted !"

"Do you doubt me ?" said Duval hotly, as, with flushed
brow he glanced defiantly at the stalwart leader of the
political plot.

"If I had the slightest doubt of you I should never have
thought of engaging you in the matter."

"Why that implied threat, then ?"

"Merely to warn you in case others might attempt to
decoy you from allegiance to those you have sworn to serve."

"You do not know me thoroughly, Monsieur Pierre La
Roche ! My word once given to friend or foe is my bond,
highwayman though I be !"

"I believe you, Duval; your hand !" Seizing our hero's
extended hand he here shook it warmly, a grasp that Claude
as freely returned.

Handing him a heavy purse, telling him that he might
want the contents ere he returned to England, Pierre La
Roche, now bidding him good night, retired, as a man with
a lamp entered the room intimated to Claude that his couch
was prepared, at the same time presenting some warm spiced
wine.

Draining the welcome goblet, Claude, worn out with
excitement and fatigue, retired, following his conductor
into a neat and pretty bedroom.

Scarce had he closed the door upon the servant ere he
was seized with a heavy feeling of sleep, that, dressed as he
was, he staggered to the couch, soon in a heavy slumber being
lost to all sense of his strange position.

It was with a dull aching head that Claude at length woke
up.

With a dreamy stare he gazed around him :
Rubbing his eyes he turned uneasily in his couch :
It was hard and uncomfortable :
With a wild stare he glared round his chamber :
Was he mad or still dreaming ?

He well remembered the soft easy couch upon which he
had thrown himself when so overcome with slumber.

But different, far different, was the one upon which he
now reclined.

The whole aspect of the chamber had changed.

The small confined place he was in was lighted only by a
sickly oil lamp :

A lamp that cast only a faint dull flicker through the place,
and smelt rancid and foul.

"Where the deuce am I ?" he gasped.

Thoroughly aroused, Claude now sat up.

Scarce could he believe his eyes :

He was no longer in the snug bedroom to which he had
been conducted by the man-servant of Pierre La Roche :

He was now, he discovered, with intensest surprise, in the
cabin of a small vessel, the uneasy rolling motion of which
told him they were out at sea.

Jumping out of his berth, for such it was, Claude now
hurried up a rope ladder :

In a few minutes, confused, dazed, and bewildered by
the strangeness of his situation, he gained the deck.

As he suspected, he was on board a vessel far out at sea.

The moon, high in the heavens, shone bright and clear
over the heaving waters.

The wind blowing almost a gale, the little barque rolled,
heaved, and pitched heavily.

Involuntarily, Claude placed his hands in his vest as he
asked himself, Was it all a dream ?

But a thrill passed through his frame as his fingers came
in contact with a packet of papers.

He was the victim of no dream :

He well remembered the converse with Pierre La Roche :
The strict injunctions as to the important documents :
To be handed only to the student of St. Omer :
The youth, Titus Oates !

"Nice night, but rough, Sir," said a thickset little man,
who now coming forwards invited Claude into the cabin
below.

"Are you the captain of this craft ?" exclaimed Duval, at
the same time declining courteously the invitation to descend
to the cabin.

"I am the skipper ! My name is Peter Moncrieff, and
this barque of mine is called the Lucy, and a better don't
sail the Channel !"

"Where are we bound for ?"

"Calais !"

"It may seem to you a strange question, but who brought
me on board ?"

"Oh, you forget that do you ! Hem, I thought you were
pretty well loaded ! I did'nt think you were as bad as that !"
said the little captain with a grin.

"I appeared drunk then ?"

"Appeared ! Ha, ha, ha ! Why you could not stand !"
exclaimed the merry sailor, who now hurried away.

"Ventre bleu, what an ass I am !" muttered Claude.
Of course I was drugged ; I see it all now ! Well, ma foi,
this is a strange business for a knight of the road ; but
parbleu no matter ! It will be a profitable adventure to me !
Diable ! if I make not something out of this little plot my
name ain't Duval !"

Walking the deck as steadily as he could, Claude, who
was a good seaman, gazed for some few moments thought-
fully across the moonlit waters, then, as the hurricane blew
fresher, with a shiver hurried below.

His brain confused by the rapid occurrence of events
that hurried him on in such breathless haste, he was fain
once more to turn into his berth, seeking forgetfulness in
repose.

When again making his way on deck it was to find that
the brave little barque Lucy had sighted the shore at
Calais.

Some two hours after Claude had set foot upon French
soil.

A strange thrill passed through his frame as he trod upon
his native land.

Wrapt in thought, he was bending his way towards the
principal hotel, when he was aroused from his fit of abstrac-
tion by a hand being placed upon his arm.

Starting and looking up, Claude now found standing
directly in his path a little tawny-faced man, who, bowing
and scraping, and pointing to a rickety-looking conveyance,
exclaimed :

"Pardieu ! am I not right in supposing that you are
bound for St. Omer ?"

There was a cunning twinkle in the stranger's eye as he
addressed Claude, who, staring fixedly at his interrrogator,
exclaimed :

"And supposing I am on my way to St. Omer, ma foi !
what then ?"

"Much. Monsieur will want a conveyance !"

"Granted !"

"And as I am going to his destination, morbleu ! Monsieur
can have a seat in my carriage free of expense !"

"Indeed ! And is it your usual custom to convey passengers from Calais to St. Omer for nothing ?"

"Oh ! Pardieu, no !"

"Then why, may I ask, am I the exception !"

"Monsieur is on a visit to the College of St. Omer ?"

"Perhaps," said Claude, who, though divining that his
tawny-faced acquaintance was a friend of Pierre La Roche,
yet did not care too hastily to confide in him.

"I am sure you had better travel with me ! I know monsieur's business !"

"Indeed ! Ventre bleu ! people sometimes know another
person's business more than their own !"

"Monsieur is severe ; but, sacristi ! enough of this ! You
come from Pierre La Roche, and are about to visit the
College of St. Omer to gain an interview with a young
student named Titus Oates —is it not so ?"

Keen and searching was the glance Claude cast upon his
strange-looking companion.

Pierre La Roche had not advised him that he would meet
with anyone on his journey ; yet did this wizen, tawny-
faced stranger appeared to know every particlar of his
undertaking.

Claude, accustomed in his adventurous calling to glance with eyes of suspicion on all strangers, cast a look of strong doubt upon the stranger before him.

His uneasy glance evidently noted, the stranger, now drawing close to Duval, said:

"Diable! you are suspicious of me, who would assist you on in your journey! Morbleu! I am half a mind to leave you, but that Pierre la Roche might be angered with me. Come, let us at once to my conveyance, or, pardieu! who knows, you may be attacked by some scoundrel sans-culotte, and, sacre! might be robbed of some valuables—papers and such like. Eh! eh! eh!"

A low chuckle here escaped the thin lips of the stranger!

Claude, with a lingering suspicion of his strange acquaintance, was about to turn away, when the other caught his arm exclaiming; "Your doubts at first were pardonable, but a continuance of them is an insult! I am not here to put obstacles in the way of the great plot that shall humble the followers of Rome, but to aid in its grand fulfilment."

An ejaculation of surprise at this burst from the enthusiast escaped the lips of Duval, who, now unhesitatingly linking his arm in that of his companion, followed him into the vehicle that was now drawn up to receive them.

From the manner of his fresh acquaintance he concluded that he should now learn more of the mysterious errand he was engaged upon.

A lingering to know the particulars of the hidden plot each moment gained a firmer hold on his mind.

Narrowly Claude studied the wrinkled, pinched, yellow visage of his companion.

Without much scrutiny he read in it cunning, deceit, and enthusiasm.

Determined to fathom the secret service to the bottom, Claude, with a smile as the coach drove off, exclaimed:

"Of course you have had a messenger from Pierre La Roche here before my arrival, who informed you of my coming."

"Yes! I was prepared for your visit."

"Know you who I am?"

"Yes! Your name is Claude Duval! There is a price for your apprehension in London! But you are now engaged on a service that will pay you. Ma foi! you can defy your enemies, if the great plot succeeds, and succeed it must, and will."

It was with no pleasurable feelings that Claude now learned that Pierre La Roche had informed this new acquaintance of his real name and calling. It was a breach of trust! With burning cheeks and an indignant swelling in his throat, he began to think that the leader of this secret business was using him as a tool to bend this or that way with pleasure. The whole affair—his capture in the woods, his abduction to the Crow's Nest, and even his conveyance on board the Lucy had been carried out with unscrupulous craft, without any attempt to study the feelings of their emissary. Suspecting the truth, Claude, with a husky sensation in the throat, now leaning forward and looking fixedly into the wizen features of his companion, who had been intently watching him, exclaimed:

"And just for supposition, suppose now that I, Claude Duval, highwayman and knight of the road, who am entrusted with this wonderful mission that according to Pierre La Roche's showing, may, if I am discovered, lead me to the Tower and the stake—supposing, I say, that I played false or threw up the affair?"

"You will not, my young friend, be allowed to do either!"

"How?" with an angry start Claude drew back in his seat.

"You will not be allowed to play us false or retract; but (in supposition all this is, you know), supposing you did play false, you would be hunted to the death. You would find the League worse enemies than your very particular friends the Bow-street runners!"

"Indeed! Well, I am not a man scared by trifles. And suppose, instead of playing the part of traitor, I declined to go further in this ticklish business?"

"You would not be allowed to turn back. You have embarked in the service of the plot, and must go on!"

"Must?"

"Yes, pardieu, must!"

"May I ask more fully," said Claude, controlling an earnest desire to pitch his yellow-faced companion out of the vehicle into the roadway, "may I ask a few particular of this secret service?"

"I scarcely know that I am right in satisfying your curiosity; but, as it is somewhat pardonable now that you are fairly embarked with us, I do not see that it signifies your being made acquainted with the fact that a secret convocation of Jesuits has been discovered in London. This meeting was found out, no matter how, by him you are about to see, even Titus Oates. Know, Claude Duval, that it is purposed by the Romish idolators to destroy the Protestant religion. But this must not be. Our grand plot, now on the tapis, will crush these Popish worshippers! We must be rid of this childless Queen, this Catherine of Braganza, and the Duke of York! 'Tis a grand cause that you are embarked in, young man—'tis a grand cause!"

"You will excuse me if I do not concur with you in that opinion."

"How! surely you are not one of those who would bow to this Popish Queen?"

"Indeed, but I am! The unfortunate lady has, methinks, been sorely tried by her monarch husband, who, in his infatuation for the Duchess of Portsmouth and other harlots, forgets that respect which is due to an honest wife!"

His face flushed crimson with passion at discovering the vile service he was engaged upon. Duval, fearless of consequences, now in a fury of rage took the papers from his vest, placed there by the man Pierre La Roche, and, tearing them to shreds, threw them at the bottom of the carriage, trampling them beneath his feet.

A dull leaden pallor stole on the features of his companion as he witnessed this ebullition of temper; then, with a spiteful malicious grin he tapped at the carriage window, when, to the astonishment of Duval, several horsemen appeared.

Throwing down the sash of the vehicle, the little wizen stranger now shouted to the leader of the troop without to make with all speed to the residence of Monsieur La Touche and not the College of St. Omar, as he had first ordered.

Boiling with passion Claude fell back in his seat.

He had, upon glancing without, descried no less than a dozen mounted men.

Escape was impossible!

With a scowl of defiance, however, he glared upon the wizen-faced stranger, who with a low chuckle exclaimed:

"'Tis well you have spoken out! You are, it seems, though a highwayman, tainted with a liking for these Popish idolators. You are a brand fit for the burning! In England you would eventually have been hanged, Claude Duval—dashing, daring Claude Duval! but we will find a more lingering death for you here! The greatest tortures shall you suffer for your act of the past hour! The destruction of these papers with which you were entrusted —papers that were worth a thousand such lives as thine— will entail no end of delay and trouble to the workers of the great plot."

"I am delighted to hear it," said Duval, smiling with utmost coolness at his enraged companion, who now turned livid with passion.

"Have you no fear of the horrors to which you will be subjected?"

"Fear is known but by name, man, to Dashing Duval," said Claude defiantly.

"Hem! we shall see! Wait till you behold Monsieur La Touche!"

"If he is as ugly and yellow-skinned as you are, I shall not be fascinated with him!"

"I don't think you will be fascinated with him, though, perhaps, you may be with his chateau!"

"His chateau?" There was a hidden sarcasm in the man's tones that Claude did not like.

"Yes, his chateau! The lone Chateau of St. Ardens! It is surrounded with forest; you'll have a happy time of it there; and you can reflect upon the folly of man whilst in your pretty stone chamber! La Touche has a special apartment for his friends! Ma foi! the cells of Newgate are pretty, doubtless, Claude Duval; but, pardieu! they are nothing to the dungeons of the Chateau St. Ardens! Parbleu! you will doubtless agree with me when you see them!"

"When I see them! But you have to get me there first!" said Duval, who having warily watched his foe now threw himself upon him, and placing his hand upon his mouth stopped the utterance of a single cry.

To drag his astounded victim to the bottom of the carriage was to Claude the work of a moment, then, as a low cry burst from his lips, Duval with an oath dashed his fist with all his force in his face, at the same time bringing the back of his head violently upon the hard wood of the carriage flooring.

Stunned and bleeding the wizen-faced stranger was now helpless.

The rattle of the wheels had drowned all noise of the brief struggle to the ears of the driver and escort without.

Despite the perilous position he was in, Claude now coolly searched the body of his victim, not a paper or article of value, however, did he find upon him.

With a curse he rose to his feet.

His peril was now extreme.

Revolving in his brain the best chance of escape, he was now startled by the stoppage of the vehicle.

In grim despair he gazed round.

Slowly, softly, he now pulled at the door of the carriage on his left hand.

It yielded to his touch.

But in the roadway without four of the escort had drawn up.

There seemed but little hope.

Nothing, however, was there before him but to make a bold dash for it.

About to leap out, Claude was now startled by the sudden appearance of the ghastly horrible face of a man that peered in at the window opposite to the door through which he had meditated flight.

Hideous in its ugliness was this face that with a demoniac grin glared in upon Duval.

With the complexion of a mulatto, the man had the features of a negro; whilst eyebrows meeting over the nose, of a jetty blackness, added to the ugliness of the stranger, whose hideous aspect was rendered perfectly demoniac by the presence of only one eye:

One eye, that gleamed under its jetty fringe like a piece of live coal.

With a wild stare of astonishment and disgust did Claude gaze upon the hideous being, who now mockingly raised his cap and exclaimed, "I am Monsieur Andrea La Touche. Welcome, to St. Omer, Claude Duval!"

Infuriate but helpless, surrounded as he was, Duval, at a sign from his malicious-looking foe, now descended from the carriage:

The senseless proprietor, who at this moment began to give token of returning conciousness, being carried in before them into the hall of a large gloomy-looking stone mansion, the door of which had been thrown open on the first arrival of the mounted escort.

Glaring defiance at his enemies, all of whom gazed savagely upon him, Claude now made his way into the house, preceded by its evil-eyed owner, Monsieur Andrea La Touche.

Opening the door of a chamber on the right of the hall, Claude's grim foe, bidding him follow, now entered.

A glance as he passed the threshold showed our hero that no chance of flight or trickery was left him:

Half-a-dozen brawny rough-looking fellow grouping about just without the door.

With a nervous thrill he could not restrain, Claude now found himself in a large room the flooring and walls of which were rough hewn stone, whilst an iron grating was its only casement.

More like a prison chamber was the place than aught else.

In surprise did our hero gaze around him.

Not for long was he left to scrutinise the place.

Scarce had Andrea La Touche closed the door behind them ere it was again opened.

With a shout and exclamation of rage Duval drew back.

His enemy, the man who had accosted him at Calais, before whom he had behaved he was now obliged to confess to himself somewhat rashly, with grim cadaverous face stood before him.

A slight bandage round his head, from which the blood still oozed, rendered his tawny ill-looking features still more repulsive.

A low chuckle now escaped his lips, as, placing his hand upon the arm of La Touche, he exclaimed:

"Monsieur Duval, there, wishes to see your chateau in Normandy! Can you without inconvenience send him there?"

"If it is your wish, Petro Delorme!"

"It is my wish!"

"Good! then he shall go! You think there is nothing to be done with him?"

"Nothing! He destroyed the papers sent over from La Roche before my very eyes whilst on our journey hither! He avowed friendship for the Popish Queen, Catherine, and openly defied us!"

"How came La Roche to entrust the business to such an emissary?"

"Ma foi! he thought as the fellow was a common thief and hunted by the laws of his own country, that he would be glad to give his services in futherance of the grand plot in hand."

Biting his lip till the blood came, Claude stood listening to the conversation carried on before him; then, as glaring defiantly at his two evil-looking foes, he exclaimed:

"Parbleu! Gentlemen, methinks your grand conspiracy must lack true-hearted supporters, since the fellow La Roche was glad to seek the services of a thief!"

"You were selected as one that was bold, daring, and at war with the laws of his country. If you had been discovered by those against whom we are warring, your life, sacre! would have mattered not."

"Ma foi! Thanks, gentlemen! I see I was entrusted with this enterprise because you considered my existence valueless!" said Claude, returning with a smile the look of deadly hate that flashed from the eyes of the two men before him.

"You have said right, Claude Duval! The work we have in hand will bring proud heads to the block, and the scaffold is no child's play! The part allotted you might have, very doubtless would have, sent you to the gallows; but to that end your own acts have already condemned you--thus Pierre La Roche argued that you were a man to whom we could entrust the dangerous portion of our enterprise! However, common thief as you are, you professed to have opinions, and dared to destroy the precious documents entrusted to your charge, and also to avow the cause of those against whom you were supposed to willingly act the rebel. You shall now meet with the reward of your temerity and audacity! Your English Newgate, and the gallows without its doors, were Paradise to the fate to which you will now be condemned!"

"Indeed, Petro Delorme! And do you think you can do that which not the judges or English officers have effected, namely, crush and remove from your path the Dashing Claude Duval? But, sacre! we shall see!"

"We shall see! Your daring and bravado will avail you nought here, my bold highwayman! Diable! if you outlive the horrors in store for you at my country seat, in Normandy, pardieu! I'll believe thee more that mortal!" said the villanous-looking Andrea La Touche.

It was not without some alarm that Claude heard of the destination intended for him.

Bitterly he cursed the folly that had led him to enter so far into the plot of his enemies, and then to defy them whilst far away from England and his friends.

Policy should have led him to carry out his mission, and then upon his return to England act the traitor, or remain neutral in the foul plot emanating against the State.

But Claude Duval was impulsive and of strong passions; nor could he control his rage when reflecting how the man Pierre La Roche had, as it were, entrapped him into joining their cause.

In grim silence Claude now submitted to the indignity of being securely bound.

With all his daring, he knew it was useless to attempt to fight against the odds that were against him.

Throwing open the door at the voice of the wizen-faced Petro Delorme, a crowd of some dozen men had poured into the room!

At the direction of La Touche, these arrivals began the process of pinioning Claude.

With a smothered curse he submitted.

His time for action had not arrived.

Instant death was not evidently intended.

The malice of his foes decreed him to endure fearful suffering ere he perished!

"Whilst there is life there is hope!" murmured our hero to himself.

Accustomed to encounter deadly perils, Claude gave not way, as some men would have done, to despair.

He would bide his time.

An opportunity might come for a fair chance of escape

DASHING DUVAL;

OR,

THE LADIES' HIGHWAYMAN.

"SAID I NOT WE SHOULD MEET AGAIN, CLAUDE DUVAL?"

For the moment he could do naught but act passively. Submission might throw his enemies off their guard.

Daring defiance, or an attempt to struggle with his foes, would but add to his misery.

Calmly, submissively, he therefore underwent the process of being pinioned.

No word escaped his lips at the insolent chuckle of the man Delorme.

Though his face flushed and his breast heaved with a volcano of passion, he uttered no sound as the one-eyed villain, La Touche, spat in his face, and his companion, Petro Delorme, with a curse, struck him a cowardly blow full in the mouth—a blow that caused the blood to trickle in a thin stream down his chin.

"Away with him to the Chateau St. Ardeas!"

The words rung like a knell in his ears, whilst a shiver, as of the foreshadowing of some unknown evil impending over him, passed through his frame.

But in that moment, when dragged like a dog to the carriage without, Duval vowed, if he ever escaped, to wreak out a terrible revenge upon his dastard foes.

Upon one of them he speedily paid back his debt of vengeance in a terrible manner. But we anticipate.

Bound and helpless, he was now hurled into a strong carriage standing without the door.

Not the same vehicle was it that had brought him to the fatal spot.

But a conveyance evidently built for rough usage.

Thrown into a seat, he was now followed by the man Andrea La Touche.

The door closed to with a loud bang; the vehicle now dashed away.

For a moment of time Claude beheld the spiteful tawny visage of his foe, the man Delorme, turned with demonial exaltation upon him, then, as the carriage dashed away, the hideous face disappeared, whilst another, if possible more fiendly and satanically revolting, was bent over him.

Like a piece of polished steel an eye was fastened upon him:

The evil eye of the villian La Touche:

He was now alone with the hideous Frenchman:

Alone and being borne he knew not whither:

To a lone deserted chateau.

A building which, from the hints dropped, was intended for his tomb!

Playing with the handle of a stiletto or dagger he had drawn from his vest, the villain Frenchman, like a fiend, glared upon his captive.

"I could slay you now, dashing Claude Duval, as easily as a butcher a sheep in the shambles; but death were a release you must not suffer! Delorme is right! your audacious defiance merits weeks of torture; and, diable! tortures you dream not of shall be yours—do you hear me!"

"Oh, yes, I'm not deaf, One-Eye!"

"You have not lost your usual air of impudent defiance, I see!"

"No, and you are not likely to take it from me!"

"Indeed! We shall see! You will be the first if your proud defying spirit is not cowed by the horror of the torture-chamber in the Chateau St. Ardens!"

"You seem proud of that place!"

"I am."

"Parbleu! what a pity you have only got one eye!"

"How?"

"Because, if you had two, how much more you could enjoy the beauties of the domain; besides that, in the torture-chamber you boast of you've only one eye to what may be going on: you'll lose half the fun! What a pity your mother didn't have a twin like you, Andrea! you'd have had the usual allowance of two eyes, you know, then; and what a pretty pair of boys you would have made!" Claude here grinned defiantly at the scowling evil face of his enemy.

"Claude Duval, you are a bold man!"

"Morbleu! have you only just found that out?"

"Are you not afraid?" Convulsively the villain's fingers twitched at his dagger.

"Afraid! what of a hobgoblin of a Frenchman with one eye? Not I!"

"Sacre! you do well to jeer me thus, and the reason I do not slay you now is that I would behold you live to suffer; you must die a lingering death, Claude Duval!"

"Must I, indeed?"

"Yes; and I will show no mercy in its administration."

"Wait till I ask it at your hands. Parbleu! my one-eyed friend, Heaven may not yet have entirely left me to thy mercy."

"Ha, ha, ha! Ma foi! but I think it has, Claude Duval, seeing that I have but to thrust this knife of mine into your carcase when you would die like a dog as you are," exclaimed La Touche, who, maliciously, with a grin, here flourished his dagger in the face of his helpless victim.

Claude, thinking that perhaps further controversy or audacity on his part might lead his cowardly enemy to slay him while he lay thus bound and incapable of resistance, now relapsed into moody silence, nor paid heed to the taunts and invectives of his merciless foe.

Onwards meanwhile rolled the coach.

Miles upon miles were now passed. Upon one occasion, stopping at a post-house, a fierce-visaged bearded ruffian, with a huge grey moustache and hair lip, took the place of the villain La Touche beside Duval, thus proving to him that no means of flight would be left open to him.

With growing despair he now asked himself how it would all end.

Gladly would he have submitted to become the prisoner of Jonathan Anstey, rather than be thus driven he knew not to what lonesome retreat by a foreign ruffian, who, it was evident, would stop at no crime in the fulfilment of his revenge.

His limbs numbed with the tightness of his bonds, faint and weak from exhaustion and lowness of spirits, Claude now relapsed into a state of semi-unconsciousness.

In low buzzing tones he heard the voice, after a time, of his persecutor, who had once more entered the coach.

As in a dream he saw the wretch's horrible eye, fiery red and gleaming with fury, bent upon him.

Darkness anon fell upon the scene.

Still on—on rolled the coach, till with a dull dazed feeling Claude fell into a half sleep:

A sleep which, undisturbed by his enemy, ended in a heavy prolonged repose.

Worn out with the rush of incidents that had crowded upon him the last few days, despite his terrible danger Claude slept on, nor knew aught of the lapse of time as he was borne onwards by his foes.

It was with a nervous start and in inky darkness that he at length awoke.

Scarce could he realise, for a moment, his position.

The evil eye of his enemy, however, peering into his, recalled Claude fully to his peril.

They were still in the coach, which was now rolling over a thick clayey road.

Upon either side in the dark gloom of night Claude beheld the dim outline of an avenue of trees.

The wind, howling fiercely and portending a storm, screamed shrill and mournful through the branches.

The coach coming to a halt our hero was now made aware that they had arrived at their destination.

With a fierce oath the villain La Touche, seizing him by the rope that confined his limbs, dragged him roughly from the vehicle.

In a moment after he found himself half-carried half-dragged along a pathway that, full of ruts and hollows, caused his enemy to stumble at every step.

It was with a nervous thrill, and a cold icy sensation darting through his frame, that Claude now beheld looming before them in the distance a large building that looked grim and weird in the blackness of the night.

One solitary light gleaming out in the darkness alone gave note that the lone dwelling was inhabited.

With vile oaths Claude was dragged on by his savage foe.

Reaching a narrow but deep stream that crossed their path they now, unfastening the cords that bound his ankles, bade him follow them over the rude bridge—the trunk of a tree that rested on either side of the rivulet.

It was with the utmost difficulty, his limbs being cramped and stiff, that Claude staggered after his conductors, La Touche leading the way and the grim-visaged ruffian with the hair lip following in the rear, a loaded pistol pointed ominously at his head.

Walking on through a garden, overgrown with every species of undergrowth and wild plants, at one time scrambling through a mass of tangled brier, the next moment floundering in a deep rut of wet clay, the party at length gained the entrance to the lonely house.

With a grim smile the villain La Touche pointed to the weird-looking building.

It was a dreary, sombre pile.

Standing there alone embosomed apparently in a thick forest:

High up against the inky clouds the chateau reared its height:

Its grey stone walls, its mullioned casements and battlemented towers, giving notice that at one time it had been a lordly residence.

Lonely and sad now looked the deserted habitation.

In rich luxuriance, adding to the ruinous forlorn appearance of the place, a terific growth of ivy clambered up the front of the building, almost shrouding the once solid but now crumbling masonry.

In silent despair Claude gazed at the black mass of building.

Hope of escape now left him.

A shiver passed through his frame:

A shiver of dread—of utter despair!

He was miles upon miles from those he dearly loved:

Was helpless and alone:

A captive in the hands of unscrupulous foes:

Of men who would hesitate at no crime!

He was lost:

Doomed to perish at the hands of wretches 'gainst whom, after all, he had committed no great injury.

Lost in gloomy and despairing reverie he was now recalled to himself, as the villain La Touche with a loud mocking laugh placed his hand upon his shoulder exclaiming:

"Welcome, Claude Duval, to the Chateau St. Ardens! Behold your final resting-place—your tomb!"

With the hoarse laughter of his foes ringing in his ears he was now hurled rather than dragged across the threshold of the huge oaken door that had a moment before opened wide to receive them.

The strong barrier shut to awoke up dismal echoes around.

With a chill of abandonment and despair Claude now stood in the lone hall of the dwelling involved in total darkness.

For a moment of time he was left alone.

A dazed stunned feeling seized upon him.

He seemed robbed of all his usual strength and courage.

He could think only of one grim, horrid fact.

That he was far away from his friends; away from all help:

A bound and unarmed captive in a lonely chateau, which his merciless and fiendly enemy had told him was to be his tomb!

CHAPTER XVIII.

THE HORRORS OF THE LONE CHEATEAU—THE TORTURE CHAMBER—LEFT ALONE—CLAUDE'S RELEASE FROM HIS BONDS—PREPARATIONS FOR THE ENEMY—THE ARRIVAL—THE SURPRISE—THE STRUGGLE—THE EXPLOSION—TERRIBLE FATE OF ANDREA LA TOUCHE, THE MAN WITH THE EVIL EYE.

Standing in thick, heavy darkness Claude was presently confused and dazed as La Touche, hurrying from a chamber near at hand, appeared with a small lamp, the rays of which, upon approaching his victim, he let fall full upon his face.

The glare for a moment was almost painful to our hero after the inky gloom of a few moments before.

"Sacre! Diablo how like you my pretty abode? You have the advantage of me in possessing two eyes. Come, you must follow me to a room above, where your orbs of vision will be of service to you. You will there see the pretty things we keep for our friends in this our country house, the Chateau St. Ardens. Come, Cartouche, do you follow on upstairs behind our friend, Monsieur Duval. If he stumbles in his progress just assist him with the point of your sword, only don't prick him too deeply, for he will want all his strength, poor fellow, by and bye.

"Ma foi! yes," said the ruffian addressed; the same who had been with them on the journey; the repulsive-looking villain, with the bushy grey moustache and hare-lip.

With heavy heart and throbbing temples, and his blood running like ice in his veins as he thought of what horrors were before him, Claude now staggered along one hall and anon up a wide spiral kind of staircase in the footsteps of the wretch La Touche, at length gaining a second hall, or corridor, above.

On either side of this passage were several doors, whilst a massive oaken one at the further end, loaded with iron and studded with nails, appeared like the entrance way of some dungeon.

To this door, dimly perceivable to Claude by the thin rays of the lamp carried by La Touche, the latter now made his way.

Aware of the folly of resistance, Claude followed:

The ruffian Cartouche close behind him with drawn sword in one hand and loaded pistol in the other.

A low laugh, that curdled the blood in his veins, now fell upon the ears of Claude, as the wretch La Touche paused at the iron bound door.

A fiendish grin stole over the villain's face:

A grin of fierce triumph!

In another moment, placing a key in the lock, the heavy door was thrown open.

All was pitchy darkness within.

Following his terrible foe, a deadly chill seized upon Claude as he entered the room.

The air of the chamber was damp and charnel-like.

An earthy odour hung in the place.

The fitful rays of the lamp but dimly illumined the spacious apartment:

Large and gloomy!

Dark and ghostly!

With a shudder our hero gazed uneasily around.

Where was he?

What was the purpose of his foes?

He was soon answered—even as the question was revolved in his brain, his hideous enemy, pointing to a corner of the chamber, held up at arm's length the lamp, which flickered dull and ghastly through the grim apartment.

A spasm of terror he could not control seized upon Duval, as in the part of the room now more fully revealed he saw a strange collection of arms and odd-looking instruments, that, hanging on the walls and lying upon the flooring, were just discernable in the fitful gleam of light.

He could not doubt where he was.

It needed not the devilish grin of malice and exultation upon the satanic features of his enemy.

Claude with a freezing horror knew the place to which they had conducted him.

He was in the boasted torture chamber:

The torture chamber of the lone chateau.

The first horror over, a wild passion now rose in the breast of Duval:

A fierce rage.

A rage that sent the blood in a rush to his heart, whilst his temples throbbed fit to bursting.

Like whipcords the veins in his forehead rose blue and knotted.

In a wild fury he attempted to burst his bonds:

But in vain; and even as the attempt was discerned by his foes, he was felled to the ground by a coward blow from the clenched fist of the ruffian Cartouche.

With a moan of pain and fury he was struggling to rise to his feet, when he was startled by a thundering crash at the outer door of the chateau:

A loud knocking imperious and continued:

A banging clatter that awoke up a thousand echoes in the lone house!

With a fierce savage look of vexation, La Touche exclaimed:

"'Tis the Band, admit them! Curses, what brought them hither at this hour? But no matter! my revenge upon this hound here will eat cold! Au revoir, Claude Duval; I must leave you for a time! I shall, however, return anon! see that you are ready to receive me!"

For a moment the evil eye glared vindictively upon him, then was gone.

A loud jarring bang sounded in his ears, as his enemies left the horrible chamber, slamming to the heavy ironbound door after them.

He was now alone:

Alone and in darkness:

In darkness, and a prisoner in the chamber of torture!

For some few moments Claude lay listening with beating heart to the sounds from below.

Voices of men high in tumult rang in his ears; this together with the banging to of doors and occasional bursts of hoarse laughter sounding to him clear and distinct.

Eagerly he strained his ears to catch the footfall of his returning foes.

But they came not.

In a few more moments the noise from below, too, ceased.

All was quiet.

Almost could Claude hear the beating of his own heart, as he lay bound and helpless in the dark and terrible chamber.

As time passed on, and his dreaded foes returned not, he asked himself, Was there no means of escape?

Was he, Claude Duval, the daring, dashing knight of the road, to perish thus in the precincts of a lone chateau in a forest in Normandy?

His pulses quickened, and his brain throbbed, as he asked himself the question!

Hope once more revived in his bosom.

Had he not passed through dangers as great as this and yet escaped unscathed?

Might he not yet elude the vigilance of his present terrible foes?

He would try.

With Heaven's aid he might yet escape.

With these thoughts in a whirl flashing through his brain, he now staggered to his feet.

His arms and wrists bound tightly, he felt that no attempt could be made at flight unless he got them free.

With deep drawn breath he now groped his way to the further end of the chamber.

There, where the rays of the lamp, when held by the villain La Touche a short time before, had revealed to him the ghastly implements of torture.

An idea conceived by Claude, he now proceeded to carry out.

One of the sharp weapons which he had seen hanging from the walls must aid to cut the ropes that confined his hands and arms.

Groping round the chamber he at length paused as a something hard struck against his foot.

Stooping down he with his manacled hands felt upon the floor for the obstruction.

A shudder for a moment passed through his frame as his fingers now came in contact with a something icy-cold.

The shudder of horror and aversion passing away, a warm glow succeeded it, as he kneeling down pressed the knot that confined his wrists upon the instrument of torture, for such indeed it was.

The cold substance he had felt a moment before was a blade of steel:

A huge sword-like blade:

A blade he remembered seeing before anything else in the glare of the light thrown upon it by the fiend La Touche.

Claude from its shape had divined then its purpose.

This blade of steel, sharp and deadly, was, when wanted for the torture, depended, swinging backwards and forwards, from the roof.

The victim, strapped to a bench just beneath the scythe, had nought to gaze upon save the slowly swinging instrument of death, which at every fresh impetus lowered yet nearer to the upturned face of the victim, till with a swinging swish it flashed right into the features, perchance across the forehead or across the mouth, just as the helpless doomed one happened to be laid.

With a convulsive thrill, as he thought of the dread purpose of the deadly steel, Claude now (not without slightly cutting his wrists) severed the cords that had so long confined them by drawing them across the sharp and horrible blade.

To remove the ligatures that fastened his arms to his side took but a minute more.

His limbs were now free.

He could combat with his foes.

He was, 'tis true, unarmed, but he could dash upon his enemies and engage in conflict, not die like a sheep in the shambles.

A warm glow diffused itself through his frame.

A prayer to Heaven escaped his lips.

Hope now once more obtained full possession in his bosom.

With beating heart and reviving courage Claude now slowly crept back to the door.

He fancied he heard a footstep without.

He was not deceived.

His hearing, always acute, had not failed to detect the tramp of a man's foot in the corridor.

Drawing his form up to its full height, Claude stretched with a glow of triumph his cramped limbs.

He seemed endowed with all his usual strength.

He longed to engage with his foes.

With no suspicion of the truth they would enter without alarm the grim chamber.

Drawing in his breath like a tiger on the spring, Claude now stood behind the door.

Gaining it a moment before he had decided on his course of action.

He would drop upon his enemies as they entered the room.

If about to be dismissed to the vale of death, one or both of them should at least follow him.

With this determination, Duval, his nerve strung as in a rack, awaited the final moment of action.

It came.

The rattle of the key in the lock of the door was followed by a loud grinding, creaking noise, as it swung back.

Claude was now hidden from the intruder.

He had forgotten that the mode of egress from the dread chamber closed inwardly.

With eyes that blazed with fury he watched the moment that he could spring with deadly effect upon his foes.

A smothered exclamation now escaped his lips—a murmur of thankful surprise.

He had only one foe to contend with:

The ruffian Cartouche—the wretch with the hare-lip.

With a low chuckle the villain crept into the room.

Softly, stealthily, lamp in hand, the fiendly servant of a fiendly master made his way into the apartment.

"Oh, oh! fainted, I suppose. Oh! these fellows are mere girls; a little suffering and, diable! they die. I hope, by the bye, the smooth-faced hound has not slipped us in such fashion, for, sacre! I care not to encounter the fury of Andrea La Touche should such indeed be the case."

"Such is not the case, sweet Cartouche!"

There was one smothered oath, a fierce ejaculation of infuriate surprise, then all was still.

Springing upon his unconscious victim as he was peering round the room, Claude had borne him with a startled cry to the floor.

In a moment of time his aggressor had snatched from the ruffian's belt a loaded pistol, and with his eyes blazing with triumph pressed the cold rim of the barrel to his forehead.

"One cry of alarm, and, sacre! by your master, Satan, and by the mother that bore thee, dog, I'll scatter your brains upon the ground!" exclaimed Claude.

The lamp that had fallen from the hands of the astounded ruffian, though it had overturned, burned yet with a dull glimmer through the dread chamber.

By its rays the discomfitted ruffian perceived that the man he had left bound was now free of his ligatures:

The helpless victim of an hour before was now kneeling on his breast, his own weapon pressed heavily on his brow.

A dull leaden hue began to steal over the ruffian's face.

He knew his life was in the hands of his late victim.

There was a desperate, savage glitter in the eyes of our hero as he knelt upon the prostrate form of his foe.

Savagely pursued as he had been, Claude determined to show to his relentless persecutors no mercy.

"Cartouche, servant of the fiendly villain, Andrea La Touche, answer me that which I shall ask; and answer truly, and without prevarication, or your own bullet shall crash into your skull! Now, firstly, tell me when is he your master coming here?"

"He will not be long," gasped the ruffian, his evil features turning a livid tint as Claude pressed the barrel of the pistol (which he had put upon full cock) against his temple.

"He will not be long?"

"No!"

"You are speaking the truth?"

"Mon Dieu, yes!"

"Why come you here alone?"

"To make the preparations."

"What preparations?"

"The preparations for your torture."

"Indeed! Well, you see, having a disinclination to the performance, sweet Cartouche, I, the moment you and your dear master left me, made my preparations in getting ready for you both a surprise; I think I have succeeded; don't you, sweet Cartouche? And now tell me! Who was it that hammered so loudly and authoritatively at the door a while back?"

"It was the Band."

"The Band?—what band?"

"Why they who inhabit and rendezvous here at the chateau!"

"Free companions I suppose; leviers of black mail here in the forest I presume?"

"Well, yes!"

"Humph! I thought so. Is the fellow La Touche leader of these brave free-traders?"

"No."

"No! take care; my pistol, or rather—I beg your pardon—your own, may go off suddenly if you don't speak the truth."

"Diable! I am speaking the truth. La Touche only owns the chateau; but the lads help him."

"I see! So far so good! And, now tell me, are the Band still here?"

"No; they were leaving when I came up."

"Oh! Pray how many of them are there?"

"There are some two dozen, but only a portion came to-night."

"Indeed! and they are now gone?"

"Yes."

"And you expect Monsieur La Touche up here presently?"

"At any moment, yes."

A glitter in the ruffian's eye caused Claude to turn his head, fancying, perhaps, that the other had at that moment appeared.

Such, however, was not the case; but the treacherous ruffian, with an idea that Claude would relax his hold, made a desperate clutch at the pistol.

The event that followed the act was horrible and startling.

Claude's finger on the trigger, the weapon, when clutched at by the wretched man, its owner, with a loud report exploded, the charge entering the upturned face of the doomed villain.

No cry · no single groan issued from the fated creature's lips.

With his mouth ripped open, and every feature blackened and disfigured by the discharge, he lay a horrible, bleeding, ghastly mass, hurried to his doom in a second of time.

"Ma foi! there's one serpent the less; that's one rubbed out; now for the master fiend; I must not be taken by surprise; but, as dear Cartouche was going to do, I must make preparations. Humph! the cards seem changing hands, and Claude, dashing Claude Duval, methinks will secure the winning one," muttered our hero, who, coolly thrusting the corpse of his former foe aside, started up and made for the door, awaiting as before the appearance of his man.

Not for long was Claude kept in suspense.

The heavy tread of some one approaching now sounded in his ears.

The report of the pistol had, as Claude suspected, aroused an alarm.

With a thrill of joy he, however, noted that it was one footfall only that sounded without.

The footfall of the fiendly villain Andrea La Touche.

With a horrible oath he now, reaching the door, strode in.

Darting to the prostrate form of the wretch Cartouche, in utmost surprise he gazed at the blood bedabbled face; then, as his keen eye roving round, he discovered not his victim, a cry of alarm and fury escaped his lips:

A cry echoed by another as with all his force Claude threw himself upon him.

"Sacre, friend La Touche! you came for a pigeon, but you've found a hawk!" exclaimed Claude as with the butt of his pistol he caught his persecutor a fearful stunning blow that, for a moment, sent him reeling like a drunken man to the ground.

No feeling of mercy was there at that moment in our hero's bosom.

He would have strangled his enemy with as little compunction as he would have done a mad dog.

But it was not the hand of the injured highwayman that was to mete out the ruffian's punishment.

The infidel, for such he was (despite his aiding in the Titus Oates' plot), was justly confounded for his crimes by a higher power than of earth.

Darting with the screech of a wild animal at Claude, the villain's foot catching in the hideous form of his late assistant, he was sent with a crash upon the floor, his head striking against one of the numerous articles used for torture that were strewn about.

A low moan escaped his lips, then a convulsive shiver shook his frame, and he was presently lying helpless, and apparently dead, beside his ruffian assistant!

With a grim smile, Claude stepped over to the now senseless form of his foe.

Keenly he watched the immovable figure.

Cautious, and watching for a surprise, Claude drew close to the extended frame of Andrea La Touche.

No sign of life, however, was given.

It was no trick, as Claude had feared.

His enemy was senseless, if not dead or dying.

Scarce believing that death had claimed the villain for its own, as he had only been struck by Claude with the butt of his pistol, our hero stooped down, and turning the discomfited ruffian over, cast a keen and searching glance into his face.

The sight he saw made Claude, despite the fiendly nature of the wretch before him, shiver with horror!

When stumbling over the corpse of the miserable wretch Cartouche, he had fallen with his face against a horrible contrivance studded with dagger blades or sharp-pointed knives.

One of these had entered the villain's single orb of vision!

Ghastly, and hideous, the doomed man looked as, now now recovering from his swoon, he rose to his feet, and, wiping the blood that was oozing from his wound, glared viciously around!

In speechless horror Claude, who had taken up the lamp, stood gazing at his late dread antagonist.

More ghastly, more fiendly than ever he now looked as, with the blood streaming from his eye, he glared wildly round.

"Curses, he has put out the light! If I mind me not he will escape! Diable! Tete bleu! How dark it is! Sacre, Claude Duval! if you think to escape me by putting out the light, parbleu! you are mistaken."

"I have not put out the light, miserable man," now said Claude, with a shudder, guessing at the horrible truth.

"You've not put out the light? Lying thief! how then is it that we are in the dark?" said La Touche, who now began, with outstretched hands, and his countenance working ferociously, to make his way in the direction of Claude's voice.

"'Tis not I that am in the dark, Andrea La Touche! 'Tis you, and you only!" said Claude, solemnly.

"Curses! What do you mean? Light the lamp, this cursed darkness appals me! 'Tis thicker, denser, than I can ever remember! Sacre! Ten thousand devils, light the lamp! Let us once more confront each other boldly! You are no coward, Claude Duval. You have by some means destroyed my faithful servant, Cartouche, he who was your match in size and strength, seek not then, under cover of darkness, to elude his master; but, light the lamp, and when I can see thee, curses! I'll have at thee, and let the best win."

With a demoniac look lighting up his hideous blood-stained features, the wretched villain here bared his arm to the shoulder, wielding aloft the bright, keen blade of a dagger.

"Andrea La Touche, wretched man, hear me! Though you would have doomed me to most hideous tortures, and would have condemned me to a lingering death, I who never did thee harm. Still, I say, I cannot fight with thee."

"And for why? Sacre! why is it that you, who have destroyed the servant dare not fight with the master? If thou thinkest by any trick to escape me in the darkness, diable! you are mistaken, though we are now alone in the chateau. Claude Duval, a portion of the St. Ardens Band will presently arrive. The door below is fast locked, the key in a place known only to myself. Ha! ha! ha! Now, Dashing Duval, will you fight with me?"

"No, wretched man!"

"Coward, you fear me!"

"Fear! Andrea La Touche, did I fear the ruffian now dead at your foot?"

"A cursed mischance it was that gave you some advantage over poor Cartouche. He is dead! Ten thousand devils! I will avenge him; you shall not escape me!"

With a curse and a savage howl, the miserable villain now made a rush at Claude, groping in a state of frenzy round the terrible apartment.

Failing to place hands upon his late victim, with a strong shudder and cry of pain, La Touche now halted in the middle of the room, drawing his hand nervously over his now glassy and bloodstained orb of vision.

"Sacre! how very dark it is! My eye too burns, burns! Diable! 'tis like a coal of fire! I feel as I never felt before. Curses! What does it mean? I will go below and return hither with a lamp."

"Andrea La Touche you need not go out of this chamber, for the lamp brought hither by the ruffian Cartouche is in the room."

"Doubtless; but I have no means of lighting it up here."

"Nor do you need, 'tis burning bright and clear."

"Liar! Ventre bleu! I guess your purpose; you would follow me below; but you cannot escape, for the outer door is hard and fast! You are in my power, Claude Duval."

"Indeed! you shall now learn the truth. I am going from the chamber; follow me," Claude here treading heavily made for the door. Attempting to rush forward, with extended arms, the doomed wretch stumbled and fell.

Rising to his feet, in a low, husky voice he, in terrified accents, exclaimed: "Curses, ten thousand devils! what does all this mean? I cannot see!"

"Andrea La Touche, you will never see again! You are blind!" said Claude, as he gazed almost pityingly upon his wretched enemy.

A horrible, ghastly look now stole over the bloodstained face of La Touche the while, in a choking, gasping voice he reiterated the words of Duval.

"Blind! blind! Curses upon him, he lies! It is done to frighten me! and yet it is very dark! whilst my eye burns

like a coal of fire ! Can he be speaking truly ? No, no, no !
It cannot be !"

"Be not deluded, wretched man ! by a terrible accident
your remaining eye has been deprived of sight ! In attempting to destroy me, you have rendered yourself blind ! You
are powerless now as the worm beneath my foot ! You will
never gaze, Andrea La Touche, upon the light of heaven
more !"

A horrible screech, shrill and appalling, issued from the
lips of the miserable man, who, as the last words were
uttered by Duval, fell huddled up in a heap upon the floor,
foaming at the mouth and in strong convulsions !

About, though not without repugnance, to lift up the
doomed man and place him in a chair, Claude was startled
from his purpose by a loud banging at the chateau !

CHAPTER XIX.

A NIGHT OF TERRORS—WHAT CLAUDE SAW IN THE VAULTED
CHAMBER OF THE CHATEAU OF ST. ARDENS –THE UNDER-
GROUND PASSAGE—THE WELL HOLE –A TERRIBLE DOOM
EVADED—THE OPENING IN THE FOREST—A CUNNING
STRATAGEM—THE ESCAPE.

Bang, bang, crash ! how hollowly the knocking resounded
through the lone house !

"The members of the Band belonging to the chateau
doubtless ! Ma foi, I am not yet out of danger it seems !"
muttered Claude, who, with a last glance at the senseless
hideous figure of La Touche, hurried, lamp in hand, from
the room.

Making his way along the corridor, he presently descended
the staircase leading to the hall below.

The knocking, now more imperative, sounded dismal and
terrible in that lone dwelling !

With a shudder, as he thought of the wretched villain
above who, unaided could scarce find his way below to
admit the rude summoners, Claude, now gaining the hall,
crept softly towards the door.

The hum of voices now came plainly to his ears.

Reaching the massive, oaken door, he now placed his
face against the panels, a fresh thundering knocking
causing him to start nervously on one side.

The echoes of the noise dying away, voices high in anger
sounded without.

"What the devil can be the matter ?"

"Sacre ! what is Cartouche up to ?"

"And La Touche, parbleu, where can he be ?"

"Perhaps drunk in the cellar !"

"Or making love to Josephine de Mortemas !"

"Tête bleu ! no ; her kisses would be too cold for him !"

"Beside that, remember, she can't be very fascinating
now !"

"Never mind that ; Andrea has only got one eye
remember !"

"And he can see better with that than you can with your
two, Rodolph !"

"Well, anyone is welcome to poor Josephine now ; she
is not for me !"

"Sacre ! you don't want cold comfort !"

"Mon Dieu ! no ; not that sort !"

A loud laugh here burst from the party without, whom
Claude guessed to be some ten or a dozen in number.

In wondering surprise he listened to their converse.

A female, it appeared, was in the house.

But had not the villain La Touche said there was no one
in the chateau save themselves.

What did the converse of the bandits without mean?

That there was something meant beyond what he could
make out Claude was certain.

Once more he placed his ears against the door, whilst
again a thundering summons for admission echoed
hollowly and dismally through the building, succeeded by
the voices of the angry ruffians congregated in the forecourt.

"It's very strange !"

"Ma foi ! yes ; I cannot make it out."

"What do you think of it, Rodolph ?"

"Why, I was just asking myself whether that cursed
fellow that was brought here has proved himself more than
a match for La Touche and our comrade with the harelip."

"Bah ! nonsense ! Was not the London thief bound and
trussed like a fowl ready for the spit ?"

"Pardieu ! and so he was."

"Anyway there is something wrong !"

"Well, yes !"

"What's to be done ?"

"Sacristi ! I know not ! We can't get in through the
keyhole !"

"Not very well, Gontron."

"What do you propose, Rodolph ?"

"Well, I suppose we must get in by the secret way."

"Diable ! I don't care about that."

"Sacre ! Nor I."

"Nor I," exclaimed a chorus of voices, all evidently
averse to gaining admission by the means suggested.

Intently, breathlessly, Claude drank in every word that
fell from the lips of those without.

There was, it seemed, some means of entering the
chamber other than by the door.

If he, Claude, could find this place, his escape were
easy.

Yet how !

It appeared little likely that he should become acquainted
with the secret exit from the old house.

A pause in the converse of those without now taking
place, all was quiet.

It was at this moment, when silence rested on all around,
that Claude was startled by the sudden noise of a heavy,
staggering footfall.

With a momentary thrill of fear he turned from the
door :

Darted aside just in time to avoid coming in contact
with a grim and ghastly form :

The hideous bloodstained figure of the miserable villain,
Andrea La Touche !

Undecided what course to take, whether to drag the wretch
away or watch unseen his further actions, Claude stood
breathlessly gazing at his every movement.

With a low hoarse chuckle he now, groping about, made
his way to the door of a room situate at the further end of
the corridor.

With the stealthy tread of a cat Claude followed.

Passing the threshold of the chamber after his vindictive,
sightless foe, he found himself in an apartment involved in
complete darkness.

No casements were there in this room, or, if so, for some
cause they had been walled up.

Breathlessly Claude stood just by the entrance.

He could hear the wretch La Touche groping about the
darksome chamber.

"Looking for the key ! That key I must have !"
muttered our hero, who now drew away out into the hall.

He did not care to cause an outcry from the villain until
he actually saw if his surmise was correct— that he was
searching for the key of the outer door.

Minute after minute passed over, and again an exclamation of fury sounding in the ears of the listener.

It was when about to himself enter the chamber and
chance a struggle with his enemy that Claude beheld him
once more groping his way out.

An ejaculation of joy escaped Claude's lips.

In the hands of the blind man was a large key.

The key of the outer door.

Making up his mind as to his course, Claude had determined to secure the article that would enable him to quit
the dread chateau, and, waiting till those without had gone,
would issue forth.

This plan was now, however, dissipated :

Was rendered impracticable.

About to hurl himself on his sightless enemy, Claude
with an exclamation of fear drew back.

A loud sound of voices rang in his ears :

Voices that echoed with the tramping of many feet inside
the house.

The robbers of the Chateau of St. Ardens had by some
means made their way in.

Meditating a rush upon La Touche for the key, Claude
the next moment gave himself up for lost.

A crowd of men now appeared, making their way through
a door situate at the furthest extremity of the hall.

Without a single weapon of defence, should he be
seized he would die without being able to strike a blow.

As yet unseen, Claude with beating heart glided by La
Touche and entered the darksome chamber from whence he
had brought the key.

Not a moment too soon had he gained his hiding-place.

With loud shouts, the strangers he had seen in the hall,
now rushed up to La Touche.

Oaths, shouts, and curses, with cries of horror, fell upon

the ears of Claude, who, in a corner of the dark room, listened to the babel without.

The robbers of the chateau were furious.

Goaded on by the blind villain La Touche, they swore the man he had vowed to slay should not escape.

With a shudder, Claude, a few feet only removed from his enemies, heard the curses heaped upon his head.

Scant mercy would he have, should he fall into the hands of the ruffians.

Bitterly he now cursed the mistaken humanity that had spared the life of the demoniac and fiendly La Touche.

But for him it would have been supposed that he, Claude, had escaped!

Whereas the ruffian band were made aware that he was still in the house.

Despair once more gathered in his breast.

There seemed little chance of escape.

Was he doomed after all, to perish in that dread chateau.

He could not believe that a merciful Providence would desert him at this last moment.

It could not be.

He would yet escape.

It did not appear that his foes meant to search the chamber he was concealed in.

The wretch, La Touche, had but just left it:

Had no suspicion of his close proximity.

His well-merited blindness had prevented his seeing the form of the man he hated glide past him.

With a thrill of joy, Claude now heard the ruffian band rush from the hall to the staircase leading to that dread room above.

The hideous torture chamber.

La Touche, leading the way, imagined his victim was still above.

With a beating heart and with a nervous thrill, Claude now softly crept up to the door of his hiding-place.

The hall was deserted.

No one was there.

The last figure of the flying horde met his sight as it was disappearing on the summit of the stairs.

With a rush, Claude now made for the other end of the hall.

There, where a short time before he had beheld the robber band start forth.

With joyful surprise, he now discovered a door partly open, and revealing a short flight of steps.

To dart down these was to Claude the work of a moment.

Banging the door after him, in total darkness he had rushed down the steps, and was presently threading the mazes of a long, narrow passage, the flooring of stone giving out strange hollow echoes to his flying footsteps.

Heedless to whither the path he was following might lead him he hurried on.

Well he knew that to fall into the hands of the robbers of the lone chateau was to meet instant death.

In wild haste he darted down the secret way.

Presently pausing, as he reached a turn in the passage, for a moment of time he stood undecided how to act.

He had now arrived at a point where the narrow turning branched off in two directions:

One to the left, enveloped in black and impenetrable gloom the other to the right, down which shone a thin ray of light.

Hesitating but for a moment he chose the latter as more cheerful and as likely for aught he knew to give him liberty as the grim and dark one.

Every minute he knew was fraught with peril.

Failing to find him in the upper part of the old building the ruffian foe would search below.

He had not a moment to lose.

In feverish haste he darted on.

Wondering whence the light proceeded that illuminated the passage he now came to a halt, as he reached a door at the top of which was an opening some two feet in depth.

Through this orifice streamed a broad ray of light:

The yellow gleam of a lamp.

Placing his hand upon the door—as he had hardly dared to hope—it yielded to his touch.

A glow from a lamp swinging from the roof of the chamber he now entered flashing in his eyes, caused Claude for a few moments to behold everything as through a gauze.

The glare, after the late darkness caused all things around to appear dim and indistinct.

Recovering from this Claude eagerly scanned the apartment he was now in.

An ejaculation of annoyance escaped him.

He found that his further progress was arrested.

He could go no further.

The chamber he had reached was small, and without door or exit of any sort.

It was a gloomy, dreary-looking place:

More resembling a vault than anything else, the flooring and walls being of stone, whilst, to the surprise of Claude, he observed the roof, from which the lamp depended, was formed of huge beams or planks of oak.

Not an article of furniture was there in the dismal dungeon-like apartment.

With a shudder he turned to go!

There was a something charnel-like in the air and appearance of the underground chamber.

A stifling, earthy, disagreeable, odour hung in the place.

It was only as he turned to go that Claude started as his eyes happened to fall upon an object in the corner:

A something lying upon the stone flooring covered over with a large sheet:

An object that bore the grim outline of a human form.

With a shudder Claude drew near and pulled the covering aside.

As he suspected the victim of assassination was revealed to his horrified gaze:

A wretched woman, apparently of middle age.

Grim and ghastly the poor creature looked.

The eyes staring up horribly in the face of the intruder!

With a sickening feeling of faintness creeping over him, Claude threw the sheet over the corpse (the head of which he noted was nearly severed from the body), and moved away to the door by which he had entered.

An exclamation of rage and despair now escaped his lips.

With a thrill he heard the heavy tread of men without.

His foes had tracked him out:

Had traced him to the vault of death:

No time had he for planning an escape.

His merciless foes were close at hand.

Their voices, as he shrank up against the wall by the door, sounded plain in his ears.

"Tonnerre de ciel! I like not this task of removing Madame Josephine."

"Nor I, Mille Combes. George, I'd sooner be of the party who are hunting the fellow who has settled poor Cartouche."

The two men here pushing open the door walked into the vaulted chamber proceeding straight over to where lay the hideous corpse.

Claude, scarce daring to breathe, with clenched teeth, finding he had but two adversaries to deal with, unarmed as he was, regained his wonted courage.

The men stooping over the corpse of the wretched woman in the corner noted not a figure that now stole lightly forth and disappeared in the passage without.

Scarce could Claude credit his good fortune as he found himself safe out of the terrible chamber of the dead.

About to dart away down the dark passages he now paused.

A sudden thought flashed through his brain, that by staying he might overhear something fall from the lips of the two men in the vaulted chamber that might aid him to a means of escape.

They evidently had no suspicion that he was in the underground portion of the chateau.

The search by the Robber Band was going on in the habitable portion of the building.

With bated breath Claude stood motionless up against the wall of the passage just without the door:

Every word uttered by the two companions in the cell falling plain to his ears.

"Now then, Cardoudal, catch hold of her feet, I'll see to her head. The sooner we get this job over, sacre, the better I shall like it."

"We convey her to the well, don't we?"

"Such are Rodolph's orders."

"Good! We shall not come back this way."

"No! Diablo! you forget we are to guard the pass into the woods in case that slippery customer that has settled La Touche by depriving him of the only eye he had left, should happen to have found out the secret path. But, allons, let us go!"

Darting away as he heard the ruffians tramping with their load out of the horrible vault, Claude now made his way along the passage till he reached that part where it diverged off.

Here he stood for a moment irresolute.

He began to think that he ought, when there half an hour before, to have taken the passage that lay now before him:

The turning that was involved in impenetrable darkness:

The lighter one had but led him to the evident receptacle of the dead:

The place where for a time the Chateau Band left their victims!

Whilst debating on his course, the tramp, tramp of the two men behind him came plain to his ears!

About to plunge into the gloomy passage that was wrapped in such inky darkness, Claude suddenly drew back, and darted a few yards down that which led the way to the hall of the chateau.

He would follow in the footsteps of the approaching foe.

There were but two, and they encumbered with their ghastly load.

Better policy Claude felt it would be to hang in their rear instead of hastening on at their head he knew not whither, as he had been doing.

He had scarce decided on this course of action when the ruffians and their terrible burthen drew near.

Passing him, and uttering vile oaths and rude jests upon their load, the two men unhesitatingly entered the dark passage.

Claude, chuckling at the success of his device, followed.

He now felt more confidence.

He had no fear of a false step on the summit of a staircase, or a fall over a sudden projection in the flooring, or the fatal result of meeting with a closed door.

Treading softly, with bated breath, he hastened on in the darkness, guided by the heavy tramp of the two robbers, and their voices sounded deep and hollow in that subterranean way.

"We are near the well, George!"

"Pesto, yes!"

"Take care, bear more to the left!"

"Bah! I know the spot."

"That's all very well; but you know how Petit Camboul got his coup de congé."

"Sacre, yes! he bore too much to the right, one night, tumbled into the well, and for once in his life took water with his spirits!"

"Mon Dieu, yes! poor Petit Camboul! Well, he was very drunk upon that occasion, for a certainty."

"Bah! was he ever sober? But, diantre, here we are; I can just see the brink of the well."

With a shudder, as he overheard this converse of the men, Claude came to a halt.

Here was a peril he had never foreseen.

A cold sweat burst out like dew upon his brow as he thought of what he had escaped.

Surely Providence was watching over him!

Had he hastened on down that fearful subterranean way, as he first intended, he would have been lost:

In a moment of time would have been hurried into eternity:

Would have perished, and in such a way, drowning in a darksome pit, used evidently by the band of the lone chateau as a burial-place for their victims:

Sick, faint, and giddy, Claude stood up against the wall of the passage.

Thick, heavy darkness hung over all; but, his eyes accustomed now to the gloom, Claude could just discern hovering ahead the outline of two human forms.

For a moment of time all was silence.

A silence presently broken by a loud splash!

Scarce could Claude avoid an exclamation of horror as the sound fell upon his ears:

The sound of a heavy body splashing deep down into a mass of water!

His blood chilled within him as he thought of the horrible death he had escaped.

For a moment he stood frozen statue-like with horror, then, recalled to himself by the sound of tramping feet, he once more glided on.

Relieved of their ghastly burden, the two men, with rapid steps, were hastening away.

Keeping to the left of the passage, Claude passed in, catching his breath, short and thick, as he presently discerned, in the opposite side of the subterranean way, a yawning cavity, the brink within a yard and a half of where he stood.

The two ruffians, who had so piteously consigned their victim to her dread resting-place, were now so far ahead that Claude could hardly hear their footsteps.

With a horror of another such danger as he had just escaped lying perchance in his path, he ran on, presently finding himself again within a few feet of the companions.

The thick, impenetrable darkness was now somewhat dispelled.

It was getting lighter.

Clearly they were nearing some outlet.

Claude now dropped more into the rear.

With no suspicion of his vicinity, the two robbers hastened on.

No sound now emanated from their footsteps.

The ground at this point, upon glancing to his feet, Claude found was wet and soft.

Here and there, small pools of water had collected.

Looking up to the roof of the underground passage, to his surprise he discovered it was quite moist, and dripping with water.

Water in thin threads, at this point, trickled down the walls.

In wondering surprise, Claude now passed on, presently pausing in his progress.

The two men, in whose footsteps he was treading, had come to a halt.

The foremost he discerned making his way up some rude steps, the latter only just distinguished by Claude, as he had been obliged to fall far back in the rear, fearing his enemies might glance round and discover him.

To the astonishment of Claude, the fellow who had mounted the steps, now passed through some opening above.

As his bulky form passed out of sight, a broad stream of daylight pouring into the subterranean way.

His companion presently following, Claude was free to hurry forwards.

Slowly, cautiously, however, he traversed the remainder of the passage.

At any moment the enemy might return.

All was quiet, however.

Save the drip, drip, of the water, as it trickled from the roof in his rear, all was still.

With a sigh of relief, Claude now gained the steps, at the summit of which, the members of the robber band had disappeared.

Casting his glance upwards, he discovered, near the wall of earth, at this point, a large opening.

The passage ending at this spot, the exit was through the opening.

With clenched teeth, and with deep-drawn breath, ready prepared for a struggle should he now be intercepted, Claude made his way up the steps.

It was not without a nervous thrill, accompanied by a devouring curiosity, that he mounted the rude ladder. Gaining the topmost round, to his surprise he encountered a thick mass of brambles:

A thick growth of wild plants and bramble bushes.

With a low chuckle of delight, he read the secret.

The exit from this underground passage opened out in the forest which surrounded the chateau.

Claude now prepared for the coming struggle:

A struggle that he knew was inevitable.

He could hear the voices of the two men who had unknowingly led him through the secret way.

They were guarding the subterranean path.

Guarding it, in case he should have discovered it, and attempt an escape.

A low laugh escaped Claude's lips.

He had no fear of his foes.

His presence so close was not dreamt of.

There was every chance of his falling upon them, and surprising them.

Slowly, cautiously, with the stealthy cunning of a beast of prey, Claude now pushed his way through the tangled brushwood.

He heeded not the prickly thorns that (had he like his foes plunged quickly through) would not have harmed him:

CLINGING TO THE GUNWALE OF THE BOAT, CLAUDE GLARED WILDLY AT THE FIENDLY VAUGHAN.

He cared not for the sharp, pricking, needle-like tendrils of the brambles; but slowly, slowly drew his form through the thick and tangled mass, till at length, himself unseen, he was able to gaze around, taking in with quick, searching gaze the advantages open to him for an escape, or for a surprise of his enemies.

To his delight and surprise, Claude now found that he was at the bottom of a hollow or glade in the woods.

All around the sides of the hollow were clothed with bushes and wild vegetation, the same as that amongst which he lay concealed.

Some ten yards from his place of concealment stood the two robbers he had followed through the secret passage.

These fellows were swearing and talking loudly.

Both were armed, swords depending from their waists, and pistols in their belts.

Huge, stalwart ruffians were they, their faces bronzed and covered with a forest of hair, rendering their appearance rather formidable.

With compressed lips Claude drew a deep breath.

He saw in an open encounter with these ruffians, unarmed as he was, he stood but little chance.

Should he suddenly make his appearance, ere he could rush upon them, they might shoot him down like a dog.

It was now broad day, the early morning sun, in a golden glow, bathing all in its rich light.

For a moment or two Claude lay thinking over the best course to be pursued.

To openly rush out upon his enemies, was not to be thought of, unless he was actually driven to it.

Unarmed as he was, stratagem was his best course:

And stratagem he decided on.

It was a bold and cunning plan that which Claude now decided to pursue.

Taking his cap from his head, he proceeded to stuff it with portions of the wild plants that grew all around him.

This done, he, pushing his way forwards till he was almost protruding from his hiding-place, thrust his cap just without the shrubbery, resting it so that any one at a few yards distant, would naturally imagine it was some one who, hiding in the vegetation, was preparing to make his way into the hollow.

"That will do it, I fancy! Now then, my friends, for the other part of the performance!" muttered Claude, who, with a grin, now struggled through the thick bushes some two yards away from the opening to the underground passage.

It was not without much pain and trouble, that he accomplished this, nor scarce had he gone as far as he purposed, ere he noted that the voices and laughter of the two robbers, in the centre of the hollow, had ceased.

"Mai foi! they sight the cap. Ventre bleu! they think the head is in it. What asses these fellows are!" muttered Claude, who, his face now in a broad grin, peered through the shrubbery at his foes.

Standing side by side, the ruffians were evidently undecided how to act.

They had fallen into the trap set by our hero.

They had sighted the cap.

But, herculean armed ruffians as they were, they evidently hesitated at dashing forwards.

In spite of his danger, Claude could scarce restrain a roar of laughter at the words and actions of the bandits.

"Sacre! that's the cursed devil who slew our comrade in the torture chamber:"

"Who has blinded La Touche for life:"

"He has found out the secret way!"

"Diable! yes."

"I say, Cardondal, go and fetch him out!"

"Mon Dieu! not likely. Depend upon it he is watching us."

"Parbleu! yes. Let's fire at him!"

"That's it! Then we will rush in upon him."

Sacre, yes! and put our swords in him. Ten thousand devils! he shan't laugh at us!"

"Sacristi, no! Now then, let him have it!"

"We'll both fire."

"Parbleu, yes!"

"Are you ready?"

"Yes."

Bang! bang! simultaneously the report rang in the air.

With wild shouts, the cowardly ruffians then dashed forward.

Both threw themselves headlong into the thicket.

Whilst Claude, with a low laugh, stealing forth, darted across the hollow, in a couple of minutes gaining, unseen, the opposite side.

His device had proved more successful than he had hoped:

He had thought to draw the fire of his enemies, and then rush upon them standing the chance of a struggle; but their furious onslaught and his attempted capture in the brushwood he had not foreseen.

For one moment Claude stood upon the edge of the hollow to glance back; then, as he heard a perfect howl of fury and behold one of his enemies frantically waving aloft his cap, he turned and bounded away with the fleetness of a fawn into the mazes of the forest:

As he bounded on, ever and again giving vent to a scream of mirth at the success of his stratagem.

CHAPTER XX.

THE FLIGHT THROUGH THE WOODS—STRANGE ADVENTURES—ARRIVAL AT BARFLEUR—THE SAUCY KIT AND THE SMUGGLER KING—THE SECRET CAVE—A CAROUSAL.

Hurrying on through the woods, Claude paused not till, spent with fatigue and out of breath, he felt he could go no further.

He had now arrived at a part of the French forest almost impervious:

So thickly grew the wild vegetation, so numerous were the giant trees, that he found he could hardly force his way on.

Glad of a pretext for a rest, he threw himself upon the greensward that flourished green and beautiful in the tiny glade where he had halted.

Like some spot artfully devised by man, not a freak of nature, was it that Claude had gained:

Surrounded with forest growth of every description, the spot upon which he now rested from his fright was lighted up by the full rays of the sun.

The nearest trees failed with their outspreading branches to shut out the orb of day from this fairy-like glen.

Reclining at length upon the sward a soft, dozy feeling crept over Claude.

Like a wild dream, a phantasmagoria, seemed the hideous scenes he had gone through since missing his comrade, Gentleman Jack, in the pinetree grove near Highgate.

Almost could he now fancy himself there, as the birds, fluttering from branch to branch, chirruped merrily their sweet notes, reminding him of England's forest glades.

With the mirthful songs of the feathered songsters trilling thus in his ears, and all around in peaceful happiness, the only sounds beyond the carolling of the birds, the sighing, gentle murmur of the soft breeze that, laden with perfume, stirred the branches of the trees, our hero, thoroughly exhausted by his late trials, dropped off into a quiet sleep, that ended in a heavy and prolonged slumber.

How long he had actually lain there Claude knew not, but on awakening was surprised to find the sun was gradually sinking in the skies; from this he gathered that he must have rested in that quiet retreat many hours.

Rising to his feet, his limbs stiff and cramped, he now prepared to hurry on.

Not without dismay he glanced around him:

His position, though safe from the accursed chateau, was anything but a pleasant one:

In the fastnesses of a lone forest in Normandy unarmed, and not yet many miles from the haunt of crime, where he had near met a terrible death.

"Humph! I would I were safe at Calais, making my way on board some vessel to be safely landed once more in the land that shelters all I hold dear on earth! Curses on the villain Philip La Roche, that sent me here with his plotting papers! If I got back sound in wind and limb! Sacre, my friend of the brotherhood of the Cross and Dagger! if I don't make England too hot to hold you, my name ain't Claude Duval! Mon Dieu! I must push on. I care not for a night in these wilds, though unaided how I am to make my way out of them is a mystery. Ma foi! the sun sinks lower yet lower in the sky. Parbleu! I must get out of this, or darkness will render me a prisoner till the morn."

Dashing forwards Claude now dived once more through the thick mazes of the forest:

Whilst darker yet darker grew the shades of night.

Uneasily he glanced around him as he tore his way on.

Hunger and thirst now assailed him.

Not for hours had he tasted food.

It was imperative that he should, by some means, now appease the ravening demands of nature.

Passing out from the thick undergrowth he had been traversing, he stumbled across a brawling stream, the limpid waters of which immediately relieved his thirst; but, as he again hurried on, the gnawing pangs of want and an earnest longing for food pressed him sorely.

It was with much alarm that Claude now observed the shadows growing darker and darker around him.

With a shiver of nervous fear he hurried on.

The vast and silent solitude by which he was surrounded, the deep, solemn, and oppressive stillness which pervaded the forest, unnerved and depressed him.

"Pleasant, this, very! Parbleu! from all appearances I'll have to rough it in these wilds for the night! Sacre! I would not care if I were armed; but to travel on thus, at the mercy of any fellow who may choose to assail me, is little to my liking!" muttered Claude, as he pushed on down a dark avenue of trees, the thick branches of which, interlaced overhead, shut out the dying sunbeams. It was upon emerging from this darksome track that he was startled by the sudden appearance of a man, who, with a bundle of faggots on his shoulders, might have been taken, by one less astute than our hero, for a simple woodcutter; but there was a villanous expression in the stranger's face, together with the startling and sudden way in which he had appeared, that told Claude the fellow was not what he seemed, causing him to draw aside in distrust, and with a determination to keep a watchful eye upon this companion, who so mysteriously had crossed his path.

"Hallo! who the deuce may you be who travel thus alone? Art not afraid, man?" Rough and hoarse was the stranger's speech, whilst a cunning smile wreathed his features, the ugliness of which was enhanced by the vivid scar of a sabre wound, which stretched from the left brow to the chin, giving a sinister look to the face.

Keenly eyeing his interrogator, Claude, with a laugh, exclaimed:

"As to your query of who I am, I have an instant answer—find out; for your second remark—Ma foi! I do not want to boast, but I am one who know fear but by name; and if anyone, thinking by my appearance that I am likely to prove an easy victim should violence be intended, ventre bleu! they will be most egregiously mistaken!"

Coo', calm, and defiant, Claude here, at the verge of the avenue, in the gathering gloom faced the burly form of the stranger; he noted a savage glitter in the man's eyes, and a ferocious expression in the forbidding countenance that foretold hostilities; nor was his suspicion as to the fellow's intentions incorrect, for with a curse he now threw down his bundle of faggots, and, with a hoarse laugh, bared a sinewy arm, which bristled with long black hair to the shoulders, whilst the huge brawny fist he clenched was hard enough to fell an ox.

"Ha, ha, ha! you don't know me! I'm the Butcher!"

"You're the Butcher, are you? Ma foi! the intelligence does not much interest me," said Claude, with a cool, defiant smile.

"Don't it? Perhaps something else will interest you that I have to tell you? I'm going to St. Ardens!"

"Indeed! and where the devil may that be?" said Claude, who could not help a slight start of nervousness as he detected the gleaming eyes of his herculean adversary glaring viciously into his.

"Hem! you don't know anything of St. Ardens?"

"No."

"Not the chateau?"

"What chateau?" A slight shiver here again shook Claude's frame.

"Why the lone chateau owned by a Monsieur La Touche, of St. Omer! Ah, I see you know that party!"

Claude, finding a suspicion, conceived a few seconds before correct, that he had fallen across a member of the Bandits of the Forest, had started back with clenched hands, nerving himself for a struggle with the man before him that he knew must soon take place.

"Well, I didn't think this morning, when I heard of you and your clever performance, that my luck would send you plump into my grasp, Monsieur Claude Duval; do you know that of all the Band of the lone chateau I am the strongest and most feared?"

"Are you, indeed? How long, my dear Butcher, may I ask, has your trumpeter been defunct?"

"Claude Duval!"

"That's I, Butcher!"

"You are a bold man and a pretty one; but I think I'll spoil your beauty."

"Sorry, Butcher, that I shall not be able to return the compliment, seeing you've no beauty to spoil; like our sweet friend La Touche you belong to the family of Ugly Mugs. By the bye! how does Monsieur progress? I had forgotten it's a case with him of 'I wish I could see, but I can't!' what a capital hand he will make at blind man's buff! he was lovely with one eye, how trancedently handsome he must look with none!"

"Don't hallo! perhaps you'll have none presently."

"How so, dear Butcher?"

"Why, curse me, if I don't have your peepers out of your head; the moon now rising shall be the last of light that you shall behold, Claude Duval. Mon Dieu! I'll lead you back to the Band without your eyes, curse me if I don't!"

A ferocious chuckle here escaped the ruffian's lips, who, making sure in his great strength of easily conquering his slim antagonist, had remained intently eyeing his victim.

Claude, however, had been warily watching an opportunity to spring in an unguarded moment upon his herculean foe.

He had observed thrust in the ruffian's belt a pair of pistols and a large knife; these, disclosed as the blouse he wore was blown aside by the breeze, our hero determined if possible to secure.

He knew that failure in this would be death, or something worse.

The ruffian would doubtless carry out his threat:

Would deprive him of sight:

Leading him back thus mutilated to perish slowly by horrible tortures in the dreadful building from which he had escaped the preceding day.

The thought of this horror nerved Claude with fictitious strength.

He must conquer by cunning and audacity his herculean foe, or he would be lost.

In a fair encounter he felt he would have no chance.

About then to bound boldly upon the stalwart ruffian who in his towering strength stood before him, Claude was diverted from his purpose by a low, fierce, growl.

Starting back with an exclamation of alarm, he now beheld emerging from a thick clump of copse a huge boar:

A wild boar of the largest size.

Like balls of fire shone the eyes of the monster; whilst its white tusks, fully revealed as it stood bristling with rage at the human figures before him, shone ominously in the deepening gloom.

Swaying its huge frame backwards and forwards, it now prepared to spring at its prey.

The click of the pistol, that the ruffian Butcher had pulled from his belt, falling on the animal's ears, drove it to frenzy.

A moment after there was a loud report, that woke up echoes in the forest: a report that was followed by a wild growl of terrible import.

For a minute or two, Claude beheld the huge beast convulsively tearing up the turf as it rolled over and over on the earth; then the bandit, who had successfully launched his bullet into the brain of the wretched beast, now stood over it and plunged the broad bright blade of his knife up to the haft in its throat, from which the blood in a second, gushed forth in a torrent.

Chuckling as he bent over the beast, the ruffian had forgotten his human victim.

Flight was open to Duval.

The woods were now involved in darkness.

A dash into the thicket and he might escape the villain who had crossed him.

But our hero, as history has told, was a bold determined man.

The ruffian of the Chateau Band was off his guard.

Claude saw his opportunity:

He would not coward-like flee:

He would boldly attack him.

Like lightning these thoughts revolved through his brain.

Drawing his knife out of the boar's throat, the stranger was now about to rise, when his forgotten foe threw himself upon him.

Snatching at the remaining pistol in the ruffian's belt, Claude, using all his strength, succeeded in hurling him to the ground.

No words issued from the mouths of the enraged antagonists.

Locked in a deadly embrace, Duval being seized in the other's herculean grasp, both were presently rolling on the sward.

Anon, a fierce oath escaped the lips of the ruffian bandit.

He had succeeded in launching Claude beneath him.

Wildly the villain now searched for his knife that had dropped in the scuffle.

"Ho, ho, ho! so you thought to take me unawares? Ha, ha, ha! you thought you could overcome the Butcher? Sacre! let me get my knife, I'll make something of you presently, my clever young friend. I have you now; you can't escape!"

Sighting the knife, which, covered with blood, lay by the body of the boar, the ruffian sprang up to secure it.

In a moment of time Claude cocked the pistol his enemy had forgotten, and, starting to his feet, fired in the ruffian's face, as with horrible oaths he bounded forwards with the knife.

With a howl of fury that echoed strangely through the woods, the huge herculean bandit staggered back, falling heavily to the earth.

A low gurgling sob succeeded the frantic yell, then a convulsive shiver shook the huge bulk which rolled over on its side.

Then all was still!

The moon now lighting up the woods threw a pale silvery radiance over the scene of death.

Like one in a dream, Claude glared at a pool of blood that was gathering horribly about his feet.

Side by side lay the ravening boar and its executioner.

With a thrill Claude stooped down and peered into the countenance of his late foe:

The man who, in all his boasted strength, had been vanquished by his slim and agile victim.

A livid look had stolen over the face of the robber:

No longer the eyes gleamed with savage passion.

A film had already stolen over them:

The film of death!

The bullet-hole in the forehead told where the fatal shot had sped.

Buried in the ruffian's brain, death had been instantaneous.

"So the wretched villain has gone to his account! Well; mai foi! it was his life or mine. Luck was against you, Butcher. Parbleu! you will butcher no more upon this earth, that's certain. But I must thank thee for finding me in weapons of defence, having left me sole heir to your property. Morbleu! I will stow my unexpected wealth about me, and then see about getting something to recruit my strength. After which, diable! I will show this infernal forest a clean pair of heels," said Claude, who now coolly secured the pistols and powder-flask, and a heavy purse that he found on his dead foe, and, turning round, went over the carcase of the boar.

"A supper of wild boar's meat won't be so bad, and, sacre! I'm so infernal hungry I could almost eat it raw, but I see no reason why I shouldn't have a fire. I must bivouac in the woods, so I may as well make myself as comfortable as circumstances will permit."

Having cut a steak from the dead beast, and severing one of the feet, Claude, presently after, tramped from the spot, and, walking on, halted at length underneath the wide-spreading branches of an aged oak that reared its height beside a little brawling, meandering stream that rippled and bubbled through this part of the forest.

Gathering some dry sticks and a quantity of bramble and furze, he now prepared to camp for the night.

By means of his pistols, snapping some powder in the pans, he soon ignited his fire.

Placing the steak of the boar over the blazing embers, his nostrils were soon saluted with a, to him, most savoury odour.

Charred and black as it was on the outer surface, without bread, salt, or other condiment, Claude presently partook ravenously of his rude fare.

Tortured with direst hunger, he thought he had never in his life made so delicious a meal, though upon ordinary occasions he would have tossed his boar's steak to a dog as not fit to be eaten.

"Mai foi! hunger is a good sauce," he muttered; finishing his primitive meal, he sat by the embers of his fire, ever and again peering round searchingly into the mazes of the wood.

Well armed, and his appetite appeased, he now cared not.

He felt not the fear that had oppressed him an hour before.

He was now in a position to face any enemy he might meet with, either of the human or brute form.

Determining to go no further till the early dawn, he heaped more brushwood on his fire, and, with no inclination for sleep, watched anxiously for the light of another day.

It was a strange scene to Claude:

There alone in that French forest:

The ruddy glare from the fire casting fantastic shadows around.

Thinking of the friends so far away, wondering if all was going well, asking himself if the pretty Maude was at that moment dreaming or thinking of him, our hero, alone by his watch-fire, sat moodily, impatiently awaiting the approaching dawn.

Thick darkness now overhung the woods.

Save the immediate spot around his bivouac fire, all was wrapped in impenetrable gloom:

A gloom, thick, heavy, and dense.

Like diamonds the stars twinkled and glittered in the sky.

The moon presently rising high up, shone with a shimmering light over the vast forest.

A nervous sensation, a creeping crawling of the flesh, passed through the frame of the lone watcher as he sat gazing up at the silvery moon.

His thoughts had reverted suddenly to the wretch Vaughan.

Where was the wretch at that moment?

Was his dearest Maude safe with Jack and Paul, or had aught of harm befallen her?

Thinking thus, it was with throbbing heart and burning temples that Claude at length started to his feet:

Started to his feet as a low mournful wail sounded through the woods:

The wail or cry as of some wretched being in a dying agony or deadly fear!

Intently Claude listened.

Was he deceived?

Yet no; in a second of time again the mournful sound thrilled in his ears:

A cry of pain, of abject terror:

A cry echoing hollowly and mournfully through the forest!

With a nervous grip Claude clutched the barrels of his pistol.

Then his fingers sought the haft of the deadly weapon he had picked up beside the dead boar.

It was all right.

The dangerous instrument was safe.

Thus armed he cared for nought.

Boldly, as again the sad wailing cry sounded in his ears, he left the spot.

Carefully, slowly, he made his way through the woods.

Once or twice he halted and gazed back at a reflection of light through the trees:

The dying shadows of his watch-fire;

But no sound of alarm, no shout of concealed foe rang in his ears.

Once the thought flashed through the mind of Claude as to whether the cry of pain that had aroused him was but a trick of his foes to lure him to their sides.

Then, as again the mournful wail rang in the night air, this idea was abandoned.

The terrible cry was one of real pain:

Emanating from a creature in dire peril!

Cautiously Claude pressed on.

With keen searching glances he peered into every thicket.

Following the direction of the cry that had alarmed him and aroused his pity, he now paused as once more, this time with startling distinctness, the sound echoed in the woods:

Echoed close beside him:

Sounded within hail!

About to shout out to give warning of his presence, he paused, and remained mute.

Should foes be near at hand, a cry from him would bring them to his side.

He must be wary:

Cautious, and cunning!

Claude's repeated dangers had rendered him as wily as the American savage:

As cunning as the fox!

With a grim smile he placed his knife ready to his hand, and drew both pistols from his belt.

The latter, in full cock, were ready for immediate service.

Armed thus, his pistols presented ready to fire at any foe that might appear, Claude now again crept forwards.

He had now reached a thick, tangled mass of copse.

So thick was the undergrowth all around him that he could scarce proceed.

Pausing irresolutely again, he was startled by the smothered mournful cry for aid,

"Help, help!"

Plain, though fainter in volume, came the cry in his ears.

He was close to the sufferer, who was evidently about to cease the mournful note of alarm.

Once more the cry echoed in the silent air, fainter, and more feeble.

Then all was silence.

Intently Claude listened.

But the sad wail ceased.

Save the sighing murmur of the breeze as it rustled the forest trees, or the occasional noise of some animal dashing through the thickets, all was still.

"It's strange, very strange!" muttered Claude, who now, slowly and cautiously, tore his way through the brushwood, at length, after some pains, emerging out upon an open space in the woods :

A large open space some quarter of a mile in extent :

An open space surrounded with dense forest.

With a quick, searching glance, Claude cast his eyes around.

For a moment nothing out-of-the-way appeared to meet his inquiring gaze.

The moon, bright and clear, shone full over the open tract in the woods.

A dark shadow, in a far corner, now attracted Claude's attention :

The dark shadow of a building.

For a moment or two he thought his eyes had deceived him.

But no ; on going a little forwards, he now made out the object before him.

It was that of a lone hut :

A rude tenement, of rough-hewn logs :

The abode of some poor woodcutter or charcoal-burner.

Clearly, plainly, was the tenement revealed in the shimmering steel blue rays of the moon.

Slowly, cautiously, our hero began to approach the lone habitation.

With a start, and nearly letting fall the pistols he held in his grasp, Claude was now horrified by another wild shriek for aid, awaking up the stillness around.

Glaring round, he searched in vain for the sufferer.

Warily he now approached the hut.

He began to think the awful cry proceeded from thence.

With his nerves on the rack, and watching for any sudden surprise, he now made for the lone dwelling.

An oppressive stillness now rested over the woods :

A quiet, the more depressing after the former harrowing shrieks echoing in the air.

Without meeting interruption, Claude now gained the hut.

Breathlessly he listened for a renewal of the strange harrowing cry.

But none came.

All was oppressively still.

The bright moon shone lustrously overhead, lighting up the open glade ; but no strange form, no hidden foe started forth upon the lone intruder.

Nervously Claude now, first glancing keenly round, made for the door of the hut.

All was still as death within.

Not a sound broke the stillness of the scene.

Almost would it have been a relief to hear again the wailing cry for help.

But it came not.

Like a city of the dead was the vast solitude.

Gaining the door of the rude hut, Claude, not without trepidation, placed his hand upon the latch.

To his surprise the door, unbarred, at once opened to his touch.

Starting back with levelled pistols he now watched anxiously for any persons who might issue forth.

Two, three, four minutes Claude stood, statue-like, by the threshold of the lone hut.

But no human figure came forth.

The pale moonbeams in a sea of silvery light poured in through the open door, now swinging back wide on its hinges ; but no stranger came from within to confront the wanderer of the night.

His curiosity now thoroughly aroused, Claude unhesitatingly passed through the open door.

All was quiet within the hut.

No harrowing sight met his gaze.

No victim of foul murder, weltering in his blood, lay stretched before him.

There was no living thing in the rude dwelling.

The lone hut was empty.

The interior, fully revealed by the lamp that shone with its blue glare in the azure sky above, Claude in an instant discovered harboured no living thing.

In surprise and awe he eagerly searched the habitation.

Nothing, however, rewarded his scrutiny. Save a cotton blouse, a worsted cap, and a woodman's axe, he found nothing to excite alarm or suspicion.

"It's very strange ! What can it mean ?"

Striding forth once more into the glade, Claude now casually raised his eyes to the roof of the dwelling.

With a start he uttered an exclamation of surprise and horror !

The sight that met his riveted gaze was a terrible and novel one !

The bough of a tree that grew at the back of the hut projected completely over the roof.

Doubtless the rude dwelling had been built purposely beneath the leafy foliage, which served to protect it from winter storms and summer sun.

The projecting branch of the tree it was that now fixed Claude's gaze.

Swaying to and fro from this limb was the body of a man :

A man completely nude :

Stripped to the skin !

No victim of hanging, however, was this.

The fatal rope was circled not round the neck.

The victim, so grotesque and grim, depended from the branch of the tree by a rope passed beneath his arms.

Swaying backwards and forwards over the roof of the habitation below, the wretched man looked strange and terrible, the unwonted sight intensified by a kind of horrible burlesque attaching to it.

Fastened to the wretched victim's waist was the tail of some wild animal, this dependage floating down behind causing almost a laugh to issue from the lips of the beholder, as the unhappy victim of refined cruelty swung too and fro.

"Well, this is a go ! Mon Dieu ! Poor wretch, 'twas his cries, it's certain, that I heard ; but now, I wonder whether he still lives, or whether fright and exposure have indeed destroyed him ! How the deuce shall I get him down ? If he is not dead and I cut the rope, the fall, the height he is into the roof, and from thence to the ground, will about do for him ! Confound it, I don't know what to be up to ! I can't leave him there, and life yet in him ! Sacre ! I have it ! I must lengthen the rope and lower him down, that's the ticket ! Ma fci ! I must be quick, too ; the dawn will soon break, and I must make all speed to the coast, for, sacristi ! the sooner I get on board some bark to carry me to merry Eulaud the better I shall like it ; though if I lose hours over this job, it is not the creed of Claude Duval to leave any fellow being in distress where he can aid him !"

Hastening now into the hut, Claude presently issued forth with the blouse, a sack, and one or two other articles he had before discerned when searching the place. To tear these things into strips did not consume much time, and in about half an hour he had fashioned a very decent kind of rope.

Glancing, ever and again, up at the strange figure depending from the tree, Claude began to think life had left the victim.

No cry pealed forth from the lips of the wretched man.

It seemed as though the fiat of doom had gone forth.

Hurrying his preparations, Duval now, in feverish haste, made his way to the back of the hut.

Not without difficulty he then began to ascend the tree.

Bare of branches below, his task of ascending the trunk was no easy one.

Slowly and laboriously, he at length, however, conquered :

Was at length stretched upon the projecting bough that hung over the roof of the hut :

The bough, from the further end of which depended a human form.

Very cautiously Claude now went about the conclusion of his task.

It was with a nervous tremor that he noted his weight, as he crawled far out upon the limb of the tree, bent the branch ominously down.

At any moment the limb might break off from the parent stem.

The height to the ground below was many feet.

A fall might cause a painful death.

Hesitating, Claude ceased to make his way out any further.

He fancied he heard an ominous creaking noise.

Another foot in advance and, like the stem of a pipe between the fingers, the branch might snap in twain !

"It won't do ; I must give it up !"

Scarce had these words left his lips ere Claude was startled by a wild piercing scream :

A scream so sudden and so startling that he nearly let go.

his hold of the branch upon which he reclined at full length. Recovering his equanimity and his balance, with terrified gaze Claude peered down below.

A few feet further out, and hanging half the distance to the roof below, he beheld the form of the unhappy stranger.

The face of the wretched man was ghastly pale.

With wild staring eyes he was glaring up at the tree.

He had evidently noticed that the bough was much bent:

Was much nearer to the roof:

And was giving signs of breaking!

Wild agony shone in the face of the doomed man!

"Help, help! Mon Dieu! no help is nigh! I'm lost, lost!"

"No; despair not, my poor fellow; I'll risk my own life to save you. Diable! here goes, it is but a tumble."

A shriek of joy now rang in the air as Claude shouted out that he was prepared to render aid.

Daringly, with his usual reckless defiance of danger, our hero now, like a huge snake, wriggled his way to the extremity of the branch.

Creaking and groaning the limb appeared each moment as though about to snap from the trunk.

Wildly a livid face was now upturned to Claude's.

A pair of eyes, glistening with terror and hope combined, met his.

A murmured blessing on his head, and a wild prayer for aid from the one above, broke from the pale blue lips of the stranger.

His arms pinioned behind his back he was incapable of rendering the slightest service to his adventurous and daring friend.

Claude now, as coolly and calmly as though resting on the ground, unwinding his ingeniously contrived rope, fastened it to that which was looped round the bough of the tree.

With frenzied gaze his every action was watched by the wretched man below.

"You must look out now, my friend, I'm going to cut the rope and lower you down."

"Mon Dieu! Heaven bless you, stranger! If I forget this aid may the Lord forget me!" sobbed the unfortunate.

Having made fast the fresh coil of rope, Claude now cut the one fastened round the tree.

He shivered slightly as the bough bent and creaked.

But keeping his nerve he allowed the rope to slowly uncoil itself, whilst he held one end firmly in his grasp.

Slowly, but surely, as the rope was allowed by Claude to pay out, the form of the helpless man was lowered towards the ground.

Anon his feet touched the roof of the hut.

With a loud cry he now bade Claude to look to himself. A fall from the roof would harm him not, he said.

Dreading each instant that the friendly branch might part, Claude, nothing loth, now left the stranger to slide from the hut to the ground, whilst he made his way back to the trunk of the tree.

Perspiring with fear and exertion, it was with exquisite relief that he at length in safety gained the trunk.

To descend now to the ground was an easy task, and in another five minutes he was bending over the body of the ill-fated stranger, who had boldly rolled himself from the roof of the hut a moment before.

With a knife Claude's first act was to cut the thongs that bound the wretched man's hands and feet.

Scarce was this accomplished ere he was on his knees before our hero, and with sobs and prayers of thankfulness was kissing the hands that had saved him from a lingering torturous death.

Dawn had now broken upon them:

The bright and crimson tint of the early morning sun shining with golden glory upon the heads of our hero and the wretched man whom he had snatched from death.

"How—how can I ever repay this debt of a life?" gasped the stranger, as, with Claude, he now entered the hut.

"Talk not thus! 'twas my duty, man! Sacre! do you think I could have gone on and left you to perish? But tell me, prythee, how came you in such a plight?"

"I was strung up as you saw me by a fiend, a demi-devil —one of the bandit crew that haunt these woods, making their rendezvous at the old Chateau of St. Ardens, some few leagues from this!"

"Indeed! is it possible that I have rescued you from the malice of one of those accursed thieves?"

"Even so, stranger! You know the band then—have perchance been prisoner amongst them?"

"I have; and have left them a memento mori of my visit.'

"How? what mean you?"

"Simply that I have helped make their accursed chief, a man called La Touche, hopelessly blind, for it was in attempting my life the wretch lost the sight of his only eye!"

"Mon Dieu! this is great news, stranger; well I know the villain La Touche, and I can but thank Heaven that he is now incapable of doing further harm. He is properly punished by the power at which he scoffs."

"Ma foi! yes; you say aright! and now tell me, know you one of the accursed band called the Butcher?"

With a start the stranger he had saved, a young man of some four or five and twenty, paused in the act of arraying himself in some articles of clothing he had drawn from a hidden receptacle in the hut and glared with livid face upon Claude: the while his eyes fairly blazed with fury as he exclaimed—

"Know that fiend—the Butcher as he proudly calls himself? who does not know him for miles around?—he who in his evil deeds spares neither man nor child? he whose hands are red with the blood of hundreds? he, that fiend beside whom the wretch La Touche is almost an angel?"

"A pretty character, truly! Parbleu! a nice young man; you know him, then?"

"Diable! yes; he murdered my brother—my only one; and it was he who, yesterday, strung me up over the roof of my hut to perish, with fiendish gibes bidding me, when I was tired, cut myself down. I am almost inclined to think the monster bears a charmed life so often hath he escaped the doom intended for him."

"I can set your mind at rest about the fellow, my dear young friend; I can, if you like, give you a convincing proof that he does not bear a charmed life."

"How—what mean you?"

"Why, the wretch is dead!"

"Dead? impossible!"

"No impossibility at all about it!"

"Are you sure of this, stranger?" exclaimed the young man eagerly.

"As sure as that you and I are standing here."

"How came he to perish?"

"By receiving a bullet from one of his own pistols in his brain."

"You saw him die?"

"Certainly I did! for 'twas my hand that fired the shot."

"Yours?"

"Even so."

"Mon Dieu! how were you able to cope with his fearful brute strength?"

"By matching against it wit and cunning."

"And your hand it was that gave him his coup de coup?"

"Yes, he is dead enough; I left him some hours back taking a sweet siesta beside the carcase of a defunct boar: the Butcher shot the beast and I shot the Butcher!"

"And he is gone—dead?"

"Yes; unless a fellow can live with a hole drilled through his forehead, and an ounce of lead in his brain, dead he most decidedly is!"

"Thank Heaven!"

"Yes. Ma foi! I think Heaven is to be thanked that aided me to rid the earth of a villain such as our mutual friend, the Butcher. But, come! you spoke but now of repaying to me the debt of gratitude for the preservation of your life; you can, in your turn, assist me at once."

"How? Oh, name the means—my life is yours!"

"Nay, the service I require will not, I fancy, imperil that; 'tis but to guide me out of this forest, the paths of which you are doubtless familiar with, and further, to aid me, if in your power, to reach the seacoast."

"Oh yes! this I can do, dear friend, and more: I have a cousin, an Englishman, owner of a vessel that runs short trips to the British Isle; and we will go to his favourite retreat off the coast at Barfleur, and at my request you will be conveyed to England without delay; but I must inform you that my cousin is one who deals in merchandise that pays no duty."

"He is a smuggler, then," said Claude with a smile.

"Ma foi! yes, and a bold and daring one."

"Then he is the man for me! I doubt not we shall soon be friends and true comrades; and now, when do you propose to start for Barfleur?"

"At once! immediately!"

"Good! The sooner the better for me."

"Allons! then, dear friend, follow! The sun is well up, we will begin our journey forthwith!"

Making his way out of the hut, Claude followed, the two presently after marching with rapid strides through the forest.

For hours they pursued their journey, meeting with no obstacle to their progress.

The paths, as Claude had suspected, well-known to his new-found friend, were traversed without let or hindrance.

Stopping as the shades of night began to fall at a little village cabaret, the companions procured rest and refreshment, of which they then stood much in need.

Up betimes the following morning, their journey was resumed.

It was with a sigh of intense relief that, as the sun began to decline in the horizon at the end of their second day's march, Claude was informed by his companion that another half-hour would bring them to their destination.

"Tonnerre de guerre! I care not how soon I face the bold smuggler, your cousin. But are you sure of his presence at this time?"

"Morbleu, yes! I know when he is at Barfleur, and when he is away."

"Dost ever assist him, Landri?" said Claude with a smile at his companion.

"Par St. Denis, yes; and would have joined his merry crew ere this! But he has told me land-lubbers are but poor seadogs, and will have none of me."

"Perhaps you are more useful to him on land?"

"Ma foi, yes, Claude, that is it! I have once or twice given timely warning of impending danger, and also helped to make good bargains with some, whom cousin Ben would have only quarrelled with, for he is hot and hasty and quick of temper. But we are near the haunt; do you not find the wind blow fresh and strong as we mount this height?"

"Aye; I guessed, a while back, that we were approaching the coast," said Claude, pausing to gather breath as, less active than his companion, he hung somewhat behind.

Mounting the precipitous sides of a rocky eminence, clothed to the summit with coarse vegetation and huge pine trees, Claude had noted the air around was keen and brackish.

A cry of astonishment presently escaped his lips as, with his companion, he gained the summit of the height, up which they had for an hour and more been toiling.

Before them now lay a wide open expanse of ocean.

Hundreds of feet below where they stood was the rocky ironbound beach.

Even at that height, Claude could hear the dash of the waves as they thundered against the rocks.

The wind with a tempestuous roar bellowed in the ears of the wanderers, threatening with violence to blow them off their feet.

In awe and admiration Claude gazed at the scene before him:

A scene of wild grandeur:

Of majestic beauty.

A white line of froth below showed the treacherous breakers, whilst the moon, just rising from her bed, appeared as though emerging from the depths of the ocean, the waters of which the moon tipped with a silvery lustre.

It was a splendid prospect.

As far as the eye could reach stretched the rocky line of coast on either hand.

With searching gaze, Claude swept his eyes around in quest of a vessel.

But not a single sail was in sight.

"You are looking for the Saucy Kit, but you will not sight my cousin's barque from this rocky height," said Landri.

"I was, I confess, looking out for a sail."

"Parbleu! and a sail you shall see ere the morn, my dear preserver! But, come, we must push on—a mile or more yet separates us from our final halting place, and our pathway is none of the safest; you must follow in my steps, treading firm and sure."

"Have no fear: I am quick of eye and possess nerves of steel," said Claude with a smile, as he prepared to follow his companion along a range of rocks which to their left went with a slight decline towards the depth below.

Night now falling, the task of threading their way along the giddy height was no easy one.

The moon, however, shining brightly lighted the bold adventurers on in their journey.

Gradually Claude soon discovered they were nearing the rocky beach below.

At every step they went lower yet lower, they discerned, down the precipitous sides of the eminence.

Once or twice a single false step would have led to their destruction.

But boldly, fearlessly, the two adventured on.

There was a sublimity to him about the journey that put to flight all thought of danger from the mind of our hero. Claude heeded not the beetling crags or howling winds, but followed resolutely on:

On, on, down the blackened frowning cliffs till the roar of waters below almost drowned the sound of his voice as he addressed his companion.

When so far down that the salt spray dashed in their faces and the inky waters seemed about to start up and engulph them, Claude's youthful leader turned sharp round an abutting portion of rock, and, making his way along a narrow path, approached a portion of the beach which, composed of sand, offered no resistance to the waters, which here at their will heaved and rolled in calm regular motion upon the shore.

In surprise, Claude now gazed around him.

Stretching afar out before him was the expanse of open sea.

To the left, high up, towered the rocks, upon the summit of which he had stood shortly before.

To the right, and distant about a mile, arose another mass of beetling crags, whilst at the back was a range of forest and open country.

At the point where he now stood Claude discovered a natural bay:

On either side frowning rocky heights:

Whilst for a mile or more was a beautiful sandy beach.

"Do you see anything out at sea now, Claude?"

"I perceive an object in the distance that in the moon's rays one might almost imagine was a bird; but that 'tis no bird that wings it's way hither I am aware: 'tis a bonny barque manned by bold mariners!"

"You are right, Claude; that dim speck your eye detects upon the waters is my cousin's vessel, the Saucy Kit!"

"And he, your cousin, where is he?"

"Carousing in the retreat!"

"Retreat! what retreat?"

"Why the Blue Cave!"

"The Blue Cave! is that rendezvous near here?"

"Yes!"

"You will lead me thither?"

"Aye?"

"It will not be necessary to warn your cousin of our approach?"

"No; we shall come across some one ere we gain the close vicinity of the cave."

"Ma foi! I understand, a sentinel!"

"Just so. They keep a watch here never fear! Ben Staysail ain't to be caught like a rat in a trap!"

"I suppose not; he were not a fit hand at his calling if he were not to be ever ready for a surprise."

"Ventre bleu, yes! Ben could give you some queer yarns if he were minded. He has not earned his title of the Smuggler King without encountering a few escapades, I can tell you."

"Parbleu! I expect not, Landri! But let us to the cave! I am all anxiety to meet the bold rover. I have told you I am a knight of the road. Haste to present me to a new comrade, the knight of the deep blue sea!" said Claude, with a laugh.

The two presently, after leaving the beach behind them (Claude in the rear), made for the rocks they had left shortly before, and which, for some distance, extended towards the wooded tract facing the sandy shore.

Halting before a huge boulder of stone covered with moss and creeping plants, our hero's conductor now paused.

Further progress seemed impossible in this direction.

In surprise, Claude gazed around him, as his companion gave utterance to a shrill cry that sounded like the note of some wild bird, as it rang in the night air.

This summons was answered in a mysterious manner.

To the intense astonishment of Duval, a portion of the rock before which they stood now suddenly gave way.

A huge cavity opened in the apparently impenetrable mass.

In the centre of this solid wall of rock now appeared a door.

Without hesitation Claude followed his companion, stooping down and passing the low narrow entry.

All was now pitchy darkness before them.

The bright silvery rays of the moon without were now lost to them.

All was dark—dark as Erebus:

A darkness thick and black.

Apparently well acquainted with the pathway, the young man Landri went inwards, bidding Claude beware of the masses of rock which hung in their way, and over which our hero, with a curse, once or twice stumbled and fell on his knees.

Slowly, and in utmost surprise, he followed his companion; at length, halting for a moment as they emerged from the narrow passage they had been traversing into a vault or subterranean way, some thirty by seventy feet in circumference.

A pale light shone in his place:

A light from a flickering oil lamp, that stood in a bracket by the side of the cave.

Ghastly and spectral were its rays.

So pale and thin was its yellow gleam, that it scarce sufficed to dispel the pitchy darkness that hung around.

Passing onward, and avoiding a stream of water of apparently a good depth, that pursued its course through this outer cave, being lost, as it wound its way into an opening on the left, the youth Landri now paused, coming to a halt once more before a mass of solid rock :

The wall of the cave.

Again he gave utterance to his shrill warning cry.

Scarce had its echoes died away ere an opening appeared before them :

A huge solid block of the rock wall slipping away as by enchantment.

A glare of light now darted forth:

A strong dazzling light, that caused Claude's eyes to ache after the recent darkness.

With a low laugh his young friend now darted down the narrow opening before them :

An archway of some five feet in length :

An archway leading to a huge cave.

Following his companion, Claude was presently standing in a huge natural cavern of immense extent.

A strange scene presented itself to his eyes.

Light, warm, and cheerful was this cave by the sea.

A huge iron tripod hung from the roof, in which were some dozen oil lamps :

Lamps upon brackets at the side of the cave gave out a flood of yellow light through the subterranean retreat.

Barrels, bales, small casks, and merchandise of every description were piled against the wall.

A fire burning at the further end of the cave gave out a cheerful blaze and warmth, the smoke curling up to a rude opening or rent in the rocky roof above.

It was to Claude a strange wild scene, that smugglers' haunt on the French coast.

Around the fire were grouped some ten or dozen men, all of whom were laughing, talking, and smoking.

From this noisy crowd a dark-faced, sunburnt, weather-beaten man of about forty years of age hastened forwards as the two friends appeared.

"What, Landri, is it thou ? What cheer, lad ? hast any news ? What brings you here so late, boy ? We sail within the hour; the Saucy Kit with a good cargo is bound for the white cliffs of Britain."

"I know it ! I thought I should catch you ere you sailed. I have brought you a passenger."

"A passenger ?" The bold smuggler here cast a keen and searching glance upon Claude, who now found himself surrounded by the strangers, all of whom eyed him curiously.

"Cousin Ben, you must take this young man to England; he has saved my life !"

"Topsail halyard blocks ! if that's so, Landri, he shall be carried over whene'er he will, though perhaps a voyage in a vessel not manned by lawless men would be your friend's safest course."

"Parbleu ! no, Cousin Ben ! My friend has outraged his country's laws, and of his own choice wishes to go back to England in your bonny craft, the Saucy Kit."

"Landri speaks truth, captain ; I am he whom men call Claude Duval."

"What the scourge of the road ? the knight of the highway, about whom I have heard so much ?"

"The same," said Claude, returning the hearty grip of the bold smuggler, who had seized his hand and wrung it warmly.

"And you have saved Landri's life, lad ! By my brave barque, the Saucy Kit, there is nothing I will not do for you ! Command me and mine to the death ! We have heard of your exploits, Claude Duval; and our strange meeting will, believe me, live long in my memory. I am fonder of my land-lubber of a cousin there than if I was his brother. You have, he says, saved his life ; and I, Ben Staysail, known as the Smuggler King, will be thy sworn friend for ever, Claude Duval ! But, come, we must have a carousal ere we start upon our voyage, and, whilst over our supper, you can spin the yarn of how you came to render service to Cousin Landri there—a service for which we cannot do too much ! What ho, boys ! broach another cask ! Fill your cans, and drink to your captain, the Smuggler King, and the bold Knight of the Road, Dashing Duval !"

Loud and long was the cheer that now rang through the cavern :

A cheer that, in that subterranean retreat, woke up a thousand echoes.

Seated at a rude bench surrounded by the smuggler crew, all of whom strove to win his friendship, Claude was now compelled to enter heartily into the carousal that took place— a carousal that only ceased as the order was given to make their way on board the Saucy Kit, at that moment anchored in the bay awaiting their arrival.

CHAPTER XXI.

OUT AT SEA—SAILORS' YARNS—WHAT ARE VAMPYRES ?—A STRANGE SAIL—THE PALE FACE ON DECK—A LOVER'S DESPAIR—A BOLD RESOLVE—ON THE DECK OF THE PIRATE—SUDDEN APPEARANCE OF VAN VAUGHAN.

Like a wild dream did it all appear to Claude, when, some two hours after, he found himself pacing the deck of the smugglers' barque.

Out at sea, the land a dim cloud, once more our hero was on his return to those friends from whom he had been so strangely parted.

More anxious and nervous he now became as to the fate of those he loved.

Pacing the deck in moody thought, his friend the Smuggler King busy looking to the working of his bonnie barque, Claude was left undisturbed to his reflections.

The excitement of his late adventures now past, he was all feverish impatience to be once more with his friends :

To again gaze with love and joy into the liquid depths of his lovely Maude's bright eyes :

To hear the ringing hearty voices of his comrades, Gentleman Jack and Paul Clifford.

Thinking thus of his absent friends, Claude was pacing the deck, lost to all around, when he was suddenly arrested by a chance word that fell from the lips of a knot of some half-dozen smugglers, who, by the light of the moon, were sitting upon deck recounting sundry yarns.

With a thrill, Claude halted by the spot where the sailors were congregated.

They were talking respecting the superstitions of different countries.

"What are vampyres, Jem ?" such was the interrogation that had startled Claude and that now again fell from the lips of one of the men.

"Vampyres are men who subsist by drawing the life-blood from the veins of their victims !"

"What a cussed horrid idea !"

"It is a horrid idea, and it's true, too !"

"I say Jem, arn't you throwing the hatchet ?"

"I am speaking the truth, so help my Davy !"

"You believe in the critters then ?"

"I do, Charley ! Vampyres exist, there's no doubt about it !"

"I have been over in India and have seen vampyre bats," said a tall, dark seaman, who, rolling a quid in his mouth, gazed somewhat incredulously at the head man of the group, a big, brawny fellow, who spoke so sturdily his belief in the horrible superstition they were conversing upon.

DASHING DUVAL;

OR,

THE LADIES' HIGHWAYMAN.

JACK ASTONISHES THE REPRESENTATIVE OF MAJESTY.

"Vampyre bats be blowed! them's nothing! I knows all about them, Harry Halyard. They fastens on your toe at night, and fans yer to sleep with their damned great wings! Them's natural cusses, they is; but what I was argufying about is unnatural. That's real vampyres—critters that it takes a precious sight of killing to get rid of!"

"What do you mean, Jem?"

"Why, that it ain't easy to kill vampyres."

"Ain't it?"

"Have you ever tried?" said the unbelieving tar.

"No, I ain't, Harry; but I knows it's a fact, nevertheless. If as how you was a vampyre, and I shot yer down on the deck there, dead as a doornail, yer'd come to life again, that's if we left yer to lie there in the rays of the moon!"

"Pretty idea, that!" said the incredulous one, sneeringly.

"That's as it may be. It's a fact, I can tell. And there's another thing, too, about the darned confounded critters, those as is bit by them also becomes vampyres after death!"

"That's a fact, too, Jem, is it?" said the man Halyard.

"It is; but it arn't no good talking to you; you doesn't believe in vampyres!"

"No, I don't!"

"Well, don't boast on it; it will only show your hignorance," said the indignant Jem, who, at one time, would have much amused our hero by his pertinacity as to the existence of the hideous thing they were talking of.

A terrible anxiety seized upon him respecting the safety of his loved Maude.

No. 11 & 12.   Price One Penny.

Had all gone well in his absence?

Was she safe with his friends?

Had ought of ill happened to her?

A terrible foreboding, a kind of foreshadowing of some dread danger seized upon him, and only was he startled from his gloomy reverie by a cry of a man in the top,

"A sail! a sail!"

Such were the words that now caused the knot of idlers to stand forwards and gather round the bulwarks.

It was a beautiful night, the moon shining bright and lustrous overhead; one faint streak of cloud only to be traced in the horizon.

To this cloud, speck as it was, however, the sailor Harry Halyard pointed to as the foreteller of a storm.

"We shall have it afore the night is out, captain!"

"Yes; we'll have the sails in by-and-bye. I don't like the look of it, Harry," said the Smuggler King, who, walking up to Claude, had his attention drawn to the sky by his mate.

"Well, Duval, my bold knight of the road, how do you like sailoring? I suppose you'd prefer the saddle of your bonny mare to the deck of the Saucy Kit?"

"Since you ask me, my dear friend; well, yes!"

"You seem downhearted, Claude; topsail halyard blocks! don't grieve for those at home, you will soon be with them! Unless we are driven much out of our course we shall land you at Folkstone on the morrow!" said the sailor, to whom, some little time before, Duval had related how he had left his friends, a week before.

"I was thinking of them, I must confess, captain!" exclaimed Claude; "I am most anxious to get to England! I fear lest anything should have gone wrong in my absence."

"Nay, trouble not your head with such thoughts! My word for it, you'll find all right on your return! Hem! I thought I knew the rakish cut of yonder craft—there goes Black Hawk!"

"And who may that be?" said Claude, as the rover here pointed to the stranger, now close alongside his own vessel.

"Why, that bark is, like this, a smuggler! but its captain, unlike Ben Staysail, does not confine himself wholly to the trick of cheating the customs."

"You would intimate that he has no objection to a little piracy, I suppose!"

"Well, yes; but I fancy nothing comes amiss to Captain Hawk! I avoid the fellow as much as I can; but we often come across each other."

"You do not like him?"

"No; to be candid, Duval, I wouldn't mind if I saw him hung up at the fore-yard-arm."

"You think he deserves such a fate?"

"I do! and you would agree with me if you knew as much of the scoundrel as I do!"

About to speak again to his friend, the Smuggler King, Claude now, leaning over the bulwarks, suddenly started, and uttered a cry of astonishment and alarm.

A sick, giddy feeling seized upon him, the while, with frantic grip, he held on to the arm of the captain.

His face, a livid hue. The smuggler, in alarm, asked him if he were ill.

A low gasping cry was Claude's only answer.

A sight upon the deck of the Black Hawk had turned his blood to ice:

Had caused him to reel back like a drunken man!

His brain seemed as if on fire.

Scarce could he command his tongue to utterance; and when at length able to use his speech, his voice sounded husky and hoarse with rage and terror.

"Captain Staysail, do you see that pale, beautiful girl upon the deck of yonder vessel?"

Claude here, shaking as with an ague, pointed out the form of a young and beautiful girl, who, leaning against the taffrail of the Black Hawk, seemed meditating a plunge into the briny deep.

Sad, drear, and woe-begone looked the pale-faced girl.

The lineaments of deep sorrow and despair could be traced upon her features.

The vessels of the smugglers almost side by side, and the moon shining upon all as bright as day, revealed each person congregated upon the other's deck.

"Do you know that lady, Claude Duval?"

"As I know myself! God of heaven, what means it?" gasped our hero, as he stood pale and trembling upon the deck of the Saucy Kit.

Never, during the dread horrors he had lately gone through, did he feel as now.

A sensation, as of utter madness seized upon him.

For in the pallid, sad face of the beautiful maiden on board the Black Hawk, he had recognised lineaments that were engraven in his memory for ever:

Those of Maude Mayburn!

Scarce could he credit the dread sight; and would have thought himself the victim of a wild delusion, a heat-oppressed brain; but the Smuggler King had also noted the form of the lovely captive! By some means she had been conveyed on board the craft now sailing for he knew not where!

But who had done this?

By whose agency had the unhappy girl been brought away from home and friends?

With lightning-like rapidity these thoughts flashed through the dazed brain of our hero, who, as the vessel began to pass their own on its outward-bound voyage, suddenly woke into activity and life.

With wild gleaming eyes, he exclaimed:

"Ben Staysail, can you, for a time, stay that vessel in its course?"

"Perhaps, lad! though I won't answer for it that Black Hawk will lie to; he is a curious character, and there is little love lost between us."

"But you will try?"

"Assuredly! Hoist a signal, Harry Halyard, I want Hawk to lie to!"

"Aye, aye, captain!" said the sailor, who, in a moment after, run up a flag that caused their neighbour to stop his course, whilst a voice, loud and clear, rang over the moonlit waters.

With trembling eagerness, Claude now pointed to a boat hanging by the davits, exclaiming:

"Lower that boat alongside, I must at once on board that ship!"

In wildest agitation, he here pointed to the stranger, the captain of which was now exchanging speech with the sailor, Harry Halyard.

"Claude Duval, I dare not let you do as you desire; it would be as much as your life is worth to leave my barque! a storm is brewing, though the night seems so fair; and, besides, I know not what may happen should you succeed in your wish of gaining the deck of the Black Hawk!"

"No matter; if I meet my death, I must! I will on board that accursed craft! It contains one for whom I would give my life!"

"Well, since you are determined, be it so; I will get some volunteers to join you, though, in the event of a quarrel with Black Hawk, we have little chance of victory, for his crew double mine, and all are bold determined men!"

"There shall be no risk of an action betwixt you, Ben Staysail; alone I wish to visit that craft! If she whom I love is in the power of the being I dare not name, I alone can save her; nor do I think that the captain of that ship will take part against me when I have had speech with him!"

"What mean you, Duval? I know of nothing that could win you sympathy from Black Hawk; unless you would out-bid any foe in the price of that he may have undertaken!"

"I can do that, and more; sailors, smugglers, or pirates are all superstitious, are they not!"

"Well, yes;" said Staysail, who was gazing in much concern at the pallid excited features of his companion.

"Good! then, if I prove to Black Hawk that he has trifled with a being not of this world, he may cease to aid my foe!"

In real alarm the Smuggler King now gazed at Claude, who, observing the looks of concern and divining their meaning, exclaimed:

"Nay, do not think me mad! Some day we may meet again, when I will explain all! I dare not longer stay here! Black Hawk is lying to, in heaven's name I pray you lower your boat, that I may go on board!"

"As you will! Lower that gig from the davits, Halyard! My friend Duval, here, is bent upon paying a visit to Black Hawk!"

"Yes, Halyard! But there is a friend on board whom he wishes to converse with."

"Humph, well I hope he will get safe back; shall I go with him?"

"No, I can't spare you; a sudden squall may arise. You may be wanted here; besides, I have not forgotten that there is an old feud between you and Black Hawk."

"It matters not, I require no one with me !"

"Ten thousand devils ! you don't suppose I am going to let you leave our ship alone ? But that I fear a fight between the rival crews, I would send all hands with you ; but I dare not risk it ! however, Jem Barnacle shall go with you, and he is the only one I can safely trust, and, now I think of it, Jem upon one occasion was of service to Master Hawk, and the fellow swore at the time he would grant him any favour he might ask ! Confound my thick head, I never thought of that till now ! Hurry up, Jem ! we will lie to till you both return !"

The boat now lowered was dancing upon the heaving bosom of the ocean.

In eager haste Claude clambered over the side, and without misadventure was presently, with Jem Barnacle, seated safely in the frail craft.

It was only as the boat was pulled away from the frowning hull of the Saucy Kit, that Claude glancing into the face of his comrade, recognised in him the sailor who had evinced such faith in the existence of vampyres.

A cold chill as of ice darted through his frame as he asked himself if his dread suspicion, that Maude was once more in the power of that demon Van Vaughan, was correct.

Lying to, awaiting their approach, Claude eagerly looked up at the deck of the Black Hawk in an endeavour once again to catch a glimpse of the pale face that had caused him to risk his present peril.

The moon now covered by a bank of heavy cloud that had crept up from windward, the ocean became in a second of time involved in darkness.

Both their own vessel and that of Black Hawk was almost invisible.

The waters, now covered with white foam, rose and fell tumultuously, whilst the gathering blast shrieked wildly over the open waste.

Nervously, anxiously, the sailor peered around, as he strained vigorously at the oars.

"I'm afraid we'll have it now, Muster Duval, afore we gets alongside that damned pirate !"

"What's that white light ahead ?"

"Oh ! that's a lantern run up by the party as we is going to see ! a wonderful piece of civility on the part of Captain Hawk ! I should guess he is in a good humour for once !"

"You have rendered him a favour, have you not ?"

"Yes ! saved his neck from the halter ! the worst day's work I ever did, cuss him !"

"Nay, it may not prove so, my good fellow ! it may be in your power presently to assist me by gaining the friendly aid of this man Hawk, who, unless he be vile indeed, will scarce refuse a favour to you, though to me, a stranger, it would be instantly denied." In a few words Claude here made his companion acquainted with the strange appearance of his mistress upon the deck of the stranger.

"You are sartin it were her ?" exclaimed the burly tar as Claude finished his relation of the mysterious incident.

"As certain as that we are both now in this boat !"

"Humph ! it's very strange ; mayhap some enemy of your'n is going to take the girl to some furrin part !"

"Such was my thought when I asked your captain to allow me to board the Black Hawk."

"I see ! and it warn't a bad move of your'n neither."

"Think you we shall reach the vessel all right ?"

"If the squall as is creeping up on us don't bust, yes !"

"And if it does ?"

"Well, I expect we'd pretty soon be a divin' among the fi-hes !"

"Heaven forbid ! not my own life I value ; but she whom I seek is in the power of a fiend, Jem Barnacle ! If all goes well, I will confide to you a secret !"

"I feel highly honoured, Muster Duval ; and if I warn't a salt, damme but I'd turn highwaymen directly !"

"Are we far, think you, from the vessel we wish to board ?" said Claude, now straining his eyes over the inky waters, that rising and tossing each moment more angrily, threatened to submerge their frail craft.

"Does yer see that black thing ahead there ?"

"A little to the left ?"

"Yes !"

"Well, that's it !"

"What, the Black Hawk ?"

"Yes ! and there goes a blue light ! Damn me if they arn't off !" A wild shout here burst from the lips of the alarmed seaman : a shout, however, scarce heard above the howling of the wind, which was now increasing to a hurricane.

"If we arn't on board in another minute it's all over with us, Duval ! Hallo, here we is under their bowsprit ! seize on to that line there ! that's it ! I think we are all right ! they knows we are alongside !"

Seizing hold of a rope trailing in the frothy sea, Claude, now undismayed by the howling tempest, helped to urge their frail vessel beneath the dark looming hull of the smugglers' barque.

Blue lights burning on the rover's deck cast a pale ghastly glare over the inky boiling waters.

By this spectral light Claude, starting up in the boat, behold a crowd of human figures leaning over the bulwarks above and glaring down upon them.

One, a pale herculean man, his swart dark features nearly concealed by a bushy beard, whiskers, and moustache, leaning far out, exclaimed :

"Are you two madmen ? What the blazes brings you on a visit to me, with a squall coming on that will utterly prevent your return to your own vessel ; I've got hands enough on board, I don't want any chicken-hearted white-livered lubbers from old Ben Staysail ! Go the way you came ! You don't board Black Hawk to-night, my brave boys !"

"Captain Hawk, don't you know me ?" Excitedly the sailor-companion of Claude here started up in the boat which was tossing dangerously upon the heaving waters, which threatened every moment to dash her with a crash against the dark hull of the rover."

"Blood and thunder ! is that you, Jem Barnacle ? Bear a hand here, men ; help those fellows on board !"

In another moment all was bustle and excitement by the smugglers.

Ropes were lowered and every assistance rendered to the two bold men in the open boat, who, not without considerable danger, at length in safety gained the deck of Black Hawk.

Blue lights still burning in the rigging of the rover, a pale spectral glare was cast upon all around.

By this glare Claude beheld a crowd of fierce savage men.

Not the forbidding features of the crew of the half-smuggler, half-pirate, however, was it that arrested the attention of Duval.

A tall ungainly figure, with livid face and steel-like eyes, it was that caused him to stagger back with a gasp of horror.

A low sardonic laugh now rang in his ears, whilst, with arms extended, the man who had strode forth from amidst the motly crew exclaimed :

"Said I not we should meet again, Claude Duval ?"

With wide staring eyes and his limbs frozen with rage and terror, Claude glared speechless at the demoniac figure before him :

None other than the wretch Van Vaughan :

Vaughan the Vampyre !

It was a strange wild scene :

The lurid light, the howling tempest, the ruffian crew gathered round, making up a picture fit for Bale !

CHAPTER XXII.

ON BOARD THE BLACK HAWK—CLAUDE'S PERIL—SUDDEN APPEARANCE OF MAUDE MAYBURN—A TERRIBLE DUEL—THE DAGGER FIGHT—THE STRUGGLE—THE VAMPYRE'S DOOM—THE SUNKEN ROCK—WRECK OF THE PIRATE.

Wildly Claude glared around at the fierce crowd ; turning his eyes away with a shudder from the hideous form of the Vampyre.

Even the ruffian faces of the pirate crew caused less alarm and horror in his breast than the sight of the fiendly features so waxen, livid, and ghastly that confronted him.

Though for a moment with his head turned aside, a strong shiver shook Claude's frame as he felt that the long steel-like orbs of his demon foe were fixed exultingly upon him.

"Ha, ha, ha ! you are surprised to see me once again, Claude Duval ! you thought you had rid yourself for ever of your rival to the hand of the lovely Maud ; but you see I have survived your bullet, recovered your dastard shot in the woods at Highgate, and live, Claude Duval, to make the girl you fondly love irrevocably mine ! Ha ha, ha ! who triumphs now ?" A hoarse shout of exultation here burst from the lips of the fiendly Vaughan.

"Look that your triumph is not short-lived !" said Claude, as he now, once more regaining his wonted courage, glared with rage and scorn upon his vindictive enemy. "Know you whom you have on board?" he then added, turning to Captain Hawk, who, in surprise had been looking on at the two who had strangely met on board his vessel.

"By chain shot and canister! I neither know nor care what he is! The fellow has paid a princely sum for the passage of himself and his fair companion; and, by Satan and all his fiends, I care not what he may be!" exclaimed the fierce-looking rover.

"Indeed! Captain Hawk, you are, I doubt not, a bold man?"

"Aye! who dare gainsay that I am other?"

"Parbleu! not I captain! As a rover, braving the law and the vasty deep, you must perforce be a man of daring and courage: so too am I, who, by the heavens above us, fear no human being; but, i'faith, I require all my nerve in facing that demi-devil there!"

"You know each other, it seems!"

"Aye, and are sworn foes to the death!"

"You have said aright, Claude Duval; but your death will be compassed, not mine! By the fiend, thou shalt not live to see thy friends again!—Captain Hawk, let me fight this bragging highwayman! Ha, ha, ha! let there be a duel off your quarter-deck; We will fight with bright steel blades, Claude Duval! Oh, oh, oh! I have one ready and thirsting for your blood!" With his eyes gleaming like live coals, the wretch here drew from his vest a sharp-pointed stiletto, the blue blade of which flashed in the lurid rays of the lights that swung from the yards.

With a grim smile the captain of the rovers glanced first at Duval and then at the livid contorted features of the villain Vaughan.

The proposition of a fight was received by acclamations from his crew, and did not fail to meet with his own approval.

"You hear your enemy, Claude Duval; and if, as I have always heard, you be bold, daring, and dauntless, you will accept his defiance and fight him to the death!"

"No! no! no!" A wild piercing scream here echoed above the howling winds.

For a moment Claude, dazed and confounded, beheld a fair form, robed in white, flying across the deck, anon darting fearlessly through the dusky crowd, and falling almost lifeless at his feet.

"Maude! Maude! dearest girl, go below! this is no scene for thee!"

Wildly our hero gasped these words, as raising the form of her he so fondly loved in his arms, he glared round, driven to frenzy by their imminent peril.

Pale, wan, and ghastly looked the unfortunate Maude Mayburn; for she indeed it was who now rested in his half-embrace.

A baleful glitter shone in the eyes of Van Vaughan, who now, turning to Captain Hawk, exclaimed:

"I command you by our compact to see that girl at once removed below! You swore to safely convey me and my lovely charge to another land! You bargained to shield me from any foes that might attempt to intercept my flight. This you swore to do ere we left the port of London. See that you fail not in your compact!"

"Never fear! Thunder and lightning! Captain Hawk is not the man to shirk any task he may have undertaken! Claude Duval, I am sorry to be compelled to come betwixt you and that young lady there! I have received a goodly sum—two hundred pounds—to safely convey your enemy and his companion to their destination! I care not though he has torn her from her home and friends! I must carry out my agreement. At the same time, I am sorry, in doing so, that I evidently cause annoyance to one who, like myself, is a bold and daring man!"

Claude, bowing to the compliment of the rover, and delivering the now senseless Maude into the hands of a mulatto woman, who had darted forwards, crossed over to the captain, and pointing to the grinning face of his hideous foe exclaimed:

"For every guinea he has handed you I will give you four, if you give up the girl he has snatched from me in my absence!"

"It may not be! Cospetto! he knows too much. I cannot betray him!' muttered the man Hawk in a whisper, the while he glanced uneasily at Vaughan, who remained, dagger in hand, glaring upon them.

"You cannot betray him?"

"No; he would put the sharks upon me when next I sailed into British waters!"

"But how if he never returns?"

"He has left instructions with members of his band in London, that if I bring not back to them a sealed packet he will deliver to me when landing upon the shores of France, that they are to consider I have played him false."

"Ma foi! and what then?"

"Why, I shall be betrayed to the authorities!"

"Parbleu! and suppose I kill him in this duel he has proposed, what then?"

"Grapeshot and canister! I did not think of that! Perhaps he imagines that it will be impossible for you to slay him!"

"Likely enough; but I don't think he will escape me this time!"

"How do you mean this time?"

"Why, I will take care he has no chance of returning again to life!"

"Returning again to life?"

"Just so!"

"Ten thousand devils! what mean you?"

"I had forgotten; you do not know the nature of my enemy."

"I take him to be a bold unscrupulous hand, and, from what I have heard, an ugly customer to deal with."

"And so he is; Van Vaughan is no ordinary foe! He is a vampyre!"

"A what?"

"A vampyre!"

"Claude Duval!"

"Well!"

"I am not a man to be fooled!"

"I never thought you were!"

"It is ill jesting with Black Hawk!"

"I am not jesting, captain; I was never more serious in my life!"

"The devil!"

"Exactly; that is just it! Our friend Vaughan, there, who is eyeing us now so suspiciously, is either the devil himself, or his first cousin!"

Staring, first at Claude, in wondering surprise, and then at the wretch Vaughan, who, during the above colloquy had been grinding his wolfish tusk-like teeth and nervously clutching at his dagger, the captain of the pirate craft now walked over to the grim form that, like a denizen of another world, glared in wild fury around.

Intently Claude watched his foe, as the rover drew him aside. For some minutes the two conversed apart.

Ever and again, the wretch Vaughan would cast his steel-like eyes upon Claude, who smiled in derision as he clutched his dagger, at the same time giving utterance to a kind of angry snarl of fierce rage.

A few moments' more converse between the captain and his strange passenger ended apparently in an understanding; for, with a smile, the former received a packet, which he placed carefully in his vest, making his way directly after to Claude.

"He swears he'll have your life! he says you cannot escape. His knife is poisoned, he tells me, so a scratch will kill! I tell you this, Claude Duval; for, curse me, if I admire the man who would act so dastard a part! Smuggler, pirate, buccaneer, I may be; but, ten thousand devils! such a trick as using a poisoned knife on a foe I would ne'er attempt!"

"I am sure you would not, Captain Hawk! But, tell me, am I not right? Have you not succeeded in securing those papers?"

"I have; I told him I would not allow the conflict to take place unless I was made perfectly safe."

"Good! You can now defy him!"

"Aye, and will! He has dared to threaten me, and must now learn that I am not one to be held in any man's hands. Kill him, Duval, if you can; and I will land you and the girl where'er you will."

"Morbleu, captain! thou hast turned out a friend, and I will pay thee both in thanks and gold! And now, as the tempest appears likely to end in a hurricane, I will even at once enter into conflict with this fiend—for fiend he is!"

"Well, he has a look about him I like not! I care not to openly defy him, or act so treacherous a part even to him as to shoot him down like a dog, so will let the matter terminate as agreed! You know the worst. Let not his dagger's point touch thy skin, or, by the devils! thou art lost; and I would sooner heave his corpse over the side than thine, Claude Duval!"

The crew of the rover, who during this had been whispering in groups about the deck, were now called together by the captain, who acquainted them that a duel was settled to take place at once, betwixt the new-comer Claude Duval and the mysterious passenger who had sailed with them from London a few days before, and whom Jem Barnacle now informed our hero had not, by his ferocious overbearing manners and unsociable disposition, made friends amongst the rough pirate crew.

"They will all be glad to see you wipe him out! Rush in at him; and luck go with you Duval!" said the jolly tar, who, with a shrug of his shoulders, added, "To my thinking he's some corpse or t'other as has got out of his grave and failed to find his way back again!"

"You are not far out there, Jem, my boy!" said Claude, who at that moment received from the captain a broad Spanish knife, some six inches in length, the blade bright and glittering as silver.

"There you are, Duval—a piece of steel that will not fail you! Drive it well home!" said the captain, with a grim smile.

"Morbeu, never fear! the weapon shall find it's sheath! I know my enemy. To be forewarned is to be forearmed," said Claude, with a meaning glance at the rover.

All now being ready, the whole of the pirate crew that had gathered round drew back.

It was a strange scene:

The preparations for that duel to the death!

With a smile wreathing his handsome features, Duval, dagger upraised, coolly advanced towards his antagonist.

Vampyre Vaughan, his ghastly livid face contorted with passion, glared ferociously with his fiery bead-like eyes upon his foe.

It was to be a duel a la morte:

One or both must must die!

The crew of the pirate ship in utmost excitement gazed upon the combatants:

The terrible duel with knives was a scene that suited them!

It was an awe-inspiring scene:

Nor were the elements wanting to complete the wild picture.

The wind, in howling gusts, tore through the rigging of the good ship, which bounded over the tempestuous seas like a huge bird.

Black heavy clouds hung low overhead, through which at intervals the moon would break forth, her pale silvery light serving for a short space to show all the horrors around.

It was a wild scene—a scene in which one of the principal actors stood forth not without a nervous thrill.

Claude Duval, as he strode forward to his enemy, could not forget that he was about to combat with no earthly foe:

He was about to engage with a hideous being not of this world!

The nature of the wretch Vaughan could not be doubted.

He proved that there was truth in a horrible ghastly superstition:

A superstition that went beyond the grave!

With a wild thrill Claude now stood facing the demoniac Vaughan.

Fierce and bright shone the steel-like eyes.

Two tiny red spots on either cheek served but to increase the horror of the corpse-like livid face.

The black beetling brows lowered over the fiery orbs; the wolfish tusk-like teeth, fully exposed as the lips were drawn back in an angry snarl, rendered the appearance of the fiendly foe positively awful and unearthly.

Not without a shudder:

Not without a feeling as though all the blood in his body was turning to ice, did Claude draw near to his antagonist.

Eagerly, and in intense excitement, the pirates looked on.

The scene was new and novel:

Thrilling and awe-inspiring!

"Ha, ha, ha, Claude Duval! why dost thou dally? Come on, man! you are doomed! Fate hath decreed against thee; thou art to perish, and thy promised bride will be mine!"

No answer did Claude give to the daunt.

Murmuring a prayer to Heaven to nerve his arm in the conflict against the fiend before him, he slowly moved round his antagonist, wily and cautiously, as a leopard in the crest wilds.

He knew a scratch from the glittering blade of his foe would be death.

With this knowledge he slowly and cautiously engaged with the fiend before him.

With stealthy catlike step, his eye fixed upon every movement of his enemy, he walked round and round him.

Snarling and snapping like an angry dog, the wretch Vaughan grew restive and impatient at Claude's cool, quiet, demeanour.

Again and again, with jeering taunts, he strove to force him to rush in.

But with wary eye Claude awaited a favourable moment for attack.

The moment came.

The very elements seemed to aid him against the fiendly villain.

About with a wild screech of fury, to bound upon Claude, Van Vaughan was for a second of time blinded and confused by a sudden blue vivid glare of lightning that darted forth from the inky clouds.

Staggering back, the upraised hand clasping the fatal knife fell to his side.

In a moment Claude was upon him.

Wild cries now echoed from the excited lookers-on.

The final test had arrived.

Locked in a deadly grip of hate the antagonists staggered to and fro:

A wild screech bursting from the lips of the frenzied villain Vaughan as Claude hurling him against the bulwarks, leant his whole weight upon him, bending him back till he yelled with rage and pain.

Nervously Claude clutched the wrist of the villain, the hand of which gripped with deadly hate the haft of the knife.

With all his force Claude bent the wretch's wrist completely round.

A wild shout now burst from the lookers-on as the dagger, slipping from the ruffian's grasp, fell upon deck.

"You have him now!"

"Brave Claude!"

"Knife him, Duval!"

"Death and blazes, let him have it!"

"Over the side with him!"

"He's a vampyre!"

"Down with the Vampyre!"

"Slay him, kill him!"

Such were the babel of cries that rang in the ears of Duval, who still in the death grip of his foe was now incapable of slaying the wretch, as in the fierce struggle between them his own knife fell from his hand over the side of the vessel, being lost in the swirling waters below.

A deep-breathed curse now escaped from Claude!

Exerting all his strength, flushed and excited by the applause of those around him, he now fairly lifted Vaughan completely off his feet, dashing him upon the deck.

A perfect cheer now rang above the howling of the blast.

The feat won the favour of all.

Half-stunned the villain Vaughan had just staggered to his feet, when, with a shout of triumph, Claude was again upon him:

Now armed:

Wielding high above his head a large sharp-pointed dagger:

The weapon of death held a moment or two before by his adversary!

A demoniac screech escaped the lips of the wretch Vaughan as Duval dashed upon him.

"Who triumphs now, fiend? Heaven, you see, has aided in your defeat!"

Staggering back against the bulwarks, convulsively the villain threw up his hands as though to ward off the impending blow.

For a second of time the blade of the deadly weapon flashed in the air, and then was buried to the haft in the breast of its former owner.

Again and again in wild fury Claude plunged the blade reeking with blood into the heart of his fiendly foe, who, with a convulsive shiver and with eyes now glassy in death, sank with a dull thud upon the deck!

A wild cheer now broke once more from the lawless crew, who gathered round the victor in excited crowds.

But high above the shouts of the pirate crew sounded a strange grinding noise:

A grinding noise followed by a startling crash:

A crash that echoed high above the howling winds that now roared wildly over the vessel !

The fiendly Vaughan forgotten in a moment of time, the crew of Black Hawk stared round them in horror and dismay.

In the excitement of the duel the ship had for a time been forgotten.

Driven by the tempest out of her course, she had struck upon a rock.

The pirate ship was doomed !

Lividly pale grew the swart features of the bold seamen, as a dull rushing noise now sounded in their ears :

The rushing noise of water :

Water that in huge volumes was rushing into the hold below !

Grating upon a rock, the ship's bottom was stove completely in.

The vessel was a total wreck !

Wildly screamed the hurricane over the doomed ship, the storm fiend seeming to revel in the ruin he had caused.

Fierce hoarse shouts now echoed above the howling blast.

The pirate crew, like demented beings, flew wildly hither and thither about the deck.

A low ominous settling in the waters of the brave ship was now discerned by all.

The pirate vessel was sinking fast !

Quickly preparing to dive into her watery tomb !

There was no chance of escape:

None !

All discipline now was at an end.

With wild shouts, cursing and swearing like fiends, some few of the smugglers appeared with bottles and jugs in their hands.

With death staring them in the face, they, gaining the spirit room, sought to stupefy their senses by the fiery alcohol.

It was an awful scene :

One for years recalled with a shudder by the bold knight of the road, who, the moment the ship was known to be struck, had dashed like a madman below.

Wildly had Claude searched the cabins for the one to preserve whom he had risked his life.

Excitedly he had shouted the name of his beloved, till, with a thrill, he heard above the rushing noise of the waters an answering cry.

On her knees, in an attitude of prayer, in a cabin flooded with water, he found the terrified Maude.

Her lovely face, blanched with terror, broke out in a smile as Claude caught her in his arms.

"Dear, dear Claude, are you safe ?"

"Yes, dearest ; but I fear we must prepare to die together ! The vessel has struck upon a sunken rock, and we are sinking fast !

"And he, that monster, that fiend ! oh, Claude, what of him ?"

"He is rigid in death ; I buried his own weapon in his heart !"

"Think you he will really never cross us more ?"

"Mon Dieu ! I trust not dear Maude. I do not think the fiendly villain will escape the raging waters which are now his shroud. But come, let us on deck, the waters each moment leap higher yet higher around us !" exclaimed our hero with a shudder, as he noted the black swirling mass, now on a level with the tables in the cabin.

Lifting the fair girl up in his arms, Claude now hastened upon deck.

Here a wild dreadful scene met his gaze.

The storm at its height howled fierce and terrible over the doomed ship. The blue blaze of lightning, that every moment flashed from the inky skies, lighting up in ghastly glare the boiling seething waters that now washed over the deck.

A wild startled cry now escaped the lips of Claude :

A cry that was echoed by the terror-stricken Maude !

In terror and amaze, both glared around them.

With horror and alarm, they found that the ship was deserted.

The pirate crew had disappeared !

Their long-boat, dancing upon the inky waters, was now some distance from the doomed vessel.

Whilst in the cabin below, Claude, forgotten by the seamen, had, with the lovely Maude, been left behind.

They were now alone :

Alone upon the deck of the doomed ship !

Alone upon the wreck !

CHAPTER XXIII.

LEFT ALONE—SINKING OF THE BLACK HAWK—A LAST RESOURCE—LASHED TO THE MAIN TOP—AT FACE WITH DEATH—THE BODY ON THE ROCK—WHAT CLAUDE SAW IN THE MOONLIGHT—A SAIL—AN ESCAPE.

It was with a sick, dizzy feeling that Claude, with his arm clasped round the waist of the trembling Maude, gazed at the fast receding boat.

There was no chance of escape now.

They were doomed to perish :

To sink down in the turbulent waters with the ill-fated ship.

The sky, black as ink, hung over them like a pall.

With eyes of despair, Claude could not but keep his gaze riveted upon the boat, which grew smaller yet smaller, as it increased its distance from the ship.

The lightning, incessant, lighted up the wild waste of waters for miles round.

Only in the pauses between each flash of the electric fluid did Duval lose sight of the boat.

The ocean, enveloped in inky gloom for a second of time, naught could be distinguished on its surface.

Fascinated by the horror of their position, Claude found that he could not keep his gaze from the boat :

The boat which, but for the delay in the cabin, would have borne them also from the wreck !

"Cursed be the fate that kept us here for death !" In wild despair, as he gazed over the inky waters, these words escaped his lips, then, as another vivid flash darted from the storm-riven clouds, he started and stared wildly round.

Far away the waters were lit up by the blue glare.

But the boat ! the boat that he had been cursing Providence for letting go without him, was no longer to be seen !

It had vanished :

Had sunk like a stone into the vasty deep :

Overcrowded, and caught in a fresh, furious gale, the little vessel had capsized ; its living burthen being hurled into their watery graves !

"They are gone, then ! all perished ! May Heaven have mercy on their souls and on ours ! for we, too, soon shall join them !"

"Claude, is there no hope of escape ?"

These words, uttered softly in his ears in a pause of the tempest, caused our hero to cast a searching glance around.

Much to his surprise the vessel had not yet sunk, though every instant now he knew was fraught with peril ; any minute might see the pirate ship buried in her watery shroud :

With one wild frenzied glance, he saw no single thing upon which he dared attempt to trust themselves.

Boats there were none ; and had there been, the fate of the first told him that it would be a dangerous and hopeless chance.

The hurricane now dying out, the waves ceased to beat with thundering roar over the deck upon which they stood.

With a wild thrill of hope, Claude now beheld the light of morn creeping over the ocean.

The terrible night was at an end !

With a muttered prayer to Heaven, that had as yet spared them, he now noted that the waters were subsiding :

The fierce winds were dying away in soft murmurs.

Yet with a thrill, Claude noticed that the vessel was now settling slowly down.

Heaving from side to side, it was preparing to rush down into the liquid gulf.

With a cry of despair, he now dragged Maude hastily along, and made for the mast.

He had noticed a minute before, in the quickly gathering light of day, that huge pieces of rock were appearing all round him :

From this he was made aware that the ship was stove in on a rocky beach :

Had, in the darkness and the tempest of the preceding night, been driven ashore :

The tide now running out might perchance leave part of the vessel above water !

With a last wild gleam of hope, these thoughts had flashed through his brain.

In a moment of time Duval had decided on his course.

He determined to make for the mast:

To ascend the rigging!

To remain on deck, was to await a speedy death:

To perish in the vortex of waters that would presently swirl around the sinking ship!

Whispering words of hope, and informing her of his project, Claude now assisted Maude to follow him up the rigging.

It was a dangerous task, the ship lying over partly on her beam ends; but with a sigh of relief our hero, with his fair companion, at length gained the top.

With a knife Claude now cut away some of the ropes, and lashed Maude securely to the mast.

"We will live or die together, dear girl!" he whispered, as, finishing his task, he held on wildly to the frail support, as with a sudden lurch the good ship sank down into the waters, settling upon the rocky, sandy bed below.

A wild scream escaped the lips of Maude, as she felt the vessel settling down.

A moment more and the waves were lapping about her feet as though angry that she had for a time escaped them.

Claude's timely act had saved them.

The maintop to which they clung was upright, some ten feet above the water.

"Shall we sink no further, dear Claude!"

"No, Maude; the ship's bottom now rests upon the rocks that destroyed her!"

"We are safe then till a vessel comes by?"

"Yes, dearest!"

Claude told her not that their fate depended upon the tides.

He could not prevail upon himself to tell the poor girl that if a ship passed them not ere the rising of the tide, they would perish:

That the greedy waters would rise higher and higher till they were both, with the topmast, completely submerged; buried in the vasty deep!

The hurricane now at an end, the waters ceased to beat in such wild fury upon the rocks.

With the rising of the sun Claude found that during the night they had been driven into a kind of rocky bay.

Rocks on either side jutted far out into the ocean.

Eagerly Claude cast his eyes over the tract of waters.

No vessel was there, however, in sight.

They were alone with the wreck:

Alone, clinging despairingly to the rigging of the doomed ship:

Awaiting what?

Perchance death at last!

A shiver shook Claude's frame as he now gazed into the pallid face of Maude.

Would she, after all, survive?

Should a ship fortunately pass and rescue them, would her strength hold out, or, giving way, doom her to death?

Pale and wan she looked as, her fair arms clinging to the mast, she gazed wearily round at the waste of waters.

Slowly, torturously, the hours sped on.

Faint from exposure and want, poor Maude relapsed at midday into partial insensibility:

Lost for a time to her sad, her perilous position!

With wild, eager gaze Claude kept his eyes riveted on the ocean.

Not a single sail, however, appeared in sight.

A burning thirst now seized upon him:

A thirst that at times tempted him to the maddening idea of drinking of the briny waters that lapped his feet.

Mastering the dread temptation, he then turned his eyes upon the pale form beside him.

Like a beautiful corpse looked the young girl as, lashed to the mast, her long fair hair swept about her neck and brow as it was dishevelled by the breeze that wafted over them.

Like a wild, wild dream did his meeting with the loved girl now appear to our hero.

In a sort of dreamy stupor he recalled the scene upon the deck of the pirate the night before:

His duel with the fiend Vaughan, he who had brought his promised bride to her present dire peril!

Then his thoughts reverted to the friends at home:

How had his loved Maude been torn away?

What had become of Jack, Paul, and pretty Kate?

Would he never see them more?

Was he, with his loved and cherished Maude, to perish out there with the wreck of the doomed pirate?

His thoughts, then changing, reverted to the man La Roche, he of the Secret Band, he, the primary cause of all:

For had he, Claude, been in England, perchance Maude might not have fallen so easy a victim to the fiend Vaughan!

Such were the thoughts that floated through the brain of our hero as he clung in wild despair to the mast of the sunken ship:

Awaiting the fiat of fate:

Death or release!

Slowly the hours wore on.

The sun like a ball of fire poured down upon his head till it seemed to Claude as though his brain would be turned to madness.

Once Maude Mayburn opened wide her eyes:

Then with a low sigh breathing the words, "Lost, lost!" relapsed once more into insensibility.

With a dazed wild look Claude gazed upon the pallid face.

Then again he swept the ocean with despairing gaze:

But nought appeared in sight!

They were still alone upon that cruel beach:

Not a single sail in sight:

No sign of rescue!

Half-stupefied, the hours wore slowly on to Claude.

In his agony as he clung there to the mast, he almost wished for death:

Would have slipped down into the waters, but for the fair lifeless form beside him.

But for her he would have given up the struggle.

Like a wild dream in after years did that scene upon the wreck recur to Claude.

Wearily scanning the ocean for a sail, a species of vertigo or madness now seized upon him.

He fancied the declining sun was the mouth of a huge furnace, over which he was hung head downwards.

Then the masses of rock all around assumed human shapes, were transformed into human figures:

And the sun changed mysteriously from a golden to a silvery tint.

The burning furnace now disappeared.

The sense of burning heat upon his brain was removed, and with a sigh Claude once more returned to the full consciousness of his position.

His temporary delirium had passed away.

He found himself clinging with a death-grip to the mast:

Maude totally unconscious beside him:

The queen of night in a cloudless sky lighting up the dread scene around them:

The moon, bright, lustrous and at the full, shone directly over the wreck.

With a despairing cry, Claude by her light found they were still alone.

No sail was in sight.

It seemed as though nought but death awaited them!

Clinging to the mast and praying for the end, whate'er it might be, Claude was suddenly startled by two objects that now caught his gaze:

One, the figure of a man, lying upon a mass of rock, left uncovered by the waters:

The other a large unwieldy thing that was slowly drifting upon the waves towards the wreck.

With fixed staring eyes, Claude, almost fancying he was still the victim of delirium, watched the mass that drifted slowly on upon the bosom of the waters and the figure of the wretched creature on the rock.

The moon, bright and full, shone clear on all around:

Lighting up the whole ocean.

By its silvery sheen, Claude now made out that the stranger upon the rock was apparently dead.

Listlessly he gazed at the stiff rigid form, as it lay its full length reclining upon the rocks:

The moon pouring its silvery lustre fully upon it.

For a moment Claude now turned his eyes away to gaze upon the drifting mass that danced upon the waters, slowly but surely nearing the wreck.

A wild cry now escaped his lips:

A cry of joy!

The object drifting surely towards the wreck was a boat:

A boat, keel upwards:

Slowly drifting in towards the shore.

A wild thrill of joy passed through the frame of Duval.

They might yet escape !

The rapidly heaving boat might afford refuge till a vessel hove in sight, or might enable them to quit the wreck and gain the rocky shore some quarter of a mile ahead.

All his former strength now seemed restored to him.

With frenzied gaze he watched the boat.

With a thrill he now noted that the waters were rising :

Were rapidly encircling them.

In a few minutes, their feet resting upon some lanyards, were covered with the encroaching tide.

In half-an-hour, perhaps less, Claude felt assured the waters would cover the head of the mast.

They must quit their resting-place or perish !

With throbbing heart, Claude now watched the boat.

The same, he doubted not, that had quitted the vessel the night before.

On, on it drifted :

Whilst higher, yet higher, rose the waters !

The tide was rushing in with fearful velocity :

Was now up to their waists !

With a cry of joy Duval now perceived that Maude was once more restored to her senses.

In wild terror she glared at the rising waters, and then at her companion.

"Claude, Claude ! I have had a fearful dream ! I thought we were drowning; oh, help, help !" Wild and shrill the poor girl's screams rang over the waters, which now lapped greedily around them.

"Have no fear, dear Maude, we are saved !"

"Saved ?"

"Aye ; a kind and merciful Providence has sent us a means of quitting the wreck. Come, dearest, prepare to leave the mast ; hold on whilst I cut the lashings !"

A loud thud now sounded in their ears, as the boat Claude had described came with a crash full against the top.

To lower himself into this providential support was to our hero only the work of a moment.

Having cut loose the ropes that held the hapless Maude, he next assisted her on to the boat, and both clinging wildly to it, were presently drifting quickly away from the wreck.

With a smile of joy, Claude soon perceived that the upturned boat was being by the current driven towards a mass of rocks, which still showed above the rising waters.

A cry of thankfulness escaped his lips as a moment after his feet touched the ground.

With a fearful lurch the next wave cast the boat upon the rocks.

Unknowing whether the tide at the highest covered their present retreat, Claude, now exerting all his strength, by a superhuman effort contrived to turn the boat over on its side.

As he had suspected, it was the same unfortunate vessel that had left the ship the night before.

By a merciful dispensation of Providence, after it had capsized, it drifted back to the wreck :

Opening a means of escape to the unfortunates that had given themselves up for lost !

Having righted the vessel, Claude now bade Maude sit inside whilst he gave a look round the small island, for such it proved to be.

His survey was soon accomplished.

The rocky eminence, which shot up out of the sea, was about a quarter of a mile in circumference.

Not the slightest sign of vegetation was there on the barren spot.

The tiny island was a bare range of bleak rock :

A range of rock almost covered at high tide.

With a convulsive shiver Claude, now glancing towards the wreck, noticed that the topmast had disappeared :

Was quite lost to sight in the rising waters.

But for the boat, he and his loved one he now knew would have perished.

About to hasten back to Maude, who was standing up in the vessel anxiously watching him, Claude was startled by observing a human form, which, reclining upon the rocks near the water, had at first escaped his notice.

With an exclamation of pity he started forwards.

He now remembered the figure he had seen when clinging to the mast.

This must be the same :

Some poor creature from the wreck,

Now lying stark and stiff in death !

No not yet dead ! even as he stood hesitating to rush forward, the wretched victim of the wreck began to move.

He was then still alive !

The waters rising higher, yet higher, warned Duval that he had no time to spare.

At any moment the boat in which his loved one awaited him, might, by the rising tide drift suddenly away ; drift away without him.

The very thought chilled the lifeblood in his veins.

Yet could he act so dastard a part as to leave the wretched seaman, pirate though he might be, to perish ?

No ! he could not, would not do it.

With a loud cry Claude was about to risk all by darting forwards, when, to his surprise, the stranger, staggering to his feet, gave utterance to a hoarse frantic yell and rushed madly away in the direction of the boat.

With a fear of he knew not what, Claude followed.

The tall gaunt figure of the stranger, with fearful bounds, darted over the rocks.

Grim and weird looked his shadow, as it was thrown in giant size behind his flying form by the bright lustrous rays of the moon.

He knew not why or wherefore, yet had Claude a horror of this strange man :

This stranger who was now dashing up to the boat !

In vain Claude called upon the man to stop.

Flying on in advance he now neared the little vessel.

Ere, however, he had gained its side, a wild heartrending scream rang in the air :

A scream that issued from the lips of Maude who was caught in the arms of the stranger !

In a moment after, and before the echo of the young girl's scream for help had died away, Claude had bounded forwards.

Mad with fury he sprang upon the unknown :

A curse and cry of horror escaping his lips as his eyes alighted upon the countenance of the stranger :

A face ghastly and horrible :

Hideous and unearthly :

Corpse-like and deadly livid :

The livid hue of the grave !

Eyes, that shone like polished steel, were now fixed with deadly hate upon Claude, the while his blood, like ice, coursed through his veins, as in his ghastly assailant he recognised his demoniac foe :

The accursed of the other world :

The wretch Vaughan :

He whom he had left for dead upon the deck of the pirate the night before :

Van Vaughan—

The Vampyre !

A low, guttural laugh now sounded in Claude's ears :

A laugh of fiendish malice—of ferocious exultation !

The next moment he was struggling violently with his antagonist.

Locked in a deadly embrace, the two, with a crash, fell upon the sharp pointed rocks.

Claude, his head striking with fearful force against the gunwale of the boat, was now rendered partially unconscious.

With a dull, dizzy feeling he sank down half in the waters that were rapidly rising.

As in a dream, he beheld the boat being pushed away from the rocks.

Like a grim, dread vision, the wretch Vaughan appeared to his dazed bewildered senses hovering before him.

Then, as a wild shout rang in his ears, he beheld the boat moving, slipping away :

Gradually being pushed from off the rocks !

A moment after, a tall, gaunt figure towered before him :

A tall figure, weird and savage-looking, holding in its arms a young girl !

A wild, piercing, heart-rending shriek, now echoing over the waters, recalled Claude once more to reason.

Sick and dizzy, he staggered to his feet.

Wildly he dashed at the boat :

Now some yards from the rocks.

A good swimmer, Claude, as a hoarse laugh rang in his ears, struck manfully out.

The cold waters revived him !

Aided to restore to him his senses that for a time had deserted him, from the effects of the fearful blow he had received when falling on the rocks !

THE MOB WITH A WILD RUSH NOW ATTACKED THE CART, WHICH, SWAYING TO AND FRO FOR A MOMENT, WENT OVER WITH A CRASH.

With wild effort, he made for the boat.

His fiendly foe—his captive, the hapless Maude, entwined in his loathsome arms—standing up in the frail craft, gave utterance to a demoniac shout of triumph as the open sea was gained.

But even as the hoarse, chuckling laugh echoed over the waters, Claude, by a desperate effort, gained the boat.

Seizing one end, he now half-rose up out of the briny deep, hurling defiance at the exulting enemy.

With a blasphemous oath, Vaughan now, relinquishing the hapless Maude, darted forwards and savagely struck his helpless victim in the face.

The blow, a fearful one, nearly caused Claude to sink back into the raging mass of waters that in wild eddies swirled by.

"Ha, ha, ha! you are doomed, in vain you fight against fate; thou canst not destroy me; fool, the moon's rays always return me to life, dost hear, man? Ha, ha! thy loved one shall become the Vampyre's bride! Oh, oh! the lifeblood in her veins shall give me new existence! She is mine, mine, Claude Duval! Now can thy boasted Heaven save her?"

"Liar, it saves her now!" gasped Claude.

A moment after the grinning fiend who thus defied the powers above was struggling in the waves:

Leaning over, glaring viciously at his victim, he beheld not the figure of the brave girl, who, creeping up behind him suddenly seized him in her grasp; her tiny strength sufficing to heave him over the side.

Whilst battling with the strong current the wretch was

carried some few yards from the boat, into which Claude had now successfully made his way.

With a wild scream, a scream demoniac and horrible in its piercing shrillness, Vaughan now with a few rapid strokes gained the tiny vessel.

Claude with clenched teeth and knitted brow was, however, ready for his adversary.

Even as he reached the side, Duval raised high above his head his knife that he had drawn from his vest:

For a moment of time the blade shone in the moonlight, then was plunged with fearful violence in the upturned face of the accursed.

There was one wild scream, an eldritch yell, followed by the gurgling rush of the waters.

Claude then, gazing over the boat's side, beheld the dark struggling figure of the Vampyre swirling away with the current.

His horrible foe had once more disappeared!

A moment after two figures were kneeling side by side in that open boat with hands uplifted, raised to the blue vault above:

Raised in thankfulness and prayer to the All-wise Power who had saved them from the wreck:

Who had released them of their fiendly enemy.

Long and devoutly that pale faced girl and bold unscrupulous knight of the road remained upon their knees offering their prayer to Heaven and asking further aid that they might be rescued from the stormy seas!

Their prayers were heard.

Hours after, when the dreadful rocks upon which the smuggler vessel had been lost were no longer in sight, when all around was a mass of open sea, a wild cry of joy escaped the lips of Maude Mayburn.

"A sail! a sail!" she gasped. "Oh, Claude, we are saved, saved!"

Then, overcome by the horrors she had gone through, the pale-faced girl sank back like a stone into the bottom of the boat:

In a death faint and lost to all around!

With a wild stare Claude now, as the moon disappearing the grey light of another day began to steal over the ocean, beheld some half-mile away a vessel sailing on the waters, and from her course evidently bearing down upon them.

In a short time the boat with its shipwrecked souls would be seen:

Would be rescued from their peril!

Tears of joy now coursed down the face of our hero as, kneeling down, he clasped the loved Maude to his arms.

All past dangers were forgotten.

Help was nigh.

A few moments more would see them safe on board the good ship upon whose deck Claude could now make out the forms of her crew.

The sun in a ruddy glow now rose from its bed tinging the waters with its golden rays:

By its light Claude perceived that they had been seen.

The sailors on the stranger's deck had noted the tiny craft dancing on the waves.

Nearer yet nearer came the good ship.

With a wild thrill of joy Claude beheld a boat lowered.

In a few moments, at marvellous speed, the little craft was making for his own.

Urged by strong rowers, soon the boat's crew arrived within hail.

Standing up in the vessel belonging to the wreck, Claude now shouted in wild joy.

Cheering words came back to him over the vasty deep.

"Hold on, mate!"

"It's all right, my poor fellow!"

"You are saved, lad, saved! Hurrah! give way my men!"

Even as these last words rang in his ears, a true British cheer echoing over the water, Claude, exhausted with cold, hunger, and fatigue, sank senseless beside the still corpse-like figure of the hapless Maude!

<hr>

CHAPTER XXV.

A BLACK MONDAY AT THE OLD BAILEY—AN OLD FRIEND IN PERIL—THE JOURNEY TO TYBURN—GENTLEMAN JACK SHOWS THE AUTHORITIES THAT ALL ARE NOT LOST WHO ARE IN DANGER—A RIOT—AND A RESCUE.

Shifting the scene of our life romance from the coast of fair France to Bonnie England, we must for a time leave our adventurous hero and return once more to his friends, Paul Clifford, Gentleman Jack, and the pretty Kate Annersley.

St. Sepulchre's clock had just struck nine, and a drizzly shower was falling, as such a motley assemblage as London rarely saw turned from the Old Bailey into Snow-hill! There was a party of mounted officers with cutlasses in their hands, and formidable holster pistols stuck in their girdles. One of the sheriffs of London, looking anything but delighted with the business he was upon, rode, pale and agitated, after the officers; and then came a cart drawn by a thick-set powerful horse, blind of one eye, and of very doubtful vision with the other. By the stolid indifference with which the horse proceeded, despite the ringing shouts that arose from the throats of about five thousand people, we might conclude that deafness likewise was among his infirmities.

By each side of the cart rode men armed to the teeth; whilst following these came another party of officers, so that the escort was a strong one and large.

But it is to the occupants of the cart we would direct the most special attention.

First, there was a coffin not a very ornamental one certainly, but still the hideous box for the dead, it was decorated with a double row of glaring white nails down each side of the lid. It was placed right across the front part of the cart, so that its ends projected some half a foot each way, and it thus formed a prominent object above the heads of the crowd.

And what a crowd was that:

An immense concourse of the dregs of London streets!

All eyes were turned upwards to the grim vehicle and its hideous load.

In the cart was a brawny-looking, thick-set man, whose bullet head was covered with a crop cut very close of fiery red hair! This man, without coat, his shirt sleeves rolled up, complacently glanced down at the howling mob, solacing himself by smoking a very dirty, grimy, clay pipe.

Looks of disgust and horror on all hands were directed at him.

He was known by all in that rude mob:

Hated and detested:

It was the public executioner:

Jack Ketch!

Little cared the savage-looking ruffian for the wild yelling of the mob.

As little did he care for the glances of hate and disgust cast upon him, as the half-blind horse that drew the dread vehicle.

Near to the hangman stood a tall, thin, cadaverous-faced man, dressed in full canonicals, with prayer-book in hand.

He was reading aloud to one who stood with folded arms in the centre of the cart.

Little heed, however, did the prisoner, for such he was, pay to the exhortations of the chaplain beside him.

He was glancing, with a half-smile upon his handsome features, at the sea of upturned faces that met his gaze all around.

Cool, indifferent, callous as to his fate, appeared that victim of the law, as he stood bold and defiant in the cart glancing at the wild mob that followed it.

His arms folded with easy grace, he stood upright, swaying gently to and fro to the movement of the vehicle as it jostled on over the rough uneven road.

Young and handsome was the criminal now being led to death.

He was above the middle height, and rather slim in figure; his hair jet-black hung in massive folds down his shoulders; his eyes were brilliantly dark, and but for the paleness of his face (a paleness approaching to the pallor of the grave) he might have passed for a handsome, gay cavalier, and not a criminal condemned to hang at Tyburn Tree.

Gaily and well-dressed was the doomed man.

He wore a buff-coloured coat, within which could be seen a vest of scarlet silk, that, when the coat at times blew aside for a moment had a rather startling effect.

A cravat of white silk, with a fringe of deep point lace, was round his neck, one end of which was tucked carelessly into his waistcoat.

Wearing tall, horsemanlike boots, and bareheaded, the wretched man was the beau ideal of a gay daring cavalier.

As we have said, the clock of St. Sepulchre's struck nine as this cortege hurried from the Old Bailey into Snow-hill, and slowly took its way towards Holborn.

The shout that the mob (that gigantic mob that, early as was the hour, had been long collecting) set up was absolutely deafening.

It was Monday:

Hanging Monday; and Smithfield had poured forth all its crowds to witness the procession.

Field-lane and the frightful rookeries beyond it and upon each side of it—to Gray's-inn-road on the one hand, and right away to St. Bartholomew's on the other—had supplied a strong force.

Alsatia, Petty France, Westminster, and St. Giles's, with Southwark, all alike contributed their quota of sight-seers.

A noted criminal had been condemned to death:

Was going to be hanged at Tyburn!

Rich and poor, gamin and aristocrat, alike thronged to the scene.

A highwayman, a bold, dashing, daring highwayman, was going to be hanged!

John Johnson, better known by his appearance and suavity of manner as Gentleman Jack, was on his way to Tyburn!

Such was, indeed, the doom that had been given out to the bosom friend of Dashing Duval.

Ever and again as Jack (for he indeed it was) thought of his absent companion a flush of anxiety, despite his own impending doom, passed over his face.

Even on the road to a fearful doom, he thought of that friend who had gone he knew not whither:

The companion of whom he had heard nought since his departure for the Isle of France:

Thinking thus of the friend he now might hope never more to behold, Jack was startled from his momentary reverie by a sudden stoppage of the vehicle.

The head of the procession, reaching Holborn-hill, had been forced to come to a stand.

The yells and other cries, shouts, shrieks, and every variety of noise and execration which the human voice was capable of giving utterance to, now transcended all description.

The officers pressed more closely round the cart, whilst the clergyman dropped his book in trepidation, and the stolid, villanous hangman drew his pipe from his mouth.

Jack, with his arms folded across his breast, alone stood unmoved by all the riot and racket that was taking place around.

"Push on!" now cried the sheriff, whose fat, puffy, sodden face turned pale as the wild shouts and yells of the mob rang in his ears. "Push on! push on!—this won't do!"

The man who had been on foot guiding the horse, now finding that the sheriff was both angry and alarmed, proceeded to use his whip, and holding the animal by the bridle contrived once more to get the cart upon the move, the cavalcade again pressing on slowly through the throng of people up Holborn-hill.

The mounted officers now using their cutlasses flatwise, after a scuffle with the foremost of the crowd, a way was cleared, the cavalcade anon passing slowly by St. Andrew's Church.

The most ticklish spot was now considered to be past; for it was where Field-lane on one side, and Fleet-market and Shoe-lane on the other, sent forth their streams of rabble that the officers feared, if an attempt at all at the rescue of the prisoner should take place, it would be there carried out.

That something of the sort had been apprehended was evidenced by the unusual strength of the escort on the occasion.

The mob, however, appeared more inclined for cheering than rescue:

Loud shouts of applause ringing in the highwayman's ears as he was led on the route to death.

It is a rather remarkable circumstance that in no one solitary instance did the immense mobs collected upon the occasion of popular favourites being taken to death at Tyburn really rescue any one; and yet, in twenty cases at the least, the populace assembled in force sufficient enough to have walked over the escort.

"Keep up, Jack!"

"Die game, old fellow!"

"You arn't dead yet!"

"Hurrah for Gentleman Jack!"

Such were the cries and vociferations that rang in the air.

The procession now reaching the Gray's-inn-road another stoppage took place.

One of the horses belonging to an officer fell, throwing its rider, and, instead of helping the man to rise, the mob rolled over him, a melée beginning that threatened to end seriously.

The screams of women and children, the shouts and outcries of men, and the clatter of the horses' feet making up a medley of sounds that was fearful to listen to.

By a vigorous charge, heedless of the amount of mischief they did, the officers succeeded in snatching their comrade from the howling mob.

His clothes torn to tatters, his face disguised in mud and gore, the wretched man, near dead, was placed in the cart.

"Great heavens! this is very disgraceful!" said the clergyman, who, here directing Jack's attention to the wounded man, added "You, you wretched criminal, are the cause of all this; you are the real author of this riot! It is shocking to find you so callous and hard of heart, even now, when every step bringeth thee nearer to death!"

Jack, now waving his hand, deigned only to cast a smile upon the divine! but the mob, taking the act as a salutation to them, now rent the air afresh with their shouts.

"Bravo! Hurrah!"

"Hurrah, Gentleman Jack!"

It was in the lull after this ringing shout—such a lull as was sure to follow it, when every one who had joined his breath to it stopped to rest from the exertion—that one clear note on a bugle horn struck upon the ear.

Nobody knew where this note came from, and yet every one heard it and looked around for the author of the sound; but the effect it produced on Jack was noticed by all.

The moment the sound of the bugle struck upon his ear a vivid flush came over his hitherto pale face, and his eyes lighted up with a brilliancy that for a moment was dazzling. It was only for a moment though that the condemned one suffered anyone to see how deeply he was interested in the bugle note.

"What's the meaning of that?" said the sheriff to the officer who rode nearest to him.

"I don't know, sir. but I don't like it; it sounds like a signal of some some sort!"

"A signal! then it can only be a signal that John Johnson, familiarly known as Gentleman Jack, is going to be hanged at Tyburn!"

"I hope so, sir!"

"You hope so; well, that is a good idea, when you see him in the cart, Mr. Officer. There will be no attempt at rescue, much as it was threatened by I don't know how many letters at Newgate. People who mean to embark in such a course don't bark so much beforehand!"

The officer, the man Blue Peters, grinned an acquiescence in the sentiment, and then, with a nod, exclaimed, "If they try on anything, sir, it will be by St. Giles's Church; but it ain't at all likely!"

"Certainly not! Now come on quicker there, will you, with the cart! are we to be all day reaching Tyburn?"

A groan from the mob, levelled at the sheriff, showed how they appreciated his services on this occasion, and a pebble now thrown in the cart struck the executioner upon the nose; a feature of his face rather large, and red as his hair.

"Ten guineas reward, for the man who threw that!" cried the sheriff furiously.

"How much for the woman?" cried a shrieking female voice in the crowd.

This produced a roar of at the expense of the sheriff, who, although he thought he actually saw the face of the virago who had uttered the words, did not deem it prudent to attempt her capture, but, upon the maxim of always finishing the business you have on hand first before you begin anything else, he rode on now in gloomy anger.

The appearance of Gentleman Jack now struck some of his friends in the crowd as rather strange.

He had again, after a brief gesture to the chaplain by way of answer to renewed exhortation, folded his arms accross his chest, and, although he kept his head rather down, it was tolerably evident was scanning with bent brows the outskirts of the mob.

The officers, who were keenly upon the watch for the slightest movement, did not fail to notice his change of demeanour. What it portended they had not the means of guessing, however.

Contrary to all supposition on the point, the cavalcade now passed on through St. Giles's without any demonstration in favour of the prisoner, beyond the usual yelling and shouting that had accompanied him all the way from Newgate.

The procession now turning into Oxford-street proceeded quicker.

The majority of the mob feeling now assured that the execution would take place without let or hindrance, with loud shouts set off at a race for Tyburn Gate.

All were eager to secure a good place before the victim should arrive.

"Well, Jack! ever daring audacious Gentleman Jack! it's all up with you now, I take it!" said the hangman, "I hope as you won't feel no malice!" he added, as he coolly knocked the ashes out of his pipe; "I hope you won't feel hard against me, Jack, as you go out of the world? I only does my duty! You know if I did'nt do the job some one else would!"

"Wait till it's done!"

"Wait till it's done! Humph it won't matter, I take it, then, Gentleman Jack! Do you recollect what the Recorder said when he sentenced you to dance upon nothing at Tyburn?"

"Yes, perfectly! you do well to remind me. He said he was very sorry to part me from my dear friends, Dashing Claude Duval, who has strangely disappeared, and Paul Clifford, who is in the Stone Jug; but that he would, he hoped, be able to send them both after me next Session. Was not that it?"

"Ha, ha, ha! Ecod! it was, and sartin I am as I'll have to top Paul, natty little Paul! and Duval, I doesn't doubt, will turn up again!"

"I hope he may; I want to see him."

"Oh, oh, oh! Perhaps you'd like him to turn up now?"

A loud laugh here broke from the lips of the hangman.

"Silence!" exclaimed the chaplain. "How dare you indulge in such mirth at such a time as this?"

Drawing back in the cart the jocose executioner was now with all else startled by a fresh clear note of the strange bugle that rang at this instant upon the damp morning air.

Sheriff, officers, and mob all looked round in surprise.

What did it mean?

Whence came the sound?

Who was this mysterious bugler?

In rage and alarm the sheriff glared at Jack, who, at the moment the bugle note again sounded, had caught his breath nervously—instantly after, however, subduing every appearance of unwonted emotion.

The officers around looked rather perplexed; but, although they raised themselves in their stirrups and took long and wistful glances about them, they could not see anyone who seemed at all a likely person to have made the sound.

"There's more in this than meets the eye or the ear, either, sir," said one of the mounted men to the sheriff.

"Ah! what does it mean?"

"I don't know, sir."

"Indeed, I could have told you as much as that; but pass the word among your comrades to look to their pistols. I don't know yet what may happen; but this I do know, that if Gentleman Jack sees twelve o'clock again in this world I will never ride as a sheriff to a hanging more!"

"What will you take for the bay horse?" said Jack, as he looked calmly into the sheriff's face.

"This horse do you mean?"

"Yes to be sure, Mr. Sheriff! For, if you never ride to a hanging again, I don't at all see what you will want with him!"

The sheriff with a frown here shook his head.

Jack's coolness and audacity surprised him.

"You carry it off boldly," he exclaimed; "but perhaps when you get a hempen cravat round your neck instead of a silken one, you will sing to another tune!"

"Don't be too sure of that, Mr. Sheriff," said Jack, with a smile. "Over-confidence is the ruin of many."

"Well! we shall see; just look ahead, Gentleman Jack, and tell me what you can see now!"

Jack did not look ahead.

He knew quite well to what the sheriff alluded.

With a heightened colour he, looking the man of the law defiantly in the face, exclaimed—"I know well that from first to last, from my capture by your myrmidons Jonathan Anstey and his runners, to my condemnation, I have had your bad word; he, the villain Anstey, has made oath to bring myself, Duval, and Paul Clifford to the scaffold; but though now in sight of Tyburn Tree, I care not! I have your enmity, I know not why, for I have never taken a penny piece from you or yours! I am of a forgiving disposition, Mr. Sheriff: but there are are times

and seasons when people go a little too far with me—take care you don't do so!"

"That! for your times and seasons!" said the sheriff, as he hero snapped his fingers close to Jack's face; "I don't mean to deny that you are a daring rascal, and that if you and I were upon Hounslow Heath I should pay some attention to what you might say; but your career is over now! Look about you, Gentleman Jack, and take a last glance at London!"

"Very good!" said Jack.

"Ha, ha! It is very good! Push on, will you, with the horse, there! What do you mean by crawling on in such a way, sir?"

The man who had charge of the horse's head was one of the under turnkeys at Newgate, or probably he might not have taken the rough reproof of the sheriff as meekly as he did; as it was, however, he gave the beast drawing the grim vehicle one or two savage cuts with the whip that quickly started it into activity, the whole cavalcade presently starting on at a trot.

Notwithstanding a great portion of the crowd had gone on in advance of the cart, yet the mob that followed and still surrounded it was very great.

Itinerant ballad-singers chanted quite close to the officers the exploits of Gentleman Jack and his comrade Claude Duval.

One mendicant, in stentorian accents, was shouting out the living victim's last dying speech and confession, which, certainly, under the circumstances, was rather premature.

With wild cries the yelling mob now followed the lugubrious procession.

The terrible gallows was now in sight.

Grim and weird looked the tree of death·

That tree from the stout branch of which would presently dangle a living form:

A figure of a fellow-creature writhing and struggling in mortal agony:

Twisting round and swinging in convulsions over the heads of the crowd who, in their thousands, were waiting to gloat upon the sight:

It was a terrible sight!

Oh, those good old times!

Those Christian-like merry days in merry England:

Those charitable times—those glorious days of old when a man would be strangled upon the gallows for petty robbery!

Better the too lenient justice of the present day than the hideous Black Monday slaughter in the olden time:

The olden time, when hanging was a pastime:

When a dozen men would be strung up at once.

Oh, those glorious old days!

But to resume.

With all his undaunted courage Jack cared not to sight the fatal tree.

With his back to the horse he beheld it not looming before him.

A loud tremendous shout, however, now warned him it was close at hand.

The vehicle was now stopped with a sharp jerk:

The fatal tree was reached:

That dread tree famed alike in verse and prose.

Wildly swept the wind over the open country. A thin mist or drizzling rain that had been falling all the journey now seeming to increase as it whirled in fog-like wreaths over the open spot.

The voice of the sheriff now sounded high and clear above the din.

"All right, officers! Clear the way for the cart! Humph! we are in good time!" he here glanced at his watch, giving a grim smile, for he did not now entertain the shadow of a doubt of the execution taking place according to arrangement.

Jack's face was now a little flushed, and that flush lent him quite a rare beauty. He had never in all his life—though to be sure that was not a long time, for he was only three-and-twenty—looked so decidedly handsome as he did at that moment, when death appeared to be before him, and when everyone in that vast assemblage fully believed that it would have been no great effort of arithmetic to have counted his mortal life in minutes.

The officers who were foremost now made themselves into a kind of compact wedge, and began to push a path for the horse and cart through the closely packed throng of people.

It seemed marvellous, how by any possible amount of

violence a passage could be at all procurable for the caval-cade; but it was after a time so procured, and at the expense of fewer broken heads than any one would have supposed.

A mob after being squeezed as tightly as you would fancy it possible for it to go, will yet bear a little more compres-sion, and so in a tortuous way Gentleman Jack was led to the fatal spot where so many had perished before him.

The vociferations of the people were perfectly deafening during the slow progress of the cart.

Wildly all manner of cries now rang in the air:

Some called upon Jack to die game; others shouted, they knew not why, but that they had heard the saying some-where, that he was worth fifty dead ones yet. The women cried shame upon the law for hanging so pretty a man, and one or two stones now thrown at the officers gave indica-tion that there were many in the crowd who only wanted a little egging on to make a regular riot of it.

The officers who were struck by the missiles handled their pistols viciously:

The act procuring a terrific groan from the lookers on:

The sheriff frowning and biting his lips, now turning to the men, exclaimed, "Wait a bit, my lads! wait a bit! let us get business over, and then, perhaps, we need not take things so easy!"

The officers understood their chief and nodded their satis-faction.

They gloried in the thought that, the hanging over, they could put spurs to their steeds and trample among the mob.

Another moment and the cart halted beneath the gallows.

With an adroitness that practice and a total heedlessness of the consequences to any one who might be in the way had given them, the officers now with their drawn cutlasses formed round the cart and the gallows.

The last hour of gentleman Jack now appeared to have arrived.

The hangman rising up, from around his waist proceeded to uncoil the rope which was to do the work of death; whilst the chaplain, with his hand upon Jack's shoulder, earnestly exhorted him:

"Let us all hope, John Johnson, that you now repent! that you, in this death hour, see the error of your ways! Repent! repent, wretched youth, ere it is too late! You now stand upon the brink of that eternity into which when you have plunged you will find—"

"Yes," said Jack, interrupting the chaplain, "I know all about that; but do you think you can reconcile a man to death by such talking? I tell you, as I told the judge when he condemned me—and he was well pleased to do it—that although I was guilty of many things, I was innocent of the charge I was condemned upon. The villain thieftaker hath sworn away my life; but retribution will yet fall upon the head of the wretch who has sent me here! Jonathan Anstey will find that Claude Duval will exact a terrible revenge for this morning's work!"

"Talk not of revenge, lost sinner, even here at the gallows!"

"And why not? However, I daresay you mean well. I will not quarrel with you! I wish to die in peace."

"And thou wilt die in the faith of the Established Church, by law set up, and kept up, in this country?"

"Come, come!" at this moment exclaimed the sheriff, "all is ready!"

"Die game, Jack!" shouted a voice from the crowd.

"Give him a cheer on his journey!"

"Hip, hip, hip, hurrah!"

"Three cheers for Gentleman Jack!"

Amid the deafening roar that was echoed over the plain, the hangman intimated, by holding up one end of the rope, that he was quite ready for his part of the job.

He had fastened one end of the fatal hemp to the bough of the tree, and, by hanging his whole weight upon it for a moment, had satisfied himself that all was quite safe.

The mob perceiving these grim preparations, had groaned and hissed vociferously.

Various were the pieces of advice given to the hangman whilst testing the cord.

"Put your neck in it, old boy!"

"We'll pull your legs!"

"Don't be afraid!"

"Let's hang the sheriff!"

This last suggestion was greeted with a roar of laughter. Scowlingly the object of the mirth glared around him. The sheriff did not, it was evident, appreciate the joke:

He could not see the fun in it!

"Laugh on, idiots, canaille!" he muttered. "Maybe, when your thieving favourite is done for and the horses of the escort among ye, you will laugh less loudly!"

Jack now, with ghastly pallid face, glared anxiously around.

Far back he cast his gaze upon the outskirts of the crowd.

Nought, however, met his eager, swift, and nervous glance.

"Now, Mr. Executioner," exclaimed the sheriff, "what are you waiting for?"

"For me," said Jack, by a great effort controlling the emotion that racked his bosom. "But ere you would behold the fiat of the law carried out, I would address a few words to the assembly."

"Oh, ho, ho! what can you have to say?"

"That's quite impossible for you to know till I speak, Mr. Sheriff! you wish the matter over; but I never yet heard of a fellow being turned off at Tyburn until he had had his say!"

"Be quick with your speech, Gentleman Jack! I suspect with all your boldness, 'tis but a trick to avoid the inevitable end."

Paying no heed to this sneering remark, Jack now stepped onto the edge of the cart.

Before him was the vast sea of heads.

Thousands of upturned faces met his gaze.

For some few moments there was a perfect babel of sounds:

Screeching, yelling, and groaning.

"Hats off!" cried a hundred voices. "Hear, hear! Bravo, Gentleman Jack! Die game, lad! He's going to speak! hurrah!"

These, and a thousand other discordant noises made up such a tumult that for some few minutes Jack was obliged to remain silent.

During the wild and noisy scene he ever kept his eyes upon the skirts of the crowd.

With white pallid face he awaited the appearance of a friend!

But no one came!

It was a strange scene to behold that mere youth await-ing a subsidence in the tumult around to address a crowd of human beings ere he was launched into eternity, no pitying hand stretched forth to save him.

The wild outcries now at last ceasing, comparative quiet reigned over the spot.

In a loud clear voice Jack addressed the living mass before him.

Rich and melodious was his voice, sounding clear and distinct, without a tremor in its tones.

To the furthermost margin of the crowd every word he uttered was audible.

"Friends, all you have come here to see me die! I can't say how much I feel the compliment you pay me in assembling here in your thousands, for well I know 'tis not merely to behold a man give up his last breath that brings you here, your principal object being to have a last look at poor Gentleman Jack, who in all his life never took a penny piece from a poor man, but who many a time has poured gold into the lap of the widows and the fatherless!"

"Bravo! hurrah!" shouted the mob.

"Bring him away," said the sheriff with a frown; "this kind of thing won't do!"

"Hold yet one moment," cried Jack, as violent hands were laid upon him; "I am going to confess!"

"As that is the case," said the chaplain, "he must pro-ceed!" The officers were here waved back.

Wild, excited, were the yells of the crowd which now, however, again subsided as Jack raised his hand in token that he asked for silence.

How strange that that man, a knight of the road, an idol with a multitude of some five or six thousand people, should be brought to be hanged before all their faces by thirty men at most!

So much for a London mob.

"I said I would confess, my friends; so I will."

"Hear, hear! bravo, Jack!"

"I confess, my friends," said Jack, as this fresh burst subsided, "that many a time I have stopped upon the high-way some sleek and portly sinner, perhaps a lawyer, perhaps a parson, and lightened him of his purse; I confess that!"

"Hurrah!"

"Bravo, Jack!"

"Proceed with the execution! this man is a lost sinner! a brand fit for the burning!" said the chaplain, who at Jack's last words had drawn back in horror.

"Nay, hear me out! I will now tell you the truth! I have a friend in the Parliament, who, I know, has made application for my pardon."

"What?" cried the sheriff in indignant amaze.

"Why, I have a friend who promised to procure me a pardon! Do you understand that?"

"Yes, Gentleman Jack, I do; but if a pardon comes for you I'll eat the gallows! that's all, my fine fellow! But I will have no more of this; there has been sufficient delay already. Swing him off! let there be an end of the affair! I tell you Jack, that this is your last minute! It is of no use your dallying with your fate; this is what you, and such as you, must all come to, you know, sooner or later!"

The hangman now, in obedience to a signal from the sheriff, seized hold of the victim by the arms and proceeded to place them behind his back, so as to tie his hands together; but Jack, suddenly turning round butted his head in the stomach of his horrible companion tilting him in a moment out of the cart.

Half a dozen officers, now seizing Jack, prevented all chance of flight should he have meditated a leap among the mob.

"Hold him tight my men! let him not escape! hold him tight," cried the enraged sheriff, who glared fiercely at Jack, as he added, "This comes of bringing a prisoner to Tyburn unpinioned; but my colleague, Sheriff Knowall, would have it so, to show forsooth that we were not afraid of him! Hold on to him, my men! don't shoot him! don't kill him! Hanged he came to be, and hanged he shall be!"

At that moment, it is likely enough, if any leader had started up from the crowd, such was the state of popular excitement, that Gentleman Jack would have been rescued; but although the dense mass of people swayed to and fro, and groaned, and hissed, and yelled their disapprobation of the proceedings of the authorities, not one hand was actually raised to resist them!

The hangman was severely bruised by his fall, and with a face as pale as death, save where a streak of blood from a wound on the left temple came across it, he was helped into the cart again by the officers. He shook so, however, that it was quite evident he was, for the next few moments, incapable of performing his repulsive functions.

The roaring yell with which he was greeted by the crowd unnerved him:

With livid face he drew back and sank down in the cart, his lips moving in tremulous alarm.

The sheriff upon beholding the terror of the wretched creature grew purple in the face with passion.

"To your work, fool! dolt! idiot! Art afraid of a yelping rabble? They have all come to see a hanging! and if it took not place, I warrant they would be disappointed about it! To your work then, fool! and get it done quickly!"

Thus exhorted, the hangman plucked up a little courage, and as the officers kept a firm hold of Jack, and such another tumble as he a moment or two before had had was not likely again to befall him, he pounced upon his victim with savage earnestness.

"That's the way to do it," cried the sheriff. "Now you will have him! All's right! How do you feel now, Gentleman Jack?"

The very lips of the hangman were now blanched white.

No reply did Jack give to the sheriff's taunt.

All hope left him!

A plan arranged for his escape had failed!

He was doomed:

Fated to hang on Tyburn Tree:

Never more to gaze upon the faces of those he loved!

His eyes, with a fixed rigid stare, wandered far away to the outskirts of the mob.

Every other eye in that vast assemblage was fixed upon the scaffold.

The cord, now about to be placed around his neck, caused Jack to give a convulsive shudder.

His eyes, fixed and staring, were now startled by a heaving to and fro of the mob.

Like the ocean in a storm, the huge mass, the living tide, heaved and tossed.

Afar off a single horseman now appeared!

A yell from five thousand throats at sight of the stranger burst forth!

At mad speed the horseman tore on:

Holding aloft a cane to which was fastened a white handkerchief, the stranger urged his horse through the dusky crowd.

One word now rang in a volume over the open waste:

Reprieve! Reprieve!

Again and again the word echoed from the mob the while the bold horseman slowly pushed on.

With what a pleasant tingle that one word fell upon the ear of Gentleman Jack!

Had he expected it?

Yes! but the time had gone past when he thought it would ring in his ears, and despair had begun to settle round his heart; but when he heard the joyous shout of the mob, new life entered into his frame, and the warm blood once more rushed to his face.

What a ringing shout it was that the people set up, and how the sheriff bit his lip as the man on horseback approached nearer yet nearer to the fatal tree!

The executioner looked amazed, whilst the chaplain shut up his book with an abstracted air, as much as to say, Who would have thought it?

The sheriff, raising himself in his stirrups, looked angrily at the approaching horseman, with a deep frown, turning in his saddle and exclaiming to Jack, "Should this indeed prove to be a reprieve, then is the gallows-tree robbed of its due!"

"Ah, that's your idea, but it ain't mine! You have pursued me in this affair with relentless rigour, Mr. Sheriff! I doubt not you are friends with the runner Jonathan Anstey! I bid you both at this hour look to it; we shall meet again!"

"I hope so, and at the same place as now, Gentleman Jack."

"Fate knoweth best! We shall see!" said Jack scornfully.

The stranger with the reprieve, at this moment reached the fatal spot, the crowd shouting and yelling wildly round him.

He was young and exceedingly good-looking, this young man, who now, with a white handkerchief flourishing over his head, called upon the mob to draw back from his horse's head.

The young stranger, upon whom all eyes were turned, was dressed in a suit of the prevailing fashion. His own hair which was of a handsome brown, hung in luxuriant curls down upon his shoulders; and but for a certain white and red complexion, that was not very manly, he looked like one who had been brought up a child of fortune.

"Well, sir! said the sheriff gruffly—well, sir, what is it?"

"What is it, sir? Why a reprieve for the condemned man there! Jack Johnson alias Gentleman Jack, you are saved!"

"Not quite so fast, young man; where are the reprieve papers?"

"I have them here! Let me see! In this pocket? No! in my hat! Confound it, where the deuce has it gone?" In evident perplexity the stranger here searched his clothes diligently for the required paper.

A grim smile wreathed the coarse purpled visage of the sheriff.

"This is too absurd!" he exclaimed, "This is a cheat! You have no reprieve, sir! Officers, you will take this person into custody, and let the execution proceed!"

A startling yell from the mob followed these words.

Glaring savagely round, the purple faced sheriff looked somewhat scared and alarmed.

"Ha, ha, ha!" now shouted the young stranger, the while his parted lips disclosed a set of even and pearly teeth.

"Here is the reprieve, after all, Mr. Sheriff! I knew I had it somewhere; but when I found I was late, you see, I slipped it into the first pocket I could get at!"

He here handed over an epistle upon which there was rather a massive seal.

The sheriff, with evident and undisguished reluctance, received the papers.

A deep frown settled upon his brow.

He had hoped the talked-of reprieve would not be forthcoming, or had been lost by the carelessness of its bearer.

"Who are you, sir?" he exclaimed angrily, as he now

recognised the Seal of the Secretary of State upon the papers he held in his hand.

"I am a messenger from those higher in authority than yourself, sir! You will please peruse those documents and see if all be correct," replied the young stranger haughtily.

Dashing open the letter, the sheriff now, in a mumbling voice, read aloud its contents:—

Sir, I have to inform you that his Majesty is graciously pleased to grant a reprieve during his Royal pleasure to John Johnson, convicted of highway robbery at the last sessions of Oyer and Terminer, holden in the City of London, and to request that you will cause the said John Johnson to be forthwith liberated from custody.

I am, Sir, your obedient servant,
ARLINGTON AND MAYHEW.

The sheriff turned the letter over and over three or four times. It seemed as if he hoped to find in some obscure corner a postscript that might contradict the substance of the epistle. He even held it up to the light and looked through it. But there it was staring him in the face—a reprieve signed by Lord Arlington and Mayhew, the Secretary of State.

There was no flaw; the paper seemed real.

Before the sheriff sat the young stranger, who, with an airy laugh, asked him how much longer he meant to prolong the interview.

"I will end it at once, sir! Of course this fellow, Gentleman Jack, is reprieved! It pleases the Secretary of State to send him on the road again, and it's no business of mine—none in the least—oh, dear, no! Ha, ha!"

"Its funny though, ain't it?" said the clerk. "Ha, ha!"

"Very funny, deuced good joke! a ride with an escort and no charges!" exclaimed Jack with a grin.

The mob now fairly roared:

The wildest shouts rending the air.

In indignant fury the sheriff, securing the precious document he had received, now turned fiercely upon him who had brought it and exclaimed "Well we must get back to Newgate, and there, Gentleman Jack, you will be released in due form. Officers, close round the cart, we will away at once!"

"I beg your pardon. Excuse me, but if it's all the same to you, I'll get out here," said Jack.

"Of course! you have the reprieve, Mr. Sheriff, release your prisoner," ejaculated the stranger.

"He will be released upon returning to Newgate, not before."

In a frenzy of rage the sheriff here ordered the cart to move on.

"Hold! Am I to understand you refuse to act upon those papers?"

The young stranger here urged his horse threateningly close alongside of the vehicle, in which stood the bold highwayman.

"There are certain forms, sir, to be gone through! I neither know nor care who you are; but, understand me clearly, my prisoner goes not out of my charge until we gain the precincts of Newgate!"

"He shan't go back!" cried a stentorian voice in the crowd.

"No, no! release him!"

"He's got his reprieve!"

"Let him go!"

"Three cheers for gentleman Jack!"

"Down with the cart!"

"Hang the sheriff!"

A perfect babel of cries now rang in the air.

The angry mob, now fairly aroused, swayed wildly too and fro.

Its leader was at their head.

The young stranger, who had brought the reprieve, had won the hearts of all.

A word, a nod from him, would produce a riot.

With flushed face, the young and handsome youth—for he appeared nothing more—saw the crowd were ripe for revolt.

Too late, the enraged sheriff perceived that he had gone too far.

With blanched visage he now saw danger looming over him.

"Hang the sheriff! Hang the sheriff!" was now the universal cry.

Wildly the officers now tried to close around their chief, but in vain.

With a terrific rush, the mob swept forward:

Swept forward like an avalanche, bearing everything away before it!

It was a fearful scene.

In vain the officers tried to rally and keep together. The fate of two or three who struck at the people, and who, on the moment, were dragged from their horses and trampled under foot, was a warning to the rest.

In utmost terror the sheriff and his men now only fought for their own safety.

A perfect howl; a roar that rang for a mile around now took place, as the mob, rushing forwards, upset the cart!

Officers, sheriff, and the cart with its load were now in a moment whirled along by the crowd!

In the wild melée that now took place, it was with difficulty that the bold young stranger kept near the man he had come to save.

Contriving to keep his seat upon his horse, he now prayed the crowd to give him room.

"Back! back, good people! and in the confusion we may escape! I place myself and him I have sworn to save in your hands; the reprieve is a clever forgery! If taken, I, too, may hang for my daring!"

"Curse me, you never shall, young master!" said a brawny smith, to whom, with others near, the stranger in highest excitement had laid bare his bold plot:

A plot to cheat the gallows of its prey:

A skilful device so cunningly got up that it had deceived the sheriff.

The success of the bold scheme won the applause of the wild mob.

Bandied round from mouth to mouth, the matter soon became known.

Wild cheers were showered at the bold and handsome youth who alone had carried out successfully an audacious trick.

The daring and impudent fraud received the highest encomiums of the mob.

With wild shouts Jack was now extricated from the living tide, and was presently seated upon the young stranger's saddle.

Slowly the horse was driven through the excited people, that drew aside on all hands to make way.

Hundreds of the mischievous crowd were now actively engaged in pelting the sheriff and his men with mud.

It was fine fun to pelt a real live sheriff:

Many a young pickpocket had his throw at an officer that morning:

It's so nice in a crowd to throw a stone at your victim, if you are only sure you won't be caught!

Of course if you are seized and and punished it spoils all the sport:

There's no fun in it then!

But on this eventful occasion there was no chance of being caught, so the gamins, the pickpockets, the gutter birds, and the mobility had a jolly fine time of it!

With the officers of course it was all the other way.

During the skirmishing that was going on with the mob and their victims, Jack and his young friend were not idle.

The vast throng readily divided to allow their horse to pass, showering the while upon them uproarious applause.

It was a magnificent steed they bestrode:

A dark bay, with a coat glossy as satin, grace and majesty in every action; the brave beast itself gained the encomiums of the crowd as it bore onwards its double burthen.

Jack now taking the reins urged the beautiful animal in the direction of the Edgware-road:

At each step now the crowd got thinner and thinner.

A good portion of the howling mob had now followed the terrified officers, fairly hunting them as they hurried off.

This left the path for Jack rather clear, as of course, he went in a direct opposite to the road taken by the flying officers.

Jack with his young friend had now got quite to the straggling outskirts of the crowd by the Edgware-road:

Glancing back he now with much emotion murmured the words, "Saved! saved!"

"Aye, saved, dear Jack! said I not I would do it!" said his companion winding a plump pair of arms around his waist.

"Yes, I owe to you my life, bonny Kate!" exclaimed Jack, turning round and pressing his lips to those of his companion, none other than the pretty Kate Annersley.

CHAPTER XXVI.

THE RACE ON THE WESTERN ROAD—THE KING'S HEAD, HENDON—THE RUNNERS—THE SPY—FURTHER ADVENTURES OF JACK AND KATE—THE HERMIT'S CAVE AT FINCHLEY, AND WHAT HAPPENED THERE.

No time had Jack and his daring mistress for further converse, loud shouts just at hand warning them both that not yet were they quite out of danger.

"Make way, make way!" cried a voice. "Down with all who oppose you! Push on! he can't escape! We shall have them both! Push on, I say!"

Shrieks, cries, and groans now issued from the mob.

Jack, who had paused for a moment upon gazing back, now discerned three mounted officers, with their drawn cutlasses in their hands, making their way towards him, and cutting down every one who opposed their progress.

"It won't do, Jack; you must give in; your clever trick has but saved you for a time!" shouted Claude's old enemy, the man Blue Peters, the foremost of the mounted officers.

"Will you have me now, or wait till you get me?"

Kate, with a cry of defiance, here, to the astonishment of the runners, handed to her companion a pair of pistols.

Not more than twenty yards behind, the enraged officers paused.

They knew their victim was an unerring shot, and neither fancied facing the glistening tube now pointed at them.

This hesitation on their part was invaluable to Jack; who, now clear of the crowd, gave his mare the rein, and lightly touched her flanks with his heels.

This was enough for the sagacious brute, who, though with a double burthen, dashed at lightning speed from the spot.

"Ha, ha, ha! Hurrah for the road! Stop me who dare!"

"Follow, follow! Curses, let them not escape!" yelled the officers, plucking up courage and darting forwards, as Jack's defiant shout rang in their ears.

Shots were here fired at the fugitives, but without effect.

The people who witnessed the bold escape seemed to have a good idea of the capabilities of Jack's beautiful mare, and made up their minds in whose favour the race would be, the officers being greeted with a derisive shout as they started off in pursuit.

Onwards dashed Jack at mad speed down the Edgware-road.

The Edgware-road, in the days of which we write, bore not the remotest resemblance to that of these times.

The long row of houses extending for miles had then no existence; and, save a few mansions of the nobility close to the Oxford-road, there were no houses until you got to the little village of Kilburn.

The road though, as now, was one of the best out of London; and Gentleman Jack's mare went along it gallantly, despite her double load.

That he should distance his pursuers he had no doubt; but just as Kilburn came in sight a new danger presented itself.

Coming in the opposite direction, Jack discerned some mounted men.

Here was a malapropos occurrence which Jack had not calculated upon; and if these men, who were rapidly meeting him, should take it into their heads to be troublesome, his position would be anything but satisfactory.

They might, however, take no further than a passing glance at him.

With this hope, Jack kept on:

Kate, seated behind with her arms around his waist, gazing nervously around.

On went the bonny mare with her double load; but above the clatter of her hoofs now came a startling cry:

A cry that caused Jack's heart to thump rather rapidly in his bosom.

"Stop him! stop him! A highwayman! Stop him!"

These were the cries that now rang in the air.

The approaching horsemen, four in number, now drew up.

Looking at each other, and then at Jack's approaching steed, they seemed rather doubtful as to how they should act.

Again came the wild shouts of the officers:

"Stop him! A highwayman! a highwayman!"

The strangers, to Jack's dismay, now showed a disposition to block up the road.

With knitted brow, he coolly cocked his pistols, and, presenting at those in front, dashed boldly forwards.

This was a state of things that the strangers did not seem to relish, for as Jack dashed forwards they cleared out of the way with wonderful expedition. One of them, much to the pretty Kate's amusement, decking head to his horse's mane as Jack flew by.

"Cowards!" presently after shouted the enraged officers, as they dashed past the four rather bewildered horsemen in the road.

"Cowards: you might have stopped them; it's Gentleman Jack, the highwayman, you have let go by!"

"That's all very fine, Mr. Officer," muttered one of the strangers, as the officer's words rang in his ears; "but it would not have been very agreeable or conducive to my health to have been shot through the head by an infuriated highwayman. No, no, Peter Potkins knows his book better than that; you're paid, my fine fellows, to hunt that sort of game; but we ain't. Come on, boys, I think we are best out of that!

The speaker, followed by his companions, now resumed his journey; whilst Gentleman Jack and his pursuers were by this half-a-mile off, Kilburn being dashed through at terrific pace, to the great detriment and terror of a regiment of geese that happened to be just waddling over the road at the time.

Jack slackened his pace just a little as he got through the village, for he had not quite made up his mind whether to make a dash into the green lanes to the left that led to Wilsdon and Marsdown, or go right on. There was not much time, however, for making up his mind on the subject, and after a moment or two given to thought, he determined upon keeping straight on until, at all events, he had distanced the officers more than he had already done.

"Jack, our good fortune befriends us!" excitedly at this moment cried Kate, as, turning her head, she gazed back at their foes.

"What is it, dearest?"

"Why the wretch, Blue Peters, the officer, is down!"

"What, has his horse thrown him?"

"Yes, and has sent him clean into a ditch!"

"Which he won't come out very clean from, Kate."

"No, Blue Peters will become Black Peters!"

"Just so, my bonny darling!"

"What shall we do now, Jack?"

"The other fellows are coming on?"

"Yes, Jack!"

"Very good; then we will wait for them!"

Jack, now pulling up his brave steed, turned round and coolly faced his pursuers, at the same time presenting his pistols full upon them.

This was a manœuvre that the officers evidently so little expected, that it quite took them by surprise.

Stopping short some twenty or thirty yards from the man they were hunting to the death, they appeared for a moment or two undecided how to act.

"Bravo, lads! now we've got him! On to him! seize him!" yelled a voice in the rear of the runners.

A loud shout of laughter burst now from the lips of Jack and Kate.

Dashing forwards appeared the unfortunate officer, Peters.

Smothered in black mud from head to foot, even his own men could scarce control their countenances as he dashed in amongst them.

"Give up, Jack!" he yelled excitedly; "we must have you! It's no use trying to fight it out with us! We must and will have you!"

"Very good, then; come and take me!" An ominous click here sounded in the ears of his enemies as Jack put his pistols on full cock.

"Am I to understand that you refuse to surrender?"

"Just so! But I say, Peters—"

"Well, what is it?" eagerly said the officer, who fancied his prey was going to give in.

"How long is it since you took up with the mudlark business?"

"Damn it! On to him! seize him, lads!"

The lads, however, didn't somehow appear to care about it.

They all hung back.

They did not care to rush forward with two steel barrels pointed at them!

Each one feared a bullet in his brains!

"On to him, cowards! are you frightened at one man?"

"No, governor; it's not him as we funks on, it's his pistols!

DASHING DUVAL;

OR,

THE LADIES' HIGHWAYMAN.

A LOUD CRY ESCAPED THE OFFICER AS HE FELL INTO THE GURGLING WATERS!

"Yes, that's jest it ! and as you're at the head on us and our superior hofficer, why don't you set us the example and rush in at him ?"

"Damn it, I can't see !"

"Can't see, governor ?" said another of the men, with a sly grin.

"No, curse it, my eyes are full of mud !"

"Ah, it's bad when you're like that, Peters ; how are you off for soap !" cried Jack, who had remained gazing defiantly at his enemies.

A wild, savage glare shone in the eyes of the officer.

Jack's last taunt stung him into madness.

With a deep-breathed curse, he now stealthily drew from his vest a holster pistol.

The sly act was, however, discerned by his victim.

Not for a moment did Jack lose sight of his foes.

Such a sinister mode of attack as that evidently meditated did not cause a very friendly feeling to swell in the bosom of our bold knight of the road.

He perceived that Peters, who had drawn up behind one of his men, meant to take a cool aim at him.

This did not suit our young highwayman.

In a hurried random discharge there was a good chance of not being hit ; but sighted, as Peters evidently intended, the bullet might find its mark.

Though Jack could not now see his actions, as he had drawn up behind the huge, burly form of one of his men, he knew his deadly purpose.

He did not like to fire upon the unsuspecting men who faced him, yet to remain inactive might be to meet his death:

To be shot down like a dog !

Whilst, with his own pistols presented unwilling to fire, Jack and Kate were now startled by a loud bang :

A loud banging report and cry of pain !

In another moment Jack beheld Blue Peters looking aghast at the figure of one of his men who, having fallen from his horse, was rolling about in dying agony.

"You've done it this time, clever Blue Peters ! You've missed the bird and shot your dog ! Ha, ha, ha !"

A jeering laugh here burst from the lips of Jack, who had read the scene before him at a glance.

The pistol raised to fire at him suddenly exploding. the charge had entered the back of the wretched man, behind whom the villain Peters had placed himself.

In horror at the accident, the officers leaped from the steeds to gather round their comrade.

The highwayman was forgotten.

In a moment of time Jack, turning round once more, galloped off.

Too much horror-stricken, his foes remained behind.

Not for a few minutes would they be likely to renew the pursuit.

These few minutes Jack hoped might enable him, like a hare, to double on his enemies.

"Poor wretch ! how horrid to be thus shot down by his own comrade !" said Kate.

"Aye, Kate ! the villain Peters is rightly served ; that bullet, meant for me, has doubtless robbed of life one of his own men !"

"Poor wretch, yes ! Think you they will now follow us, Jack !"

"After a time, undoubtedly ; when they have got over that mishap, they will be after us ; more savage and determined that ever."

"You think so ?"

"I am sure of it, Kate."

"Where do you propose to go ? This is the road to Hendon, is it not, Jack ?"

"Yes ; and to Hendon we are going."

"Shall we be safe there ?"

"As safe as anywhere."

"Know you anybody in that place ?"

"Yes, dearest ; I have a friend who will do his best for us."

"What is he ?"

"Oh, a jolly fellow ! true as steel—the landlord of an old inn, well-known to our fraternity, Kate."

"And this inn is at Hendon ?"

"Well, yes."

"And we are going there now, Jack ?"

"Aye, Kate ! as fast as my bonny mare, Starlight Nell, will carry us !"

Touching the flanks of his bold steed with his heels, despite her double burthen, the superb animal tore on at renewed speed.

Their foes, the officers, were now entirely lost to sight.

All alarm, for the moment, of pursuit was at an end.

For a time they were safe.

Wild, excited shouts of triumph now pealed from the mouth of Jack.

He had escaped the hangman's hands :

Through the aid of the bold girl who now clung so lovingly to him as he dashed on, he had evaded the doom to which his country's laws had condemned him !

"But for you, Kate, by this I should have been no more," he said, as he turned and gazed lovingly in his companion's face.

"Nay, talk not thus, dear Jack ! May I not as well say, but for you and dear Claude, I should ere this have been either the bride of the fiend Jonathan Austey, or of the grave ?" exclaimed Kate, with a shudder.

"Ah, your escape from that villain was due to my loved pal, Claude ! Would he were with us now ! I miss him sadly."

"Do you think that aught of harm has come to him ?" in tremulous accents these words fell from the lips of the pretty Kate, the while tears dimmed her bright blue eyes.

"I must admit that I feel deep anxiety on Claude's account and that of Maude. I cannot understand this silence and continued absence."

"Would it not be well to try and find out the whereabouts of the man Philip la Roche—he who sent dear Claude to France ?"

"I had intended, darling, to do this ; but my unfortunate capture prevented my carrying out the project."

"But you are now free, dear Jack !"

"Aye, thanks to your boldness, Kate ! — now that I am at liberty, we must not forget that another pines in captivity. We must have Paul Clifford out of the Jug, or our work is but half-accomplished."

"Yes, dear Jack. Poor Paul ! he is a merry fellow ; would he and Claude were with us now !"

Their enemies the officers nowhere to be seen, the highwayman with his bold young mistress cantered on leisurely along the road, until the then village of Hendon was in sight.

"There's our destination, Kate !"

"And whereabouts is the inn ?"

"On the other side of the village."

"We have to pass right through it, then ?"

"Yes, without we make a detour, and that is not necessary."

"Oh, dear, no ! Muddy Blue Peters and his men are far behind us, I expect !"

A merry laugh here issued from the rosy mouth of the pretty Kate as she thought of the officer who after his misadventure had presented such a filthy and draggled appearance.

Cantering quickly through the village, not without a stare of astonishment from the rustics that happened to meet them, they at length gained the extreme end.

Here, standing almost alone, was a rambling, old-fashioned inn :

An old inn, with white stuccoed front and a huge blackened beam embedded in the wall running right across, giving to the building a quaint and solid appearance.

Jack, now leaping from his horse, assisted his fair charge to descend, then walked into the house, not without thanking his lucky stars that had led him to arrive when not a soul was in the place :

The time, about eleven in the morning, the usual frequenters of the King's Head were away in the fields.

Scarce had Jack passed the threshold ere he was met by the host, who, first staring at him in utmost amaze, then seized his hands and shook them warmly.

"What, Jack ! daring, cunning Gentleman Jack ! Am I awake, mad, or dreaming ? Why I heard that they had run you down, and that your career was at an end, and was just getting the blue devils at the thought that I should never see you more."

"But here I am, Sammy Green, well in health and jolly in temper !"

"Well, I need not say how delighted I am to see you alive and well, Jack ! We must breach a couple of bottles of my best wine over this escapade ! But who is the young gentleman you have with you ?"

"No gentleman at all, Sammy, but a brave girl to whom I owe my life ! Nay, blush not, Kate ! Sam is an old friend, and I may safely confide all to him."

Jack here, despite Kate's warning glances and gesticulations, recounted to the landlord facts already known to our readers.

In astonishment, and with eyes of admiration fixed upon the lovely girl (who in her male attire looked more saucy and winning than in her feminine dress), the worthy Sam Green heard how boldly and skilfully the plan for Jack's rescue had been carried out.

"Well, it's the most daring trick I ever heard of, Jack !"

"Yes ; and it succeeded !"

"As it deserved ; but how got you the Seal of the State ?"

"By a little cajolery my dear Kate won upon a spooney clerk in the Home Office to get her an impression."

"I see ; and the rest was a capital forgery."

"Just so !"

"Well, it's the neatest thing I have heard for a long while ! and now to business. I suppose you did not pursue your journey here alone ?"

"How do you mean ?"

"Why you had some friends in the rear ?"

"Oh, ah ! yes !"

"Exactly ! and they may drop in here any minute ?"

"Well, yes !"

"Good ! then we must get ready for them !"

"It would be as well !"

"I should say it would ! They would make it warm for you if they copped you now, old boy !"

"Daresay they would ! But what do you propose, Sam ?"

"Why, first, let Miss Kate go into my daughter's room

(she and the missus are both out). She can array herself in my Phœbe's Sunday things, and can come down here in the bar parlour!"

"Capital, capital, Sam! that gets rid of the clever young man from the Home Secretary who brought the reprieve!" said Jack with a grin at Kate.

"Exactly! And now as your friends may drop in upon us at any minute, we will at once get ready for them!"

"Well, yes; it would be as well!"

"Hark, Jack! I hear the ring of horses' hoofs even now on the road!" exclaimed Kate, her pretty face slightly paling.

"And so do I! but it may be only a casual traveller on the road!" Jack here was about to hurry out from the bar where they had been standing when he was restrained and held back by the landlord.

"Are you mad, Jack? If it be not an officer, the approaching horseman might be one who attended the public meeting at Tyburn an hour or two back!"

"By Jove, you are right! What shall we do, Sam?"

"Why, make your way up into the dining-room, first floor front, you know! While you are gone, I will to the door and interrogate the traveller when he comes up!"

"Good!"

"Mind, if 'tis an officer, or anything is wrong, I'll whistle; you'll hear me, as the casement window of the dining-room is open!"

"All right, Sam!" exclaimed Jack, who, with Kate, now hastened out of the parlour, the two, making their way up a flight of stairs, being presently stationed near the window of a large room in which on market days the neighbouring farmers were wont to dine.

Motionless and quiet now stood Kate and Jack, intently listening for the slightest sound.

The clattering of horses' hoofs that had alarmed them had ceased.

The traveller had arrived at the King's Head:

Had halted at the inn door.

Plainly, on leaning forwards, Jack and his fair companion heard the sound of voices without.

"Anybody particular been by your house, Mr. Landlord?" exclaimed the stranger, whose voice Jack failed to recognise.

"No one very particular has been by, sir! there was a cart with a couple of men in it that were not the handsomest fellows I've ever seen, and there has been a waggon with a few trusses of straw!"

"Is that all?"

"Yes, all that I saw; and living, as a body may say, in a sort of road that ain't over full of people, it would be hard for anyone to pass and me not see them! I heard your horse a goodish while before you came up!"

"Well, I advise you to keep your eyes open, landlord," said the stranger; "for between you and I there's fifty guineas going a-begging.

"You don't say so?"

"It's a fact!"

"The devil it is?"

"Yes! Would'nt you like to have 'em?"

"Would a starved horse like beans?"

"Well, then, you may earn them if you keep your eyes open."

"I'll go halves if you tell us the secret."

"Oh, it ain't no secret! Listen to me: if there should chance to come past here two persons mounted on one horse—as beautiful a bay as ever you clapped eyes on—there's fifty pounds' reward for them. Gentleman Jack, the highwayman, is one of them; no one knows who the other is; but the Sheriff of London will give twenty guineas to any one who will lodge him in Newgate!"

"But I don't understand! I thought the highwayman you speak of was to be hung this morning at Tyburn?"

"He was to be, but he got away by a trick! It's too long a story to tell just now; but you'll soon hear all about it. I am one of several who are going along all the roads out of London to give notice of his escape and of the reward offered for the fellow's capture, so if you keep a good look out the fifty guineas may be yours, which, I calculate, for you, old boy, wouldn't be such a bad day's work."

"Not at all—not at all! I fancy my old gal would rather like it—it would pay!"

"I should say it would, rather better than retailing sour ale and bad spirits! Ta, ta, old man!" With a loud laugh the stranger, here putting spurs to his horse, galloped along,

Jack plainly discerning him as he peeped cautiously through the casement.

In a moment or two after the landlord hurried into the room.

"I suppose you heard all, Jack?"

"Guess I did!"

"What do you think of it?"

"Well, it looks as if they meant it!"

"It does so; but I think we can baulk them."

"Well, with your aid, dear Sam, I have every faith in eluding the vigilance of my foes."

"I don't think they will find you out easy now you are with me, Jack. Hallo! what do you want?"

A lad, about seventeen, who had here opened the door closed by the landlord a moment before, exclaimed, "Please, Measter Green, the goat has slipped her chain off her neck, somehow, and has gone down the road!"

"Gone down the road? Confound her! and will be getting in someone's garden again, and I shall have I don't know what to pay for damages; damn the goat! Be off after her, Bill! And, stay! you put that bay mare in the stable when this gentleman came, half an hour ago, didn't you?"

"Yes, measter."

"Good! now be off!"

"Shall I take the pony? I don't know how long the goat has been gone; she may be a mile away by this, I reckon!"

"Well, you had better ride then, Bill, and when you have found her make haste back."

"All right, Measter Green, I won't be long!"

In a moment after, the lad was heard descending the stairs at a tremendous rate, scarce a minute elapsing before the clatter of the pony's hoofs which he had secured leave to take were rattling upon the road.

"Infernal careless boy, that of mine, Jack! I'd wager fifty guineas it's his fault the goat is at large! Damn it, I wish there was no boys! they are only a nuisance, especially such lazy worthless clodhoppers as my boy, Bill! Damn him and the goat too! Stop here, Jack, while I go and get some mulled wine; I think all is safe for the present!"

With a smile at Kate the worthy landlord now left the room.

Scarce had he disappeared ere Jack made his way hastily to the window.

Glancing out he found the road deserted.

Not a creature was in sight.

With a somewhat troubled countenance he now turned away.

In affectionate solicitude Kate placed her hand upon his arm, at the same time glancing nervously at the door.

"Jack, dear!"

"Well!"

"What do you think of that boy, and his story of the goat?"

"What do I think, Kate?"

"Yes; what was your impression concerning that boy? If you believe he is honest, I do not; his face is a dark and lowering one"

"What would you insinuate, Kate?"

"That he is acting falsely; that his story of the escaped goat is a lie, a wicked lie, to gain leave to quit the inn."

"Your suspicion, Kate, is mine; I believe he has heard all, and has gone to give information to our enemies."

"Should he do so, we are lost!"

"No; we will away from here at once."

"Yes, Jack, the King's Head is no longer an abiding place for us."

"No, Kate, dearest!"

"Think you the landlord is honest?"

"I would stake my life upon it. Hush! he comes! he is here!"

Just at this moment the host appeared with rather a troubled look:

An uneasy look in his face that told he was both annoyed and alarmed.

"Jack, Mistress Kate, I fear there is treachery in the camp!"

"Treachery!" echoed both the highwayman and his fair companion.

"Yes; the goat that my cursed boy told me had broken loose and gone down the road is now gambolling in the paddock."

"Was that lad near when you were conversing with the strange horseman, Sam?"

"He was, Jack!"

"I suspected as much! He overheard the fifty guineas' reward and has gone to claim it!"

"I fear 'tis so, and have hastened here to tell you."

"We had our suspicions, Sam, and were talking about the boy just before you came up."

"Well, if I ain't even with him for this, cut me for the simples, that's all; but I think I'll prove one too many for them all, even now! Kate, my dear, do you hasten up to my wife's room and instantly change your clothes: that will be one good thing done."

"Yes; I can make an appearance then!"

"And help to mystify the enemy."

"Yes; the officers will look for two of us," said Jack, with a smile, now growing more hopeful.

"Exactly; and we know they will have no chance of lighting on the young man!"

"Not the ghost!"

With a low rippling laugh Kate now hurried from the room, their kind host explaining the way to the bed-chamber above.

"Now what is the next move, Sam?" exclaimed Jack as the pretty Kate disappeared.

"Why, I must keep you out of sight of those who will doubtless soon be here, and swear hard and fast that you are gone."

"But how the devil will you do that?"

"Easy! I had Galloping Dick, he that is transported now, here for four days in safe hiding."

"Diable! Where did you put him?"

"I'll show you presently; you got into danger through coming to my house, Jack, and I feel in a manner bound to see you out of your peril! Now, if you will be entirely guided by me, we will baffle the grabs beautifully!"

"Right you are, Sammy! But hark! is that the pony coming back with that cursed boy? I hear the clattering of feet upon the road!"

"No, no! the pony don't make a noise like that, Jack! It's some horse. We can see from the window easy enough. Ah! it's the stranger coming back!" exclaimed the landlord, who was now peering out of the casement; "he has had information that you are here from that young ruffian, Bill."

"He won't stop here, Sam!"

"You think not?"

"I am sure of it; he won't care to tackle me alone!"

"You are right; he has galloped past the inn on the London road."

"Of course; he has gone for assistance!"

"Very good! Then, whilst he has gone, we can get ready to put a mystifier upon them when they come back. Come on, Jack! follow me and I'll show you where I purpose to put your mare, so that, if anything happens that you want to get her in a hurry, you will know where to find her!"

The kindhearted host, now hurrying out of the room, made his way downstairs at great speed, and presently, followed by Jack, reached the stables where, quietly feasting on some fresh hay, was bonny Starlight Nell.

Taking her out, Jack, first fixing upon her the saddle and bridle, the landlord hastened into the yard and through a gate into a meadow.

Right across the meadow was a thick plantation, something in the character of a preserve; through this, when reached, Sammy Green, who was leading Jack's beautiful steed, unhesitatingly hurried, chuckling loudly as he went.

"All's right! I don't think anyone has seen us, Jack; and if we crossed the meadow without any prying eye upon us, we are safe! You must know that this copse and the meadow as well belong to a house that is to let, and has been to let I don't know how long; they asked me to have the particulars of the place in my bar, so folks are referred to me about it, and so you see, Jack, I have access to the house and grounds. Now, close at hand there is a small building that was erected for pheasants; there is plenty of litter in it, and it will hold a horse as comfortable as any stable that ever you saw; you had better take the reins now, Jack — your mare is more used to you than me!"

"Rather!" said Jack, with a laugh, who now, taking his bonny steed, guided her through the copse, the landlord of the inn going on in advance, and presently pausing at the door of a little fanciful building with a thickly thatched roof.

The door of the place opening with a touch, Jack (whose brave and sagacious mare followed them, stooping down at a jerk of the reins) found himself in a neat, warm, cosy place, thickly laid with straw, and forming a quiet, safe retreat for the brave beast, the loss of which to Jack might lead to death.

"Now, Jack, if it were not that there is such an infernal hue and cry about you, I should have advised that you and Kate had made a mount of it and bolted; but I feel convinced that for some time the roads will be blocked up against you in every way, and it is a thousand times better for you to keep yourself quiet for a day or two, if necessary, than to go out and be nabbed."

"I feel the force of your reasoning. I suppose I am to stay here with the horse?"

"Oh dear no, Jack! We must have two chances for you, not one."

"How do you mean?"

"Why, if the mare should happen to be found here it will by no means add to your identity or aid in your discovery."

"Well, no!"

"Very good; and if you are hunted out in the hiding-place to which I shall take you, it won't jeopardise your mare."

"Of course not! Then you mean to have one retreat for me, and another for my bonny Starlight Nell?"

"Exactly."

"Well, I leave all to you."

"Right, Jack! Now if—I use the word if, mind—you should be smoked out where I shall hide you, you will make a dash for it and come here!"

"Just so!"

"Very good! Now we will leave the horseflesh here and get back to the King's Head."

Closing to the door of the little snuggery, the two now hastened through the copse, and soon after gained the inn.

Entering cautiously the house, and met by blushing Kate in the passage, they found that all had been quiet in their brief absence.

No one had been:

And the villain boy Bill, the spy and traitor, had not returned!

"All goes well then for a time, Jack. Now come upstairs with me, and you, Mistress Annersley, can get into the bar. If any one comes, call me down; I shan't be a minute!" exclaimed the landlord, who now darted up the stairs, followed after a moment by Jack, who first stayed to catch a kiss from the rosy lips of his brave girl, who watched his departure above with eyes that beamed with love.

Sammy Green, upon gaining the top of the staircase hurried on, and opening a door to the left conducted Jack into a small bedchamber.

"This is your retreat!"

"The devil it is!"

"You don't think it a safe one?"

"Well really, Sam, I don't."

"Ah, there you are wrong; look here!" The landlord, with a smile, now walked over to a cupboard.

Throwing open its door, with a grin, he then looked up into the face of his companion.

"There you are; ain't that a proper hiding-place!"

"Can't say I see it! Why any dunderheaded runner would look into a cupboard!"

"Of course he would; there's the beauty of it!"

"Not if I was fool enough to stop in it!"

"Of course not; but you would not stop in it!"

"I shouldn't, that's certain, if they found me there!"

"I don't mean that, Master Jack. Now, look here, I'll tell you a secret; the bottom of this cupboard is false!"

"The deuce it is!"

"Yes; and below is the cupboard of the bar-parlour."

"The devil!"

"Exactly; though mind you, his satanic majesty, as far as I can see, has nothing to do with it. Well, you see, Jack, there is a rope below, that, sliding carefully down it, will bring you to the roof of the cupboard in the bar-parlour."

"I see!"

"Very good; then when you are there you must know that, lifting up a portion of your standing place, in a moment of time you have ensconced yourself in retreat number two!"

"Where I may be pounced upon any minute!"

"No, Jack, you are wrong! Now listen to me. In my time I have had a few moonlight riders here, and have kept them in safe hiding! I have seen the officers make too many searches not to know how they set about it. They make a mark upon the door of every closet they open, after having had a good look in; sometimes even asking for the keys and locking them up. Now, don't you see how easy and safe a contrivance this is; your foes, for instance, arrive here by and bye; they search for you in this room; you are in this closet, and you make your way to the parlour cupboard; then when they are downstairs you clamber back to your former place, and the officers are done!"

"Yes; it's not a bad game!"

"I should think it ain't; I have seen it played many a time!"

"Well, I'll see if I can't cheat my friends at it by and bye!"

"You understand how to work it?"

"Oh, yes! I shall wait here till they arrive, and when they come upstairs will get into the cupboard."

"That's the ticket! And make your way into the one below, which will have been searched?"

"How if it has not?"

"Well, you will get up here again when they have left the room! I will warn you by letting off a pistol in the parlour; that will be a signal you cannot fail to hear."

"Nor the officers?"

"Oh, damn them! I'll tell them it went off by accident! And, by all that's infernal, Jack, there they are!"

A loud banging noise now sounded from below:

A loud noise followed by the sound of angry voices.

"There they are, Jack! Keep up your spirits, we shall do them yet!"

With a smile of utmost confidence the landlord now left the bedroom.

Jack was now alone:

Alone, intently listening to the jar of voices below!

A dark shadow gathered over his brow as the voice of the officer Blue Peters rang in his ears!

This man, this ready willing tool of the villain Jonathan Anstey, followed him up persistently.

"Keep the door, and blow out the brains of the first person that interferes with you!" he cried. "Now then, Sam Green, we know our man is here! Stand aside! We are going to search the house!"

These words of the runner sounded plain and distinct to Jack, who now, with a grim smile, got into the closet.

As might well be supposed, situated as he was, with his life hanging as it were by a thread, Jack was nervously and excitedly anxious now to hear all that was going on.

He strained his hearing to the utmost to catch the faintest echo of the sounds from below!

All, however, was a confused hubbub:

A medley of sounds confused and indistinct!

Leaving him now for a few minutes in his secret hiding-place, let us rejoin the landlord his friend:

The worthy Sammy Green, who was doing all in his power to defeat his foes.

At the time that Jack was endeavouring to catch the purport of what was going on below, his kind host was standing in the hall conversing with the officer Peters!

"Now, Mr. Sam Green, landlord of the King's Head, do you mean to tell me you don't know me?"

"I certainly have not that pleasure!"

"Ah! hem! my name is Peters, fellow!—Blue Peters!"

"You may be Blue, Black, Yellow, or Green Peters, but I tell you I don't know you."

"Mr. Green?"

"Well!"

"Do you think that I'm a green 'un?"

"How can I when you say you're blue?"

"Oh, go it! I see how it is, I'll have to lock you up!"

"Indeed! and what for?"

"For insulting an officer, and aiding and abetting a highwayman!"

"Me bet with a highwayman! Allow me, sir, to inform you that I never betted anyone in my life!

"Oh, go it, go it! you are funny; a funny man you are! Curse me, I like funny people, I do!"

The furious look Master Peters here gave the stolid-featured Sam Green, however, belied the words he uttered, or else he had a strange way of testifying his delight at anything.

"I'm glad you like funny people, because we have plenty this way."

"Have you, indeed? Perhaps you think Gentleman Jack, the knight of the road, a funny man?"

"He may be, for aught I know."

"Perhaps you think it was funny, his escape from hanging this morning?"

"What was that, Mr. Peters, I haven't heard it?" said the landlord, assuming a look of utmost innocence.

"Why he was standing beneath Tyburn Tree, yes, exactly beneath it, the rope all ready, when at the last moment up dashes a young fellow shouting 'Reprieve!'"

"A reprieve! Then the highwayman was saved?"

"Yes, saved by a daring audacious fraud! The reprieve was a humbug, a swindle, a sham, a cursed hoax!"

The enraged Blue Peters here fairly stamped with passion at the remembrance of the scene at Tyburn, where we may here mention he gained in a conflict with the mob some slight tokens, such as a cut lip, a flattened and bruised olfactory organ, together with fearful impressions of heavy boots on his favourite corns.

"And if the reprieve was a forgery, may I ask how the deuce Gentleman Jack and his friend the young stranger escaped?"

"Why they bolted in the excitement, assisted by the mob! But we shall have them; there's fifty guineas' reward out, and twenty added to it by the sheriff. Now, look here! your boy tells us that you have had two suspicious-looking characters here. Let me warn you to give them up at once."

"What did you say the reward was?"

"Fifty guineas! But if we find them here you'll have to square it with your boy, as he gave the tip."

"I can't."

"Can't what?"

"Have the reward, or any portion of it."

"How so?"

"Because the people you speak of, if they are Gentleman Jack and his friend, have gone."

"Gone?"

"Yes, they went soon after my Bill."

"Oh, I see! I say, Sam Green!"

"Well?"

"Do you see any green in my eye?"

"Can't say I do; I see a bit of mud where you have been fishing for tadpoles!"

"I say, Nat, and you, Bendigo!" (two stout officers here stepped forward) "search the house; look into every hole and corner! Our man is here; and when you find him, clap the darbies on our funny landlord here; he is aiding an escaped criminal to elude the majesty of the law!"

"Is he? That's what you say!"

"I dare say you think yourself very clever, Sam Green?"

"Well I do, rather; my old mother had eleven of us, all boys; they were all fools except me!"

"Oh, indeed, poor devils! what became of them, funny Sam Green?"

"Why, they all turned Bow-street runners!"

With a grin the landlord now darted away as, with a deep-breathed curse, Blue Peters made a dash at him.

With rude oaths, slamming to of doors, and other noises, the officers above meanwhile continued a rigid search throughout the house.

Of course their efforts were fruitless.

As had been arranged, Jack upon hearing the enemy tramp up to the bedroom, slipped at once through the trap he had ready raised down to the cupboard below, returning to his former retreat the moment he heard the runners conversing in the lower part of the house.

"Well; can't you find him, my men!" said the amused and delighted landlord, who was rubbing his hands at the success of the secret hiding-place.

"He ain't here, Mr. Peters," said one of the men, turning his back to the grinning Boniface.

"Are you sure he ain't here? Have you looked in the beer barrels? Dear me! I've a horrid idea; perhaps he's hiding in a butt of ale; or, who knows, may have concealed himself in the flue?"

"He may have done that latter! perhaps you'll prove a leetle, a very leetle bit too clever, Sam Green!" exclaimed Peters, who noting a look of alarm and concern put on by the landlord, rushed madly to the fireplace.

"Look here, officers! Come away, it's absurd, no man would attempt to get up the chimney!"

"Wouldn't he? Allow me to differ with you! I think our particular man would!"

"But I'm sure you are mistaken."

"Excuse me, I don't think I am! It's all right, Adams! I think we've got him now; get ready the bracelets!"

Peters now spoke excitedly and confidently.

The appearance of dismay put on by Green thoroughly deceived him.

He made sure now that he had found out his victim's hiding-place.

Striding up to the kitchen firegrate, for it was in the taproom that the conference between Green and the officer had taken place, Peters now pulled out a brace of pistols and putting them on full cock, with a malicious grin pointed the barrels up the wide-mouthed orifice.

"Now I think as this will about bring him down!" a grin of satanic malice and devilish joy here stole over the face of the officer (who as the landlord rushed forward with clasped hands) fired, bang! bang!

With deafening report the weapons were discharged.

Blue Peters eagerly bent forwards.

He had said his firearms would bring something down: And so they did!

Not the blackened wounded figure of the highwayman was it, however, that came with a thundering crash and a rumble down the chimney; but about two dozen bricks, and a blinding shower of soot; some of the latter smothering the confounded Peters, and the former causing him to yell with dire agony as they fell upon his feet; the toes of which were scarce yet recovered from the ill usage of the morning, in their conflict with the hob-nailed boots of the mob at Tyburn.

"Oh! oh! oh! Asteuch! asteuch! asteuch! Oh, murder! oh, my foot is smashed to a jelly! Ten thousand curses on that infernal highwayman! oh, won't I—asteuch! won't—asteuch! I—asteuch! make you pay! asteuch! for this!"

In wild fury, sneezing, spitting, coughing, groaning, and swearing, Blue Peters staggered out of the kitchen making his way quickly from the inn, followed by the jeering cries and shouts of the delighted Sam.

"I say, Mr. Peters, will you have another fire?"

"Curses!"

"You ain't blue now, old man!"

"Damn!"

"Do you want a bath?"

"Laugh on, Sam Green. Make the most of it. Asteuch! I'll have revenge!"

"How will you have it, baked or boiled?"

"Go on! Oh, shouldn't I like to strangle you? Asteuch!"

"Don't put yourself out, Peters; but go and buy some soap!"

"Forward, men, that cursed innkeeper is laughing at us! Damn him, he'll drive me mad! and if I stay for much more, I shall put a bullet in him!" yelled Peters, now beside himself with fury.

Loud and long was the peal of laughter that burst from the mouth of Sammy Green, as the officers pell-mell dashed away.

A laugh, presently echoed by another, as the last of the runners disappearing, Gentleman Jack stole cautiously forwards:

"Done them, Sam?"

"Yes; clean and fair!"

"A clean sell?"

"Rather!"

"How the devil came the fool to fire up the chimney?"

"Because I led him to suppose you were there."

"Well; if he didn't find me he found some soot for his pains."

"Yes, and brickbats, Jack!" the landlord here indulged in a grin.

"Seen anything of that sweet youth?"

"The boy Bill?"

"Yes!"

"No; the varmint ain't shown up."

"I suppose you'll come across him again?"

"I've no doubt about the matter."

"I suppose you'll give the interesting youth a memento?"

"Rather; one he won't forget to his dying day!"

"I fancy he will keep out of your way!"

"That's very likely; but I'm bound to come across him."

"Well, he certainly deserves something!"

"He does; he ain't got fifty guineas, but he'll have something in lieu of the gold that he won't get rid of quite so easy."

"Well, Sam, I must own I should like you to lay hands upon the young villain; through him I must clear out, for it will not be safe to stop here!"

"Certainly not, Jack; any moment may bring the foe back."

"Just so! When do you propose for us to start?"

"At once! The day is waning away, and we shall soon have the evening glooming, and then darkness."

"Is Kate ready to go?"

"Yes; the wife and daughter have both returned, and the pretty Mistress Annersley waits but the signal of departure."

"Good! Where do you propose for us to go?"

"To a secret place, which, I would stake my life, your enemies will never find out!"

"You intend us to go to this retreat to-night?"

"Yes, Jack. You see, the best thing for you to do now is to remain quiet. The racket, and hue, and cry after you will not last long; but while it does it will be hot, and the best thing you can do is to hide somewhere, and I'll take my oath that no London crib will be as safe as the country one I'll show you."

"Where is this place, Sam?"

"Do you know Finchley Common?"

"Yes; certainly I do."

"Very well, then; you must know that a little way to the right of it, among the meadows, there is a clump of trees— quite a little wood, in fact."

"I know the spot well."

The landlord now hesitated, and Jack was puzzled to know what stopped him from going on in his narration of the advantages of the little wood by Finchley Common; at length after an apparent struggle, whilst his face grew slightly pale, he exclaimed "Well, well, you shall know it; the knowledge may serve you in good stead!"

"What do you mean, Sam, dear friend, you seem strangely put out?"

"Why you see, Jack, the place I am going to conduct you to revives old memories within me! I once had a son, who like the pious people that go to church on a Sunday to rub off the sins of the whole week and be as great rogues as ever on the Monday, did those things he ought not to have done, and left undone those things which he ought to have done, and so he was at a game of hide and seek with the officers for a long time, poor fellow!"

"I understand!"

"Of course it was my business to hide him, and do the best I could for him, as he was my own flesh and blood?"

"Of course!"

"Well he and I together quite by accident found out a capital hiding-place in the little wood that lies so close to Finchley Common, and which I am going to take you to, where I think if you like you may be quite safe for a while!"

"I shall be greatly beholden to you, Sam; for, to tell the truth, I do require a rest! My sojourn in Newgate was not a very pleasant one, and a man must have strong nerves that is paraded from the Old Bailey to Tyburn to be hung and not feel it a little!"

"He must indeed!"

"Well, I suppose we had best be off?"

"Yes; and I've just bethought me, Jack, I think it will be safer if I go ahead!"

"How do you mean?"

"Why, if I go first, and the officers are ever so much in ambush, they wont stop me! Depend upon it, this house is watched. Now, what I propose is this: I will go now, and you with Miss Annersley—for whom you'll find a mount in the stable—can come on to Finchley Common in, say, an hour."

"Not a bad idea, Sam!"

"All you will have to do when you start will be to ride down from here to Finchley Common; and then, when you are quite sure you are unobserved, cross the meadow to the little clump of wood that I have mentioned, where you will find me awaiting you."

"Capital! 'tis an excellent arrangement, Sam! We will go acquaint Kate of our plans immediately."

The two now, hurrying upstairs to a private room, where the brave girl was recounting her bold adventure to the landlady and her daughter, at once informed her of their project.

About an hour after, mounted upon two horses belonging to the friendly landlord, they left the inn.

The evening twilight had now deepened into the shades of night.

A few bright stars twinkling in the skies, no moon being visible, the night was a dark one.

All this told in favour of the fugitives.

Gentleman Jack had a hope, but not an expectation, of getting to the little wood that the landlord had spoken of without interruption. He did not think the officers were likely to give up the chase quite so easily as they appeared to do; and, if they did waylay him, Jack felt that it would be rather a ticklish affair.

For his own sake he felt not so particularly anxious; but it was something that touched him now to think what might happen to her to whom he owed so much, and who was now endeared to him by every tie that could unite one person to another.

Kate was not blind to the thoughts and feelings of Jack, and, as they cantered along the road, tried to laugh him out of his somewhat desponding mood.

"Now, Jack, 'prythee do not look so glum! Cheer up, sir! Is this the way you treat a lady, forsooth, with head hung down as though you were being led back to Newgate?"

Then, striking him on the shoulder playfully with her whip, the young girl in a more serious tone added—

"You see we have met with no one; and I begin to think that I am right in my conjecture that your friends, the officers, have given the affair up as a bad job!"

"I hope so, with all my heart, dear Kate!"

These words had scarce left the lips of Jack ere himself and his fair companion were startled by the sudden appearance of a horseman, who now darted out from the shadow of a clump of trees.

"Hold! Who are you—whither go you?"

"Danger, Jack!" whispered Kate, as she drew her horse close to the side of her lover.

The only answer vouchsafed by the knight of the road was to pull out his pistols, a proceeding that caused the adventurous stranger to draw away, the while he shouted wildly—

"Here he is; it's our man! I have him! I have him!"

"Have you, really!" cried Jack, as he spurred his horse forwards, and passing the yelling stranger at a gallop caught him by the neck, as he did so fairly lifting him out of his saddle and dropping him into the road.

"Help, help! Murder! fire! thieves! Oh, I'm killed!"

With wild yells the bruised and terrified stranger, the victim to Jack's strength and audacity, woke up echoes in the silent night.

Unheeding the frantic shouts of this new enemy, Jack, shouting to Kate to give her horse the spur, galloped at mad speed along the road.

At terrific speed the lovers dashed away.

Turning his head, as they galloped on in the murky darkness of the night, Jack now beheld a crowd of some dozen horsemen starting out into the road from the adjacent meadow.

"An ambush, Kate; they are after us, but be not alarmed. I feared this ere we started. However, if we can by any means throw them off the track and reach the hiding-place where Sam awaits us, we are all right. We will give them a race. They mean it. Hark, the clatter of their horses' hoofs! They have lost no time; but we have the start through my hurling that fool into the road. Have you your pistols ready, Kate?"

"I have!"

"Well, it is our lives they seek, so we must do the best we can and defend ourselves! It is they who force us to the fight, not we them!"

"Right, Jack! I will spare them not! Woman though I am, I will boldly face them!"

"Bravo, Kate! Thou art a true bride for a knight of the road!"

Bang, bang! ping! went a couple of bullets at this moment from the pistols of their foes!

"Are you hit, Kate?" cried Jack nervously, as he felt the whish, ping, ping of the bullet as it passed close to his ears.

They were unpleasantly close to the enemy.

"I'm all right, Jack; but I'm afraid if we don't get further ahead their next fire may do some damage."

"By heaven, yes! We must urge these beasts of Sam's to their utmost."

"Yes; or else become targets for the Bow-street runners to practice on!"

"A thing I have a decided objection to, Kate!"

"And I!"

Both now urged their steeds to renewed exertion.

Their enemies, Jack soon became aware, were much better mounted than himself and Kate.

One thing told in their favour: the officers were endeavouring to keep together.

All had not got good horses, and those who could go fast waited for those who could not.

They made sure of their prize, and allowed the chase to continue.

Like a cat with a mouse they played with their prize till they lost it; but we anticipate.

Tearing on, Jack with Kate now used both whip and spur.

It was a chase to them of life or death.

"Do you know the road, Jack?" gasped Kate as they flew on.

"Yes; every inch of it!"

"Then tell me, is there a turning anywhere near at hand? as, if so, we must play them a trick!"

"Yes; I fancy that there is a turn in the road some two miles further on!"

"Mon Dieu, that is too far!"

"How so?"

"Why, I am sure my beast will never keep up!"

"Never mind! I remember there is a cluster of houses a little way ahead, round which the road turns, and they hide it for nearly half a mile there!"

"The very thing, Jack! we must get just past those houses, and then we must dismount and let our cattle go on without us!"

"That may do! 'tis a good device, Kate. There they go! stoop low in your saddle, dearest!"

Bang, bang! Again the loud report of firearms rang in the air.

"On, on, Kate! the cluster of houses lies just before us now!"

The officers were now so close upon them that the sound of their horses' feet came painfully sharp upon their ears.

"A highwayman, a highwayman! stop him, stop him!"

Loud and clear these cries rang in the night air.

Like yelling fiends the officers came tearing on: Hunting their human prey.

In another minute Jack and Kate each gave a sigh of relief:

They had reached the cluster of cottages.

The road diverged at this point.

Not too soon had the fugitives gained the spot: Their horses were giving in.

Unused to such fearful speed, the beasts now stumbled and staggered at every step.

"Get your feet out of the stirrups, Kate!"

"All right, Jack!"

With his right hand her lover now held her horse by his head, causing the brute to come to a stand, and in another moment they were both safe out of their saddles, whilst the jaded beasts, relieved of their riders, and saluted with a smart cut from a whip, again bounded on in the darkness.

"So far, so good; come on, Kate!" exclaimed Jack in a whisper as he caught the fair soft hand of his companion in his own, and led her into the pathway near.

The spot at which they had both dismounted was close to a garden wall, which threw a very deep shadow into the roadway.

About a dozen feet or so from this place was a whitewashed cottage, from the casement of which there came a stream of light.

"Hallo! what's the matter?" now cried a voice from the door of the cottage.

The shouts of the officers, and the report of their pistols, had raised an alarm.

In crouching attitudes, with beating hearts, Jack and Kate sank down in the shadow of the wall.

With wild cries the officers now dashed up.

The horses of those whom they were thus hunting to the death flying on ahead deceived them.

The ruse practised by Jack and Kate had met with success.

With loud cries of "Stop 'em, stop 'em!" the mounted officers swept pell-mell by.

For a time Jack and his companion were safe.

The outcry of the men of law, much to the annoyance of the fugitives, of course, aroused all the inhabitants of the hamlet.

The different owners of the cluster of cottages came looking out in excited alarm.

"What is it?"

"It be a highwayman!"

"Where be he?"

"He be gone!"

"Did thee see the officers?"

"My! didn't they make a clatter?"

"Hullo! who be this?"

A countryman here pounced upon Jack, who, followed by Kate, had now stepped boldly forward.

They knew it was no use to remain crouched up in the shadow of the wall, so, putting a bold face on it, they both made their way up to the villagers.

"Who be you?"

"Where dost come from?"

"Hast seen the highwayman?"

"Yes, confound him, and have lost my gold repeater and diamond ring," said Jack with cool sangfroid as the posse of chawbacons congregated around him inundating him with questions.

"Dang it, stranger, hast he robbed 'un?"

"He has so, the villain! and stole the horses of myself and wife."

"Oh, he did, did he? Hem! ha! I will see to this, sir," exclaimed a stout, fat, podgy man, who here bustled forwards:

"Now what did you get robbed of, sir, ahem! I'm a constable; listen everybody while I interrogate these people! Now if you please, sir, what did this audacious highwayman rob you of, that is what the law asks?"

"He stole my purse, with five guineas in it," said Kate with a smile.

"And my gold repeater and diamond ring!"

"Ahem! ha! Anything more?—listen everybody!"

"Well, yes; I think he took out of my waistcoat pocket a bent sixpence and a silver whistle."

"Oh! was that all?"

"Yes; and quite enough too, I think, old fellow!"

"Come, come! don't call me an old follow. I beg to tell you that I am, in this place, which is a village in a manner of speaking, the representative of the Sovereign of these realms, King Charles Stuart!"

"If that be so, as we are not used to such high society, we will wish you good night!" said Kate with a laugh.

"Exactly! we don't feel comfortable with so great a personage. Ta, ta! good bye, old pump!"

Jack, with Kate, who was now laughing loudly, began to walk away.

"Oh, the world must be surely at an end, and this blessed village and Finchley too will be swallowed up! I'm called an old pump!"

In horrified amaze the village constable here stared around at those who, open-mouthed, had stood listening to his converse with Jack.

The two fugitives meanwhile were hurrying away:

Both wished to get clear of the village.

Finchley Common, Jack knew, was close at hand.

His object now was to make his way thither, and find out the appointed place of meeting with Sam Green:

The little clump of wood across the meadows.

Pushing on rapidly down the road, dreading the return of the officers at any moment, the lovers were now startled by a loud cry:

A loud voice calling upon them to stop.

"Who on earth can this be?" said Kate, somewhat alarmed.

"Not those whom we fear; he who calls is on foot! I think, whoever it is, our best plan will be to wait; it would be foolish, situated as we are, to quicken our steps or disregard this fellow, whoever he may be."

"Hillo! hi, hi, stop!"

"Well, we have stopped; what's the matter?" said Jack, as their pursuer, panting and breathless, came up with them.

"Nothing particular is the matter, good sir; only I am glad to see you have stayed your progress at the call of legal authority. I'm, ahem, a constable, a legal representative of majesty!"

"Oh, yes; you are the man whom we met just now!" said Jack, as he recognised the podgy form before him.

"Well, you must allow me to say that I think your time would be better employed in looking after the two highwaymen, instead of racing after me and my wife!"

"Oh, you do, do you? Very good, then, sir; I have to tell you that I have seen my missus since I spoke to you yonder."

"I can only pity or congratulate you, as the case may be," said Jack. "I hope she is quite well."

"Sir, she is quite well; that I can inform you, sir."

"I'm glad to hear it."

"I can assure you, sir, that my wife is a very surprising woman."

"Is she, indeed?"

"Yes! Hem, ha! She is a clever woman, too! Do you know she saw you pass her window?"

"Well, sir!"

"But it ain't well, sir! My wife considers that you are both suspicious characters, and orders me—no, she don't order me, but she suggests, gently and humbly suggests, the propriety of taking you both up."

"Indeed!"

"Aye, you may say indeed as much as you like!"

"Pshaw!"

"Yes, and you may pshaw too, sir!"

"Pooh, pooh!"

"Very good, very good! If it pleases you to pooh-pooh a constable, do so! But the man, sir—the individual, sir—that pooh-poohs a constable can't be any good, sir! There, sir! what do you think of that?"

"Why, I think, Mr. Constable, that you are an ass!"

"A—a—a what?"

"An ass, an unmitigated ass!"

"Me an ass?"

"Most decidedly you are; and, if you don't pretty soon clear out, I doubt whether you will get away with a whole skin."

"Not get away with a whole skin! Sir, do you know you speak to his Majesty when you speak to me? Do you know that when I produce this staff you ought to humble? When you see this little crown at the end of it, you ought to shake in your shoes, that you ought! Do you see it?"

"Yes, we do," said Kate, with a laugh, as the fat man shook his insignia of office in their faces; "we do see it; and I rather fancy that, unless you scramble over that hedge, you will never see it again." The bold girl here snatched the staff out of the hands of the man of law and hurled it away.

"Is I a constable? Am I awake?"

"Perhaps that will satisfy you on these points," exclaimed Jack, who had much to Kate's amusement, sent out his right foot upon a portion of the fat man's rotundity that must be nameless.

The representative of Majesty was so confounded at this insulting act of unparalled audacity, that for the space of about half a minute he stood transfixed; then, applying his hand to his dishonoured person, he ran away howling at the top of his lungs.

"This will never do, Kate; that fool will bring our enemies upon us in a moment if they should return."

"What shall we do?"

"Why I must go after him, curse him!"

With a bound, Jack now started after the fat constable, who had stopped his cries merely for want of breath.

An expert runner, it took Jack only a few moments to catch up with him.

Seizing him in a powerful grip, he now unwound a thick scarf that was fastened round the throat of the terrified functionary, and using it as a gag, at once stopped the yells that were issuing from his lips.

Tying together his hands, Jack now using all his strength lifted the unfortunate representative of Majesty fairly off his feet, hurling him with a crash into a thick-set hedge of hawthorn and blackberry:

A stifled, smothered kind of groan informing Jack that the prickly portions of the bed he had alighted on had found their way into something belonging to his victim, whom he now left to his fate as he hurried back to Kate.

A few minutes after the fugitives unmolested were making their way across some adjacent fields.

"I think we shall gain Sam's retreat, after all, Kate!"

"I hope so, dear Jack! are you sure you know the place the landlord spoke of?"

"As sure as I know my right hand from my left."

Both now came to a halt.

In the darkness of the night they had fallen with a thump full against a gate:

"THEY HAVE BEEN WALLED UP AND LEFT TO PERISH, PAUL!"

A gate that divided the meadow they had crossed, from another that lay before them :

A gate that was rendered as inaccessible as possible by branches of furze being placed in and out between the bars, as a sign that the meadow was shut in for grass.

This obstacle did not long deter Jack, who pulling out the furze helped Kate over, himself following after.

"Wait a moment, I will leave no token that we have been here behind us," said the cautious knight of the road, who now carefully replaced the furze that he a minute before had pulled out of the bars.

Finishing his task, both then once more hurried on.

The grass was very thick and was by no means easy walking ; but their lives depending they knew upon their speed, both hurried on.

Passing over the meadow a large tract of thick conse or wood loomed before them.

"Here we are, Kate !"

"Heaven be praised !"

"Hallo ! who's there !" cried a voice close at hand.

"Friends !" replied Jack, with a thrill of joy, as he ran forward and gripped the hand of a man who had started up in their path, no other than their staunch assistant, Sammy Green.

"Well ; you have both got here all right !"

"Not without extreme danger !"

"How ?"

"We have been pursued !"

"The devil you have !"

"And escaped only by a clever ruse !"

"Sly fox! you are the one to slip the grabs! But where are the horses?"

"Well, Sam, not knowing I can't say!"

"What! have the officers collared the steeds instead of the highwayman?" said Sam, with a laugh.

"They may have done that, for aught I know!"

"Well, no matter if they have, Jack; I warrant they won't take them to Newgate."

"No, nor this child either, yet awhile, I'm thinking!"

"Well, I don't want to be an alarmist, but the best chance of avoiding that contingency, Jack, will be for you to get into a snug retreat at once."

"Right you are, Sam!"

"It strikes me, Jack, that the sooner you are both in the old cave the better, as the country is getting all alive with Bow-street runners after you!"

The landlord now leading the way, Jack, with the soft hand of Kate clasped in his, followed closely, and in the course of a very few minutes, they reached the outskirts of the wood.

It seemed to Jack that the moment they got under the shadow of the trees they were safe.

"This will do!" he exclaimed. "Who the deuce will find us here?"

"Your foes would not be long ferreting you out in the woods merely, take my word! No, no, Jack, we must not halt here! I must see you safe underground!"

"But is this cavern you speak of quite deserted, Mr. Green?" exclaimed Kate.

"For all that I know it is. It is known by only a few to exist, and is, or was called the Hermit's Cave; but I don't believe that since I and he whom I mentioned to you, Jack, had the charge of it, that a human foot has passed it."

"I suppose not! My dear absent pal, Claude Duval, and myself found a cave in the woods near Highgate, and I suppose this place is something like it."

"Very likely! However, the Highgate one wouldn't serve you this turn, Jack! You'd be safe to be collared before you got half way there."

"Yes; I rather fancy I should!"

Following the landlord, a halt was presently made by the side of a huge chesnut tree.

Close to this monarch of the woods it appeared was the cave.

It was, Jack admitted, one of the most ingeniously got up places for concealment he had ever seen.

Near the chesnut tree was a spring of very clear, pure water, and so esteemed had one time been this bubbling stream, that an excavation had been made, and a little basin of brickwork formed to hold it.

The descent to this basin was by a very short flight of three rude steps, whilst beyond it was a kind of excavation, in which it was said that an old man had lived for many years by assisting those who came to taste the waters of the spring.

"Is this the place?" said Jack.

There was a tone of disappointment in the words that was instantly noted by the landlord.

"Yes, this is the crib; and I see you don't think much of it; but don't be in a hurry, wait till you've seen all!"

"Oh, if there is anything more to be seen, that's enough, Sam. I thought this cavity fronting us was your cave!"

"Did you? then you thought wrong! The place I'll show you into in another minute, saved one who was as well hunted as anything—human or brute—could be! It saved him, Jack, and will save you! Come down!"

They all three now descended the little steps that led to the spring; and, skirting the edge of the basin that had been made for its reception, they found themselves in the excavation beyond it.

The place was involved in darkness.

A pitchy inky gloom hung in the secret cavity!

"We now want a light; but we will soon have it, Jack, and then you will see where you are!" Bidding them stand still their friend now, after some delay, lighted a small wax taper that he had pulled from his pocket.

Handing the light to Kate, with folded arms the landlord with a grim smile now exclaimed: "Well, Jack, here you are! Now what do you think of it?"

The taper with its dull yellow faint glimmer only partially revealed the cavity, and casting a hurried glance around Jack, pointing to a number of pieces of planking, exclaimed: "It's an odd enough place! I suppose those blocks of timber are shored up to support the roof?"

"They are so!"

"It seems to me pretty clear that the roof would soon tumble in without them," said Kate. "Why there's at least a dozen of them!"

"Just so!" said the landlord. "And now tell me candidly, if you had come to this place and looked about you, would you have had any idea that anything else was to be discovered in it?"

"Certainly not!" exclaimed Jack.

"Decidedly not! There is nothing more to be seen is there?" said Kate, wonderingly.

"Yes, but there is though! Now you shall both see something that not an officer in London would think of! The last thing that anybody in his senses while in this place would think of doing, you would say, would be to remove the rough planking that shores up the roof and keeps the walls from all tumbling in together!"

"I should think it would!"

"Very well then, here goes!"

No sooner had these words escaped from his friend's lips than Jack with Kate darted towards the spring!

To their astonishment and alarm Sam Green began tugging violently at a huge piece of timber in a corner of the cavity:

One of the most solid blocks apparently in the place!

"He's mad!"

"Come away, Jack!"

About to dart out both were arrested in their flight by a loud laugh from their friend.

"Oh, oh, oh! I had you that time!" The landlord, who had now pulled away the piece of timber, pointed to an opening in the wall behind where it had rested, disclosing to the wondering eyes of the fugitives a space just large enough to admit the body of one person!

"Here's the secret, Jack! What a clever contrivance!" said Kate.

In wonder and admiration Jack drew near.

"There you are! ain't this a safe retreat?" exclaimed the landlord. "That narrow opening leads to a much larger cave than the one we are now in, and you can see that there is a thick rope and a bar at the end of it, by which means you can fasten up the plank securely on the inside, so that there can be no indication left without of its use!"

"Diable! what a fine idea! Let us go in."

One after the other the three now passed into the little narrow passage, the landlord leading the way, and Kate following last with the light.

The passage proved to be well constructed, the walls being well flattened and the flooring of clay smooth and hard.

After traversing the secret way for some twelve feet, to the surprise of Kate and Jack, they emerged into a spacious cavern, which seemed really for a place of the sort to be one of the most airy and comfortable that could be well imagined.

The walls of the cave were well flattened like those of the passage leading to it; but the most curious thing connected with these walls was to see the myriads of roots of trees that ran over them and intersected each other in all possible directions, making a complete network that one could hardly suppose was other than a work of art.

The floor was very hard and compact, and to Jack's surprise he saw various articles of rough-looking furniture in the place.

What astonished Kate, however, was the purity and goodness of the air, upon which she made a remark to the landlord.

"Yes," he said, "it is always so; and if a fire be lighted the smoke gets out quick. There must be some openings in the roof to the wood above that we cannot see, as well as some sort of means by which air gets in at the sides of the old place. How do you like it?"

"Much," replied Kate, who was gazing admiringly around.

"It's capital, Sam! It almost beats our own cave at Highgate!"

"Well, as long as it serves your turn, Jack, I'm satisfied."

"How long would you advise us to stop here Sam?"

"Well, I should say a couple of days. Your friends outside will be tired of looking for you by that time!"

"So I should think!"

"You can make yourselves comfortable, you know, I will bring you plenty of provisions to-morrow, and you will soon find the eight and forty hours slip away!"

About to put a question to the kind-hearted landlord, Jack was now startled by the sound of a man's voice :

A voice that sounded close beside them :

As though proceeding from a corner of the cavern.

With a scared look, Kate almost dropped the light, whilst Jack instinctively clutched the butts of his pistols !

"Who on earth is that ?"

"Is there danger ?" gasped Kate.

"Hush !" said Green, who evinced no alarm. "Be still ! The fact is, the roof of this cavern is not twelve inches thick, and it is only kept up by the roots of the old trees. You may always hear every word that any one says above. Hark ! let us listen, I think your foes are even now in the woods above, Jack !"

CHAPTER XXVII.

A TERRIBLE FOE—THE LIVING TOMB—THE CAVE OF DEATH —THE RISING OF THE WATERS—DESPAIR AND HORROR — A LAST RESOURCE—THE ATTACK UPON THE ROOF—THE ESCAPE TO THE WOODS—THE STRUGGLE WITH THE WATCH —THE FLIGHT—THE PURSUIT.

Breathless, and in hushed silence, the three friends now stood in the old cave.

The landlord was quite right, Jack found, when he said that converse from without could be heard.

Whilst standing in the dimly lighted cave, breathlessly awaiting any sounds from above, a man's voice came plain and clear to them.

"They can't be far off. We will not leave the woods, friends, till we see something of them."

"Very well, sir !" said another voice.

"Is Jackson here ?"

"Yes, sir !"

"Where's Peters ?"

"Watching in the meadows !"

"Good ! you are quite sure, Smithson, that you saw them go over the ploughed field ?"

"Not over it, sir, in a manner of speaking ; but they went round it by the hedge path you see, sir ; there they got over the stile and made for the wood, and me and my mate has been too much on the look out round about the skirts of it for 'em to leave it and we not know of it, you see, sir !"

"Very good ! Now you all understand that the reward will be equally divided amongst you. The authorities are determined to capture this audacious scoundrel Gentleman Jack and the party by whose fraud he this morning cheated Tyburn Tree of its due. He was by the laws of his country condemned to be hanged, and hanged he must be ! Now, keep a sharp look out, for the fellow is as cunning as a fox, and may even now be hiding in the hollow of a tree hearing every word I say !"

A low smothered laugh here escaped from Jack, in which indication of mirth he was joined by the landlord and Kate.

A trampling of feet overhead and the sound of voices ceasing, the friends now became aware that the foe had moved off.

"A narrow escape, Jack," said the landlord. "Had we been talking loudly here they would have heard us as plainly, almost, as we heard them."

"I suppose so ; however, as it happens, we are all right, and now that myself and Kate know that any noise might be detected, we will keep silent in the cave."

Good ! Well, I will be off now !"

"Had you not better wait a little ?" said Kate. "May not the foe be now hanging about ?"

"Well, you see, Miss Kate, I must chance it. If I am to get back to the inn, it must be at once. Your enemies have not yet settled their plans ; and perhaps when they do, one arrangement may be to surround the wood. I had better be off at once. If I meet an officer I'll swear I've been hunting for you. I've a good tale to tell in the robbery of my horses."

"So you have, Sammy," said Jack with a grin.

"Then you will leave us immediately, Mr. Green ?"

"Yes, my dear young lady. I can do no good stopping here."

"Well, no."

"I shall be off now, and will come back in the morning with some wine and provisions."

"Ah, don't forget that, Sam ! An empty sack won't stand, you know," said Jack.

"Just so, my bonny knight of the road ! Now, Miss Kate, if you will stay here in the cave a moment Jack had

better go with me to the outer one. I want to see if he understands how to close the piece of timber properly, so that it is hard and fast in its place, and not likely to give way at an accidental touch "

"Right you are, Sam ! go ahead ! Kate, I shall be back in a moment !"

The two, now quitting the cave, made their way down the short narrow passage, passing out into the outer excavation.

The landlord, now seeing Jack understood how to put the plank in its place by the aid of the rope and iron bar, prepared to go.

"Now, Jack, ere I cut stick back to the inn, if anything should happen to make this retreat disagreeable to you, you know where to find your horse."

"I do ; and if the worst should come to the worst, I will at last seek safety in the saddle rather than on foot."

"It will be your best plan ; and now good bye ! I advise you not to come out of this place without strong reasons fo so doing."

"Never fear, Sam ! I'm safe here ; and here I'll remain for awhile. Ta, ta, brave heart ! I shan't be sorry to see you back !"

"I will be with you in the early morning. Now let me see you put the plank in its place."

The landlord, here stepping back, waited whilst Jack turned again into the narrow passage.

With very little trouble he now, by aid of the rope and bar, fixed the heavy timber against the small outlet.

The passage was now shut off from the outer excavation.

Muffled and hollow sounded the voice of the landlord as he bade the highwayman good night.

Anxious now to rejoin Kate, as the minutes had flown by since they had left her in the inner cave, Jack was groping his way along the darksome passage when a wild thrill of alarm darted through his frame as he heard a loud thundering crash without.

A roaring rumbling sound like thunder afar off, followed by a strange rushing noise, whilst the ground of the secret passage trembled beneath his feet.

With a wild thrill of horror, his blood turning icy cold in his veins, Jack whilst listening to the rumbling noise which was now dying away, felt the soft hand of Kate suddenly grasping his.

Leaving the lamp in the inner cave, she on hearing the strange and alarming noise, had darted down the passage.

"Thank heaven, you are not hurt, dear Jack ! I feared harm had come to you !" she gasped, then whilst her voice trembled with alarm and excitement, she exclaimed, "What is it, Jack ? Oh ! what has happened ?"

"Heaven knows, Kate ! Hark, do your hear anything ?"

With beating hearts, the lovers now stood close together in the dark secret passage listening to a strange rushing noise, that sounded singularly horrible in that underground place :

The rushing, plashing sound of water !

With a thrill of wild terror Jack instinctively guessed the fatal truth :

The outer excavation had fallen in :

They were prisoners :

Entombed alive !

A cold icy perspiration broke like dew over his forehead as he listened to the rushing sound without.

"Kate ! Kate, dearest ! return at once to the cave ! I will join you presently !" Husky and choking the words escaped his lips ; whilst the young girl, clinging to him confidingly, exclaimed, "No, Jack, I cannot, will not, leave you ! Oh, tell me what do you think has happened ?"

"I fear the worst, darling !"

"You would intimate that we are prisoners here ?"

"Well ; yes, I fear so !"

"Then we shall die in this horrid place, Jack ?" Wildly the poor girl clung to her lover, nestling to him as it were for protection.

"Nay, darling, we may yet escape !"

"What do you suppose has happened ?"

"Do you not suspect, dearest ?"

"No, dear Jack ! What means that continual rushing noise ?"

"'Tis the waters of the spring, Kate, which have burst their bounds and flooded the outer cave !"

"Great heavens ! then we are lost !" A low moan of horror here burst from the young girl's lips.

"Nay, do not yet give way to despair ! Providence may

upon to us a means of escape! But do you, darling, return to the cave. I wish to find out what has actually happened."

At the solicitation of her lover, the trembling girl now allowed herself to be taken down the passage back to the inner cave.

All was as they had left it:

Save, however, that the lamp was burning low and dim; whilst the air seemed less pleasant, carrying a cold damp chill with it.

Bidding Kate wait his return, Jack now once more groped his way down the passage.

Holding up the lamp which he had brought with him, his eyes were raised to the roof.

For the first moment he saw nothing to alarm him.

But as he stepped on he started and uttered an exclamation of terror.

Stooping down he now found that the flooring of the passage was no longer hard and dry.

The clay was soft and wet.

Water in a stream was coursing down the narrow pathway.

It was with no surprise, no fresh feeling of horror, that Jack, making two or three more steps forwards, found he could go no further.

The secret passage was blocked up half its length.

Blocked up with a mass of mud and earth.

The roof near the outer excavation had fallen in.

In one solid mass had the earth from the roof of the secret way fallen into the passage.

An escape out of their prison by this way, Jack saw was impossible.

With heavy heart he now hastened back to Kate.

With white pallid face the young girl met him at the entrance of the passage.

"Well! well! What, oh what is it, Jack?" she gasped, clutching nervously at his arm as he made his way into the cavern.

"As I suspected, Kate, the roof of the passage has fallen in!"

"Great heavens!"

"Yes; the spring has overflowed, deluged the outer cave, and reaching the roof, has brought it down in one mass."

"And we are caged here, as it were, in the bowels of the earth? Oh, Jack, what a fearful death is before us!"

"Nay, dearest, we may yet escape!"

"How?"

"Why, by the roof!"

Casting his eyes upwards at the network of roots, like a flash, it occurred to the brain of Jack to make their way from thence out into the woods.

Better captivity, better death upon the fatal gallows, than meet it there in that horrible tomb, condemning her he loved also to perish.

No cry of joy escaped the lips of Kate as her lover pointed out the way of escape.

With ashen features she looked up in his face, her bright eyes swimming in tears, as she exclaimed "No, no, dear Jack, it may not be! Escape by the roof will give you into the hands of your enemies, who will drag you, my loved one, to the scaffold! No, we must stop here, and die together!"

A shudder here passed through the young girl's frame as, glancing down, she observed in the dim light a thin black stream creeping serpent-like out of the passage.

The water that was to be their shroud was forcing an entrance.

The cave in a short time would be flooded.

Winding his arms around her slender form, Jack pressed the dear girl convulsively to him.

He feared an attempt to escape by the roof would lead to immediate capture, yet was this their only chance.

To stay much longer in the cave would be to perish:

To drown horribly in the black muddy waters.

The taper now flickered faint and dull in the cave of death.

The atmosphere, damp and stifling, was affecting the light.

Choked up, the passage now admitted no air from without:

The only air to the cavernous retreat being that which gained an entry by the crevices in the roof.

With wild despairing eyes Jack glanced around.

There seemed no hope.

The only way to liberty would, in all probability, lead to prison and Tyburn Tree:

Yet, despite Kate's repugnance, Jack determined to chance it.

They might, by good fortune, evade their enemies;

But to remain in the cave was to face instant death.

Even now, the water pouring in, covered the floor of the cave, increasing in volume.

With a shudder Jack beheld the black stream with a rush dashing in.

The barrier without loosened, the water would soon fill the cave.

With a fixed, stony stare Kate gazed at the inky mass as it, with a surging rush, poured in upon them.

They were standing now ankle deep in the horrible black-looking stream.

Without resistance, Kate permitted her lover to lift her on to the rough-hewn table, himself following a moment after.

"Kate, dearest, 'tis useless stopping here; we must brave the worst; we must escape by the roof!"

"And I shall then behold you seized and led into captivity!"

"Perhaps not, Kate! We may succeed in baffling the foe in the woods; but there is no resisting the enemy in the cave here," said Jack, who now pulling out from his vest a huge clasp knife, opened it, and began vigorously to attack the roof, which almost touched his head as he stood on the table.

Kate, who saw that her lover was right, and that at all events an escape out of their horrible tomb, even though they fell into the hands of the officers, was better than waiting to perish in the dark, dreadful cave, amid the gurgling waters, now clung to him as he hacked vigorously at the roof with his knife.

The way that the bold girl clung to Jack rather assisted him in his task as she steadied his form as he stood on the table.

The clay forming the roof soon began to fall about their heads in jagged bits as the knife cut its way.

Jack, with a thrill of dismay, found his task not such an easy one as he had expected:

The clay forming the roof was hard as iron, being, as it were, baked by the fires that had so oft been kindled in the place.

In a perspiration of fear he hacked away at the hard mass.

A shrill scream now escaped the lips of Kate as they became in a moment of time enveloped in utter darkness.

The taper with a sudden puff had expired.

The air in the cave was now close and stifling.

Horribly the water now gurgled and plashed as some two or three feet in depth it dashed against the walls.

With a thrill of horror Jack saw that if they did not within another quarter of an hour make their escape, that death would claim them for its own!

With the energy of despair he renewed his attack upon the roof.

Wildly he hacked at the roots and clay.

In large masses the earth, as he laboured on, fell about him.

Striking on wildly Jack suddenly uttered a cry of horror!

"Kate, dearest Kate, we are lost—doomed!"

"What mean you?" ejaculated the young girl, as she clung with a shiver to his side.

"I can no longer pursue my task."

"How so, dearest?"

"Why, my knife has broken. Accursed be this cave, for it will be our tomb!"

"Pray, Jack, do not say so! Why I can see the light from without!" said Kate with a cry of joy. "We are saved, saved!"

Jack, who had bowed his head down in despair, now looked up as the joyful shouts of the young girl rang in his ears.

An ejaculation of surprise and delight escaped his lips!

Kate was right.

A thin ray of bright moonlight shone in upon them from the roof.

A huge piece of clayey soil had come down with the last stroke of his knife, and had left bare the thick root of a tree!

This piece of root, which was as thick as a man's arm, hanging down, Jack, with a cry of joy, seized in his grasp.

Giving to his fair companion a warning cry, he now, using all his strength, pulled at the root.

As he expected, down came a shower of clay, stones, and grass:

One huge piece almost striking him down from the table into the muddy stream below.

A broad flood of moonlight now poured in upon them.

With an exclamation of triumph Jack found he had made a rent in the earth above some two or three feet in straggling width !

Oh how delicious it was to the captives to breathe once more the fresh pure air of heaven:

To gaze again upon the bright silvery moon !

With a shudder Jack and Kate now stood for a moment in silent horror listening to terrible sounds in the cave:

The roar and rush of water !

The cave was now half full !

In a few minutes more all would have been over !

With a prayer to Heaven for their escape Jack now prepared for their exit from the dread place.

The table on which they stood now began to sidle backwards and forwards !

Jack knew well the meaning of this.

The rising water, but for their weight, would set it floating.

With a cold shiver as he thought of what they had escaped, he now bade Kate get ready to climb out of their terrible prison.

"But how are we to get out, dear Jack, now the opening is made ?" said the young girl with a nervous shudder.

"Easily, Kate ! Be not alarmed; we are safe enough now. You are young and active, and I am strong; so we shall manage."

"Now let me help you to climb on my shoulders; from thence you can quickly scramble through the opening and be safe out in the woods."

"And you, dear Jack ?"

"Will follow on after."

"How ?"

"By aid of the root you see hanging down !" Jack here pointed to the snake-like arm that dangled over their heads, his strong pull at which had opened to them a few minutes before the way to liberty and life.

By the assistance of her lover, the bold girl, after some little exertion, now managed successfully to emerge from the grim cavern into the open woods above.

No sooner, however, was the table released from her weight than it shifted with a jerk from beneath Jack's feet.

This contingency he was prepared for.

With a strong grip he had seized hold of the root of the tree that hung over his head.

Putting out all his strength, he now began to pull himself through the opening:

Kate, with pallid nervous face, bending over him from above.

The tree, the root of which Jack clung to, was a Pollard oak, that stood some yard and a half from the broken roof of the cave.

But for this denizen of the woods the whole mass of earth that covered the retreat would have fallen in.

The network of roots, however, saved the clayey soil from crumbling away.

But for this, Jack might have been, after all, buried alive.

This fear it was that blanched the lovely face of Kate Annesley, who, with wild eyes, watched her lover as he struggled up through the huge rent in the earth at her feet.

Intent upon escape from the horrible cave, their foes had by both been forgotten.

As Kate bent over the figure of her lover, who was now half-way out of his late dread prison, she saw not, heard not, the stealthy step of a man in the brushwood near.

Jack, intent solely upon getting clear from the well-hole the cave had now changed to, had quite lost the remembrance of his foes:

A startled cry escaping his lips, as finally struggling forth and staggering to his feet, he found himself gripped in a strong pair of arms.

A deep-breathed curse escaped his lips, followed by a muffled shriek from Kate, who was clasped in the arms of a stranger, who at the moment of Jack's capture had stolen up behind her.

"We have done it, Jackson !"

"We have so; I've got him !"

"Then, mind you keep him !"

With an exclamation of rage, Jack, here contriving to slip eel-like from his captor's grasp, hurled him with a crash to the ground.

A wild startled cry escaped the officer's lips, who now, to the surprise of his companion, who was holding Kate, suddenly disappeared:

Disappeared, uttering a shriek of horror !

Releasing his fair prisoner, the remaining officer rushed forwards:

Rushed forwards to where a second or two before he had seen his wretched comrade disappear !

A wild cry of terror escaped the man's lips as he beheld a huge rent in the earth, from whence welled forth a black, inky stream; then, as horrified shouts for help escaped him, Jack and Kate unseen glided away—

Unnoted—forgotten: the officer, lost in horror at the dread peril of his companion, whom he now saw struggling in the muddy waters at his feet.

With the fleetness of fawns, Jack and Kate darted through the woods:

For many minutes they heard the wild shouts of the officers they had escaped from echoing in the air.

Jack smiled grimly at the sounds.

"Let him hallo himself hoarse, Kate; it will be all the better for us !"

"How so, Jack ?"

"Why, it will draw all other watchers in the woods to the spot."

"So it will ! I hope that poor wretch won't drown in that horrid hole !"

"Not he, Kate; his comrades will have him out ! But he will be no loss; there's plenty of the cursed manhunters left without him," said Jack, who, we must admit, was very indifferent as to whether his late captor escaped from the cave or not.

Hurrying on through the thick copse without molestation, the highwayman began to think that he should get clear away without further trouble.

Stopping ever and again to listen, he now, with Kate following on beside him, made less haste through the copse.

Jack felt that caution was extremely necessary.

At any moment they might stumble across some one hidden in the brushwood that flourished around them on all sides.

"What a beautiful night, Jack !" at length, murmured Kate, the first to break the silence they had kept up between them during their flight. "How beautiful is the moon !"

"Yes; I confess I love her ladyship's light, Kate ! I love the soft, cool, and gentle moonlight above all other lights ! How bright and beautiful it is as it shines down through the little openings in the trees !"

"Yes, Jack; and see upon the ground here, how bright it is, while the shadow of the leaves looks like some pattern in silver and dim grey worked upon the earth of the little forest !"

"Yes, it's very beautiful, Kate; 'tis a lovely night; though, for that matter, we ought to pray for darkness; for the moon we so much admire may give us to our foes ! Hist ! hold on, Kate ! I fancied I heard a noise close at hand !"

Both, now, not without a nervous tremor intervening, listened for any sounds in the woods.

Plainly to their ears, as they stood statue-like in the copse, anon came the sound of footsteps of a man.

Jack had not been deceived.

Some one was close upon them in the woods.

Tramp, tramp ! A man's footfall, safe enough:

Sounding upon the other side of some bushes near which they were standing, and upon which the moon they had been admiring glinted bright and beautifully, frosting the foliage as with silver !

The sound of the footsteps that now fell upon the ears of the companions was precisely what one would suppose would result from some person going to and fro upon some sentinel-like duty, and tended to confirm Jack's suspicion that the wood in which he and Kate now were had round it a cordon of watchers.

"It is as I thought, Kate !" he murmured in a whisper; "my enemies are keeping guard all round the wood; and probably, when daylight arrives, they will take measures bring affairs to a crisis !"

"Then we must bring matters to a crisis by getting out of the woods while night hangs over us !"

"Right, Kate !"

"There is but one man here, Jack ! Can we not get the better of him—and that without doing the fellow an injury ?"

"It must be tried, Kate ; in the woods here we dare not stop ! The watcher is still marching to and fro on his post. What say you, dearest, to our creeping forwards to the line of bushes that separates us from him, and, listening to him closer, we may perhaps get a look at the fellow and see the sort of customer we have to deal with ?"

Agreed, Jack ! come on !"

Our two adventurers, who had been sitting upon the roots of a chesnut tree, now in a silent and cautious manner crept slowly fowards to where the sentinel was keeping his lonely watch.

The line of bushes that separated them from him was about eight or ten feet in height, and here and there a tall tree shot up among them in the night sky, giving them an irregularity of aspect that added much to their picturesque beauty.

As the moon was situated in the heavens, the side of the bushes next to Jack and Kate was illuminated, and the other side, the friends doubted not, was in strong shadow.

This was against them, as there would be some difficulty in their seeing the sentinel ; whilst he, gazing out of darkness into light, would very easily see them.

This chance of discovery they had to run.

Just as they, treading softly the line of hedge, reached the further end, the man stopped suddenly in his march to and fro !

Jack, fearful he had seen them, whispered Kate to lie down.

Then, crawling onwards, he at length gained a portion of the hedge where a large gap enabled him to look through.

To his great surprise Jack now found that this thicket terminated the wood in that direction !

All beyond that point was to the eye—at that time, when the moonlight, although it shone brightly in some places, greatly confused the landscape by the abrupt shadows that it produced in others—a field of apparently great extent.

Cautiously Jack now peered at the man on the watch :

A huge burly fellow, broad-shouldered and herculean in appearance, no mean antagonist in a scuffle, that Jack saw at a glance !

"Well, this is a game I don't like ! Curse me if I wouldn't sooner be at the old game—

"'For its my delight, on a shiny night,
In the season of the year !'"

The watcher whom Jack did not fail to anathematise here struck out into several cadences, in which he explained to the trees and shrubs, and a passing rabbit that scampered along in the brushwood, the delights of poaching.

Finishing his vocal performance the fellow now, who seemed pretty tired of the task allotted him, opened his huge mouth and gave such a yawn that Jack thought he was never going to close it again !

"Curse me if this watching for that chap hasn't made me sleepy ! I'll doze for ten minutes and chance it ! They wouldn't have got me on this caper if it hadn't been for the lummy reward they offered—twenty guineas if I nail him, or ten for his dead body ! Well, if I comes across him, I'll make a safe game of it, and go in for the ten ; there's no trouble over that ! I've just got to let him have the contents of my gun, and if he gets away after that, he'll be in luck. If I collars him I might get a dig from his cheese-cutter in my bread-basket, which wouldn't at all agree with the health of Reuben Muggins !"

The man, with another yawn, now settling down with his back against the hedge, composed himself to doze :

Jack, with glistening eye, watching his every movement !

A dark frown gathered over the highwayman's face as he glared upon his enemy—this big, burly, ruffian, who for gain, who for a paltry ten guineas had avowed his intention of shooting him down like a dog !

"Well, Mr. Muggins, if I don't make your mug a little plainer than it already is before I've done with you, it's a caution !" muttered Jack, who, now joined by Kate, whispered what he had heard.

A smile flashed over the pretty face of the young girl. Glancing through the gap in the hedge she saw that the burly sentinel was now fast asleep !

"It's all right, Jack !"

"What's all right ?"

"Why, Reuben Muggins !"

"He's gone to sleep ?"

"As fast as though he'd had a dose of morphine !"

"Good ! My name ain't John if I don't operate on the beggar, Kate, before we go !"

"You don't intend so hurt him ?"

"Oh, dear, no !"

"You wouldn't deprive the poor man of ten guineas ?"

"By no manner of means !"

"Shall I wake him up ?"

"No ; that would be cruel !"

"Why so ?"

"Because the poor chap is tired !"

"So he is ! Don't he snore ?"

"Rather ! I think he don't lie comfortable ; his head is too low ; go and raise it for him, Kate !"

"I can't—I've got a pain in my foot !"

"It strikes me Reuben Muggins will have a pain somewhere presently, Kate !"

"I've not the least doubt of it !"

"He spoke just now about giving me the contents of his gun !"

"Which you don't care about accepting ?"

"Well, I don't know, Kate ; I don't think I'd mind having the weapon ; perhaps he'd give me that too ?"

"He might !"

"I don't like to disturb him or I'd ask him !"

"Well, there is only one course open to you, Jack !"

"And that——"

"Is to take it !"

"But he might be cross if he woke up !"

"Well, you can apologise !"

"So I can, with the barrel pointed at his head !" said Jack with a grin, who now, followed by Kate, began to make for the other side of the hedge, the same upon which reposed their foe, who slumbered on in blissful ignorance of the proximity of the fugitives he had been put there to watch.

The great difficulty before Jack and his mistress was to get quickly through the hedge without disturbing the herculean slumberer.

Not without causing a slight crackling noise, Jack, however, succeeded in bending down the large stems of one of the bushes without awaking their foe.

There was now a tolerably clear space for him and Kate to pass through.

"I trust there is no other watcher near, Jack !" said the young girl, as, stooping down, she passed out of the wood into the field on the other side, and, proceeding, her companion quickly followed.

No sooner were they fairly in the field, standing in the full glare of the moon's rays, than both looked searchingly round.

All, however, was quiet.

No living being was in sight.

Jack now, with noiseless tread, approached the sleeping sentinel.

He had determined to secure the fellow's gun.

For Jack to resolve upon a thing was to execute it.

He was aware that the aspect of affairs would be wonderfully altered if he had the loaded weapon instead of his enemy.

The cards would then have changed hands.

He would hold the winning one :

The gun was the trump card.

The game they were playing was a heavy one :
Death !

Should he secure the firearm of the enemy, Jack felt he would be safe ; the game would be in his own hands.

Breathlessly he drew near the sleeper.

The coveted weapon lay in the hollow of the man's arm.

There was great danger of awakening the sleeper in securing it.

This danger, however, Jack determined to brave.

It was an anxious moment for Kate, who stood statue-like watching her lover's movement.

First assuring himself that the man was still in heavy repose, Jack now placed his hand upon the barrel of the gun, which rested partly on the sleeper's shoulder.

Slowly he began to draw it forth.

Ceasing, however, as he suddenly discovered that the stock was held hard and fast in the fellow's arm.

Stooping down Jack now found that the lock had caught in the sleeve of the sentinel.

There appeared no chance of securing the weapon without awaking its proprietor.

Jack was in a bit of a dilemma:

He could not make up his mind how to act.

Whilst debating thus the man turned round on his side, moaned in his sleep, then went off again, apparently heavier than before:

This time with the gun resting under him.

With a deep muttered curse, Jack drew away.

He cared not to arouse the sleeper.

Joining Kate, who was standing near and had seen all, they both decided to hurry at once away.

"We will go, Jack; the fellow is little likely to awaken before we are out of the field."

"That's true, Kate!"

"Once we are out of his sight we are safe."

"Well, yes. But I'd have liked to have had that gun from him, nevertheless."

"With Kate's arm in his, Jack now moved away."

Scarce had they taken, however, a dozen steps before they were startled by a loud exclamation behind them.

With a curse, Jack turned his head.

A cry of fury escaped his lips.

His huge burly form at its full height, the coveted gun at the Present, stood the sentinel.

"Hold! if you don't stop, if yer move another step, I'll put a bullet in yer as sure as my name's Reuben Muggins!"

"Hold, man, hear me!"

"Well, what is it? No tricks; it won't do for me!"

"What will you have for slaying me?"

"Ten guineas."

"And for this you'd shoot me down like a dog?"

"Aye, with as little compunction as I'd strangle a rabbit! But I'll spare yer life if you give in quiet and come along with me?"

"Indeed! you are very kind! Perhaps you'll get more for my capture than you would for my carcase, sweet, handsome, fascinating Reuben!"

"Look here, if I have any more of that chaff, I'll let fly! I'd have shot you before if I hadn't seen you'd got a gal!"

"The gal is greatly thankful to you, dear Reuben!"

"Are you going to give in? If so, I'll not fire, but will merely hand you over to those as wants yer?"

"How good you are, hands me Reuben Muggins!"

"And when you're gone, if the gal likes, I'll take your place!" said the ruffian who here shouted out a word so coarse and base that the hearing it sent the warm blood in a tide of crimson to the face, neck, and brow of Kate.

With his blood seething in his veins, Jack, who during the above colcquy had been devising a means to throw the ruffian off his guard, waited to hear no more, but with a cry of fury bounded forwards.

The filthy and brutal insult offered to the girl, for whom he was prepared to give up life, fairly maddened him.

A horrible imprecation escaped the man's lips as Jack dashed forwards:

Levelling his gun the weapon missed fire:

In a moment more the highwayman was upon him.

His blood at boiling point, Jack was endued with a fictitious strength.

For the time he was the equal of the giant he was opposed to.

Clubbing the weapon that had flashed in the pan, the ruffian, as Jack dashed in, aimed it at his head.

Stopping nimbly aside, the knight of the road avoided the fierce blow and closed with his gigantic foe.

Wildly the two now struggled:

Gripped in a deadly embrace:

An embrace of deadly hate!

The gun falling on the ground, the two combatants, without knives or other weapons, struggled wildly to gain the mastery.

With a thrill of horror after his first burst of passion was over, Jack found that the herculean ruffian he was struggling with was by nature endowed with thrice his strength.

In the fierce embrace of the wretch, he could hardly breathe.

Panting and breathless, Jack presently was borne with a crash to the ground.

With a dull thud, he fell with fearful violence on his back.

In a moment his adversary was upon him:

His brawny herculean form pressed heavily on his chest.

Twining his huge, coarse, bony hands in Jack's neckerchief, he gripped him round the throat till he gasped for breath.

Bending his bloated sensual face close to his, the ruffian now uttered words that drove him almost mad.

"I'll strangle yer like a pup! I'll have ten guineas for your carcase; and I'll have your gal into the bargain!"

"Excuse me, but I don't think you will!" cried a voice that Jack, half strangled as he was, and fast losing consciousness, immediately recognised as that of his friend, the landlord, Sammy Green.

For a moment Jack saw something wielded in the air, then, as his foe started up, there was the sound of a sickening blow, and stunned and bleeding the ruffian, robbed of his brutal strength, fell to the ground an inert mass.

"Humph! I owed you that, Mr. Reuben Muggins, for your insults to my daughter, a week or two ago!" said Sam Green, who here coolly wiped the blood off the stock of the gun he had struck the ruffian down with, and handed it to Jack, who, rising to his feet, now ran to Kate, who, in a half-swoon, was resting against the hedge.

"Thank Heaven, you are saved! O, Jack dear Jack, I thought you would be murdered by that villain!"

Kate here grew deadly pale, and shivered with terror as she beheld the man Muggins move slightly, whilst a low moan issued from his lips.

"Don't be alarmed, Kate, my dear! I warrant he won't be worth much yet awhile. I gave him a very tidy tap on the head! I don't think he will see clear for an hour or so! But come, Jack, we must away; for your friends, the runners, are as plentiful about this wood as flies round a honey pot!"

"How on earth did you find us here?" gasped Jack.

"Why, my dear fellow, I couldn't rest quiet when I got back to the inn, but, daring all, hastened back to the cave with a couple of bottles of wine and some cigars, thinking we would have a night of it, and, to my surprise, when I reached the spring, I found the caves were flooded. Coming across a posse of officers, I, telling them I was hunting for my stolen steeds, learned from them that you had both come out of some hole in the ground, into which you had pitched afterwards one of their mates. This fellow, with much difficulty and half-dead, they managed to fish up. Of course I guessed at once what had occurred, and how you had escaped!"

"Then you did not know when you left me that the cave had burst in!"

"No, dear boy; or be assured I should have aided your escape out of it, in spite of all the officers in the kingdom! Before you had fairly put the plank back in its place I was off; I heard footsteps in the woods and ran from the spot with all speed."

"When and how did you quit the officers?"

"Oh, I left them half an hour ago watching by the old cave. They can't make out that matter; it's a mystery to them! Some of them, Jack, don't scruple to say that you have dealings with the devil!"

"The deuce! Well, that don't matter; it will only cause them to be more careful of me when we meet."

"Exactly; that's what I thought, Jack. Depend upon it they will only venture to attack you if they are in a body."

"Just so; I don't think I need fear one or two if I should come across them!"

"No; I fancy they would show you their heels. But come, Jack, you had better get out of this!"

"Can you advise us where to go for safety?"

"Well, yes; I think I can! You see it won't do for you to try and leave the neighbourhood yet."

"I suppose not."

"Take my word for it, Jack, you would be nabbed should you attempt it! The road is alive with people after you!"

"The devil it is?"

"Yes; you see you are rather notorious just now."

"An unenviable notoriety!"

"Well, yes; you see your escape when you had, as one may say, the rope round your neck, has made you the talk of the town!"

"I see!"

"Consequently there are hundreds on the watch for you."

"I am much obliged to them."

"What do you propose for us to do, Mr. Green?" said Kate, in a nervous trembling voice.

"Why I first beg to suggest that we get away from here. I will take Jack to a safe hiding-place, and you, Miss Kate, can go home with me."

"And leave Jack? No!"

"Well, you see, I think that your staying with him will hamper him in evading his foes; if he knows you are safe with my wife and daughter, he will have more confidence in his powers. You must see what I say is right, if you will only think it over."

"What say you, dear Jack, to this?" exclaimed Kate, as she gazed lovingly into the eyes of her companion.

"Loth as I am that we should part, even for a time, I feel that Sam is right, Kate. Should I have to take to horse I could with much more facility elude my pursuers on the road than if I had you, dear girl, in company. Your peril would unnerve me, Kate. It shall be as our good friend has proposed. We part but for a time; in two or three days at latest we shall be together, and by then, who knows, may be rejoined by Claude, whose prolonged absence troubles me. Take her, Sam; I can find my way to the pheasantry, where I have left my bonny Starlight Nell! I will dare all, and take at once to the road!"

"As you will! Though I had proposed for you a safe retreat and hiding-place in which you could have remained until the heat of pursuit was over."

"And where is this place of which you speak so confidently?"

"Close at hand!"

"Parbleu! what, another cave?" Jack here winked mischievously at the landlord.

No, it's no cave, master Jack, but a house!"

"A house?"

"Yes, a house, which is to let!"

"And you propose me for a tenant?"

"Exactly!"

"Well, it ain't a bad idea!"

"I shouldn't think it was, seeing that the building is avoided by all who live near.

"Indeed! how is that?"

"Why, it bears an evil repute, Jack!"

"The devil it does?"

"Yes, that's why it don't let!"

"I see; what is it about the crib?"

"Why, they say it's haunted, Jack!"

"Oh!"

"That won't prevent you taking up your abode there for a couple of days?"

"I guess not! I don't fear the damned redbreasts (officers), and I'm sure I don't ghosts, male or female!"

"Good! then you will alter your plans?"

"How do you mean?"

"Why, you will go into the haunted house instead of on to the road?"

"Well, yes, I think I will!"

"It will be the best!"

"You are right, Sam, though this hiding business is not what I like!"

"It's better than the cells of Newgate, or Tyburn Tree, Jack!"

"Well, yes!"

"During this colloquy the worthy landlord had led his companions across the field, and now, passing through a gate, hurried them along the high road presently without encountering anyone, turning off down a narrow lane, that was bordered on either side by a thick hedge or preserve.

"Are you going to the house now, Sam?" said Jack, as they hurried on.

"Yes, my flower! we will see you safe, and then I and Kate can make tracks for the inn!"

"Good! I shall be light of heart and merry as a cricket when I know my girl is safe!"

Kate here looked gratefully at Jack, who, unheeding the landlord, clasped his arms around her, kissing her eyes, her rosy mouth, and peach-like cheeks, a proceeding that produced a faint "Oh, don't, Jack!" from the pretty Kate, and a loud laugh from Sammy Green.

Reaching the end of the narrow lane, the little party now came to a halt.

Before them were some large iron gates, whilst, far as the eye could reach, on either hand was a row of low wooden railings.

Just through the gates was a long avenue, some quarter of a mile in extent.

This avenue, bordered on either side by a row of fine beech trees, was, Jack afterwards found, a rookery, myriads of the nests of these birds being perceivable in daylight.

The moon's rays shut out by the trees, the avenue was dark and gruesome looking.

It was, as the friends had halted at the gates, that a loud "Hallo!" followed by the loud report of a gun rang upon the night air.

"Hallo! there's your foes; curse them, what brings them so close?" muttered Green, who, for the moment, seemed quite staggered at the proximity of the enemy.

"That gun was fired as a signal, depend upon it!" said Kate.

"You are right, my girl; and the sooner we get away the better!"

"Think you we have been traced here, Sam?"

"No! No one in the village would come near this place. The Hemlock Grange bears too bad a name!"

"What do you propose now, Sam?"

"Why, I must alter our programme. I meant to have shown you into the house, but must leave you to enter it alone!"

"Oh! I can manage that. You are sure I shall be safe?"

"Aye, lad; as undisturbed as though you were in your grave, I warrant!"

"Very well; you'd better be off! That gun was evidently a signal; it has not been fired again!"

"No! Well I will get back to the inn with Kate, and will join you in the morning. Here is a taper, and a means of lighting it! If you make your way into one or two of the upper rooms of the house you will find them partly furnished. There is a very nice bedroom in which you can rest if you don't fear the ghost!"

"Devil a ghost will frighten me, Sam!"

Shaking hands with the landlord, and embracing the pretty Kate, at the same time chiding her for her tear-dimmed eyes, Jack now passed boldly through the iron gates, which he found opened to the touch, and was presently making his way along the darksome avenue of trees!

For a few minutes he beheld the form of her he so fondly loved standing with the kind-hearted Sam at the end of the avenue.

Then, as he hurried on, they turned away, being lost to sight in the gloom!

Jack was now alone:

Alone in the long walk, as 'twas called, of the haunted house!

It was not without a chill and a feeling of awe that Jack walked in.

The avenue, as we have said, was very dark, the moon's rays being quite shut out by the foliage of the trees.

Though aware that his enemies could scarce be lurking about the dark walk, yet did Jack pull out a brace of pocket pistols, given him shortly before by Sam, and see to the locks.

They were loaded and ready for use, and with one of these in his hands he walked on with less of nervousness than he had done.

He knew it was folly; yet, as he proceeded on through the avenue, he expected a man to dash out upon him, and bid him stand, every moment.

No such occurrence of course took place, and, unmolested save by one or two bats that dashed disagreeably in his face, Jack at length came to the end of the walk.

He now found himself upon the verge of a large lawn:

The moon, bright and luminous, throwing her silvery rays on all around!

CHAPTER XXVIII.

WHAT JACK SAW IN THE HAUNTED HOUSE—THE SHADOW IN THE MOONLIGHT—THE SUMMONS WITHOUT—OLD FRIENDS—ARRIVAL OF THE RUNNERS—THE WHISTLING GHOST—A PISTOL SHOT AND A DISCOVERY—THE SECRET PASSAGE—THE HORRORS OF THE TAPESTRIED CHAMBER.

In awe, and with a nervous kind of feeling, Jack stood for a few moments inactive on the lawn.

It might have been the intense stillness of the place, or the feelings inspired by the mass of building that was before him. But be it what it might, certainly a sensation akin to alarm crept over him as he stood there in the white light of the moon gazing up at the old house.

DASHING DUVAL;

OR,

THE LADIES' HIGHWAYMAN.

JACK ASTONISHES BLUE PETERS AND HIS MEN IN THE HAUNTED HOUSE.

There is, we believe, a universal sensation of creeping, crawling dread felt by every one who is left alone in or near a building reputed to be the haunt of spectres or the scene of crime!

Conquering the sensation of fear that had been stealing over him, Jack now boldly crossed the lawn.

Should any person pass by the gates, he knew that he might be descried in the luminous glare that shone around.

Hastening forwards he now determined to enter the house.

Reaching a portion of what he guessed had been the domestic offices, he now descried a little old-fashioned Elizabethan window so close to the ground that he was able to look in.

The casement he found communicated with a scullery or outhouse, and he doubted not that it was connected with the kitchens.

With little difficulty Jack now made his way through the casement, which he discovered lifted up readily.

Entering the little stone scullery he next passed through a half-open door into a large kitchen.

All was dark, drear, and chilling!

The windows looking out into the gardens at the back of the house being covered with dust and dirt, the moon's rays shone in but partially, throwing a dull, hazy kind of light in the place.

A damp, mouldy, mildewy smell was in the kitchen that did not at all please Jack, who at once made his way out of it.

Traversing a long passage and passing in and out of one or two rooms, in some of which a scampering of tiny feet across the boards told of the vicinity of numerous rats, Jack at length gained the hall of the old house.

Glancing up he now observed before him a grand old staircase, with balustrade of solid mahogany; on the summit a casement of coloured glass threw a light down into the hall below.

Up this staircase Jack unhesitatingly made his way.

There was something touching and profound in the stillness of the place.

The very air seemed to have a strange, lazy kind of motion!

The same kind of damp mildewy smell he had noticed in the kitchen, he detected on the staircase.

With a shiver he hurried on, his boots raising dismal melancholy echoes in the place!

Gaining the topmost stair, Jack was now brought to a standstill by an unexpected sound in the old house:

The sound as of a man whistling!

With all the blood in his body stagnant with terror, he stood there at the top of the staircase, listening to the strange unwonted noise.

He could not be mistaken!

Plain and shrill came the sound:

The sound of a man whistling an old air—the strains of which were peculiarly awful to hear in that old house.

His brow, damp with the perspiration of fear, the bold knight of the road felt almost like taking a headlong rush down to the hall below!

Then, as the sounds suddenly ceased, he began to regain his wonted courage.

It was some human being he had to cope with:

Some person besides himself was in the house!

It was the strong, loud whistling of a man that had so startled him:

Some man in the rooms above!

This stranger could be no officer!

Perchance some bold, prying fellow, who, for a wager or out of a spirit of bravado, had made his way into the building:

The building reported to be the haunt of beings of another world!

It must be so!

Revolving this in his mind, Jack once more strode forwards.

He would boldly seek this man:

He must, by threats or otherwise, win upon him not to betray his, Jack's, presence in the house!

To let the stranger meet him, and then allow him to quit, with the intelligence to the first one he encountered that he was in the place, Jack felt would never do.

This man must be seen and awed into silence.

Passing down a corridor he now reached a second flight of stairs.

Whilst debating as to whether he should ascend these the strange whistling sound once more echoed through the house:

The sound coming from a room on the left hand of the corridor in which he stood.

With beating heart, and a chill of fear he could not repress, Jack listened to the noise.

A wild melancholy air was it that sounded in his ears.

Spellbound the highwayman stood, for a moment, frozen with terror; then, with an effort throwing off the feeling of alarm and horror that had seized upon him, he boldly strode to the door of the room from which the sound proceeded.

Shrill and clear the notes rang in the air.

Placing his hand upon the lock of the strong oaken door Jack endeavoured to open it.

To his surprise it was hard and fast, refusing to stir.

With a thrill of horror he now found it was locked:

The key, touched by his fingers, causing a nervous feeling of alarm to seize upon him.

The strange whistling still went on:

The man within being a prisoner;

For the door leading into the chamber was locked from the outside.

The knowledge of this it was that astounded and terrified the bold knight of the road.

Unless he had entered the room by some secret means, how came the stranger to be within?

Was he a prisoner?

But no! this could not be!

Who would choose a room in the old House to Let for a captive?

And if this was not the case, who, what could it be?

The strange whistling now ceasing, the silence that ensued was more terrible to Jack than the noise.

He could not bear it!

The horrible deathlike stillness froze the blood in his veins!

With a creeping, crawling shudder he now turned the key in the lock:

He would fathom this mystery, come what would!

Gentleman Jack, as we have before seen, was a bold, daring man;

But as he stood without the door, as he slowly swung it open, a cold, icy chill stole all over him!

Standing on the threshold of the door, as it opened before him, he saw a large, splendid apartment, hung with oil paintings and partly furnished.

A broad ray of moonlight shone in the chamber.

A sickening feeling crept over Jack, as, in this pale glare of the luminary of night, he beheld a shadow:

The tall shadow of a man.

This shadow for a moment was fully revealed, then, in a second of time, disappeared.

No noise of footsteps, no sound came from the chamber, yet was Jack now aware that the figure of a man was before him:

Standing just opposite to him:

His face bent forwards close to his own:

And such a face.

Livid as that of a corpse:

The eyes bright and gleaming, the white teeth projecting from the blue lips, and the demoniac grin of Mephistopheles in the thin haggard features.

His hand involuntarily glided to his pistols; Jack was about to make a clutch at the grim-looking figure before him when he was startled by a loud crash below:

A loud crash and sound of broken glass:

"Great heavens! what is that!" he gasped, as he darted back.

Then, about to address the man before him, an exclamation of wild affright escaped his lips.

The stranger was no longer there:

Had mysteriously vanished!

With a crawling shiver, and a feeling as of ice-cold water being thrown down his back, Jack, making a step forwards, cast one glance around the vast chamber.

Fully lighted by the rays of the moon, that poured in a stream of silvery lustre anyone, within would have been revealed.

But no human form met Jack's inquiring startled gaze.

The room was tenantless!

About to dash in, with a feeling of terror and rage combined, for the thought that he was being juggled with flashed through his brain, he was diverted from his purpose by a repetition of noises in the lower part of the house.

"Diable! what does all this mean! Sacre, Master Green! I begin to think that there is some truth in the report that this cursed place is haunted!" exclaimed Jack, as, with a pistol ready cocked in each hand, he now, hurrying from the room, made for the staircase he had ascended shortly before.

It was with utmost alarm, upon glancing down, that he beheld the figure of a man:

A stranger, standing in the hall, apparently irresolute as to whether he should mount the staircase.

"By Jove! someone is in the house then, and it's no ghost after all! Damn them, they wanted to hoax me! There is, I suppose, some secret means of leaving that room, and the fellow I saw a moment ago has now descended into the lower regions! Very good! if I don't mark them for playing their cursed tricks on me, my name ain't what it is, that's all!"

With a chuckle, Jack now, leaning over to balustrade, peered down at the figure in the hall.

In the shadow of the corridor Jack could not be seen.

He, however, was able to watch every movement of the stranger.

A curse escaped his lips as he now beheld the man examining the priming of a formidable pair of holster pistols.

"Oh, oh, my flower! that's your game, is it! Well two

can play at that fun, I reckon! If you think you are going to put Gentleman Jack, you are most deliciously and decidedly mistaken! Damn him, here he comes, crawling up the staircase as though it was made of eggshells! Well, you had me just now when on your whistling game, and I'll just see if I can't startle you, my friend! Let me see, how shall I astonish his weak nerves? Oh, I have it! Capital! If this don't give him shiverem-shakems, I'm a Dutchman, and no knight of the road!"

With a grin, Jack, who had been keenly watching the stranger, now caught sight of a piece of old wainscoting that rested against the wall of the corridor.

Made of oak and studded with rusty iron nails, though rotten with age, it was yet not a nice-looking thing to throw at anybody.

Jack, however, had decided to pitch it upon the head of the stranger, who was so quietly and cautiously ascending the staircase.

It might be the fellow who had been practising on his fears, or it might be a Bow-street runner who had followed him into the house; but, whoever it was, Jack determined to astonish his nerves, and he certainly did.

He succeeded to perfection.

Just as the man had got half-way up the stairs, Jack, leaning over at the top, threw down the piece of old wood, at the same time giving utterance to a wild yell or diabolical screech, an admixture of ha, ha, ha! and the he-haw! he-haw! of a jackass.

The crash of the wood as it thundered clattering down the stairs, and the horrid yell combined, caused the man who had been ascending the staircase to roll down them with a shout of terror.

The piece of timber Jack saw, with disappointment, had missed him, falling not on his head as he had intended, but striking against the balustrade, and thence with a clatter dashing into the hall.

"Humph, that did astonish him! Tit for tat! Perhaps you'll try another whistle, my hearty!" With a grin Jack here bent over, watching once more the actions of the stranger.

Staggering to his feet—for he had rolled down the stairs when so astounded at Jack's yell—he now, with pistols presented, advanced as if bent upon again ascending them.

This rather nonplussed Jack.

He was in hopes the enemy would have retired.

But no; coolly, courageously the man, a tall strapping fellow, now began slowly and cautiously to once more mount the stairs.

"Damn him, he's got pluck! Confound him, what shall I do? He's evidently alone! Perhaps a greedy hound who thinks by my capture to procure the whole of the reward to himself! Hallo! why he's at the whistling game again; and—yet—no! It can't be him, for he is only half-way up the staircase, and the whistling, as before, sounds from that infernal room! Damn it, what does it mean?"

In mingled surprise and alarm, Jack now stood listening to the mysterious whistling that again resounded through the house.

The stranger, to the astonishment of Jack, now retreated down into the hall again.

"He don't like it any more than I, 'tis evident, and therefore cannot be an accomplice! Unless his descending the stairs is to draw me forth, placing me as 'twere between two fires! I'll go into the room again, ghost or man, I care not! they shall not find Gentleman Jack a fellow to be played with!"

Grim and defiant, the young highwayman now strode along the corridor.

In a few moments he gained the door of the room he had unlocked shortly before.

It was wide open, as he had left it.

From within the apartment loud and shrill came the whistling noise.

Not without awe and a chill of fear Jack peeped into the room.

There were three large windows at the further end.

Through the centre one poured a flood of moonlight:

A bright, lustrous, silvery shimmer, that threw deep shadows in the far corners.

Standing gazing up at the luminary that rode high, like a silver shield, in the skies, Jack, with a spasm of fear, beheld the tall, gaunt figure of the stranger whom he had first seen on the threshold of the chamber.

This man it was whose loud whistle echoed through the house.

Who—what could he be?

One thing Jack was now sure of:

The man upon the staircase must be an accomplice.

With a thrill of fear and rage, he stood glaring at the stranger, who, whistling on, gazed at the bright silvery moon, standing motionless and erect as a statue.

"It's some cursed jugglery, and, by the devil, I'll fathom it!" about, as these words fell from his lips, to dash forwards to the casement, he was seized from behind and violently thrown to the floor.

A curse of fury escaped him, as he fell with a crash by the door.

Locked in the powerful grasp of his assailant, who had crept upon him from behind unseen, he in vain attempted to snatch at one of his pistols that had fallen in his surprise from his hands.

To his alarm, he found himself incapable of getting either of the weapons.

He was powerless in the embrace of his antagonist.

Expecting a bullet in his brain or a knife in his side, Jack was now astounded by his captor suddenly leaping up, with a cry of astonishment.

Instead of attempting to secure him, he bade him rise.

"Get up, old fellow! Don't you know me?"

Staggering to his feet in wild surprise, Jack gazed at his strange antagonist.

The moonlight shining full upon him revealed features well known.

With delight and astonishment Jack recognised in his late assailant an old friend.

"Paul, Paul," he gasped, "is it you?"

"Yes, old pal! Don't look at me as if I was one of the infernal ghosts; but give us your fist, and let me thank you for that little bit of fun you practised just now; though, mind you, if that piece of timber had fallen on my nut, it might have given me something worse than a headache!" said Paul Clifford, for it was he, who, now stepping forwards, seized the hands of his astounded friend in his.

"We will leave this room, Paul, dear boy, and will get down stairs!" With a cold shiver Jack here made for the door.

Glancing round he no longer beheld the strange figure at the casement:

The whistler had again disappeared.

The two friends were alone:

Alone, in what Jack began to believe was a haunted room.

Followed by his new-found friend he now hastened down the staircase, both presently after entering the scullery, and, clambering through the small casement, gaining the lawn in front of the house.

"Now that we are out once more in the open air I breathe freely! Now tell me, Paul—for I feel like one in a dream—how, in the name of heaven, came you here, when I imagined you were caged a prisoner in Newgate?"

Incredulously Jack here gazed upon the form of his companion, who, with a light laugh, exclaimed "Well, I will for the present make my story short, Jack, for I fear the grabs will be here presently! You must know that I yesterday escaped from my cell, and evade I successfully the pursuit after me, and, instead of seeking refuge in a London crib, made for the old Tree Cave at Highgate! Here I learned that no one had been near; poor Luke, that half-mad boy of Claude's, being in a state of frenzy at his continued absence from the old Tree Cave! I then took to the Western Road, as I learned you had taken to it after yours and Kate's clever exploit at Tyburn! I, knowing that Sam Green was a friend to all moonlight riders, then made for the King's Head! Here I heard of your dreadful adventure at the Hermit's Spring, and leaving the Bonny Kate and Sammy Green half-an-hour ago, sought you here, where, I am sorry to say, I have been followed by the cursed runners, who, mistaking me for you, twigged me in the copse, and only lost sight of me as I gained the gates leading to the beech tree avenue of this queer old den!"

"You are sure my foes traced you here, Paul?"

"I am sorry to say I am certain they know I am in the neighbourhood of the house!"

"Confound them, that's awkward!"

"It is, Jack! Won't they grin if they happen on both of us?"

"Yes, it would be a bonbouche for them!"

"Rather; they would kill two birds with one stone with a vengeance!"

"Or, to speak more to the purpose would hang two highwayman on one tree!"

"Exactly, Jack; but, damn it, we ain't going to be collared like that?"

"Not likely; I don't seem to care for anything now you are here with me, Paul; it was so miserable being in this lonely old house all by one's self!"

"I should fancy it was, Jack, though my companionship has brought the enemy upon us!"

"Oh, bother them; we will get out of their hands somehow!"

"It won't do for us to quit the place?"

"No; I should be afraid to chance it!"

"You see, Jack, they are all mad with rage at your escape! and with the knowledge that you're somewhere in the neighbourhood they are hanging about like bees round a hive!"

"Just so! Well, I suppose we had better get into the house?"

"I fancy we had!"

"I don't like the place!"

"Nor I; it smells earthy and charnel-like!"

"Well, so it does; but it ain't the smell I care about; it's the cursed mysterious noises! You heard that whistling?"

"I did, Jack, and stood on the stairs with an idea at first that something was wrong; then I fancied it was you having a lark, and to settle my doubts I dashed softly up the stairs, and saw you staring at the centre window in that picture chamber as though you had seen a ghost!"

"And I had!"

"Good heavens!"

"Yes, I saw a figure as plain as I see yours now!"

"I saw nothing! When I dashed in upon you, uncertain whether it was you or not, I made sure of my own safety by making you prisoner!"

"Just so, Master Paul; I perfectly remember; but do you mean to tell me you saw no human form but mine?"

"I did not, Jack!"

"You heard the sound of a man whistling?"

"Oh, yes; as plain as I now hear the breeze in the beeches yonder!"

"But you saw no one?"

"I saw no one!"

"'Tis very strange!"

"It is so, Jack; but see, by heavens, there's our enemies!"

"Where?"

"There, the other side of the lawn!"

Paul, who with his companion, was standing under the shadow of the walls of the old house, here pointed to a posse of some seven or eight men, who, in an excited group, had just emerged from the avenue of trees.

"That's the officers, sure enough;" said Jack with a curse.

"What shall we do?" exclaimed Paul, who with knitted brows cocked one of his pistols.

"Why, get into the house!"

"It's our only plan!"

"Of course it is!"

"We can't tackle that lot!"

"No, and if we did, and worsted them, depend upon it there's more at the gates!"

"Very true; come on, Jack!"

Paul now, approaching the casement, was about to scramble through, when again came the loud whistling of a man inside the house.

In nervous haste the highwayman drew back.

"Damn it, Jack, did you hear that?"

"I did!"

"What on earth can it be?"

"I know not; but, be it man or devil, we must face it; we dare not stop here!"

"Well no, better the ghosts, if such things indeed be, than the infernal runners!"

"Right you are, Paul! Do you follow me! See, by heavens, our foes are now walking across the lawn!"

"So they are, by Jove!" said Paul, who, glancing back, beheld four or five officers hastening towards the house.

In another moment, without further hesitation, the comrades of the road had clambered through the little casement.

Shutting the window to, Jack, now leading the way, made for the door of the scullery leading to the kitchen. Closely Paul followed.

About to quit the little apartment, they paused by the door.

A dark shadow was thrown on the window they had just before closed!

Their enemies had gained the walls of the house!

Their murmuring voices came plain to the ears of the friends.

"I tell yer, I don't believe he is in the house!" said one.

"And I believe he is, so there's the difference! The fact is, you are afraid of the ghosts, Tomkins!" said another.

"Well, I own I doesn't care for spectres! I doesn't mind a highwayman, though he face me with loaded pistols; but, darn me, I can't abear spectres!"

"And you are convinced this old house is haunted, Tomkins?"

"Haunted? In course it is! that's why it don't let!"

"Bosh!"

"Oh, is it bosh? All right! go in and see the ghost of old Dan Hewson, him as murdered his brother, his wife, and their child, to get the property; and then come and tell me it's bosh!"

"Who the devil is Dan Hewson?"

"Why the spectre, to be sure! You're safe to hear him if you don't see him!"

"Hear him, Tomkins! hell and the devil! what do you mean? Does your ghost talk?"

"No, he don't, he whistles! Hark! O Lord, save us, there he is!"

A loud scampering of feet now sounded from without as Paul, nudging Jack's arm, whistled softly.

A cold prespiration, however, broke over the brow of the young highwayman as a whistle, loud and shrill, answered as an echo to his own in the upper part of the house.

"There's some cursed jugglery in all this, Paul! follow me, ghost or devil I care not, I'll fathom this mystery, come what may!"

Wildly, excitedly, Jack rushed from the chamber: Followed closely by his companion.

It was with no small alarm that Paul noted, as they dashed out of the scullery, that the officers had returned.

The unclosing of the casement, which opened with a creaking noise, sounding in the ears of the friends as they rushed away.

"By all the fiends, they seem upon chancing the ghost! they are in the house, Jack!"

"I hear them!"

"Where are you going?"

"To the picture-room!" gasped Jack, as he darted once more up the old-fashioned staircase.

Paul quickly followed his friend however, some yard or so in advance of him.

Again, to the horror of the companions, the shrill, weird, melancholy, notes of the whistle fell upon their ears: Followed by a wild cry below, and the banging of a door!

"The officers have bolted, Jack!" gasped Paul, as the commotion below reached him.

"The curs! they can hunt a living man, and flee from a being of another world; not so will Gentleman Jack! I will see what all this means, Paul, come what will; follow me; here we are!"

With a wild rush Jack darted to the door of the haunted chamber.

No sooner had he gained the threshold than with a loud cry he fired a pistol.

"I had him there, Paul! I've hit the cursed ghost! Come in, lad! I think I've laid the shadow of Dan Hewson!" Excitedly the words fell from the lips of Jack, whom Paul, upon hastening forwards, found standing by the door of the vast chamber staring round wildly, the moon shining upon the glistening steel barrel of the firearm he had discharged the moment before.

"In the name of all that's holy, Jack, what have you shot?"

With awe and surprise Paul now stared around him.

He found they were upon the threshold of a large square room, the walls of which were thickly panelled, and in each panel hung a portrait. There were grim-looking knights clad in complete steel, and there were grave and solemn-looking judges and churchmen; but one portrait immediately opposite to the door of the room attracted at once the greatest share of Paul Clifford's attention.

His friend Jack, too, was keenly gazing with a mystified air at this picture.

The portrait was that of a man in a hunting dress of an age long gone past. The figure had a pointed beard and a coal-black moustache, and the dark lustrous eyes in the steel-blue glare of the moonlight seemed life-like and bending frowningly in anger upon the companions as they stood upon the threshold of the chamber.

"A grim-looking fellow that, Jack! But tell me what was it you fired at but now?"

"A something that faced me, Paul, as I darted up to the door."

"A something! What, the deuce, do you mean! What was it?"

"A figure that hovered before me like a shadow, a grizzly, ghastly figure, Paul, that all but turned my brain to madness to look upon!"

"And you fired upon it?"

"Yes, full in its face! Whether the creature be of this world or the next I know not; but I can tell you this, I never took a fairer shot at anything in my life!"

"I believe you, Jack; and I fancy you hit your man!"

"Diable, I am sure of it! Yet, where is he?"

"There he is, Jack!"

"Where?" cried the startled highwayman, as his companion gripped him by the arm.

"Why, there!" Paul here pointed with a smile at the portrait facing them.

With a loud cry Jack darted forwards.

His friend was right.

His bullet had found a mark.

Through the centre of the brow of the portrait was a round jagged hole, a plain indication of where the shot he had fired had taken its course.

"Well, old pal, what do you think of your phantom now?"

"I am fairly staggered, Paul."

"The matter is easily understood, Jack! In the shimmering light of the moon you mistook the portrait there for a ghost; you fired and hit it!" Paul, who had stepped up to the picture, here put his finger to the bullet-hole, starting back with an exclamation of surprise.

"What's up now! what is it?" cried Jack, eagerly making his way to the panel.

"Why there is a space behind the portrait! Don't you hear how hollow the wall sounds? The young knight of the road here tapped with the butt of his pistol against the panelling, which, as he said, gave out a dull reverberation.

"I don't think anything of that, Paul. It is usual enough for the wainscoting to be some inches unconnected from the wall in houses of this class," exclaimed Jack.

"Yes, some inches, but not some feet," said Clifford, who here passed his ramrod through the orifice in the picture, without it meeting with any obstacle.

This is very strange, Paul!" said his companion as he keenly watched his proceedings.

"Yes! Do you know, Jack, I think your chance shot will lead to a discovery!"

"If it indeed be so, as I begin to suspect, by Jove, we may bid defiance to our enemies!"

"Just so, that was what I was thinking! I have an idea that the whole of this panel in which the picture is set can be made to move out!"

Both eagerly now examined the corners of the portrait, but no vestige of a fastening could be discovered.

If the panel upon which the picture was painted was indeed moveable, the companions were fain to admit that it was very cleverly constructed.

"There must be some mechanical means, if any, of removing it, Paul, depend upon it!"

"Of course, Jack!" exclaimed his companion, who had been roving with his hand over the painting till his fingers touching the handle of a sword worn by the figure he uttered a cry of surprise.

"Here, we have it!"

"What?"

"Why, the secret!"

With a smile Paul here drew Jack's attention to a small brass knob that was let into that part of the painting representing the sword borne by the portrait.

At a first glance this brass knob presented to the eye the appearance of paint being very freely laid on.

Jack now pressing forward placed his thumb heavily upon the spot, when, as he expected, the panel in one mass slowly slid aside, disclosing a long black space beyond it!

"Hallo, Jack! we are getting at the secrets of the House to Let! You may depend upon it that there is not an old palatial residence such as this in England but what has its secret passages, and its concealed doors, and staircases winding within the walls! Come, I feel delighted over this discovery! There is one thing very certain, that we can defy the officers while we are in this haunted crib!"

"It looks like it certainly! How confounded dark it is behind the panel!"

"Of course it is! You have got a taper, have you not, Jack?"

"Yes."

"Then light it. At any moment our foes may gather courage enough to search the house."

"So they may, Paul!"

Jack now, after some little delay, procuring a light, which he got from a flint and steel he carried, now, with his friend, peered into the recess behind the picture.

The companions, who were both bold, daring men upon the road or when in danger, shuddered and drew back as they glanced into the darksome cavity:

All was so black, drear, and ghastly:

The secret way being involved in impenetrable gloom.

"You don't like the look of it, Jack?"

"No, curse me if I do!"

"Yet, I think it were as well to take advantage of our discovery!"

"Well, yes, so do I! Hark!"

Intently the companions, light in hand, now stood by the panel, straining to catch a repetition of a sound they had heard below:

The sound of men's feet:

The tramp of some four or five men in the hall of the house.

"It's our fellows, Jack!"

"Yes, confound them, they have made their way into the house!"

"Well, I thought they would not give up the chase without searching the building!"

"As it happens it don't matter, Paul!"

"No; your pistol bullet at your supposed phantom has saved us!"

"Well, yes, it looks like it."

"There wouldn't have been much chance for us, in flitting from room to room, Jack!"

"No; I think we should run great peril of capture. But in you go, they may come up here any moment!"

"So they may, confound them!" said Paul, who now stepped into the recess, Jack following, and closing to the secret door.

They were both now for the time safe from discovery.

"Well, I suppose it's a century or more since any living being was here, Jack. Look at the dust how it clings to one's feet; it looks like wool!"

"It does; and the accumulation of a century would not be more, methinks, than sufficient to give it such an appearance."

Both now gazed around them in awe and surprise.

With intense interest Jack, holding up the light, beheld to the left nothing but a mass of rough wall.

"The passage runs to the right, Paul; the wall stops it here to the left."

"Well, I suppose we may as well find where the secret way will lead us?"

"Decidedly; we are safe enough from our foes here, and can laugh them to scorn."

"Just so, Jack! only we must take care the laugh ain't too loud, or it might betray us."

"Exactly; but I spoke in metaphor, clever Paul!"

"Oh! I see."

Do you? then it's more than I can, even with this light!" said Jack, with a grin.

"Well, depend upon it, old pal, if we keep on we shall light upon something presently!"

"Very possibly; there is one thing in the affair, Paul, and that is that we cannot by any chance miss our way, for the passage is so narrow that we can't stray from it if we were ever so much inclined to do so!"

"No, I suppose not, Jack. How cursed musty it smells here!"

"Yes, I could do some of Sammy's nut brown ale now."

"Don't talk about it !"

"I'm half-choked !"

"So am I !"

Clouds of dust rose in the narrow way as the companions walked on.

The passage, as Jack said, went to the right only, and appeared to be in altitude about the same as the room they had both left, but its width was certainly not more than two feet.

The dust was not the least remarkable phenomenon of the place; it lay upon the floor so thickly that it completely deadened their footsteps as they trod on it, nor did it fly, as they expected, about them like ordinary dust, but seemed to have consolidated itself into a woolly substance.

There was one thing, however, which gave Jack more annoyance than he liked to admit, and that was the gigantic spiders' webs that were in the place, and which really were so large and strong that they might well make anyone shrink from encountering them.

Jack ducked every now and then to avoid these; but Paul, who followed, being in the shadow, could not very well see the nature of the obstacles before him ; at length, in a voice of dismay and disgust, he exclaimed—

"Hold hard, old pal ! Blest if I can stand this !"

"What's the matter ?"

"Well, that's what I want to know ! Hold the light ; there's some cursed insect on my face ! Ugh ! damn the thing, it makes me shiver !"

Jack, turning with the light now on his companion's cheek, observed a hideous spider, the size of a nut, whilst a remnant of the creature's web rested like a crape mask over his features.

With a sweep of his handkerchief, Jack cleared away the disagreeable mass, exclaiming, with a laugh—

"It was only a harmless weaver, Paul !"

"A what ?"

"A weaver, that was all !"

"Confound it, we are in a complete nest of the beastly insects !" said Paul, as glancing down he observed three or four bloated old fellows perambulating over his boot-tops.

"Well, we are certainly visitors to a colony, it appears !" said Jack. "They are, with their webs, hanging about me like a set of curtains ! and I have more than an idea that there is one of our new acquaintances, as big as a walnut, crawling down my back ! Ugh, damn the things !"

"I say, Jack !"

"Well, what is it ?"

"We have other company than the spiders ! Something has just run over my boots !"

"What was it, Paul ?"

"Why, a rat as big as a kitten !"

"The devil !"

"Yes, the sooner we get out of this the better I shall like it !"

"I suppose so ; but better rats and spiders than Bow-street runners !"

"Well, yes ; the former run from us, but the latter run after us !"

"Exactly ; the tenantry in this passage are as eager to get away from us as we are to cut from the grabs !"

"Just so ! How much further do you mean to go, Jack ?"

"I hardly know what to do ; but I think we had better push on than turn back ; the passage must have an end. Hallo ! what, in the name of all that's wonderful, have we here ?"

Holding up the light, Jack now, with his friend, was startled by their having come suddenly upon a piece of iron mechanism, apparently fastened to the wall ; it was covered with dust, and but for the sound as he rapped it with the butt of his pistol, Jack would not have discovered that the obstruction before them was made of metal.

"A queer affair that ; what do you think it is ?"

"Why, the mechanical contrivance to open another door, depend upon it, Paul !"

"By Jove, yes ! you're right !"

"Right ! of course I am !"

"Hadn't I better hold the taper whilst you tackle the machinery, Jack ?"

"Well, yes, I think you had !"

Jack now giving his companion the light, began to grope among the ironwork ; after some considerable time, which tried the patience of them both, finding a little lever, which pressing upon, a little door in the wall of the passage to their left slid aside.

All was darkness in the chamber or cavity beyond !

Holding the little taper out at arm's length, Jack now, followed by his companion, stepped out of the secret passage:

Drawing the panel slightly to, they now, with much curiosity, surveyed the chamber they had entered :

A small room, hung with tapestry, and completely furnished.

In awe and surprise, the companions gazed around !

But a faint light emanated from the taper held by Jack, who now slowly with Paul walked round the little room they had so strangely made their way into.

The furniture, rich and costly, was covered inches thick in dust.

For many, many years must this secret chamber have been closed.

Approaching a table, the drawer of which was open, an exclamation escaped the lips of Jack :

An exclamation of surprise and delight !

At the further end of the open drawer lay in little heaps some glittering metal.

Taking some of these out, Jack, to the intense delight of himself and his friend, found that they were gold coins:

Tarnished with lying by, and bearing the date, as Jack with some trouble made out, of two centuries before !

"Well, this is a go !"

"Yes, Paul ; and blest if we go from here empty-handed as we came !"

"No fear ! Why there is a hundred at least of these pieces of gold !"

"Quite right," said Jack, who began forthwith to bestow the precious metal he took out of the drawer into his pockets, a process of transfer in which he was assisted by Paul.

Having effected this task in a few moments, they resumed their search through the chamber.

For a century or more must the room have been left alone ; for upon closer scrutiny the friends found that the tapestry was decaying and falling to pieces, on the walls a swarm of moths fluttering out of it as they held up the lamp.

The floor originally, they discovered, of polished oak, was now carpeted inches thick with a coating of black dust.

No sound was there as they trod the secret chamber :

In awe and wonder, the companions gazed around them !

There was a weird, grave-like silence in the place, whilst the air smelt close and musty.

"Well, this is a curious crib, Jack !"

"Yes. I don't much like it, though I ought to, considering what I've got in my pocket out of it !"

"You ought so ! I consider we are in luck ; we've out-witted the officers and come across some gold pieces without looking for them on the road !"

"So we have. I say, Paul ?"

"Well !"

"Don't you think there is a musty-fusty smell here ?"

"There is so ! You see there is no window or door in the place !"

"Yes, there is a door !"

"Where ?"

"Why, here !"

Jack, lifting up the hangings, in a corner of the room, now disclosed a small door.

Such an exit from the apartment he had been looking for ever and again, as he passed round the chamber, drawing aside the hangings, till his perseverance was at length rewarded.

"There you are, Paul ; there is, you see, a means of leaving the room other than by the secret passage !"

"Well, yes, it looks like it ; though perhaps this door may only open to another rat and spider territory !"

"That we will soon see ! Hold this lamp !"

"Right you are !"

Jack now searching for the means of opening the door, could discover none :

There was no handle or other way by which it could be opened.

"It's no door after all, Jack !"

"Yes it is ; hark !" Tapping with his knuckles a hollow sound was returned.

"It must open with a spring."

"It does ; I've found it !" Jack here, stooping down, pressed a nail he saw projecting from the woodwork. As he expected, this nail was connected with a spring, which, with a loud click now acted, the door slowly swinging open.

Holding the lamp high up, Paul, standing behind his friend, peered into the cavity they had discovered.

A cry of horror now escaped their lips :

A cry that was followed by a rushing scampering noise, as some score of rats dashed out from the cavity and flew across the room.

Not the rats was it, however, that caused the cries of terror to issue from the lips of the friends.

Transfixed with horror, with distended eyes they glared into the recess before them.

The cavity now disclosed was, it appeared, a very small inner chamber belonging to the one they were in.

In the centre of the tiny apartment was a small table and two chairs.

In these chairs, as though in life, sat two figures :

One habited in the costume of a lady, a string of pearls fastened round the neck, was leaning with her elbows upon the table, her ghastly skeleton hands clasped as though in prayer.

The figure facing her, that of a cavalier, was clasping in its bony grip a small black substance as though in the act of handing it to his unfortunate companion. Upon the floor at their feet was a broken pitcher ; whilst upon the very centre of the table stuck a jewel-hilted dagger, which fastened, it appeared, a scrap of paper or parchment to the wood.

In wild horror for a few moments the friends gazed at those grim human forms.

Rich velvet robes still hung about the ghastly female figure, whilst the dress of years before yet clung in fluttering fragments to the grizzly skeleton of her companion.

"God of Heaven, how dreadful, Jack !"

"Dreadful, indeed !"

"What on earth does it mean ?"

"Can you not guess ?"

"No !"

"Why those poor unfortunates have been imprisoned in that tiny chamber and left to starve !"

"Great Heavens, yes ! what a death !"

"A terrible death indeed, Paul !"

"Can you summon courage to enter ?"

"Yes, poor unhappy remnants of mortality, why should we shrink from them ; for to their complexion must we too come at last ?"

With unhesitating steps, Jack now advanced into the dread cell of death and, leaning over the table, plucked forth the dagger, seizing in his grasp the piece of paper that had adhered to its point.

The paper was yellow with age and covered with dust.

Drawing back into the apartment, Jack now held the scrap of paper up to the light.

A few lines, faint and almost indistinct, were with much difficulty now deciphered by the bold highwayman :

A few lines of terrible import ; a testimony of dire horrible revenge.

In a low hushed voice, as though in fear of awaking the dead from their ghastly sleep of many years, Jack read out to his companion the contents of the paper :

"Having decided to wipe out the dishonour put upon me by thy death, I leave thee, Godfrey De Lorme, to perish with my wife, thy guilty paramour ! Her child, nor the light of heaven, she will see never more ! In soft dalliance, if thou wilt, thou canst pass thy last hours ! The lamp I leave you will burn for three days ! The crust of bread and water will last you one ! You will both recover from the opiate I have administered to you some two hours after you have been placed in the secret closet of the tapestried chamber ! The house will be shut up, your death cries will be heard by none ! Thus perish the adulterer and his victim !—Signed, AVENGER."

With a cry of horror, Jack here allowed the terrible paper to flutter from his grasp :

The comrades instinctively, both with pitying eyes, turning their gaze once more upon the dead.

"How horrible !"

"A fearful, terrible revenge, Paul !"

"Aye ! the thought of what those unfortunates must have suffered makes my blood crawl like ice through my veins ! Come, we will go ! I feel as if I could hardly get my breath in this dreadful place !"

"And I am the same, Jack ! Do you know I fancied awhile back that there was a horrible, musty, fœtid odour—a smell as of the grave—in the terrible apartment !"

"And so did I, Paul !"

Giving a last shuddering glance at the doomed ones, the companions now closed to the secret panel, and, finding nothing more to be discovered in the tapestried chamber,

passed through the little door they had left ajar, entering again the darksome passage.

"What is the next move, Jack ?"

"Well, I suppose we can only return whence we came ?"

"That's about it !"

"It's no use stopping here !"

"No ! we have got a good haul of the needful, and, therefore, need not grumble at having dared the passage of cobweb alley !"

"Exactly, Paul ! Come on, I long to get back to the portrait-room !"

"So do I ! Ugh ! the horrors of that closet have turned my inside inside out !"

Slowly, carefully, the friends, now conversing in whispers, traversed the secret way.

In a shorter time than they had taken to reach the tapestried chamber, they gained the secret panel, opening into what they had christened the portrait-room.

With a knowledge of the labyrinth, they were able to hasten their return, and in five minutes from their departure from the chamber of death, they had gained the end of the passage. they were now standing on the inner side of the picture Jack had fired at !

Intently the companions listened for any sound from within !

But none came :

All was quiet !

"I think it's all right, Paul !"

"So do I ! but you can soon see if the coast is clear !"

"How ?"

"Why, do you forget you made a hole in the wall !"

"By Jove, yes ! I can look into the room through my bullet hole !"

"Of course you can !"

"Good, dear Paul !"

"I should say it was ; you'd be lost without me !"

"Oh, yes ; however, my prince of highwaymen, I must admit you're not a half sort of bad pal," said Jack, with a low laugh, as he now, climbing on his friend's shoulders, placed his eye to the small hole his bullet had made in the picture, when he had fired at it some time before.

Jack now made the discovery that day had broken.

A thin ray of the early morning sun was shining through the window of the portrait-room, tinging the walls with a golden, ruddy, tint.

One hurried glance through the orifice sufficed to show Jack that the room was empty.

"It's all right, old pal !" he exclaimed, as he slid from the other's back, "There is no one there. I think the enemy must have decamped."

"Well, we will live in hopes of such being the case ; decidedly we can do better without than with those sweet interesting fellows who are so eager to come across us Jack !"

"I eventuate we can !"

After some little delay and trouble the companions at length succeeding in opening the secret panel, passed out of the dark grim passage, and stood once more in the large old-fashioned chamber of the haunted house.

"Here we are, safe and sound !"

"Right and tight !"

"Plenty of dirt, Jack !"

"And gold, Paul, my hearty, don't forget that !" said Jack, as he chinked the precious metal he had crammed into his pockets when in the tapestried chamber.

"Do you know, I feel quite another chap now we are out of that horrid place ?"

"I expect you do !"

"It's quite a treat to see the sun again !"

"It is so !"

"I wonder if our friends have gone ?"

"We must find out !"

"We ain't going to stop here !"

"Well, no ! though we can bid defiance to the redbreasts by means of cobweb alley."

"We could so ; but do you know I'm getting infernally hungry ?"

"So am I, Jack !"

"And thirsty ?"

"Don't talk about it !"

"Those cursed spiders' webs have got down my throat."

"Ditto ; I could do a jug of ale now."

"I suppose you could ; and both being agreed on that point we'll see if we can't get what we want !"

Jack leading the way, the companions, leaving the room, now cautiously descended the stairs without.

Unmolested, undisturbed, by any noise or intimation of All was intensely quiet in the old house, not a sound intensely quiet could be heard. the presence of their foes, they gained the hall below.

"All seems pretty right, Jack !"

"Yes; I think our beauties have tired of their job, and turned it up !"

"That's my idea."

"Well, I think we'll make for the scullery !"

"The way by which we entered !"

"Yes !"

"I don't see we can do better !"

"Nor I ; we can't stop here and starve."

"I certainly don't care about it ! What the deuce is up with Sammy Green, I wonder !"

"He was to come here with some grub !"

"Just so ; but he hasn't !"

"Depend upon it that is no fault of Sam's !"

"I think not !"

"I'm sure of it ; I suppose the cursed runners have kept him away !"

"That's about it !"

"Well, runners or no runners, we'll get out of this !"

"Yes ; I've had enough of the haunted house !"

"So have I, though I don't consider we have done so bad in it !"

"Well, no ; it's been a lucky crib to us !"

"It has so !"

Cautiously making their way through the domestic offices, the two companions now gained the little chamber, the narrow casement of which opened out upon the grounds in front of the house.

Here they paused.

The utmost caution was now necessary.

Should their enemies still be lurking in the precincts of the old house they might be surprised.

It was with a cold thrill of fear and a quick nervous start that they now heard the heavy foot of a man sounding on the gravelled walk without.

Reaching the little casement through which they had scrambled the night before, they had been going to take a look out in the grounds, when the sudden intimation of the proximity of a stranger startled them and caused them to draw back in the shadow of the wall.

"Curse them, they are not yet gone !" said Paul in a whisper.

"It looks like it ; get your barking irons ready !"

"Right you are, Jack !"

"If they want a blue pill, they must have it !"

"Just so ; we'll oblige them !"

"We will so ! Hush ! they are here !"

A dark shadow now obscured the sun's rays that had glinted in through the casement.

With keen eyes the two friends now watched unseen the actions of the stranger.

An arm being thrust through the window, a heavy package was dropped on the floor, whilst, a moment after, a leg began to follow the appearance of the arm.

With a broad grin, Jack now seized the parcel and stealthily crept from the chamber, Paul following wonderingly in the rear.

Gaining the adjacent kitchen, Jack paused, giving utterance to a low chuckle, as a cry of astonishment echoed from the scullery.

"Damn my rags; this is funny ! I dropped the parcel I have had such trouble to get here in before me, and now, curse me, if it ain't gone !"

A loud laugh as these words fell from the lips of the stranger escaped from Jack—a laugh in which he was joined by his friend.

A moment after the noise of a hasty footstep sounded in the scullery, then as Jack, who had torn open the package, taking from it a pork pie, began greedily to devour it, a burly form appeared before them.

Paul, his mouth crammed with ham sandwiches he had pounced upon as his companion half-untied the parcel, looked up with a grin as a voice shouted in his ears the words of Macbeth : "' May good digestion wait on appetite, and health on both !' Gents, I hope you like it !"

"Yes, we do like it, Sammy; don't you make no mistake !" Jack here began an attack upon a second pork pie, as the true-hearted and friendly Sammy Green, for it was he, came forward with a laugh, pulling from his pocket a couple of black bottles.

"When you have done your feed, here's some fine old port, lads, to wash it down !"

"Sam, you're a brick !"

"He's a regular pantile !"

"He is so !"

"I should think he was !"

"This is fine ham !"

"The pork pie is immense !"

"Well, Sam ought to go to heaven if it's only for this one act of charity !"

"Just so ; but I'd rather he would stop where he is while he serves out such jolly fine pork pies !"

"You don't like it !"

"No ; I can't keep the gravy from running out of the corners of my mouth !"

"Well, this ham slides down my gullot, Jack, like suds down a sink-hole !"

A loud laugh burst from the landlord at these encomiums upon the food were passed by the hungry highwaymen; then, as they finished the repast brought to them, washing the good things down with some first-rate old port, they turned to their friend of the King's Head and eagerly questioned him as to their foes.

"How about the grabs, Sam !"

"Are they hanging about the House to Let !"

"They'd better Let it alone !"

"How did you get here, Sam !"

"How's Kate !"

"Do you think it will be safe for us to leave this damned house !"

"How shall I answer your questions ? One at the time ! I'm thinking the pork pies and ham has got up in your heads !" said the worthy Sam with a smile, as the queries of the two excited friends were rained into his ears.

"Well, you see, we are anxious !"

"If the grabs are gone, we want to be off !"

"We don't like this house !"

"It's haunted !"

"Oh, you've seen the ghost, have you !" said Green, with an attempt at a smile, though with a cold shiver. Jack noted an uneasy look in the face of their friend as the words fell from his lips.

"We have seen the ghosts, or ghost, of this old house, Sam, now," said Jack seriously; "and, what's more, we have, I suspect, seen what you, I'd stake my life, never have !"

"And what's that !"

"Why, the hideous, horrible skeletons of two wretched creatures, who, shut up in a secret closet, must have perished by a lingering death years back !"

"What mean you !"

"I will tell you, Green, though the thought of repeating to you that which we have seen makes my flesh creep and crawl upon my bones !"

Jack here in a low, hushed voice, the while he gazed furtively around the gloomy, dark kitchen in which they stood, related that which is already known to our readers.

For a moment deep silence followed Jack's narration.

The landlord, Sam Green, was startled.

He, in answer to the nervous inquiries of the friends, admitted that he had never been in the tapestried chambers, nor knew of the secret passage. He had, he said, a belief that the house was the abode of beings of another world, and this it was kept the lone building empty. "For the very reason of its bearing the repute of being haunted, I made sure of the old house keeping you in safe hiding from your enemies. This tale of the scene you have witnessed goes to give me firmer faith in spectres than anything I have ever heard ! As 'tis not a pleasant place to remain in now that you have your pockets full of gold, I should say bid goodbye to it; but I do not think it is safe just yet !"

"Are our foes so near ?"

"Yes, Jack ; they are hanging all about the grounds !"

"The devil they are !"

"They don't think of entering the house ?"

"No, they tried it on last night, and had enough of it !"

"They were frightened at something ?"

"Yes !"

THE LEAP FOR LIFE!

"And yet they cling to the idea that we are on the premises?"

"Well, yes?"

"They give us credit, then, for more pluck than they own to possess themselves?"

"Oh, their argument is, that you prefer a spectre of a dead man to a live one with a yard or two of rope in his hand?"

"Oh, they say that, do they, Sam?"

"Yes, Jack; and to my mind you are fools if you don't own they are right!"

"Well, certainly the ghosts are better company than Bow-street runners and hangmen!"

"Just so!"

"Of course, you advise us to stick here a little longer?"

"Decidedly; they will get tired of their fun by to-night, I warrant!"

"Do you? then we can venture out to-night?"

"Well, yes! You see if they are still on the watch they will be getting lazy and sick of it."

"So they will!"

"Of course they will! I have brought you the two bottles of wine; what you have not drunk, with the remainder of the pies and other things, will last you till nightfall; and then, when the ghosts walk, you can run!"

"Taking care we don't cut from the shadow and cop substance!" said Paul with a smile.

"Well, yes; but I fancy, if you are cautious, you'll get away all right?"

"We must have a try!"

16

"Rather; I for one don't care for another night here, Jack!"

"Nor I, Paul! And now tell me, Sam, what do you advise?"

"Why, that you sneak out of the house when it's dark; the later you make it the better."

"Well, and where do you think we had better make to?"

"Why the pheasantry, Jack; I've put a fine prad there for you, Paul, along with your pal's. Mounted on your steeds make all haste away to Highgate!"

"Highgate, Sam?"

"Yes; Kate Annersley desired me to tell you that she will be at the old Tree Cave, the favourite retreat of poor Claude Duval, to-night, at twelve."

"Parbleu! as my dear absent chum would say, then I'll be there!"

"You see Kate's idea is that you will be safer from the grabs there than anywhere."

"And she is right, Sam; once at the retreat in Highgate woods I care not; the cave is known to none."

"Good! then I should say get there with all speed and lie by for a week."

"Just what I shall do, Sammy; but now, I say, old fellow, I and Paul here arranged a little while back to divide the swag we got out of the tapestried chamber along with you; so we will go into that business at once, as we may not have the opportunity again."

"Excuse me, Jack, I must decline!"

"Decline what?"

"Why, the offer to share the swag as you call it."

"But you must; nay, damme! you shall take it!"

"I shall do nothing of the sort, Gentleman Jack!"

"And may I ask why you reject the coin, Mr. Green?"

"Certainly, Mr. Highwayman," said Sam, assuming the other's offended tone; "because I cannot think, as a respectable publican, of accepting the proceeds of a robbery!"

Jack, who here saw that the kindhearted landlord meant having his own way, laughed loudly—a burst of hilarity in which he was joined by Paul and Sam Green himself.

"That point being settled, my daring High Tobies, I will now leave you to yourselves," exclaimd the jovial host. "It was with a sight of twisting, turning, and doubling that I got here; and I expect I'll have the same job to get back! Now remember, Jack, Miss Kate's appointment—midnight, at the old Tree Cave at Highgate! You will find your steeds in old the pheasantry in the woods near! And now good bye!" The worthy landlord, here shaking the hands of the highwaymen, turned from the kitchen, and in another minute had left the house.

The two friends were now once more alone:

Alone in the haunted house!

"Well, here we are, Paul, once more all alone in our glory!"

"Yes; and the sooner we are quit of such glory the better I shall like it!"

Well; I must say I should prefer a ride over a springy heath, with the sweet air of heaven fanning our brows, to the dim, gloomy, horrible shades of this dreadful house, the very air of which seems tainted with death and the charnel vault of decaying mortality!"

"That's it! The very air we breath is like that of a charnel house, Jack!"

"There's no denying it, Paul! But we must grin and bear it!"

"Yes; thanks to those cursed runners! But hark, Jack! I could have sworn I heard some one in the scullery!"

At this moment, plain to the ears of both, sounded a heavy footfall:

A heavy footfall in the outer chamber!

In a second, the companions darted to the kitchen door leading to the passage that was connected with the other domestic offices.

Scarce had they gained this exit from the place, ere the figures of four or five officers appeared before them.

To dash away into the dark passage outside the kitchen, and slam to the door after them, was, to Jack and Paul, the work of a second.

Loud yells and wildest shouts followed their disappearance.

"We've got them!"

"Here they are!"

"Damn the ghost!"

"Down with the highwaymen!"

"Hurrah, hurrah! we've got them!"

Such were the cries that reached the ears of the two friends as they darted away.

Up one passage down another they flew!

Great advantages had the two adventurers over their foes.

Every apartment of the old house below was known to them.

Whilst the exulting officers were darting in and out of the domestic offices, Jack and Paul had succeeded in gaining the staircase.

"All right now, Jack!"

"Rather!"

"We will just have a game with these fellows!"

"We will, Paul! a good idea that! We will come ghost over them!"

"Exactly; come on! I ain't sorry they have stormed the lions in their den!"

"No; we will roar like thunder!"

"Just so! Give them filings!"

"Yes; if we don't get them to give this house a wide berth, I'm wonderfully sucked in!"

"So am I!"

Both had now gained the summit of the staircase:

In about the middle of the corridor: from thence, it will be remembered, was the entrance to the portrait chamber.

To this room the adventurers now darted.

All was as they had left it.

The secret panel in the hall of cobwebs, as Paul termed it, was still open.

"I think we can about mystify our friends now, Jack!"

"Just what we can do! Did you recognise one of those voices that shouted after us, Paul?"

"I fancied I did; Blue Peters is one of the gang, ain't he?"

"Yes; I thought you'd recognise the rough, harsh, grating sound of his voice!"

"You were right, he always cries out like a bear with a cold!"

"I never heard a bear with a cold, Paul!"

"Well, you can imagine the growl of one of those animals if he was afflicted with a cold in the head. Well, Peters's voice is like it! But I say, Jack!"

"Well, what is it?"

"When an enemy is beseiged in his castle, what does he do to the daring invaders?"

"Why, drives them back if he can!"

"Of course, by such playful means as molten lead from the castle walls, pieces of rock, and such like little mementoes, being rattled down on the foe!"

"Exactly!"

"Very well; we must do the same thing, Jack!"

"Not a bad idea; but we've got no molten lead or rocks!"

"Well, we can find a substitute!"

"I didn't think of that!" said Jack, with a grin, as Paul, striding across the room, went up to the old ruined casement, and, with an exertion of strength, lifting it partly up tore one half of it clean away.

"I've got something to astonish them with!"

"What are you going to do with that, Paul?"

"Why, as the coves downstairs tumble up, this half of the old sash will tumble down!"

"Oh, lord! what a game!"

Jack here laughed loud and long, then leaning out of the broken casement he seized hold of a piece of coping-stone which, crumbling to decay, was readily removed from its place. Armed with this, he hastened out of the room.

Paul, who had darted away a moment before with his implement of warfare, he now discovered standing at the edge of the stairs.

Jack, as he gained the side of his companion, peered down, a grim smile wreathing his features as he observed a little mob below:

A little knot of some half dozen men:

The foremost, a big burly fellow, wearing a cocked hat, a red coat, and a nasal organ as red as his garment!

"There's Blue Peters, Paul!"

"I see the beggar!"

"What are they doing?"

"Canvassing the advisability of coming up!"

"I fancy they will soon see the advisability of stopping where they are!"

"Calculate they will, Jack! I see you've got a shot!"

"I have so, a regular nobbler!"

"Mind, I fire first!"

"All right, old man! We won't waste our ammunition! I'll hold my seventy-four pounder in reserve!"

"Good, Jack! Hallo, they twig us!"

A loud shout now rang from below:

A shout that echoed strangely through the old house.

The companions, who had placed their implements of warfare behind them against the walls of the corridor, now leant forwards boldly.

They had no desire to keep out of sight.

They proposed to annoy their foes and at last to seek safety in the secret passage.

Here they knew they would be perfectly safe from capture.

The officers having entered the house, was rather a relief than otherwise.

It might give them a better chance of quitting it, and at all events it did not add to their danger of being taken.

The foremost officer now stepping forwards shouted out coaxingly and threateningly to them:

"Gentleman Jack, and you, Paul Clifford, are you going to give in? You know you are wanted—we must have you—so instead of attempting to escape you'd better come down!"

"Certainly, Blue Peters, we might do so! As you say, we are wanted and you must have us, we might come down; only don't you think, Blue Peters, that if we did, you would reckon us as remarkably green, Heh, Blue Peters?"

"Gentleman Jack!"

"What is it, old man?"

"You shall smart for this!"

"You don't mean it?"

"I daresay you think you'll escape us; but you won't if I watch the house for six months, or burn it over your heads!"

"Ah, you're a bad man, a very bad man, Blue Peters! you don't know of a barber's round here, do you?"

"Pshaw!"

"Because I was going to advise you to have your head shaved; you're very bad!"

"Forward, men! I'll stand no more of this! Fire upon them!"

"Here they come! let fly, Paul!"

Jack, who had, with his friend, been leaning over the stairs, now drew back.

His disappearance for a moment was taken as a signal that he had made for another part of the house.

In a wild yelling crowd up the staircase poured the officers, headed by the enraged Blue Peters.

When half-way on their journey, Paul stepping forwards with the part of the old sash in his hands, raised it up over his head and sent it, with a crash, down below.

Such a crashing, deafening, din, now rang through the old house as surely had never been heard there before.

The report of pistols, the crash of broken glass, the cries of pain and yells of fury from the runners, making up a babel of sounds.

With a loud laugh the two friends now peeped down at the foe.

Standing at the foot of the staircase, surrounded with splintered wood and broken glass, were grouped the enraged runners.

Blue Peters, in their midst, was employed mopping a thin trickling stream from his nose which obstinately persisted in running from it.

"You've tapped his claret, Paul!"

"Yes, I've drawn first blood!"

"I say, Peters, how do you feel, old man?"

"Will you have another window frame?"

"'I'm on Tom Tiddler's ground, picking up gold and silver," cried Jack, laughing at the menace and frantic gesticulations of his foes.

"Now then, gentlemen, come on; be in time; we have a few more shots! Come on, Peters, don't look blue on it, old man! rush to the assault! 'None but the brave deserve the fair,' you know! That's the style—all together! Ready, Jack, with the seventy-four pounder! here they come like yelling fiends! they will have it! Fire."

Scarce had the last words issued from Paul's lips ere Jack, with knitted brow, stepping forwards, hurled at the shrieking, yelling crowd, the heavy stone.

There was a dreadful sickening smash, then a howl of pain, succeeded by a stillness that, after the fierce tumult, was almost wondrous!

"I think that has settled some poor wretch, Jack!"

"Well! if they will hunt us like wild beasts they must expect us to turn and save ourselves! 'Tis our lives or theirs!"

"You are right there, old pal! By Jove, your shot has done fell work, though!"

Leaning over the staircase a sickening sight now met the eyes of the highwaymen.

Extended at length in the hall below was a man with his head stove completely in!

The stone hurled by Jack had fallen with a smash full upon the wretched officer's upturned face!

Toppling down the stairs he had rolled into the passage.

One groan—one little shiver—and all was over!

The wretched officer was dead!

He, who a moment before had shouted wildly for the death of the highwaymen, was now himself a corse!

"Well, he has gone his road! Such is the fate of the man-hunter!" exclaimed Jack, who, now leaning forwards, shouted defiantly to the alarmed and enraged runners.

"Look you, Blue Peters; 'tis your lives or ours! You hunt us like beasts of prey. So be it. Expect the reprisal of the tiger or the leopard! We will not tamely submit like curs to be dragged to the scaffold. Our hands have never been stained in blood save in self-defence. He, your comrade, for gain would but now have shot us down like dogs, or led us captives to Tyburn. The world, I think, Blue Peters, is made up of fools and rogues. Excuse me, but I think you, by your savage onslaught upon two desperate men, prove yourself one of the fools! And now take the warning of the rogue: Depart as you came; for as surely as you follow us about this house, so surely shall you suffer for your temerity! We know the intricacies of the old house, and you don't. Take my advice, Blue Peters, and clear out!"

"What, at the order of one who has tricked—audaciously cheated—the gallows? Give up! Go, when I have you all but in my grasp? No, no, Gentleman Jack! I leave not this house till I have you safe, dead or alive!"

"I am afraid your stay then will be a long one, old man!"

"Lease the house, Peters, you may have your wish then!"

"Wait till night!"

"You'll find it all a lark!"

Jeeringly the companions now shouted at their foes, who apparently in doubt as to what they should next do, stood at the bottom of the stairs, glaring with ferocious looks at the men who so coolly defied them.

"Do you see what they're up to, Jack?" exclaimed Paul, who now drew back preparatory to seeking safety in the portrait chamber.

"They are all looking to the priming of their pistols, and with drawn cutlasses seem as though bent upon a desperate rush!"

"That's just what they mean to do! We had better step it!"

"Well, I think so; discretion is the better part of valour!"

"Just so! We have given them a good dose!"

"Yes, and rubbed one of them out!"

"Well, as you say, it's their lives or ours!"

"Of course it is!"

"And as we decline to become dead to please them and the law, why they must either let us alone or take the consequences!"

"Exactly; but as they mean a rush we will give them the go-by and rush first!"

"Right you are, Jack; go ahead!"

In another moment the comrades had gained the portrait-room:

Not a minute too soon were they.

With fierce cries their foes had bounded up the stairs.

Loud yells of triumph escaped the lips of the officers as they found that there was no opposition.

"We shall have them now!"

"Down with them!"

"Revenge Bill Simmons!"

"Death to the highwaymen!"

Such were the cries that rang in the ears of the two bold adventurers, as they made their way once more behind the secret panel:

This time all in darkness.

They dared not use a light until they had progressed some way down the passage, as the glare might, they knew, be seen through the orifice, for the sun no longer shining in the picture chamber, a semi-darkness hung in parts of the room.

"Well, here we are in Cobweb Hall again, Jack!"

"Cobweb Alley, Paul; don't call things out of their names!"

"I say, Jack!"

"Well!"

"What will Blue Peters say now?"

"He'll look very blue on it, I fancy! Hush! by heavens, they are in the room!'

"They ain't here, Mr. Peters!"

"Damn it; I could have sworn I saw them dart through the door of this chamber!"

"So could I, sir; but it could not have been, 'cause there arn't room to hide a mouse; and if they had bolted in here, why, in course, they would be here now!"

"A genius that!" said Jack, in a whisper.

"Yes; I wonder whether his mother had any more like him?"

"It's to be hoped not; there are too many clever people in the world now! Hark! I think they have gone, haven't they?"

"I fancy so; but of course you won't quit Cobweb Alley just yet?"

"Not likely!"

"I say, Jack!"

"What is it?"

"There's a cursed spider crawling up my leg!"

"Never mind that, old pal; better a spider on your leg than a runner on your back!"

"W   ves; but I say, Jack; hadn't we better creep on down the passage, and light the taper? To my fancy the tapestried chamber would be better than this!"

"I don't know but what you're right; and, since we are compelled, in a manner of speaking, to return there, we will just turn the place inside out; who knows, we may find something worth having!"

"So we might, Jack! Go on ahead and let us get there at once; for, curse me, if I like this! Damned if there isn't a r..., or something, trying to make a meal off the toe of my boot!"

Treading carefully along the darksome passage, expressions of loathing and disgust escaping them as they heard, ever and again, a squeaking noise accompanied by a scampering of feet, the friends at length gained a portion of the secret way where they thought it would be safe to light their taper.

For some few moments in silence Jack felt in his pocket for the means of obtaining light, an anathema of rage and annoyance at length escaping him.

"What's the matter, Jack?"

"An infernal accident!"

"What is it?"

"Why, I have lost the bit of taper!"

"The devil, you have?"

"Yes; I must have dropped it either in the portrait chamber or the other one!"

"What other one?"

"Why, the tapestried room where we got the money!"

"It can't be there!"

"How so?"

'Because I remember you had the light when we went back!"

"Of course I did! What a fool I am! but what a cursed mishap!"

"Well, yes, it is awkward, as we dare not show up yet, whilst our foes are in the house!"

"Of course not, and here we are penned in this horrible place in pitchy darkness!"

"Can't be helped, Jack, we must make the best of it!"

"Well, I'm glad, since it is due to my infernal carelessness, that you take it so easy, Paul!"

"What's the use of doing anything else?" said Clifford, who, however, we must own, did not feel as comfortable as he would have his friend believe.

The dreadful things they had witnessed, the strong proof that the old house was in reality haunted, combined to render Paul fidgetty and nervous in the extreme, as he stood there by his companion in that gloomy pitch-dark secret way.

"Well, I don't believe in standing here; suppose we make our way back?"

"All right, Jack!"

About to retrace their steps, the adventurers were now startled by a loud cry:

A cry that sounded strange and hollow:

A cry that echoed wildly in that grim passage!

A moment after there was a little bead of light shining in the eyes of the alarmed and amazed companions!

Paul, who had been following behind Jack and had turned to retrace his steps, was the first to gather in the meaning of the strange light:

A light that each instant grew brighter, stronger!

Gripping Jack by the arm, in a husky whisper he bade him hasten with all speed to the end of the passage.

"What is it, Paul?"

"Why, our cursed enemies have by some accident or other found out the secret of the picture panel and are now preparing to enter the passage!"

"The devil, they are?"

"Yes; the light you see there, glimmering as though fastened in the flooring, is held by one of our foes!"

"Luck is leaving us, Paul!"

"It looks confoundedly like it!"

"Well, we had better seek the tapestried chamber!"

"Yes, though in darkness it's not a nice place to enter!"

"Well, no; it's less disagreeable than a cell in Newgate, Paul!"

"So it is, the dead can harm us not, whilst the living are prepared to, and can if we do not outwit them, send us to perdition!"

"Exactly! But come on, for, by Jove, you are right; Blue Peters is about to enter the passage with his followers. Curse them! how, in the name of all that's damnable, came they to find it out?"

With beating heart, in rage and alarm, Jack now stumbled on, gaining at length the ironwork that was connected with the secret panel opening into the chamber adjacent to that of the dead.

With a cold shiver, Jack, searching out with his fingers the spring, pressed it hard, the little door as before opening slowly with a creaking, grinding noise, that gave them both a kind of thrill through all their frames as they heard it there in the dark gloom.

"Come on, Paul!"

"All right!"

"Is that you holding my coat?"

"Yes; what did you think it was?"

"Ugh, I don't know! I'm nervous as a child in this cursed place!"

"I wish we were well out of it!"

"So do I, dear Jack! Its broad day still out of doors, and yet here you can't see your hand before your face!"

"No; and, pugh, what a horrid smell!"

"Don't talk about it!"

Passing through the narrow little opening, the companions now carefully closed it after them.

Snap went the spring, causing them both to give a nervous start.

They were now once again in the tapestried chamber.

There, close to the victims of a terrible revenge!

With clasped hands, the highwaymen, side by side, stood in that drear and terrible chamber, both intently listening for the slightest sound.

All, however, was silence:

A stillness so deep, so intense that each could hear the beating of the other's heart!

Jack, the first to break the silence, in a hoarse husky voice exclaimed—

"Do you think our infernal foes have gone back, Paul?"

"I doubt it, Jack!"

"But we can hear nothing of them?"

"Well, no! But, depend upon it, they will be very careful how they search for us in these secret places!"

"So they will, I did not think of that!"

"They know that we are armed!"

"Of course!"

"And may have the fear at any moment of our dropping upon them with our bulldogs!"

"Diable! yes, Paul; when I think of that, this silence of our foes bodes ill for us!"

"Well; it don't argue that they have given up the search!"

"Certainly not!"

"That being the case, any moment we may hear them at the panel!"

"Confound them, yes; they might even now be on the other side of it!"

"They are, Jack!"

Husky and hollow sounded the whisper of Paul, as he, pressing his companion by the arm, drew him across the room.

A strange scraping, rasping noise now sounded in their ears:

The sound as of a file grating upon iron.

In downright alarm the friends stood in that grim, dark chamber with beating hearts and foreheads damp with the perspiration of fear.

Still the strange rasping, grinding sound went on.

A strange peculiarity struck both the friends, one whispering his thoughts to the other.

Their enemies, who they conceived were trying to open the spring door, executed their work in silence.

Not a single exclamation reached the ears of the startled friends.

Not a sound of human voice awoke the stillness of that dread chamber:

Only that strange rasping, grinding noise.

"What on earth is it, Jack!"

"God of Heaven knows! I would we were well out of this house!"

"So do I! What shall we do!"

"I know not what course to take, Paul; there are no means that we are aware of that will enable us to quit this chamber save by the secret passage!"

"No; and that bit we are debarred from!"

"Just so!"

"What do you advise!"

"I'm all abroad, Paul; I don't know what to be up to! Hark! that strange noise has stopped!"

During the above brief colloquy the companions had been standing by the secret panel, which still remained as they had left it—fast shut.

The mysterious grinding noise, however, had now ceased.

The total stillness that ensued was oppressive in the extreme.

Breathless, and alarmed at their novel and perilous situation, the companions remained rooted to the spot, awaiting a repetition of the strange noise from without that a few minutes before had so startled them.

No sound, however, now fell upon their ears.

All was silence:

The silence as of the grave!

Involved in impenetrable darkness, with the knowledge of the dreadful horror that lay concealed in the secret recess, it was in shuddering terror the friends remained there in that lone chamber of the haunted house.

Each in the deep silence of the place could hear the beating of his own heart.

For a few moments neither broke the stillness; then, at length, Jack, gripping Paul by the arm, in a hoarse, husky voice bade him see to his firearms.

"What is your purpose, Jack!"

"To get out of this; I can't stand it! better a struggle with our foes; better Newgate itself than the horrors of this lone house!"

"I agree with you there! What do you mean to do!"

"Why, open the panel!"

"Suppose our enemies are on the other side!"

"Why, we must attack them!"

"Very good! We have the advantage over them of knowing the secrets of the place, whilst they don't!"

"Exactly! Now, I'm going to open the panel, get your barking-irons ready!"

"I'm all ready!"

"Good! Now, when I throw the door open, you move a little back on your side, and I will do so on mine; our foes will then rush in, we can dart out, bang too the secret panel, and then bolt them in!"

"Capital! glorious! I never thought of that!"

"Well, I did! Now then, ready! my hand is on the spring!"

There was now a sharp click as Jack opened the panel.

With beating hearts and bated breath, the companions awaited the result.

None, however, came.

To the astonishment and surprise of the friends no cry rang in their ears—no flash of light illumined the darkness!

There was, apparently, no living being without.

All was inky darkness with the silence of a church vault.

Had their enemies gone!

Or was this a trick—a trap to lure them forth?

Each afraid to break the stillness around, the knights of the road stood by the open panel, peering into the gloom of the secret passage without.

Jack at length, unable to bear the torture of suspense, boldly determined to step forth.

In a hoarse whisper he informed Paul of his purpose.

With Jack to resolve was to execute.

In another moment he had one foot out in the passage.

A startled cry now escaped his lips.

"What is it, Jack!" In wild terror, Paul here clutched him by the arm.

Why, I've trod on something soft! Curse it, I would we were well out of this infernal house!" Stooping down as these words escaped his lips he now groped with his hands upon the floor of the passage.

A thrill of horror darted through his veins, whilst an exclamation of terror escaped him.

His hand had lighted upon a something clammy and cold:

An ice-cold face:

The face of a corpse!

CHAPTER XXIX.

MORE MYSTERY—THE STRANGE VAPOUR—PERIL OF THE ADVENTURERS—AT FACE WITH DEATH—THE FLIGHT ON TO THE ROOF—A LEAP FOR LIFE.

"What is it, Jack! What fresh infernal horror have you discovered now!" gasped Paul, as his friend's startled cry echoed through the little chamber.

"Why, here is a corpse just without here! How it came here Lord knows!"

"It must be one of our enemies!"

"I suppose it is!"

"How the deuce came it there!"

"That is the marvellous part of it!"

"It's very strange, Jack!"

"It is so; but I suppose we must reckon that we are in luck, as we have only one dead enemy instead of, as we expected, half-a-dozen live ones!"

"Exactly; but it mystifies me how the deuce our friend came to his end just outside here!"

"Well, it is very strange, Paul; but I'm getting used to mysterious things in this infernal house; perhaps the whistling spectre strangled the poor beggar!"

"Don't, Jack; I feel as if cold water was running down my back at the idea!"

"Well, come on, let us get out of this!"

About here to step over the horrible obstruction in the passage, Jack drew back, at the same time clutching his friend nervously by the arm.

"No, Paul; but—but——"

"Well, when you've done butting——"

"I have come over very queer, old pal; it's no larks! I feel as if I had got a wet handkerchief over my mouth!"

"Curse it, Jack, and I just begin to feel the same!"

"I can hardly draw breath!"

"Nor I!"

"God of heaven, what can it be!"

"The air seems charged with some noxious vapour!"

"Yes, Paul; hot, stifling, and deadly!"

"What can it be!"

"Lord in heaven only knows! follow me, or we shall be like those poor victims in the recess!"

In haste the two friends here stepped out into the passage, starting back, however, in a moment, uttering gasping cries of horror and alarm.

"Oh, Jack, what does it all mean!"

"I know not!"

"I couldn't breathe at all, outside."

"Nor I; the whole passage is choked up with some noxious foul air!"

"And yet this passage is our only means of escape!"

"Yes; this room is getting full of the noxious vapour now!"

"It is; I feel as if I should choke!"

"And so we both shall if we don't soon get out of this!"

"What, in the name of heaven, are we to do!"

"Why, we must make our way along the passage."

"But we can't draw breath!"

"Walking upright, no; but we must crawl along on our hands and knees."

"You are right, Jack; for heaven's sake, let us go at once, my brain is dizzy! I feel sick, faint, and can scarce breathe!"

"I will go first, Paul, do you follow!"

"All right, dear pal!"

Sinking down upon their hands and knees they now crept out into the grim funereal-like passage without.

The foul mephitic vapour that so oppressed their lungs, as Jack had suspected, was now less discernible.

Still very bad, it was with a choking, gasping sensation that the two friends crawled along.

Thicker, denser, seemed to grow the atmosphere as they advanced.

With their faces close to the floor of the secret way, yet were the companions nigh suffocated with the strange and noxious air.

Gaining the vicinity of the picture-gallery, from which they had first entered the passage, Jack was startled by observing a thin ray of light.

The panel leading into the portrait-room was open:

Had been left wide open by their foes.

From this aperture came a glare of light.

Approaching nearer, Jack noted a thin blue haze pouring into the passage:

A bluish vapour, that emanated from the portrait chamber!

In wondering surprise, sick and giddy with the foul air they were breathing, the friends at length gained the end of their journey.

With stifled cries they bounded into the chamber!

Scattering wide with their heels a mass of burning charcoal that, placed in a pan by the secret entrance had poured it deadly fumes into the passage.

The first impulse of the companions was to dash to the neighbouring casement:

Each, with avidity, drinking in the pure, sweet breeze as it rushed into the chamber.

"Well, what do you think of it now, Paul?"

"Why, that our fiendly foes, the runners, who hit upon the method of stifling us with their charcoal dodge, are sold again!"

"That's it, curse them; it was a devilish idea!"

"Aye! quite worthy of the man-hunters!"

"Yes; but it seems we are not doomed to die like dogs just yet! But how the day has slipped away, Paul! Why the sun has set, and it is getting quite dark!"

"It is so, and I vote we cut stick from this horrid house at once!"

"We can't do so very well at present, Paul!"

"Why so?"

"Look down there!"

Jack here pointed to the lawn in front of the house, upon which were grouped some dozen or more Bow-street runners.

"A regular blockade!"

"Yes!"

"We've got to stand a siege it seems!"

"Well, yes; it looks like it!"

"What do you propose to do now, Jack?"

"I don't know; the enemy seem determined to have us this time!"

"They do so!"

"I say, Paul, do you notice that, although we have scattered the charcoal fire about the room, that a very heavy and oppressive atmosphere still remains!"

"Yes; the room looks as if it was filling with smoke!"

"So it is!"

"Nonsense, it cannot be!"

"But it is so, Paul!—Hark! What is that?"

Intently the startled companions now listened:

Listened to a roaring, rushing noise below:

A roaring and crackling as of burning wood!

With pallid features Jack and his friend stared wildly, first at their foes and then at the door of the room.

The officers were pointing with exulting shouts towards the house.

Turning their gaze from their foes to the door of the portrait chamber, which was shut to, the highwaymen noted a mass of smoke curling its way into the room from beneath!

"They are bent upon our destruction, Paul!" exclaimed Jack, in a thick, husky voice of passion.

"Yes! Is there no escape from this fresh horror?"

"Heaven knows, Paul!"

"Heaven have mercy upon us, Jack!"

"Aye; for man will not!"

"No! But, come, even though our fiendly foes have fired the house, we will not yet despair!"

"Bravely said, Jack! Lead on, dear pal; and if we are to perish, we shall at least die together!"

"Nor gratify the enemy by a single death cry!"

"No, they shall not hear a sound save the noise of our funeral pyre as it consumes the quick and the dead!"

"Right, Paul! Come, stick close to me, I am going to make my way to the upper part of the house!"

"Right you are, Jack! Heaven grant us aid! To perish in a burning house, and such a house, is a fearful ending!"

A moan of despair here escaped the lips of the young highwaymen, who began to lose all hope in their fresh dread peril.

Striding over to the door Jack, now stooping low down, a precaution followed by his companion, threw it open.

In a moment dense volumes of thick black smoke poured into the room.

The roaring, crackling noise of burning wood now came plainer than ever to their ears.

They had divined the dreadful truth:

Their enemies purposely or by accident had fired the house.

The haunted house was doomed!

The lower chambers were a mass of flame!

Crawling on their knees the friends noted that the smoke below was of a ruddy red tint:

Less dense, brighter, and more glaring than that which in thick clouds poured up the staircase.

"There is no escape down the stairs, Paul. We must make our way to the top of the house!"

"All right, Jack, lead on, I'll follow! And, if we escape, from this time forth I'll have no mercy on our cowardly enemies; when I meet a Bow-street officer I'll shoot him down like a dog!"

"Aye, 'tis war to the death for the future!" muttered Jack savagely, who now with mad haste dashed along the corridor and gaining another staircase at once ascended it.

Reaching the summit of this flight the smoke they found was less dense.

Rushing in with a shudder, as he thought how little was the chance of final escape, Jack, closely followed by Paul, now dashed along a dark passage.

At the end of this was a door.

Upon trying it the companions found it was locked; with a rush however against it, they caused it to fly open.

The friends now discovered that they were in a chamber at the top of the old house.

The pale blue rays of the moon just rising in the heavens stole in through a tiny diamond-paned casement, lighting up with a ghostly light the small apartment!

In the centre of this room Jack and Paul discerned a pair of steps leading to a trap above.

This trap was open:

A rush of cold air wafting in upon the heads of the highwaymen!

"We must go up that ladder, Paul!"

"All right! You are captain, lead on!"

"Can you guess where that trap will conduct us to?"

"The roof, I suppose."

"Well, not exactly! But I fancy there is only a loft overhead!"

"Just so, and out of that you will be on the roof!"

"I expect so!"

"Well, we had better make for it: it's no use stopping here!"

"Not a bit; come on! All are not lost who are in danger!"

"Right, Jack; our day is marked out for us in the book of fate I take it!"

"Exactly; and if we don't burn or drown—"

"Why, we shall hang!"

"That's about it!"

Tripping lightly up the ladder, Jack now passed through the open trap.

Both in a few minutes after were standing, not in a loft, as they had supposed they would, but in a small belfry tower:

A place in which of yore had hung a bell:

A bell that had oft rung its chimes when the old house was tenanted.

The belfry tower, however, now no longer owned the bell; the timbers upon which it had hung suspended alone remained.

With a wild stare of alarm the companions gazed round them.

Many feet below were the grounds of the old house, the trees of which were now bathed in the shimmering light of the moon.

Motionless, speechless, the friends stood there, high up in the old belfry tower.

The hope of escaping a terrible death seemed lost to them.

Below them was a ruddy blood-red glare:

A ruddy glow that lighted up the grounds in a dazzling brilliancy.

The fire in the old house was burning fast and furious.

Showers of sparks and ruddy smoke poured out from the casements below.

In the belfry tower all was quiet.

Half an hour or more Jack calculated it would take for the flames to reach them where they stood.

And then—

A strong shiver passed through the frame of the bold highwayman, as he asked himself what hope had he and his friend of evading the dread doom that was before them.

Ever and again a huge bat would dash into the faces of the friends, whilst the hooting of an old owl added to the horrors of the grim scene.

"It's all up, Jack!"

"Looks infernally like it!"

"We may just as well have stopped in the house!"

"I don't see that!"

"There's no escaping from here!"

"Perhaps not; but we have half an hour more life up here than we should have had down below!"

"Granted; but if we are to die, the sooner the struggle is over the better!"

"But while there's life, you know, there's hope, Paul!"

"I see no hope here!"

"Maybe you don't; but I may presently, if you will only have patience!"

Jack spoke so calm and confident that his companion really began to think he had discovered a means of escape.

Eagerly he glanced round.

No apparent opening was there, however, of getting from their perilous position.

With a sigh and exclamation of despair Paul, with folded arms, stood gazing moodily up at the bright lustrous moon.

With a shudder he asked himself where would he and his friend be when that moon sank to rest.

Dead! Burnt to cinders perchance!

Calcined to dust by the cruel flames!

"Are there no means of escape, Jack!" he gasped, as these thoughts surged through his brain.

"Yes, Paul, dear boy; we have a chance, 'tis a dangerous one, but yet I think practicable!" exclaimed Jack, who, whilst Paul had been wrapped in his terrible musings, had been searching about for a plan of escape.

As he had said, he had hit upon one.

Dangerous, but yet a chance that might rescue them from the doom that menaced them.

Bidding Paul follow him, Jack now descended through the trap into the apartment below.

Here the companions found the air hot and stifling.

The fire was gaining ground:

Was eating its way up to the roof of the house!

Thick smoke now filled every passage and chamber.

With heads bent low, however, the two friends boldly passed from the room leading to the belfry tower, returning down the passage to the staircase up which they had made their way shortly before.

Reaching these, Jack paused.

Dense volumes of smoke, tinged a firy-red, pouring up, drove them both back.

"Do you want to go down those stairs!"

"Yes, Paul!"

"Then I am afraid it can't be done!"

"It must be tried!"

"Very good, lead on!" gasped Paul, who, on his hands and knees, could scarce draw breath in the thick, furnace-like clouds that rolled around them.

Jack, with a warning to be careful first addressed to his companion, now unhesitatingly slid down the stairs.

Reaching the passage at the bottom, the roar of the flames in the lower part of the house was dreadful to hear.

Unheeding this or the yellow-forked flames that licked up from below, Jack, gliding like a snake along the floor, now made his way for one of several doors that stood on the right hand.

Pushing the first of those open, a current of air at once relieved the adventurers.

Through the smoke that hung in the apartment Jack was able to discern a casement.

By this it was the wind from without, that had dashed in their faces as they pushed open the door, was making its way into the apartment.

Rising to his feet, Jack bounded forwards to this window.

"Thank heaven!" he gasped. "Thank heaven! Paul, I was right! We are saved!" he exclaimed, as he leant half out of the window.

"Saved! how!" said Paul, his brain fairly in a whirl as his friend's words fell upon his ears.

"Why, just look out here and tell me what you see!"

Eagerly, excitedly, Paul leant forth.

In some surprise he found that they were now in a back room of the old house.

Many feet below was the garden, now fully revealed in the ruddy glare of the fire and the silvery moonbeams.

Not the grounds, with their forests of brambles and thickets, however, was it that caused Paul to utter an exclamation of delight.

He saw in a moment Jack's purposed means of flight.

Close to the house, rearing its height up from the garden below, was a fine old beech tree.

The topmost branches of this tree were on a level with the casement out of which Paul was now leaning.

So close to the casement was the beech, that a jump forth would send them into its branches.

By this means Paul saw an escape from the burning house could be effected.

No prying eyes were below.

The officers were all congregated in the front of the house.

Flight by the trees seemed easy.

The risk of not catching a successful hold of the branches after a leap into them of course must be chanced.

"Well, old man, what do you think of! I see you tumble to my plan!"

"I do so, Jack! I only hope we shan't tumble to the ground after we do our leap!"

"No fear; the branches are too thick, we are bound to catch hold of one of them."

"Well, I think so."

"Of course we shall!"

"Any way we must chance it!"

"Rather! the old house is getting too hot to hold us!"

"It is so! How and when did you think of this plan, Jack?"

"When we were up in the belfry tower I caught sight of the tree. I knew a lower chamber at the back of the house would look out upon it; but I did not think we should so immediately find our way into the room that is closest to it of any other apartment."

"There's our luck, Jack! Thank heaven, our cursed foes are baulked of their fiendly design this time!"

"Yes, they won't make a roast of us this journey! But come, now for it! I will leap first, do you follow; don't hurry; it looks very easy, but still it's all a bit to do! If we fall short it's a case!"

"Just so, Jack, a case of smash!"

"Well, yes; we should'nt be up to much if we fell from here into the grounds!"

"Knock the wind out of us, old pal!"

"Guess it would!"

Leaning far out of the casement no inconvenience did the friends now experience from the smoke, though the roaring rush of the flames and the crackling of the wood gave token of the fierce ravages of the fire, the boards of the room in which they stood now bursting up from the effects of the furnace below.

"Time's up, Paul; here goes!" said Jack, not without a shudder gazing back at a sheet of flame that at that moment burst into the room from the door and floor.

Scrambling out on to the sill of the window, Jack, now measuring carefully the distance between the house and the tree, swaying his arms to and fro to give impetus to his body, took the daring leap.

For a moment of time Paul beheld his friend's form in the air, then a crashing of branches and a cry of delight from Jack told him all was well.

Screened by the thick foliage, Paul only knew by the voice of his companion that he was safe; then, giving a warning shout that he was coming, he also essayed the leap for life.

It was with a thrill of fear that he felt himself whirl through the air, a sickening faintness seizing upon him as for a second he thought he had jumped short; then, as he alighted among the branches, catching wildly at a giant arm he felt the hand of his friend upon his neck, and half strangled he was drawn by his neckerchief safe on to the limb of the tree which a moment before he had been clinging to with a nervous despairing grip.

A murmur of thankfulness to Heaven escaped the lips of Paul, as standing beside his companion in the old tree he found that they had both escaped:

Had in safety eluded the dread fate intended for them:

A horrible death in the burning house:

The old house now one mass of flame!

Not a moment too soon had they escaped.

With a thundering explosion some of the old walls now fell in, whilst a part of the roof shooting up into the air, amid a myriad shower of sparks, told them that had they been in the house, they would by this have perished.

But a merciful Providence had aided them.

By a miracle almost had they escaped!

But both, as they stood with glaring eyes gazing upon the flaming ruins, vowed to have revenge upon the cruel foe who had mercilessly doomed them to so dreadful a death!

CHAPTER XXX.

THE STRUGGLE IN THE SHRUBBERY—DEATH OF THE RUN-NER—THE FLIGHT THROUGH THE GROUNDS—THE LONDON MAIL—DARING EXPEDIENT OF THE HIGHWAYMEN—A COMICAL ADVENTURE—IN THE HIGHFLYER—THE ROBBERY—ONCE MORE UPON THE ROAD.

For some minutes the friends remained ensconced in the branches of the old beech, gazing at the ruins which, when in the belfry tower, they feared would have been their shroud.

"Well, we are safe out off that, Jack!"

"Thank heaven! yes, it was a close shave!"

"It was so; and having got safe out of the cursed house, I now vote we get as quickly as possible as far as we can from it!"

"Very good, Paul, I'm with you in that! Well, come on,"

Both now made all haste to descend from the tree, and, in a few moments, were landed safe on terra firma.

Slowly, cautiously, they now prepared to get out of the grounds:

Jack taking the lead, Paul followed on behind, both keeping a wary look out.

"I don't think there is much chance of our foes interfering with us," said Paul, as they tore on through the thick brushwood.

"You see, Jack, they fancy it's all over with us!"

"Well, yes; ain't they doing a grin now?"

"Rather on the wrong side of the mouth though!"

"Yes; wouldn't they stare if they saw us?"

"I guess they would that! they would not see anything more in this world after, though,"

"You'd put a bullet in them?"

"As mercilessly as I'd put one in a mad dog!"

"So too would I, Paul; the runners will find Gentleman Jack a rough one to deal with in future!"

Conversing thus in low tones, the friends, pushing their way through the wild growth of bushes that over ran the gardens, now arrived at a paling that separated it at this part from the high road.

The moon bright and clear, all was light as day.

Standing by the rude low fence the companions, glancing back, beheld the skies, though the fire was dying partly out, still tinged a blood-red.

With a nervous shudder as they thought of what they had escaped, both now at a bound leapt over the palings.

Just upon the other side was a mound of earth, covered with grass and bramble, whilst at the bottom of this ran a little rivulet.

Into this tiny stream both our friends soused.

Scrambling to their feet, for they had not noticed the palings were fixed upon this mound, they were, with a merry laugh, making from the spot, when their ears were startled by the utterance of cries of astonishment and rage:

Cries that a moment after were succeeded by the sharp report of firearms.

"Damnation! Satan aids them! they have escaped after all!"

"Down with them!"

"Keep your man, Jackson! we well soon have up the other!"

"Will you! I rather doubt it," said Jack, who, seizing the speaker (who after firing was about to dart away) with all his force, struck him with the butt of his pistol a blow between the eyes that sent the officer with a crash on to the ground.

"So much for you, my boy! Now, Paul, how are you getting on?" Jack, here leaving his late antagonist, who lay stunned and bleeding in the hedge, made towards his friend, who, kneeling upon the officer who had attacked him, and whom he had thrown to the ground, was gripping him with savage ferocity and with both hands by the throat.

Paul Clifford, mad with passion, and with the remembrance of the terrible death to which the officers had one and all condemned them, mercilessly clung to the wretched man beneath him, turning a deaf ear to his companion's warning that they had better get away.

Only when, with a convulsive shiver and a face purpled with strangulation, his foe he so vengefully gripped to the death ceased to struggle did Paul rise to his feet.

"I told you what I would do. Every cursed officer that crosses my path now I will serve the same," he muttered savagely, as he kicked the corpse aside.

Paul Clifford was fairly mad with fury; had Jack's late antagonist, who lay where he had fallen half-stunned, given sign of life, there would have been but a small chance for him.

"I do not wonder at your rage, Paul; but we must not let passion lead us into danger. We must away at once, or that fellow's death may cost us dear; the pistol shots have caused an alarm Hark to those shouts, even now they a hunting the neighbouring woods! Those infernal beggars there have apprised the others by the report of their firearms of our escape from the burning house!"

As Jack, speaking excitedly to his companion, drew him away from the scene of the encounter, loud cries with the firing of pistols echoed in the air.

The runners had indeed been warned of the escape of their victims.

Like bloodhounds they were again on their track.

With knitted brows the two friends, as they dashed away, beheld in the distance a posse of officers making for the scene of the late struggle.

Jack was right; the sharp report of the pistols had given them note of what was passing.

"Confound those fellows, but for them we should have got clear away!" he gasped, as with Paul by his side he flew rather than ran down the road.

"Well, one of them has paid dear for his attack!"

"Yes, he won't run any more, that's certain, Paul."

"No; he's gone a journey now where Bow-street runners are not required."

"Just so! But hark, did you hear that, old pal?"

Jack here, pausing in their mad race, halted by the wayside.

Distinctly at this moment was borne upon the breeze the sound of a horn.

"Do you know what that is?"

"Guess I do, Jack! it's a coach."

"Yes, the mail for London."

"Exactly; but I don't see what it matters to us! We can't very well go in for business now," said Paul, with a grim smile.

"No; but I tell you what we can do."

"What, Jack?"

"Why, stop the mail, and get inside."

"The devil! Do you mean to say you'll offer to go as passenger?"

"Just what I do mean."

"By Jove, it's an audacious move!"

"Exactly! and therefore more likely to succeed!"

"You propose to hail the coach?"

"That's it!"

"And go to London?"

"Yes; or part of the journey!"

"By that means we shall effectually escape our enemies?"

"Exactly; the coach, if stopped at all, will be searched by our foes before it gets to us!"

"So it will!"

DASHING DUVAL;
OR,
THE LADIES' HIGHWAYMAN.

GAILY CLAUDE LED FORTH THE LOVELY GIRL IN THE IMPROMPTU DANCE ON THE HEATH.

"Very good! then when it comes up we hail and take our places!"

"A capital idea, Jack!"

"I should say it was!"

"I don't think I'd go all the way to the long village—London!"

"No; our destination must first be the old Tree Cave!"

"Yes; and then we can send Luke down to Sam Green for Kate!"

"You forget Kate is to be at Highgate to-night!"

"True, I had forgotten that! There's one thing I have to propose, Jack, though!"

"Well, what is it?"

"Why, that we levy a toll on all the passengers in the mail before we bid them good-bye!"

Well, that must be according to circumstances; and now, before the drag arrives, let us disguise ourselves as much as possible!"

This proposition of Jack's was speedily and immediately carried out; and what with their hair drawn over their brows, handkerchiefs muffled over their mouths, and coat-collars drawn up, a great change was certainly effected in the appearance of the highwaymen.

It was only just as they had completed their operations that again, loud and clear, came the note from the horn of the guard on the night air:

The mail coach for London was close upon them.

"Here it comes, Paul; we shall be at Highgate in half an hour!"

Both now hailed the coach, which came rattling on at

No. 17 & 18.   **Price One Penny.**

great speed, and when it drew up the coachman called out—

"Full outside, gentlemen! but there are two places inside, if you like to take them!"

"That will do!" said Jack.

Upon this the guard dismounted from the roof and opened the coach door for the two inside. And in the course of another half minute, the "All right" of the guard notified to the coachman that he might start again, and off they went.

Jack and Paul now began to look around them at their companions in the coach, which consisted of three persons. One a rather elderly lady, the other two being of the male sex.

One of these latter was a red-whiskered, coarse-featured man, with a very low forehead and tiny eyes, that might have been supposed to have been taken out of the head of a doll, so small and glassy-looking were they!

Beside this passenger sat a timid-looking man, with light wavy hair, the colour of tow; whilst his face bore a soddened kind of appearance, the colour of the flesh being as much like that of a suety-pudding made of coarse flour as anything; whilst a pair of gold spectacles, that rested on a very large nose, increased the outré look of the man.

"A fine night, gentlemen!" now said the red-whiskered passenger.

"Yes, it is a very fine night!" exclaimed Jack.

"Gentlemen," said the old lady, as she looked over at the two friends with anxiety impressed on her features, "is it true that that horrid man who wouldn't be hanged, Gentleman Jack, as he is called, and another dreadful robber, named Paul Clifford, are really on the road!"

"Well, madam," said Jack, with a smile, "we don't know of our own knowledge; but we did hear something of the sort at the King's Head, an inn a little distance from here!"

"You really did, sir!"

"Yes, madam, but it may be merely nothing but rumour after all!"

"It makes one nervous, it really does!" exclaimed the large-nosed gentleman, who here began to wipe his spectacles, looking at the same time in a scared manner around him. "It's makes one nervous, and nervousness is bad for the health; it injures the digestion! I do wish they would hang all highwayman right off without trial or anything else; that would free the country of the fellows, I warrant!"

"You are quite right, sir; you speak with the profoundest wisdom. I am delighted to hear such sentiments fall from your lips. I shall be happy to boast that I have ridden in a coach with a gentleman who giveth thus out to the world his beautiful, delicious project for ridding the world of baseborn robbers!" Jack here, to the astonishment of the pudding-faced man, seized his hands and squeezed them so hard that he brought tears into the eyes of his victim.

"Well, it is, I must confess, a good idea of this gentleman; all those wretches ought to be hung, that they ought, directly they are caught," said the old lady; "and really the danger of travelling ought to make everyone attend to their spiritual concerns. Amid all the terrors of the road it is a great consolation to me that I have with me in my hand at this moment a volume of those beautiful hymns by Graspall and Cantem, which are so greatly admired!"

"Damn it, madam," said the red-whiskered individual, "I don't see any cause for fear at all, hang me if I do; do you, gentlemen!"

"Not the least, sir!" said Paul.

"Fear, absurd! ridiculous! monstrous!" echoed Jack.

"That's just my opinion, gentlemen! The most extraordinary thing in all the world is how anybody allows himself to be robbed by a highwayman; hang me up like a mad dog if that don't get the better of me!"

"It is odd!" said Jack.

"Very; quite comical!" said Paul, with a half grin.

"Well, I don't know, gentlemen," said the gent with the spectacles; "but when a horse pistol comes up to you and presents a loaded highwayman at your head, what are you to do!"

"Dear me, sir," exclaimed the old lady, "you are making dreadful mistakes in what you are saying; do you know you have put the cart before the horse!"

"Did I, madam! What cart, madam!"

"Well, really, you are quite an absent man!"

"It's on account of my nervousness, madam; I assure you I come of a nervous family, and it's quite evident that I really cannot help it; but what did I say! I hope no offence!"

"Oh dear no, sir!" exclaimed Jack, who began to think he was the companion of lunatics.

"Well, if I did, I humbly apologise; but already I am very nervous, and the thought of those villains of highwaymen has quite upset me!"

"Ah, nervousness is, allow me to say, damn it, a thing I only know by name!" exclaimed the red-whiskered passenger. "I met a highwayman once; but the fellow, damn it, did not make me nervous; sink me, split me if he did; they found out that they had caught a Tartar!"

"So I should think!" said Jack. "Who was it tried to rob you!"

"Oh, damn it, Claude Duval—Dashing Duval, as his friends call him; but, sink me, I took the dash out of him, and if you like to hear it I'll tell you how it was!"

"I should like to hear about the affair very much!" said Jack with unmoved countenance, at the same time administering to Paul a severe kick on the shins, as that young gentleman was giving every indication of bursting out into a roar of laughter.

"You would like to hear how I served the vagabond, damn it, sink me, smother me, so you shall!" said the whiskered one. "And let me tell you all as long as I am in the coach you need be under no apprehension about Claude Duval, ha, ha!"

"I rather think the sight of me would be sufficient for him! If he were only to see me I rather fancy he would be off quicker than he came, sink me, split me! ha, ha!"

"I feel decidedly more comfortably than I did," said Jack, "after your assurance; for I have heard that this Duval they speak so much about is a desperate fellow, and that he is not so easily got rid of!"

"All a mistake, damn it! sink me, burn me, quite a delusion, lad! I settled worse than he is; the fellow, his companion, who cheated the hangman at Tyburn yesterday, why, split me, smother me, I—I was stopt by him once. I soon settled the vagabond!"

"The deuce you did!" said Jack, now more than ever interested in the red-whiskered passenger.

"Yes, it's a fact, sir! I was stopped by the fellow, Gentleman Jack, and I'll, damn it, be bound he won't forget me till the day of his death!"

"And you encountered that highwayman, and got off without being robbed of anything!"

"Yes, damn it, smother me, sink me, it's a fact!"

"I can scarce credit it!" said Jack with assumed amaze.

"I daresay not, sir; but, lord, these fellows are all curs!"

"Oh, I believe that!"

"So do I!" said Paul, who here began to stuff his pocket-handkerchief into his mouth.

"Will you mind telling us about this occurrence!"

"Damn it, yes; when I think of it, split me, burn me, if it ain't better to hear than the adventure with Duval! You must know, gentlemen, I was crossing Hampstead Heath on my road to Highgate by Swains-lane about the dusk of the evening, just getting, damn it, a bit darkish, you know!"

"Oh, dear me, yes," said the old lady, "how dreadfully exciting!"

"It makes one nervous!" exclaimed the gent with the spectacles.

"Well," continued the red-whiskered man, who was evidently quite delighted at the effect he was producing, "you must know I was in a gig, and just as I got to a rather lonely part of the road, by Lord Montford's park wall, there came out of the shade a man on horseback; but split me, bury me, damn it, I didn't quiver a muscle!"

"Good gracious! I should have died. A man on horseback!"

"Yes, madam, a man on horseback, and riding up to the side of the gig he said 'Halt! your money or you life!'"

"What did you do, sir!"

"Why, I pulled up my mare, and I said to the fellow in quite an off-handed sort of way 'Who are you!' 'Oh,' said he, 'I am Gentleman Jack, and if you don't hand over to me your watch, jewellery, and money, I will send a brace of bullets through your head!'"

"Sir," interrupted the gent with the spectacles, "do you mean to tell me you were not nervous then?"

"No, sir; damn it, no!"

"Then you don't come of a nervous family, it's quite clear!"

"But what did you do?" said the old lady.

"Aye, how did you settle him?" said Jack, nudging Paul.

"Yes; what did you do with him?"

"Did you sink, smother, or, damn it, burn him?"

"I'm coming to that," said Red Whiskers, frowning at Clifford, whom he could not fail to notice was taking him off; "if you don't interrupt me, I'll tell you how I settled the ruffian. You must know the fellow presented a pistol at my head, and I said to him 'Well, Gentleman Jack, if you will be contented with my pocket-book, it is at your service, on one condition!' 'Be quick,' he said, and he gave the pistol a kind of shake, and put it rather nearer to me, which was just what I wanted, you see!"

"Dear me, sir; you don't say that?"

"Yes, madam, that's just what I wanted; for, you see, it enabled me to lay hold of it, and with one wrench to get it out of his hand. In another moment I was standing up in the gig, and had his own pistol levelled at his head!"

"Capital! Bravo!" said Jack.

"Damn it! what a bold trick!" exclaimed Paul.

"And he wasn't nervous?"

"My blood runs cold," ejaculated the old lady, lifting up his hands; "what happened next! Pray go on, sir!"

"Well, ma'am, when he found I was one too many for him he cried out, 'Spare my life!' 'No, villian! said I, I have you now at my mercy; stir hand or foot and I fire! I feel that I ought to rid society of you—damn it, I do! But, sink me, burn me, smother me, no! I promised you my pocket-book, and my pocket-book you shall have; but there's nothing in it; and sink me, burn me, you shall eat it!'"

"Eat it?" cried the old lady.

"Eat it?" gasped the old gent with the spectacles; "he made a highwayman eat his pocket-book; he is certainly not a nervous man!"

"And did he really eat it?" said Jack.

"Ha, ha! you shall hear. When he found he had got such a determined customer to deal with he began to beg himself off, you see, as well as he could, and presently he took the pocket-book in his hand and placed it actually in his mouth. The tears were in his eyes, then, as he said, 'Oh, sir, are you satisfied? pray let me go!' and then, while I pretended to be looking another way, for, to tell you the truth, I wanted to get rid of the rascal as I was in a bit of a hurry, off he went, and I don't believe he stopped till he had placed a good five miles between us!"

"What a coward!" said Jack.

"Damn him! sink me, he ought to have been smothered for bolting!" exclaimed Paul.

"I wonder how long he took to digest the pocket-book!"

"Well, I'm a nervous man, I couldn't have tackled the fellow like that; but he must have been frightened!"

"Frightened! he must have been a regular cur," said Jack.

"As all these fellows are," said the red-whiskered gent, who here cast a stern glance at Paul; "all you have to do is to face the villains boldly, as I always do, and they will invariably, you will find, knuckle under. Sink me! I care no more for a highwayman than I do for meeting a donkey or a pig in the road."

"He is a wonderful man, and not at all nervous!"

"Was it a large pocket-book you swore you'd make Gentleman Jack put into his bread-basket, sir?" said Paul.

"Not very large; about this size!" the red-whiskered one here produced a small morrocco case, "and if I hadn't felt compunction for the fellow, damn it, he should have eaten it, sir," he exclaimed, glaring fiercely at Paul, who was now obliged to burst out into a roar of laughter.

About to give vent to some angry exclamation the gent's rage was subdued by a sudden stopping of the coach, a voice without crying, "Hold!"

In a moment the brave passenger sank far back in his seat, squeezing himself into as small a space as possible behind the old lady, who gave utterance to a shrill scream; whilst the nervous gentleman, with a gasp and a groan, slid off his seat at the feet of his fellow-travellers.

It was with a rather unpleasant tremor that he heard the loud cry to halt.

They had a shrewd suspicion as to the cause.

They suspected it was their foes.

The sudden demand upon the part of a stranger, who with a stentorian voice had bade the coachman pull up, startled both Jack and Paul, recalling them at once to their true position.

In their amusement with the bragging passenger they had forgotten their late peril.

"Now, then, what is it? who are you that dare stop the Highflyer?" shouted the gruff voice of the guard.

"We are officers of police."

"What a mercy! We are saved!" said the old lady.

"Ain't they highwaymen? Oh, what a thing it is to be nervous!"

"Damn it! there's no blood after all," said Red Whiskers, now starting forwards and shoving his head out of the window of the door, which he presently after, much to Jack's rage and annoyance, opened and ventured to peer forth.

"What passengers have you, coachman?" said the foremost officer, a man whose features Jack was glad to find he did not recognise.

"We have five insides and three out."

"Good! I must take the liberty of looking at them; we are after a couple of highwaymen. Of course they are not here, but as a matter of form I must search the coach."

"Certainly; right you are! You may look away, but you won't find the birds you want have made a nest of the Highflyer!" said the coachman with a loud laugh.

It was with rather an uncomfortable feeling that Jack and Paul heard this colloquy.

They both felt that their present position was not the safest in the world:

Any moment might discover them to their foes.

Their only resource, they knew, was to keep quiet.

The officers were in too strong force to resist; they, too, were mounted, whilst Jack and Paul in an attempt at flight could only flee on foot.

There was nothing for it but to sit it out.

There was now a great flashing of lanterns and in another minute the officer who had addressed the driver of the mail stepped forwards and peered in at the door.

"Sorry to trouble you, gentlemen," he exclaimed, as he flashed the lantern he held in his hand upon its occupants.

"Oh, pray don't mention it, it's no trouble!" said the nervous man. "Indeed, I'm a nervous man, and—and I'm much obliged for your visit!"

"Damn it! it makes no difference to me," said Red Whiskers; "I've made up my mind to shoot the first high-wayman I may meet, sink me! burn me, if I don't!"

"Ah, I see my men ain't here!" said the officer with a laugh, gazing into the face of the valiant hero, whose spirit of braggadocio Jack was now most thankful for, as it drew away the attention of the runners from the other insides, who now procured but a cursory glance from the man of law.

The lantern was now withdrawn; Jack and Paul, who had sunk far back in their seats, giving a sigh of relief as the officer who had it turned away.

"Oh, dear me!" ejaculated the old lady, "how glad I shall be when we get to London; I'm sure all this is enough to frighten every one of us to death!"

"Madam!" said the red-whiskered man, this sort of thing may frighten old ladies; it may frighten insolent gentlemen (here a withering look was cast upon Paul); it may frighten a nervous man; but it don't affect me in the least, sink me! burn me, if it does!"

"Well, I don't know anything about sinking and burning, sir, I can only express my surprise that when the alarm first fell upon us you squeezed so close into my corner that I was almost blused, in a manner of speaking," said the old lady; "I'm sure as you were in as great a fright as any of us!" she added, indignantly tossing up her head.

"Me frightened, ma'am? Sink me, smother me, if you were a man, I'd—I'd, damn it, yes, I would, annihilate you, sink me!"

"Don't go on like that; it ain't Christian-like; remember what the delightful Graspall and Cantem say in the 254th Hymn!"

"Confound it, ma'am, I don't read hymns! Damn it! hang all the world! sink me, if a man had looked me in the face and said half you have said, I would have eaten him—eaten him, I would, by Jove!"

"But it is quite true what the lady said; you did try to

hide yourself, sir, I saw you do it," said Jack, with a smile; "now, do you know, my opinion is that you are about as big a coward as ever I came across!"

"That's just what he is," said Paul, who, as the coach now free of their foes rattled on, enjoyed the sport with the whiskered braggart.

With a would-be fierce look, the fellow glared at the two friends, but no exclamation of anger escaped him, Jack's sudden interference seemed to dumbfound him.

"Now, I have listened attentively to all you have been saying," said Jack, "and now hear my opinion of you, which is this—that you are what is vulgarly called a thundering liar! I don't believe one word of your story about the highwayman and the pocket-book! I feel quite certain that you are one of those threatening faint-hearted bullies, who go through the world swearing and shouting and frightening timid people, but who are in reality the greatest cowards out!"

"Curse me, sink me, I ain't going to stand this! Blood must flow in bucketfuls! I am sorry, very sorry; but, damn it, I'll have to smash you!"

"Very good!" said Jack, with a grin. "How are you going to begin?"

"Well, damn it! smother me, if a lady was not in the coach, I—"

"Oh, don't mind me!" said the female passenger, who saw through the fellow and seemed to enjoy the fun. "I beg that you won't mind me!"

"You hear what the good lady says, sir! Now for this smashing business! When are you going to begin?"

"Well, when I come to think of it, damn it! I shall, as a gentleman, treat your insults with contempt—with bitter contempt sir, I shall show you that you are quite beneath my notice!"

"Oh, but I must take offence at that! and now I won't let the matter rest till you have begged my pardon for daring to say you would treat me with contempt! If you won't apologise, I shall insist on fighting you! Here are my pistols, and you can choose which you please. They have both a full charge in them and never miss fire, so that it is quite a matter of indifference to me which of them you take!"

"Oh, no murder! I beg pardon; damn it, I didn't mean anything! I'll do anything you wish for peace and quietness! I don't intend to fight about a mere joke! Oh, dear no! Upon my life, sir! Sink me, stifle me, if you ain't the funniest gentleman I ever saw!"

"I cannot allow you or any man to call me funny! Retract, sir!"

"Oh, I do! Oh, certainly, with all my heart! Curse me, anything you like!"

"Very good; now where is that pocket-book you say you tendered to the highwayman, Gentleman Jack?"

"Sink me, burn me, I ain't got it!"

"Well, you have some other!"

"Oh, ah! damn it, yes!"

"Very good; just oblige me with it for a moment!"

Jack, here, who held one of his pistols in his hand, raised it rather threateningly in a line with the red whiskered man's face, who at once pulled from his vest a small pocket-book, handing it over with a bewildered, frightened, idiotic stare.

With an exclamation of terror at the sight of the pistol, the nervous gentleman sank down all of a heap at the feet of the old lady, who, with rather a dubious expression of countenance, was intently watching the proceedings of the stranger.

"Now, was it an article like this you offered Gentleman Jack, the highwayman, to eat?"

"Well, a—yes! something like!" said the braggart, who, shivering as with an ague, stared wildly at Jack, who put the pocket-book in his pocket.

"Well, as you confessed he didn't put away the other, I'll make him manage this one!"

"You!"

"Yes; the knight of the road you so audaciously told such lies about is a friend of mine!"

"Murder!"

"I shall give him your pocket-book!"

"Fire!"

"With your purse, watch, and rings, which I request you to hand over!"

"Ha, ha, ha! Damn it, yes! A capital joke! Only, sink me, burn me, you—you do it so real!" gasped the red-haired one, as he forced a sickly smile.

"You will find it very unpleasantly real if you don't quickly hand over your valuables!"

With a face the colour of putty, the wretched victim at once placed in the hands of Jack the articles he had asked for a moment before.

With a dazed, wondering stare, the old lady watched the exchange of property, whilst the nervous one lay moaning and groaning at her feet.

Securing his booty, Jack, now lifting his hat, addressed himself to the astonished female, who, open-mouthed, drank in every word.

"Look you, madam!" he exclaimed, "when next you travel with a fellow like that, don't believe all he may say, and now, ere I go, allow me to inform you that I am the very highwayman he told his lies about! Nay, be not alarmed, dear madam, both yourself and the nervous gentleman are perfectly safe! I wouldn't hurt a hair of your heads; but for our worthy braggart here, if I had a pair of shears, I'd have off his whiskers and, damme, make him swallow them! As it is, I must leave him, carrying away with me a sweet memento of our meeting! I and my comrade, Paul Clifford, are now about to quit the coach! Au revoir, a pleasant end to your journey, and, now, one word of caution to the three of you! If you give the slightest hint of who we are to the guard or the coachman, we will, ere we are made prisoners, blow out your brains: so take timely warning! What ho, guard! We will get down here! our friend, Lord Snuffleton's shooting box is near at hand!" shouted Jack, who had thrust his head out of the window.

"Get down here, sir! Lord Snuffleton! Yes, sir! certainly, sir!" said the obsequious hornblower, as, having clambered down from his seat, he opened the door.

In a moment Jack and Paul jumped out, first turning and glancing menacingly at their late companions.

Giving the guard a guinea, which about doubled their fare, they then both plunged into a thick copse that lined the roadside, scarce having entered the shrubbery ere the winding of the horn and the rattle of the wheels told them that the mail for London, the Highflyer, was once more on its journey!

CHAPTER XXXI.

AGAIN ON THE ROAD—THE MOUNTED RIDE—THE BATH MAIL—A ROBBERY—OFF WITH YOUR BOOTS—THE MOUNTED DRAGOONS—THE FLIGHT TO THE WOODS AT HIGHGATE—THE OLD TREE CAVE—JACK AND PAUL MEET AN OLD FRIEND—DASHING DUVAL TELLS A STRANGE STORY.

Loud and long the companions laughed, as they dashed through the copse by the wayside.

They had effectually outwitted their late fellow passengers:

And had thrown their foes, the Bow-street runners, off their track.

Bounding on for a time through the thick copse, they presently again, by a sudden detour, came out on the high road.

Both now pausing, looked each other in the face, and then burst out into renewed laughter.

"Ha, ha, ha! I say, Jack!"

"Well, old pal! what is it?"

"Well, I should fancy the next time he talks about me it will be truth, not lies, that will come out of his mouth!"

"Exactly; oh Lord, oh dear! shall I ever forget the face of the fellow as you hold out your hand for the valuables?"

"Didn't he look comic?"

"Yes; as a kinchin on his first visit to the stone jug!"

"He won't forget me in a hurry, Paul!"

"I don't suppose he will! But I say, Jack, what are we to be up to now?"

"Why I think we had better see if we can't get our prads (horses)."

"The very thing I was thinking of!"

"Without them we are, in a manner of speaking, at the mercy of our foes!"

"Exactly; and that ain't at all to my liking!"

"No; nor to mine!"

"Very good! then we will see if we can reach the pheasantry where Sam has placed our steeds!"

"Right you are; come on!"

At a quick pace the two friends now hastened along the road, presently diving again into some thick woods.

They were aware that they had some distance to go, as they had ridden some miles in the Highflyer; but upon canvassing the matter over, they thought it better to procure their steeds ere they made for the secret cave at Highgate, as the animals might prove a source of trouble and annoyance to their mutual friend, Sam Green, if they were not presently removed.

Having, therefore, decided to procure their steeds, the companions, with all haste, made for the place where they expected to find them:

The woods near the haunted house: the old ruin now a calcined heap of ashes.

It was with a strange nervous thrill some two hours after their determination to secure their horses, that the highwaymen stood in the avenue of trees that led to the grounds of the old house.

All was quiet, no sound of alarm fell upon their ears.

The foe they had cause to dread was no longer there.

Standing in the centre of the avenue, the bare walls of the old house could just be sighted by the friends.

For some few moments the companions remained in silence gazing at the place where they had encountered such dire perils; Paul, the first to speak, with an involuntary shudder, exclaiming—

"Let's get away, Jack; and tell me what do you think about what we saw last night in that horrid habitation?"

"I know not what to think!"

"Do you believe in spirits, Jack?"

"Those contained in a bottle? Decidedly I do!"

"Pray be serious! Do you think that there are such things as immaterial beings?"

"Well, Paul, to answer you in sober seriousness, I do not see why spirits, as they are called, should not be! Say it is inexplicable to me: so is our existence. Is not all around us a great mystery!—the earth, the bright blue skies above, the burning sun, the silvery moon now shining upon us, the diamond-like stars—are not all alike wondrous to our limited understanding?"

"Yes, Jack; all that sort of thing has puzzled some of those men, whose brain-pans have had more in them than mine or yours! But come, what do you think of that figure of the whistler we saw in the lone house?"

"I scarce know what to think of it, and can but believe that it was a supernatural visitant from the other world!"

"Such is my belief, Jack!"

"Well, I suppose it won't haunt the place any more now!"

"No; the house is burnt down!"

"And his ghostship is burnt out!"

"Exactly so, Jack!"

Walking cautiously on during their converse, the companions had now gained the woods in which, it will be remembered, was situate the little building where the worthy landlord, Sam Green, had conducted Jack with his horse when they had first left the King's Head.

With very little trouble this place was found out by the companions.

Jack, who had taken the lead as he neared the shed, drew back with an exclamation of alarm.

"What is it? What's up?" said Paul in a whisper.

"Why, damn it, there's some one there!"

"Where?"

"Why in the pheasantry!"

"The deuce there is! Who can it be?"

"That's just what I should like to know!"

"It can't be our enemies?"

"I don't know; it might be!"

"Shall we step it?"

"Without our prads, after we have come all this way back for them? not if I know it!"

"Very good; then we had better boldly open the door of the shanty, and walk in!"

"The very thing I have decided upon!"

"All right, old pal! forward's the word!"

"Got you barking-irons all right, Paul?"

"I have so!"

"Good! keep close to me, and in another moment we'll have out the horseflesh!"

"That's your style!"

Slowly and cautiously the two now made for the little thatched building, that in the soft moonlight looked the cosiest of snug retreats.

As they approached the door, the sound of a man's voice came plain to their ears.

"There is only one to deal with, Jack!"

"Yes; and no matter who he may be, we will soon settle him!"

"Just so; if he is quiet, and behaves properly, we'll give him a guinea!"

"Yes; and if he comes the running dodge, we must give him one for his nob!"

"Exactly, Jack; a tap on the head to teach him manners!"

"Hallo! who's there?"

So suddenly the voice sounded in the ears of the two friends, that they both started back.

A head, thrust out of the doorway of the shed, was now fully revealed in the rays of the moon.

In speechless amaze, the two highwaymen gazed at the object before them.

The head, followed by the body, a little short stunted figure, now stood just without the pheasantry:

A little itré figure of a man with a fat face, a shock of red hair, one eye, and one of his ears gone.

"Hallo, who is it? Be that you, mearster!"

In wondering amaze, Jack and Paul gazed at the strange figure before them, a low laugh escaping them as a volley of oaths were uttered by the stranger.

"What do you call that, Jack?"

"The Old Man of the Woods!"

"Is he guarding our steeds?"

"He may be; but if he is, he will soon be relieved of the responsibility!"

"I guess he will!"

Both the highwaymen now made a step forwards, a proceeding that brought forth another volley of oaths from the little one-eyed man.

"Look here, if yer both on yer don't step it pretty smart, smash me in a pumpkin if I don't gie yer summat yer won't forget, as sure as my name's Mike!"

With an exclamation of rage, the friends drew back.

They saw two things that enraged them:

One was a brace of pistols, presented by the diminutive stranger; and the other, a sight of their horses, which were both fastened up in the little building.

"Now, it's no manner of use looking vicious, if as how you wants to collar these prads! Cuss me! you'll have to do it over my body!" said the stranger.

"Who, the devil, are you?" exclaimed Jack, who was meditating a rush forwards, though the pistols held by the little stout man were pointed ominously at his head.

"Ha! who are you? that's it!" said Paul.

"Why, I'm old Mike! One-eyed Mike, as they calls me! but my one optic is good enough for you two; don't you make no mistake!"

"Indeed! and may I ask One-eyed Mike what you're up to with those horses?"

"I'm minding on 'em!"

"Oh, you are here to see the steeds ain't taken away?"

"That's just it!"

"And who put you here?"

"Him as owns 'em!"

"And who may he be?"

"That's my business!"

"Is it? Now, do you know I think it's as much mine!"

"How so?"

"Because I happen to be the owner of the bay mare!"

"That's an infernal lie! Nay, stand back, or I'll put a bullet in yer!"

Grating his teeth with rage, Jack glared viciously at the stranger.

There was that in the fellow's look that told he meant keeping his word, and though Jack would have thrown himself fearlessly upon a dozen Bow-street runners, he did not care to risk being shot down like a dog by an elfish-looking stranger in those silent woods.

"I say, Jack, I can't stand this!"

"Nor I, Paul!"

"On to him! never mind his barking irons!"

"Hold!"

Loud and clear the man's voice rang in the ears of the friends as they were about to dash upon him.

"Hold! What may be your names? Surely you ain't both escaped the flames! It ain't possible that you are Sam Green's high-toby friends, Gentleman Jack and Paul Clifford?"

The stranger, in doubt and surprise, here lowered his weapons.

With a loud laugh, Jack stepped forwards and held out his hand, a proceeding in which he was joined by Paul.

"It's all right, Mike! we are the knights of the road whom the cursed runners would have treated to a roast, but we were too clever for them ; we got safe out of the burning house, leaving the spectres to enjoy the blaze ! We met with an adventure on the road, and came back here after our prads, which you have so well guarded !" said Jack, who, with another laugh, here handed the man a guinea, the while he seized upon and led out his brave mare, which had treated him a moment before to a whinnying sound of recognition.

Paul, securing the other horse, a noble, handsome steed, the two friends, followed by their late strange adversary, made way at once through the woods in the direction of the high road.

"And so poor Sam thought we were frizzed up !" said Jack, with a laugh, as they hurried on.

"Indeed he did ; and in a dreadful state I left him, I can tell you ! Howsomever, gentlemen, now I find you are safe and sound, I'll hurry to the inn and make Sam acquainted with the fact of your escape. He'll be main glad to hear it, I know !"

"We should be glad to show up in person, Mike, but that it might be dangerous !" said Paul.

"Well, it would be a kind of walking into the lion's den !"

"How do you mean ?"

"Why, some of the Bow-street runners, them as set fire to the Grange, are baiting now at the inn !"

"The devil they are ?"

"Then the sooner we get on the road, Jack, the better !"

"Yes ; here we are out of the woods, and now for a run to Highgate !"

"To the old Tree Cave ?"

"Yes ; for pretty Kate will think something has gone wrong if I don't soon show up !"

"So she will, Jack ! Ta, ta, Mike, you will haste to Sam Green !"

"Yes ; the sooner he hears the good news the better !"

"Right you are, Mike ! Farewell !"

Having gained the high road, the highwaymen, now vaulting into their saddles, gave their steeds the rein and were presently dashing away at good speed.

Shrill shouts of exultant glee now burst from the mouths of the companions.

They were once more safe in their saddles :

Free of their enemies, the Bow-street runners !

"Hurrah for the road !" shouted Paul. A warm glow diffused through his frame as he was borne along.

"A moonlight ride ; a traveller with a well-filled purse ; and rosy lips to greet one's return !" shouted Jack.

"Hillio, away !"

"We are free !"

"As air !"

"And care for nought !"

"A fig for the grabs !"

"Hurrah for the road !"

"Who cares for Tyburn Tree ?"

"We can die but once !"

"Hurrah ! Ha, ha, ha ! Hurrah for the road !"

Wildly the two friends shouted thus to each other as they were borne along.

At terrific pace the steeds dashed on.

The animals were fresh ; their riders bold, defiant, exhilarated.

On they rushed !

A village was reached and passed at lightning speed !

Like a panorama it flitted by the eyes of the daring night-riders.

The Gothic-built ivied tower of the little village church for a moment caught the eye of the friends, and then was lost to view.

Again they were tearing along the open road.

Heath, copse, meadow, and common seemed to flit by the riders like a phantasmagoria :

So fast they rode !

Anon, in the silence of the night, other sounds than the clattering of their own horses' hoofs reached the ears of the companions.

"Hold, Paul !"

Jack pulling up his steed now gazed at the scene before them.

"Did you hear nothing a moment ago ?"

"Yes, Jack, the rattle of wheels."

"Exactly ! Hark !" The sound of a horn afar off now echoed faintly in the air.

Far away in their rear the friends glancing back beheld a vehicle upon the road :

Behold it just as it passed a turn in the highway.

Quite a mile off the vehicle could only just be discerned in the shimmering rays of the moon.

"Well, Jack, my flower, what do you intend to do ?"

"Why stop that drag to be sure !"

"Just what I thought you were up to ! What do you take the affair to be ?"

"A long drag."

"No ?"

"Yes ?"

"Are you sure ?"

"I am convinced of it."

"Then it must be——"

Jack here hesitated as he, leaning forwards in his saddle, took another stare at the approaching vehicle."

"It's the Bath Mail, Paul, and nothing else !"

"The devil ! And you propose——"

"To stop it ; just so ?"

"Well, it will be a cool trick !"

"A trick that I will execute, Paul !"

"As you will ! I'm on. If we have any luck we shall make enough to lie by for a week or two !"

"We shall so !"

Jack now motionless in his saddle gazed intently at the coach behind them.

Again the echoes of the guard's horn sounded along the road :

Sounded cheerful and joyous as it rang on the night air.

The noise of the wheels of the mail and the loud clatter of the horses' hoofs presently fell clear upon the ears of the friends.

"Paul, get your barking irons ready !"

"All right, my flower !"

"Do you take the off-side !"

"Right you are !"

"I will intimidate the driver and the guard : do you cut the traces of the leaders !"

"The very ticket !"

"Threaten with your barker, but don't fire unless self-preservation demands it."

"All right, Jack, my daisy !"

"I'll see to the passengers !"

"Ease them of their superfluous cash !"

"Just so !"

"You won't hurt them if they ain't disagreeable ?"

"By no means !"

"You will do the business in a gentlemanly and scientific manner !"

"I will so !"

"In fact, make them all feel it pleasant to be robbed ?"

"Just so !"

"Like a real knight of the road and high-toby man !"

"Decidedly ; but our friends approach, and I fancy we shall be the happy recipients presently of plenty of gold-finches (guineas). Oliver (moon) is somewhat too bright ; but, no matter, our particular and solicitous friends, the grabs, are far away, and we will see, if we cannot give them something fresh to talk about. Here comes the drag, By Jove, Paul, there's nothing like the high-toby business ! Here they are ! Get ready to give them a hearty welcome !"

With another blast from the horn of the guard, the Bath Mail now dashed up.

"Hold ! or, damme, I'll send a bullet in your skull !"

Confounded at the sudden interruption in their course, the driver of the coach hesitated, casting a glance of wild surprise at the figure of the well-dressed horseman, who with a pistol in each hand, sat upon his steed, barring their progress. Loud shrieks of women, oaths and curses of men, sounded from within and without the coach.

"Drive over him !"

"It's a highwayman !"

"Where's the guard ?"

"Blow out the brains of the robber !"

"Murder, fire !"

"Thieves, help !"

These, and such like cries escaped the lips of the passengers of the Bath Mail ; whilst, Gentleman Jack, cutting the traces of the leaders, sent them bounding away, then daringly leaping off his saddle on to the box, he coolly seized the driver by the collar of the coat and tumbled him into the roadway.

Shrieks, cries, and pistol shots now rang in the air !

"Ha, ha, ha ! Mr. Highwayman, take that !"

There was a loud report.

The next moment the coach was dragged with the utmost violence for some dozen yards, and then overturned, whilst another of the horses tearing from the traces dashed at wild speed from the spot, leaving a trail of dark crimson in its flight.

The bullet from the pistol of the passenger on the roof intended for the skull of Gentleman Jack had buried itself in the flank of the horse !

"Well meant, but you didn't do the trick that time ! Over you go ; look out below !"

Despite his shrieks and cries of rage, Jack, exerting all his strength lifted the passenger who had fired at him off the roof of the coach and pitched him with a curse at the feet of Paul, who had now dismounted from his horse and was gallantly handing out from inside three ladies.

Scrambling down, Jack now joined his companion !

Chuckling as he caught sight of some rich gold chains hanging round the necks of the females, he exclaimed to the foremost, "Sorry to trouble you, my dear lady ; but really those flashing eyes require no jewels to mar their lustre. That necklace, too, with the diamond cross, is shamed by the snow-white neck it is intended to adorn !"

"Wretch, villain, robber, take them !"

A maiden lady of some seventy years of age, with an ill grace here took off a beautifully chased necklace of gold and diamonds, handing it to the highwayman.

"Those rings, dear madam, they do not look well without the necklace, believe me !"

With cries of rage and fury, the lady, here pulling off the jewels from her brown shrivelled fingers, handed them to Jack, who put them in his pocket with a smile.

"I say Mr. Highwayman, can you do anything with that ! Ha, ha, ha ! I guess that's done it !"

With a loud chuckle the guard, who had been forgotten by Jack and Paul, now leant over from the roof of the coach, behind which he had crouched concealed, and presented at the heads of our friends a wide bell-mouthed blunderbuss.

Scarce had the echoes of his laugh of exultation died upon his lips ere it was followed by a deafening report and a howl of pain :

The facetious and funny guard had, indeed, as he had said, done it :

But not in the way he had expected :

Not the head of the highwayman was it that was blown in the air :

But his own terrific weapon :

The bell-mouthed blunderbuss had burst, and with a howl of pain the unfortunate guard fell to the ground surrounded by the ruins of his firearm.

"So much for the guard !" said Jack with a shout of laughter ; "Who'll have another fire !"

"Yes, friend, that verily will I !"

A fat rubicund-tinted face now appeared from behind the coach. The bright barrel of a pistol gleaming in the moonlight caught the eye of Jack, then, ere he could start aside, there was a sharp ringing report the ping and swish of a bullet whistling by his ear, his hat in a second of time whirling off his head into the air :

Perforated with a bullet it fell to the ground.

Jack, coolly picking it up, once more placed it on his head, exclaiming, "Bravo, Broadbrim ! a little more and you would have done the trick ; but you see powder and shot is of no use against me !"

"How so, friend ?"

"Nay, I cannot die by the bullet, because I'm born to be hanged !"

"Verily, I think such will be thy fate !"

The Quaker, now dragged forwards by Paul, began to empty his pockets, handing their contents to Jack.

With a smile the highwayman gazed at the wealth handed to him, which consisted of a few coppers, a wooden snuff box, and the horn handle of a walking stick.

"Is that all you have to give me ?"

"Yes, friend !"

"Paul !"

"Yes, captain !"

"Hand us over one of your barking irons ?"

The rubicund face of the Quaker now turned a pasty yellowish tint.

"Is this loaded all right !" said Jack, as Paul handed him a pistol.

"Oh yes, captain, there's two slugs in it !"

"Good ! Now then, Broadbrim, listen to me !"

"Verily, friend, I will attend ; speak on !" gasped the Quaker, his face now the colour of an underdone muffin.

"Are you listening !"

"Ye—s !"

"Now it may appear strange to you ; but I was one of your fraternity once !"

The face of the Quaker now brightened a little.

"Yes, I was a Friend once ; but I was read out because I was poor !"

"Yea !"

"Since the time that I was kicked out from the Society for being destitute, I have sworn never to go without money !"

"Yea !"

"And, therefore, being now in reduced circumstances call upon you to hand over to me your valuables !"

"Friend, I have nought more to give thee !"

"Friend, thou liest !"

"Yea, verily ; thou art a sinful man ; I tell thee thou hast my all !"

"All right ; forgive me for doubting you ; on to him, Paul ! Skin him !"

Amidst the laughter of some of the outside passengers, who indeed had nothing to lose, the Quaker was now thrown upon the ground, and, despite his cries for mercy and threats of vengeance, was eased of a pocket-book thickly stuffed with bank notes, a handsome gold repeater, and a small canvas bag filled with guineas.

Rising to his feet after he had rifled the unfortunate Quaker of all he possessed, Jack stood literally choking with laughter at the fury of his victim who, stamping with rage, almost foamed at the mouth at his loss.

"You shall hang, villain ; yea ! verily, thou shalt hang if there be law in the land ; I will not be robbed ; a goodly reward will I offer for thy apprehension ; thou shalt hang, dog ! thou shalt hang for this !"

"I say, Jack, are we going to stand this impudence !"

"Not much !"

"Have you got all his valuables !"

"I have so !"

"Very well, then I'll have his clothes !"

Shouting with laughter, Paul here seized the unfortunate Quaker in his arms, and, despite his struggles, succeeded in tearing nearly every article off his back. Then, all but reduced to his underclothing, he tore from his enemies.

Jack, as he took his flight, saluted him with a kick upon a portion of his anatomy which must be nameless.

Howling with fury, the victim dashed wildly away, shouting himself hoarse for help.

The two companions, laughing heartily at the man's flight, now turned their attention to the few outside passengers, who, awed by the pistols in the hands of the highwaymen, stood in a little terrified group by the overturned coach.

Upon questioning this party, Jack found they consisted of a stout farming man, a poor governess, a strolling player, and one or two others, who gave proof that they had no means or anything to be robbed of.

Seizing hold of the player, Jack in fun now, presenting a pistol at his head, called upon him to hand over his money.

"Take my all, O robber ! 'He who steals my purse steals trash : 'tis something—nothing !'"

"There's nothing here, certainly !" said Jack, as he opened a little greasy leathern purse handed him by the actor. "Whither are you bound, my friend !" he added, gazing pityingly at the other's threadbare suit.

"To London, fair sir, where I hope through the influence of Mistress Nell Gwynne at the Duke's Theatre to procure an engagement as juvenile tragedian !"

"And you are going to London without a copper in your possession !"

"Unhappily, yes, 'tis so ! little of the world's dross hath at present fallen to my share !"

"Well, here are five guineas—late the property of old Broadbrim—take them, and when you get to London drink a cup of wine to the health of Gentleman Jack !"

"That will I, brave heart ! I accept your gift, but, believe me, am poor in thanks ; thy name, however, shall be engraved on the tablets of my memory for ever ; by yon bright moon I swear it !"

Upon questioning the other outsiders, Jack, discovering that they had but little means at their command, set them free, merely snatching a kiss from a pretty little servant maid who stood giggling in a corner of the wayside.

"Now then, Paul, clear out is the word!"

"Hold on, Jack!"

"Well, what is it!"

"Why, do you see that fellow cowering down in that hedge there!"

"Yes; well, what of it!"

"Why, I owe him one!"

"What for!"

"Why, while you were busy on the roof a little time back he had a pop at me; his pistol missed fire, but that was not his fault, it was my luck!"

"Just so; well!"

"Well, I want to do as we did with old Broadbrim!"

"What, skin him!"

"Yes!"

"Well, all right, only be quick about it!"

"Leave me alone! I'll make short work of the beggar!"

With a laugh Paul now darted to a thickset hedge that here grew by the wayside, and in which was cowering the form of one of the travellers by the Mail—a tall thin cadaverous-faced man, who wildly howled for mercy as Paul dragged him from his hiding-place.

"Please, Mr. Highwayman, let me alone! Murder! Fire! Thieves! I've got nothing, indeed I havn't; I'm only a poor man!"

Paying no heed to his victim's cries, Paul turned all his pockets inside out:

But nothing of value could be found upon him.

Paul uttered a curse of disappointment.

He had fancied from the fellow's alarm that he had got money.

But not a single article of value could be found on his person.

The traveller now, with a subdued chuckle, turned to go.

Paul eyed his lean, lank victim with no friendly feeling.

Jack had now mounted his horse.

The guard and driver of the Mail were seeing to the continuance of their journey.

The player, whom Jack had befriended, now hurried up to Paul, as his victim was about to start away.

"Hist!" said the actor, clutching Clifford by the arm, "perdition seize upon me if I do let that man escape! Friend, companion of Gentleman Jack, let not that fellow escape, or, an thou wilt let him depart, first search—search his boots!"

With a grin the player here drew on one side:

Drew near to the coach as Paul seized once more upon the man.

"Hold, my friend; don't be in such a hurry; the Mail ain't ready for you yet!"

"Please, Mr. Robber, I ain't going to wait for it; if you please, I am going to walk!"

"Oh dear, no; you can't do that!"

"Why not!"

"Because I require your boots!"

"My—my what!"

"Your boots!"

"Ha, ha! good, Mr. Robber, how funny you are!"

"You think so, do you! It's my humble opinion you'll change your tune presently; but come, we waste time; off with your boots!"

"You're joking!"

"No, curse me if I am! I've got bad feet; your boots look larger than mine, so we will change!"

"I—I—I'd rather not!"

"But you must!"

"I couldn't get yours on—indeed I couldn't!"

"You'll have to try!"

"But I'm sure they won't fit!"

"Then you must pursue your journey without any; your boots I've taken a fancy too, and your boots, curse me, I'll have!"

"Help, help! Murder!"

Wildly the victim struggled with Paul, who, dexterously throwing him, proceeded to pull off his boots.

"Help! Mercy! Spare my life! Don't rob me of my shoes! Fire! Thieves! Robbers!"

"What are you making all that noise about?" said Jack, who had now alighted from his horse; "he only wants your boots!"

"But I shan't be able to walk!"

"Who says you will! Ain't you going to ride!"

"But I shall catch my death of cold!"

"Not at all; wrap your feet in flannel, or shove them in a nosebag!" said Paul, choking with laughter as he tugged at the coveted boots.

Despite the struggles and cries of his victim, Paul at length secured his prize:

He succeeded in pulling off the boots of his victim.

Oaths and shrieks of savage fury now escaped the lips of the owner:

Cries of rage that were echoed by shouts of laughter from the highwaymen.

With a chuckle, Paul now drew from the fatal boots a roll of bank-notes, a gold chain, and some loose gold.

"Ha, ha, ha! an expensive pair of pumps! I say old fellow, how are your poor feet? Well, well, never mind! Upon second thoughts, I won't rob you; there's your boots back, I have only taken out the pebbles; they might cause blisters!"

"Curses!"

"Don't swear, it's a bad habit!"

"You shall hang!"

"That's what the Quaker said; that's not news; I know all about that; tell us something I don't know!"

"I'll—I'll—follow you to the gallows!"

"You are very kind, when that time comes we'll have a glass together!"

"Thief, robber, give me back my gold!"

With a wild yell of demoniac fury, the enraged man now dashed at Paul, and clutching him by the throat endeavoured to hurl him in the road:

There was the sound of a brief struggle and a heavy blow:

Then, stunned and bleeding, the enraged traveller was thrown senseless at the feet of his antagonist.

"He asked for it, and he's got it!" exclaimed Paul, turning to Jack, whom he observed intently gazing along the road in the direction of London.

During the last few minutes the passengers by the Mail had been engaged getting it ready to resume its journey.

The horses had been brought back, the broken harness repaired, and things began to look more like a continuance of the route.

It was at this moment, while their victims were busy with the coach, that the highwaymen were startled by an unwelcome sight.

Half a dozen horsemen with all speed were making for the spot:

One in the rear with scarce a rag to cover his nakedness was shrieking wildly and urging the rest to increase their speed.

Despite their danger, Jack and Paul, could not keep from shouting with laughter as they gazed upon this figure:

The well remembered one of the Quaker:

The Quaker who had vowed revenge:

The man of peace whom they had denuded of his covering:

Whose podgy portly frame was exposed to the cruel blast!

"Our friend seemeth bent on vengeance, Jack!"

"Yea, thou art right, Paul, and it behoveth us as the officers are with him to depart!"

"Yea, verily Jack, thou art right!"

With loud shouts of renewed laughter the companions now vaulted into their saddles:

Both loaded with plunder—being presently once more upon the road.

Scarce, however, had they progressed a few hundred yards from the scene of the robbery, ere they were startled by a noise in front:

The clatter of horses' hoofs and clanging of steel!

"Damn it, Jack, look ahead!"

"Mounted dragoons by all that's unfortunate!"

"We are hemmed in!"

"By Jove, yes! Officers behind and soldiers in front, things look serious, Paul!"

"Rather!"

"This is awkward!"

"Very!"

"What's to be done?"

"Ten thousand devils, I don't know!"

"Confound it! how that infernal Quaker keeps yelling in our rear!"

"Yes, he is bent on trying his vocal abilities!"

"I shall give him a blue pill if he get's close enough!"

"Well, I think one would do him good! We must alter our course, Paul."

THE MIDNIGHT BURIAL IN THE CROSS ROADS.

"Yes, I think so! With the officers in our rear and the dragoons in front we dare not go straight for the old Tree Cave!"

"No fear; we must make a detour!"

"That's it! Already you see the soldiery are taking heed of the howling Quaker!"

"Confound him, yes! We had better take that hedge there, and gallop over the fields that lie on the other side."

"Yes; it's our only chance!"

Turning their horses' heads and giving them the whip both as though shot out of a cannon now flew over the hedge of hawthorn, finding themselves a moment after in a large meadow.

Across this the highwaymen galloped at mad speed.

Wild shouts and a babel of cries sounded behind them.

Glancing back when half-way across the meadow the companions discovered that the soldiery had taken the hedge :

The redcoats were in hot pursuit :

Their shouts and the clanking of their sabres sounding unpleasantly distinct to the ears of the companions !

At lightning speed the highwaymen dashed on :

The moon high over head shining full upon them !

In silence the friends galloped over the meadow, passing an open gate upon the other side, and then making their way into what seemed like some large park belonging to a neighbouring estate :

The clang of the dragoons' sabres as they followed in pursuit with the officers ever and again sounding in their ears.

"We made a good haul stopping the long drag (mail coach) at length," said Jack, "and it would be too bad to be collared by the grabs now! It will never do to lose the gold mine we have secured, and be conveyed to the stone jug into the bargain!"

"Confound it, no! I wouldn't care if we could get to the old Tree Cave without our foes being too close on our heels!"

"It's what we must try and do, Paul! I think we are distancing them!"

"Yes, our horseflesh beats theirs, that's pretty certain!"

"What place is this?"

"Some park or other!"

"I can sight a fence there to the left!"

"Yes, I see it."

"Shall we take the horses over it?"

"Well, I think we may as well!"

"At it then! At once if we can get over without being seen we may double on the hounds!"

"'Sblood, yes! I'm nervously anxious to get away! Now we have such a haul about our persons it would be cruel to be robbed of it!"

"So it would, Paul; and those thieves of officers would take all our store with very little compunction!"

"They would so!"

"Yes, and laugh at us into the bargain!"

"Of course they would!"

"They are a bad set of men!"

"Yes, a hard-hearted lot!"

"No milk of human kindness!"

"Not a halfpennyworth."

With a loud shout the companions, who during this colloquy had made for the fence that bounded the park, leapt their steeds over it and came out once more into the high road.

To their delight their foes were no longer to be seen!

They were hidden in the mazes of the park.

With a loud hilloa the companions now giving their brave steeds the rein, dashed at lightning speed along the road.

Laughing heartily at their escape, they soon left the park far behind!

Their foes had failed to track them:

They had at length eluded their search.

Wild shouts of triumph escaped the lips of the companions as they discovered that they were no longer pursued.

"Done the grabs this time, Paul!"

"We have so!"

"I did'nt think we should shake them off so easy!"

"No; nor I."

"I expect they are still wandering about the park!"

"Very likely!"

"I say, Paul!"

"Well?"

"It strikes me that we can't be far from our destination!"

"What, the Highgate woods!"

"Yes."

"Well no; we must be handy there now, I fancy!"

"Of course we are! Hallo! Whew! What do you call this?" With a loud whistle of astonishment Jack now drew his mare up by the wayside, Paul following his example, and uttering an exclamation of surprise!

They had now arrived at an open spot near a large heath:

Here four different roads joined.

Near the end of the one they had been travelling stood by the wayside a ghastly, horrible object:

A grim, horrible gallows, in the iron chains from which hung a blanched and grizzly skeleton!

In awe and disgust the two friends gazed at the loathed object that stood so grim and ghastly-looking by the wayside.

Not so much the hideous gallows was it, however, that had evoked the surprised exclamations from the two friends, and that caused them both to draw up.

There was something very strange and unwonted about the place!

Near the gallows by the crossroads was dug a newly-made grave:

An open grave dug a depth of some five feet or more!

This of course was a rather strange thing to find near such

In amazement the companions glanced around them:

"Well, Jack, what do you think of this, old pal?" said Clifford, the first to break the silence that in their awe had fallen upon them.

"I don't know what to think of it. It's very strange!"

"It is so! What the deuce has the grave been dug there for?"

"Perhaps some relative of that poor wretch who has hung so many years intends to bury him!"

"That must be it, Jack!"

"Yes, I fancy so!"

"I suppose whoever dug the grave has been surprised in his task, and had to make a bolt of it!"

"That's about it; of course such friends as we left behind us in that park would have interfered in this!"

"Just so, and perhaps the poor devil who dug that hole has got into trouble!"

"It's more than likely, but come, we will leave the place, it ain't the most inviting in the world!"

"No; I don't care how soon we get away!"

"Come on then, Paul, we are not more than a mile from the Highgate woods; I know these crossroads—that one to the left there is ours! Come on, dear pal, in half an hour we shall be safe in the old Tree Cave!"

With a last glance at the strange scene before them, the adventurers now gave their horses the rein, and dashed from the spot.

As Jack had said, they were near their journey's end.

In a little more than a quarter of an hour after leaving the gallows by the crossroads, they came up with a thick copse:

A thick copse or tract of woods.

Leaving the high road, Gentleman Jack plunged into this thicket, quickly followed by Paul.

Not far had they penetrated into the woods ere they were arrested by the loud hooting of an owl.

It was now broad day.

The dawn of another day in a golden glow rested over the woods.

An exclamation of delight escaped the lips of Jack, as the hoot of the owl rang through the woods.

"That's him, we are all right, Paul!"

"That's who, Jack! what do you mean!"

"Why, that owl, is no owl at all!"

"You are coming the Irishman over me, Jack, what the devil do you mean?"

"Why, that the boy Luke has sighted us! Ah, here he is!"

With a loud whoop and a gymnastic performance that caused the horses to rear up in affright, Duval's lad, the watcher by the Tree Cave, now plunged into the little glade where the highwaymen had drawn up.

"Welcome, Gentleman Jack! Hurrah! I've brave news! There are two doves waiting you in the cave; and, oh, oh, oh! another whom I think you'll be glad to see! Come on, my brave knights of the road, there are strange sights for you, and wondrous things for you to hear in the old Tree Cave!" shouted Luke, who, bounding about, seemed half-mad with delight.

"A curious character!" said Paul, with a laugh.

"Well, yes; but poor Luke is a faithful fellow!" exclaimed Jack, who, with wonder as to the words uttered by the boy, now having dismounted, hurried on in the direction of the cave.

Leaving their charges to be cared for by Luke, the two highwaymen made at once for the retreat.

With beating heart, Jack pondered upon the words that had fallen from the lips of the strange boy.

"There were two doves in the cave, and strange things to hear!" What did he mean?

In anxiety and suspense, Jack, closely followed by his companion, hurried on.

The nearer they approached the vicinity of the cave, the greater became his anxiety to know what awaited him.

It was just as they had gained the back entrance to the cave that Jack was startled by a human form springing out of the brushwood upon him:

The figure of a man:

A tall, handsome cavalier, the lineaments of whose classical cut features were in an instant recognised.

A loud cry of delight escaped the lips of Jack, who in a moment after was locked in the embrace of the stranger.

Shouts of surprise and delight burst from Paul.

"What! Duval! Well, this is glorious!" he cried.

"Dear old pal! I began to think we should never see

you more !" gasped Jack, as he stood beside his old friend, for it was indeed our hero whom we have lost sight of so long that had burst so suddenly upon him near the old Tree Cave.

"Ah, Jack, dear boy, many a time since I saw you last I never thought to reach dear old England more ! But come, dear pals, let us enter the retreat ! I have much to tell you, and much to do ere the morrow's sun rises ! Thank heaven, you are both here ! I have prayed fervently, Jack, that you might arrive in time to join in a task I have in hand, and, mon Dieu, my prayer has been heard, you are here ! but come with me into the cave, nor start at that which I have to show !"

"Lead on, Duval, dear friend ! but tell me, where is Maude and my dear Kate ?"

"Both are with Jenny Dunning at The Cat and Her Kittens !"

"Why are they staying at the inn, instead of the cave, Claude ?"

"Because I have something here it were not well for them to see, Jack !"

"When will they visit the cave ?"

"To-morrow morning at about this time."

"I shall not see Kate to-night, then !"

"Well, no ; but I promised Luke should hasten to the inn and inform her of your arrival, Jack ; I can understand, dear friend, your wish to meet with her, but you will agree with me that it was impossible for those dear girls to remain in the cave until the completion of the task I have in hand."

"What task, Claude ?" said Jack, gazing in wonder at the grim countenance of his new-found friend, whose brow, as he made his way into the cave, was overcast and clouded with a vindictive frown.

"A task, Jack, that you are more fitted to carry out than I ; look there and tell me what you see !"

Halting at the opening of the outer cave Claude now pointed to an object in the corner.

An oil-lamp depending from the roof gave but a dim light in the underground chamber.

A strange shiver shook the frame of Jack, as, clutching Duval by the arm he glared at the dark object in the corner of the cave.

Well he divined the nature of the thing.

The object to which Claude had drawn his attention was a human form.

Resting upon the ground, a piece of sackcloth thrown over it, Jack, with a shudder made out in the dim light of the lamp the outline of the corpse.

The thing that lay so still and immovable was a dead body.

"Damn it, Claude, I don't know why, but I somehow feel as if I knew who it was you had there !" gasped Jack, who now, darting forward, boldly stooped down and drew the sackcloth from the face of the corpse, a loud cry escaping his lips as the features were revealed.

"God of heaven ! Vaughan the Vampyre !" he gasped.

"The Vampyre ! and here in the old Tree Cave !" ejaculated Paul.

"Yes, dear pals, 'tis even so ; and I think you'll find Dashing Duval will, upon this occasion, effectually, and for ever, rid the earth of a monster !"

"But how, in the name of heaven, came that wretch here ?"

"Well, 'tis a long story I have to tell you, Jack ; but I can, for the present, sum all up in a few words, at a more opportune moment giving you in full detail the marvellous adventures and hair-breadth escapes I have had since I saw you last. I will pass over at present, then, my adventures in fair France, and explain to you how that fiend there crossed my path." (Claude here related facts already known to our readers, giving to his surprised companions an account of his wild adventure with the wretch Vaughan up to the time when he had rescued Maude and struggled in the open ocean till saved by the seamen of a British ship on her way to a distant port.) We will now give, in our hero's own words an account of his further strange perils and escapes.

"Saved by the hearts of oak belonging to the merchant ship, the North Star, myself and my loved Maude received every attention—an outward-bound vessel, however, we were borne yet further from the land I was to anxious to gain. In three days after our rescue a small brig London bound passing us, our kind rescuers transferred us on board. All went well, a pleasant trip ending in our once more sighting the white cliffs of Dover. At this little port I and Maude landed ; from thence without misadventure we reached London, and, at once leaving the City, made all haste to Highgate, for at the old Tree Cave it struck me I was more likely to hear of you, dear friends, than anywhere else."

"Exactly ; you could not have done better, dear Claude !"

"That was my idea ; reaching our retreat here, from Luke's lips I heard of your clever escape from Tyburn."

"An escape due to Kate's daring and ingenuity."

"Well, yes, bless her heart ! Parbleu ! I don't think you would have managed upon that occasion without her. However, to finish my narrative. Finding you were at hide-and-seek I conducted Maude to The Cat and her Kittens, determined to seek you out, with strict injunctions to Luke to keep a watchful eye in the woods ; I then left and was about to start off upon the western road, the one I heard you had taken, when I was diverted from my intention by meeting with an old foe."

"He who now lies so rigid in death before us ?"

"Yes, Jack, even that fiend, Vampyre Vaughan, whom I last saw struggling in the open ocean ! With a knowledge that it was no common mortal I had to contend with, it was no surprise to me to meet the wretch as I did in the woods yesterday, prowling about and bent upon my destruction !"

"Was he alone ?"

"No ; he had made all sure for my capture !"

"How ?"

"By e'en bringing down with him from London a dozen runners, headed by my late enemy, Jonathan Anstey !"

"Your late enemy ! Damn it, Claude ! you don't mean to tell me that implacable, remorseless villain is dead !"

"He's dead as a man with a bullet-hole in his temple and the leaden missile resting in his brain can be !"

"Ten thousand devils ! and how came that about ? 'Twas your hand that slew him ?"

"No !"

"The deuce ! Then who was the clever spark that laid him low ?"

"No spark at all ! Jonathan Anstey, the vicious, merciless Bow-street officer, perished at the hands of a woman !"

"At the hands of a woman ?"

"Yes, Jack ; a young lady well known to you !"

"Known to me !" In utmost amaze, Jack reiterated his companion's words.

"Yes, my dear boy ; and it is even-handed justice that ordained the ruffian should die by the hands of the girl whom he would have so basely injured !"

"Great heavens ! you allude to my Kate ?"

"Just so !"

"And she shot Jonathan Anstey !"

"Yes, Jack ; the bullet in the brain of the thief-taker, was sent upon its errand of death by Kate Annersley !"

"But how was this !" fairly gasped Jack.

"Why, you must know, that having left Luke with strict injunctions as to the guarding of our secret retreat here, I, last evening, as the shades of night had wrapped all in gloom, hurried through the copse, in my confusion and hurry falling like a rat in a trap into the hands of my two deadliest enemies—Anstey and the Vampyre, who were concealed in the woods ! A loud yell of triumph burst from the lips of the runner, who, gripping me fiercely by the throat, exclaimed, ' I have you at last, Dashing Duval, and ere a week is over you shall swing on the gallows !' Scarce had these words left his lips, ere there was a stunning report, and with a bullet in his brain, Jonathan Anstey, who had been kneeling on my breast, fell back stone dead ! What followed appears to me now like a dream. Struggling to my feet, I saw a young girl with a pistol in her hand, from the barrel of which the smoke of a recent discharge yet wreathed ! I beheld the bold Amazon strike a grim-looking stranger near a fearful blow with the butt end between the eyes, that sent him down in a heap beside the dead officer, then, as some half a dozen figures dashed forward in the gloom, I pounced upon the half-senseless man struck down a moment before, and dashed through the brushwood followed by my preserver ! Cries of rage and alarm echoed in our ears as we dived into the thick masses of the copse. The followers of the deceased runner having stumbled over his body, their surprise at the discovery caused a delay in our pursuit, and I safely, with my prisoner and preserver, gained unseen the cave here ! By the light of that lamp hanging from the roof here I then discovered that my escape from capture was due to

Kate Annersley, whilst he whom I had dragged with me was no other than Vampyre Vaughan!"

"After the first few moments of surprise were over, pressing the dear girl to my bosom, I then bade her hasten to the inner cave, and then, with as little compunction as though I were slaying a mad dog, I threw myself upon the fiend before me, and, with these hands strangled the life out of his half-senseless frame; a low gasping hiss once escaped his lips, and the choking accents, 'We shall meet again!' fell upon my ears. In another moment all was still, but even then I, with rage and terror, left not the body till I had buried my knife in the breast of the fiend. Covering the corpse over, I, joining Kate in the habitation cave, bade the dear girl has'en to The Cat and her Kittens, telling her that there she would find my Maude. Leaving Luke to watch over the fiendly dead, I made my way boldly, first secreting a spade by the crossroads, about a mile from here!"

"You then it was who dug a grave near to the gibbet on the heath!"

"Aye, Jack; but how know you this?"

"Why, myself and Paul noticed the unusual circumstance, and thought some poor wretch wanted to bury the skeleton of the murderer swinging in his chains!"

"No, Jack, I it was who, with frantic haste, dug that receptacle for the dead!"

"And your object?"

"That I might bury the Vampyre!"

"Just so; 'tis a sure means of ridding the earth of the monster!"

"So I had heard you say, Jack!"

"Yes! Let me see, you have dug the grave near the crossroads?"

"I have!"

"Good! When did you begin your task?"

"At midnight!"

"Were you disturbed?"

"No; not a soul passed the spot!"

"You are aware that the body must be placed in its grave during the midnight hour!"

"Yes; and knowing that, I left, after finishing the grave, making up my mind to return with Luke at the proper hour with my fiendly foe and a sharp-pointed stake!"

"To thrust through the body? Right; I am glad I am here, and having heard your news, will tell you the escapes of myself and Paul, for we, too, have had our dangers, dear Claude; I am happy to say, however, that we have plenty of the needful; but come, let us leave this abode of the fiendly dead, and in the other cave we will have refreshments!"

"Right, Jack; you can there recount to me your adventures. When the morning is fully advanced I will send Luke over to the girls. We had better keep quiet during the day in the cave, and at night carry out our dread task!"

"Just so, Claude; well, your two worst enemies are now removed from your path!"

"Yes; and that being so, I have thoughts of giving up the road, and leaving England with my darling Maude for ever!"

"Well, we will talk that over, Duval; I myself am tired of our dangerous profession!"

"And I rather fancy the backwoods in the Far West would be better than a dance upon nothing some fine morning at Tyburn Tree or outside old Newgate!" said Paul.

Little did the three friends then guess that a terrible tragedy in futurity would cause them to recklessly follow their present dangerous and adventurous career.

But none can see into the future:

A wise dispensation of Providence!

For who that knew the cares, toils, and dangers in our course through life would patiently live to meet them!

It was about midday that the boy Luke (having been despatched an hour before) returned with the two girls from the inn at Highgate, The Cat and her Kittens.

Joyful was the meeting in that secret cave in the woods between the highwaymen and their mistresses.

Having shaken hands warmly with the two maidens, Paul Clifford suddenly remembered he had left something in the outer cave.

With a feeling of chagrin he began to think he was one too many in the group.

Soon, however, was Paul made happy by the presence of pretty Jenny Dunning, who, by permission of her father, had come to the cave to spend a few hours with Kate and Maude, the three arranging to return to the inn as soon as the shadows of night had fallen.

With wine and refreshments at command the little party passed a happy day in the old Tree Cave.

Recounting to each other their adventures and escapes, time flew on till the faithful watcher without, the boy Luke informed them that evening was drawing nigh.

It was with a cold nervous thrill that Claude heard this.

Was it the task before them!—he burial at the cross-roads, or a feeling of an impending ill that caused him to shudder as with an ague? he asked himself, as with a lover's fondness he gazed into the bright eyes of his mistress, the pretty Maude.

Trying to shake off the nervous feeling that weighed upon him, Claude succeeded so far that his expression passed unnoticed by his friends.

With fond words of farewell the three girls now hastened from the cave:

Under the charge of Luke they returned to the inn:

The highwaymen with downcast looks remaining in the secret retreat:

The cave in which they had passed as happy a day as ever they remembered!

CHAPTER XXXII.

THE BURIAL OF THE VAMPYRE AT THE CROSS ROADS—AN ALARM—THE DEPARTURE—ARRIVAL AT THE HAUNTED LANE—THE THREE HIGHWAYMEN MEET WITH A STRANGE ADVENTURE.

"I don't feel remarkably well!"

"Nor I, Jack!" replied Duval, as his friend gazed rather lugubriously around.

"Well, I don't see how we can expect to!" said Paul; "we have just been deserted by three angels in petticoats, and are now alone with the dead body of a cursed being, that if he was laid out in the moonbeams would jump up into life again!"

"You are right, Paul, to remind us of our task, for we have much to do between this and midnight!" said Duval, who now, with his companions, made his way out into the other cave:

The outer cave, where rested the corpse of the fiend Vaughan.

All was as they had left it.

No sign of life was there in the ghastly object that lay so still in the corner of the cave.

With a grim fierce frown, Duval gazed upon the corse.

"'Tis a strange, horribly thing the mystery that enshrouds the wretch!" he muttered.

"Yes, 'tis a ghastly, terrible superstition; and never did I when a boy in Hungary, expect to meet with a cursed vampyre in matter-of-fact, unbelieving, material England!" exclaimed Jack, as he eyed the corpse of the villain Vaughan suspiciously, as though in fear that it would start up into life before him.

"Well, I suppose the burial by-and-bye will finish him!"

"Oh, yes, Paul; I don't think Claude will ever come across the fiend again once we have him safely laid in his unhallowed grave by the crossroads!"

"He's a pretty subject!" said Paul, giving the body a vicious kick. "I wonder how he'll look with a stake through his ugly infernal carcase!"

"About as handsome as Jonathan Anstey after he had got Kate's bullet in his skull!" said Claude.

"Well, I suppose the pair have met by this time!"

"Not at all unlikely!"

"Perhaps drinking our very good health out of red-hot goblets of brimstone wine!"

"Or having a supper off lava and cinders!" exclaimed Paul with a grin.

Turning from the hideous corpse, preparations were now begun for the terrible task they had before them.

Gentleman Jack having manufactured a sack, the body was thrust into it, Duval unceremoniously and boldly seizing hold of the rigid form without any sign of disgust or alarm.

"It's no time to stand upon trifles, he muttered; the fiend tortured me too much in life for me to fear him now."

Procuring a sharp-pointed stake that he had fashioned that morning, Claude now intimated that it was time to depart.

"It has gone eleven, and by the time we get to our journey's end it will be near twelve o'clock!"

"All right, Claude; you lead the way, I and Paul will follow with the stiff-un!"

Jack here seized hold of the sack, and, assisted by his friend, dragged it along the floor of the cave.

"I say, Claude!"

"Well?"

"The cursed beggar is very heavy; I should have fancied desiccation ought to have set in by now!"

"So it would, Jack, were it an ordinary body!" said Claude, with a shudder.

The three friends had now left the cave, and with their ghastly load were presently threading the mazes of the woods.

With much annoyance Claude found that it was a beautiful moonlight night.

He feared they might be interrupted in their task.

No one would believe the dreadful tale they had to tell.

Were they not in fear of the law's officials, boldly Duval would have courted inquiry.

As it was, an interruption in their task might lead to the escape of the evil, horrible being.

In anxious suspense as to the result of their project, Claude, followed by Jack and Paul, who dragged their burthen along behind them, now hurried on, reaching the extremity of the copse.

Here they were joined by Luke with their horses.

Mounting these, Duval, throwing the corpse of Vaughan in front of his saddle, the friends dashed away.

In silence the knights of the road pursued their path.

The task before them was a solemn and terrible one.

With no mortal foe were they contending.

With his hideous burthen in front of him, Claude, with one hand on the reins, held fast the terrible load with the other.

Bright and lustrous the queen of night shone in the blue vault above:

Flooding heath, hill, and dale in a spectral glare.

Cantering on without a word an exclamation at length escaped the lips of Claude:

An exclamation of terror.

His hand resting on the sack was suddenly drawn away as if stung by a serpent.

With a cry of horror he hurled the horrible burthen into the road.

In a moment his companions had drawn up.

"What is the matter, Claude?"

"What is it?"

"There's the gibbet; we are only two minutes now from the crossroads!" said Jack, who gazed rather alarmed at the pallid face of his friend, that shone deadly white in the moon's ray.

"Jack, Jack," he gasped, "for God's sake, let us get our task over!"

"That won't take us long, my dear boy; but what is it that has frightened you?"

The three had now leaped from their saddles, and were standing by the sack thrown in the road a moment before.

Pointing to this, Claude, in a husky voice of terror, exclaimed "Jack, dear pal, as my hand rested upon that hideous thing a moment ago, I felt it move!"

"God of Heaven!"

"Yes; see, see, Jack, the Vampyre even now is re-endued with life!"

"By heavens, yes! the moon's rays penetrate through the thin covering that enshrouds the corpse!" said Jack, who here with a curse drew a pistol from his belt and made for the terrible sack, that now, to the horror of all, had rolled out from the centre to the side of the road.

Stooping down, Gentleman Jack now feeling for the head within with an oath fired his pistol.

For an instant the sack rose up and down as if a living being inside was striving to get free, then all was as before:

Save that a dark crimson stain shone upon the turf by the wayside:

The crimson stain of blood!

"This is horrible!" gasped Claude.

"I feel like a woman: as if I was going to faint," said Paul, who, watching Jack, drew back with dismay as he beheld him about to untie the mouth of the sack.

"It's all right now, pals!"

"What do you mean, Jack?"

"Why, my bullet planted in the head of the beggar has stopped the game! Diable, I said so! look here!" Jack here, coolly tearing open the sack, pointed to the horrible face of the Vampyre.

With a thrill of terror Claude and Paul stooped down.

They now saw a fresh and terrible wound.

A bullet had gone right through the jaw-bone, crushing and flattening in the skull behind.

A thin stream of blood, as from a living being, was oozing from the ghastly wound.

"And an hour back the creature was rigid in death!" said Claude.

"But we will take care he don't come to life any more, old pal," said Jack, who, now the boldest of the three, seized the hideous corpse, and dragged it along to the cross-roads, now distant some hundred yards.

The newly-made grave, as it had been left, still yawned near the gibbet, the full moon shining upon it revealing the wet clay five feet down.

"Now then, Claude, give me that stake! I'll soon settle this gentleman!"

Seizing a thick billet of wood that was sharpened to a point at one end, Jack now placed it with the sharp end upon the chest of the corpse.

With a heavy hammer given him by Paul he then struck the wood, which in a second tore its way into the bosom of the dead, crashing away the ribs with a horrible noise in its progress.

Sick and giddy, dizzy and faint, grew Paul and Claude as they gazed upon the scene.

Jack, his teeth set, countenance frowning and grim pursued his task, no word of terror escaping his lips.

No cry of alarm issued from him, as, striking at the sharp-pointed stake, he drove it clean through the body, the while the eyes of the hideous being slowly opened, glaring up wildly at the bright moon.

"Ha, ha, ha, fiend! Being accursed! stare up at that luminary of night that can never save thee more! Go to Satan, and tell him I sent you!" Hysterically these words were shouted by Jack, who now, completing his horrible task, hurled the bleeding, disfigured frame into the open grave.

"Now then, Paul! now, Duval! fill in; you have seen the last of Vampyre Vaughan!"

Frantically Jack here began to shovel a mass of earth upon the corpse, that rigid, blood-stained, and stiff, lay in its unhallowed grave.

Recovering from the stupor of horror that had enthralled them his companions now set to and aided in the work.

Half an hour after not a sign was left of the newly-made grave.

The earth stamped down, some fresh sods of grass laid over the top, no one passing would imagine that the ground had been opened.

"There, the job is done! Off and away is the word, and not too soon, for, by all that's infernal, here is a posse of mounted police!" exclaimed Jack, as he pointed to a dark cluster of horsemen some two miles away, and who by the broad light of the moon it could be seen were making straight for the crossroads.

In a moment of time the three friends were once more in the saddle, and at lightning speed were dashing from the spot.

The spirits of the three now rose as they left the cross-roads behind them.

The horrible task was over!

They believed firmly that they had effectually destroyed the accursed being, Vampyre Vaughan!

With light hearts they bounded on.

The night, a lovely one, in the pleasure of their moonlight ride the recent horrors were forgotten.

Speeding on across the open country, they at length turned down a narrow road.

On both sides of this grew a thick and lofty hedge.

All three now drew up:

They did not care to go on further down this, and the hedge was a rather nasty jump.

"Stop a minute!" said Duval, leaping from his saddle.

"I'll just look over the hedge and try and see where we are!"

"Right you are, Claude! I think those officers we saw have turned it up, so we need not do anything risky!"

"Certainly not!"

Duval, now climbing up into a small linden tree, cast a glance over the hedge.

"There's nothing to see but a shady lane!"

"Is there much of a bank there, Claude?"

"Oh, dear no; hardly any!"

"All right, then; we will break our way through; that, I think, will be our best caper!"

"Well, yes, so do I, Jack! We don't want to turn back, nor go further down this road!"

"No; and it ain't worth while to leap a hedge like that without the Philistines are behind you!"

"Of course not! Get down and let us scramble through, we can break a passage for the horses!"

"Just so!"

Duval now, with the assistance of Paul, soon broke a way through the hedge large enough to permit the passage of themselves and their steeds, the three adventurers and their beasts presently all standing in the lane, which was one of the most damp and shady ones they had ever seen.

"Well, we shouldn't do much in the way of business here if we wanted to!" exclaimed Jack, as he glanced round.

"No; the place is one rather avoided. I know it now I'm in it!"

"You do, eh, Claude?"

"Yes; it's called Redhand Lane. A murder of peculiar atrocity was committed in it some years ago; and owing to some strange circumstances connected with the discovery of the deed of blood, the lane has got its name! I recognise the place by that little spring which you can see gushing out of the bank there by that old willow tree!"

Jack and Paul looked in the direction pointed out by their friend, and they now both saw and heard a little rivulet that like some shining snake, wound its glittering way amid the luxuriant vegetation that grew by the hedge of the lane.

"It's a pretty place, mind you, in broad day!" said Duval.

"I don't doubt it, old pal, for by moonlight it has many beauties."

"Yes; and it's a pity the place has got the name it has!"

"I should fancy, from the appearance of the ground and the straggling vegetation, that the solitude of the lane is seldom disturbed!"

"You are right, Paul, it is not! I don't suppose there is anyone in the neighbourhood who would come here at this hour for any money!"

"Where does it lead to, Claude?"

"In one direction, to a crossroad not far from Finchley; and in the other, to some waste land adjoining a farmhouse. So you see the temptation for anyone to pursue the tortuous windings of the lane is by no means very great. I think, before we leave it, I will have a taste of the water of the spring!"

Stepping forwards, Claude now threw himself down on his knees, and, hot and feverish from the events of the past hour, placed his mouth with delight in the cool gushing waters of the rivulet.

It was as he rose up considerably refreshed that he was rather startled by a stone striking him with some force on the forehead.

"Hillio! what the deuce is that!"

"Did you speak?" said Jack, who, with Paul, had remained by the gap in the hedge.

Duval, returning no answer to his companions, now snatched a pistol from his pocket, and stooping down fired at a piece of copse, as a second stone winged by unpleasantly close to his head.

Scarce had the echo of the report died away, ere there came a strange unearthly yell or laugh upon the still air!

Jack and Paul now dashed up to the side of their friend.

"What's up, Claude?"

"Who did you fire at?"

"Sacre, I don't know! I was drinking here as you know, and was startled by a blow from a stone, and as a second one came, I thought I'd return the compliment to the sender by the discharge of a bullet!"

"It's very strange!"

"It is so!"

"What a cursed horrible laugh that was!"

"Yes, parbleu! they won't laugh much if I come across them!" muttered Claude, savagely.

Their nerves unhinged by the dread business of the early part of the night, the highwaymen were more startled by the present occurrence than they would otherwise have been.

"Well, as I don't see the use of stopping here, my advice is that we step it off!" said Paul. "You said, Claude, that we could get from this lane to the Finchley-road!"

"Yes; we can!"

"Very good; let's be off!"

"Allons, I'm with you, brothers!"

All three, now mounting their steeds, leisurely cantered off.

A short trot of about half a mile brought them to the mouth of the lane, and then they found that there was to the right of it a rather deep pit, from which gravel and sand had been taken in vast quantities, for the pit was in parts exceedingly deep.

A rather miserable rotten-looking railing at the edge of the pit next to the road, was the only protection to travellers from falling into it in the dark.

"An awkward place, Claude?"

"Very; but no doubt the road is but little frequented! Only fancy a pair of restive horses in a carriage backing up against that rotten-looking railing!"

"A nice catastrophe!"

"Rather! Hallo!"

"What is it now, Claude?"

"Why, I thought I saw something move at the bottom of the pit!"

Day at this moment beginning to break, a white light shone over the place.

The three friends now leaning forwards, glared eagerly and curiously into the recess before them.

Nothing, however, met their steadfast gaze.

There was a little vegetation here and there—yellow furze far down, and some bushes, too, of brambles, as well as some broom, growing wild and luxuriant in patches; but all seemed still enough.

"What was it you fancied you saw, Claude?"

"Well, a something seemed to glide as it were along the bottom of the pit, but the form or figure was too ill-defined for me to make out what it was!"

"You are sure you saw something?"

"Certainly; but what it was I cannot tell!"

"Perhaps it was a hare or a rabbit!"

"It might have been! Hallo, who are you?"

From behind the shattered trunk of an old tree, there now crept forth a woman, attired in the usually squalid garb of gipsy or beggar.

Soap and water had not certainly been acquainted with her visage for sometime.

Age appeared nearly to have bent her double; the hag supported herself by the aid of a thick blackthorn stick, of about eight or nine feet in length.

A cloak, that had once been red, fluttered in rags around her; and the rest of her apparel strongly resembled an old sack with a hole in it, through which she had thrust her head, and around which hung the dishevelled locks of her grey hairs.

Holding out a dirty and shrivelled paw, in whining accents she exclaimed—

"Charity, good gentlemen, charity!"

"I say, Claude?"

"Well?"

"What do you think of the old gal?"

"Not much!"

"I think, to my mind, a bath would about suit her," said Paul.

"She wouldn't be any the worse for it!"

"Give a trifle and start her!"

"She don't appreciate our company; she is going," said Jack, with a laugh, as the hag, with a muttered curse, turned away.

"Don't swear, old lady, its wicked!"

"How are you off for soap, mother?"

"It's a dear article out here, ain't it?"

"All right, you villains! rail at me with your ill-timed jests; but, mark me, you will all come to the same end, the gallows! Oh, oh, oh! the gallows, you gaol-birds!" yelled the old hag, as, in a tempest of rage, she turned and quitted the spot, hobbling with her staff with wondrous speed down the lane.

"I say, Jack, are we going to stand this?"

"No; after her!"

"Parbleu! that's no woman!"

"That's my idea!" said Paul.

All three, with loud voices, now dashed up the lane after the hag.

To the astonishment of the friends she had disappeared: Was nowhere to be seen !

"Well, this is a rum go, Claude !"

"Diable ! yes."

"Where the deuce has the old hag gone ?"

"Up a tree ?"

"Not likely !"

"I don't believe it was a woman at all," said Paul.

"You're about right there; I'm of the same opinion," exclaimed Jack, who was peering inquisitively round.

"Well; whoever or whatever it was, they have made a clean bolt of it !"

"Yes; they have vanished clean away !"

"Exactly; and to my minds, pals, we had better go too !"

With a wild start and a stare of astonishment the friends now found themselves confronted by a short stunted man, with a face the colour of coffee and a huge nose of the hue of a picked cabbage.

Where the fellow had come from, or how, unobserved, he had got so close to them in the lane, was to the astounded comrades as great a mystery as the sudden disappearance of the old hag a moment before.

Duval, the first to recover from his surprise, now turning round upon the stranger in gruff accents (for he was much annoyed they should have been taken unawares), exclaimed—

"And pray, friend with the red nose, who the devil may you be ?"

"Oh, I'm Hookey, I am ! Mother Demdike told me you were here ! The Owls are out !"

"So you said just now; and, as the sun is getting up, I should think the owls had better get in."

"They won't go in till they have settled you and your chums !"

"Won't they, indeed, Mr. — Mr. ——"

"Hookey !"

"Ah, yes, I remember ! Well, now do you know, if you study your good health, Mr. Hookey, I should advise you to Hookey Walker out of this !" said Claude, significantly, pulling a pistol from his belt.

"Oh, it's no use you showing fight, it ain't; there's too many for you to cope against, unless you three put yourselves down as a match for a dozen Owls !"

"It depends upon the sort of birds we have to contend with," said Claude, who, with his friends, began to grow rather uneasy.

They could not make out where the fellow before them had started from.

His sudden appearance had startled them out of their usual daring.

They stood for a moment undecided how to act.

This indecision apparently encouraged the strange red-nosed man, who now said—

"You'd better follow me quickly; it will be better for you !"

"And where the devil do you want to take us ?" exclaimed Jack, who, with Claude, thought it best to temporise and learn something more before they attempted any act of an aggresive character.

There was such a cool style about Mr. Hookey, that the friends, though somewhat alarmed by his innuendoes, were also amused.

"Yes, where do you want us to go ?" said Claude, reiterrting Jack's question.

"Before the Owls !"

"Is that all ?"

"Yes !"

"I say, Jack," said Claude in a half-whisper, "is this fellow mad ?"

"Curse me if I know; it's a rum go !"

"It is so; and I see no harm in humouring the fellow a little !"

"Well, no; though I should like to knock him on the head !"

"Oh, we can do that any moment after we have seen the Owls !"

"So we can ! Tell him we are ready !"

The man, who had been coolly leaning against a pollard oak at the end of the lane during the above brief colloquy, now started, as Claude called upon him that they were ready to go.

"Now, Hookey, we are quite ready; lead on !"

"Ah ! I thought you were no fools when I looked at you ! If you had been, you, seeing I was only one, would have tried to knock me over; and if you had, as sure as eyes are eyes, you'd have been run up to dry in the sun; for the Owls don't stand much nonsense, I can tell you ! But, come on !"

"First, how far are we going ?" said Duval.

"To the other end of the lane !"

"The other end ?"

"Yes; there where the stream runs by the willow !"

"Why that's where we came from an hour or two ago !"

"I am perfectly well aware of it !"

"The devil you are ! You're like the little boy that stole the sugarplums—you seem to know all about it !"

"I know how you came to enter the lane; and, mind you, as a servant to the Owls, you would have done better if you hadn't entered it at all !"

"That's your opinion ?"

"Yes !"

"Is it a deadly offence then for strangers to come into Red Hand-lane ?"

"When they come in as spies, yes !"

"Spies ! Have a care, or, sacre ! I'll put a bullet in your head !" exclaimed our hero, the blood rushing to his face in a hot flush as the insulting epithet escaped the fellow's lips.

A grim smile only crossed the man's features as Claude pointed his pistol at his head, and a moment after, to the surprise and alarm of the knights of the road, at least a dozen stalwart, sturdy men started up from behind a mass of brushwood near, all of whom looked menacingly upon the friends.

"You see, strangers, that you are in our power; if we willed it, we could effectually remove you from our path; but we are here for another purpose than to trouble with every inquisitive fool that may think proper to pry in these woods; there's your road !"

The foremost of the mysterious assemblage who had been addressing himself to Claude here pointed to the lane down which he, with his companions, had made their way shortly before.

"And you wish myself and friends without further parley to go the way we came; eh, is that it ?" said Claude.

"That's it !" said the stranger.

"And what if we refuse ?"

"You dare not !"

"Dare not ?"

"No ! If there is any more hesitation, I will have you all three hanged from the branches of the nearest tree !"

"Dear me ! Allow me to suggest that you might not find that a very easy task; 'tis true you outnumber us by four to one, but that won't frighten Gentleman Jack, Paul Clifford, and Claude Duval !"

"Ha, ha, ha !"

"Oh, you may ha, ha, as much as you like; you'll find what I've said is the truth !"

"It's not about your being frightened respecting our numbers that made me laugh," said the stranger, who here gazed at Claude and his companions rather dubiously.

"What was it then, may I ask, that excited your friends ?"

"Why, your giving the names you did just now !"

"What names ?"

"Why the names of three noted knights of the road !"

"Oh, I see; you doubt my assertion that we are those parties ?"

"Most certainly I do !"

"And would it make any difference in your conduct towards us if I can prove in any way that we are indeed the parties I have named ?"

"Most certainly it would !"

"Indeed ! and as I neither know nor care if your knowledge will render you friends or foes, I beg to assure you that we are the redoubtable highwaymen whom I have named, and that we shall do just as we like about going or stopping here ! Jack, Paul, get ready your barking-irons !"

"Hold !"

Starting forwards, the stranger here, as Claude and his friends assumed a determined attitude, raised his arm, his own troupe, with angry exclamations and frowning countenances, putting their hands to their vests as though to draw forth their pistols, the butts of which could be plainly seen by the highwaymen.

"Hold! Stay your purpose, my men! Stand back! And now listen to me! Claude Duval, for from your mien and tone I believe you are he whom travellers fear and the law has banned! for your own safety's sake you had better get away! We are a political party here, who have a hiding place in the old chalk-pit and a neighbouring farmhouse. Only yesterday was it that by a villain who has served us we were betrayed to the authorities, and from intelligence we have gleamed we expect every hour to come in contact with an armed troop of dragoons! We have all vowed not to be taken, and shall fight with our enemies a fight, à la morte, to the death! Watching you unseen a little time back, I fancied you were spies sent forward to reconnoitre our strength. My men were for shooting you down like dogs, but I would not have it, and am rejoiced that I willed it so; for I have heard, despite your calling, that you are a bold and chivalrous man! And now, Claude Duval, I would urge upon you to depart, for at any moment our foes may arrive and your position might then become a perilous one, as you would be doubtless recognised and secured! Go, then, in safety while yet you may!"

"I say, Jack, and you, Paul!"

"Well!"

"You hear what our friend here says!"

"We do!"

"Well, what do you think about it!"

"As to our getting away, do you mean!"

"Yes!"

"Well, I, for one, shan't go!" said Jack.

"Nor I!" echoed Paul.

"You hear my companions, stranger!" said Duval, with a smile, as he turned round to the leader of the political band.

"I heard them refuse to depart, and cannot understand why they should desire to remain after what I have said."

"Well, I will tell you. You said just now you thought we were spies."

"When I first saw you prowling about I certainly did so."

"Very good; and your companions were for shooting us without question!"

"Well, yes!"

"And you would not have it so!"

"No; I did not think it right, without giving you a hearing: the end has proved I was correct!"

"Just so; and therefore to you we owe our lives! Now, those lives are at your service!"

"How do you mean!"

"Why, you expect every moment to be attacked by mounted dragoons!"

"Yes!"

"Very well; in such a case you mean showing fight!"

"Aye, to the death!"

"Exactly; you have sworn not to be taken prisoners!"

"We have!"

"Very good; then as you intend to fight, an extra three pair of hands will be of service!"

"How!"

"Why, I and my companions will join you; we have often fought upon our own account, now we will fight on some one else's!"

"Claude Duval," exclaimed the stranger as he seized his hand with an iron grip in his own, "Claude Duval, highwayman though you be, you are a noble fellow!"

"Pshaw!"

"Nay, it is so; and at the same time that I thank you in the name of all of us for your generous proffered aid, it may not be!"

"And why!"

"For more than one reason!"

"State them!"

"I will. First, we are a political party; we fight only for our honour and opinions."

"Yes!"

"Very well then! If you were to join us you would condemn yourselves, if taken, to immediate execution, and we should have it said that we had been so reduced as to enlist the aid of strangers."

"But I don't see how either of these reasons should prevent your acceptance of my proffer. For the first, if taken by our relentless enemies, the Bow-street runners, death on the scaffold would be our sentence. For your second

reason, it will never be known that we came together as friends; we may have been your prisoners for aught the world can tell!"

"Still, Claude Duval, I would rather we fought this battle out alone! But hark, the tramping of a troop of horses! By heaven, it is too late, and you are lost!"

"Not at all; we ain't found yet," said Claude with a light laugh:

A laugh that presently after died away on his lips, being succeeded by an exclamation of alarm, as, glancing down Red Hand-lane, he beheld some two dozen soldiers advancing on foot, whilst some mounted hussars at a quick trot came rattling along the adjacent high road.

A deadly pallor overspread the face of the leader of the political band as he noted how they were hemmed in:

There was no chance; no opening for retreat if even it were thought of.

Whilst their foes were so numerous, resistance was little short of downright madness.

Nevertheless, the mysterious assemblage, with grim looks of rage and despair, each drew from beneath his clothes holster and other pistols and short rapiers and cutlasses.

"Don't give yourself up, Montford! We will fight as we agreed to the death!" they cried, as they crowded enthusiastically round their leader.

With pallid features and knitted brow, the man, a tall handsome military-looking personage, drawing a sword, exclaimed, "Be it so, friends! We will show this Charles Stuart how his political foes can die! He shall not find the Puritan party willingly bow the knee to his popish Queen! Ha, ha! they are here! Now then, let us meet them with a bold charge; and remember all, 'tis a fight to the death!"

"To the death!" shouted the little band as it boldly rushed forward down Red Hand-lane, to meet the infantry, that with levelled muskets advanced towards them.

Meanwhile, on galloped the hussars, who, reaching the spot where Claude and his companions were standing by their steeds, called upon them to surrender.

"And for what are we to give ourselves up!" said Claude, as he addressed the officer of the troop.

"Why you are members of the Rye House Plot Band, are you not!"

"Sacre! no; you are mistaken, worthy captain, those brave and desperate men, who are now rushing down that lane there so determinately to destruction, I with my friends here met a little time back. We were arrested as spies, but, proving we were none such, were informed we could go on our way!"

"Indeed! Well you may be speaking the truth or otherwise; but, in the meantime, you must give yourselves up as prisoners!"

"Sacre, never!" cried Claude, as he sprang in his saddle, a proceeding that Paul and Jack imitated.

About to close round the companions, things would have gone bad with the knights of the road, but that a roar of musketry and a yell of fury rang at that moment from the lane.

The conspirators and infantry had met:

Were engaged in a desperate conflict!

"Come on, Sir Harry, delay not with these fellows; we know them not! Let us secure Colonel Montford if possible alive. He is leading on his friends in the attack yonder. I can discern his tall form over all others!" cried a young hussar.

Without paying any further heed to Claude or his companions, the troop, at a mad gallop, dashed down Red Hand-lane.

"There they go. Those poor political beggars will be cut up like chaff!"

"Yes, Jack! Mon dieu! it is all over with them!"

"Red Hand-lane will be red enough to-day!"

"Parbleu! yes, Paul! Poor devils, how they shout!"

"They are determined to die game!"

"Mafoi, yes; there's no giving in about them!"

"No, some of the soldiers will bite the dust!"

"Yes! Well I suppose we had better get away while we can!"

"We had so!"

"We have nothing to gain by stopping here!"

"No!"

"It was a close shave just now!"

"Yes!"

THE LAST ADVENTURE OF THE KNIGHTS OF THE ROAD.

"Very good ; then we will now clear out. Off and away is the word !"

"That's it, Claude !"

In another moment, with a loud hillio, the three friends, once more safe in the saddle, were dashing along the high road in the direction of London :

Their hilarious shouts echoing cheerily in the air !

CHAPTER XXXIII.
THE STORM—THE OLD MILL—THE MEETING WITH THE RUNNERS—A CAPTURE.

Galloping on, ever and again giving an encouraging shout to their steeds—onward dashed the bold highwaymen.

For a time neither of the three noticed a gathering darkness :

A darkness as of night that fell over heath and road.

The wind, in low hollow gusts, moaned across the open waste, whilst from the inky clouds that had so momently collected fell some heavy drops of rain.

"Hallo ! we shall be in for it presently, Claude !"

"Yes, we are going to have a thunderstorm ! Parbleu ! we were wise to get under shelter !"

"If a shelter can be found !"

"There's no hostelry nearer than a mile or two !"

"More than that, I take it !" said Paul.

"Yes, you are right !" said Jack, as, with a shrug of the shoulders, he watched the great black clouds that, like a huge pall, hung overhead. "There is no inn for less than three miles !"

"Sacre ! then in that case we are in for it !"

"Damn it, yes; and here comes the beginning of it!" said Jack, as a vivid flash of lightning darted from the inky clouds, whilst a deluge of rain showered down upon them.

"Well, this is rich!"

"By Jove, yes!"

"I'm soaked to the skin!"

"So am I!"

"If the storm don't abate, or we don't get shelter, parbleu! we shall get half-drowned."

"Half drowned? whole you mean," exclaimed Jack, with mumbled curse, as a blinding flash of lightning so startled his horse that the boast nearly threw him from the saddle as it reared upon its haunches.

"Hurrah! It's all right!" now shouted Paul, who was a little in advance of his companions.

"What's all right—what is it, Paul?" they both shouted as they dashed forwards.

"Why, look ahead; don't you see anything?"

"Blessed if I can see anything but the pouring rain that comes down as though it meant a second deluge!"

"Perhaps it does; but no matter to us, pals, for there's our ark!"

With a laugh Paul here pointed out to his friends a building he had sighted on the common they were passing over a few minutes ago.

With loud shouts the three were presently making with the utmost speed for this place, which, on getting closer to, they discovered was an old mill.

An exclamation of surprise escaped the lips of Claude as they gained the old building:

A grim sad-looking pile, falling to ruin and decay:

An old water mill, the stream of which was already swollen to overflowing by the rain that, in one steady downpour, kept on.

"Well, Claude, what do you think of it? You don't seem to like it," said Paul, as he unhesitatingly led his steed in through a huge rent in the side of the ruin.

"Well, he certainly don't seem to relish your ark," exclaimed Jack, who now followed his companion.

"I do not like the cursed place, I own, and would almost sooner remain in the storm bad as it is than seek shelter with you," said Claude as, with a gloomy brow, he passed into the mill.

"Why, what has come over you, old pal? What is there about the mill you don't like?" said Jack, noting the sombre look upon the countenance of his friend.

"You don't know this old building, do you, Claude?"

"Yes, I do, Paul; it was in here that I first met the cursed wretch, Vaughan!"

"Oh, Lord! then I don't wonder you object to the shanty."

"Nor I!" said Jack, who now looked nervously round as a fresh blinding flash of blue forked lightning streamed into the mill.

"Confound it! I wish we had kept on."

"So do I! I am sorry I saw the place," ejaculated Paul, shivering with cold and nervousness.

The lone ruined mill (the roaring thunder and rush of the rain with the screaming wind sounding without) was certainly not a nice abiding-place when they came to reflect that 'twas there upon a former occasion the hideous Vampyre had shown himself.

"Shall we stop it, Claude?"

"Aye! shall we boldly face and brave the pelting of the pitiless storm?"

"No, Jack! no, Paul! We are here, and here we will remain until the rain ceases."

"And that won't be yet awhile, I swear!" exclaimed Paul.

"No, the clouds are still as black as ink. Ugh! there's a crash!" said Jack, as a roar of thunder reverberated overhead, that shook the sides of the old mill and made it tremble to its foundations.

"Well, this is very nice, I must say!" muttered Jack, ruefully.

"I'd sooner be in the old Tree Cave than here."

"I dare say you would, Paul, who wouldn't?"

"Hark, pals!"

"Well, what is it?" they both cried nervously, as Claude motioned with his hand for silence.

"Why, I could have sworn I heard voices whispering in the chamber above!"

"The devil you did!"

"Yes; and I think we had better just crawl up that ladder and see if we really are alone!" Claude here pointed to the old rotten steps up which he had made an ascent upon the occasion of his first visit to the old ruin.

To this decayed and insecure ladder Paul, being the nearest, at once darted.

All three now plainly heard the tramp of feet overhead! Claude was right:

They were not alone in the ruined mill.

Intent upon the steps up which Paul had now half made way, the three friends discerned not four or five stalwart men whose figures at this moment appeared at the front entrance of the mill.

"We've got 'em!"

"Here's a bit of luck!"

"All three on 'em at one go!" Such were the cries that now sounded in the ears of the astounded companions.

"Seize the cursed Frenchman, 'twas he who killed my uncle; never mind the others!" shouted a voice that in shrillness and vindictiveness rang high above the rest.

Exclamations of astonishment and rage now escaped the lips of the highwaymen.

They had unwittingly fallen into a trap.

The ruined mill at the time of their arrival was sheltering their most inveterate foes:

A posse of Bow-street runners, who were at that very time searching for them on the road, had sought the shelter of the mill!

Wildly the three highwaymen now struggled with their enemies!

Taken by surprise they were at a disadvantage!

The runners had pounced so suddenly upon them that they were fairly amazed, and lost their usual wit and cunning.

In the wild melée that now took place, two of the adventurers, however, succeeded in escaping out of the mill.

Dashing Duval, to secure whom the most strenuous efforts were made, was unable to escape:

Dragged to the ground by three of the foe, he was made captive.

His companions, who meanwhile had successfully gained their horses' backs, were about to return and attempt a rescue, when a mounted troop of soldiery dashing up they were with heavy hearts compelled to flee:

The hussars they had left an hour before arriving upon the scene, the capture of their friend was effectually carried out:

Dashing Duval became a prisoner:

Was once more safe in the hands of his merciless foes:

The cunning limbs of the law, the Bow-street runners!

On his journey to London it was that Claude learnt that the officer heading the runners was none other than a relative of the deceased Jonathan Anstey.

This man with a chuckle told Claude that he had vowed to bring him to the scaffold.

How he succeeded will be seen in our next chapter.

CHAPTER XXXIV.

THE ESCAPE NEAR NEWGATE—THE FLIGHT TO THE SILENT HIGHWAY—THE RACE ON THE WATERS—A FIGHT ON A BARGE—THE WHARF—THE ESCAPE—THE MEETING NEAR THE OLD MINT IN SOUTHWARK.

One o'clock boomed out from the dome of St. Paul's.

The streets of London are solitary and deserted.

A strange quiet rests upon the city.

How different to the scene of bustle a few hours before!

The plodding citizens, the merchants, the clerks and the labourers at the warehouses and wharves are all gone.

The hive of busy London is silent:

Save the tread of the City watch, or shout of some intoxicated reprobate, not a sound disturbs the stillness of the night.

Anon the rattle of a vehicle wakes up echoes in the neighbourhood of the Old Bailey.

An obstruction not seen by the driver causes the coach as it crashes against it to fall over.

Then follow the loud shouts of enraged and infuriated men.

Oaths and curses ring on the night air.

"Stop him! Stop him!"

How the wild cry echoes, as a flying desperate man rushes towards an adjacent turning near the scene of the accident, that leads to the water-side:

Presently a flight of stone steps are gained:

Greasy, green, and covered thick with the mud and slime of the river:

Down these the hunted victim flies :

A party of four or five dash up as he disappears.

A few watchmen now creep forwards, some following the pursuers down to the water's edge.

"What is the matter !"

"Anyone drowned ?"

"Have they discovered a dead body ?"

"What's it all about !"

"Where are the City Watch ?"

These and such like cries are uttered by the little crowd as they gather on the steps and gaze eagerly across the dark waters of the river.

There is no moon.

The Thames, like a sea of ink, surges on its waters, looking black and hideous in the darkness of the night.

Anon, there is the sound of oars in the rushing waters.

A boat pushes from the steps.

In it are seated four Bow-street runners.

"Runners arter a cove !" muttered a ragged creature, who stood upon the lowest step, gazing after the rapidly receding boat.

With strenuous exertions the pursuers of the escaped criminal pulled out into the centre of the stream.

For a few minutes there was silence among the occupants of this wherry—a silence at length broken by a man at the rudder.

"Steady, steady, lads ! By heavens, we shall have him yet ! Accursed be the mischance that overturned the coach ! the very fates seem to assist and protect this infernal Frenchman ! Had it not been for the accident, Claude Duval ere this would have been safely caged in Newgate ! Can you sight him, Bolt ?"

"Yes, Mr. Groves ; he's pulling like a devil ! I can just discern him in the thick gloom !" said a man who, leaning forwards, was peering over the rolling tide.

"Give way, lads ! he must not escape us, I have sworn by my uncle's corse to bring Claude Duval to the leafless tree, and I'll keep my oath !" said the leader of the pursuers, a tall thickset man, who sat in the stern of the boat.

A dark object looming right before them now caused them to utter exclamations of alarm.

"Where away !" shouted the leader, "or we shall fall foul of something in this infernal darkness !"

"Hold on to your oars !" a moment after shouted the runner excitedly. "By heavens, the slippery hound has left his wherry and has scrambled up into a barge !"

The officers now, arresting their boat, pulled up at the side of the dark mass that had loomed upon them a moment before, and up the sides of which their leader had beheld the figure of a man climbing.

On to this barge the occupants of the boat now proceeded to follow their victim.

Like grim spectres, they appeared as though emerging from the dark waters of the Thames, as they left their frail boat for the larger vessel.

As the determined runners gained, at length, the side of the barge, a dark figure, with a curse, started up at the further end.

"So, so ! I have failed to double on them ! But, for all that, I won't give in ! I'm not yet, I think, booked for the stone jug !"

Claude, for it was indeed he, now raised an iron bar that lay at his feet, and gripped it with a fierce oath.

He made a vow to escape or perish.

Near to our hero lay the body of a man bound and helpless.

This was the unfortunate bargekeeper, whom he surprised a moment before.

A low groan escaped this man as he saw the officers mount the side of his vessel.

He feared further ill-treatment.

But the runners, heeding not his extended form, bounded up to where stood their victim, stern, grim, and defiant.

With a fierce oath Claude glared upon his enemy.

With vengeful grip he held on to the iron bar :

A fearful instrument in the hands of a determined man !

The foremost of his foes, the leader of the runners, the nephew of the late thief-taker, Jonathan Anstey, now called upon Duval to surrender.

"It's no use, my French buck ; you're trapped this time ; we happened on you nicely at the old Mill down at Highgate, and you don't suppose you're going to escape us now ! Come, drop that weapon and give in !"

"Give in ? Give in now ? And what should I get by it ?

Do you take me for a double-distilled ass !" said Claude with a jeering laugh.

"Well you had better give in, and not show fight, Duval ; we have got you hard and fast !"

"No—excuse me Mr. Groves—not yet ! Ah, Bolt, how d'ye do ? Sacre ! it's a dark night, ain't it ? Ah, parbleu ! and are you there too, M'Nabem ! and Smithson, I declare, along with old Cherrynose ! Pity my old friend, Blue Peters is not here to make up the party ! Damn it ! I ought to be proud—so many daring officers so anxious as to my welfare that they even follow me, on a dark night, on the bosom of old Father Thames ! Do you know I think I'll place my autograph on Newgate stone when you get me there !"

"And that will not be long first ! But come, Duval, enough of this ; come on, and quietly ; you have been wanted for some time !"

"Have I really ? Well, now the want is supplied, ain't it ? Sacre ! come and take me !"

Duval here threateningly raised the iron bar.

"Claude Duval, am I to understand you intend to resist your capture ?"

"That's just what I do intend to do, Mr. Groves ! Your uncle was not clever enough to hang me ; and, do you know, I don't fancy his nephew who follows in his steps will be able to do it ; although he has sworn to ! You see this iron bar ; attempt to raise your barking-irons and I'll smash your head in like an egg-shell ; your finger on the trigger shall be your death-warrant !

There was a fierce savage glitter in the eye of Claude that told his enemies he meant resisting to the last.

"It's no use your showing fight, Duval !" exclaimed the officer Groves angrily ; "we must have you in the end."

"Come and take me, then !"

"Do you persist in your intention to resist us ?"

"The exact card I'm bent on playing : you've hit it !"

"Curses !"

"Don't swear like that, or you'll corrupt my morals and those of your followers."

The runner Groves, paying no heed to this last taunt, turned away, conversing in an undertone with his men as to their best plan of attack in securing their victim.

Duval was known by all to be a man of his word :

Bold, daring, and, in urgent cases, unscrupulous.

He had said he would use the fearful-looking bar of iron, and there was no doubt in the minds of the officers but what he would.

Well they knew his courage and daring defiance of danger.

The five men all gave a nervous shhudder as, standing upon the edge of the barge, they beheld the bold highwayman gripping with deadly purpose his powerful weapon.

It was more than probable that at least a couple of them in a scuffle would fall :

Fall with broken arm or head into the dark rolling waters.

It behoved them to attack their man with caution.

Groves, uneasily casting a glance at Claude, began once more to parley with him, the barge, meanwhile, without guidance of any kind drifting on with the tide.

"What object do you expect to attain by thus resisting our authority, Duval ?"

"Why, your defeat, of course, and consequently my escape !"

"Humph ! you match yourself, one, against us that are five ?"

"No, three ; and I can tackle three Bow-street runners any day !"

"Three ? how do you count us three !" said Groves, who was willing to gain time, with the hope of some controversy taking place that might lead to the safe capture of the bold highwayman.

"Why, I count you three thus—when you fire at me, I shall make a dash at you, and send you over the side and Bolt there after you ; thus there will be three only to contend with, not five ; poor Cherrynose there I hardly count at all ; a struggle with Smithson and M'Nabem will soon finish the affair, and a bath at midnight in old Father Thames will wind up the attempted capture of Dashing Duval. Now are you ready, friend Groves ? if so, come on !"

"Very clever ! and I daresay you think by this bravado to frighten us, but you are deluding yourself ; nought can save you ! you can't escape. If you think to effectually elude us and avoid the bracelets (handcuffs) and a lodging in the stone mansion, Newgate, you are mistaken; as to easily settling myself and Bolt, I think you are in error! Now then, lads, we must on to him; curses, he's laughing at us!" Infuriated, as he saw Claude raise the iron bar, Grove, here levelling his pistol, fired.

The sharp ringing report that followed was the signal for attack.

In another moment the daring knight of the road was struggling with his determined foes.

In a second of time one of the runners disappeared with a plash over the side, and was presently battling with the rolling, heaving waters, with some difficulty gaining a boat that dragged behind the barge.

Meanwhile the fearful struggle with Claude and his enemies went on.

The thought that his friends were in safety, and the agony that his loved Maude must be suffering at his capture, maddened him.

Wildly he combatted with the runners.

His peril endued him with fictitious strength.

He knew that if taken to Newgate all was at an end.

Tyburn Tree or the outside of the gaol would be his doom.

"Cherrynose," he shouted, flushed and heated as he found he was successfully avoiding a capture—"Cherrynose! join Smithson, he wants company; cool your inflamed proboscis in the water, old man!"

There was a wild cry of horror as the runner named, who had been hanging bulldog-like on to the highwayman, was suddenly lifted off his feet and hurled into the stream.

"Help, help, help!" shouted the affrighted wretch.

The unfortunate man, who couldn't swim, was in danger of drowning.

No remorse, however, had Claude as he heard the wild cry for aid pealing from the lips of the half-drowned man.

It was his life or theirs.

It was at this moment, while the howling of the drowning officer was gradually getting weaker and fainter, that Groves succeeded in hurling Claude upon his back.

In a second, with a cry of triumph, he was kneeling on his chest:

"Slip the darbies on, M'Nabem!"

"How is he going to do it?" yelled Claude, who like a huge serpent twisted and writhed in the iron grip of his assailants.

"On with the bracelets, curse yer, or he'll have me off!"

"All right, Mr. Groves, I think we can do the trick now!"

"M'Nabem here drew from his pocket a pair of handcuffs, and endeavoured to thrust them on the wrists of the panting highwayman.

Claude, who had been husbanding his strength, now with a deep-drawn breath suddenly shot up his knees, and with a sharp, quick jerk sent the astounded officer over the side.

Seizing the man Groves in his arms he then rolled over, and succeeded in getting free from his grip, with a yell of triumph staggering to his feet.

Now master of the field, Claude darted to the other end of the barge.

With a cry of surprise and joy, he found the vessel had drifted close to the water's edge:

Was now resting against a quanity of logs, that were like a huge raft heaving up and down on the waters.

To bound on to these, was to Claude, the work of a moment.

Darting on he came to a wharf.

Making his way to this, he, unheeding the cry of a startled watchman, hurried on to a pair of large iron gates.

On the other side of these was a public street.

With an exclamation of delight, Claude rushed to the gates:

They were locked.

In rage and fury he, for a moment, hesitated what to do; then, as the yells of the officers, who had escaped from the river and were now close at his heels, sounded in his ears, he, squirrel-like, mounted the obstacle before him, presently in safety gaining the other side.

With frantic haste, he now sped down the dark street before him:

A thoroughfare that brought him out, he found, into the neighbourhood of the Borough.

The barge had drifted to the Surrey side of the river.

This Claude was delighted at.

In a moment he decided where to go:

He would haste at once to the Old Mint.

Once there he was safe.

Several habitations there would hide him from his foes.

Wildly Claude dashed on:

The yells of his pursuers ringing like a death-knell in his ears.

How would it after all end:

In capture and death, or freedom?

A cold shudder crept through the frame of Claude as he dashed on with his foes like bloodhounds at his heels.

Upon how many occasions had he not thus been compelled to run for his life?

His life, that by his own acts, he had made forfeit to the laws.

During his race that morn, the early light of another day falling upon the silent streets, Claude vowed, if he escaped the foes who were now hanging on his flying steps, to for ever give up the calling that had so often perilled his existence.

He kept his vow.

Dashing on, followed by the yelling officers, he now, dashing down a bye-street, came full against some stranger, who, by the force of the collision, was nearly jerked off his feet.

"Hullo, lad! whither away so fast? flying from the grave? If so, come with me, for Gentleman Jack—Claude, by heavens!" gasped his friend (for it was he), who here, catching sight of Duval's features, gazed at him with an incredulous stare.

"Thank heaven, dear old pal, we have met! But if you know a hiding-place hereabouts at once conduct me to it, for Anstey's infernal nephew and his men are hard upon my heels."

"Damn 'em, yes; I can hear them. But follow me, Claude; we'll put a fog on them presently."

At mad speed the two now dashed away.

Panting, gasping for breath, they tore on.

"Have we far to go, Jack!"

"No; I suppose you're pretty nigh done up."

"Well, I am near spent, I confess."

"Never mind, old fellow; you'll be safe enough presently. Lord, what a treat the girls will have when we meet to-night! But here we are; hold on!"

Jack now paused as they opened the door of an old inn, in the front of which hung the curious sign of "The Cat and Fiddle." Giving three very loud and sharp raps for admission, his summons in a moment after was answered by the sudden appearance of a head from a first-floor window, a loud, gruff voice halloing, "Who's there?"

"Hawks in distress!" replied Jack.

"Grabs at hand?"

"Yes, Joe; and if you ain't considerable smart we shall be collared!"

The head, as these words left Jack's lips, was drawn in, and a few seconds after the door of "The Cat and Fiddle" was slowly and cautiously opened, the two friends at once, with a sigh of relief, stepping in.

For a time at least they were safe!

CHAPTER XXXV.

AN ADVENTURE AT "THE CAT AND FIDDLE"—IN THE OLD MINT AT SOUTHWARK—THE OFFICERS BAFFLED—THE ESCAPE OF THE HIGHWAYMEN.

"Any of the family here, Joe?" exclaimed Jack, as the door of the inn closed to.

"No; not a soul! and jolly wild they'll be when they learns that Dashing Claude Duval and his pal, Gentleman Jack, have honoured "The Cat and Fiddle" in their absence. But—hallo! are the Philistines so near at hand, my rum culls?" exclaimed the landlord, as a loud bang at that moment sounded on the door:

A loud summons for admission, followed by a chorus of yells!

The officers had succeeded in tracking the highwaymen to the inn.

Bang, bang! crash! The old door fairly groaned under the rude attack.

"Go it, you beauties! You don't come in here yet; not if I know it! We are all deaf and can't hear! The Cat is playing on her Fiddle, and we don't hear nothink!"

"Where are you going to shove us, Joe !"

"In the old place !"

"All right, lead on ! It ain't the first time you've helped Gentleman Jack out of a fix."

Crash ! Bang !

"They are arter forcing my door, I fancies !"

"Yes ; and I'm blessed if they won't succeed presently, Joe, if they go on like that !"

"Oh no, not it ! That there door will take a power of hard knocks, it's used to it."

"So I suppose !"

"In course it is ! But, come on ! This way, boys ! We'll fog the grabs yet, double on 'em, and leave no trace behind ! Come on !"

Joe, the landlord, followed by the two friends, now hurried down a passage, and opening a door at the further end, passed out into a yard at the back of the house.

"Here we is, boys, the finest hiding crib out, bar none !"

"What, in this yard ?" Incredulously Claude gazed around him.

"Yes, Mr. Duval, in this blessed yard, and nowhere else !"

The landlord, with a grin, here gave a knowing wink at Jack, who was smiling at Claude's blank looks.

"Why, confound it, there's only the dustbin and the water-butt !" said Duval.

"In course, that's just it ! That's the blessed snuggery where I bet no grab, let him be ever so artful, would find you, once you're inside !"

"Inside the dusthole ?" said Claude, in disgust. "Thank you, I'd rather not !"

"I doesn't suggest the dustbin, Muster Duval ; the water-butt is the caper !"

"Confound it, landlord, a joke with us at this moment, with the enemy hammering and yelling like fiends at the door, is out of place. Why, the butt is full of water !"

As Claude had said the butt was full, full to overflowing, the water running over the top, trickling down its sides, and falling with a plash on the stones beneath !

"It's all right, Duval, my flower, you needn't fear a cold bath !" The landlord now pulling out a plug some three feet from the top, the water gushed out with a loud gurgle for a few moments, then ceased.

"Now then, in with yer, we arn't got no time to lose !"

Claude, now, guessing there was a trick in the affair, rushed forwards, and upon examining the butt found, three feet from the top, a false bottom.

Lifting this up with some difficulty, for it was closed and even fitted to the sides of the butt, Duval as he suspected discovered that all beneath was dry and hollow.

Unhesitatingly scrambling in he was followed by Jack !

"All right, lads ?"

"As a bird in her nest ;" said Claude with a smile.

"Very good ; now you can stop there, like a couple of blessed turtle doves, till I come back : blarm'em, how they are hammering at that door, blowed if they won't have it in after all !"

As these words fell from the lips of the landlord, the friends, even in their strange hiding-place, heard the loud banging without.

Having now replaced the trap, the landlord ere he hurried away, turned on some fresh water ; the friends two minutes after, in their dark abiding place, hearing the plashing noise caused by the fluid as it trickled over the top all down the sides of the butt, on to the stones beneath.

For a few minutes only the plashing of the water was heard by the two companions ; but at length the silence was rudely broken by the noise of angry voices !

Joe, the landlord, with the officers were in the yard.

"He ain't here, gentlemen, so help me, nor his pals neither ; I ain't seen either on 'em !" now said the voice of the landlord. Loud and clear the voices without sounded to the ears of the friends.

"You lie, Joe Nobbers ! we know you before to day !" said the man Groves, whose husky voice Claude with a thrill at once recognised. "Your assertion that you have not seen that confounded French robber don't go down with me ; but I'll watch your premises for a month but what I'll have him, and his pal Gentleman Jack too ! You've stowed them away some where, I am certain !"

"Have I though ? Law ! what a funny man you are, Mr. Groves, to think as how I'd put away two big real live highwaymen ! Lord ! perhaps you fancy I've got the gentlemen in my pocket ? Ha, ha, ha ! perhaps you may think I have even shoved 'em into the water-butt or dustbin ?"

"As likely as not Jenkins, look in that place ! Your cursed funny style won't get over me, Joe Nobbers, I can tell you you !" said the officer Groves passionately.

The hidden friends in breathless silence, immured in their retreat, now heard the lid of the dust-hole raised and shut !

Then followed a loud jeering laugh from the landlord, who facetiously invited the runners to have a peep into the waterbutt !"

Uttering volleys of oaths and curses, the concealed highwaymen now heard the officers leaving the yard :

Then all was silent.

Nought fell upon the ears of the companions in captivity save the trickling of the waters and the dull plash as they fell upon the stones beneath the butt.

A quarter of an hour passed away :

An age to Duval and Jack, who, cramped and unable to move were enduring torture in this prison.

At length came to their ears the sound of cautious foot-steps in the yard :

Presently followed the loud rush of waters :

A few minutes after the covering above their heads was removed :

The golden rays of the early morning's sun shining full upon them :

A broad stream of daylight that fairly dazzled their eyes !

The next moment the friends, looking, saw the features of Joe Nobbers peering over them.

"Well, Claude Duval, Dashing Duval, what does yer think of the water-butt now, old fellow ! fine caper ain't it ?"

"It is so ; but it's confounded close quarters for two, Joe," said Duval, as now, followed by Jack, he scrambled out of their retreat.

Both immediately, much to the amusement of the landlord, began stumping up and down the yard to relieve their stiffened limbs.

"Ha, ha ! I expect you're a little stiff, lads ; but better a cramp in your limbs than a crick in the neck at Tyburn or outside Newgate ! But come on into the house, boys, the grabs have cleared out ; there's nothing to fear ; and, ere you go, damme, we'll drink confusion to all Bow-street runners."

Re-adjusting the mysterious apparatus that had so effectually hidden the companions from their enemies, Joe Nobbers hastened into the house.

Here, over some refreshments which they washed down with some good old port, the companions with their jolly friend the landlord laughed heartily as they talked over their recent escape.

CHAPTER XXXVI.

THE MEETING AT THE OLD TREE CAVE—CLAUDE'S RESOLVE
—A VOW WELL KEPT—DASHING DUVAL'S FAREWELL TO
ENGLAND, AND RETURN TO LA BELLE FRANCE—CONCLU-
SION.

Stopping in their hiding place at "The Cat and Fiddle" until the shades of night once more descended, Claude and his companion Jack passed a very comfortable and pleasant day ; and just as the goddess of night, the silvery moon, was tinting with her radiance the red-tiled roofs of the tumble-down ramshackle tenements in the Old Mint at Southwark, the friends, bidding good bye to honest old Joe Nobbers, hurried away.

It was a bright and beautiful night.

A sweet lovely calm seemed to the bold highwaymen to rest on all around.

Contrasting his then position with that of the perilous night before, Claude began to reflect upon the vow he had made whilst being hunted by the emissaries of the law :

The vow to give up his dangerous and dishonent calling.

The sweet angelic face of the fair Maude, guardian-angel like, rose up before him.

He thought of what must have been her pain, her agony, when hearing that again had he become a captive.

As these reflections passed through his brain, Claude again registered the vow to heaven of the night before :

The vow to give up the road, to leave England, the scene of his crimes, for ever !

Thinking over this it was in moody silence that Claude sat in the coach that was now bearing himself and Jack to Highgate.

Reaching at length their journey's end the companions at once hastened with all speed for the adjacent woods :

The woods in which was situate the old Tree Cave.

Bright and lustrous shone the luminary of night.

With a shudder Claude gazed up at the radiant moon as he passed the pinetree grove, near the cave :

That place where he had first, in deadly encounter, met the fiend, Vampyre Vaughan.

Then again came the remembrance of the morning when he was captured in those very woods by the conspirators ed by the man La Roche.

His voyage to France, his perils at the lone chateau—all passed vividly before him.

But a brief lapse of time—and yet what wild scenes of adventure had he not gone through !

Like a phantasmagoria the shadows of the past flitted before him.

Lost in this reverie of the past was Claude when, with Jack by his side, he once more halted by the entrance of the old Tree Cave.

A wild scream of delight now rang in the air as he strode into the secret retreat.

In hysteric joy the lovely Maude, who had darted forwards, clung to the man who the day before she had thought never to see again.

With the fond girl in his arms, Jack, Paul Clifford, and the pretty Kate Annersley gazing delightfully upon him, Claude now surprised them all by, in firm decided tones, affirming that he meant to give up the road and, making for his native land, endeavour by honest industry to redeem the past.

Shades of astonishment and pain flitted across the faces of Jack and Paul at their companion's project for the future.

" You really think of leaving us ?"

" Of giving up the road ?"

" Aye ; I have sworn it ! I registered a vow to heaven that I would endeavour to retrieve the past ! I will keep my oath !"

" Nay, you surely jest ?"

" No, dear pals ; my resolution is irrevocable ! I am fixed in my resolve !"

" And whither do you intend to migrate ?" said Jack, who saw that no persuasion would induce Claude to forego his project.

" Why, I shall, without delay, make for the land of my birth !"

" France ?"

" Yes ; and with the sum that I possess I shall purchase some little residence in Normandy ; or, perchance, may hit upon a cosy retreat near to the Pyrenees, where, unknown, I may succeed in time in attaining an honourable position amongst my fellow men !"

" And for us—myself and Paul—have you no advice to give as to our future movements ?"

" Well, as to that, Jack, you must act on your own discretion. Because I am about to quit England, and for ever give up my past lawless profession, I would not by word, thought, or deed, seek to imbue you with my notions !"

" That's like you, dear Claude However, since you have determined to leave the country where we have encountered such perils, so too will I. But, as I do not care for France, I shall with my dear Kate make way to the New World, and in the backwoods build myself a home, forsaking the Road for the Prairie."

" And as I, Paul Clifford, don't care to be left behind, I'll go with you, Jack ; and as Jenny Dunning has got her father's consent to become mine, why there will be a companion for Kate whilst you are out buffalo-hunting."

A laugh here escaped the lips of the friends as the pretty Jenny at that moment came tripping into the cave.

A long and merry evening was that spent by the highwaymen and their future brides in that snug retreat :

The last night was it in the old Tree Cave.

On the morrow, Claude, well disguised, went up to London, accompanied by Maude and the faithful servant the boy Luke.

Here, bidding adieu to his companions, he that same night sailed away for the land of his birth, La Belle France.

Jack and Paul Clifford, leaving London, made a journey to Liverpool, and from that port, a week after Claude Duval's departure for France, sailed away for the Far West.

Our Life Romance is now finished :
Nothing more remains to be told.

Our hero, Dashing Duval, was one of those few who, by his brave and good resolution to become an honest man, escaped the hideous scaffold. His name appeareth not in the dread calendar of crime ; the record of those who perished by the hangman's hands, mentions not the chivalrous Dashing Claude Duval. Gentleman Jack and Paul Clifford, with their friend, also escaped an untimely death upon the gibbet !

On the rolling boundless prairies of the Far West, on the Canadian rivers, in the Rocky Mountains, many were the dangers they encountered in their after life ; but never did they experience such misery and horror as when, outraging their country's laws, they were Knights of the Road !

Successful in speculations, and by sobriety and industry securing a moderate competence, Claude Duval purchased an old chateau in Normandy, and here with his fondly loved Maude and a numerous progeny ceased in time to remember those days of peril he passed when he was known only as Dashing Duval, or the Ladies' Highwayman !

FINIS.